An only child, Madge Swindells was born in Dover, England. Her father was a romantic Irish deep sea diver and her mother a thoroughly practical Londoner. The desire to write, she says, has been her one and only lifeline during a tumultuous and changeable life which has led her through four husbands, several countries, numerous liaisons and a varied career ranging from social work and poultry farming to financial journalism. For the past fifteen years she has published and edited magazines for a readership as diverse as commercial fishermen, sports retailers, school children and businessmen.

She lives in Johannesburg with a hard-headed Scots accountant, her daughter and numerous cats and dogs.

'When we partake of joy, we partake of God and to reject joy is to reject God.' Herbert Richer

MADGE SWINDELLS

Futura
Macdonald & Co
London & Sydney

A Futura Book

Acknowledgements to Lawrie Mackintosh, Nellie Swindells,
Jeffrey Sharpe, Vivian Moses, Greg Morris and particularly to
Lana Odell for invaluable assistance.

*The characters in this novel, and their actions, are purely imaginary.
Their names and experiences have no relation to those of actual
people, except by coincidence.*

First published in Great Britain in 1983
by Macdonald & Co (Publishers) Ltd
London & Sydney

This Futura edition published in 1984
Reprinted 1984 (twice)

ISBN 0 7088 2528 1

Reproduced, printed and bound in Great Britain by
Hazell Watson & Viney Limited,
Member of the BPCC Group,
Aylesbury, Bucks

Futura Publications
A Division of
Macdonald & Co (Publishers) Ltd
Maxwell House
74 Worship Street
London EC2A 2EN
A BPCC plc Company

Part One

1

THE CAPE OF GOOD HOPE, February 1938

The last of the road ran westwards along the south side of the lagoon to peter out towards the sea, traversing a desolate area too stony for the plough, too sandy for wheat, a place of reeds and wild bush where you could graze one sheep to five morgen and set pigs and goats roaming, but little else. Beyond the gravel road lay one more farm, called Modderfontein, which means 'mud spring'. It stretched north-east to the Atlantic Ocean and north-west as far as the lagoon where seagulls nested in marshes.

Across the lagoon you could see the whaling station and when the wind blew nor-westerly the stench of decomposing blubber would waft over the lands, but today there was no wind. It was almost noon; torpid sheep were prone under the bushes and even the seagulls had stilled their raucous cries.

Yet the surface of the lagoon was ruffled as an empty paraffin drum raced over the waters, north to south, east to west, leaving a trail of white spray and evanescent rainbows in its wake.

On the horizon a cloud of yellow stained the blue and, beneath, a worn-out van rattled towards the point where the lagoon almost met the road. There it skidded to a halt and the driver, covered in yellow dust, clambered down, stretched and tried to wipe the dust from his eyes with the back of his dusty knuckles.

He was a giant of a man; twenty-four, but looking older, his face weather-beaten by the dry heat of the land and the biting cold of the Antarctic, he stood six foot three in his bare feet, his hair brilliant red, eyes emerald green, laughing now as he watched the barrel skim by. It was three days since he had harpooned the shark and secured it to the empty drum; standing thigh deep in the lagoon he had thrust home the shaft, penetrating the shark's side so deeply that the creature could not tear loose and reluctant to move, unable to dive, it starved slowly in shallow water.

Simon Smit had been born and bred on Modderfontein, which he had inherited in his teens, and since then he had led a dualistic existence. From May until November he planted and harvested his meagre wheat crop on the north side of the low hills where the soil was less sandy; after harvest he signed on as a harpoonist returning late in April with cash enough to buy seed and fertilizer. This year, his foreman had left and Simon was unable to sign on. The harvest had been poorer than usual, the rains nonexistent and he wondered uneasily how he would pay his debts.

Modderfontein was ten miles beyond the small village of Saldanha Bay, a remote, near-miss of a place, situated on the sou'-westerly side of the African Cape, refuge for goats and a few outlandish farmers, descendants of shipwrecked settlers. Yet the bay was one of the world's two A1 grade natural harbours on London's Admiralty Charts and would have become the major port of the Cape, but for the lack of fresh water.

The time was late February, 1938, a year of cataclysmic events in Europe, a year when Hitler became Germany's supreme military commander and marched into Austria 'to quell civil disorder', the year of the Munich Agreement and the Crystal Night, but while tidal waves of impending doom engulfed the western world, not an eddy reached Saldanha Bay. There, disaster was measured in inches of rainfall, and time was merely the measure of seasons.

Simon climbed into his van and drove towards the Cape. Two sows were squealing in the back under a hastily erected wooden frame and in the corner, separated from the pigs by a roll of wire netting, sat a young girl of seventeen, clutching a stick to clout the pigs.

Her name was Sophie and she was scared. Conceived under

8

a longboat on a whaler in dry dock, spawned in a ditch at Modderfontein, she never knew her mother or her father. She was a hybrid of two kinds of needs and in her veins ran Swedish, Hottentot, English, Indian, Portuguese, Russian and Chinese blood. This mongrel mix had produced a girl of extraordinary beauty which had faded with the tough farm life.

Sophie had been found abandoned by Simon's mother and reared to follow the turkeys over the land. Day after day, year after year, she had wandered behind the flock to retrieve the eggs from their secret nests.

There had been one milestone in Sophie's life and that was the death of Simon's mother. Sophie was fourteen at the time and she had wept when the turkeys were sold. Lately she had decided to leave the farm to find work in the city and that morning she had begged a lift from the master.

Some distance past Malmesbury, Simon braked under an oak tree. Climbing through the fence he set off towards a small stream. He scowled as he heard a plaintive call from the van.

'Master! Don't forget me, master.'

'I'll be back, Sophie.' He hurried on.

'Master, I'm thirsty.' Her wail went unheeded, but she managed to open the wooden door and a few minutes later he heard her running through the undergrowth behind him.

'Bugger off,' he grumbled and she veered to the right, making for a clump of trees bordering the river.

Simon slithered down mud slopes into a cool, enchanted place where sunlight came dappled through leaves and bushes thick with birds' nests. Enviously he noted that the stream flowed strongly in spite of the dry summer and he wondered why God had singled him out for special punishment, for although the rains had been sparse, only one area had been neglected and that was Saldanha Bay. Even as he soaked his head in the crystal water and drank deeply, he felt angry with God.

His anger turned to irritation as he sat gnawing a stick of biltong, watching the water flow past, but bad temper without an audience is the height of frustration, so when he heard

9

Sophie splashing downstream, he went in search of her. She was lying in a pool, hair streaming in the current, only her nose, big toes and two rounded breasts showed above the brackish water. Her breasts were strangely white, brown nipples erect, and Simon wondered what parentage had produced so light-skinned a daughter.

She was no longer a child and he felt desire rising until he became ramrod hard.

He felt ashamed and then angry with Sophie for inspiring his guilt, and seeing her clothes lying in a heap beside his feet he flung them into the branches.

Eyes closed, Sophie was singing to herself.

'Sophie, let's go,' he called slyly and, retreating a few paces, sat on a rock at the water's edge.

She opened her eyes and sat up with a start, clutching her hands over her breasts. 'Heavens, you gave me a fright, master,' she called in her unattractive sing-song accent.

'Come on.' Impatiently. 'Can't wait any longer.'

'The master must look away while I get dressed,' she said nervously.

'Who wants to look at you?' he retorted and grinned when he heard the expected cry of despair.

'Master, my clothes is gone.'

'Are you coming or staying?' He moved upstream, but a moment later she tugged his arm.

'Master can't leave me here.' She was both shy and desperate and trapped between two emotions, her features contorted with anguish. Simon felt blood rushing to his face; there was a tight feeling in his chest. He had never seen Sophie when she was not covered in dust and dirt; how smooth her skin was, soft and inviting. She looked so much like Janet Gaynor, he thought. He had seen her in *Seventh Heaven* at the cinema.

As desire supplanted guilt he wished he had left her clothes alone. 'There's your things,' he said, nodding curtly towards the top of the tree. 'Perhaps a bird tried to steal them.'

Sophie's eyes glinted angrily as she turned away but she was too scared to complain and too short to reach. Laughing

10

to himself Simon sat on the ground and watched her buttocks, breasts, and the tangled forest of hair between her legs as she climbed the tree. Scratched and sobbing with humiliation, eventually she managed to retrieve her precious garments.

Simon's frustration had become unbearable. He thought he would explode. It was a sin, he reasoned, but who was God to chastise him when He, Himself, had neglected to send the rains?

As Sophie reached the ground he grasped her arm and, pushing her down, flung himself on top of her.

She yelped with pain as she landed in the mud, but after a brief moment of incredulity, fought like a wild-cat. Simon caught her wrists and forced them up and over her head to the ground, with the other hand he seized her buttocks and pulled them up, while his knees pushed her thighs open. When he came, a few seconds later, he cried out with the agonizing pleasure of it.

Simon had not come upon a virgin before, but he had heard enough stories to recognize the situation. He was shocked and felt soiled by her. He shuddered and climbed the slope quickly. When he looked back she was still crying as she washed herself. She would be bound to make trouble for him. On impulse he sprinted to the van, abandoning Sophie to the fields and flowers.

For a while he drove with his foot on the accelerator, nervously glancing over his shoulder from time to time. It was not Sophie he feared, but the avenging hand of God. Instinctively he knew that an evil seed thrust into fate's fertile soil would flourish and his crop would be disaster.

Four hours later Simon reached Stellenbosch and delivered his pigs. They were fine stock and he sold them for a good price, glad to be rid of them. Two years before, in spite of warnings from local farmers, he had invested in 'Large White' sows and a boar, but the first litter had been a disaster, for the price they fetched had not covered the cost of their food and with their sun-sensitive skins they could not be turned out to scavenge.

He felt better when he had disposed of his squealing cargo

and the cash was in his pocket. He decided to inspect the local farms, a pastime that always depressed him.

He could hardly control his envy as he admired sleek cattle, aristocratic horses, lush grazing and the swollen udders of the Jersey cows. Above all the vineyards fascinated him and he sat drooling at the glossy black grapes that hung in abundance from every branch. Behind the vineyards were stately farmhouses, gabled, shuttered, reeking of riches, surrounded with paddocks, lawns and oaklined avenues.

One day he would own just such a house, he promised himself, but how? Twenty years' deprivation in the Antarctic would not pay a half of it.

Feeling cheated Simon raced to the village, but a few miles on halted with screeching brakes before the most beautiful homestead of all. The sign read: Fontainebleu and underneath: *A.T. van Achtenburgh*. The farm dominated the surrounding countryside with its air of stateliness and abundance. Simon sighed and eventually drove on in a chastened mood.

He parked in front of the village café, pushed his battered Stetson back and chose a seat by the window. He had nearly finished his Coke when he heard a clatter of hooves. A moment later a superb, pure-bred Arab mare cantered past. The rider was a young girl of about eighteen in jodhpurs and white silk blouse. He caught a glimpse of her profile, brown hair flying. A cat dashed across the road and the mare reared, ears back, showing the whites of its eyes. Too nervous, he decided and wondered without really caring if the girl could manage. She coped magnificently and a second later horse and rider passed out of sight.

'What a beauty,' he said aloud and whistled.

'The horse or the girl?' the café owner asked, winking at him.

'Why, the horse.' Simon was surprised he asked, but on second thoughts he decided that the girl ran a close second. She had a look about her that he could only label as 'class'. Thoroughbreds both of them!

'Who's she?' he asked idly.

'Van Achtenburgh's daughter. Richest family round these parts, but there's only one daughter, no sons.'

'Van Achtenburgh from Fontainebleu?' The hairs were rising on the back of his neck.

'You know them?'

'Sold them stock,' he lied.

'If I had their fortune I'd find something better to do than fool around with horses all day. That's all they think about — horses,' he said contemptuously.

Simon leaned back and began to dream of owning just such a horse, for although his own mare, Vixen, was probably the best schooled horse in the Cape Province, she was nothing to look at. After a while, his dreams began to encompass stables and eventually the entire Fontainebleu estate. He returned to reality when the barman tapped him on the shoulder and asked for sixpence for the Coke.

'You a farmer round these parts?' the café proprietor asked.

'Sure,' Simon lied. 'Malmesbury way.'

'S'pose you'll be queuing up with rest of 'em to try your luck with van Achtenburgh's daughter?' he giggled nervously.

'No time for that sort of thing.' Simon felt as if an electric shock had passed down his spine. In all the hundreds of ambitious schemes he had devised lying awake at night, marrying money was the one solution that had never occurred to him. Suddenly his dreams seemed that much more promising.

'You folks have a horse show around here?' he asked as he flipped a coin on the counter.

'Next month,' the man told him. 'She'll be there, that's for sure.' He winked again. 'She wins all the trophies regular as clockwork.'

2

Autumntime. The Cape sizzled in the third week of an Indian summer. The nights brought little relief for the Berg wind sprang up from the mountains, bringing the heat of the Karroo desert and choking the air with dust and the tang of veld herbs. Now the wind had dropped, but the air was still warm. A dangerous, light-headed night.

Simon Smit felt light-headed, too, as he climbed through the fence into the vineyard. His senses were heightened and exaggerated; the moon was a brilliant globe near enough to touch; the hills crouched menacingly over him. Beyond the vines the Fontainebleu homestead shone dazzling white in the moonlight.

Simon's bare feet sank ankle deep into the fertile soil that oozed between his toes. Soft and sensuous soil.

Even the air was different here. Sweeter! Scent of roses from the garden; water on damp earth from the river; drift of wood smoke; honeysuckle in fences and new mown grass from Fontainebleu's wasteful lawns. Rich man's air. He sucked it in greedily, filling his lungs to bursting and felt the richer for it.

He took a bunch of grapes; crushed it against his skin; thrust them into his mouth and bit sensuously. The juice ran down his cheeks and neck. Oh God, he was hungry. Hungry for life, for the soil, for the water flowing wastefully over stones and overwhelmingly for Anna.

He bent down and grabbed a handful of soil, rubbing it between his fingers. Not soil – gold dust. Here lay the difference between them and he? Were they better? Did they love the soil more? Or work harder? Did they freeze their balls

14

in the ice four months a year to pay for fertilizer? No, by God! The difference lay here in his hands. This soil. This rich and fertile patch. All that they had – it sprang from this. The soil ran through his fingers. He smeared his hand on his trousers and walked towards the house.

As he approached the garden he veered to the left, to the east wing where the vines grew to the balcony. A familiar route.

Anna's dog bounded out of its kennel and licked his hand. They were old friends by now. Anna's room was in darkness. He fondled the dog and waited on the top step. The front of the house was a blaze of lights, but he must stand in the shadows like a thief. He would have it out with Anna, for once and for all. She said she loved him, so why was she so afraid?

Then he noticed a sheet of paper rammed in the window. Square, bold handwriting. Not Anna's, surely? But it was. Mama was entertaining the Jouberts, old family friends. Could he wait? She was sorry.

He sighed.

For two pins he would go home, but just as quickly he rejected the idea. Keeping to the shadows he skirted the house, Wagter at his heel.

The patio was wide and imposing. Snatches of voices came through the open windows. As he watched, the glass door nearest to him was flung open by a maid in striped uniform. Simon jumped back into the shadows and collided with a gnarled tree trunk. He looked up. Boughs as thick as his body. It had stood there for a hundred years or more.

Simon pulled himself into the branches until eventually he was lying only yards from the open door. A grandstand view!

The room took his breath away. He gawped at the long yellowwood table choked with silver and cut glass. The walls were cluttered with portraits in heavy gilt frames. Carafes of wine gleamed ruby red.

Anna's mother hurried into the room. Simon had met her at the horse show and he still smarted from her spite. Now she was primping herself in front of the mirror. A vain and difficult woman, he thought. God forbid Anna would grow like her mother; though to give her her due she was still handsome, with black hair piled up on her head and sharp but even features. The maid was summoned and appeared seconds later.

'Is dinner ready?' Maria van Achtenburgh demanded.

'Yes, Ma'am.'

She flicked an impatient glance around the room and hurried off.

The maid went to the sideboard, poured a glass of sherry, knocked it back and pushed the tumbler in her pocket.

Now the family were coming on to the patio. Mrs van Achtenburgh was a good head taller than her companion, a stocky man, Joubert presumably, with cerise face and short white hair. 'Anna's such a talented girl,' Simon heard from her mother as they passed.

But why the procession? Simon wondered.

Next came Anna's father with a middle-aged woman clutching his arm. Jewels glittered from every spare piece of skin. 'André, have you noticed what a perfectly lovely couple they make,' she whispered and glanced over her shoulder.

So they were trying to marry Anna to Piet Joubert. There he was hanging around the doorway waiting for Anna. Even at that distance he looked arrogant. It was something to do with the way he held his head poking forward like a turtle. Mean, sloping shoulders and spindly legs. A sneaky son of a bitch.

When Anna burst out, Simon's mouth dried and he nearly lost his balance. Since their first encounter at the horse show they had seen each other nightly for three weeks, but she had worn only slacks or jodhpurs. Now she was wearing a long blue silk dress, cut low in front and flaring out around her ankles. It revealed every curve of her body and her taut breasts were half exposed. Piet could not tear his eyes away. Simon gritted his teeth and hung on. But what a weed he was. He dismissed Piet with a laugh.

They walked solemnly into the dining-room. André van Achtenburgh filled the wine glasses. Then he took a Bible from the sideboard and went to the head of the table.

'We'll have a short reading from the book,' he said, opening it.

'Children, obey your parents in the Lord: for this is right. Honour thy father and mother (which is the first commandment with promise); That it may be well with thee ...'

A familiar passage; it brought back memories of his father who had read the Bible nightly as they sat around the rough wooden table. His mother had strained to mend their clothes by candlelight, while his father's voice droned on and on.

André van Achtenburgh gazed around briefly. He knew the book by heart, no need to follow the words. He glanced uneasily at Anna. She was his only child and now she was gazing out of the window with an expression of rapt wonder. Her sudden transition from girl to woman frightened and upset him. He had grown used to girlish laughter, braided hair and prim school tunics. This dress was a disaster. Maria's fault, for here she was trying to hawk the girl to their richest friends as if she were a Christmas goose. He would have something to say to her later. Right now Maria was dreaming. The frailty of women. They could never listen to the holy words, always thinking of dresses and shopping. Except his Anna. She was different. More like a boy really. As for that milksop, Piet, over his dead body ...

Maria van Achtenburgh was considering the waywardness of her daughter who had been cold to the point of rudeness to their guests. God knows she had tried hard enough with her, but sometimes Anna made her so uneasy. She had watched her daughter ripen early under the hot African sun, reaching puberty when barely eleven, with budding breasts and a pragmatic attitude towards sex which farm children acquire early. For years she had waited for her wilful tomboy to mature and become more feminine, and when this had not occurred she had eventually enrolled her in the most exclusive school in the Cape. Now school was over and Anna seemed content to help her father run the farm, school the horses and teach piano in the village. Yet lately she had changed. Always dreaming. Look at the silly child now, gazing out of the window at the moon.

17

She watched her daughter dispassionately. Her features were fine and regular, much as her own had been at her age, but there was a difference, a certain sensuousness; you could see it in her eyes, her full lips and the smooth high line of her cheeks. The sooner she was married the better.

She glanced sidelong at Louise who nodded back.

Louise was already regarding Anna with an acquisitive eye. She was well aware of the reason for the dinner and, in fact, she heartily approved of the match which the two women were conniving, although neither of them had voiced their intentions. Anna was a headstrong, wilful girl, as everyone knew, but there were no other children on either side and together the two estates would be worth a fortune.

The guests were getting restless, Simon noted. Her Pa was going to read on all night. He was thinking of something else, that was clear. How mean he had been at the horse show, giving him short shrift when he tried to take Anna for a hamburger. Between the two of them they had won all the trophies. Yet looking at her Pa now he couldn't dislike him. A good man to go whaling with, he decided. Tough and reliable.

Pa stopped at last. The maid tripped in with lobster salad, glasses were refilled, the conversation rose and fell.

When he saw the food, Simon remembered how hungry he was. There had been so little time. Little enough for sleeping, let alone eating. Each morning he had been on the lands, cultivating the soil well before dawn in order to steal the hours to visit Anna. Then driving back through the night and starting all over again four hours later. He could not remember when he had last eaten, but Anna was eating enough for two.

The plates were removed, the glasses refilled and in came the tray again, this time loaded with a small wild boar, roasted whole, an apple in its mouth. Simon nearly fell off his perch.

'My word, this is a treat,' Joubert called out. 'I haven't tasted wild boar for over a decade. It's the finest meat in the world. I've always said that.'

'Uncle Acker shot it for us,' Anna said. 'We get a good deal of game from South-West Africa.'

'My brother is a karakul sheep farmer,' Maria explained. 'He's Anna's favourite uncle. She used to spend her holidays there. There's nothing you can teach her about hunting.'

Anna shot a look of resentment at her mother. She felt overcome with shame. Here was her own mother showing her off as blatantly as Pa and she showed their prize bullocks. She glanced desperately at Pa, who winked.

I've a right to pick my own friends, she thought angrily. Where was Simon now? She had arranged to meet him in the vineyard. Her mother had told her of the dinner party only at lunch. It was a surprise, she had said. A disagreeable surprise! Anna remembered Piet from school although he had been four years ahead of her. He had been head boy in his last year and she had disliked him even then.

Piet decided to breach the awkward silence. 'Come now Anna. You must give me some moral support. I can't persuade your father to plant a few acres of Pinot Noir grapes for dry red wine. He'll be sorry. He thinks there's no market for red wine, but he's wrong.'

Louise eyed her son critically. He seemed to have no sense with women. No wonder he had no girlfriends. 'Come Piet, what would a beautiful young woman like Anna know about wine?'

'Why Anna knows as much as her father,' Maria threw in.

Louise ignored her. 'Tell Anna about the swimming pool we're constructing.'

'Yes, mother,' Piet said automatically. He coughed self-consciously. 'Actually it's kidney-shaped and fifty metres ...'

'Do you like swimming, Anna?' Louise broke in.

'Anna won a cup for diving at school,' Maria replied.

Anna stared stonily out of the window and to her horror saw Simon's eyes staring at her. He was laughing. A disembodied face amongst the oak leaves.

She flushed, jumped and knocked her wine headlong. The red stain spread over Ma's best lace tablecloth.

'Never mind, dear,' Maria said, eyes glittering as she tipped the salt cellar on to the stain.

19

The remains of the boar were removed and a milk tart took its place, Willem Joubert's favourite. He eyed it greedily. Louise recited excerpts from Piet's thesis between large mouthfuls. They all drank too much wine and Piet's face became swollen and ugly. Suddenly Anna felt his hand on her thigh. She kicked him sharply and looked up to see Simon's agonized green eyes. She smiled wickedly.

'We're having a tennis day on Saturday,' Louise said, watching her shrewdly. 'Do you play?'

'Why yes, I'd love to come,' she said, surprising everyone. She put one hand on Piet's shoulder. 'Do you play, Piet? Splendid.'

After dinner, when they were sitting on the patio with coffee, the conversation was still revolving around Piet's academic successes. Simon was having difficulty keeping awake. The maid tripped in and out refilling cups. She had knocked off more of the sherry, Simon could see from the way she walked.

They were leaving at last and taking long enough about it. The parents went inside, too obviously, leaving Piet with Anna for a few minutes.

'Don't mind Mother,' he said. 'She's all right really. My word, you've improved.' He placed his hands on her shoulders. 'In fact, you're beautiful.' He drew forward to kiss her and jumped as an acorn hit his cheek.

'Autumn hazard,' he said, laughing puzzledly.

Another sharp hit on the head.

'It's a baboon,' Anna told him. 'A renegade. Haunts the place. I expect it's up in the tree.'

Piet looked up in alarm.

'A baboon is a dangerous animal,' he said seriously.

'Oh yes,' she said. 'Pa intends to shoot it on sight.'

'Enough!' Simon exploded when Anna ran into the vineyard soon afterwards. 'Enough of this nonsense. I'm sick of hanging around here. If you think I'm not good enough for you, Anna, then to hell with you. We'll break off now before it's too late.'

'How can you say such a thing?' she retorted. 'Last night

you said you loved me. Fine sort of love to talk of breaking up the very next day.'

'There are limits to my endurance,' he said sulkily. 'If you love me then you must tell your parents about us.'

'Isn't it fun like this? Our own secret.'

'Not for me. I'm tired and hungry.' He scowled at her. 'Besides it doesn't feel right. Either you tell them and I call on you like a civilized person, or it's over between us.'

How old-fashioned he could be at times. But how could she tell her parents? Pa had been furious at the horse show. At the same time she could not face the prospect of losing Simon.

She shivered and pressed closer against him.

Simon tilted her chin and pressed his mouth against her soft, smooth cheek moving his lips softly over her face until they reached hers; swiftly he thrust his tongue into her mouth.

Anna could not resist the onslaught of Simon's masculinity and the brutality she sensed in the man. He was exciting, compelling and terrifying at the same time and she adored him.

'How about riding on Saturday?' he said, hugging her closer.

'But the tennis party ... ' she murmured.

'Forget it! Saturday or never.'

'Not riding,' she said, trying to regain the initiative. 'We'll go for a drive. You may call for me at two.'

Simon was still angry. He kissed her briefly and left.

Anna sat on the steps in front of her bedroom long after he left. She was aching with loneliness and the need to be with Simon.

The Berg wind was blowing up again, a restless, whining wind that banished sleep. The farm workers were still singing; bullfrogs were croaking in the river.

Not a night to be alone.

Anna was filled with a strange new restlessness. She could not bear to go indoors. 'Simon, oh Simon,' she whispered. Was he yearning for her as she longed for him?

3

Simon was worried. His clapped-out van would not make a good impression on Sunday. He had set his heart on the second-hand bakkie which the co-op were selling for old van Niekerk, but they would not accept a penny less than fifty pounds and he could not imagine how to raise the money.

He had plenty of time to think about it on the five-hour journey to Saldanha Bay.

The route led through the Stellenbosch vineyards towards the Cape, passing fields of fruit and vegetables and the fine dairy herds of Durbanville.

Five miles from Cape Town he turned north towards Malmesbury, a rich wheat and dairy area and, as usual, viewed the fertile farms on either side with longing.

Lambing season. White fleeces gleamed in the moonlight. Planting would start soon and by July the young sprouts would be thick and lush, each stem packed close to the next, a dense, waving sea of green which made Simon sick with envy. The farmhouses stood a mile or two apart from each other, stark and white in the moonlight. Content and affluent, they watched haughtily as Simon's old truck rattled past.

On the outskirts of Malmesbury the road veered left towards Saldanha Bay. Sandy soil and scrawny sheep. The farmhouses were meaner; five miles or more between neighbours. Simon concentrated on the road ahead, looking neither to left nor right as he imagined himself master of Fontainebleu. The dream was absorbing; he passed the lagoon and whaling station without noticing the smell. At last he reached Modderfontein, where five generations of Smits had wrested a living from the soil and the sea.

Simon stopped the van, opened the gate and frowned.

If rain did not come soon he would have to put the sheep into the lucerne and that would be a disaster. He drove to the crest of the first hill and, struck by the poverty-stricken nature of his farm, cursed quietly.

Between the sea and cultivated land were hills of bush and stones, home of lynxes and troops of baboons. Tonight the baboons were barking wildly in the wind.

Simon wondered if he could trap enough to pay for his van. He usually sold them to a Cape Town laboratory for five pounds each, but they were crafty and he never found more than one in the same trap. He had only caught five in the past year.

At last he reached the homestead. Parking his van in the shed, he checked the dairy. It reeked of sour milk. He would kick Jan's arse in the morning. The cows had been milked and were grazing round the dam, so without bothering further he went into the house and, kicking off his boots, flung himself headlong on the bed.

Saturday began as it always began with the cocks crowing at dawn and the lowing of the cows impatient to be milked, but to Anna every sound had a special significance. It was as if the roots of her existence were inextricably linked with these homely sounds. The fleeting premonition that she would awake one morning and not hear them kept her shivering in bed.

The familiar clatter of Flora's heavy feet and coffee cups rattling helped to calm her rising fears.

The morning hung around twice as long as usual. Eventually Anna went to prune the roses; a task she had been putting off for days.

'I don't know why you insist on doing this.' Maria frowned at her daughter's hands when at last she found her in the garden.

'Because I do it properly,' Anna retorted, 'and Jacob doesn't.'

23

'What time is Piet calling?'

'Ma, I'm not going to the Jouberts' tennis party. I'm going out.' She spoke sullenly.

Maria stared suspiciously at her daughter: 'I don't know why you have to be so mysterious about everything, unless you're feeling ashamed of yourself.'

Anna flushed and glared at her mother. 'I know dozens of men I like more than Piet.'

'And this one is ...?'

'Simon Smit,' she blurted. 'I must get ready.' She hurried to the house feeling ashamed of being such a coward while Maria went to find André.

An hour later Simon raced into the courtyard in his brand-new van, scattering the chickens and Maria's pet peacock.

André was pacing his study, wondering how to deal with the boy. He could not understand his daughter; she had the pick of the neighbourhood. At the same time he admitted that he knew little about the Smit boy and perhaps he was not as bad as he had imagined. When he saw Wagter wagging his tail, André's lips compressed in anger. So Simon had been there before. When? he wondered. Not in daylight hours or he would have seen him and for the first time André, too, felt a twinge of unease. He strolled into the courtyard wondering whether to shake hands, and then thought better of it.

'Ah, young Smit, isn't it?' he began.

'We've met before, sir, at the horse show.'

'I'm rather surprised to see you, I'll be honest about it. Well, since you're here, perhaps you'd like some cider while you wait for Anna. She's always late, you know. Come into my study, my boy.'

It took only a few minutes to discover that Simon was even more unsuitable than he had feared. The boy was little more than a poor white.

His parents had died leaving him penniless except for a barren farm which, it seemed, was good for a few sheep, but little else. The boy seemed to be living on his wits, whaling four months a year to keep the farm from the bailiffs. He hardly knew how to tell him of the absurdity of calling on his daughter. Finally he decided to shirk the task and speak to Anna when she returned.

By this time Simon had priced every item in the study, and even imagined himself directing the farm from this room. When Anna appeared, looking radiant in blue silk slacks with a matching blouse and a white straw bag flung over her shoulder, Simon beamed happily. Her father watched with misgiving. Anna was so young and inexperienced. She would be a target for every fortune-hunter in the Cape.

He summoned Flora to call Maria.

'Well, this is a pretty kettle of fish,' he told her. 'I can't help thinking that she's doing this to get her own back. After all, you were rather obvious about Piet, weren't you, eh?'

Maria was furious.

'Since you've decided to blame me for this fiasco, you may as well know she's been seeing Simon in the village every day since she met him at the horse show.

André scowled and stared out of the window.

'Did she tell you this?' he said at last.

'I have my sources of information.'

'Ah well,' André sat down looking gloomy. 'I suppose I'll have to see Smit when he comes back. He won't come here twice – I'll see to that.'

The van skidded along the gravel while its two occupants sat awkward and tongue-tied, each engrossed with their own problems.

Simon was fuming because Anna had not complimented him on his new van, but even Simon had to enjoy himself on such a perfect afternoon and eventually he forgot about the sheep he had sold for the down payment and began to relax.

Simon had decided that they would picnic on the banks of the Hex River amongst the mountains. It was a spot he knew well, situated on a friend's farm and he had brought a Thermos of strong black coffee and some fruit.

It was a lazy, somnolent afternoon, hot, yet not unpleasantly so. They sat on the sandy beach by the river and listened to the water splashing over mossy rocks, the drone of insects and the call of the piet-my-vrou bird from a nearby tree.

They had little to say to each other. When Simon reached out and put his arm around her she felt happy beyond anything she could remember. She sat breathless, watching a dragonfly swoop over the water.

'This is the happiest afternoon of my life,' Anna said eventually. She smiled at him and he felt entranced by her and pulled her roughly towards him, crushing her against his chest. They sat still for a long time, obsessed with the nearness of each other. It became hotter and the ice-cold mountain water gurgled invitingly.

'Let's ... ' they both began.

'Could you swim with your eyes closed?' she murmured.

'Naturally. I always swim with my eyes closed.' He closed them tightly and took off his shirt and trousers. When he kicked off his pants and stood naked, Anna gasped.

How huge he was; how handsome! His muscular chest was tanned to a deep brown, but his buttocks and thighs were pure white. Anna was consumed with curiosity. She had never seen a man naked.

Simon opened his eyes and laughed lazily. 'Cheating are you?' he said. 'I'm going to swim. You please yourself.'

Anna went behind a rock and thought about it. 'Shall I?' she asked herself wistfully. She peeped over the rock to where Simon was splashing in crystal water. 'No,' she said firmly, but for some strange reason she was removing her clothes piece by piece. Nakedness; a strange yet familiar feeling; the breeze caressed her skin; the sun soaked in; the elements seemed to be in collusion to arouse her. She felt old – as old as womankind. Here was her man, she had chosen him. That was all.

Simon was lying on his back in shallow water. Anna bent over him and kissed him.

He sighed and pushed her away. 'Don't. Please don't do that or I'll lose control.'

His voice was so hoarse she could not recognize it.

Simon sat up and considered her. He felt both aroused and

26

alarmed; physical need was drowning his mind. Once he had let passion take over. He forced himself to remember Sophie crying at the water's edge. Guilt diminished his passion.

He had not enjoyed the remorse and disgust that had followed the act. Besides, Sophie had not enjoyed it either. Obviously women did not like sex. Anna must love him; he hung on to that thought and gritted his teeth.

White teeth, green eyes and the murmur of water falling on stones. Anna would never forget the afternoon as long as she lived. She lay smiling trustingly, for this was home. It was as if she had been always married to Simon and merely parted by some accident of birth.

The afternoon flashed past while they lay in each other's arms. They hardly noticed the sun sink behind the mountains. Suddenly it was dark, but they could not bear to leave.

The silence that enveloped them on the long drive home was pregnant with unspoken questions and answers.

It was late and Anna's thoughts turned uneasily to her parents. She sighed. Simon wound his arm around her, pulling her closely against him.

'What's the matter?'

'Oh, it's just – I don't know.' It would take more than an afternoon to explain how her parents viewed Simon and his world. Why could they only see as far as his red van and his terrible haircut?

They returned at midnight to find her father pacing the courtyard. Simon parked with squealing brakes and a shower of dust. Glancing sideways, Anna noticed that Simon's neck and chin had turned mottled red and there was a twitch at the side of his cheek.

'Anna, go to your room,' her father barked.

Simon walked around the van, opened the door and helped her down. 'Thank you for a lovely day,' he said slowly. 'I'll see you tomorrow.'

She could not believe that her father would speak to her in this tone. Indignation overcame embarrassment. 'Good heavens, Father, you'd think I'd been missing for a week. Why are you snapping at me?'

She would have argued further but Simon took her by the arm and whispered: 'Don't worry, I'll sort this out. I'll phone you in the morning.'

Anna paused for a moment, undecided, then went to bed.

'I wish to speak to you, young man.' André walked stiffly to his study and sat at his desk. He looked up to see Simon standing in the centre of the room, huge and implacable.

'Sit down, sit down,' he snapped at Simon. 'You're wasting your time with my daughter. She's only nineteen. It's another fourteen months before she comes of age and I'll take care she never marries you. It's easy to see she's taken with you, although for the life of me I can't see why.'

Simon pulled up a chair without answering. For a while the two men sat in silence. André gave in first. 'I'd like your word that you will not see my daughter again.'

'No, sir,' Simon said. 'I love Anna and she loves me.'

André's blue eyes became colder and meaner looking as he sized up his adversary. He leaned back and laughed curtly. 'I'm sure you would like to marry Anna. Who wouldn't? She will inherit most of my fortune. Let me tell you, young man,' he went on angrily, 'I've been doing some checking on you this afternoon. You have little more than sand dunes and half-starved sheep. Anna on the other hand is one of the most eligible young women in the district and by far the most beautiful. She can look forward to a brilliant marriage and a carefree future, which is what I have always intended for her.'

Simon leaned back, feeling relaxed. Anna would marry whoever she pleased. He was not going to worry about threats from an enraged father, who was behaving like the baboons he caught in his traps. Give him time and he'll tire himself out, he thought as he stood up. 'I'll go,' he said turning towards the door, but he felt a hand on his arm, and turning looked down into the anguished blue eyes of his adversary.

André's voice was hoarse with frustration: 'I'll tell you this, Simon. If you should succeed in marrying Anna I will cut her out of my will. Don't think I'll give in because I've never been crossed by any man without getting my own back. I'll see you

28

in hell before you get a penny of mine. You think you've won, don't you? I can see it in your face. Well, believe me, you've lost, because the two of you won't last five minutes on your tuppeny-ha'penny sand dunes.' Grimly he went back to his desk and picked up the paper.

Simon, who was a good judge of character, knew André meant what he said and he arrived home feeling disturbed.

When Anna came for breakfast the following morning there was no sign of Pa. Her mother always slept late and her father was in the stable tending a sick horse, Flora told her.

Eventually Anna went to find him.

'Want some help?'

André nodded without answering and for a while the two of them rubbed linament into Ponty's stiff hind legs.

'Pa, I want to talk about last night,' Anna began with difficulty. 'You've never shouted at me before; behaving as if you were ... I mean as if I was ... ' She sat back and thought about it. 'Behaving as if we aren't friends,' she went on eventually. 'I'm not a child and it's not as if I haven't been out till midnight before. Why only ...'

'Anna, Anna, give over,' he said. 'Things are different now. You're growing up. The more's the pity. If I had my way things would stay as they've been.' He sighed. 'You're a young woman now, Anna. An heiress. You've got responsibilities. You can't go out with any Tom, Dick or Harry, just because you like the look of them.'

He smiled sadly at her. 'You've always been a bright girl, but maybe we sheltered you too much,' he said as he packed the medicines into an old wooden box. 'What's more you're turning into a very beautiful woman, but I don't think you're mature enough to handle it yet.

'When you were a kid we never cared who you played with from school – rich or poor – they were all welcome here, but now it's got to change. I know you won't like it, so before you go making a fool of yourself in the neighbourhood I want to send you away. How would you like to go to that highfalutin school you and your mother have been on about?' He tried to muster a smile. He would miss her.

She stood moodily kicking her foot against the wall.

'It's the top Swiss finishing school and I've heard the music education is superb. Not that I know much about that, but your mother's been inquiring.

'Well, how about it?' André glanced at his daughter and sighed. He knew that expression; bottom lip gripped by her teeth, eyes narrowed as she searched for the means to get her own way.

'I won't stop seeing Simon,' she began.

'You've no choice,' he said. 'I'm sorry, Anna, but that's the way it is.'

Anna scowled at him. 'Of course I've a choice. I'll do what I like.'

'Listen Anna. Without my money Simon won't want to marry you.' He grimaced. 'It's the money he's after, I'll bet my last penny on that.'

'It's not the money,' she retorted hotly. 'Simon has a farm.'

Her father snorted.

'You've been checking on him.'

'Of course I have. He wouldn't ask you to marry him if he thought for one minute he'd have to support you.'

'That's a beastly thing to say,' Anna said, her temper rising. 'Particularly since he isn't here to speak for himself.'

'We'll see,' he said infuriatingly. Standing up, the two eyed each other warily. 'I'm warning you, like I warned him, Anna, and you know me for a man of my word. If you marry Simon you'll not get a penny from me, so let's see what he does.'

How could Pa be so blind, she wondered? She was sure she would see Simon that afternoon.

But Simon did not come. For days she wasted hours in the café where they usually met. Big shadows appeared under her eyes and she walked around listlessly, filling the house with gloom until even Wagter moped around with drooping head, his tail drawn into his haunches.

Anna was badly shaken. It was her first love affair and she had loved passionately. Now she felt worthless. Unlovable!

30

By the end of the third week Anna's parents were beginning to worry about her.

'She'll get over it,' André told Maria daily.

It was autumn. For Anna the days passed slowly; the wind was colder than ever; life took on a bleaker aspect. Pa's offer of the Swiss school became more inviting. One morning she searched for her father and found him by the river supervising the construction of a new bridge.

'Hi, you're just in time to give me a hand,' he called when Anna walked moodily along the river bank. For an hour the two worked together as they had done often in the past, for Anna had been brought up like a boy. She knew how to construct a shed, build a farm road, supervise the wine-making and anything else a farmer would need to know. When they were walking back to the house she said:

'Pa, I'll take you up on that offer of Switzerland.'

André was glad she had come to her senses.

That night Anna could not sleep. How could she have allowed herself to be so humiliated by this oaf, just because his green eyes glinted when he laughed and his red hair burned in the sun? As she pictured him, tears stung her eyes. She stood up, wrapped a rug round her shoulders and stared out of the window. Blowing up for a storm, she thought.

Wagter was curled in his kennel outside the door, his tail beat the patio lethargically when he saw her. Anna was about to draw the curtains when Wagter shot out of his kennel, teeth bared, the hair on his back standing erect.

She opened the door. 'What is it, Wagter?' she called, but the dog wagged his tail and raced off. Then her heart began to beat wildly and a moment later she saw Simon standing there, smiling up at her.

The grinning oaf. Did he think nothing had changed?

She flung back the door, raced into the vineyard and slapped Simon's face with a crack. 'Cruel, cruel ... ' she spluttered. 'Detestable!'

Simon caught her wrists and pushed her away.

'I hate you,' she sobbed. 'You made a fool of me, pretending

31

that you loved me and then leaving when you found out ... '
She broke off, unable to say the ugly words.

'Don't you want to know where I've been?' He was teasing
her again.

'No,' she said firmly.

'I wanted to buy you a ring,' he said quietly, 'but I had to go
fishing to earn the cash to pay for it. I've just got back. Here,
have it if you want it, it's no use to me.' He tossed the box on
the patio and strode through the vineyard with Wagter
whining at his heels.

Anna found the ring and fled to her room, slamming the
door behind her. For a moment she was so confused she could
hardly think, but overwhelmingly she was relieved. All this
misery for nothing. After a while she sat on the bed, opened
the box and stared at the ring. An amethyst set in silver.
Tasteless, but she loved it anyway.

A few minutes later she heard tapping. Simon crept into the
room. He put a finger to his mouth.

'Shh,' he whispered. Tiptoeing across the room he switched
off the light and locked the door.

She heard his footsteps approaching then he sat on the bed
beside her. 'Can I stay and talk to you?'

'You don't have to whisper,' she said aloud. 'Everyone's in
bed. Their rooms are down the end of the passage.' She tried
to quell the feeling of excitement surging through her body.
'You don't have to put the light out either, there's no one in
the vineyard at this time of night.'

'I wouldn't like to take a chance,' Simon said quietly. He
put his arm around her shoulder and pulled her close.

'Go away,' she said miserably.

'I've missed you, Anna. At sea I had plenty of time to think
about us. Your father's dead set against me. We'll have to wait
until you come of age, but you're worth waiting for.'

'Well, I'm not sure you're worth waiting for,' she said.
'Anyway,' she sighed, 'I've agreed to go to Switzerland for a
year.'

He tried to conceal his anger. After a year overseas Anna
would forget him. The thought was chilling.

'You don't love me,' he said churlishly.

'Oh, I do love you,' Anna cried out. 'You know I do, but that doesn't change anything.'

He bent down swiftly, caught her shoulders and, pushing her back, kissed her savagely, pushing his tongue hard into her mouth and holding her face with his hand.

There was a streak of lightning, followed by thunder.

'Listen, it's starting to rain,' he whispered. 'Thank God for that.'

'You must go,' she said urgently.

He stared down at her, listening to the rain which was fast becoming a deluge.

'Can't I wait until the storm passes?'

She nodded, feeling guilty, but not really wanting him to go.

'So this is our last night,' he murmured. His hand fumbled under her nightdress and found her breast and began to fondle her nipple.

'No, stop.' She caught his hand, tried to push it away, then pushed it back on her stomach.

Bending forward abruptly, he caught her nipple in his mouth and sucked gently, licking the tip with his tongue.

She moaned softly. 'Simon, this is a madness,' she whispered. 'You must go. I swear I'll scream.'

'Scream,' he murmured. His mouth wandered over her skin to her belly, discovering every part of her. Impatiently he fumbled with her nightdress until she lay naked on the quilt. Bending over he whispered, 'You belong to me. Can't you feel it?'

She gasped, shocked at her need. She wound her arms around his neck and pulled herself up to him until she could feel the warmth of his hard body against her.

'Oh Simon, love me, love me,' she murmured.

'Oh Jesus! Sweet Jesus!' Simon gasped. Thrusting her legs apart he pushed into her. Anna recoiled with pain, but seconds later she reacted to his rhythmic thrusts. Forgetting the pain, she abandoned herself to the all-consuming joy of belonging and loving and when, minutes later, she felt him climax inside her she cried out with happiness.

Simon clamped his hand over her mouth and for a few seconds they lay listening as they heard a door open and shut and footsteps approaching down the passage.

'Anna.' It was her mother. She rattled the door handle.

'Anna.'

'Yes, Ma.'

'Are you all right?'

'I had a nightmare,' Anna called. 'The storm. Sorry to wake you. Good night.'

Her mother's footsteps receded. Then her door shut.

'Phew.' Simon let out his breath, sank down next to her and, to her astonishment, fell asleep while Anna began to cry, great, silent sobs that racked her body.

4

The first winter rains fell heavily during the night and when Simon left at five a.m. it was dark and still hammering down. Anna fell asleep and awoke later to find her coffee cold beside the bed and the rain splashing the windows.

Wagter was whining in his kennel, she opened the door to let him in and his muddy paws left marks on the carpet. Flora would be bound to grumble at her. She tiptoed back to bed and was horrified to see the red, telltale stain on her sheets and for a moment she was panic-stricken, but then she realized that she could wait until her mother went shopping and change the sheets. The knowledge that she was forced into deceit filled her with misgivings and she sat on the end of the bed feeling dejected.

Her sense of guilt was soon forgotten and for Anna life returned to its former reassuring routine of shopping, farming, tennis parties and outings with friends. Anna was farm-bred enough to know that with rains so late this year Simon would have to finish planting the wheat in record time or risk a late harvest. Because she no longer felt rejected she began to look better, her cheeks regained their former glow and filled out and the shadows disappeared from under her eyes.

Maria and André congratulated each other on overcoming the crisis with the minimum of discomfort.

For Anna, this period away from Simon was a relief; she had been flung into an emotional relationship for which she was not prepared and as the days passed the memory of their night together became unreal, until she almost forgot about it. Consequently, no one was more surprised than Anna when, at a tennis party three weeks later, she fainted and had to be carried to the chemist around the corner where he revived her with smelling salts and a glass of cold water.

A week later she woke up feeling sick, but blamed it on the crayfish mayonnaise which they had eaten for supper, but when her nausea continued every morning for the next few days she began to remember stories she had heard which terrified her. Rather than approach her mother she planned to visit their family doctor, but took fright in the waiting room and returned home without seeing him.

The following morning she made an appointment with a doctor in Paarl which she felt was far enough away to protect her secret, if indeed she had a secret. She borrowed her mother's car and drove five miles to Paarl feeling sick with embarrassment.

Anna was grateful that the doctor was old and fatherly-looking, and after a brief examination he told her she was pregnant. She returned home in a state of dread, unable to face the future, and walked around the garden for hours wondering what to do. Towards evening she telephoned Simon, but there was no reply and soon afterwards her mother arrived and her father returned from the stables, so she was unable to try again.

The next morning after a sleepless night she crept along the passage to her father's study and, shutting the door behind her, dialled Simon's number. The telephone seemed to ring for hours until at last she heard his voice, but then she felt strangely reassured.

'Simon, something's happened and I must see you. It's very important,' she said.

'What is it?'

'No, I can't explain, you must come, Simon.'

'Man, I've got one more patch to plough. Can't it wait another day?' He sounded exasperated.

Anna felt a twinge of unease. For the first time she came to terms with her dependence upon him and felt frightened.

'It's urgent,' she said hoarsely.

Silence! Then he said: 'It can't be as urgent as the

ploughing. I'll be over as soon as I've finished. See you.'

As she heard the telephone replaced, panic engulfed her. Anna's upbringing had been cloistered and she had never had to fall back on her own reserves or test the quality of her strength. Now that she could not rely on her parents she felt unable to cope. She forced herself to go back to her room and plan her future, but when she thought about it her alternatives appeared pitifully few. She decided to tell her parents and wondered how to set about it. Finally she did nothing, but wandered around the house and as she had expected Simon did not come.

The following morning at breakfast Maria casually suggested that they invite the Jouberts over for tennis and a barbecue on the following Sunday, but Anna said timidly: 'Mother, I think it's time you gave up. I'm going to marry Simon.' Then she leaned back and waited for the explosion.

Her mother gasped and clutched her napkin to her face, while her father turned white. His eyes looked very mean and very hard.

'You'll not be marrying Simon,' he said quietly. 'I've a mind to go down to the Magistrate's Court and get an order restraining him from seeing you. If you won't listen to common sense you'll learn by force, my girl.'

'If you won't give your permission I shall apply to the courts,' she said evenly, amazed that her voice could sound so calm when she was filled with dread.

'Ah ha, courts now, is it?' He towered over her and shook his fist in her face. 'And what about your promise to go to Switzerland?'

'André, leave Anna alone,' she heard her mother gasp.

André thrust his hands into his pockets and stared out of the window. 'You can't say I wasn't fair to you, Anna. I told you to wait a while.' Adding: 'I'm not an unreasonable man.'

She wanted to call out: 'Father, I'm pregnant, for God's sake help me,' but the words stuck in her throat and for something to do she picked up her spoon and took a mouthful of porridge, but had difficulty swallowing it.

When her father turned back to her, he appeared to be in a

more conciliatory mood as he said: 'Anna, be reasonable. The courts would never give you permission to marry. You're only nineteen, Simon hasn't a penny and he can't support you. I don't like the boy and I flatly refuse to keep him for the rest of my life.' He broke off and thought about it and then burst out: 'No, not under any circumstances.'

Anna sighed and put down her spoon. 'Father, I'm sorry to have to tell you this,' she said, and in spite of her resolve her mouth was dry and her hands were shaking. 'I have to marry Simon.'

She was not prepared for the outburst that her words provoked. While Maria wailed, André in a fit of fury slapped her face with all his force, bellowed like an enraged bull and stamped out of the room with Maria behind him, leaving Anna with her cheek stinging, wondering if she had a black eye to add to her problems.

Shortly afterwards she heard her parents arguing in the study. It was the first time she remembered them fighting and her mother's voice was screeching in a manner that she had not considered possible, while her father was yelling back. Then she heard her mother erupt into a flood of hysterical tears, but still she sat staring at the table. It all seemed unreal, a bad dream that she was forced to endure.

After a while the telephone rang and Flora came hurrying into the room. She picked up the receiver and then she said: 'It's for you, Miss Anna.'

It was Simon and at the sound of his voice her heart went soaring like a lark released from a cage. 'I've finished the ploughing,' he told her. 'Now we can pray for more rain. I'll see you tomorrow probably.'

'Simon, you must come,' she gasped. 'I'm pregnant and Pa's in a fury.'

'I'll be over,' he said briefly.

Her parents' fight went on for most of that morning. Anna felt miserable and guilty and wandered off to the rose garden where she sat beside the fountain pretending to read a book, and that was where her mother eventually found her. Maria looked dreadful with a blotchy face and swollen eyes. Anna was surprised. She had always seemed so remote.

'André's right,' she began. 'I'm to blame. I never told you ... never warned you ... What do you know about men? All they want to do is get you into bed. What a fool you are.' She gave a long sniff and buried her face in her hands.

'I've never talked to you about sex,' she flinched as she said the word. 'I've never been able to bring myself to. Putting up with their ... their nasty ways. It's not something one wants to talk about. But my God, you don't do it for nothing. You get a wedding ring first, a settlement, money, jewellery ... Even then ... ' She broke off and began to cry again.

'You've disgraced us all and if the servants heard it will be all over the neighbourhood. Ah well! You and I will go for a holiday. Arrange an abortion. Afterwards we'll tell your father you fell downstairs and had a miscarriage.'

'What does Father say?' Anna asked.

Maria sighed. 'He insists that you go to Johannesburg and stay with Aunt Cassie. Put the child up for adoption. He's quite inflexible once he makes up his mind. Either that, he says, or marry Simon, in which case he'll disinherit you.'

Anna shook her head, unwilling to face any of the alternatives. Feeling strangely sorry and embarrassed for her mother, she went to her room to wait for Simon.

Simon did not come that day or the next, although the family hung around the house, each pretending to be absorbed in their duties. Maria embarked on a gigantic spring-cleaning project with the maids running around in circles flapping feather dusters, brooms and brushes and taking down the curtains, while Jacob was summoned to clean the windows. André decided to do his accounts, which was a task he reserved for impossibly tedious days. Anna passed the time roaming around the farm with Wagter. Over the past few days she had realized how much she loved her home.

In many ways she was more like a man than a woman with her love of the soil and her pride of ownership, which she felt as a deep, emotional need. She had always considered the farm to be half hers and her father's threat to disinherit her was a blow which she felt keenly, although she was loath to admit this.

The farm stretched for well over two thousand morgen of the most fertile land in the district. The van Achtenburghs were known for their Palomino grapes, which made the finest white wine in the district; their export quality Hanepoot grapes could not be bettered; their stables were renowned for the prize Arab mares which they bred and their Jersey cows took the trophies at the cattle show every year. It was Anna's greatest joy to help her father lead the cattle around the arena. Besides the vineyards, they had two thousand morgen of wheat in Malmesbury which was managed by a foreman, and even their pigs were sold as breeding stock to local farmers.

The van Achtenburghs' land stretched to the hill slopes where glades of oaks had stood for over a hundred years and three rivers ran amongst wild proteas, and on that day Anna walked through the oaks and up the hill and wandered for hours, feeling downcast at the prospect of losing her home.

Anna was not a religious girl. Although she had inherited the Presbyterian religion from her parents, she accepted it as she did the laws of the land and the social conventions with which she had been reared, as something necessary, but external to her real self. Her conviction of the rightness and wrongness of things sprang from deep within and it was from there that she learned about life itself. She needed no rules to tell her that it was wrong to have an abortion or to have her child adopted.

Anna returned to the farm at sunset, feeling hurt and frightened because Simon had not come and that night she lay awake until dawn. Consequently, she was still in bed next morning when Simon arrived at eight. She heard his van skid to a halt in front of the house and Wagter's barks change to yelps of welcome when he recognized Simon. Then she heard her father's voice, which sounded curt and unusually high-pitched, as he ordered Simon to the study.

Not long afterwards there was a knock at her door and Flora called out: 'The baas says for you to come to his study now.' Then she giggled.

They all knew her problem, Anna thought miserably. She

40

looked in the mirror to comb her hair, noticing that her face looked too white, there were shadows under her eyes, while her hair hung lustreless. Miserably, she went to the study where Simon was standing pale-faced and tight-lipped in the corner, glowering at her father. His face did not change as she walked into the study. He merely flicked an impatient glance at her and looked away again.

Anna's chin went out defiantly and she pursed her lips together, looking very much like her father at that moment.

Simon sat on the straight-backed chair looking ridiculous. He was dressed in his khaki farm trousers which were torn at the knee, and his khaki shirt, a relic from army days, which was too tight over his bulging chest and had several buttons missing. His hands were huge and suntanned as they rested on his knees. Yet in spite of his rough clothes and his huge strength his face was almost perfect, Anna decided, like a statue of a Greek god topped by a mass of red curls.

'Well, sir,' her father demanded angrily. 'What have you got to say for yourself?'

There was a long silence while Simon hunched his shoulders and thrust his hands deep into his pockets as he leaned forward. Then he said: 'Sir, the last time I saw you I asked permission to marry Anna and you were extremely rude. Since then I have become resigned to your decision.'

Anna gasped and said, 'But, Simon …'

Simon interrupted sharply. 'Anna, why don't you leave your father and I to discuss this because there's very little you can do about it.'

Anna forced herself to sit still, up to her ears in humiliation.

'The situation has changed, Simon, and you're the reason for it. I don't know when or how you found the opportunity to make Anna pregnant, but I'll see you pay for it, sir. You took advantage of a young and innocent girl.'

The twitch in Simon's cheek was very much in evidence as he struggled to control his temper. 'Let's get one thing straight. You can't force me to marry Anna and I assure you I didn't rape her.'

Anna gasped and reddened.

41

André was white with rage. 'You'll marry my daughter without further delay and you won't get a penny for it. She's made her choice, she's disobeyed me, brought disgrace on the family name,' he shot a scathing glance at Anna, 'and now she'll take the consequences.'

'And what about her dowry then?' Simon stared mulishly at his feet, refusing to meet Anna's eyes.

'There'll be no dowry,' her father retorted. 'If she had waited like a decent woman it would have been different. The two of you behaved no better than pigs rutting by the river.'

'Pa!' Anna's anguished voice cut in on the conversation, but the two men appeared to be quite oblivious to her as they squared up like fighting cocks.

'A girl in her position always has a dowry,' Simon said obstinately.

André looked meaningfully at Maria as if to say: I told you what sort of fellow he was and now you can see for yourself.

'Not a penny,' he repeated obstinately.

Anna could not control a sob that hiccupped out. 'Stop it, stop it, the pair of you. We don't want a penny of your money, Pa.'

'I told you to keep out of it,' Simon said coarsely. He scowled and strode angrily out of the study and the family watched in consternation as he drove off with screeching tyres in a cloud of dust. For a long time they stared out of the window and then her father said heavily: 'Well, good riddance to bad rubbish. That's the last we'll see of him.

'Anna,' he went on, looking obstinately in the other direction, 'you can say goodbye to a marriage in these parts. By now the word'll be all over the district, but since your taste seems to run to hoodlums I don't suppose that will be worrying you much.'

'As for you, Maria,' he scowled at her mother, 'I hold you responsible for this unfortunate affair. You had nothing else to do but look after your daughter but it seems that it's too much trouble, so you can take the consequences and go with Anna to Johannesburg.'

He strode out of the room, frowning angrily, and Anna bit

her lip. She had never known her father to be so set against her.

'I'm sorry, Mama,' she said, 'but I'll be going to marry Simon.' And with that she ran to her bedroom, where she locked the door and leaned against it, just wishing for peace. Soon afterwards her mother was knocking on her door and reluctantly Anna let her in. For an hour Maria tried to persuade her daughter to give up her plan, but Anna was determined. In spite of the way Simon had behaved she felt that she loved him. Besides, she could not face the prospect of abortion or adoption and she knew that life with her family would be unbearable now.

'Well, if you're determined on this mad plan of yours I'll do what I can with your father.' Wiping her eyes Maria hurried off, and for the rest of the morning Anna heard them shouting in the study.

Eventually she heard her father's footsteps stamping angrily along the passage with her mother hurrying behind murmuring: 'No, André, please, André,' and a second later her door was thrown open and her father stood towering in the doorway. He looked haggard and old, Anna thought. His eyes looked small and bloodshot and although he was obviously suffering Anna felt that she hated him. He refused to look at her and fixed his eyes on the window behind as he said:

'If you leave this house to go to that man I'm finished with you. You'll never set foot here again and I'll never have your name spoken in this family. I've forbidden your mother to visit you, so don't try to wheedle your way round her when you find yourself in trouble. Your mother has persuaded me to give you some money,' he went on, 'and I'm giving it to you, not because I owe it to you but because you're going to need it.' He put an envelope on the dressing table and walked out.

Her mother sat on the bed looking dazed.

Anna was blinking back tears of rage. She picked up the envelope and tossed it into her mother's lap. 'You can give Pa this,' she said. 'I don't need it. He thinks he owns everyone. You can tell him from me that I won't be wheedling round the family for anything.' She made a great effort to control herself,

43

but her mother turned on her angrily.

'You must be the stupidest daughter any mother had,' she said bitterly. 'It's only two hundred pounds. I'd give more, but André controls every last penny, I don't even have my own bank account. A good deal of the money's mine, you know, but I can't get hold of it. Pa's invested it all.'

Maria hurried from the room feeling that her heart was bursting with sorrow and then she thought: there must be so many things which I could pack for her, and frantically she began to pull out the spare sheets and towels and the more she found for Anna to take the better she felt. Then she remembered the furniture in Anna's room which assuredly belonged to the girl, and by noon she needed the lorry to pack everything.

When the lorry was filled to overflowing, Maria sent Jacob hurrying to the fields to collect labourers to unload the lorry and start packing again to make extra room. In the middle of it André came stamping out in a temper and asked her what she thought she was doing and for once in her life she stood up to him.

'I'll take no more bullying from you, André,' she said sternly. 'I'll give Anna exactly what I wish and don't you try to interfere,' she said with a loud sniff.

André stared in amazement and hurried back to his study where he watched surreptitiously, but Maria who was feeling ill hurried back to her bedroom and lay down. Lately she had been feeling so tired and today she was exhausted.

Anna set off at eight the following morning in the small bakkie which had been delivered from the village as a present from her mother. In the back were six hens in a crate, her Siamese cat, Ming, in a cat basket, and Wagter, looking puzzled. Anna had refused to take her horse, for she knew that she would not be able to care for it properly.

'She's better off here,' she said sadly when she went down to say goodbye to Jessop. Her father had made a point of leaving early that morning so that she could not say goodbye to him; only her mother was standing in the courtyard, clutching a handkerchief to her face.

44

'I'll be all right, Mother,' she said. 'I promise you that. Simon and I will work hard and we'll save and soon we'll be able to buy a farm in a better area.'

'You don't know what you're talking about,' Maria said. 'There's no way out of that sort of poverty.'

5

Her mother's words drummed in Anna's ears on the five-hour drive to Saldanha Bay and she could not help feeling apprehensive, but it was a beautiful autumn morning and after a while her mood lightened.

Four hours later she reached the outskirts of Malmesbury. In the distance she could see the hills of Riebeek Kasteel, but she turned towards Langebaan and from then on the soil became less fertile. Soon she was skirting low hills of black scrub and beyond them the road curved north-west and she could smell the sea. The road became rougher, the van skidded and bumped over deep ruts. Occasionally she glanced over her shoulder for the reassuring sight of Jacob and the lorry, her last link with home.

It was noon when she reached the small village of Saldanha Bay and parked in front of the only store in the only street.

Gideon Olivier's Farm Store, the sign read. Anna glanced inside anxiously, while Wagter leaped out of the van and watched the local population with mistrust. Ming awoke and set up a cacophonous wailing.

The farm could not possibly be near here, Anna decided, for the village stood in the midst of windswept, sandy lands which stretched as far as the eye could see where nothing better than weeds or scrub would ever grow. Although she could not see the lagoon nor the whaling station from where she stood, she could certainly smell it, and she found the bitter-sweet smell nauseating.

She hurried into the store and asked the way to Modderfontein.

'So you'd be the young lady that's coming from Stellenbosch to marry Simon then?' Olivier said. 'Ah, there's nothing secret here once you start talking on the telephone.

'It's a party line, you see, and folks here got nothing better to do but listen to the calls.' Noting Anna's distress he said more kindly: 'Right now you've missed him. Gone out after a whale. They saw the whale blowing up westerly yesterday and Simon got the mad idea to go after it in a pilchard boat, which was all that was available, the rest being out, you see.'

The voice droned on recounting the story while Anna stood stunned with disappointment.

'How long do you think he'll be?' she asked.

Olivier shrugged. 'Depends. Likely they'll come back without it, but if he spears it he'll have a bit of cash in his pocket. Maybe a week, who knows? You take my advice, dear. Go back to your parents.'

'Will you show me the way to Modderfontein?' she asked, biting her lip with temper.

'That's easy, you just keep going. Follow your nose as far as the road goes and when it comes to an end you'll see the gate.'

It became increasingly difficult to drive as the road fell into disrepair. The land was dry in spite of the rain and dust rose from the track until Anna was nearly choked.

Eventually the road became impassable, but as she braked she saw a gate set into a wire fence. The sign next to it had been freshly painted and read: *Modderfontein* and underneath *Simon Smit*.

Anna climbed out, stretched and coughed, trying to clear her lungs. There was nothing to see but hills and valleys of scrub with no sign of life except, just beyond the gate, a pile of sheep dung with a few flies buzzing angrily over it. Well, at least he had one sheep, she thought sadly, for it was every bit as bad as her father had promised. She scrambled to the top of a nearby hill and from there could see for miles. Only a small portion of Simon's land was cultivated, about five hundred morgen, she estimated, while the rest was covered in bush scrub. It was poor soil and as she thought of Simon stubbornly planting his wheat year after year she felt that she could forgive him for viewing Fontainebleu with a covetous eye. There were about five hundred sheep in sight and pitifully few lambs. With a sinking feeling in the pit of her stomach she climbed down the hill.

6

The farm road was a nightmare and Anna wondered if she had taken a disused track, for the further she went the more desolate the place looked. If the farm lay this way then it was at least ten miles from its nearest neighbour. There were no trees and, apart from the occasional sheep, no sign of life and she began to despair of ever finding the house. Eventually, two miles from the gate, she manoeuvred a dangerous curve, crested a hill and nearly crashed into three ugly pigsties made of flattened paraffin tins haphazardly nailed together. She braked and approached slowly, alarmed by the frantic squealing, thinking that such hideous structures would never have been permitted at Fontainebleu. When she peered over the wall she was charged by an enraged sow guarding her litter and in the next sty there was another, covered in scabs. They had no water or feed and there were three dead piglets from a total of fifteen.

She stepped back feeling shocked and angry. There was no sign of a tap or feedstuff, but in the valley she could see a cluster of roofs, and when she walked to the edge of the hill she saw a small farmhouse facing a courtyard, ringed with outhouses. On the left was a corrugated iron shed and beyond the kraal a dam.

Anna returned to her van and set off on the long drive to the valley and when she reached the courtyard did her best to imitate Simon's screeching brakes, but there were no chickens to flap out of her way, no maids came scurrying towards her, not even a dog barked – the farm was deserted. Anna climbed out of the van, slammed the door and stood uncertainly until

Jacob arrived and parked the lorry behind her. His face was glistening wet in the sun as he wiped the sweat off his forehead with the back of his sleeve.

'That was a bad road, Ma'am,' he said and she hid a smile at his staid understatement. There was a lowing from the kraal that sounded ominous.

'The cows are in pain and the place seems deserted, I wonder ...' she broke off, trying to conceal her dismay.

In the kraal the farm's neglect was even more apparent. There were ten cows, udders full to bursting, heads hanging dejectedly, and presumably they had stood there since the previous evening.

'He should be shot,' she blurted out and then regretted her hasty words which Jacob was sure to repeat. 'He's gone whaling, you see,' she explained. 'Someone must be in charge. How could he?' she murmured to herself as she quickly turned a bucket upside down and took the nearest udders in her hands. The milk spurted out and the cow let out a contented grunt.

'First things first, Jacob. Take a bucket and carry water up to the pigs.'

'But, Ma'am ...'

'I know it's a long way, Jacob, but I don't think there's a tap up there.'

Jacob went off sullenly.

'There must be someone here,' Anna said aloud. 'He can't just go off and leave the place, the cows would be stolen. I'm sure Simon wouldn't do that.'

When the cows were milked she led them down to the dam and left them to graze. There was a sudden commotion in the shed. She could hear Wagter snarling and muffled shouts. She arrived breathless to find a drunk man sprawled on bales of feedstuff trying to fend off Wagter.

'Heel,' Anna called and investigated the stinking figure. 'Who are you?'

'Jan,' he grunted.

She bent over him and gagged – the eternal stench of farm workers, sour wine, tobacco, woodsmoke and filth.

49

Anna was glad to hear Jacob running to the shed.

'You work here?' she asked, hoping that he did not.

'Foreman.' He grinned evilly and his only tooth, which was brown and pitted, jutted from the middle of his top jaw. His face was yellow and wrinkled and she guessed he was mainly of Hottentot blood, one of the few remaining inheritors of an almost extinct race.

'Farm foreman – that's a joke,' she said incredulously. 'Chuck him in the dam, Jacob, that will sober him.'

The protesting drunk was propelled down the hillside to the dam where he landed with a splash and at first seemed content to lie and drown, but eventually he came out spluttering and covered in mud and flew at Jacob in a frenzy. Jacob picked him up as easily as a dog with a hare and flung him back again, and the third time Jan came out submissive and fairly sober and ambled off to his hut, which stood on the far side of the dam.

Anna returned to the van and sat in the driver's seat trying to pluck up courage to enter the house. The wind was getting up, the door squeaking as it swung in the breeze. Presumably there was nothing worth stealing in the house or Simon would have locked it. When she saw Jacob coming down the hill she walked inside.

After the glare of sunlight on whitewashed walls Anna could not see, but when her eyes adjusted to the gloom she found she was standing in a hovel. Except for an old stove, the room was empty, walls blackened by smoke, the rough cement floor pitted with cracks and craters like an eroded riverbed. The ceiling was of heavy timbers, low enough to touch, the walls a foot thick, made of mud and stones and pitted with thousands of ant holes. Lying in one corner was a blackened saucepan and a primus. There were no shelves or cupboards and worst of all – no tap.

It was a very old cottage, she decided. Half the kitchen had once been a bread oven, for the huge chimney covered half the ceiling and was roughly blocked with corrugated iron sheets. No doubt the timber had been salvaged from a shipwreck well over a hundred years ago, she thought nervously. After a while she plucked up courage to explore the rest of the cottage. There were two bedrooms and a living room plus a small room leading from the kitchen which once must have been a pantry.

In one room stood an iron bedstead with a mattress and a blanket. A nail driven into the wall held a coathanger with one suit. In the second bedroom two rough-dried shirts hung from another nail beside a telephone. There was no toilet or bathroom, no electricity, not even a tap outside and with so many broken windows, the house was icy cold.

When Anna heard Jacob knocking she tried to pull herself together.

'I'll unload the lorry now, Ma'am.' His voice was disdainful. 'I must be getting back.'

The thought of being left alone in this nightmare shack filled her with despair. But it was her home now, she reminded herself. Hers and Simon's and she would have to make it bearable. The first thing she would build was a toilet, she decided, and went outside to search for taps and water.

Eventually she found a pump operated by a windmill behind the eucalyptus grove a hundred yards from the house. Apart from the fresh water tank in the centre of the courtyard fed by gutters from the surrounding roofs, there was no other water supply.

By nightfall Jacob and Jan had carried her possessions into the cottage and the spare bedroom was packed high with crates. Even the bedroom looked more like home, with her bed, wardrobe and dressing table perched precariously on the uneven floor. Her mother had packed some garden furniture which Anna set out in the lounge.

She was tired and hungry. 'I suppose you'll be going now,' she said awkwardly to Jacob. 'Would you show me how to light this primus stove?'

It was not difficult, but messy; then Jacob found a lantern and a hammer in the dairy. He hung the lantern from a hook in the ceiling.

'You'd best have my matches,' he added awkwardly, taking them out of his pocket. 'The chickens are up in the loft, so don't forget to let them out in the morning, your cat is in the house.' He was anxious to be gone.

'Yes, thank you, Jacob.' She sat on a crate in the corner listening to the lorry drive away. She was cold and too miserable to move, but eventually she made an effort and said to herself: 'Well, this won't do,' and picking up the lantern she hurried nervously from room to room, wishing she had curtains to cover the windows and the means to warm the house.

The wind was getting up, belching icy drafts through broken windows. The lamps flickered, the candles blew out and Anna began to talk to herself for company.

'The thing to do,' she said, 'is to get the kitchen in order and after that the rest will be easy.'

Sensing her distress, Wagter crawled under the bed and lay whining, while Anna opened the crates.

It was past ten when she heard a commotion from the loft; the hens were clucking and beating their wings; heavy footsteps sounded overhead. Wagter sprang to the door growling while Anna cowered in the corner of the kitchen, but when she heard one of her precious hens having its neck wrung, anger replaced fear.

She raced out of the cottage to the stone steps leading to the loft and arrived breathless at the top, just as Jan crept out holding the dead fowl in his hands.

'You thief,' she sobbed as she grabbed the chicken. She gave him a blow with the hammer and he hurtled down the stone steps to the ground.

Anna sat on the steps and burst into tears. Jan was the only human being within ten miles and she had killed him. She was freezing, but afraid to go down.

After a while Jan sat up, rubbed the back of his head and grinned evilly.

'Missus, I'm hungry,' he whined. 'Don't be afraid. It was just old Jan trying to get something to eat.'

'I'm not afraid of you,' she retorted. 'Wagter, see him off!' The dog sank his teeth into Jan's leg and Jan howled, and set off at a trot with Wagter snapping behind.

Clearly she was not safe from that thieving rascal, Anna

decided, and spent the next few minutes pushing several heavy trunks against the door.

Anna nearly cried with joy when she found the packing case filled with provisions. There were dog biscuits and a tin of fish for Ming, but her cat had vanished.

Towards midnight the Sou'Easter reached gale force, blasting the cottage with sea spray. Anna could hear the roar of the breakers and tried not to think of Simon miles out in this storm, chasing a whale in a pilchard boat. Madness! Her paraffin lamp flickered; the flame dwindled and died. Empty!

Anna burst into tears of frustration. Kicking off her shoes she wrapped herself in a blanket, longing for morning.

Strange sounds and the fearful loneliness of it all banished sleep. She heard ewes calling their young and soon she could identify the different cries. One lamb had no answering call and she wondered if it was lost or perhaps the ewe had died.

She too, was utterly lost and abandoned.

Much later she fell into a restless state of half-sleeping, half-waking and, turning, saw a face at the window staring at her. A second later Jan was gone and she was left shivering and even more determined to repair the windows and buy locks for the doors first thing in the morning.

Old Jan, who had woken in the night with a burning throat and a head full of cement, tiptoed around the house peering in every window to see if the young Missus had any wine. The house was filled with countless useless objects but no wine that he could see, and after a while he ambled to the borehole and plunged his head into the pool. The water glittered and when he looked up the wheat stubble shone like rods of silver in the moonlight, blinding his eyes and dazzling his mind with the incredible beauty of it.

'Poor old Jan,' he muttered to himself. 'No food, nothing to drink.' He remembered the half-smoked reefer in his pocket and pulling it out, cupped his hands around the cigarette to protect the flame as he puffed greedily. Soon he began to feel the craving for wine and tension drain out of him as his blood coursed through his body, warm, reassuring, bringing a sense of well-being. He felt his skin come alive and his toes and fingernails began to sprout as if bursting into leaves. Suddenly he remembered old tunes from his youth and started to dance as he sang to himself, his lean buttocks jerking in time to the rhythm.

The noise disturbed an owl. With a piercing shriek it abandoned its prey and soared past into the night sky. Jan overbalanced with shock and sat on the ground, swearing and shaking his fist at the owl, omen of death. Abruptly he sat down and puffed nervously at his cigarette until it disintegrated, then he leaned against a tree trunk, eyes closed, a gentle smile on his face as he listened to the music made by water tinkling into the borehole and the sound of wind in the leaves. Lastly he thought of the beautiful young Missus, who reminded him so much of the mother whom he had never seen but whom he knew had been beautiful. As he pictured her huge blue eyes and her pure skin he felt no anger for the blow she had dealt him. After all, she had a right to look after her hens and at that moment he felt that he would cheerfully die for her as he fell into a deep, contented sleep.

Anna was awakened before dawn by the sound of knocking in the next room. She leapt out of bed in terror and fumbled for matches as Wagter came snarling. As the flame flared she saw green eyes shining and her cat, looking ferocious, holding a rat. Anna screamed and dropped the match. Wagter darted forward and the cat fled into the spare room. She slammed the door and stood shaking with terror and relief. Ming was safe. What's more, he had caught his supper. She padded back to bed in the dark, stubbing her foot against the boxes, and rolled herself in the blanket, but sleep evaded her as she listened to the cry of the lost lamb, which was more feeble now. She longed to rescue the lamb, as if by doing so in some strange way she could rescue herself. Eventually she thought, nothing could be worse than lying in the dark imagining the worst. I shall get up and find the lamb. And having made the decision she felt better.

It was far less frightening outside than inside and her fears evaporated.

Eventually, from a hilltop, in the first soft light of dawn, she saw blurred white shapes scattered over the land. She could hear her lamb clearly now, but when she walked towards the flock they began to shift away as if drifting in the early morning mists, calling their lambs, jostling and pushing. The faster she went the greater distance the sheep kept between her and them. A hopeless quest. She sat on a rock under a bush and waited for light. Then, in spite of her discomfort, she must have dozed because she awoke suddenly to find the sky had lightened in the east and the fields looked incredibly beautiful, with the mist drifting in the valleys and the hilltops bathed in a rosy glow. She wondered what had wakened her and then realized that it was the stillness. The sheep were still and huddled together, staring over their shoulders in the same direction. She saw her lamb clearly now. It was scarcely three days old and easily identifiable by a large yellow stain which covered the back of its rump. It was ill and tottering badly as it dashed from ewe to ewe trying to suckle, but each time was rewarded with a kick. Only the lamb seemed oblivious to the danger that was stalking in the bushes on the other side of the flock, for now Anna could see a lynx, ears flattened, tail pointing as it crouched on its belly and moved forward in short, sharp bursts of speed.

Her first thought was one of dismay and fear, she was too late to save the lamb. Then she leapt to her feet with a roar of rage, stumbled with stiffness, and rushed headlong down the hill shouting and waving her arms. The flock were wary of her but terrified of the lynx and they moved and jostled, unable to decide which way to go, while the lynx kept moving closer to the lamb. Anna stooped, picked up a stone and flung it at the cat, missed, but not by much and the animal stood still, snarling angrily at her, unable to choose between fear and hunger. She picked up another stone, hurled it and this time managed to get it on the rump. Spitting and snarling, the cat began to back away. Now she could see its yellow flecked eyes filled with spite and its pointed ears. It was a glossy creature, well fed and strong; no doubt gorged on Modderfontein's lambs.

The lynx turned and sped up the hill and an instant later

was out of sight amongst the bushes. Anna lunged forward and grasped the lamb by its back leg, hauled it to her and tucked it under her arm. The lamb let out a pitiful bleat and then gave up the struggle and nestled close to her for warmth, sucking her finger enthusiastically, no longer afraid.

When she arrived at the homestead she was surprised to find Jan hard at work looking none the worse for his fall. He had milked the cows, separated the milk, and Anna took a jug of skim milk for the lamb, but soon became weary of dipping her fingers into it for him to suck. What she needed was a bottle with a teat and she decided to drive to the village and buy one. Even the horrid black walls, the broken windows, the uneven floors and the filth of the farmhouse that depressed her so much could all be rectified, she thought, and Simon would be pleased if the cottage were transformed into a livable, clean home. She would just have to delve into the money Pa had given her, but when she sat down to make her shopping list she became alarmed at the quantity of goods she needed.

Anna could not help longing for home. She missed her parents badly, but comforted herself with the prospect of the coming baby and the return of Simon, whom she loved in spite of his strange behaviour. She could not begin to understand him. Why did he work so hard on the farm, yet live in squalor?

There was no point in dwelling on her problem, instead she threw herself into the task of transforming the cottage and building a toilet and, as an afterthought, added new pigsties to the list of urgent jobs.

The next two weeks were filled with activity. The walls were cleaned and painted; the loft was cleared of cobwebs; the kitchen floor recemented; ceiling timbers varnished. Floors and ceilings sloped towards the valley, while the distance from floor to ceiling differed by as much as a foot, but with rugs and curtains the cottage was miraculously transformed and when she had finished Anna felt proud of her antique home.

With Jan's help she planted and fenced a field for vegetables, but Jan presented a problem which troubled her daily. He had been born at Modderfontein and probably his parents before him. There was no telling how long Jan's family had lived there, eeking an existence from the sea and the land. He had never learned anything, never been to school, nor could he drive the tractor. He was irresponsible and fit for only the most menial tasks. Besides, he had been reared on the dop system. For breakfast, lunch and supper he received a large mug of strong sweet wine which kept him in a permanent state of semi-intoxication. He exchanged his labour for the right to live on the land and keep a few fowls sleeping in a hovel which stank as badly as he did. Anna guessed he was paid a pittance, plus a sack of mealie-meal and the offal when a sheep was slaughtered. His days were spent passing the time between one mug of wine and the next. To Anna's mind it was a demeaning system for both employers and employees. She intended to change it.

Yet in spite of his diminutive size and evil appearance he was a good worker, but he stank so it was unbearable to be near him. Eventually she plucked up courage and said, 'Jan, if I bought you new shirts and pants, would you wash?'

Jan looked up grinning evilly. 'Missus?' His face wrinkled as he strove for comprehension.

'Jan, you smell,' she said. 'You must wash.'

He laughed in surprise, wondering why anyone would care whether he washed or not, but she persisted with her promise of new clothes and the necessity for him to be clean.

White people were full of nonsense, he thought, grumbling to himself, but the thought that she spoke to him and promised new clothes was disturbing. Then he grinned again. 'Yes, Missus,' he said.

The next time Anna went to the village she bought Jan some khaki trousers and shirts and seeing a notice in Olivier's window of a poultry sale nearby, she went to the auction and acquired eight turkeys, six geese and a dozen laying hens quite cheaply.

The days passed in a flurry of activity, but when night fell the same terrors came surging back: Where was Simon? Would he ever return? What if he had drowned at sea? Perhaps he would not marry her now she was penniless? Who would want her anyway? Certainly not her parents, for her mother had not telephoned. She was alone and destitute, miles from the nearest neighbour. Then she would hear strange noises outside, crackling branches, scuffling leaves from the eucalyptus grove, the barking of baboons would sound unnaturally loud and it seemed to Anna that she was alone and unwanted in the final outpost of civilization.

Worst of all were fears for the future, for she had to admit Pa had been right. This land would yield little and the five hundred morgen of wheat Simon had planted was sparse and weak. Jobs were few and far between for ruined farmers. She had spent half of the money Pa had given her and she was determined to keep the last hundred pounds for the baby. With her candle blown out for economy's sake, she would huddle in bed and pray for morning.

When work is the only refuge from anxiety, an enormous amount is quickly accomplished. In no time Anna had finished all the tasks which she had planned and she turned her attention to the farm. One morning she sent Jan to saddle Vixen and set off to explore.

It was a depressing ride, for besides the poor quality of the wheat she found fifty carcasses of lambs killed by lynxes. Anna decided to round up the sheep and pen the pregnant and milking ewes in the lucerne camp.

On the morning of 30 July at ten a.m. the wind changed and began to blow from the north-west, a sure sign of rain, and instead of the fresh tang of the sea came the stench from the fish factory. Anna became violently sick and afterwards she thought: They're butchering a whale. She caught her breath as she realized Simon was back, and stood flushed and snared with indecision. Then she cried out with excitement and raced back to the house, wondering if she could bathe and change before Simon arrived.

Soon she was sitting in the tub on the kitchen floor scrubbing herself, pausing only to wonder at the change in her body, for although she was only three months pregnant her waist had gone and her stomach was thickening while her breasts were large and upright.

Remembering the night she had spent with Simon and

anticipating the reunion, her skin tingled and icy shivers plunged through her stomach. What would he be like? she wondered. 'Simon, oh Simon,' she murmured aloud and suddenly she was filled with longing. She pictured Simon's delight at the transformed cottage and an evening of domestic bliss, but what could she cook? One of her precious hens would have to be slaughtered, she decided.

Wrapping a towel round her, she hurried to the bedroom and stared anxiously in the mirror. She nearly cried with vexation for her face was rough and red, eyelids swollen, while her hair hung lank and shapeless.

She sighed and reached for her best blue dress but when she tried it on it was too small. Had she ever been that slender? In mounting panic she tried all her dresses, but not one fitted. Then she remebered the trunk of old maternity clothes her mother had sent, flung it open and rifled amongst them.

By lunchtime the chicken was simmering on the wood stove and Anna was looking fairly presentable, for she had plaited her hair and wound it round her head, powdered her face and was wearing a pretty flowered smock.

Anna spent the rest of the day hurrying from the bedroom mirror to the kraal, where Jan was building new pigsties, and back to the stove. When the sun set she set about her evening chores, feet leaden with disappointment. She locked up the lamb and the chicken, chased the turkeys into the barn, lit a candle at the table and sat in a deckchair.

Now and then she thought she heard the sound of an approaching van and hurried to the door, only to be disappointed. Eventually she fell asleep and awoke to the sound of rain beating against the windows. It was midnight. She felt cold and stiff. Filled with disappointment she went to bed.

It was dusk when Simon left the fish factory and as he walked to his van he was caught in a squall and thoroughly drenched. He grinned and patted his pocket where the fifty pounds felt bulky and reassuring. Luck was on his side. All he needed was rain and he'd show that damned cynical bank manager that

Modderfontein could raise a good crop of wheat. He longed to go home, but there was Anna to think about. By now she and her hard-headed father would have reconsidered the matter of Anna's dowry and he felt sure that the coming interview would be more in his favour. Anna was probably thickening and worrying where he was and whether or not he was going to marry her. He grinned again. It had been a stroke of luck sighting that whale, for the cash would pay towards his new van while the three weeks spent at sea would vastly increase his bargaining power.

He drove without concentrating as he re-lived the magnificent chase of the sperm whale in a boat no bigger than his prey. They had chased her day and night, through storms and rough seas, for two weeks and it was Simon who had fired the harpoon, mortally wounding her with the first shot. That was the life for him, he decided. He had a damn good mind to sell the farm and invest in whaling – that was where the money lay. But who would want Modderfontein? It was a sobering thought which dampened his enthusiasm and after that he drove more carefully until he reached Fontainebleu.

He parked the van at the far side of the courtyard and crept around the side of the house to Anna's window. He knocked quietly, but there was no reply. Even the kennel was empty. Simon felt puzzled and disappointed. He retraced his footsteps and knocked loudly on the front door. It was some time before Jacob arrived, blinking and rubbing his eyes.

'I want to speak to Anna,' Simon said aggressively to hide his embarrassment.

Jacob looked surly as he showed him into the hall. Simon listened. He heard knocking and the sound of a door opening. Low, muffled voices. Seconds later André hurried along the passage, clasping a shotgun which he was waving dangerously.

'Get out – get out of this house and never come back.' André looked hard and mean, his small blue eyes glinting, his face white with anger.

Simon wondered how such a mean man could have a

daughter like Anna. 'I must speak to her.' His voice sounded hoarse.

The shotgun moved up slightly. Simon stared into the barrel.

'Get out.'

Simon took a step backwards. 'Where is she?'

'Get out.'

Simon strode to the door, slamming it behind him. He wondered what to do next, feeling suddenly soaked and depressed. Until then he had not realized how much he was looking forward to seeing Anna. He decided to wake the servants and find out where she was, but he could get no response when he rapped at their doors. Eventually he gave up and drove home.

At Modderfontein Simon's despair reached lower depths, for he had to climb out of the van five times to open and shut the gates. The rain which he had longed for with all his heart was too hard and too sudden; it fell as if unleashed from a gigantic reservoir overhead, solid sheets of water, beating the land unmercifully, washing away the topsoil, the new, tender shoots of grass, the fertilizer. 'God damn you,' he shouted into the heedless night. He should have contoured the slopes, but there was no money for luxuries. The land was eroding in front of his eyes and his van slithered and skidded over ravines and cracks.

When Simon reached the crest of the hill overlooking the homestead he was shocked to see that the pigsties had vanished and for a foolish moment he imagined that the rain had washed them clean away. He slammed on the brakes and went to investigate, but there was no sign of pigs or pigsties and not even the manure remained. Had Jan abandoned the farm and stolen the pigs? Or perhaps thieves had moved in and helped themselves, but why was the manure gone? He forgot the pigs and his stomach recoiled with a pang as he thought of his cows and for a moment he was too upset to drive. He went careering down the hill, slammed on the brakes and ran into the cowshed.

Thank God the sheds had been freshly cleaned and filled with straw and the cows were munching contentedly. Still it was strange for Jan to do any extra work, particularly when Simon was away. When he reached the farmhouse he found the kitchen door bolted and his anger surged. He was about to kick it down when he noticed curtains at the windows and at the same time heard Wagter whining and the sudden realization that Anna was there stunned him.

'Anna, Anna,' he called hoarsely and, running to the bedroom window, knocked loudly.

A match flared and then he saw the candle glow dimly through the curtains.

Anna was filled with alarm. It must be Jan; something was wrong. Then she remembered Simon and her sad evening and she flung back the curtains. Sure enough it was Simon, but he looked so strange. Gone was the thick halo of bright red curls for now his hair was wet and plastered flat to his skull. For the first time she noticed the brutishness of the man, for his face looked wider, his head flatter, there was a coarseness about him that she had not seen before. He grinned oafishly. She opened the window.

'Oh, Simon,' she said.

The draught blew out the candle and she hastily closed the window and fumbled for the matches while a thousand treacherous thoughts raced through her mind. Who was this man? She hardly knew him! What insane desire had led her to this strange cottage? Reaching for her dressing gown, she hurried to unlock the back door.

Simon stepped inside and shook himself like a dog, spattering Anna who shrieked: 'Oh, how cold,' and then they stared at each other, embarrassed and silent.

'I've just come from Fontainebleu,' Simon said and as she heard the name Anna winced. Fontainebleu was from another era.

'What did Mama say?' she stammered.

'I didn't see her. Your father nearly shot me.' He stepped forward and grasped her shoulders roughly. Some of the old magic was coming back and Anna felt irresistibly drawn to him as she smelt the familiar smell and felt his warm, hard hands holding her closely against him.

'Why did you come here?' Simon asked.

Anna felt confused. Surely he understood? 'Where else could I go?' she began and burst into tears.

Simon pulled her closer and pressed his lips on her forehead. 'Poor Anna, poor darling. Did they turn you out?'

'No,' Anna said carefully. How was she to explain? 'I had to make a choice, you see.'

Simon sighed, peeled off his wet clothes, pausing briefly to examine the kitchen and glance into the lounge as he did so.

'Looks nice,' he said.

Anna felt disappointed, she had expected much more. 'The floors are re-done.'

'Hmm, so I see. Is there any hot water?'

She pointed to the stove. 'And the loft is cleaned.'

'That's nice.'

'Don't you like it?'

'I'll see better in the morning.'

She felt let down. Irritable. 'The place is completely renovated.'

'I can see it cost a packet,' he replied. 'Where did you get the cash?'

'Pa gave me some money.' Why should she feel so guilty, she wondered.

'How much?'

'Two hundred pounds.'

He snorted. 'That won't go far. You've spent most of it?'

She nodded. 'We couldn't live in a pigsty.'

There was a long silence as Simon stood naked, glancing at the ceiling where the beams shone varnished in the candlelight. Then he shrugged and taking the bucket of warm water, flung it into the galvanized tub, splashing the floor. He was so big that he filled the kitchen. His huge shoulders rippled in the lamplight. She felt intimidated and wondered why. He should be grateful, she reminded herself.

'Well, Anna,' he said, hunched in the tub. 'Life is tough here. I hope you knew what you were doing. There's no money, just wheat and sheep, so you can start praying for rain.'

63

'You should have thought of that when you asked me to marry you,' she replied tartly and went to bed sulkily.

Miserably she listened to sounds in the kitchen. Simon was helping himself to cold chicken and cutting bread. Eventually she heard his footsteps along the passage.

'Man, that was great,' he said as he walked in carrying the candle. He leaned over Anna who was pretending to be asleep.

'There's no need to be angry. I was only telling the truth. It's a tough life you have ahead of you, but my Ma survived so I guess you will.'

He bent down and stroked her cheek softly and when Anna looked up his face had softened and he seemed filled with tenderness.

'Do you love me?' She could not help asking the age-old, inevitable question.

'Of course I do. I've thought of nothing but you since we met.'

Bending down Simon kissed her gently on her neck and her cheeks, moving his lips softly over her smooth skin. Reaching down he began tugging at her nightdress, but Anna hung on to the hem, wrapping it tightly around her knees.

'No, no, I'm shy.' She did not know whether to laugh or burst into tears.

'Too late for shyness,' he said and, clasping her hands behind her back with one hand, he pulled the nightdress over her head. Her breasts were larger than he remembered and they glowed pink and white in the candlelight. He began to suck urgently and then his lips moved over the tight skin of her belly.

She sighed. Well, she was his now, for better or worse, and he was hers and he had cost her dearly. She reached up and grasped him hungrily and pulled him down, kissing his neck and his chin and his shoulder as he made love gently and tenderly.

'I love you,' she said afterwards. 'I shall always love you. You wanted me to come, you wanted the baby didn't you? We'll be happy, won't we?'

She waited for his reassuring reply, but there were no words to calm her fears for Simon was already asleep.

7

Anna woke late next morning to find the light glowing brightly through the curtains. She snuggled under the blankets, pushing herself closely against Simon's back for he radiated heat like a wood stove, but he stirred restlessly and murmured:

'Is it morning? Go and make coffee,' adding as an afterthought: 'love, will you?' and his large arm came over and patted her on the rump.

This was the big division that wealth made, she thought. The rich could afford to put their women on pedestals while the poor turned their wives into servants. She scrambled out of bed, put on her dressing gown and went into the kitchen.

She was late, her new acquisitions were setting up a commotion and Wagter was whining to go out. She ran into the yard and let the fowls, the geese and the turkeys out of their pens and Hansi, the pet lamb, came bleating behind her.

When Simon looked out of the window he saw a stout, red-faced girl, wrapped in an old tweed dressing gown, tripping across the cobblestones followed by the lamb, turkeys, geese and chickens and last of all, the dog. He swore quietly to himself and tried to quell his mounting irritation. How was it possible that he could win the best-looking bird in the Cape from the richest family what's more, and return three weeks later to find that she had turned into a dowdy, homespun and rather inefficient version of the local farm wives that he could have chosen from any of the neighbours, and with a bit of land to go with her? He pulled on his boots and stumbled into the courtyard, rubbing his eyes sleepily.

'Have you never kept turkeys?' he asked curtly.

'No, why?' She looked up laughing and was surprised to see so hard an expression.

'Because any damn fool knows you don't shut up turkeys,' he said. 'They're wild birds: they roost in the trees and roam over the land gleaning insects and they nest in secret. I bet you've even put nesting boxes in their hokkie,' he smiled and stamped over to look. The next moment she heard his cruel laughter pealing out. When he returned he was still grinning and Anna was white-faced and furious.

'So how do you get their eggs?' she asked.

'Man, that's the big problem,' he said slowly. 'Most of the women hereabouts keep a little girl to run behind them and spy on them. Didn't your mother keep turkeys?'

'No,' Anna said looking upset. 'She didn't have to.'

'My Ma used to have a little girl she found abandoned who spent her days following the turkeys and collecting the eggs.' He stopped short as he remembered Sophie when he had last seen her. Then he strode back to the house.

Anna following him, trying to quell her mounting anger. 'I may not know how to rear turkeys, but I certainly know how to look after sheep a damn sight better than you do. I found at least fifty lambs dead over the land and rescued this one within seconds of it getting killed by a lynx.'

'It would be better off dead than shitting all over the courtyard,' he retorted.

Surely they couldn't fight on the very first morning, Anna thought desperately, and she made an effort to control herself. 'I drove the sheep and the lambs into the lucerne camp,' she said calmly. 'I'll let them out when the lambs are stronger.'

Simon turned and stared at her and his eyes looked mean. 'Why don't you mind your own damn business and stick to the house and the chickens like other wives round these parts, instead of poking your nose into men's affairs?'

'Men's affairs!' she flared. 'My God, when I arrived the cows' udders were about to burst and the pigs hadn't been fed for two days and Jan was lying dead drunk in the feed ... ' She broke off and bit her lip.

66

'Let's get one thing straight,' she went on. 'I'm not putting up with the farm being badly managed. I'll run it while you're at sea and when you're at home you can run it yourself – as long as you run it properly,' she added as an afterthought. 'If you don't like the arrangement you can say so now. We'll part before we get married.'

He threw back his head and laughed again. 'You're in no position to dictate terms,' he said. 'Look at you, belly sprouting like an overripe pomegranate. Where would you go?'

'I'd have the baby adopted and start again,' she said icily.

Simon watched her narrowly. It seemed to him that he had underestimated her. She had a lot of her old man in her. Stubborn will and nasty temper to boot, but he could not help admiring her spirit. Well, he'd knock the sharp edges off her one of these days and in the meantime there was always the chance that her father might relent and give her a field or two.

'Do what you like,' he said. 'I've been breaking my neck trying to get the farm to pay. The lucerne was for the cows.'

'Plant some more,' she said softly.

He wondered why he had not done that in the first place.

Anna took a basin of mealies and scattered them over the field behind the yard. When the geese and the turkeys had finished pecking the last grains, the geese waddled to the dam and the turkeys set off in single file to graze over the hills. Then Anna hurried to the kitchen to make breakfast, which was fried eggs from her own chickens, thick slices of home-made bread and thick, salty butter which Jan had made. She put a cloth over the garden table and they sat on garden chairs in the sitting room and Simon could not help noticing that she was well organized. Perhaps a wife would be useful after all, he wondered, apart from the obvious advantages. He reached out suddenly and pulled her towards him.

'Simon, I've work to do,' she protested.

'Listen, it's raining,' he said as he carried her to the bedroom. 'No one works on a farm when it's raining.'

Anna's honeymoon lasted for three days. Apart from tending

the cows Simon had little to do, so hung around the house finding any excuse to catch Anna as she passed and carry her off to bed. How gloomy it was outside, how delicious to pull the blankets over their heads and dive into their own secret world. Curled up in the gloom they would gaze passionately at each other; make plans for the future; whisper promises and murmur of love until desire mounted. Then their single bed would slither and slide in a frenzy over the slippery wooden floor; while icy torrents of rain poured unceasingly over the land, churning the ground to mud, depressing the cattle and sheep who, with heads hanging low, slithered and sloshed through the mire in search of pasture. The deluge sent the turkeys huddling together in the branches of the eucalyptus trees where they hid their heads under their wings and sulked; while Hansi, the pet lamb, cried so piteously at the back door that Anna pulled his box into the pantry. Only the geese were happy frolicking in the dam.

On the fourth day they woke to find the clouds had blown away and the sky was crystal blue. Only the mist lingered in the valleys and hung around the dam. The whole world was sparkling fresh and smelling deliciously of damp earth, fresh grass and wet leaves. The ravenous turkeys set off early and trailed in single file far over the land to the hills where baboons roamed and Anna watched them anxiously until they were out of sight, wondering if they would return unharmed.

The next three weeks were lonely ones. Each morning Simon would wake at five, sleepily dress and take the Thermos and sandwiches from the kitchen. She would hear the door slam and his footsteps cross the yard. Not long afterwards the sound of the tractor echoed in the shed. Then she would see searchlights rake the room and Simon would drive through the courtyard past the borehole, over the hills, to where he was raking the fallow land almost two miles away. She would get up and busy herself with jobs she had created until nightfall when she would cook the supper. Long after dark, two pinpoints of light would slowly return and Anna would check that the tins of hot water were warming on the stove. Half an hour later Simon would come roaring through the courtyard, put the tractor away, check the cows and stumble wearily into the cottage. Then he would crouch in the galvanized iron tub on the kitchen floor and tell her of the soul-destroying, monotonous grind of driving a straight furrow hour after hour, day after day.

At the beginning of August Simon calmly announced that they would be married the following week and he drove to Bellville to obtain the licence from the Magistrate's Court.

Anna could not help remembering what might have been when she stood in the bare room for the simple ceremony which lasted three minutes with two cleaning girls as witnesses. Her mother had always planned a white wedding with a guest list running to a thousand, but it was best not to think about the past, she decided, as she pledged her life to Simon.

We're married and that's that; now we'll feel closer Anna decided on the long drive home, but from then on Simon became cold and distant. Anna could not understand why and she worried about it. Clearly he was disappointed with her and who could blame him? She was so plain now, repulsive even, with no waistline, a red face and chapped skin. She felt sure that the attraction had been her father's fortune and now she was poor he found her a burden. So she went on castigating herself, feeling unloved and unlovable.

Truth was, during the ceremony Simon had awoken with a jolt to his responsibilities, and was consumed with worry both for Anna and the coming child, for what if the rains did not come? It would be September soon – springtime; and there had been only fourteen days of rain, the driest winter he could remember. The rain tanks were only half full, the ground dry, the wheat sparse. What if the harvest were a failure? How could he feed her? Simon felt the frustration of a small child who plucks a flower for its beauty and then pulls it to pieces. When he saw Anna scrubbing floors, or dressed in ill-fitting hand-me-down maternity gowns, or plucking a chicken outside the kitchen door, he could die for shame.

There she sat, Anna van Achtenburgh, pick of the district, who could have had so much, up to her elbows in chicken shit and sneezing from the feathers. But guilt is a very hard feeling to sustain, it scurries away like a hermit crab seeking a shell and takes refuge in anger or callousness. Simon chose anger – with himself, with Anna and, above all, with God who had brought him to this miserable state by His meagre pittance of rain, which, after all cost Him nothing.

A week later Anna experienced her first real rift with Simon. He was late for lunch so she went looking for him and found him behind the cowshed at the back of the kraal castrating the young lambs, and to her horror his mouth was gory. She watched unbelievingly as he picked up the young lambs, bit off their testicles and spat them on the ground. Feeling wooden-legged she ran into the barn and for ten minutes she was unable to stand as she heaved into the straw. When Simon found her she was red-eyed and white-faced, convulsed with cramps and clutching her stomach.

'Don't ever make love to me again,' she sobbed. 'Don't ever touch me ... ' she broke off and hiccuped.

'You don't understand,' Simon said coldly. 'It's quicker and it hurts the least. All the farmers do it that way, it's been done for generations and anyway it's the only way I know. My father taught me and his father taught him.'

'It's obscene,' she stammered. 'You're a bunch of savages.' She ran back to the house and shut herself in the bedroom feeling that the end of the world had come. She was living with a savage, an oaf, a peasant. A man with no more feeling than the baboons in the hills. She cried all that afternoon until she fell asleep, and when she awoke she was late to feed the hens and the turkeys and the lamb was bleating piteously outside her window, so she got up and went about her chores silently.

From then on there was a coolness between them which neither of them could overcome. Anna was intentionally aloof and Simon hated her for it. She reminded him constantly of the way they ran the farm at home and Fontainebleu seemed to figure in every sentence she uttered. Simon began to feel low, ill-mannered and ignorant and he dreaded mealtimes, for then she was sure to comment on the shortfalls in his manners.

'Fontainebleu is best forgotten, put it behind you,' he

growled frequently, but she would not.

Simon longed to put her in her place, assume his rightful male prerogative of being loved, honoured and obeyed in his own home but Anna's superior ways kept him slinking through the house as if he had no right to be there. Worst of all was her silent acceptance of the deprivation she endured.

Her cat, Ming, was not so silent about it, and it seemed like a living reminder of all that Anna had lost. It was so superior and aristocratic with its ice-cold, crystal blue eyes, its pale chocolate fur, its long black whiskers and its arrogant manner, all of which seemed to shriek Fontainebleu and money.

At first Simon tried to woo the cat with pieces of cheese, eggs and even some chicken in desperation, but the cat would have nothing to do with him and when he touched it, it would lunge out spitefully, drawing blood. This was Simon's first failure with an animal and he hated the cat beyond endurance. Each morning Ming would leap on their bed before dawn and yowl for his breakfast, deliberately digging his claws into Simon. When breakfast came it was never to his liking and he would sniff disdainfully, take his place on the kitchen cupboard and glare balefully at Simon as he munched his bread and coffee. His eyes seemed to say: 'That's all right for oafs like you but I'm used to something better.'

One day Anna was ironing in the kitchen when she heard a shot ring out from behind the henhouse and, leaving the iron on the stove, she ran to see what had happened, only to find Ming writhing on the ground, although he was clearly dead with a bullethole through his brain.

She screamed and bent over the poor creature. 'Why, why, why?' she wailed.

Simon pointed angrily to the mangled feathers of the dead hen beside the cat and then stalked back to the farmhouse.

Anna blinked back her tears until the cat lay still and then she gathered the poor creature in her arms and went to bury it.

When Simon returned late that evening there was no supper and no water on the stove for his bath. He showered at the pump and returned blue with cold in a filthy temper.

71

'Where's supper then?' He frowned at the opposite wall, unwilling to look at her.

'You can get it yourself.'

Simon cut himself some thick slices of bread and butter and bolted the food in silence. Then he looked at Anna calmly, as if the anger had gone out of him.

'It's different here, you see, it's not like rich people. Everything works. Cats, dogs, women. We don't carry passengers, not in a poor place like this. Something you've got to get into your head, you're not rich any more.'

Anna went to bed in a temper but realized belatedly that she had forgotten to put a lock on the bedroom door and she was unable to keep Simon out, so she turned her back and pretended to be asleep when he came to bed.

For a while Simon fidgeted and sighed, but eventually he reached out and roughly pulled her on to her back.

She dug her elbows hard into his ribs. To her surprise he clambered over her pushing her legs apart with his knees.

'I don't feel like making love.'

Pinning her arms on to the pillow, he lunged into her.

'No!' She uttered one despairing wail for lost illusions, for trust dishonoured, for something precious irretrievably squandered. The cry of innocence destroyed.

8

In the morning Anna lay shivering in bed too miserable to get up, wondering what Simon was doing, for usually she would hear the tractor or the sound of his voice shouting at Jan. After a while she began to worry about the turkeys and the geese clucking outside so she set about her morning chores, and when she saw Jan she called out: 'Where's the baas?'

Jan grinned revoltingly and said: 'Baas gone fishing, two-three weeks. He said to tell the Missus.'

She felt a sick feeling in the pit of her stomach for while she felt she hated him, fighting was better than loneliness.

The next few days passed in misery as her loneliness increased, for she had none of the hope that had sustained her before. Besides, she was out of provisions and having spent the first hundred pounds Pa had given her she was unwilling to break into the rest. The money stood between her and destitution and for want of a better place she kept it hidden under the flour in the tin.

Two weeks passed while Anna tended her fowls, supervised the farm and went for long walks over the hills with Wagter.

By the end of August it was bitterly cold, but there had been no rain for over a month; the driest winter ever recorded and the farmers around were full of misgivings, recalling previous years of ruined harvests and starving sheep. When she met her neighbours in Olivier's shop or at the co-op they would pour out their woes, which were always the same, debts and more debts because of the drought.

'Where's young Simon, then?' old man Mostert asked Anna one morning when she was collecting pig feed at the co-op.

73

'Fishing,' she replied, trying to look light-hearted about it.

He shook his head. 'A farm won't prosper if the farmer's always chasing fish,' he said ominously. 'He should be raking the fallow land, like the rest of us. It's baked hard, you see.'

When Anna inquired for a tractor driver Mr Mostert agreed to lend her one to help out for a week.

It was on the third day when calamity overtook them. The farm was criss-crossed with deep ravines where, in previous years, the rivers had cut deep into the soil, causing narrow crevices of up to a hundred feet obscured by bushes which grew thickly along the edges. The tractor driver, who was raking too close to the bush, caught the rear wheel of the tractor in the donga and when he found that he was slipping into it he jumped and left the tractor to hurtle into the depths.

The driver ran off and was not seen again and Jan trudged back to tell Anna the bad news. With a sinking heart Anna accompanied him to where the tractor had fallen. It was fifty feet down, wedged hard three feet from the bottom where a few stagnant pools were all that was left of the stream.

Anna drove to the village and engaged the local crane driver to pull out the tractor for twenty pounds, but although he brought a gang of workers and hauled on the tractor with a chain for over a day he could not shift it and eventually he told her, 'No one's ever gonna get that tractor out of there, Ma'am. Eventually it'll rust to bits.'

At the end of August Simon returned, full of good humour with twenty pounds in his pocket, and he seemed to have forgotten their fight three weeks before. Anna met him in the courtyard and told him her news.

Retribution was swift. With a single blow he knocked her headlong to the cobblestones where she bumped her head on the edge of the water tank. For a moment she was too dazed and horrified to move, but when she picked herself up and saw Simon bending over the engine of his van, quite unconcerned as to whether he had hurt her or not, she picked up a brick from the side of the tank and hit him hard on the head.

Simon crumpled and lay prone.

Anna could not believe that she had knocked him out so

easily. She prodded him gently with her toe and then a bit harder. 'Get up,' she said. 'You can't fool me.' But still he lay there without moving and she wondered what to do. Then she decided to do nothing, so she went to the kitchen, shut the door, took a bucket of cold water and began to bathe her face. When she looked in the mirror she saw that her cheek was swollen.

Ten minutes later Simon arrived at the door looking dazed.

'Next time you hit me I'll shoot you,' she said, too angry to be afraid.

Simon went out again without replying and Anna felt she had learned a valuable lesson, for she would stand up for herself in future.

When night came and still Simon had not returned she went to Jan who was cleaning the dairy.

'He's with the tractor, Ma'am,' Jan told her, so she took the lantern and walked over the fields to the donga. In the dark she nearly missed the place, but eventually she saw a light glowing deep down below the bushes and, carefully holding on to the branches, she peered over the edge. Simon was slowly dismantling the wheels of the tractor and as she watched him the hairs on the back of her neck began to tingle for the tractor was precariously placed and Simon was lying beneath it. What if the walls of the donga should give under the stress? Surely Simon would be killed? She repressed a desire to call out to him and trudged back to the cottage.

That night she made mutton and pumpkin stew and left it boiling on the stove, but still Simon did not come and eventually she went to bed. In spite of her fears she fell into a deep, dreamless sleep and only awakened at dawn when she discovered that Simon had not returned. She dressed, fed the lamb and the poultry and set off over the hills with a flask of coffee and a bag of sandwiches.

When she arrived she saw what looked like a pile of junk spread out on a groundsheet at the top of the donga, and Jan scrambling up and down the steep slopes like a monkey bringing out the spare parts as Simon dismantled the tractor. She could not help marvelling at them both for they had

75

worked all night. She leaned over the edge and called out, 'I've brought you some sandwiches and coffee.'

'Thanks,' was the brief reply from beneath the half-dismantled tractor.

'I don't think you're safe there,' she called out, but there was no reply and she felt foolish. 'Well, is there anything else you want?'

Simon looked up and grinned at her and suddenly she felt a wave of warmth in spite of their fights and she smiled down,

'Lunch,' he yelled, 'later, and meantime much more coffee.'

For two days Anna carried food over the hills for Simon and Jan; fed the pigs and milked the cows. Simon returned at midnight and left at four each morning until the tractor was dismantled and carried to the surface. Then he reassembled it in the shed.

'In fact it's better,' he told her, 'because it's been oiled and cleaned and a couple of spare parts that were about to break have been replaced.'

She wondered why he was breaking his back trying to make the farm pay when he had a good living in his hands fixing and repairing farming implements.

For the next two weeks they lived together like strangers, polite and cautious, each attending to his or her own duties.

For his part Simon had developed an uneasy respect for Anna. He had never been close to his mother, never learned to love another person. His passion, such as he could muster, was lavished on his land. Still, he reasoned, Anna was not the soft and helpless parasite he had imagined and with time and patience she might still make a good farmer's wife.

Anna was confused about her feelings for Simon. She was sure that he had never loved her. Attracted by her parents' wealth, he had been infatuated by all that she represented. Nevertheless she watched him face the challenges that would daunt a lesser man. She knew that he would die before he would shirk the back-breaking toil of wresting a living from his barren acres. For that she admired him, although she was sure that he was setting about it the wrong way.

There was little to do while Simon was at home running the

farm and Anna became increasingly depressed. Without music, friends, or her horse, she began to pine for home and her former life and before long she began to feel sick and caught a bad cold.

She fretted because they were running out of the basic provisions she had purchased and one morning she asked Simon over-casually for some money to stock up.

'We're running out of a few essentials,' she said.

'Such as?'

'Oh well, sugar, flour, soap, tea, coffee, face powder ...'

'Face powder!'

She jumped perceptibly at the way he said that.

'Plus the rest.'

'Forget it.'

They looked at each other blankly, as if creatures of different species.

'I must have these things,' she faltered.

'That's tough. I tried to tell you, tried to warn you that life here without a dowry would be difficult.'

'I spent the hundred pounds Pa gave me on the house,' Anna went on, feeling loathsome. She quivered and forced herself to continue. 'I bought wire netting, saucepans, paint, lanterns, food – and then of course I paid twenty pounds to try and get the tractor out, and what with one thing and another ...'

'That's too bad,' he said ungenerously, 'because there's no cash until harvest time.'

'But that's November,' she burst out. 'In fact, December, before you get the cheque. How will we manage?'

'Like everybody else,' he said without feeling in his voice. 'Occasionally I'll kill a sheep, you have eggs, we have milk and butter from the dairy. That's enough.'

'You must give me the money,' she exploded in temper. 'You can sell a pig.'

His fist came crashing on the fragile table. 'Not to keep you in face powder.'

Anna turned away. She felt defeated and no longer able to face the future at Modderfontein. The pains in her back and

77

her stomach were so much worse than before and she had no one to ask whether or not this was normal. She was suddenly aware how sore her throat was, how her ears ached and how wretched she felt.

During the day Anna's temperature rose and by nightfall she felt as if she was on fire, her eyes were swollen and sore, her lips cracked, when she stood up she had to hold on for support. Worst of all there was a sharp pain through her shoulderblades. When Simon came home for lunch she said: 'You must take me to the doctor, Simon, I never felt this ill before. I think I'm getting pneumonia.'

'You're talking nonsense, you've got a bad cold, that's all. It'll pass. Colds always get better whether you see a doctor or not.'

'Well, I should prefer to see a doctor,' she argued stubbornly.

'I've no money to pay for a doctor,' he said apologetically.

'You don't have to pay him now, he'll send an account.'

Simon exploded into a harsh, mirthless laugh. 'People like us don't get accounts, sweetie. You pay first.'

He went out of the kitchen slamming the door and Anna went back to bed feeling very alone. When Simon came back later that afternoon she said weakly: 'Simon, I have enough money to pay for the doctor. I'm only asking you to drive me there.'

He looked at her sullenly and sat on the edge of the bed.

'I'll get you some medicine and if you're not better by morning I'll take you to the doctor,' he said a little more gently. 'Where's the money?'

'I'll get it,' she said miserably and pulling herself to her feet she walked unsteadily to the kitchen, reached into the flour tin, pulled out two pound notes and gave them to Simon. 'Well there you are then,' she said and went back to bed.

Simon was gone for hours and Anna was unable to quell a feeling of unease. She had exactly seventy-eight pounds left, which she was saving for doctors' fees and the necessities for the baby. Eventually she went into the kitchen, and reached into the flour tin. She felt sick as her hand encountered only

78

the bottom and stupidly she fumbled around and even tried the rice and the sugar, but she knew that the money had been under the flour. Clearly Simon had taken it. Tears rolled down her cheeks as she went back to bed and waited for Simon. Night fell and she awoke to the sound of her geese and turkeys flapping outside the door. Pulling a blanket around her she gave them their mealies and called Jan to shut the fowls in the pens for her.

When Simon eventually returned he was met by a white-faced Anna, wrapped in a blanket, waiting in the kitchen.

'You stole my money,' she said the moment he came in.

'Stole?' He looked at her in amazement. 'How can a husband steal from a wife? I am the legal custodian of everything that you own and I decided that our money was best invested in lucerne seed. It's there in the lorry if you want to know. Here's your medicine.'

Obviously he had rehearsed his speech on the way home. He pushed a paper parcel towards her and she took it reluctantly and went to bed.

Next morning she heard the cows bellowing from the other side of the dam. It sounded as if they were in the field where she had planted her previous vegetables and, scrambling out of bed, she peered through the window. Sure enough, the cows were in the vegetable patch and forgetting how ill she was she ran into the courtyard.

'Jan, Jan,' she cried. 'The cows are trampling the seedlings. Go and drive them out.'

Jan watched her sadly. His crinkled, yellow face was twisted into his usual lopsided grin, but his eyes shone with compassion. 'Master did put the cows in the vegetables,' he said. 'Master said there's no water for vegetables.'

Anna felt defeated. When Simon came back she was sitting in bed hunched over her knees, gasping for breath with the blankets pulled round her.

'You put the cows on my vegetables,' she accused him.

'It's not your vegetable patch, it's my farm,' he said as if in a good humour. 'I don't want a vegetable patch there. In fact, I

79

don't want a vegetable patch anywhere because there isn't enough water.'

'That camp cost a lot of money,' she sobbed, 'the seeds and the fence and all the time I took.'

'Then you wasted your money,' he replied. 'I plan things my way and the sooner you get that into your head the better.'

Anna began to shake as great sobs racked her body and made her cough and splutter and the tears rolled out of her swollen eyes until she thought she would burst. Simon sat beside her and put an arm round her shoulder and pulled her close to him.

'Anna, when are you going to settle down to being Mrs Smit, running the house, doing the washing, and keeping a few chickens for your Christmas money? Man, I think your father brought you up as a boy. You don't seem to know how girls should carry on at all. There, there,' he patted her shoulder awkwardly and snuggled down into the bed beside her, kicking his shoes across the floor. 'There, there, there,' he said as her sobs grew louder. 'It's just that you act so odd. Why would you be wanting to plant vegetables? That's my job, isn't it? And the sheep and the cows and the farm, that's all my business too.'

'But you're never here,' she sobbed miserably.

'Hush, don't argue, that's another thing you'll have to learn,' he said softly. 'Wives around these parts don't argue with their husbands. Of course I know it's a big change for you,' he added generously.

Anna clung to him, wrapping her arms around his neck as her sobs gradually quieted. A part of her so desperately needed warmth and love, just anyone who would care whether she was sick or well, but another part of her deep inside was saying: *So this is the price of love, complete capitulation.* 'Yes, yes,' she sobbed, 'Yes, yes, anything.' She sighed. 'Just love me.'

Simon, for his part, felt a surge of desire that he had not experienced for the last two weeks. This sobbing, shaking woman was after all his wife and not as fearsome as he had imagined, and pushing her knees aside he opened his trousers.

Anna, who was sure that she would never in all her life

desire sex again, accepted that this was the price she must pay for love. She would exchange sex for love, find affection only in the furtive fumblings of the bedroom. Simon could express his feelings only through the sexual act and for the rest he would take what he wanted and go his own way.

Anna lay ill with pleurisy for ten days, enduring a feeling of intense self-loathing. Surely she had sunk as low as she could go, little better than a sex slave or a beast of burden; she was a primitive, downtrodden farm wife, a peasant, and so she went on with her endless flagellation.

As she recovered she began to feel that perhaps she was not entirely to blame, for she had been cheated. She had expected love or at least comradeship, but Simon intended to be the boss and run things his own way, she thought, while she was to be reduced to a mere appendage, trotting backwards and forwards in the kitchen while her lord and master ruined their future. It was not good enough, she decided.

On the fifth day of her illness she began to take stock – it was a painful experience. She had made a terrible mistake, admittedly, but was it necessary to pursue her downhill route? For the first time she saw clearly that she was punishing herself with this morbid acceptance of her lowly status. It would end now, she vowed, that morning. Never again would she be trampled on or deprived. Love was ended and so was the need for any other human being, for it led to disaster.

Returning to her parents was unthinkable; she would be despised by the neighbourhood and leaving Simon would merely add to her list of failures.

Money was power, money meant freedom from want, money meant respect. She saw now that the rosy glow that seemed to surround Fontainebleu and her parents was the result of wealth. Wealth was a red carpet perpetually laid at your feet wherever you went. She, too, would be rich, she decided. But how? She knew that she would succeed, but the hows and the wherefores had still to be devised, so she lay in bed for days, thinking, planning, calculating, and one morning she awoke to find her plans completed to the last detail and suddenly she felt better.

9

It was mid-September, springtime, and hopes for rain had faded. A solitary peach tree burst into blossom beyond the kraal and birds began to build their nests in the bushes. Wild geese returned from the north, flying in formation over the farmhouse, uttering their strange, strangled cries and gulls were nesting by the thousand around the lagoon.

It was time to put her plan into action, but still Anna hung around, afraid to take the first step. Instead she went for long walks over the fields and up into the hills where wild flowers were blooming and baboons sat like sentinels on rocks as she passed.

Anna was watching the turkeys set off for the lands when she felt a strange stirring of life inside her. It was a new feeling, rather as if a butterfly had emerged from its cocoon to flutter its wings against her side. For a full four seconds she stood entranced and from then on the growing life inside her womb took on a new importance. Her child! She had felt it move. Suddenly the baby became a physical being, a separate person. She no longer felt lonely and the spur she needed was there.

She called Jan and together they began to pack her useless electrical appliances, her clothes, jewellery, linen, curtains, rugs, garden furniture, in fact all that she owned on to Simon's lorry.

'I'll have to make two trips,' she murmured more to herself than Jan, 'and I'll need help with the furniture.'

Jan looked downcast. When she climbed into the van he said: 'Missus leaving?'

'No, Jan, just starting a new life,' she said doubtfully. 'I'll be back by evening.'

She could not help feeling afraid as she drove to the first prosperous farm she could find on the road between Saldanha Bay and Malmesbury. It was the Mosterts' farm, she read, and they owned an impressive dairy herd. They should be able to afford something, she thought hopefully.

When she drove into the courtyard the maid came running out, followed by Mrs Mostert who was flustered to be caught with her hair in curlers. Clearly visitors were a rare event.

Anna had rehearsed her speech, but somehow she could not help stuttering.

'I don't need these things, you see,' she explained as the crowd around her thickened and she became more embarrassed. She broke off as she heard laughter. By now the whole family had arrived. There were several small boys and two daughters with flaxen hair and bright blue eyes, a crowd of farm workers, an elderly lady, and then the farmer himself arrived and jumped on to the lorry.

'You're trying to sell your possessions?' he asked kindly.

'Not sell,' Anna explained red-faced and sweating. 'I want to swop them for laying hens, day-old chickens, turkeys. I'll take anything useful like that, you see I'm planning to start a poultry farm.'

'But good heavens, you're pregnant,' the woman said horrified. 'You drove yourself all this way in that lorry? Whatever can your husband have been thinking of?'

'If you want to buy anything ... ' Anna said, anxious to get the sale over with so that she could be on her way.

The farmer's wife introduced herself and her brood. Her name was Fanny and her husband's name was Franz. She could not resist burrowing in the chest of clothes and when she held up the beautiful Schiaparelli creation the farm workers gasped.

'Why, I know who you are, you're the van Achtenburgh girl,' she said and suddenly her eyes gleamed.

'Hang on, hang on a minute, Fanny,' her husband growled, sensing Anna's distress. 'Put it back and I'll tell you what we'll do. Is this all you want to sell?' he said, turning to Anna. 'Or is there more?'

'There's more,' she whispered, 'much more, but I couldn't move the furniture.'

'You'll sell it quite easily,' he smiled at her kindly, 'but I'm not going to let you go traipsing round the countryside. You can leave it here with me. Don't you worry,' he said, sensing her dismay, 'it'll be safe enough and I'll send a driver back with you to pick up the rest. Now you be here on Saturday morning at eight sharp and we'll sell everything. How's that?'

Anna could hardly stammer her thanks, only too grateful to be gone from this embarrassing ordeal, but they would not hear of it and she was led into the kitchen for a cup of coffee and some cake. They would not dream of letting her go, they said, until they had heard her plans down to the last detail.

When Simon came back late that night there was a thick stew simmering on the stove, but that was all. No table or chairs, no wardrobe, vases, carpets, chests, or even a bed. Anna's clothes had mysteriously disappeared with her furniture and his old iron bedstead was back in the bedroom.

Simon was sure that Anna had packed to go. At suppertime, when they sat on wooden crates to eat mutton stew in the kitchen, he found he could not find the courage to ask her. There was a lump in his throat and he was unable to swallow. Eventually he pushed his plate aside and went to oil the tractor. He worked until ten, but Anna did not appear to be leaving. At last he went inside and found her asleep in his old iron bed.

When he climbed in beside her, they found they were forced into close intimacy by the narrowness of the bed. After prodding each other with knees and elbows they discovered they both had to face the same way and turn together.

There was a cold wind blowing and Anna was glad of Simon's warm body beside her.

Simon whispered: 'Why Anna, when I saw Jan load your bed on the lorry I was sure you were leaving, but here you are.' He laughed shakily.

'I'm auctioning my things,' she said briefly.

He sighed. 'Maybe I've been a bit hard on you, Anna. The truth is you frighten me, you being so spoiled and used to the best. Do you have to sell your furniture? Maybe we should talk about it. After all, a spell of fishing brings in a bit of cash.'

'I'm buying chicks,' she told him.

He pulled her close against him. 'You don't get much at auctions. Reckon you'll be a bit disappointed. When Pa died I took all the furniture to the village and bought fertilizer with the cash – didn't amount to much.'

As he talked Anna's irritation with him turned to compassion. She could understand his need to push poverty behind him and make his farm pay. After all, she was doing the same. Any fool could see that the land would yield little, but Simon was blind to reality; he loved his land obsessively. She reached out and squeezed his hand.

After a while Simon edged on to the sharp metal frame and pulled Anna on her back. He tried to make love by balancing his knees on the steel, but the old springs groaned and sagged and Simon cut his knee. Eventually they made love on the floor.

In spite of his callousness, she loved him still. His hands on her bare skin still thrilled her; his green eyes glinting with humour, or even anger, had the power to turn her anger to warmth. She desired him as much now as she had ever done and thought she understood him better. Yet only in bed did she ever achieve the closeness that she longed for; for then Simon was truly hers and she loved him with her mind and body. Although he said little she could feel he cared, too, for his hands would grope for hers and his eyes were filled with tenderness.

'I love you,' she gasped. 'Oh Simon, I love you.'

The next morning Anna drove to the village to see the manager of the local farmers' co-operative. When she explained her plan he promised her all the feed she needed with a hundred and twenty days to pay. The money she received from the sale of the cockerels at four months would pay for the food of both the cockerels and the pullets, she told him, so she would be starting off afresh with free pullets and she was expecting five pounds a month profit for each hundred laying hens.

'It will work,' she told him enthusiastically, and caught up with her charm, her enthusiasm, and the fact he knew he could recoup any debts from her husband or her father, he agreed to supply her with all the feed she needed for a trial six-month period up to a maximum of one thousand pounds – an unheard of sum – and Anna was delighted.

Saturday morning Anna awoke early, feeling sick with fright. It was too late to change her mind and anyway, she knew that she could not, but what if her possessions were unwanted? What if she only obtained a few old hens, what if ... Her thoughts were full of forebodings and then she said to herself: 'I'm going to believe in my poultry farm, it must happen, there will be thousands and thousands of hens all over the hills and eggs going to the market by the lorryload, thousands and thousands of eggs.' And when she had visualized this multitude of eggs she felt much better.

It was a beautiful, crisp spring morning and Anna was full of hope as she drove to the Mosterts', but when she arrived she was taken aback to see so many lorries driving towards the gate, which was festooned with flags and signs. When she reached the courtyard she found it filled with trestle tables upon which all her possessions, looking pitiably few, were laid out, with the furniture stacked in the middle, while servants were running around with trays of cakes and jugs of homemade lemonade. There were nearly two hundred people examining the wares and Anna felt as if she was on display. She was so ashamed that she crept into the kitchen and huddled in a chair where she could see the courtyard through the big bay window.

Eventually Franz Mostert climbed on a table and yelled for silence.

'Well, we all know what we're here for,' he began, 'so I won't waste your time, we'll just get on with the auction. Now remember, we're not bidding in money, we're bidding chicks, and deliveries can be any time over the next four months. Is that agreed?'

There was a murmur of assent from the crowd and he nodded. 'OK, let's get started.' He held up her mother's beautiful copper saucepan which she, in turn, had inherited from her grandmother.

'This is a beautifully made example of early Afrikaans handiwork well over a hundred years old or I'm a Dutchman,' he said, which brought a few laughs from the crowd. 'Who'll open the bidding?'

A shrill, feminine voice yelled from the crowd, 'One hundred day-old chicks ready early November.'

Franz laughed. 'It's a good start, but this is worth more than that, Henrietta.'

The bidding hotted up – three hundred, four hundred, finally five hundred and fifty day-old chicks to be delivered on 1 October.

The bidding became frantic when the bed linen was offered.

'What am I bid for these silk sheets and hand-made eiderdown?' Franz called. 'Made in Germany, I can see it on the label, from the finest down.'

'Fifty turkeys.'

'Three hundred day-old chicks.'

'Fifty four-and-a-half month old white Leghorn pullets,' came a male voice from the crowd.

'That's better,' Franz said.

Anna began to feel faint, how would she cope with all this, she wondered. She had no idea what had been bid or what she had sold. Mostert's voice went on, chiding the bidders, pushing for more. How can I ever thank him, she wondered, but then she saw Fanny bidding for her bed and decided to give it to her for a gift.

Brooders, old henhouses, wood, ducks, wire netting, fertilized eggs, turkeys, geese, how would she ever cope? Perhaps the whole idea had been madness. What if they all died?

When her jewellery came on offer Anna clamped her hands

over her ears. She could not help remembering her eighteenth birthday when her parents had bought her a gold locket. There was her ring, an emerald set in platinum, and the single diamond which Uncle Acker had found once in South-West Africa, rather coarsely mounted on a heavy gold chain. Gone – all gone. Well, it was her own choice.

At last the auction was over, the people began to leave, and she heard Fanny calling her name.

'Why, you look all in,' the woman murmured sympathetically as Anna came into the courtyard. 'Well, cheer up, you haven't done too badly. Two hundred turkeys, two brooders, an assorted selection of old henhouses, five hundred month-old pullets, several dozen geese, one incubator, and let's see, how many day-old chicks was it?' she called to her husband. 'How many day-old chicks, Franz?'

'Ten thousand coming in batches over four months.'

Fanny turned back to Anna. 'There you are, see. Dear God! Franz, come quickly, the poor girl's fainted.'

10

The farmers stuck to their bargains. Hardly a day passed without a basketful of chicks arriving. Soon the hillside was dotted with chalet-type chicken houses.

Anna began work at five each morning and carried on until night fell. She and Jan spent hours carrying buckets of water from the pump to the chickens. September passed, the days lengthened and Anna was able to work longer hours.

By mid-October Anna had five thousand chicks and the grain bill was running into hundreds of pounds.

Each day Simon threatened to close the account. Only the prospect of five thousand starving chicks prevented him from keeping his word, for he knew as well as Anna that there was no market for half-grown birds.

Anna had no time for fighting with Simon and she ignored his black looks and churlish temper. The next month passed and another four thousand chicks arrived at the door and Anna was often desperate to find a place for them. More than once she housed them in a pantry until new houses could be made. The brooders were always filled to overflowing and often the chicks had to be turned out before they were old enough, but there was little danger at this time of the year.

Still the rains had not come. Occasionally the clouds would roll in fierce and heavy from the north-east, deep and purple with the promise of rain, but only a light drizzle would dampen the hillsides as if to tease the heavy-hearted farmers, and then the clouds would drift on towards Cape Town, Stellenbosch and Worcester where the sheep were up to their bellies in mud. But in the drought-ridden Langebaan district

89

the rivers began to dry, the dams were low and saline, and the scrawny sheep ranged miles over the veld, searching for pasture. The farm folk were downhearted, already counting their losses from the coming harvest.

'Damn it, it's too late now,' Simon complained to Anna during the morning breakfast break.

Anna knew, for she had walked over the fields the previous day and noticed how thin and sparse the shoots were growing, so that when you looked over the hills the view was all brown with only a shimmer of green.

'This crop won't cover the fertilizer, let alone our debts,' he said moodily. 'If the rains come now it's too late, but if they don't the whole crop will die. This place stinks. It's a lousy, rotten, sodding place and I wish to God I was rid of it.'

'I know, I know,' she said gently, feeling a strange twinge of compassion for this stranger she had married.

'But you don't know, that's the trouble. You don't know what it's like to break your back year after year trying to turn this place into a farm. You don't know what it's like down in the Antarctic, the back-breaking work, the cold, and all the time worrying about the farm. Every damn penny went into fertilizer and look at it. I've said a million times all this place needs is water and fertilizer, so I break my neck to pay for the fertilizer and then the rains don't come. Why, it's even worse than last year.' He buried his face in his hands and bent over the table. 'God's punishing me,' he moaned.

'That's a strange thing to say.' Anna wondered if she was meant to take him seriously. 'Why should God want to punish you in particular?'

Simon frowned and darted a sly glance at her. 'Because of something wrong I did,' he mumbled. 'There's a prayer meeting for the rain down at the van Ahlers',' he said as if coming to a sudden decision. 'You're to come with me, and wear something decent,' he said eyeing her dirty flowered smock with displeasure.

'Oh heavens, I don't think I could leave the chickens,' she argued. 'There's so much to be done today.'

'You're to come with me,' he repeated obstinately. 'Are you

too proud to get on your knees and pray for rain?' His green eyes burned and he clenched his fists.

'It's not that I'm too proud,' she began hesitantly. 'It's just that I don't believe praying will bring the rain any quicker.'

'If you don't believe in God ... ' he began angrily.

'Of course I do,' she cried out, 'but maybe just a different view of God.'

Simon was unsure of how to tackle the argument, then he said: 'You're my wife and it's your duty to come.'

'Very well,' she said, 'if you put it like that.'

Simon watched her, feeling irritated. She was like a blade of grass, she shivered and shook with the slightest breeze and could be flattened easily, but take your foot off and she sprang up twice as tall and strong. Well, she was Anna Smit now, for all the good it did her, and she should learn to do as she was told. He sighed – she had appeared so much more desirable when she was Anna van Achtenburgh. Then he stood up and went into the yard. As he reached the doorway he called over his shoulder, 'And put your heart into it when you're praying, you never thought to ask about the water supply when you spread those damn fool chicken houses all over the hills. The boreholes dry up as regular as clockwork every summer. What are you going to do then, eh? With a dry winter like we've just had the water probably won't make December.'

Anna gasped and felt her knees quiver beneath her. It was impossible, insane! No water? This was the one need that she had failed to investigate. All those hours of calculation and plans, but she had forgotten to take into account her need for water, imagining that it would always be there. But how could they run out of water? She had never heard of a farm running out of water. Still, this was not Stellenbosch.

As she worked out the extent of the probable disaster ahead she could hardly breathe. How many buckets a day was she using? It seemed that Jan and she spent most of their time trudging up and down the hill carrying bucket after bucket. Without water she was doomed – doomed to a life sentence as the downtrodden wife of the poorest, meanest farmer on the poorest, meanest farm in the Cape Province. She felt tears pricking her eyes and only the fear of Simon returning prevented her from breaking down. All at once she understood the full scope of the disaster for Simon and again she felt a small spark of compassion for him.

'Oh please God, send the rain,' she muttered and suddenly she was caught up by her own duplicity. She, who was too sophisticated to join the village folk at prayer meetings, was quickly muttering prayers when it hit her as hard as it was hitting them. 'God forgive me,' she muttered. 'I never understood what it was like.'

She went outside and stared earnestly up at the sky. Surely she had felt dampness on her face then? She studied the clouds with a new intensity. They were grey and thick, moving slowly from the north-west, but there had been little change in that for some days.

Suddenly she wondered if Simon was merely trying to frighten her and she decided to go and find Jan who was on the north side of the hill cleaning out manure.

She found him eventually and, leaning in the door of the chicken house she called out, 'Jan, you ever know the boreholes dry up in summer?'

'Missus?' He looked round, his yellow parchment face straining for comprehension, his eyes eager like a bird's eyes.

'The pump, and the borehole, I'm talking about our water, Jan. Is there plenty of water in summer?'

'Some summers there's plenty – sometimes nothing.' He shrugged and raised his hands, indicating the helplessness of the human condition in the face of nature's merciless plan.

'What do you do when the water's gone?'

'Well, we don't use none.'

'And the cows?'

'There's the dam.'

He came out backwards and climbed to his feet. Although his words were inadequate, his eyes glowed to show that he understood. 'There's the tanks,' he said.

She turned away so that Jan could not see how frightened she was. Jesus! How could she have been such a fool? She felt her face burning with fear and shame as she trudged off to the house. Clearly it was impossible to transport the water she needed from the village to the farm. Sheer economics would make that impracticable even if she had the time or a big enough truck.

By the time she had returned to the farmhouse she had worked out to the nearest penny what she could raise from the sale of her beloved hens as spring chicken for the table, but it was not nearly enough to cover the feed bill.

'Simon, there should be underground water here,' she said when they were leaving for the van Ahlers' prayer meeting. 'Have you tried sinking boreholes?'

'My old man tried it. Got it into his head once that he could irrigate this place in the bad years. Lost two thousand pounds sinking boreholes all over the place. Dry as a desert. Just about ruined him.'

Simon avoided looking at Anna, feeling somehow that he had failed her by not being able to provide the water that she needed so badly.

'But Modderfontein – that means Mud Spring. So where's the spring?'

'Maybe there was one once but it must have dried up. Probably wasn't ever much.'

They drove the rest of the journey in silence. Suddenly Anna felt Simon's hand reach out and take hers and she felt a little less alone. God knows she needed a friend, and she squeezed his hand in return.

'Doesn't always dry up,' he went on. 'There's still time enough. I remember five years in a row when we had good rains. Don't give up.' He turned and grinned at her. 'Just pray.'

Anna prayed. She prayed until the wood splinters penetrated her woollen stockings and rubbed her knees sore, until her back was breaking and her ears were humming with the noise of the congregation's monotonous refrains. The voice of the preacher went on and on, and the sermon seemed to last forever until eventually Anna began to feel faint and sick.

It was a nightmare – the simple people around her sweating and praying in the stuffy room and one or two women

93

sobbing into their handkerchiefs as they pleaded with the Lord to send them the rain they needed so desperately, the noise of the wind outside the windows, the preacher shouting. It was a primitive, alien scene and Anna could hardly believe that she was there. Even the sight of her own swelling belly, her red, roughened hands, her lank hair and her unfamiliar hand-me-down clothes from her mother's early youth, all these things were unbelievable. Where was Anna van Achtenburgh now? Gone for ever. To think she could have been in Switzerland studying music. She burst into tears and smothered her face with her handkerchief, but no one noticed for they were all crying for rain.

The drive home was grim with foreboding for the clouds had blown away during the prayer meeting and the sky was crystal clear, deep blue and it was hotter than ever.

That night Anna dreamed of water, streaming, falling, flooding, cascading, rolling in tidal waves down the hillside and she awoke to the sound of the wind howling in the chimney and the noise of rain beating on the corrugated iron roof. She leapt out of bed and flung the window open, but the stars were bright stabs of disappointment and there were no clouds in the merciless sky. Only the wind had whipped itself into a whirlwind, hurling stones and rubble on to the roof.

In the weeks that followed Simon became surly and sulky, alternating his moods from bullying to cajoling her to get rid of her flocks. He moaned about the crowing in the mornings, he complained about the smell when the wind blew from the south-west, and after that he grumbled about the turkeys which, he said, would take the grazing from the sheep. Most of all he fumed about the rising bill for poultry feed, wood for the henhouses and wire netting. Simon had lost his illusions about Anna, for under that soft exterior lay a steel-like resolve that both frightened and repelled him, and he sensed that she would always have the beating of him.

Anna, for her part, had little enough time to worry about Simon and his griping, for with eight thousand growing chicks, and another two thousand on the way, there was plenty of work to be done and she followed her poultry book to the letter, having designed every house according to its specification. When she offered Simon the manure as rent for the land his fury knew no bounds, but when he recovered his temper he took the manure anyway and had Jan dig it in the field he was preparing for lucerne.

By the time the harvest began Anna was well into her sixth month of pregnancy and she was round as a pomegranate, with glowing cheeks and sparkling eyes and hair that was shining and longer than usual. She walked with a spring in her step and her legs and thighs were hard as a youth's. The pains had gone and so had her sickness and she hardly noticed she was pregnant except when she caught sight of herself in the mirror.

It was back-breaking toil from morning till night and if she had a spare moment she would sit and calculate her theoretical profits from future sales of cockerels and eggs.

Only a month to go and she would sell her first table birds and pay the cash to the co-op. By Christmas the first five hundred pullets would start to lay and that should bring her more than fifteen shillings a month, and then she would smile as she thought of the turkeys, for she had three hundred which would be ready for Christmas.

The days passed and became hotter and longer and still the chicks came, more and more each day. Surely the farmers were overpaying her? When Anna looked at the hillside it was dotted not with two hundred but with two thousand chalets, while in her mind she saw her cockerels housed in huge, corrugated iron sheds, thousands upon thousands of them.

It was the same with the growing child. She could see her daughter, Katie, almost an exact replica of herself but with red hair, running over the hillside behind her and sometimes she would find herself turning and talking to the child, and then she would remember that Katie was not yet born. Her contentment with her coming child and the satisfactory condition of her business was marred by the lack of water, for there was far less coming out of the borehole than in the month before, and each morning she would stand and watch the trickling tap as Jan filled the endless procession of buckets.

Then her stomach would become knotted with fear until she forced herself to imagine the water gushing from the borehole, frothing, splashing, dampening the air around until she could feel the spray on her face and hear the hissing force of it. 'You promised, you promised,' she would murmur into the wind. 'Doesn't it say: "*things soever ye desire, when ye pray, believe that ye receive them, and ye shall have them.*" ' Then she would feel guilty for the doubts in her mind and she would say: 'Thank you, thank you for the water, but hurry.'

As the days passed Anna began to develop a new kind of regard for Simon, for she sensed his anguish and her compassion was born from understanding his terrible fight against his environment, his greed born of deprivation.

It was mid-November, time to prepare for the harvest, but it was clear that this was a disaster year and the spindly wheat heads seemed hardly worth the trouble of collecting.

So Simon brought out the ancient harvester, took it apart and put it together again; a yearly ritual, and at five a.m. on the morning of 20 November, he set off rather sadly to the nearest fields.

From then on, day after day, he would follow a circuitous route starting with the outer perimeter of the patch that he had chosen and by sunset he would be at the centre. Here there were always a few hares sheltering in the uncut wheat and when the harvester burst upon them, they would break cover and race across the lands. Simon would be sure to maim one of them with his catapult. Daily they dined on hare pie, hare stew or roast hare.

Soon the hillsides were covered in wheat stubble and by mid-December the harvest was over and Jan loaded the sacks into the lorry for Simon to drive to the millers at Malmesbury. When he returned he came into the kitchen and caught Anna by the hands and, pulling her to him, he rested his head against her breasts like a small child.

'Well, that's it,' he said. 'Five hundred pounds. The worst ever. I spent more than that in fertilizer, not counting the grain, the insecticides and the molasses. Jesus,' he sobbed. 'Jesus, but it's been a bad year. Another year like this and I'm packing up the farm and we'll go to the city and look for work.'

'It will be better next year,' Anna said. 'You'll see.'

He drank a cup of thick, black coffee and sighed. 'I'll sign on tomorrow,' he told her.

'What do you mean?' She paled. 'Sign on what?'

'Whaling of course.'

'But four months in the Antarctic?'

'That's right.' He frowned at her. 'It brings more cash than this damn farm.'

'How much do you get?' she asked.

'Depends.' He seemed absorbed with his coffee.

'Depends on what?'

'Depends on the catch, of course.' He put the coffee down. 'Now Anna, don't start anything. I always go down to the Antarctic after harvest, particularly after a bad year. I don't have any choice, you see. I have to pay the debts. You've been building up enough with your damn chickens.'

'I'll pay my own account,' she retorted. 'You can't go. You know the baby's coming. What happens if I need help?'

He laughed contemptuously. 'You need help? Ha!' With a scowl he went out of the kitchen and drove to the village and when she saw him next it was midnight and he was blind drunk.

Exactly two nights after Simon left, the borehole began to dry and the water slowed to a trickle. After four hours of waiting they had watered only a quarter of the chickens and Anna was filled with dread. 'Take the water from the freshwater tanks,' she commanded Jan in an imperious tone.

'But, Missus,' Jan protested weakly.

'Jan, take the water from the freshwater tanks or the chickens will die.'

Jan had become Anna's devoted slave, but he found it hard to obey, for the water was all that they had to last them and the cows until next winter's rains, which were a good four months away. Admittedly they would have a few summer showers, but nothing of any consequence.

Anna went back to the house with a heavy heart. 'Dear

97

God,' she whispered. 'Dear God, what am I going to do?' She felt shrunk with the weight of her sorrow. She went to the dam to examine the water, but she knew that the hens would not lay if they were given such brackish brew.

It was then that the baboons decided to lay siege to the farm. As if sensing Simon was away they openly invaded the land during daylight hours, gleaning the grains of wheat and chasing away the sheep from their pasture; they ripped out handfuls of lucerne; destroyed the peas and even killed a turkey. That night, when Anna tossed restlessly in bed worrying about water, she heard them barking close to her henhouses. They were after the eggs, she decided. She put on her shoes, took Simon's gun, and ran up the hillside firing into the air. The baboons fled.

Early next morning she drove to their nearest neighbours, the Stassens, whose farmhouse was a good ten miles away, to ask them how they kept the baboons off their land.

'We've never had trouble with them, they don't come this far,' Johan Stassen explained when Anna was sitting at the kitchen table with a cup of coffee.

'They hang around their waterhole, you see. You won't catch them far from that.'

'But there's no water on Modderfontein,' Anna told him with a catch in her voice. 'Just a borehole that's drying up, and then there's the streams in the dongas, of course, but they're as low as yours are, I'm sure. The baboons stay up in the hills most of the time.'

'Use your sense, Mrs Smit,' he said chidingly. 'There's no living beast can manage without water.'

'My husband's father spent a fortune trying to find a water supply. He sunk eight boreholes, but he never found a spring,' she said.

'Likely the baboons are more wily than old man Smit was,' he answered with a chuckle and then stopped as he caught his wife's frown. 'No disrespect meant, Ma'am.'

When she reached home Anna put on her boots to protect her from snakes, took the rifle from the peg, and went into the yard calling Wagter. Jan was looking haggard as he leaned over the tap waiting for the bucket to be filled.

'Jan, look after the farm, I'm going into the hills to look for the baboons' water supply.'

'The Missus mustn't do that,' Jan said, eyeing her bulging stomach with concern.

'Jan,' she said, trying to make him understand. 'There must be water in the hills. That's why we have so many baboons.'

Jan put down the bucket and stood frowning at her, scratching his head. His face looked sullen, his eyes uneasy and suddenly Anna realized that Jan knew where the water was. 'Jan,' she said gently. 'If I don't find that water all my chickens will die and I shall be very poor.'

Jan shook his head obstinately. 'No water,' he said. 'The baboons go down to the river.' He pointed towards the lagoon where a stream flowed into the marshes on the other side about ten miles away.

Anna sighed and set off up the hill and after a while she heard Jan's running footsteps as he caught up with her.

'Old Jan knows where the water is,' he said. 'It's been there since I was a boy.' He laughed. 'Likely it's been there forever.'

Anna felt angry. 'But Jan, you know how desperate we are for water, and the old baas before Simon. Why didn't you tell anyone?'

He looked away again and eventually he said: 'My Pa is buried there and my uncle.' Anna realized that Jan and perhaps his father, too, thought of it as their own sacred place.

'It's a long way,' he went on.

With Jan ahead and Wagter behind they trudged over the hills. When she saw the flock spread out over the land, meagre and scrawny, she felt heavy-hearted, but eventually they reached the slopes of the hills where the land had not been cultivated and the black bush grew shoulder-high, thick and interspersed with weeds and wild herbs.

Anna began to suffer from the weight of her unborn child as she climbed. Soon the bush became thicker and thorn trees made the way almost impenetrable. Thorny brambles caught at Anna's clothes and once she saw a cobra slithering away.

'It's a long time since old Jan was here, but it's not far

away,' he mumbled.

Anna felt tired, so she sat on a boulder and said to Jan: 'Go and search, Jan. I'm going to have a rest.'

Jan went up the hill, but as Anna sat listening to the sounds of the birds, the crickets, the humming of insects and the murmuring of the wind she fancied she heard water, bubbling, running, gurgling water. It was as if her dreams had materialized beneath her feet, for she could hear it as plainly as she had imagined.

She stood up and pushed her way through the dense bush and then the land seemed to slip away beneath her. She was falling down steep, slippery slopes; rolling, turning, and she only knew that somehow she must protect Katie as she fell, so she managed to turn on her back and slither down, feet-first, sixty or a hundred feet of moss-covered slopes until she found she was up to her neck in a deep pool of water. Far above her she could see sunlight sparkling through leaves which made a dappled, moving pattern against the brilliant sky, while myriad birds' nests hung from branches above. She pulled herself to the side of the pool and laughed aloud with joy and then she buried her head in the water and drank it; it tasted sweet and pure, straight out of the mountainside, for this must be the water from the drainage of the whole line of hills, she decided, and no doubt it had bubbled and gurgled here for hundreds of years, or maybe forever.

She could see the spoor of baboons, and when she heard Jan calling she yelled, 'Jan, I'm down here, in the water. Be careful, it's slippery.'

Then she saw Jan coming hand over hand like a monkey down the branches of a tree whose leaves were in the sunlight, but whose trunk was deep down in the donga.

'But where does it come from?' she asked. 'There's never a sign of water when you look up at the hills.'

Jan laughed. 'It comes out of the earth,' he told her. He led her up the gully about fifty yards to a deep, natural pool where the water was bubbling. There was watercress growing there, and tall reeds, and as they approached a heron and its mate flew up out of the donga. Anna stood staring in wonder and

100

pleasure, unable to tear herself away from this wonderful place.

'Has it ever dried up?' she asked.

'Not since I can remember,' Jan said.

'Does no one know about it?'

Jan shrugged. 'The master never knew and the young baas never found it.'

'When he was a boy, didn't he play up here?'

'He was always working,' Jan said. 'The young master never played.'

'Well, where does it go?'

Jan shrugged. 'Back in the earth.'

He was right, although Anna could hardly believe it. The water gurgled for fifty yards, filled a small pool then sank underground into a sandy area. The crevice ended there with a steep wall of rock.

'My Pa's buried up there,' Jan pointed to the top of the rocky outcrop, 'and the water's down underneath.'

Anna returned to the farmhouse feeling elated. But how could she pay for a borehole and the pipes? Well, it had to be done.

Next morning she put on her mother's best woollen smock, hat, gloves and the only pair of stockings she had left and went to see the manager of the Land Bank. The interview did not last long. Anna discovered she could neither open a bank account, nor borrow money, or even deposit her own money without her husband's permission and even if she were willing to ask Simon he was away in the Antarctic for the next four months. She decided to try the local co-operative and went to see the manager.

'It will cost you at least five hundred pounds. I can put you in touch with an engineering company specializing in boreholes,' he said. 'Reliable blokes in Malmesbury.'

'Would they want to be paid right away?' she asked timidly.

'Yes, I'm sure they would,' he said. 'In advance. Farmers round here are a bit short of money, you see.'

'Oh yes, I know that,' she said heavily and went home.

Five hundred pounds – it was beyond her. On the long drive

back her mind was feverishly calculating the money that she would receive from the sale of her poultry. She was so engrossed that she hardly noticed the shooting pains in her back and her stomach as she drove over the bumpy road. By the time she reached the homestead she felt desperately ill and close to fainting, but at the same time she had worked out how she could raise five hundred pounds by the end of January. What could she do in the meantime, she wondered, for the borehole water was as good as finished and the fresh water in the tanks would only last a week if she used it for chickens.

Jan met her at the door and as she stood up she fainted with pain and came to shortly afterwards, to find herself lying on her bed with Jan standing apologetically beside her.

'Jan, what are we going to do?' she murmured, clutching her stomach as another shooting pain contorted her face and she groaned involuntarily, but then it passed. 'What are we going to do, Jan?' she repeated. 'How can we get the water to the chickens?'

'You leave it to old Jan.' He tapped his finger on his head and went out, apparently more concerned about the chickens than her.

The following morning she heard Jan's footsteps coming down the passage. 'Missus, Missus,' he called.

'I'm here, Jan,' she called and sat up, relieved to find that she was feeling better.

'Is the Missus in trouble? Is it the baby?'

'No, not yet,' she said. 'The pains are going away.'

Jan stood looking haggard and dirty. 'Old Jan can't drive,' he said, 'but I can walk to fetch the doctor.'

'No, that won't be necessary, Jan,' she said. 'If I need the doctor I will telephone.'

Jan looked relieved and his face crinkled into a smile. 'I've moved the chickens,' he said.

'What do you mean, Jan?' she asked. 'Moved them where?'

'Up to the water,' he said and he went off again. Anna thought to herself: but that's impossible. She was so tired, she lay back and fell into a deep sleep.

She woke the next morning to hear turkeys gobbling in the

yard and the dog barking. She felt stiff and her back was aching, but the frightening pains had disappeared. For the next few weeks she would be very careful, she decided, but when she went into the courtyard and found that the chicks and hokkies had disappeared, she decided she was well enough to walk over the hills after all. When she arrived at the pea camp she saw a dozen young boys of school age finishing the runs while others were carrying buckets of water from the pool.

'But Jan,' she said aghast. 'How will I pay them?'

'Old Jan paid them with eggs,' he said simply.

'Eggs?' She looked at Jan doubtfully. 'It's not time yet.' Then she remembered the five hundred pullets she had received at the auction. 'The pullets!' she shouted. 'They've started laying.'

'Small eggs,' Jan mumbled. 'But there's three boxes ready for the co-op.'

She gasped. 'I'll have to drive them to the village,' she said happily. 'Oh Jan!'

11

On 20 December Anna sold her first cockerels and because it was nearly Christmas she received an excellent price which more than covered the food bill, both for cockerels and pullets from that batch. Several times a day Anna would examine her notebook hopefully labelled: *Anticipated Profits* and check her figures, but she could find no error and providing no ill luck befell her she could expect an average of four eggs a week per hen, or profits of five pounds a month per hundred hens, and as she had five thousand pullets ranging from week-old to four-month chicks she was hoping for a profit of two hundred and fifty pounds a month – a magnificent sum, all of which would be ploughed back into the business.

Nevertheless it was a hot, dry burden of a summer for everyone in the Cape and particularly for Anna, who toiled over the fields hampered by an extra thirty pounds of weight.

As December passed Anna became particularly homesick remembering Fontainebleu at Christmas: the gaily striped tarpaulin; gigantic tables laden with food; barrels of home-made wine; crowds of family, friends and farm workers; and carols at midnight.

Remembering the children who had helped Jan move the chicks she suggested tentatively that they might like to come for lunch, and when Christmas Day dawned Anna saw, not a dozen, but at least a hundred children traipsing along the farm path looking shy, but hungry.

Anna gave them some bread and sent them to water the poultry while Jan killed and roasted a sheep and more turkeys and Anna made bread, puddings and sweets so that instead of lunch they had their Christmas party under the stars, gathered around the fire in the courtyard. Eventually the children trudged home carrying parcels of leftovers.

By mid-January Anna was eight and a half months pregnant and feeling increasingly confused, for while she was impatient to be rid of her burden and to hold Katie in her arms she was also afraid and she had no one to turn to other than the village midwife, Mrs Engelbrecht, called 'Angie' by everyone.

Once a week Anna drove to the village to see the doctor who would tap her a few times on the stomach, listen carefully and assure her that there was absolutely nothing to having a baby.

Angie, on the other hand, viewed her increasing girth with dismay and told her she was carrying a 'big 'un' that might give her trouble. Anna did not understand, but would lie awake at night worrying about it and the more she worried the more she became a victim to cramps and pains. Soon it became impossible for her to sit down, she had either to stand or lie.

She missed her mother more than ever while her disappointment in Simon grew daily. She felt that she would never be able to forgive him for leaving her when she needed him so badly. Her anxiety increased, and not just for herself; she dreaded the moment she would be incapacitated and have to leave her poultry in Jan's care, for God knows how drunk he would get the moment she turned her back.

The long walk to inspect the poultry became more difficult and when she got there she would scan the horizon fearfully. Any number of crippling blows could come to wreck her dreams: lynxes; marauding baboons; disease, but of all her fears none obsessed her quite as much as fire, for without rain the bush-covered mountain slopes were ready to ignite from a spark and the hens were dangerously close to the bush. But how could she move them? Jan spent most of his time climbing rough-hewn steps cut into the steep slopes of the ravine, carrying a wooden pole with a full bucket of water dangling from each end.

'Surely another downpour is well overdue,' she would say

earnestly to the farmers she met in the village, and they would nod their heads and reply: 'We never had a year as bad as this.'

Her first profits, she vowed, would be spent on a borehole and pipes to carry the water far away from the hills.

Still, the time passed in a flurry of activity, for apart from the eggs which had to be washed and transported once a week to the village, and the daily poultry inspections, there were also the in-between moments of joy when she would buy a few things for Katie or get the cradle ready, but the end of January passed without any sign of the coming birth and a week later Anna was still waiting. It was a long, bitter, tortuous week and Anna longed for her mother.

One day, when she was feeling low, and worrying because the baby was overdue, she put her pride in her pocket and telephoned Fontainebleu. Eventually a strange voice answered.

'I'd like to speak to Mrs van Achtenburgh,' she said timidly.

'They've gone away,' the man replied in a gruff voice.

'Who is speaking, please?' Anna asked.

'Name's Dutoit, farm manager,' he barked.

For a moment Anna was too shocked to answer.

The voice went on: 'Who's speaking?'

'I'm a friend,' she gasped. 'Where have they gone?'

'Mrs van Achtenburgh took ill – heart trouble and then pneumonia, so they went to a clinic in Switzerland. I'm managing the farm till they get back.'

'Thank you,' she said miserably and replaced the receiver, her hopes dashed, feeling truly alone again. The news that her mother was ill stunned her, for until that moment she had thought only of herself. She wondered guiltily if her own actions had contributed to her mother's illness and at that moment she longed to be with her. No wonder her mother had not come, and like a fool she had been too proud to contact her.

As she leaned against the wall beside the telephone the first pain gripped her. It was unlike anything she had experienced before, an all-consuming pain which blocked out reason. A second later it had gone and she took a deep breath, walked into the bedroom and looked in the mirror. She looked normal, just a bit pale. Had something gone wrong? Or perhaps she had imagined the worst of it.

Twenty minutes later the second pain transformed her into a vegetable, something that bore pain, for there was nothing else of her left for conscious thought or action. Between the third and fourth pains she had the sense to go to the telephone and dial the midwife's number, and fortunately Angie was in and Anna began haltingly: 'Terrible pains, you can't imagine, beyond description. I fear there must be something badly wrong.'

Mrs Engelbrecht's voice sounded reassuring to her: 'No, dear, that's just the start of it. Now don't you fret, you'll be all right. The pains are not so bad if you lie down. It's no good trying to fight them. I'll be right along, but don't you worry, I'll be there within the hour.'

Anna replaced the receiver. An hour! How could she endure an hour? And then she felt another frightening lurch in her stomach and the next minute she was back into this other terrible world; a world where time stood still, where a second could take hours, where her ego was diminished to a small microbe crawling in a vast, pain-wracked cavern somewhere in the region of her stomach. It passed, as the others had passed, and she began to get the hang of it. There was a time between to recuperate; to build her strength; to prepare herself, she realized.

She wanted some water, but was afraid to get it and so she lay counting the minutes between the pains, becoming increasingly terrified, and when Mrs Engelbrecht arrived she found Anna clutching a sheet which was wet through, staring horrified at the ceiling, bathed in sweat and almost too stiff with fright and pain to move.

'There now, this won't do,' Mrs Engelbrecht said sternly. 'You're right at the beginning of it. If you're going to carry on like this now, what are you going to do when the real pains come?'

'Real pains?' Anna gasped. 'What do you think these are?'

'These are just for starters,' Mrs Engelbrecht said. 'But don't worry, everyone has babies and everyone recovers. You'll have forgotten all about it by morning. Now if you'll stop fretting I'll change your clothes and get you some water and when the pains come you can hang on to the bed.'

She soaked a towel in water, twisted it over the bedstead, and gave it to Anna to hold. 'Grip it tightly and it will help you,' she said.

Anna sighed, dreading the next pain, and when it came it was much worse. She lay feeling her body washed over, as if on the shore of a sea of pain in which she was slowly drowning.

By nightfall Anna was as pale as death, with staring eyes and wet plastered hair and Mrs Engelbrecht had not telephoned the doctor because, she explained, the contractions were still too far apart. For Anna time disappeared and she had entered a state of timelessness where a second could last forever. It was unearthly. Inhuman!

Dawn came and Anna was too exhausted to cry or talk. As the day wore on Jan knocked at the door occasionally to ask how the Missus was doing, but otherwise the two women stayed together waiting in the bedroom.

Saturday morning Mrs Engelbrecht telephoned the doctor, for although there was no sign of the head, the girl was slowly sinking. To Anna the world had ceased to exist. Her ego had disintegrated and when she surfaced between pains it was to wonder that she was still alive, that the mind could endure such agony.

The doctor arrived at seven a.m. and immediately summoned the ambulance which took another two hours to reach the farmhouse. Half-conscious, she jolted over the rough farm track on the half-hour journey to Malmesbury's hospital, but when they arrived there was no doctor to perform an emergency Caesarian operation and she was driven on to Bellville. Mercifully by this time she was unconscious.

Anna awoke to a sense of tremendous peace and relief, although for a while she could not think why. She opened her eyes and wondered what was so wonderful. Eventually she realized it was the absence of pain. She felt her stomach, which was smaller and covered in dressings. The baby was gone, Katie was gone, she began to murmur and groan; then she fell asleep.

When next she opened her eyes there was a nurse beside her who said, 'Don't worry, Mrs Smit, everything's all right. You must rest.'

'Where's my daughter?' Anna gasped.

'Your child is well, now go to sleep.'

Anna sighed and, realizing that the ordeal was over, she burst into sobs of relief.

'There's nothing to cry about,' the nurse said sternly. 'You're better, and your baby is a fine, strapping, ten pound boy.'

'A boy?' Anna struggled to sit up. 'There must be some mistake, I had a daughter.'

'You had a boy.' The nurse laughed. 'Now rest a while and we'll bring him to you.'

But Anna could not rest for she was filled with dismay. Where was Katie? Katie who had followed her over the hills, rounding up the sheep and feeding the chickens? Where was Katie who could sing sweeter than anyone in the world, who was bewitchingly clever and entrancingly beautiful? A son? She could not come to grips with the idea, so after a while she began to think about her chickens and the more she thought about them the more she worried, for left to himself Jan was bound to get drunk and if the chickens had no water they would die.

I've got to get back, she thought, and so strong was her presentiment of danger that she began to sweat. As she lay in bed in that strange, half-awake, half-asleep twilight state she could smell the smoke, hear the hissing and crackling as the fire raced down the mountain slopes. She called out in terror and the nurse hurried to her side.

'There's a fire on the farm,' she murmured.

The nurse laughed at her foolishness. 'There's a veld fire

down the road,' she said. 'You can smell the smoke drifting past the window. Don't think about the farm, just think about getting well.'

Anna closed her eyes and a tear drifted down her cheek. She knew there was a fire at Modderfontein.

Jan was sleeping by the donga when he caught the first scent of smoke drifting down the slopes from the bushes above. He sat up, rubbed his eyes and thought about the impossibility of getting from the bank of the stream where he lay almost unconscious to the top of the slippery slope.

He had remained faithful to Anna's wishes for two long days but on the third day when feeding the fowls, he caught two of the cockerels, wrung their necks and took them to the village where he exchanged the birds for a gallon of wine.

Jan loved Anna with a passion that was childlike in its simplicity. No one had ever befriended him; he could not remember his mother or father, simply the old baas, and the old baas before him who had given him food and a place to sleep, and in return he had herded the cows and sheep for his lifetime. Then Anna had arrived and he had feared her more than anyone for he was sure that in her frenzy to drive out the dirt and filth from the cottage he, too, would be banished, but instead she had bought him new clothes and cooked his food. Now she had abandoned him and he felt rejected. Nevertheless, part of him remained faithful to her even when he was drunk, so he had trudged from the village to the farm, staggered up the slopes to his casually erected hut in the chicken camp and fallen into a deep sleep from which he had awakened two hours later with a raging thirst and a splitting headache. Crawling on his hands and knees to the donga he had slid down the slopes and immersed himself in the running stream.

Now he felt stiff and his head seemed set in a block of cement. So great was his misery that he was hardly aware of the outside world, so the disturbing thought came and went and then came again – fire! He lifted his head, groaned and rested it on his knees.

110

There was a fire. Part of him wanted to rescue the hens, but most of him wanted to sleep, and after a few minutes of indecision he summoned the energy to climb up the steep steps. On the edge of the donga he paused incredulously to watch the awesome scene, for the flames were racing across the black hills and the heat was so intense that each bush erupted in a shower of sparks, flames and crackling even before the fire reached it. The wind was north-west and the smoke was coming across the hill slantwise, choking the chickens who, panic-stricken, were clucking, jostling and fighting each other to get out of their pens as they perceived the danger.

The Madam was ruined, he thought. The hens would choke to death long before they burned, for silly fowls always expire with the first puff of smoke. He thought about the eggs that he had failed to collect on the previous day. Well, they would be roasted, and then he thought: the Madam will never know that I neglected her fowls when the silly creatures are all dead and the eggs all roasted.

The noise of the fire was deafening and still he stood watching while a strange feeling overtook him. Was it love, compassion, pity? They were words that Jan had never heard and the feeling was one that he had never experienced. He suddenly knew that he would die if a single one of the Madam's fowls perished. But there were four thousand five hundred pullets, three thousand cockerels and the whole camp was likely to go up in flames at any moment.

Suddenly he was racing from one run to the next, with a single, swift movement he wrenched the wire netting so that the silly birds, clucking, fluttering, squawking and shaking their heads were able to race out from under the netting and down the hill in a gigantic confusion of flying feathers and flapping wings. Long before he finished dozens of shadowy shapes emerged out of the darkness and smoke to help him. With at least fifty village schoolboys it was fairly simple to remove the coops and runs to the safety of the donga.

12

Anna remained in hospital for ten days, fretting and worrying, but regaining her strength, and on the morning of the twenty-fifth the doctor paused during his routine calls to sit beside her.

'Under normal circumstances I would let you go home today,' he told her gently, 'but knowing you will be alone on the farm I'm afraid to let you go. Who will look after you with your husband at sea? Is there no one who could stay with you?'

In spite of his probing Anna remained obstinately uncommunicative and insisted on leaving that day, and eventually the doctor gave in and told her that he would send her and her son home in an ambulance.

Anna took her baby out of the cradle beside her bed and hugged him. 'I won't be alone,' she said gaily. 'I'll have Acker for company.'

'Acker?' the doctor mused. 'That's an unusual name.'

'Not really,' Anna said. 'It's a German name. I have an Uncle Acker in South-West Africa, my favourite uncle.'

The doctor smiled sadly at her, for clearly she had made an unfortunate match. He could not help feeling sorry. He hardly knew how to break the bad news, but Anna seemed happy enough as she played with her son.

'He's such a beautiful baby,' Anna said lovingly, 'and look at his hair, so long and red. He's not at all wrinkled and ugly like other babies.' She smiled at the doctor. 'I was sure I was carrying a daughter,' she said, 'I'd even named her Katherine, but now that I have a son I love him just as much. Next time I'll have my daughter.'

112

'I'm afraid there isn't going to be a next time,' the doctor said. 'We had to perform a hysterectomy.'

Anna was stunned. No daughter? No Katie? It was impossible, Katie was so real to her. In a daze she heard the doctor explain that the fall had damaged her womb.

He broke off when he saw that she was on the verge of tears. 'Mrs Smit, you must remember that you're a very lucky woman to have such a beautiful son,' he went on. 'So many women are childless and there's nothing we can do about it. I'm sorry, Anna,' he said gently. 'We had no choice.'

The drive home was full of wonder for Anna as she clutched her baby, but when the ambulance reached the farm road Anna became tense with alarm for there were black patches amongst the wheat stubble and bushland and she could see that fires had been breaking out spasmodically over the lands. Sensing her disquiet, Acker began to wail. Ten minutes later when they crested the last hill Anna felt distraught, for the entire slope from the crest of the hills to the valley below was black. The fire had ravaged an area of at least a hundred acres and she knew that she was ruined, her henhouses destroyed, her precious hens cruelly burned. Poor Acker, was he to be a poor child from the poorest of homes, going barefoot to school?

The thought was more than she could bear and she stopped the ambulance driver, telling him that she would rather walk the rest of the way. Taking her small bundle of clothes and Acker in her arms she went slowly down the hillside. Her eyes blurred with tears, her feet felt laden, and then suddenly she nearly tripped over a pullet scurrying across her path. When she rubbed the tears out of her eyes with her knuckles she saw a sight that she would never see again, for the path, the fields, the courtyard, the roofs of the farmhouse and the outhouses, the rim around the water tank, the eucalyptus trees and even the thorn bush outside the back door were white as snow. Seven thousand chickens! Somehow it looked more like seven million.

Anna dropped her suitcase and yelled loudly: 'Jan!' She would have liked to have raced down the slope, but she could hardly push her way through the chickens. Then in the courtyard she saw schoolboys catching the chickens and stuffing them into sacks.

'Jan,' she laughed. 'Jan, whatever are you doing? Why are the hens all over the place?'

Jan looked strangely humble when he saw her. 'Missus, old Jan lost some of the henhouses,' he said sadly. 'There was a fire, a very bad fire.'

'I saw that, Jan,' she said solemnly, 'and I thought that all the hens had been destroyed.'

'Ah, no, Missus.' Jan's face crinkled and he grinned for the first time. 'Old Jan let them all out. There wasn't time to catch them, you see, and I couldn't move them by myself so I just let them go. Then the boys came and we saved most of the houses. We've been feeding them down here and taking them back a few at a time.'

'But that's wonderful, Jan. In fact, you are wonderful. Thank you, my old friend. I will never be able to thank you enough.'

'I've lost most of the eggs,' Jan told her. 'Wagter he's a sly one. He loves eggs.'

'It doesn't matter. We'll make it up.'

She pulled the shawl from Acker's face. 'Look at my baby, Jan,' she said. 'Look at Acker.'

The old man was almost rude with his lack of enthusiasm. 'Why. I thought you had a daughter.'

'Well, I made a mistake,' she said.

It took two weeks of back-breaking work to restore order to the poultry farm. Anna learned to carry Acker on her back as African women do, securely strapped in a torn sheet.

One evening, when she could not sleep from worrying about her mother, she lit a candle and wrote to her, pouring out her love for Acker, her sorrow that she would not have another, her hopes for the poultry and her wish that her mother would visit her when she returned from Switzerland. '*I feel responsible for your illness and pray for your recovery,*' she wrote.

When she sold the second batch of cockerels she received three hundred and fifty pounds and, instead of paying it to the co-op, she explained her plight to the co-op manager and paid only fifty pounds. The balance covered a deposit on a borehole and pump, the balance payable over three months.

The engineering company lost no time in sinking a borehole from the hill above the mud spring, and at a depth of three hundred feet they hit an aquifer which they described as the only one they had encountered in that area. The water came bursting out at a rate of twenty thousand gallons an hour.

The work was endless; days passed in a blur. Anna lived, slept, ate and worked chickens. Each day the eggs had to be weighed, graded and scraped clean with a saucepan cleaner. She became adept at flicking eggs down the production line. In no time she could grade fifty eggs a minute on her cheap egg-grading machine; cleaning them took a little longer.

February was harvest time for the grapes and Anna began to miss her home more than ever. After days of indecision she decided to drive home and find out when her mother was returning. Once she had made up her mind she felt happier and she set off full of optimism the following morning with Acker sleeping in his cot on the front seat. He was a happy baby, she thought gratefully, and gaining weight daily.

Far off Anna saw a woman walking along the track and when she approached she saw it was a thin, bedraggled Coloured woman.

Just another farmgirl, she thought as she drew up. One of thousands, but they shared a common face – the face of deprivation. Dumb, defeated eyes. Mouths that could plead or lie. Shuffling figures on the lip of survival.

The woman was clutching a baby wrapped in a filthy blanket. The baby began to cry.

Anna felt sick as she peered at the wrinkled, wizened face covered with sores. 'What's the matter with your baby? It looks so sick.'

The girl stared sullenly without speaking.

She was unusually light-skinned, Anna thought, and her features were fine. She should have been pretty, but she was ugly.

'What's your name?' Anna asked her.

'Sophie, Ma'am,' the girl said eventually.

'And what do you want here, Sophie?' Anna asked.

'The baas. I'm looking for the baas.' Her gaze shied away like a nervous horse as she tightened her clutch on the baby.

'The baas? You mean Simon Smit?'

'Yes, Ma'am.'

'Well, he's away. He won't be back for a long time. He's gone whaling, you see.'

'Oh,' the girl wailed, too taken aback to speak for a while. At last she said, 'Who are you?'

'I'm Mrs Smit,' Anna said, trying to stem a feeling of alarm as she stared at the woman.

Abruptly she held out her bundle to Anna who took a step backwards, unwilling to touch the filthy baby.

'Help me,' the girl whined. 'It will die and it's his, you see.'

'Whose?' Anna asked.

'His.'

'Impossible,' Anna began indignantly. 'You're lying.' She turned to the van. 'Go away or I'll call the police.'

Sophie followed her and caught her arm. 'Look,' she said pulling back the shawl.

The wretched baby's hair was deep red, its skin pale under the dirt. Anna wanted to be sick. She felt ashamed, too, for the baby was obviously starving, a fragile, wizened thing, half the size of Acker.

How old was it? she wondered. She could not bring herself to ask, she was too angry and too bitter.

'I was born here,' the girl went on. 'I grew up here; I used to guard the turkeys and the sheep.'

Anna remembered Simon telling her of the girl his mother had reared and sent to work on the lands. She felt confused, stung with compassion as well as anger, hating the girl and at the same time pitying her. 'Go up to the house,' she said. 'I'll go to the village and buy things for the baby and when I come back we'll talk.'

The drive to the village was a nightmare. Memories of Simon crowded in on her; Simon with his red hair glinting in the sun; Simon naked in the tub, his broad, strong shoulders, his bottom lip so full and sensuous; the way he held her. In spite of everything that had passed between them, Anna knew that she loved him still. Now he and this woman ... She gritted her teeth. Had the two of them made love even when he was seeing her? The baby was so small, surely it could not be much older than Acker. Perhaps during that painful three weeks when he had disappeared? She nearly choked on the thought. Had Sophie lived in the cottage with him? She could have been diseased and without doubt she had lice. At the thought Anna felt contaminated and itched everywhere.

'God damn the bastard,' she muttered. 'I hope he drowns in the Antarctic. I hope he dies of the cold, slowly and painfully.' Her eyes clouded with tears, she missed the turn and swung the rear mudguard against the farm post. She braked, rubbed her eyes and peered out of the window. The post was still standing, but the mudguard was crumpled.

In the village all she could think about was Simon and Sophie while she made her purchases. She wondered if everyone in the village knew about it and, if not, how much would she have to pay to make Sophie go away and take her red-headed baby with her. That was the answer, she told herself on the drive home. All the girl wanted was money. She would pay well to be rid of her.

But when Anna reached the farm there was no sign of Sophie and Jan said he had not seen her. Anna felt relieved. No doubt she had left because Simon was married. Poor little baby, she thought belatedly. It would not last long.

When she was feeding Acker later that evening she heard wailing in the loft and, putting Acker in his crib, she raced up the stone steps, her heart thumping with anger. Sure enough, there was the filthy bundle and no sign of Sophie.

The baby's forehead was burning hot. God knows what was wrong with it. She felt she was endangering the life of her child by taking this waif into the house, but she could not let the poor thing die. She picked it up and carried it into the kitchen.

Anna was breastfeeding Acker and she had no idea how to mix the formula, but the instructions were simple enough, so

117

she sterilized a bottle, mixed the feed and pushed the teat into the baby's mouth.

The child seemed too weak to suck, but eventually with some coaxing, it managed to swallow some of the contents of the bottle, but shortly afterwards vomited.

Anna decided to bathe the baby next, and unwilling to use Acker's bath she put it into the tub. When she unwound the wrappings she was appalled to find that it was a little girl – a fragile, emaciated little girl, suffering bitterly.

The doctor was reluctant to come to the farm when he heard about the abandoned baby later that night.

'There are so many of them,' he said. 'Bring her to surgery tomorrow,' adding as an afterthought, 'if she's still alive.'

As the evening wore on it became clear that the baby would die, for it vomited all the feed it swallowed. Anna became increasingly alarmed and, putting the baby in a box in the back of the van, she drove to the village and woke the doctor. He confirmed her fears. The baby had pneumonia, was allergic to cows' milk and baby food and had no chance of survival. He refused to take it off her hands, and after giving her some medicine sent her back to the farm.

It was a long drive home in the dark. The wind came up and rocked the van; the child whimpered; it seemed to Anna that while she had been cruelly used and cheated, how much worse was the fate of this small baby who lay dying on the seat. Admittedly Simon's promiscuousness and unfaithfulness had scarred her, but through this same act a child lay suffering. It seemed that the baby and she were inextricably linked and her determination grew to try to save the child, as if by so doing she could protect herself.

Later that night she fed them and once again the baby vomited its feed. In desperation Anna thrust her nipple into its mouth. To her surprise the baby began to suck, not vigorously like Acker, but at least it was swallowing and afterwards it did not vomit.

. 'Poor thing,' she murmured, stroking the baby's cheek. 'I doubt you'll be alive tomorrow.' Sadly she wrapped it warmly and placed it in a padded crate next to the coal stove.

At one a.m. Anna was woken by wailing. She found the baby crying and carried it to bed. In the morning the little girl was lying at her side, suckling contentedly, and it seemed that her temperature was slightly better.

Anna nursed the baby for two anxious weeks. As the little girl fought for life Anna became more involved in her destiny and increasingly fond of her. She was so frail and delicate and although probably about a month older than Acker she was much smaller. Slowly she gained strength and by the end of February it was clear that she was going to recover.

Anna began to worry about her future. She was so light-skinned. Who could believe she was a Coloured child? When the sores began to clear and her hair grew longer she looked a little like Acker although Acker's eyes were green and hers were brown.

Autumn was approaching and Anna knew it was time to make a decision about Sophie's baby. There were not many options available. Anna knew that by law she could not bring up a Coloured child as her foster daughter or rear her in the house. As a Coloured, the law would not allow her to sleep in the house or sit at the table to share meals and, of course, she could not attend the local white schools. She could not even take the child to the cinema with Acker or into a restaurant for a lemonade. But what if she were to try to bring her up as the maid? Two little red-haired children reared in a master-servant relationship. Unthinkable!

As the years passed the stigma of being a non-white in a white household would corrode her and she would end up like her mother, or worse. Once again she reminded herself that the child was Simon's daughter.

She could get rid of her embarrassing problem by handing the child to a neighbouring farmer. Anyone would take it, for the child would be an assured form of labour and could make herself useful from six onwards.

One day Anna hung around the Coloureds' shacks and watched the children playing by the lagoon – a rough, tough skinny mob. When they saw Anna they swarmed around like

119

hornets, begging for pennies. No, a foster home here was out of the question.

Eventually she decided that the only answer was to place the child in an orphanage.

After hours on the telephone Anna found an orphanage for Coloured children run by nuns in Cape Town. The next day was cold and windy. Anna dressed the babies warmly and tucked them into the cradle which she placed in the front of the van. She felt sad, but determined, knowing that she had left it far too long. She felt guilty, too, for being so tardy in registering Acker's birth, but who could blame her? After all she was alone on the farm.

She found the home eventually, parked the van and, leaving Acker in the cradle, carried the baby into the main entrance of the convent where she was met by one of the nuns.

The Mother Superior arrived looking as sterile as her surroundings and after a brief glance at Anna's corduroy work trousers and mended blouse led her into the office.

'I found this baby girl abandoned in my loft,' Anna began nervously. 'No one wants her. I've been looking after her for three months, since her mother disappeared, so I thought perhaps you …'

'We are full, more than full, in fact overflowing, but we cannot turn away a child,' the nun began. Then she gasped as she bent over the baby. 'A little red-headed child and so light skinned.' She lost no time in prising the story out of Anna.

'So you would hardly welcome this child growing up in a foster home in your district,' she said severely.

'No, that's not fair,' Anna burst out. 'She'll be better off in your care. After all, she'll get an education.'

'Let me show you round,' the nun said sadly. 'We do the best we can, but the home is run entirely on charity. Children need mother love,' she went on, 'but we are so short staffed.'

It was a dismal scene, the children were either mentally defective, deaf or crippled. Obviously the misfits came here. No one else wanted them. The nursery smelled of urine, vomit and disinfectant.

'You can place the baby here,' the Mother Superior said,

pointing to a cot, but when Anna bent to place the child there she found that she was unable to do so. Her hands would not obey her head and as she struggled with herself the baby began to wail and her hands gripped Anna's as if she understood.

'Thank you for your suggestion,' she said as firmly as she could. 'I will look around for a suitable foster home.' Then she fled.

In the following nights there was little sleep for Anna for she could find no solution to her problem. If only Sophie would come and take the baby, she thought.

As if in answer to her plea, the girl arrived at the farm early one morning. She looked just as dirty and hopeless as before, and she was drunk.

'Madam, I came for my baby,' she said swaying in the doorway. Her face revealed her secret triumph.

'I don't have your child,' Anna lied without hesitating. 'It died. What did you expect, leaving it in the roof like that? Serves you right. The police are looking for you, Sophie. It's a crime to abandon your baby.'

'My little baby died?' The girl collapsed wailing on the doorstep.

Anna saw Jan hurry out of the dairy. She had forgotten about Jan. He would be sure to tell Sophie the truth.

Anna felt horrified at the prospect of handing over the baby. She fled to the bedroom and locked the door. The babies were sleeping peacefully after their feed and they looked a little alike. She lay shaking for a very long time. Yet it was strangely quiet outside. Eventually Anna went to see what was happening and saw a small figure in the distance walking along the farm track.

Jan was cleaning the dairy.

'She's gone then?' Anna said as casually as she could.

'Yes,' he said quietly. 'I showed her the grave, so she left.' He did not look round and Anna caught her breath in amazement. An unexpected accomplice, she thought uneasily.

Anna drove to the Magistrate's Court in Bellville early next morning, trying to rationalize her actions. After all it was

Simon's child and if it were not for her it would have died long ago. It was she who had nursed the child back to life, no one else had as much right to the baby as she had. Besides, she argued with herself, who else could feed the baby?

The clerk made it easy for her.

'Twins,' he said before she had time to speak. 'What a lucky girl you are.' He called his assistants and they cooed over the children. 'The little girl looks just like you,' the clerk said.

Anna nodded, too relieved to answer.

Eventually he opened his file. 'Date of birth?'

'January the thirteenth, nineteen thirty-nine.' Anna had no idea when Sophie's child was born, but they both looked the same size.

'Mrs Smit, you are supposed to register births just after the children are born.' The clerk tried to look severe.

'I was ill,' she gasped. 'I'm alone on the farm. My husband is whaling.'

'That's tough,' he said. 'And their names?'

She had forgotten about a name for the little girl. 'My son is called Acker André Smit,' she began, 'and my daughter ...' How strange it sounded, 'my daughter', but indeed she was her daughter now. 'But of course, she's called Katie,' she burst out. 'Her name is Katherine Maria Smit.'

Part Two

13

Simon's sleepless nights were filled with images: flashes of blue silk by moonlight; white breasts on river sand; chapped hands cupping mealies. Even by day, scanning the horizon for whales, he would find himself gazing into Anna's eyes.

For the first time Simon was lonely and filled with strange emotions: desire when he endured the lonely bunk; compassion when he remembered Anna's fears; aggression when he pictured that ninny Piet Joubert still after Anna and perhaps sniffing around Modderfontein in his absence. Anna was his wife, she belonged to him and from now on he would stay with her. This was love, he decided.

He regretted his decision to go whaling, abandoning Anna when she needed him, what with the baby coming and no water for her silly chickens. Poor Anna! Ruefully he admitted that he had run away, ashamed that his farm could not support a few lousy hens, but he would make it up to her, he would pay for her chicken feed without a murmur of complaint.

But how?

As if to punish him the trip had been cursed from the start, one disaster following the next. Whales had been scarce, the weather foul, they had lost three men in a storm that almost wrecked the whaler and half their catch had been savaged by sharks. He would be lucky to earn four hundred pounds. What an oaf he was!

'Hellish trip,' he muttered, pacing the deck of his floating prison as Saldanha Bay appeared reluctantly out of the morning haze.

125

When the whaler docked Simon was first over the side. Wages could wait, he told the startled pay clerk as he grabbed the keys of his van and soon he was racing towards Modderfontein.

Autumn mists drifting in valleys, green grass piercing the topsoil, birds migrating northwards and his ewes ready to drop, but Simon was oblivious to all this. Mouth dry, palms sweating, he wondered what he would find at home. His stomach knotted when he thought about his child. Was it a son, or daughter? Who cares! Just let it be healthy. Just let Anna be all right. Nothing else mattered.

Anna was in the pantry checking eggs. Five thousand almost filled the small room and she could not help gazing far longer than necessary, but eventually she forced herself to close and lock the door.

When she heard Simon's van she took fright and, slamming the bedroom door, she leaned against it trying to stop shaking.

How foolish to be afraid. Why, Katie looked just like Acker. She smoothed the blankets, watching the sleeping babies. No one would ever know, yet pangs of fear shot through her stomach as she heard the van skid to a halt in the yard. Still she hesitated, staring possessively at Katie. By now Sophie had become unreal, a nightmare; Anna knew that Katie was her child, for Simon had planted his seed in the wrong womb. She had merely taken back what was rightfully hers.

'Anna,' Simon called from the kitchen.

A voice that still had the power to make her cry. She wiped her cheek with the back of her hand and hurried to the kitchen. Simon looked pale and thin, more handsome if that were possible. Damn the man. Her heart was pounding, her breath coming in short, sharp bursts and she had to restrain an impulse to throw herself into his arms. Deliberately she resurrected his crimes. There stood the man who had left her to face childbirth alone; stolen her money; seduced her for her father's fortune while living with that Coloured whore. His crimes were endless, to love him was to love a cobra. An invitation to disaster.

Simon stared as if he wanted to retain the image forever.

126

'God, I missed you. Oh, Anna, how I missed you.' He picked her up, hugging her. 'I'm never going to leave you again.' Then he put her down gently and patted her stomach. 'You look fine, Anna, just fine,' he lied.

The truth was she looked older and tired, but she was his wife and he loved her, although she was acting rather strangely. 'Was everything okay? I mean the baby ...'

She nodded.

'A boy?'

She nodded again.

'A boy!' He punched his fist into his cupped hand. 'And you?'

'I'm all right as you can see.' Her voice sounded curiously hard.

His face folded into a slow smile. 'Where's my son, my Simon?'

'Acker,' she said firmly. 'After Uncle Acker,' the hardness now becoming ominous.

'Where's Acker?' he asked, finding the name strange and feeling alarmed by her manner.

'Sleeping,' she said.

Simon regained his spirits as he rushed down the passage, but when he opened the door there were a few seconds of silence. Then he yelled: 'Twins! Anna – twins.'

Katie began to scream as Simon gathered the babies in his arms.

'No, no,' Anna protested. 'Leave them.'

'I must,' he said, blinking back his tears, 'I must hold them. Twins. Jesus! Who would believe it? And they both look alike – just like me. Why, look, Anna, one has brown eyes and one green. Acker and ...?'

'Katie,' she said.

'A girl. It's a girl,' he said wonderingly. 'This one?' he asked, choosing correctly. She nodded.

He began rocking them around the bedroom, singing an old nursery rhyme. The twins stopped crying and began to watch him suspiciously.

'She's going to be a little beauty, Anna. Look at those eyes

127

and that hair. Where are their bottles? I'll feed them.'

Anna felt jealous. What right did he have to come here and take over? 'They don't have bottles,' she snapped. 'Their next feed is at noon.'

'You – breastfeeding? I don't believe it.' He sat down on the bed and laughed. When Katie cried again Anna felt relieved. Simon would soon tire of them.

'Since you're here you may as well look after them. They can't be left alone, and I have work to do.'

That man was a disaster, she persuaded herself. Coming back, interfering, and just when she had the farm so well organized.

The pet lamb was sprawled across the doorstep looking fat and ungainly. A damn nuisance to everyone, Anna thought for the first time, as she prodded it out of the way with her foot. A useless farm animal was ridiculous, she would turn him into chops one of these days.

Jan was scrubbing the dairy. He watched Anna curiously as she passed and fleetingly she felt uneasy. Jan knew, but surely no one would believe him, not even if he raved about Katie in one of his drunken fits. Still, she retraced her footsteps.

'Morning, Jan,' she called out.

'Morning, Missus.'

'The boss is back.'

'Old Jan saw the baas.'

'He loves the twins,' she said firmly.

He nodded, smiling, and his tooth wobbled. Would it never fall out? But perhaps he did not know what 'twins' meant.

'He's very glad I have two babies,' she said firmly.

Jan sat back on his haunches. Words baffled him and he struggled to find a way to reassure her. Overwhelmed by the long silence he scratched his head. Then he said, 'Old Jan put a cross on the grave.'

'Thank you, Jan,' she said simply and hurried away.

When she looked at her watch Anna was annoyed to find that she had wasted thirty-five minutes; valuable time scheduled for inspecting the poultry. She arrived, breathless, to find that the egg boxes were over-full and the feeders were

128

getting low, but the boys would come after school.

Only one snake lay in the nesting boxes and it was asleep, bulging with eggs. She must go and call Jan, but as she turned away she paused, thinking that the time for relying on men was over. She must kill it herself. Her thoughts ran on inexorably while she ran to the feed shed where Jan kept a forked stick handy. She had watched him often enough, but when she lunged forward she was quaking with fear.

The stick landed accurately over the reptile's neck leaving it pinned and helpless, but Anna was unprepared for its ferocious strength as its tail whipped frantically, flaying her.

Anna groped for the spade to slice off its head, but she had forgotten to place it handy. Too late she realized that she was as much a prisoner as the snake, for if she let go it would strike her.

The cobra spat and hissed, yellow eyes blinking hatred. Even a snake knows how to hate, she thought, while I keep loving those who would destroy me. She leaned harder on the stick. Then she remembered her pocket knife and, holding hard with one hand, she pulled out the knife and lunged at the snake. The first blow glanced off the side of its head and the creature found greater strength in its desperation, but the second time her aim was true. She struck again and again long after the snake lay dead. Then she took the corpse by the tail and dropped it by the feed shed. Jan would find it and bury it later.

'So much for snakes.' She laughed and it was a cruel laugh. Momentarily she frightened herself.

Later, when she returned home, she found Simon in the kitchen smiling happily as he rocked the sleeping babies.

'Where did you go?' he asked curiously.

'To the chicken camp.'

'You still have some?'

'Yes,' she said and turned away.

'Anna, I'm sorry about the water. I want you to know I'm going to pay the feed bill.' He felt better when he had said that.

'That won't be necessary, thanks.' Her voice was flat,

129

automatic. 'I'm paying it off as arranged.'

She's not as hard as she's making out, Simon decided. A little love and a little wooing and we'll be back to normal. 'How will you manage?'

'Same way I bought the furniture and the baby clothes. Did you think you'd find them wrapped in rags? You left us without a penny, surely you remember?'

'I didn't think,' Simon stammered. 'Besides, you always have your parents.' He looked at her, feeling frightened by her coldness. 'I went to earn money,' he said, appealing to her. 'You can have it all, it's only four hundred pounds, but it's yours.'

'Thanks, but you probably need it for the farm.' She opened the pantry door. 'Look, five thousand eggs. Looks more, doesn't it? I deliver this amount four times a week and I get a good price.'

Simon sat immobile for a moment, gaping at the crates. 'Impossible,' he said at last. 'What d'you do for water – and labour?' he added as an afterthought.

'I found water, and as for labour, schoolchildren help me afternoons and I pay them with eggs.'

She watched Simon's face struggling with mixed emotions: incredulity, joy, envy, fear. It was all there. He really is a country bumpkin, she thought contemptuously.

Simon saw contempt slide slyly over her face and felt intimidated. He wanted to carry her to bed, but felt bewildered in the face of her new status as mother and poultry farmer. He forgot to be glad about the water, instead he thought: It will come right in bed.

'Well,' Simon sighed and stood up awkwardly, pushing the babies towards her. 'Feeding time, I suppose.'

Anna's breasts were painfully heavy, knotted with milk that was overflowing.

'It's time the shearers came. I'll round up the sheep and inspect them.'

'They've been,' she said briefly. 'Last Wednesday.'

'And the wool?'

'Delivered to the wool buyers. No point in leaving it here.'

130

'You should've left it for me to grade,' he said making a visible effort to smile. 'We're paid more if it's graded.'

'Well, of course, any fool knows that, so I graded it. You could double your income with a better strain. Still, you'll get about two hundred pounds, or so they told me.'

He could not complain, Simon thought moodily. It was fifty pounds more than he usually received.

'It's because of the lucerne,' she told him as if reading his thoughts. 'I've been supplementing their grazing. Used up your camps and planted some more. Now we have water it's no problem.'

He still did not believe her. Perhaps one of the dongas was fuller than usual. 'And the cows?' he asked, wondering why the hell he'd left the farm to her. He'd be lucky to find a job to do.

'Just fine. I sold the bull.'

For a moment he was too angry to speak. Then he said: 'Ferdinand? What d'you do that for?'

'He wasn't special. They've got this artificial insemination service at Elsinore. Cheaper and better.'

'Of course,' he said thinking how he had loved Ferdinand. He scowled at the floor, unwilling to start a fight. 'I'll saddle Vixen and inspect the fences. There'll be a lot needs doing.'

She nodded, wishing him gone. The fences and gates had been repaired, but after all he had to do something.

'I put Vixen out to graze,' she called through the open door at his retreating back, for he was going towards the stable.

He turned and came back and she could not help noticing his sagging shoulders. 'Don't worry,' she called out. 'She's all right. A regular guts. She wanders up to the chickens and tries to pinch their food; broken in once or twice.'

'I'm hungry,' Simon said in the doorway.

She shrugged. 'Lena will fix you something.' Then she hurried off with the twins and Simon was saddened by the sound of the bedroom door slamming.

Still he hung around, unable to cope with the feeling of inadequacy. Today, overwhelmingly, Anna reminded him of old man van Achtenburgh. He would have to do something

131

extraordinary to keep his end up or he would be swamped by her.

After a while a young girl walked into the kitchen, dark as coffee, head shaved, but with a certain intelligence and grace about her.

'Are you Lena?' Simon asked.

'Yes, baas.'

'How long have you worked here?'

'A month.'

'Lena, I'm hungry.'

She smiled. 'I'll make the baas some chicken sandwiches.'

'Guess we're not short of those,' he said mournfully.

He took huge, hungry bites, filling his mouth with strong, sweet black coffee and chewing the mixture with concentration before gulping it. He felt better when he had eaten, and taking the saddle and bridle from the shed he set off over the hills to find Vixen.

When he crested the second range of hills he stopped in wonder for beneath the black slopes of virgin bush separating Modderfontein from the sea lay several fields of green, and from the various shades he recognized lupins, barley and lucerne. Below the camps were hundreds of chicken houses in neat rows and the sight made him catch his breath. He quickened his pace, but forgot about poultry for now he could see a large water storage tank beyond the fields, several taps and a long pipe stretching towards the lucerne.

Racing up to them he stared for a long time. Water, on Modderfontein, it was a miracle, but it took a van Achtenburgh to find it, he thought resentfully. Eventually he plucked up courage to turn on the taps and the force of the water amazed him. He turned them all on, letting the water run wastefully down the hillside, but the force from each tap was just as great.

'My father!' he said in wonder.

After a while he caught sight of Jan digging a hole for a dead cobra.

Still in a daze from the water, he asked, 'Where d'you find it?'

Jan shook his head. 'The Missus. She killed it. Missus angry. Look.' He held up the punctured skin for inspection.

'Jesus!' Simon whistled and looked away. All at once he caught the image of Anna, fragile, tender, smiling at him, just the way he had pictured her during long months at sea. The image faded. Irretrievably lost.

'Jan, go and find Vixen,' Simon began.

Jan stared away obstinately. 'Jan must watch the chicken feed. Boys come.' He pointed to a row of youths climbing the hill.

Restraining the impulse to cuff Jan round the ears, Simon walked away. He had lost his leadership by leaving the farm in Anna's capable hands. A stranger on his own land, but not for long, he vowed.

Vixen was nowhere in sight, but he whistled and heard her answering neigh from the donga, and when he looked over the edge he found a sloping path had been cut into the side and Vixen was rushing towards him. The mare nuzzled his shoulder. At least there was one creature glad to see him.

It was a long, lonely day as Simon checked the fences, the cattle, the sheep and marked out the areas for this year's planting. But the day was not as long as the evening, when Simon and Anna sat like strangers, groping for words to throw into the pit of silence that engulfed them.

It seemed there were a hundred jobs for Anna to do before she would go to bed, and once there she became as modest as if she were sitting on the beach, and managed to remove her clothes and put on her nightdress without showing even a portion of skin.

This was not the homecoming Simon had dreamed of during lonely nights and lonelier mornings when he woke ramrod-hard, bursting with desire.

But she had suffered and he was the guilty one so, restraining his need, he set about making Anna as amorous as he felt. She had loved to have her back stroked, so Simon pushed her nightgown straps off her shoulders revealing half of her back, which he stroked tenderly, letting the tips of his

133

fingers run softly over her taut skin. Long afterwards, when he tried to turn her towards him, he found she was sleeping and he shook her angrily.

'Oh,' she yawned. 'Oh, I'm so tired, such hard work, must sleep.'

'I'm damned if you'll sleep,' he muttered losing his temper. 'I've been waiting all day for this. Months! Damn it, Anna, you're like an iceberg. What's the matter with you?'

'Nothing,' she said and curled on her side of the bed with her back turned. 'I'm tired.'

'Get rid of the chickens if this is what it does to you.'

'Without chickens we would've starved,' she retorted, adding defensively, 'I've every right to keep chickens.'

'I've got my rights, too,' he shouted. 'You're my wife and it's your duty to love me.'

Suddenly she was wide awake. 'Duty!' she shrieked. She lit the candle and sat up holding it over her like an avenging angel. 'Duty!'

The candle tilted and hot wax fell on Simon's bare stomach and the pain, though trivial, stung him into a rage. He wrenched the candle from her hand, pinched out the flame and flung it across the room.

Pushing her down beneath him he forced her legs apart and let out a long sigh of relief, but Anna lay unmoving, cold and uninvolved, so that when Simon came it was a poor thing, a shadow of what he had hoped for. He felt cheated.

Anna lay without moving until he said, 'Well, shift over then.'

'Oh, you're finished, are you?' she retorted and turned her back on him.

'Jesus! I'll get you for that,' he muttered and turned his back too, so that they were both very uncomfortable in their single bed with their knees over the edge, and neither of them could sleep.

Simon was wondering where he had gone wrong, but he knew well enough and after a long and painful self-interrogation he blurted, 'Anna, I'll look after you and the children from now on; I'm sorry for what I've done. Let's start again.'

134

But Anna pretended to be asleep. It makes no difference to me, she was telling herself. Whatever he does to me, I shall feel nothing, he can't get through to me and I shall always despise him. She decided to buy another single bed and wondered why she had not thought of that while he was away.

Early next morning, Simon awoke first and tried to woo Anna by kissing her gently on her neck and her shoulders, but the twins began screaming and Anna rushed away, locking the nursery door behind her, not wanting to be watched as she fed them.

By the time the twins were bathed and changed, Jan had loaded the lorry and Anna carried the cradle to the front seat and started the engine.

Simon came running over from the shed. 'Where are you going?'

'To Cape Town to deliver eggs.'

He frowned at her. 'Weren't you going to say goodbye?'

'Goodbye.'

'Can't I drive the van for you?' he persisted. 'It must be awkward with the twins.'

'Not at all, I enjoy the ride,' she said. 'Besides it's really quite a job, collecting the money, finding new contracts.' She let out the clutch and the lorry swayed precariously up the rough farm track.

Bitch, he thought. She was treating him like a moron. All the same he had better hire a bulldozer and flatten that road. He could not bear the thought of an accident with his babies in the van. Anna had no right to put her business before the children's welfare, he thought, watching her anxiously out of sight.

The first rains were due and Simon decided to drive to the village to order seed, fertilizer and molasses. The manager of the co-op was unusually effusive. He hurried over, clapped Simon on the shoulder and invited him for a cup of coffee in his office. Simon feared the worst and was already explaining how he intended to pay Anna's bill when the manager said:

'Give my regards to your charming wife. What a businesswoman she is. Well, they say the apple never falls far from the tree.'

His voice droned on, but Simon, though anxious to escape, discovered that Anna had paid half her feed bill and was buying shares in the co-op. If she had spare cash she could have lent him the down-payment for a new harvester, he thought ruefully. Even Simon's bill was less than he had thought, because Anna had paid off the money she had received for Ferdinand.

There was another surprise at the village store, for Olivier who had run his own business for over thirty years, had engaged a manager.

'Jewish!' Olivier told him in a stage whisper that could be heard across the warehouse. 'One of those German refugees we're reading about in the papers. Poor bugger lost his shirt, but he got out. His English is all right, but no Afrikaans. He'll soon pick it up since he's German-speaking. Never seems to sleep, works here ten hours a day and goes round the farms collecting produce at night. Give him his due, he's never late.'

Olivier had two daughters and no son. Great hulking girls like their father with ginger hair, large bones and broad backs. So far they had remained unmarried.

'Reckon he'll chose one of them if he's got his head screwed on right,' Olivier confided. 'Half the shop goes with each of them.'

Unlikely, Simon thought watching the man curiously. He looked slender, but he was handling sacks of mealie meal as if they were feather pillows, working with an economy of movement that Simon could not help admiring. He was wearing a suit and tie which looked absurd in the store, but in spite of the heat and the manual labour, he might have just walked out from his tailor's. His hair was blond and stood up from a widow's peak in a startling frizz, and his skin was burned to a smooth golden tan which only blonds acquire. Something about his blue eyes was disturbing, analytical and observant, they were set rather too close together over strong, sharp features.

He won't last long here, Simon thought. Give him time to get his bearings and he'll be off to the city. It was clear that he understood every word Olivier had whispered and he looked amused.

On the way back from the whaling station, where he picked up his cash, three hundred and eighty-four pounds, Simon began to think about Olivier's assistant. Eventually he made up his mind, drew to a halt, turned the truck, and returned to the village where he introduced himself to the new manager who, he discovered, was called Kurt Friedland.

'Heard you're buying farm produce round about and I reckon you're starting a wholesale business.'

The bloke's a genius, Kurt thought sarcastically, but he answered civilly enough: 'If you have anything to sell I'll call after work.'

'Not me, my wife,' Simon explained. 'She has about five thousand laying hens and she's been delivering eggs to town herself.'

'You'd like me to take over?'

'Well, it's a bit difficult,' Simon said blushing. 'She runs things her way. Best if you talk to her.' He leaned over the counter and slapped Kurt on the shoulder. 'Come and eat with us, man. That way we can talk about it over a glass of wine. Maybe Anna will see reason.'

Dinner was the last thing Kurt wanted, for it would waste his evening, but he could think of no way to avoid it so he said, 'At seven then. Thanks,' and forced a smile.

Simon felt pleased with his flash of inspiration. He had found a way of keeping Anna on the farm. Besides, with a guest for dinner she would warm up a bit. Who knows what might happen afterwards.

Much later, Anna too drove home feeling satisfied with the day's work. She had delivered her five thousand eggs to the chandlers, gained new contracts for eggs from the police and fire department and now she was tired. She was behind schedule, too, for her breasts were hard and sore, leaking over her blouse, and the twins were beginning to whine.

As she crested the hill above the farm she felt reluctant to go home, so she parked the van and sat on the grass to feed the babies, abandoning herself to the sensual pleasure of milk being sucked through her nipples and the melancholy sounds of evening: cries of seabirds returning to the swamps around the lagoon; clucking of hens; cows lowing as they returned for milking; the cry of herons as they soared overhead. The baboons began barking. Something was frightening them and the sound was unusually clear. She could even hear the sea lapping against the shore, for the wind had veered to the north-west carrying the sound towards her. On a distant hill she could see young turkeys, three hundred of them, returning in single file, silhouetted against the grey-green evening sky.

As the cold autumn mist curled around her, she shivered. Winter was coming and it would be a lonely winter.

Lately Anna was overcome with a feeling of emptiness. Yet she had the farm to build, her poultry to run, her babies. What more could there be? Deep inside her she knew that one vital ingredient was missing. Joy! Somehow joy had gone out of her life. Well, that was just part of growing up, she decided. Joy, like Father Christmas, was merely an illusion.

14

To Anna, Simon's invitation was just another example of his idiocy. How could they entertain without a table and she without a dress? Besides, they were short of plates and cutlery and possessed only two mugs.

Simon was unable to understand her concern over trivialities, but did not interfere when she telephoned to cancel dinner. It was too late for there was no reply. Finally she had a brainwave, they would make a *braai* under the trees, as she had done for the children's Christmas party, and they would remain outside for the evening with tree trunks for chairs and the lantern hanging from the eucalyptus branches. She felt better and called Jan to chop wood and light the fire while Lena was set busy stuffing sausage skins with spices, minced pork and beef and preparing chops.

Since Friedland worked for Olivier it followed that he would be a country bumpkin, Anna decided, yet she could not overcome a sense of unease. Had she bothered to analyze her feelings, she would have realized that she was ashamed to meet anyone and work had become her refuge. She was cheered by the thought that this was not a social occasion; the man was calling on business, the more was the pity, since she had no intention of parting with her precious profits.

He was late, which was lucky, for the fire would take hours to cool sufficiently to cook on it. At last she saw distant headlights approaching slowly, the driver obviously alarmed by their precarious road. When the headlights were switched off Anna could make out an old grey van. The door opened and he stepped out.

Anna was poking the fire. She called, 'Over here by the lantern,' and stood up, but a moment later she was overcome with embarrassment. Her guest was tall and well-dressed in a superb grey suit. He looked distinguished and out of place. He glanced around curiously for a few moments and something in his expression made her angry. He might be visiting the zoo, she thought. He had a strange way of walking; placing his feet carefully before him as if balancing along a wall. His hands were long and delicate and he was clutching a bunch of sad red roses. He looked at them, shrugged and shook her hand with an apologetic smile, but when his eyes reached her face his expression changed. It was as if he recognized an old friend. Next minute he's going to say we've met before, she decided, but all he said was, 'Well, well.'

'Good evening,' she began holding out her hand. 'So pleased to meet you. We have planned a traditional South African *braai* for you. We love to eat under the stars.' She gestured towards the sky where clouds were gathering thick and angry and her laugh rang falsely in her ears. 'This is how our forefathers ate when they trekked through the bush,' she gabbled on, 'and it has become a tradition now.' She indicated the tree trunk on which Kurt was to sit and he glanced at it without much enthusiasm and then back to Anna, gazing at her silently for far longer than necessary until she blushed and looked away.

To Kurt the evening was becoming unreal, but whether nightmare or fairytale he had not yet decided. It had begun earlier with young Simon Smit gossiping with Olivier in the storeroom and the words Jew, refugee and penniless had cropped up repeatedly. It irked Kurt to be labelled, even though it was true.

Kurt had not yet shaken off a sense of unreality. Reality struck home only at night with memories of shouting mobs, burning homes, his father's blood congealed on paving stones.

He had left, bartering his family's ballbearing plant for a one-way ticket. Europe was doomed, tainted with a veneer of civilization that could be dissolved in seconds. He must go further, as far from Europe as he could. Were it possible he

140

would have chosen a desert island or the Antarctic, but finally the choice had narrowed to Australia or South Africa. Once in Cape Town he had found a thriving metropolis which depressed him, so he had grabbed the first job offered away from the city. Here, in Saldanha Bay, he had met a more primitive breed, people who meant what they said and had little enough to say in any event. Quiet, homespun people, kindly enough, content with their lot, obsessed with the weather and their crops.

But loneliness was like a damp winter wind, it sunk into his bone-marrow, seized his joints, dulled his brain, and when he had recovered from his initial annoyance at Simon's invitation he found he was actually looking forward to his first social occasion.

So he had set off, dressed in his only suit, on a chilly evening in mid-May. Out of habit he had purchased chocolates from the store, but flowers had proved a little more difficult until he remembered the vegetable farmer outside Malmesbury who grew cut flowers for market, and he had driven there to purchase a bunch of long-stemmed roses which had become battered on the seat over the Smit's bad road.

At dusk the wind changed abruptly, as it often did here, veering to the north-west, creating a thick sea mist which rapidly spread over the land so that his route became almost impenetrable.

He had been wrestling with the Smits' road for over twenty minutes when suddenly, in the blaze of headlights, he saw a leopard dragging a full-grown sheep across the road ahead. For several seconds it stood poised and snarling, dazzled by the light; a huge beast, glossy and powerful. Then it melted into the mist abandoning the sheep.

Kurt felt stunned and elated. Never before had he seen a wild beast outside a zoo and it seemed that he had found the outpost of civilization for which he had longed. Here predators had fangs and spotted skins and their victims were sheep and not people.

But what to do? The sheep was sprawled across the road and it hardly seemed polite to run over it. He could not help

141

grinning at his unlikely social dilemma, still, he thought, a sheep was a valuable possession to a farmer, so he climbed out of the truck and, puffing and panting, shouldered the beast into the back of the van, keenly aware of the strong stench of leopard which he could hear growling in the shadows.

Ten minutes later he parked in the courtyard feeling that he deserved a stiff drink, warm fire and a good meal, but again his sense of unreality was heightened when Anna came towards him for she was that rare phenomenon, a perfectly beautiful woman. He was unable to look away from her Grecian nose, her wide-set deep blue eyes and her hair, which was scraped back and braided around her head in a most unbecoming style, and even her ridiculous men's clothes could not diminish the shock that ran through him as he gazed at her. Here was a woman who hated her beauty and her femininity, he decided. Not that it mattered, for he was captivated by her.

'Thank you for inviting me,' he said and handed her the roses. He stood cautiously beside the tree trunk which, it seemed, was to be his chair.

Anna was tongue-tied. Kurt Friedland was the most improbable person that she could imagine running Olivier's store.

Fortunately Simon arrived and clapped Kurt on the shoulder.

'Hi, Kurt, ready for grubstakes?' he said heartily.

Kurt turned. 'Oh hello, Mr Smit. My van disturbed a leopard on your road. It had just killed a sheep, I'm afraid.'

There was a startled silence and then Simon burst into crude laughter and clapped Kurt on the shoulder again. 'Impossible, Kurt, how much have you had to drink?'

Kurt shrugged, looking slightly offended. 'I assure you … ' he began.

'Perhaps it was a lynx,' Anna cut in. 'They look very similar although, of course, a lynx is smaller, but at night, in the headlights, and accentuated by the mist, one could easily be mistaken. We have a great many casualties from lynxes.'

'Can a lynx kill a full-grown sheep?' Kurt asked.

'No, well, I suppose it could, but they don't. They go for the lambs.'

Kurt shrugged. 'Whatever it was, it was carrying a full-grown sheep in its mouth as easily as if it were a rabbit.'

Simon burst into his teasing laugh again. 'Man, if you can't tell a lamb from a sheep, then maybe you shouldn't be in the wholesale business,' he said between guffaws.

'Possibly,' Kurt said coldly. 'Anyway your sheep, or lamb, is in the back of my van, so please call your boys to remove it.'

Simon went over to the van and the laugh faded. Then he called: 'My God, look at this!'

Jan came running and hauled out the carcass and the four gathered around examining the jagged wounds.

'I think Simon owes you an apology, Mr Friedland,' Anna began. 'You see, it's years since a leopard was seen in these parts. I'm told they're almost extinct.'

'This one sure as hell will be,' Simon added. He was already running for his gun and shortly afterwards disappeared into the darkness with Jan and Wagter at his heels.

'What about the *braai*?' Anna called uselessly into the mist.

There was a long silence and for something to do Anna picked up the poker and began to rearrange the fire. How could Simon be such a fool? And now he had left her to cope alone. What if Kurt should ask for the toilet? They only had a deep hole in the ground, lime-filled, covered by a portable wooden hut concealing a rough, homemade wooden seat. When the stench became unbearable, Jan was called to fill in the hole, dig another and move the hut. Right now it was due for a move, she remembered. And then she thought: What if it rained? As if in answer to her fears, the first drop fell and sizzled briefly on hot stones. Anna shivered.

Looking sidelong at her incredible profile, Kurt sensed that he was not welcome. But why, for heaven's sake, were they to sit outside on this cold, damp autumn evening? Briefly he wondered if she were slightly deranged. He had heard stories about her around the village: Anna van Achtenburgh from Stellenbosch, who had given up a fortune to marry her penniless farmer and now dressed in men's clothes and drove

143

a tractor and a truck, to the horror of local farm wives. Some even said she worked on Sundays, which Kurt had discovered was the ultimate sin. He felt grimy from the sheep and needed a wash.

The turkeys shifted restlessly in the branches overhead and Kurt leaped sideways, but too late. A large, white drop rolled down the sleeve of his jacket. He took out a handkerchief and began to dab at the offensive stain.

'It's only turkeys,' Anna said as if that excused everything. 'You're hardly dressed for a *braai*.'

Kurt felt somehow that he was at fault here.

'The fire's going out,' Kurt said after another awkward silence.

'No, it's not. You see it has to die down before we can cook the meat or it'll be burned.' She stood up reluctantly. 'Jan was going to cook the supper, but I doubt they'll be back in time. Well, I'll fetch the meat,' she said shyly and left.

When she returned she busied herself arranging the meat and sausages on the grill. Then she said, 'It's strange but mutton never tastes so well cooked any other way.'

'Tell me about the poultry farm,' Kurt began. 'Five thousand hens – a lot of hard work.'

'Oh, I'm sorry,' Anna cut in. 'I meant to tell you earlier that you've had a wasted journey. I need the better prices I get in Cape Town. I'm sorry.'

'Don't say sorry,' Kurt said seriously. 'This is the first time I've been invited to a home in South Africa, and my first *braai*. I'm grateful.'

Anna squirmed. 'Would you like some wine?' she asked. 'It's made locally from vineyards in Stellenbosch. Of course we don't have the soil for it here.'

She poured some of Jan's wine into a tin mug and blushed as she handed it to him.

For a while they were too embarrassed to speak. Anna was overcome with shame and shyness and Kurt was caught by the spell of the strange evening. When they did speak it was simultaneously, blurting the words out so that neither heard what the other said.

They broke off and regarded each other warily.

'You were saying?' Kurt urged.

'Today – this afternoon – the baboons were making such a commotion. It must have been the leopard frightening them. How fortunate you are to have seen it.'

'I thought the same.' On impulse he reached forward and squeezed her hand. 'Anna, may I call you Anna?' He carried on without waiting for her reply. 'Please call me Kurt. I want you to know that you have nothing to fear from me. Whatever it is that's upsetting you, please don't concern yourself on my account.'

She tried to explain. 'I live here by myself most of the time. Simon goes fishing and whaling and when he's back he's on the tractor most days. We've never invited anyone home.' She swallowed and gave him a tremulous smile. 'We're not really equipped, you see.'

Kurt leaned back and gazed into the tree and to his dismay saw rows of turkey tails overhead. By now his suit was ruined, so why worry? It wouldn't have lasted forever.

Sausages sizzled, turkeys gobbled, an owl hooted. Anna drank two mugs of wine and began to feel dizzy.

The meat was cooked and Anna handed Kurt a heaped plate of chops and *boerwors* with a baked potato. The mist was thickening, but the fire kept it at bay. Anna shivered and piled more wood on the fire. She smiled apologetically. 'Eerie, isn't it? Like a cave.'

When she smiled she looked even lovelier. If she were married to me, Kurt thought, she would be smiling always. 'You're right.' He stood up and snapped off a branch. 'We are the last survivors of an expedition to the South Pole. Our supplies have run out and this is our last meal. Tomorrow we die, but still we have carried the flag. I name this outpost Modderfontein.' He thrust the branch into the ground.

Anna giggled. How young she was. He tried to think of something else to make her laugh.

'The South Pole, my goodness, you must be cold. Better

145

have some more wine.' He held up his mug and Anna filled it.

'It tastes awful really,' she confided. 'Too sweet. We keep it for Jan.'

The mist pressed in on them. Anna retrieved the rest of the meat with a long fork and piled it on to a wooden platter. 'Help yourself,' she said.

'Don't you feel a strange sense of togetherness?' Kurt asked when they had eaten.

'It's the mist and the fire.'

'To me it seems that we are together in an icy womb, waiting to be reborn into a new and alien world. I shall be tied to you forever because of our prenatal togetherness.'

'Do be serious and have some more wine.'

'No, thanks, and I'm serious.' After a while he reached forward, took the loaf, and breaking off a piece handed half to Anna. 'It's symbolic, Anna. Take it and eat it. I have the strangest feeling that you and I will be sharing for a long time.' He grinned self-consciously. 'Right now I have nothing to share, so you may have the benefit of my wit, my business brain and you will share your beauty and your *boerwors*.' He broke off and gazed up at branches shrouded in mist where they could hear drops of rain splashing on leaves. 'Please God, you will share your roof with me when it rains.'

'Oh, oh,' Anna began, suddenly too miserable to care. 'It never rains here,' she moaned angrily. 'Everywhere else the sheep wallow in the mud, the ground turns into a quagmire, but here it's dust and drought and never a drop of rain. Last year we prayed. Oh, how we prayed for rain, and now, this evening, just when it had to be hot and dry – it rains.'

'Come on, Anna, a farmer's wife should be laughing for joy.' He patted her shoulder awkwardly.

'Of course at Stellenbosch,' Anna began desperately, 'they've had a good deal of rain already. The soil is richer, ideal for grapes.' She launched into a monologue on the types of grapes grown at Fontainebleu and the wines they made. She would talk all night if she had to, until he left. Anything rather than invite him inside.

There was a sudden whoosh as a gust of wind swept

through the trees, blowing the rain off the leaves. The fire hissed and spluttered. Kurt sprang up, grabbed the plates and the meat platter and hurried to the open door where a dim light glowed. The almost empty room was presumably a kitchen for there was a cupboard and a wood stove glowing in the corner, and beside it were two upturned boxes and at the back of the stove an old paraffin tin simmered with hot water. He shuddered as he thought of Anna working there.

When he returned to the fire Anna was still crouched beside the ruins of her *braai*.

'Don't sit here in the rain, Anna. Ridiculous. Look, you're wet through.' He took her hand, but she seemed to have frozen hard on the tree trunk, so he pushed her to the kitchen.

'I'll make coffee,' she said hopelessly as Kurt huddled on a box next to the stove. 'You see I sold my furniture, clothes, everything,' she told him. Her story poured out, the auction, the chicks, the water, her hopes.

'So why the gloom? You should be happy,' he answered when the torrent of words came to a halt. 'You made a plan and it's working.'

'Yes, but I didn't count on visitors, especially someone I don't know.'

He smiled. 'I don't feel strange with you, after all we have so much in common, both penniless, and full of plans. If you came to my room you would see an iron bedstead and one table. A year ago we were both rich and in a year's time we'll be better off. We are two of life's adventurers starting out together, so why shouldn't we be friends?'

'We're friends.' She smiled and suddenly felt happier.

'Could I take my jacket off and wipe it? Perhaps it will dry over the stove.'

'Oh please, let me,' she said, and taking it she began to rub at the offending sheep's blood and turkey stains with a wet cloth.

'Strangest of all is being called "Jewish refugee",' Kurt began. 'I never thought of myself as particularly Jewish and as for refugee — that sort of thing happens to Poles and Czechs, not German industrialists. We owned a ballbearing plant. I

147

suppose I had everything easy. Right now life seems unreal. I go through the motions of being alive: eat, sleep, work. I even make plans ...'

He broke off as she said, 'The stains are out. I'll get a coathanger.'

'You can make money in this country if you're prepared to work,' he went on when she came back, not really caring whether or not she was listening. 'Food distribution, for instance. There's a fortune to be made with hard work and patience, so I work hard and have patience, but all the time I'm thinking: this is just a strange dream. I'll wake one morning to find I'm back in Germany, back at the plant.'

Anna stood on the box and hung his jacket from the hook in the ceiling.

'Tonight was particularly unreal, meeting you.'

'Tell me why your English is so perfect,' she said to change the subject.

'I went to school in England for five years. Finished there, in fact, and then a German university.' He grinned self-consciously. 'Can I have some more wine, please,' he went on. 'It's not so bad, this wine of yours.'

The liquid splashed red against the glass; ruby patterns on the ceiling.

'We heard rumours, of course, but no one believed them. People were being moved, new settlements, anti-Semitism growing. Then, one Friday, after a meeting on the common, a crowd of people came rushing along the road. Ordinary people; we knew them well enough; the shoemaker, the fishmonger, all the locals, but it wasn't them any more. They had turned into a great angry beast with fangs in Main Street and a tail wagging two blocks away.'

He shuddered. Remembering. A body sprawled on the pavement, unrecognizable. Abruptly he took the wine jar and filled his glass again.

He's going to get drunk, Anna thought.

'I'm married,' he went on. 'Or perhaps I should say "was married". By now Madeleine will have divorced me. Her mother was Jewish, but she resented her Jewishness. She made a big thing out of hating me, trotting out old grudges, but she was really scared. The capsule broke, you see, so she went to live with another man.'

'Do you always talk in riddles?' Anna asked him.

'No. People live in capsules. Surely you've noticed? Voluntary encapsulation to avoid the terror of the unknown, safe in the confines of their beliefs, routine, as it is now, and will be, forever and ever. Then things happen, terrible things, like an incurable illness, or being Jewish in Germany. People ignore them, hope they'll go away, or make up lies easy to believe. Anything rather than face the situation.'

Anna wished he would go home. She was frightened by the attraction she felt for him and the strange sense of having known him for years. She felt drained; she wanted to crawl into bed and hide there for a very long time. Emotions had ruined her life; they were never going to get the upper hand again. She said, 'Would you like some coffee?'

He smiled. 'Forgive me, I needed to talk. No coffee, thanks.' He stood up. 'I must go. Thank you for a delightful evening.' He looked a little embarrassed, as if he knew he had talked too much.

At that moment Wagter swept into the kitchen, wet and muddy. He shook himself in the middle of the floor, spattering them.

'Oh Wagter, no. Bad dog,' Anna shrieked and held his collar while Kurt retreated to his van. There was a light bobbing on the crest of the hill, but Kurt had no wish to wait for Simon's return. He drove home, gripped with the mystery of Anna. She was a wild, headstrong beautiful woman, he decided, but depressed, afraid of her own emotions and hating her femininity. She was made for laughing and loving, not money-making. No doubt she would succeed, but at what cost?

Anna stood in the doorway of her kitchen watching Kurt's van drive away. The strange feeling of togetherness which she had shared with Kurt filled her with apprehension. She would not see him again, she decided.

Minutes later Simon arrived, drenched, muddy and in a

149

foul temper.

'It's gone up in the bush,' he told her. 'Could be twenty miles away by now. Need a good tracking dog, Wagter's useless. We'll probably never see it again, but if it comes back I'll organize a hunt with the neighbours.'

15

'Arriving Monday,' the telegram had proclaimed. 'Love, Uncle Acker.'

Anna had read the telegram half a dozen times. She had been tempted to telephone him in South-West Africa, but eventually decided against it. Let him come and get it over with, she thought. She had no doubt that Uncle Acker was being sent by her parents, who were still overseas, to inspect the farm and her condition. Well, he could make what he liked of it.

After the fiasco with Kurt Friedland she had acquired two chairs, a kitchen table and a single bed from the second-hand mart in Malmesbury, but she had not seen Kurt since that evening and she avoided the store, shopping at Malmesbury itself.

Anna begrudged wasting money on furniture for she was saving for the purchase of another four thousand chicks and the past month had been a busy one, preparing brooders and planting four camps of mealies to help offset the feed bill.

Uncle Acker had given her no indication of how he was arriving, whether by bus or by train. Was he expecting to be met? Inquiries at the station had confirmed that the trains came on Tuesdays and Thursdays only, so Anna carried on with her chores of planting, cleaning and grading eggs, a task which now required fulltime help. Even so, the telegram had upset her routine and she found it difficult to concentrate. She kept thinking about him.

How she had enjoyed holidays with Uncle Acker! Although he shot only for food, he had taught her to hunt, to track and

151

to survive in the bush. Most of all she had loved to feed the variety of wild animals he had rescued and tamed, birds, bucks of all description, meercats and once a leopard cub. When he was at home, or in the bush, he was a graceful, clever man, his shyness gone, gifted with the ability to communicate with all animals. On his rare visits to Fontainebleu, he became an awkward, tongue-tied man, always tripping over things. Either way, she had loved him …

Now, for the first time in her life, she was reluctant to meet him.

Apart from telling Lena to bake a tart and roast a leg of lamb she had made no special preparation for Uncle Acker. Yet all day she had been listening for the sound of a car and several times she thought she heard it, but it was only Simon stubbornly ploughing wheat two miles off.

Foolish, stubborn Simon! They had fought long and bitterly over the wheat this year, with Anna dead set against planting. Given enough water they could develop the dairy herd and this would pay well enough, but Simon wanted a wheat farm, he had set his heart on it and had to do things his way.

When she heard a car coming she caught her breath with fright; so many emotions tumbled around. Had he heard from her mother? What were they saying about her? Surely they were anxious! Anna had never forgiven her parents for abandoning her and this, more than anything, had increased her bitterness.

The car drove into the yard and Anna rushed out of the shed only to find Kurt outside the kitchen. She bit her lip with disappointment.

'Oh, it's you.' She walked across the yard towards him.

'It's me and I've had better receptions.'

'Sorry. I thought you were my uncle. I don't know exactly when he's coming, you see.' She looked anxiously over the hills and then back to Kurt. 'I suppose you haven't seen a sign of him?'

Kurt watched her curiously. Her eyes were too large, her face too pale. She looked tired and worried. 'No, but I'll go if you want me to.'

'Well, he's not here yet.' She hesitated. 'Would you like some coffee?' She half hoped he would refuse. After their disastrous evening a month ago she had begged Simon not to invite him again, saying that she disliked him, but the truth was she was afraid, for instinctively she was drawn to him, as if they had known each other for years. He threatened the safe, emotionless cocoon into which she had fled. No place for friends, no time for wasting, just work and growth. No one must interfere with her ambitions.

'Ah, a table and chairs. The poultry business must be improving.' He sat down, laughing. 'I smell eggs and bacon.'

She smiled. 'All right.' It took only a few minutes on the hot wood stove. She watched him sidelong as she prepared breakfast. Strange how he always managed to look superb, yet it was the same suit. She had a strong suspicion it was the only thing he had to wear. His hands were beautifully kept, in spite of his rough work, the correct length of cuff always showed. He must have been a wow in Germany. Here he was a trifle too meticulous. Most women would find him too remote; eyes too cold; mouth too thin, yet his features were strong and if you glanced briefly you would say he was exceptionally handsome.

'There's going to be a war, Anna,' Kurt said as she passed him a plate. 'The Germans are about to invade Poland and if Britain comes to the aid of the Poles I shall join up.'

He watched her carefully, but she showed no sign of regret.

'When it's over Anna, I'll come back.'

'Back here, whatever for?'

'I know you feel as I do,' he said evading her question.

'And how would that be?' she asked tartly.

He shrugged uncomfortably. 'I can't believe my feelings can be entirely one-sided.' His eyes showed all too clearly how he felt.

Anna said: 'We've met once before; why, we aren't even friends and you're forgetting I'm married. I don't want to hear another word of this.'

'But you can't be happy.'

'That's none of your business.'

Watching Kurt, Anna saw his mouth had set into a tight, thin line. He had been spoilt as a child, she decided. What a cheek. A man meets you once and fancies himself in love. Still, he was lonely.

She felt impatient with him and glanced surreptitiously at her watch. A quarter to ten, damn it. Without supervision, the two hands she had hired would have slowed their pace. With seven thousand laying hens time was becoming an obsession. On average she washed, graded and delivered twenty-eight thousand eggs a week. In her rare idle moments she would find herself automatically grading eggs with her hands like a maniac. In her dreams eggs would come tumbling towards her, more and more eggs, until she woke up sweating with fright. If she stopped work for a moment anxiety would settle on her like a tick bird on a bullock and drive her back to cleaning and counting. She began to fidget and fume.

Seeing her impatience Kurt said, 'Anna, how long would it take you to obtain a contract for all your surplus eggs and chickens for the same prices you get in town?'

'Why, that's impossible,' she laughed.

'More than an hour?'

'Why, yes, of course. You're being ridiculous.'

'Then you can waste a few minutes because I've brought you that contract. It's right here,' he said, tapping his top pocket. 'For the defence force.'

'But, Kurt,' she said, suddenly contrite. 'You're in the food distribution business. Keep the contract and supply them yourself, like you do everything else.'

'I don't supply eggs and poultry. Besides I'll be gone in a few weeks.'

'You're being melodramatic,' she told him sternly. 'The war hasn't started yet. Probably it never will.'

Kurt stared at her impatiently. 'You just won't face reality, will you, Anna?'

'My reality is my children, this farm and the poultry.'

Kurt kept looking at her as if willing her to say something.

To break the embarrassing silence Anna said, 'Simon didn't

get the leopard. There's been no sign of it since that night. Just wandering through I suppose, like you.' She smiled at him, but he looked offended. He took the contract out of his pocket, placed it on the table and left.

Shrugging him off she went back to work and became so engrossed that at first she did not hear the heavy vehicle rolling towards the farmhouse. Only when it swung ponderously down the last incline did she feel eggs vibrating on the trestle table and then she ran outside and was astonished to see her father's big lorry awkwardly manoeuvring the last bend. Running to the courtyard she saw Uncle Acker.

'Oh, but it's lovely to see you again,' she called out. 'How are you? How is everyone?' When he climbed down she threw herself into his arms. He was her favourite person, but this time something went wrong.

He had always been a large man, with arms longer than normal and extra big feet. This had been offset by the sheer bulk of the man, 200 pounds of muscle; now his flesh had shrunk so that his arms hung thin and ungainly from his large, bony frame. His stubbly hair, which he always shaved once a month, had turned from blond to white and his face looked haggard. Only his eyes were unchanged: deep blue, brimming with warmth and shyness.

'My, you're so thin,' she said, stepping back and looking up at him. Had she forgotten how old he looked? She made a quick calculation. He was only fifty-two, but looking sixty. 'How are you keeping?' she asked anxiously.

'All in good time, all in good time, my girl.' He wiped his hand over his face, a gesture she remembered well. 'That was a rough ride,' he said. 'Your road's impossible. Needs fixing.' He frowned. 'I was worried about your piano.'

'Piano?' Incredulously.

'And a few other things your mother asked me to bring.'

'She's back then?' For a moment Anna felt a deep sense of joy.

'No, she's not,' Acker said. The joy faded. 'She wrote to me. But that can wait a while.'

His face darkened when he saw the rough wooden table and chairs, but he did not comment on her obvious poverty, merely telling her about the ten thousand karakul and the losses he had suffered in last year's drought while he ate a slice of milk tart and drank Anna's thick, black coffee.

The twins woke up and screamed for food. They were five months old, but not yet weaned, and Anna proudly showed them to Acker before she went to feed them.

Acker seemed pleased that the boy was named after him, but said, 'Babies don't appeal to me much, although to be honest they look healthy enough. When they get to six or seven I'll be interested.'

'I'll tell you what,' he said when she returned. 'I could use a little air. How about showing me this farm of yours and perhaps I'll meet your husband somewhere about.'

They went out in the rain and tramped over the hills to the chicken camp while Anna told him about the auction, her hopes for the poultry farm, the water she had found. Then she showed him the camps of lucerne and barley she had irrigated and the vegetable field and pointed to the distance where Simon was ploughing for wheat.

'Not wheat soil,' her uncle said ominously.

'But Simon feels that with the right manure and irrigation he will succeed,' she said uneasily.

'And you? What do you think?'

She shrugged. 'It's his farm.'

When they returned, the wood stove and warmth of the kitchen seemed twice as welcoming, but Acker had little appetite for the roast lamb, pumpkin and sweet potatoes.

'You're losing weight,' she told him. 'I don't think you're eating properly.'

'When you get older you don't need so much food,' he said. 'But where's Simon? Can't he spare an hour to have lunch with your uncle?'

'He's angry,' she admitted. 'Fed up with the lot of us. You see, Pa wouldn't give me a dowry.'

'It's not compulsory. Hardly ever done nowadays.'

'I know, but he thought with Pa being so rich and him

having next to nothing … Oh, you know the story, Uncle Acker, I'm not going to bore you with it all over again.'

'A man could be civil,' he said.

'It's more than that. I've been a disappointment to him. I'm not really what he feels a wife should be. You see, I'm making a living already and I have plans for the future. To tell the truth I'm the only one here with any money in my pocket.' She laughed.

When they had finished lunch, sensing something was wrong, she could not wait any longer. 'Don't you have a letter for me? What did Mama say to you?'

'Anna, I've come to bring you bad news,' he said. 'Your mother died in Switzerland. Three weeks ago it was, but the letter took two weeks to arrive and then I flew down here.'

'Dead and buried then?' she said stonily, but she was thinking: I killed her. If it weren't for me, she'd be alive today.

Watching her Acker felt perplexed. There was no sign of emotion on the girl's face, instead she looked like a statue, expressionless. Some people were like that with grief, he thought. They kept it bottled inside them. Far better if she cried. He sighed and handed Anna the letter from her mother.

'She wrote to you before she died and your Pa sent the letter to me.' He handed her an envelope.

'I'll read it later, Uncle Acker,' Anna said.

'Anna,' he said. 'Don't blame yourself. Maria had rheumatic fever when you were a child and it weakened her heart and you know how many heart attacks she had after that. When you left she had another and your father decided to take her to a clinic in Switzerland for a few months, but she became ill again so they stayed.' He sighed and carried on.

'Your mother wrote to me, same time as she wrote to you, giving me a long list of things to bring you from the house, but I didn't bring the horse. Thought I'd better ask you first.'

'How is Jessop?'

'Fine, but fat. Not enough exercise, but that's soon righted.'

'I don't have time, there's no leisure here, what with the poultry and the twins,' she said without expression.

'I understand,' Acker said gently.

Acker left earlier than he had intended, angered by Simon's absence.

Anna stood sadly in the yard watching him leave. It could have been worse, she thought, as the lorry disappeared from sight.

It was late that night, when Simon and the twins were sleeping, before Anna could bear to open her mother's letter. She sat at the kitchen table with the lantern beside her and smoothed the single sheet of paper.

'*Dear Anna,*' she read. '*I've been thinking a great deal about you these last few months and I have come to the conclusion that life is too short to harbour grudges. You were wilfully wrong and made a sad mistake, which I am sure you have regretted often enough, so I forgive you now, while I can.*

The doctors tell me to rest a lot, but who can rest in such a lovely place? I go for long walks and remember the walks we used to take together.

I can never feel secure with my damaged heart so I have taken the precaution of making a will. As you know the two Malmesbury farms are mine and one of them has a small house where the foreman is living now. There's a cottage in the village which is let to a German family. The children were at school with you; I expect you remember them. Then there's a few shares in the local co-op and a field Durbanville way. All the property is to be left to your children, however many you may have, to be divided equally amongst them when they come of age. I know how much you need the money, but I never trusted that Simon of yours and I am afraid he will take it from you. At least this way you know your children will have something and in terms of the will the interest can be used for their education, so that will help you a little.

When I come back, and I hope it will be soon, we will make up for lost time. I am looking forward to seeing you and my grandchild. Is it a boy or a girl? Please write soon and tell me.

With all my love.'

Anna lit a candle and burned the letter. They were the best farms in the area and currently worth about twelve thousand pounds each, but when her children inherited them they would be worth so much more. She would not tell Simon, she decided. Not now; maybe never. 'I'll succeed anyway,' she murmured. She fetched some paper and wrote a short note of condolence to her father. There was little to say and she did not expect a reply. She sealed the envelope and put it in her bag. Then she went sadly to bed.

16

From that time on Anna became even busier. She would trudge through the mud from coop to coop, injecting, inspecting, delousing – endless chores. And those eggs! Thousands of them to be collected, transported, washed, weighed, packed and delivered. And it did not end there; accounts had to be sent; cockerels plucked and cleaned; coops disinfected; manure collected.

From July onwards the weather worsened; rain, floods and icy winds. The hens hung around with wings drooping, tails trailing and moulted, as Anna had known they would, but she was unprepared for the excessive appetites they developed in cold weather. Egg production slumped and she was unable to fulfil her contracts.

At odd moments, at the supper table, or while cooking, Simon would find her jotting down figures with a worried frown.

It was a time of indecision for Anna, knowing what should be done, but unsure of how to set about it, and while she dilly-dallied the food bill soared.

She had less time for Simon, not even a minute to sit at breakfast, or talk while he bathed, for the twins were thriving and they demanded her few moments of leisure.

Simon became increasingly resentful so that they could hardly exchange two words without flaring up, and afterwards they would not remember what it was they had been fighting about.

'What the hell's got into you?' he said one morning.

'I'm worried about the hens moulting.'

'All hens moult in winter, any fool knows that.'

'Not all hens, young pullets don't moult.'

'Well, they're not young pullets.'

Thoughtfully: 'They could be. It's no good. I can't afford to feed seven thousand hens through winter.'

'For God's sake, Anna,' he exploded in temper. 'You should have thought about that before you bought seven thousand hens.'

It was mid-July before Anna made up her mind. She drove to the village to find Kurt. How depressed he was looking. Bleak eyes with bags beneath them.

'Hi, Anna, what brings you here?' Mundane words, but his face lit up when he saw her.

Anna felt the same sense of togetherness and she became that much colder.

'I have a problem, Kurt. I hope you don't mind me coming to you. I want to sell four thousand hens now, but I need a good price. Do you have any idea how I could do this?'

'Giving up?'

'No, nothing like that. It's just that they're moulting.'

Kurt could not help laughing. 'It's been known to happen to hens at this time of the year.'

'Yes, but they eat double. I'll hardly cover their feed bill with next season's eggs. There doesn't seem to be any point in keeping hens past their first laying season. I don't know why anyone does. It's crazy.'

He smiled sympathetically. 'I'll phone around, see if I can raise some buyers,' he told her.

'I'd be grateful.'

'I hope that you are not angry with me still,' he said stiffly. 'Perhaps we could meet again ... ' He broke off looking awkward. 'If we were in Vienna I would invite you to lunch,' he said. 'But alas ... I don't know of a restaurant here.'

'Please come to supper,' she said, feeling trapped. She smiled spitefully. 'We'll have a *braai*. Simon will be so pleased to see you again. Would tomorrow night be suitable?'

He nodded. 'Hopefully I will have a buyer for you.'

Anna went back to her poultry feeling slightly relieved, but when he heard the news Simon was beside himself with rage.

'You can't slaughter four thousand hens who've another three years' laying ahead,' he stormed.

'Why can't I? They're my hens.'

'It's cruel.'

'It's business.'

Anna had no patience with him; she rushed off to the grading room.

'Cruel,' she muttered to herself incredulously. A strange word to hear on his lips; the man who had shot her cat. Yet he was always drooling over the twins and to watch him you might think he was brimful of human kindness. Simon was an enigma, for why did animals and children follow him around like a lot of silly sheep? Even Wagter had taken to him from the start.

When Anna remembered Simon in the vineyard waiting with Wagter, a crack would appear in the wall she had built around her emotions and she would catch a glimpse of the anguish raging beyond. Once she had loved him. Now love was irretrievably gone and that was the worst loss of all; worse than the loss of her home. It was the cause of her despair, her aching back, the hayfever from which she suffered.

Anna's only solace was work and when sadness gripped her she would bury herself in calculations and frantic scribblings. Money was real. Love was an illusion. When she had counted her theoretical profits, she would count her savings, hidden behind a loose brick in the old bread oven. Over three hundred pounds!

For Simon it was a time of long, lonely days, but there was no shortage of work. It had rained throughout June and well into July. The wettest June for twenty-five years, they said in the village. The rivers ran strong in the dongas, sucking away fallen branches and leaves, lifting small dams that he had constructed to hamper soil erosion and sweeping them clean away. Even the borehole down by the farm was belching huge gusts of water and the rainwater tanks were overflowing and

162

flooding the yard. Everything was wet, the thatch sodden and dripping, the wooden doors so swollen they would not shut.

Simon watched the sheep plodding through unaccustomed mud, heads hanging, but sleeker and glossier than in previous years, while the ewes with their lambs stayed in the lucerne camps Anna had planted.

He sighed when he thought of all that water waiting there, flooding underground caves, unknown and unseen, century after century, while his parents and their parents before them broke their backs and their hearts for lack of water.

It had to be a van Achtenburgh who found it, he thought enviously, but who would dream of searching for water high in the hills when common sense told you it would be down in the valleys?

One drought year his father had sunk eight boreholes, wasted the gleanings of thirty years of toil, and all for nothing.

His father had believed in the water. 'It's there, as much as we need. Just waiting for the finding.' His voice hoarse from coarse, home-grown substitute tobacco.

On the old tractor they had sat together day after day, ploughing a straight furrow. The son, tall and gawky with matted, red hair; his father who, with eyes shining, nursed hope like a baby.

'In God's good time, in God's good time.'

His father's bad eye, useless and forever wandering, would turn outwards towards the land; while the other glared at him, a great, fierce black eye under heavy black brows. But on that day, that awful day in a terrible drought year, his eye had been less fierce. Uneasy.

The neighbours had come from a dozen or more farms on horses and carts and, like a flock of sheep, they had trailed behind the water diviner, the women clutching skirts and bibles, the men with spades over their shoulders.

A small, dark man, Italian they said, skipped ahead of them carrying a forked stick, like a priest with a crucifix at Lent, holding it high so that everyone could see it, and they had tramped for four hours from one valley to the next, the women wiping their faces with calico handkerchiefs.

163

On the eastern boundary the stick had begun to twitch and the diviner to shake like a man with the palsy. The women had sunk to their knees with cries of 'Thank God' and 'Alleluja' while the men had driven into the soil in a frenzy and at ten feet they had reached water, to the sounds of sobs and shouts of praise, but it was brackish, sour and salty, enough to poison sheep and the soil.

'You'll never find pure water in this area.' The words of the diviner had condemned them to poverty.

After that day his father's hair had whitened and he had grown old before his time, letting the farm fall into disrepair.

There must be a reason, Simon thought, overlooking the land as he stood in the drizzle. His face bore the marks of puzzlement as he strove to understand the strange workings of God. Around him the wheat was shooting up thick and green, just as he had always dreamed; the sprouts not more than a fingernail high, but already the ground looked green as far as you could see and interspersed with wheat were lupins, a darker green, and even on fallow land the grass was sprouting.

He twisted around and looked behind him; a scene dimly perceived through the mist like a painting he remembered in a travelling show at Malmesbury. He saw flashes of black and white as two herons beat their heavy way to the lagoon.

At dusk Simon went to the dairy to supervise the separation of the milk, but Jan seemed to have become curiously efficient. As usual Simon was reluctant to go into the house, but he could not stay outside forever and eventually he went into the kitchen, dark and empty except for the glow from the stove. He knew from the light under the bedroom door that Anna was feeding the twins and he tiptoed down the corridor, but the door was locked.

The mystery of women, he thought sadly. There was Anna, tender and sweet with the children, but a virago the rest of the time in ugly, cut-down men's clothes with her hair scraped into a bun. He could cry when he remembered Anna at Fontainebleu and the fault was his. All his life he had coveted beauty, picking flowers and moping when they died; snatching butterflies until their wings broke. Once his mother had been given a china figurine in pink and blue and Simon had worshipped it until one night, creeping from his room to gaze at it by moonlight, he had been overcome and gripped it in his grimy fist. It had shattered. He had cried for the next day, not from the beating, but from the shame of beauty impaired.

He could not help remembering the china statue when he looked at Anna.

Confused emotions tumbled through his mind as he sat by the fire, but one was overwhelmingly strong – he wanted to love Anna, be loved by her. Damn it, she was his wife, what else was there in marriage?

It was late before Anna came to bed. Long after supper, when Simon had bathed, read and finally pinched out the candle, he could hear her moving around in the kitchen. He knew every sound: the eggs being checked, the cupboard locked, the long silence while she wrote in her journal, the bath, lastly the brick being pulled out of the bread oven. Stealthy movements by candlelight. Her need to hoard confused him.

Finally she came tiptoeing down the corridor into the bedroom, sheltering the flame of the candle with one hand. She blew out the candle. She would never learn to pinch it with her fingers and always they slept in the lingering smell of burning wick. Now was the time he had waited for, but suddenly he was afraid. She was so cold. A living statue.

Eventually he went over cautiously to her bed and, pushing her aside, wriggled in. She was pretending to be asleep.

'Anna, wake up. I want to talk to you, Anna.'

'I'm awake,' she said eventually.

'Anna.' He fumbled for the words. 'Whatever it is we lost, we have to find it again. I still love you, Anna, there's many years ahead of us. Must we live like strangers? I'm sick of it.'

'There was nothing to lose. We dreamed it up one night in the moonlight.'

'I know I was wrong,' he plodded on desperately. 'I shouldn't have left you alone, but it's done now and no harm came of it. Thank God. I'm older now.' That was the truth of it. By God, he felt a good twenty years older.

'Aren't you tired?' she replied, a hint of desperation in her voice. 'Don't you want to sleep?'

The room was dark as pitch. Simon could not see as much as a gleam from the window. Tired? All she wanted from life was sleep, work and more work.

'I want to make love to you,' he said eventually and, fumbling under the blankets, he smoothed her nightgown up over her soft, white thighs. He found he was panting, fingers shaking as he pushed against her, his penis hard and bursting with desire. Yet she was so cold. He sighed. Why was she so unresponsive? After a while he turned away and lay on his back.

The room was lightening and the wind was getting up. He saw moonlight through the branches of the eucalyptus trees. Moving patterns on white walls.

Anna was like a man, single-minded and determined, no time for warmth and joy. He had become unnecessary, to Anna, to the farm, to anyone. The realization was like an unexpected cold shower and he lay quietly and considered the problem. He had to admit, grudgingly, that Anna ran a tidy shop. She employed a reliable tractor driver. Why, he even had to fight to get on his own tractor. Jan managed the cows adequately and hordes of young schoolboys fed the chickens, fixed the fences, mended the roads and herded the sheep. A man could get an inferiority complex this way.

But why would a woman want to work like a man? He blamed van Achtenburgh, bringing her up like a son. Well, maybe with patience he could turn her into a woman. It would be like taming a wild bird; like the falcon he had once caught. He reached across with his left hand and began to caress her shoulder, letting his fingers drift over her spine, up and down, around her neck, fondling the soft hairs. Her skin shuddered involuntarily and he leaned over, propping himself on one elbow as he stroked her back from her buttocks to her shoulders.

'Anna, I love you,' he whispered. 'Let's start again.' How he longed to do just that. He remembered how he had pictured her during the long months at sea. Visions of joy and plenty; the harvest golden. Abundance! And him on his harvester, filling sack after sack, while Anna tripped over the fields with jugs of lemonade. An absurd dream.

'Anna,' he whispered. 'Anna.' But there was no answer. He got out of bed and tiptoed around to her side. Her face looked ethereal in the moonlight as she stared at the window. 'What's the matter with you?' he said. His voice was choked and high-pitched.

She looked at him and burst into laughter. Then she curled into a ball, pulling the blankets around her. 'It's stopped raining. Look at the moon there.'

'Please Anna, you're driving me crazy,' he gasped. 'Show me some warmth, for God's sake.'

'Warmth?' She hated him at that moment. 'You mean desire.' She laughed. 'I've never refused since the day you raped me. What would be the point?'

She opened her legs and lay coldly, quietly acquiescent. A silent accuser, submitting, yet never conquered.

Simon fell on her in anguish, buried his mouth in her hair, grasped her hands and pushed them above her head, pinning them to the pillow. He wanted to thrust hard and deep inside her, deliberately hurt her, feel her gasp with pain if not pleasure. Any reaction. But anger and humiliation had replaced passion; his maleness had shrunk to negligible proportions and he was beside himself with rage.

This had never happened before and for a moment, in a frenzy, regardless of his lack of readiness, he tried to tunnel into the deep well where pools of oblivion awaited him, but it was no use.

After a while he rolled over and lay with his back to Anna, feeling more humiliated, guiltier than he had ever felt in his life. He was a worthless thing, no good as a farmer, no good as a man. He knew that Anna had the beating of him now and it was dawn before he fell into a restless sleep.

17

Next morning the sun rose ruddy in a clear sky. Wintertime, yet by nine the sun's heat had warmed the earth, releasing the tang of damp grass and wild herbs. By ten the thatch roof was steaming.

Simon, who had left at dawn, cantered to the house in a frenzy, his violence transmitted to Vixen who was a mess of sweat, foam and rolling eyes.

He rubbed down the mare and stamped into the kitchen where Anna pretended not to notice his mood.

'The rain has washed away the topsoil from the hills and the wheat's gone with it,' he began mournfully, spooning sugar into his coffee.

'Madness to plant it in the first place, so now you've lost it all,' Anna said impatiently.

'Not all, just the shoots on the slopes. A hilly farm should be contoured, it stands to reason.' He sighed. 'Should have done it years ago. Put a few terraces round the slopes and the soil stays put.'

What ill luck brought me here away from Fontainebleu where the thick red loam lies waiting to nourish every seed? 'The farm's good for grazing and that's that,' she retorted.

Simon did not answer. He was piling salty butter on home-made bread and cramming it into his mouth. When he had finished he said solemnly, 'I need two hundred pounds to hire a bulldozer. That's all it needs to contour every hill. The farm will be the richer for it.'

'Don't look at me like that,' Anna said, feeling mean and suddenly hating herself. 'I don't have two hundred pounds to waste on such tomfoolery.'

'Better than wasting it on chickens, moping in the rain and eating our money.'

She glared at him. 'The money comes from the chickens.'

'Well, I must have two hundred pounds.' He brought his fist crashing on the table, which startled Anna. She dropped the butter dish and this more than anything brought her temper rising.

'Then go and earn it,' she snapped, picking pieces of buttered china from the cement. 'Sell some sheep, go fishing, anything. I'll not pay for such nonsense.' There was no reply so she went on desperately. 'I'd willingly pay for a good ram, or better cows, but not for contours. You'll keep us in debt forever with your mania. You're mad.'

She looked up into a purple face, cheek twitching, but such a strange expression; humiliation, rage, disappointment, compassion. For a moment she was startled and nearly gave him the money, but the moment passed and Simon was gone. Rushing away to his van.

Goodness knows how big losses will be this winter, she rationalized. She felt uneasy and, going to the wall, prised out the brick, but the money was there.

With so much work there was no time to waste worrying about Simon. Later that afternoon the telephone rang. It was Koos, the pay clerk at the fishing factory.

'Simon's signed on,' he told her. 'He said to let you know and remind you not to forget the cows.'

As if she could forget the cows. What nonsense. She shrugged and went back to work.

Time speeded up when she was working and as the sun sank she was nowhere near finished, but she locked the egg room and went to inspect the dairy and the cows in the kraal. She was still there when she heard a voice calling.

'Over here, Kurt,' she called. 'Good heavens, it's seven. I haven't started yet. Never mind, I'll grill some chops. It won't take long. How are you?' All in one breath.

'Don't worry, I'm not hungry,' he said trailing beside her as

169

she hurried to the kitchen.

'Well, if you come to dinner you have to eat,' she said. She glanced sidelong, smiling at him, but her smile faded.

'My God, you look awful. Kurt, what's happened?' She took his arm.

Kurt's eyes, which usually gleamed with humour, were bloodshot; his mouth compressed into a thin line.

'Nothing.'

A strange man, full of moods, she thought. No doubt he would tell her later. 'Do you mind sitting in the kitchen?'

He nodded and she washed her hands, hung up her coat and began preparing supper.

'Where's Lena?' he asked moodily.

'Bathing the twins.'

'And Simon?'

'Fishing,' she replied and then wished that she had not told him. 'What about the chickens?' she went on hurriedly.

He frowned at her. 'Don't worry, you're in luck, I found a buyer. They're expecting two mailships and one troopship in harbour this month and they'll take the lot.'

'Who will?'

'The Apex Ships' Chandlers in Woodstock. You can phone them and arrange everything.'

'Kurt, you're a genius.'

Watching her eyes shining Kurt thought ruefully: Business. That was the way to Anna's heart. 'How will you cope with plucking and cleaning five thousand chickens?'

'I'll cope,' she replied.

'Then what?'

She sensed that Kurt was bored with the subject so she shrugged and smiled. She planned to use the cash to buy pullets to lay during the remaining winter months.

'Supper's ready,' she told him later. 'Let's go.' She led the way into the living room, carrying dishes on a tray.

Kurt hesitated in the doorway. 'Well, that's better,' he said, noticing the table and chairs Anna had bought the previous day.

'I found them at Malmesbury mart, genuine yellowwood,

covered in grime. Jan cleaned and polished them.'

'Well now, perhaps you'll tell me what's wrong,' she said when she had served dinner: strong sweet wine, braised lamb chops, new potatoes boiled in their skins and home-grown peas.

Kurt pushed his plate aside and drank in a gulp. 'Within a month we'll be at war with Germany.'

Anna frowned, unwilling to come to terms with this war everyone was talking about. The papers were full of it; German troops concentrated along the Polish border; Britain, France and Russia signing pacts. New words had come into being and the papers were full of them: Allies; Axis; Nazis. Every day she read the headlines at the store but never bought a paper. What had all this to do with her? It was a madness that belonged to men and to Europe, which was far away.

'You were full of it the other day. Couldn't wait to join up.'

He scowled at her. Then he blurted: 'I've been turned down.'

'By whom?'

'Everyone. I tried the air force first. I hold a pilot's licence. Then the navy. Last of all the army. They all turned me down.' He looked like a man enduring the worst that life can offer.

'Why, Kurt?' she asked, only conscious of her relief.

'Because I'm German.' He spat the words out. 'Incredible.'

'It's not that bad, is it?' she asked gently.

'Yes, or so it seems.'

'Eat your supper,' she ordered.

He picked up a fork and prodded a potato.

'Think about the future, Kurt. Go and build your wholesale business. You're always so positive. What's got into you?'

He laughed suddenly. 'For you. I'd gladly do it for you.'

'Do it for yourself. When you're rich you won't worry about an old farm wife, there'll be too many young girls after you.'

'You're a cynical bitch.'

'Realistic.'

Kurt reached forward to fill their glasses. He felt washed out. An empty shell. When he looked back he marvelled at himself. So controlled, all through the bartering, arguing, getting his sister to the States, calmly arranging the takeover of his factory. Revenge had kept him going. Suddenly he buried his face in his hands on the table. Revenge had been taken away and he had crumpled without his crutch.

Anna stood up and put her arm around him, resting her cheek on the back of his neck. 'It will all pass,' she whispered. 'You've lost everything, but you're young. Young enough to start again.'

'It's not the money,' he said wearily. 'I feel like an empty house after the floods recede. I'm still standing, but everything has gone, stripped to the cement.'

Surely everyone recovers eventually, Anna thought with the innocence of youth. The point was to survive. All he needed was a push in the right direction.

'In a year's time you'll be doing so well you won't believe you talked all this nonsense,' she said. 'It just needs guts.'

'Two things hurt me the most and to my shame it wasn't the death of my parents,' he went on, ignoring her. 'Madeleine, she was my wife. I can't forget the things she said when I tried to make her leave Germany.' He drained the glass, stood up and walked to the window. For a while he stood looking at the dark hills but not seeing them. 'Then there was Gunther, my friend.' He broke off, his faced twisted into an expression of despair.

'Gunther was at university with me and afterwards, when his father's company closed, I brought him into the plant. He was supposed to take over administration. Well, he did.' He laughed mirthlessly. 'I never knew he had joined the Nazi Party. High up, too, and all the time he and Madeleine ... ' He shook his head, and began pacing the room. 'It's the first time I've talked about it. I won't again. Promise.' He managed a smile.

'Well,' she said, trying to cheer him. 'I'm glad you aren't joining up.'

His face lit up and, bending down, he caught her wrists and pulled her to her feet, hugging her closely. 'Thanks for saying that at least.'

172

Suddenly the closeness of him caught her breath and she felt her body reacting to his strength and maleness. All her womanly instincts blazed into a passionate desire to hold him, feel his body pressing on to hers as she sensed his need. How handsome he was, tall and square-shouldered, his eyes even deeper blue in the lamplight. His face radiated intelligence and sensitivity.

'Anna, what are we going to do?' he whispered, brushing his lips against her cheek. 'I love you, Anna.'

'It's the wine talking,' she said, trying to push him away.

A sudden gust sent the oil lamp flaring.

'Damn!' Kurt said.

'The wind's come up.' She busied herself fetching a candle and finding another mantle for the lamp.

'You're not happy with Simon,' Kurt persisted, but Anna remained silent, avoiding his eyes as she pumped the lamp. 'Try to lie. Tell me you're happy.'

'Well, what good is this silly talk. I'll not leave Simon, nor the twins.'

'You don't mean that.'

'I surely do.'

'Anna,' Kurt was watching her anxiously. 'If I thought you really meant that I would leave this house and never return.'

'Then better you go now, for I do mean it. I'm married to Simon and there's an end to the matter.'

She's wrong, but she's won again, Kurt thought, as he started the engine and swung his van in the direction of the dark road. Then he braked. Perhaps she would still come out, change her mind or even wave goodbye, but he saw the lamp being carried to the bedroom and after a while he drove home.

That night he could not sleep. Anna's image kept intruding into his thoughts. She was a strange, compelling woman. There was something wildly sensuous about her, but she had not yet awoken to her own sexuality.

18

It was late spring in the Cape and after winter's deluge the wheat was sprouting tall and dense in the valleys, ears thickening and ripening under the hot African sun. Lupins were in bloom; a profusion of blue hills and valleys under the deeper blue sky. Daily, newly-hatched sea-birds ventured over the land, returning to the reeds around the lagoon: terns, oyster-catchers, gannets and the southern black-backed gull. Cormorants in formation flew to their fishing grounds, guinea fowl shared the wheat with the hares, tickbirds devoured ticks on contented cows, while larks and swallows swooped over the farmhouse and everywhere wild flowers bloomed pink and mauve. But Anna had no time to waste gazing at all this. She had work to do.

After the excitement waned, the only effect of war on the farmers was slightly increased prices for produce and they were well satisfied.

The defence force doubled their order for poultry and eggs and Anna, with the blessing of the co-op manager, spent some of his feed money on an additional five thousand pullets, an outlay which she felt was justified, in view of the growing demand. She also employed two additional farmhands, for the poultry houses were spreading over several fields.

On a particularly beautiful morning the postman clattered along the farm road in his truck. From the expression on his face and sensing his discomfort Anna knew it was bad news. It was a telegram from Windhoek. Uncle Acker was dead.

Anna crumpled the telegram in her hand, letting it drop heedlessly on the floor and trudged back to the grading shed.

Why could she not grieve for him? In another age, another

world she could have, she told herself woodenly, but now she felt only numbness. 'Poor Uncle Acker,' she said aloud several times, trying to get to grips with grief. Yet she could not help noticing the eggs were unusually large for this time of the year and the yield was better than average. But poor Uncle Acker. Her hands skimmed like lightning, packing, feeling, checking. Fancy dying at fifty-two. A tragedy! Yet, when she thought of thirty more years of grading eggs she became appalled. She began to calculate the number of eggs she would grade in that time. The figures became astronomical. Horrified, she broke off and tried to concentrate on her work.

The day dragged on, longer and more bothersome than usual. The flies seemed more aggressive; the labourers more trying; Lena burned the bread and a cobra killed three hens. Today there was no solace in work, merely drudgery.

Later that evening, when she had bathed and fed the twins and put them to bed, she sat outside on the balcony overlooking the farm, trying to remember her mother and Acker when she was young and they were happy, but she was dismayed to discover that she had walled off this part of her life. She could force herself to remember dates and events, but faces and feelings eluded her. Life at Fontainebleu seemed as real as a book or a play. I have no emotions left, she thought. Yet she felt for her twins, for they were the apex of her life, the cornerstone on which sanity rested. For the rest a frightening blank.

I am cursed, she thought, her mother and uncle dead and not a tear left to cry with, not a memory to catch hold of. The lantern flickered and went out, the moon rose, owls hooted, but Anna, filled with a sense of emptiness, sat motionless.

Kurt was surprised to find the door open, the house in darkness. The glow from the wood stove showed the kitchen empty apart from Wagter, who beat his tail lethargically on the floor. Anna must be somewhere around.

'Anna,' he called.

When he saw her supper untouched on the table he began to feel annoyed. She was not in the bedroom, nor the nursery where the twins were sleeping. Then he saw her sitting trance-like in the chair outside the front door, eyes staring, unmoving, and for a moment he thought she was dead.

'Anna,' he called. The stupid child was exhausted.

She stared eerily without answering or seeing him.

He shook her, but there was no response. He slapped her and she cringed and gasped.

'Oh, Kurt,' she said breathlessly. 'Oh, I'm so cold. I was just sitting. I must have sat there for hours. I don't even remember. What time is it? What are you doing here? Oh, Kurt, I'm so cold.'

'You can't carry on like this,' he said quietly. 'You're exhausted, drained. Money's not worth it, Anna.' He frowned at her. 'Go and get a jersey. I'll fix some eggs. Your supper's cold and ruined on the table.'

'Fancy you cooking!' she said when she had found a jersey and brushed her hair. She was beginning to feel warmer.

'Well, how do you think I eat nowadays? I have one hotplate and I make the most remarkable dishes.' He smiled at her. 'I've discovered I have a talent for it.'

How confident he looked and some of his mood seemed to infect her too, so that her depression lightened to a tolerable sadness. His eyes gleamed, a half smile played round his lips, too handsome by far, she decided. She distrusted handsome men nowadays, but still she could not help noticing how his tanned skin shone in the lamplight and his eyes seemed a deeper blue. This was a new Kurt, unexpected and disarming.

He was pottering around wearing her apron, mixing a concoction of onions, peppers and spices in the frying pan.

'I was upset because Uncle Acker died. The telegram came today.'

Kurt was humming to himself.

She blurted out, 'Kurt, you're not listening to me.'

He looked up in surprise and his face twisted into a grin of delight. 'Darling Anna, I swear I will always love you, slave for you, propose to you, but I can't always promise to listen to you.'

She shrugged. Why should she burden him with her bad

176

news and her sadness. 'You mustn't say things like that,' she said.

'I'm merely telling the truth,' he protested and, pushing the pan aside, he caught hold of her and hugged her. 'Where's your peasant husband? Fishing again, I suppose. Leaving you all alone. Someone has to look after you and it might as well be me.'

'No Kurt, let go,' she mumbled as he pressed his lips firmly on her own and, afterwards, when he stepped back and began mixing eggs in the pan she added; 'you're being a fool. This is wrong.'

'Wrong? Everything's wrong nowadays. That you and I are here at all is wrong. You know how I feel about you. Women are supposed to have an instinct about these things.'

'Instinct tells me to beware of glib men who trot out words like love just because they're lonely.'

He was still smiling, no longer caring what she said.

'You keep ignoring Simon,' she said crossly. 'It's as if he doesn't exist for you.'

That was not true, he decided. Simon was unforgettable. The discordant note in an otherwise perfect symphony.

'Why do you hang on to that oaf you married?' he said when he had put the omelette on the table and cut it in half. 'Is it some ridiculous feeling of loyalty? You know he's on the make. Or are you afraid of being divorced?'

'No,' she said. It was none of those reasons.

'If it's the twins, you know I'd love them like my own,' he persisted.

She sighed. Why did he feel he had the right to know? 'I shall depend on myself from now on. No one else, never again.'

'It's a cold, empty life you're planning.'

'When I count my savings I feel warm all over. It's a very nice feeling. I have four hundred and fifty pounds hidden behind a brick in the kitchen.' She looked up to see if he was listening, but he was reaching into his bag. 'Your omelette's getting cold,' she said.

'Don't wait, I'm coming.'

He hurried back, carrying two wine glasses which he filled with wine.

'Oh Kurt, how super.'

'I'm fed up with tin mugs.'

'To tell you the truth, so am I.' She lifted her glass. 'The wine is superb. Business must be good.'

'Yes, it is. I told you before, plenty for both of us.'

Should she divorce Simon? She wondered. Uncle Acker had suggested as much to her. Yet just thinking about it was difficult. But why? She did not love him. Far from it, for she hated him. Was she too proud to let her friends find out that she had been mistaken? If so she and Simon were tied to each other because of pride. Or was it because of the twins? Simon loved them, she knew that.

'Anyway,' she said aloud without really intending to, 'I have no grounds for divorce.'

'It doesn't matter,' he said. 'If you come away with me, Simon will eventually divorce you. He will hate you and want to get rid of you. Besides, before long he would want to marry someone else.'

The thought made her feel sick.

'No,' she blurted too quickly, and after that they ate in silence.

Later, when she was making coffee in the kitchen, Kurt caught hold of her and pulled her towards him. 'Anna,' he said gazing at her intently. 'If you won't leave Simon then you must widen your horizons, get some happiness into your life. Start riding again, play the piano. There's no joy in your life.'

The milk boiled over on the stove.

'Oh blast,' she wailed. 'Oh, what a smell.'

'Here, let me help you.' Kurt began to soak the milk with a cloth but already it was sizzling brown on the black stove.

Unexpectedly Anna found herself trembling at the nearness of his long smooth arm with shirt sleeves rolled up. She could hardly resist reaching out and touching him. She caught her breath and after a while noticed Kurt watching her.

He walked away.

When she carried the coffee to the table she saw Kurt sitting in front of the piano. He began to play a German song and when he stopped she said, 'You're not very good.'

He grinned. 'I try at least. That's more than you do.'

'Here, shift over.' She pushed him off the chair and sat down. Suddenly she missed the height of the old piano stool. How familiar the keys were. When she looked up she was shocked to see white walls instead of the pale blue Japanese printed wallpaper her mother had loved so. She sighed.

But what had happened to her fingers? She swung her right hand over the keys, trying harder, but the notes came out like a row of bricks in a driveway. 'Damn it,' she swore. 'My hands are only fit for cleaning eggs now.'

She felt embarrassed. Sitting straighter, squaring her shoulders she began the *Sunrise Concerto* which had been her favourite at school. She had played it at a school concert when she was sixteen. She remembered her mother dressed in blue and her father, stiff and upright, in an unfamiliar suit and starched white shirt, watching proudly from the front row.

How badly she played. Would it ever come back to her?

She began again, simple tunes that she had learned years ago. At last the music began to flow and she forgot Kurt, forgot that she might wake the twins. The music seemed to come, not from her hands and the piano, but out of her stomach, drawn like a diaphanous thread, her life force transposed into sound.

And with the sound, scattered images came and went. Her mother sketching. Pa's voice like wind over dry leaves, his shrewd blue eyes. Uncle Acker, grave and kindly, large-boned, clumsy-looking, yet as delicate as a forest deer when he hunted or worked.

Her thoughts kept returning to her father for the two of them had always been a team. Inseparable, until Simon came. 'Oh, Pa,' she whispered.

Hours later she stopped playing and leaned back as of old, automatically waiting for the applause, but there was none. She turned her head. Kurt was sleeping, leaning back awkwardly in the chair, mouth open, a silly smile on his face. Did he always sleep smiling?

179

Heavens, it was midnight. She had played for hours, no wonder he was sleeping. The absence of sound disturbed him and he began to stir. He sat up and grinned self-consciously.

'What's the time?'

'Midnight.'

'Sorry I slept through your second debut.'

She smiled. 'I was expecting some applause.'

'Applause? My God. It was awful. I was lucky to fall asleep.'

She laughed. 'Yes, it was awful, but towards the end it was beginning to get better.'

She stood up and closed the piano. 'I shall practise every day and then I'll give you a better recital.'

How very young she looked when she smiled. Kurt stood up, finding it almost impossible to leave her, so he said good-night quickly and gracelessly and almost ran to his van.

Anna listened to the sound of his engine slowly fading. Always a sad sound. Tonight, for once, she was not tired, but the house was unendurable. She went outside and sat on the wide, stone steps by the door. The night sky had cleared. There was no moon and the stars were extraordinarily brilliant. She could see the glow from the headlights of Kurt's van moving silently away like a bright yellow globe rolling over the hills. There were no other lights, yet houses were tucked away in valleys where families were bedded, fires glowed, husbands and wives with bodies entwined. They slept safe in the security of family constraints and bonds. Worlds within worlds. Why did she feel so alienated? A being from outer space could not feel more alone than she. The servants in their shacks were better off for they loved, fought, hated, whined and toiled, but they were not alone. Even Jan had a woman; a great, fat, hulking woman, black as night and powerful as a bull.

'Oh God,' she wailed, suddenly frantic as fear and loneliness swelled through her. She did not want to be alone. She would go after Kurt were it not for the twins. Where was Simon? Tossing on black waves in his lonely bunk. Was Simon ever lonely?

A restless night. Warm breezes from the north stirred the leaves where turkeys rustled and pushed. Cries of sheep, baboons barking. A lonely owl swooped across the yard close to her. A sudden shrill shriek of agony. Death when an owl crosses your path, if you could believe the Coloured folk.

There was a glow to the east where there should have been darkness. The yellow globe was riding back over the hills like a home movie wound the wrong way.

'You felt my thought waves willing you back,' she said five minutes later when Kurt walked into the kitchen.

'Something like that.' He watched her thoughtfully. Tears glistened on her eyelashes and her face was pale. He understood her loneliness and the fear that it inspired.

She smiled faintly and wiped her eyes on the back of her hand. So forlorn. Compassion flared and with it a fierce burning in his loins. 'You don't have to be alone,' he said and touched her shoulder briefly.

'Not tonight. Other nights perhaps, but not tonight. Please.' She looked up and her face was full of dread and pleading.

He touched her neck and fondled the soft hairs there; felt her shudder and let his hand move softly to her cheek.

She reached up and caught hold of his fingers and gripped them fiercely.

All that mattered, he thought, was that she should not be so terrified. He glanced at her apprehensively as she covered her face with her hand and shuddered.

'Shall we go to bed?' he said in a soft, expressionless voice.

Holding her arm he drew her up and led her slowly to the bedroom. She glanced shyly sideways, but his face was devoid of any emotion.

'I'll undress you,' he said softly and shut the door. His face looked pale as death in the flickering candlelight.

With a strange obedience she stood still and allowed him to remove her corduroy trousers, blouse and underclothes, shuddering as his hand touched her body, stroking so softly with deft, deliberate movements. At last there was the soft touch of his lips on her stomach and her navel.

181

He was tender and masculine at the same time and he lifted her gently and laid her on the bed as if she were a child. He stroked her back and her arms and after a while her breasts and stomach, so that eventually the sobs of sadness turned to cries of pleasure and when he made love to her she lay still, without participating, feeling a deep sense of joy.

She wondered, why was she doing this? Why was it necessary? Why did she not feel guilty, merely sad, but peaceful at last? She knew that it was not Kurt she craved, but love; any love from any man. Just to be stroked, to be needed, to shut out the loneliness of the night. Just this once! For only the second time in her life she achieved an orgasm and cried out wildly, hardly knowing what she was saying.

Afterwards, when she lay on his shoulder smiling to herself in the dark, she was surprised to discover that Kurt was tense and wide awake.

'Kurt,' she whispered.

'Yes?'

'What's wrong?'

There was a long silence and eventually he said: 'When you came you cried out "Simon". You love him, that oaf of a husband of yours, you love him although he treats you like a peasant.'

'How can I love him? I loved him once,' she added eventually.

She sat up and lit the candle and Kurt saw that she was smiling, serene and confident.

'I love you,' Kurt said. 'I love you very deeply. I shall always love you.'

She did not reply.

'Do you love Simon?' he persisted.

'No, I hate him,' she said.

'Why? Hate is such a destructive word, Anna. You are too gentle to have emotions like hatred.'

'Are you hungry?' she asked.

'Yes.'

'I'll get some biscuits and make coffee.'

When she returned she told him about Simon, about the

horse show, about Sophie and her baby. 'And I placed the baby in a foster home,' she lied. No one, not even Kurt, would find out about Katie.

'So you see, how could any one love a man like that?' she repeated. 'Only to hate him,' she broke off.

'You must come away with me,' he said urgently.

'No,' she said.

When Kurt saw the stubborn expression in her eyes and the set of her chin he decided to wait. Patience would win her, he decided. Patience and the soul-destroying toil she was enduring. No one could stand that for long. Besides, she loved him. Whatever she said, he knew that she loved him.

Morning came too quickly. When the first light of dawn appeared over the hills Kurt left.

There was no guilt in Anna when she faced Simon three days later, only a sense of sadness which she could not shake off.

19

It was November, an uneasy month when the grain begins to thicken and ripen in the sun and farmers become tense, for rain can ruin the harvest. On Modderfontein the crop was far from bountiful, but it was better than usual and would show a profit. Simon spent his days examining the sky, gazing at the weathercock or telephoning the weather bureau.

When harvest time was almost upon them, he went early one morning to Malmesbury and returned driving a new harvester, a magnificent contraption, huge and painted bright red with gadgets everywhere.

With this model, Simon explained, one man could cut the wheat, gather the grain into sacks leaving the stubble in piles, and all this in half the usual time.

Anna admired it and then asked, 'How could you afford it?'

'On our account,' he told her uneasily.

'Our account?' Incredulously. 'Your account or my account?'

'What's the difference?' he replied casually. 'Same farm, same family. Stupid to have two accounts. It's the man who's liable for every penny. If your chickens went phut it's me they'd hammer.'

'But my account was in arrears because of the pullets I bought. Good heavens. How will I buy the feed?'

Simon remained obstinately staring at the control panel. 'I've been meaning to talk to you, Anna. Okay, so you bought the chickens, but now it's too big for a woman to handle. You're neglecting the twins. I'll run the poultry from now on, so that you'll be able to spend more time in the house. As for

184

the feed, I'm sure our credit's still good. The Smits have been dealing there for generations.'

'You'll not touch my chickens,' she warned.

'Our chickens,' he retorted. 'I'll run them a damn sight better than you, slaughtering young hens and throwing away good money.'

Anna was shaking with rage as she drove recklessly to Malmesbury.

'I'll not be paying for Simon's harvester,' she told the embarrassed co-op manager. 'You'd best remember that when you're handing out credit to him.'

'My dear young lady, you place me in a most awkward situation.' He hurried her out of the main shop and into his office. 'I opened a separate account only at your insistence, but really the two accounts have always been one. I don't have to remind you, I hope, that legally you share all assets. If you were to get into debt Simon would have to pay.'

Sanctimonious old pig, Anna thought. At that moment she hated all men, but she controlled herself and said, 'Mr Jensen, when I bought the pullets you increased my credit facilities. Now how will I buy my feed?'

'It's not that bad,' he said patronizingly. 'Your Simon paid four hundred and fifty pounds this morning. I expect he'll pay the balance after harvest.'

'Four hundred and ... ' Anna felt her knees weakening and fell back into the chair. Where would Simon get that much money if not from behind the loose brick, for that was the precise amount she had saved. 'It's my money. He stole it,' she gasped.

'Mrs Smit,' Jensen said. 'I will not become involved in your domestic squabbles, but I'll remind you for the last time that economically speaking you two are a unit. I'm sure you knew the score when you married him.'

She drove home furiously. A unit were they? Well, next time she would find a better hiding place. To think that she could not start a bank account without Simon's permission. It was insane.

On the way Anna overtook the post office van and the driver

hooted. Anna drew to a halt at the side of the road and a few minutes later the postman came pounding along the path.

'Thanks for stopping. Saves me a long drive.' He handed her a bulky registered letter stamped Windhoek. It had obviously been written by Uncle Acker before he died, she thought, as she signed for it. Remembering her reaction to her mother's letter she decided to read it later.

Simon was right about one thing only, she admitted when she reached home, she was neglecting the twins. Watching them, she felt a deep surge of love, tinged with guilt. She could hardly blame them if they thought that Lena was their mother for often enough it was she who fed them, bathed them and put them to bed. The few words they could speak were kitchen Afrikaans. Still, at ten months they were delightful, with long red hair and large bright eyes. Katie was the restless one, while Acker was larger and more placid. They were starting to walk and Anna had barricaded the kitchen door. Together they crawled and staggered over the rest of the cottage, frequently getting splinters in their hands and feet from the bare wooden floors.

If she could only learn to slow down she would be able to spend time with them, she thought, for now she employed a full-time lorry driver and a handful of labourers, yet she was unable to relax unless she was working.

She must force herself to take time off for the twins, she decided, and after lunch Anna put the babies on her back and walked over the hills to the spring. There, hidden amongst the reeds and bushes, Jan had constructed a small dam.

The twins were heavy and Anna was exhausted when she arrived. She took off their clothes and sat them on the river sand to play and they were soon crawling around gurgling happily. Then she stripped naked and lay in the pure, cold water. For the first time in months Anna cast a critical eye over her body. Her arms and shoulders were brown, but the rest of her was white except her feet, which were suntanned for she often went barefoot. She was still slim, but now that the milk was finished her breasts sagged. Who cares, she thought? She had no desire to look attractive.

She leaned back on her elbows, forced herself to stop worrying about Simon and his threats and to enjoy the afternoon. Above her a colony of weaver birds were chopping reeds to weave their nests, which hung thick as grapes from every reed and branch. Turtle doves were cooing in the trees and quails scampered upstream.

After a while she moved to the sand and lay in the sun, feeling her bare skin caressed by the warm breeze. She felt languid, but after an hour her body began to take control and she succumbed to a state of restlessness, a vague but persistent longing to be loved. How long had it been since she made love with Simon? Over three months, for after two more attempts he had given up. She had the beating of him now, for an icy look was all it took to quench his passion. While nursing the twins sex had been unwelcome, but now they were weaned, Anna had begun to have amorous dreams and it was always Simon, not Kurt, who figured in these dreams.

Remembering Kurt, and how he had been that stolen night, made her face burn with embarrassment. She would gladly be rid of him, for only Kurt understood the longings and fears behind her stern exterior. A solitary witness to her weakness.

After a while she lay in the pool to wash away the sand, dried herself on her blouse and dressed. Then she took the letter from her pocket.

It was not from Uncle Acker, but from a lawyer.

It read: '*Dear Mrs Anna Smit, Please accept our deepest condolences on the death of your uncle, Acker Klaus du Toit, and rest assured that we will do our utmost to act for you with the same wholehearted endeavour with which we served your uncle for thirty years.*'

Anna was puzzled. Why ever would she need them?

'*You are no doubt aware that you are the sole beneficiary of your uncle's will (copy of which is enclosed herewith) and therefore the owner of a twenty thousand hectare karakul farm, called Bosluis, two hundred miles north of Windhoek, plus five thousand head of karakul sheep, farmhouse and personal effects.*

In your absence we have employed a farm manager, Mr Nick Foley, who is available on a temporary basis as he is about to start his own farm in the same area.

187

Before he died, Mr du Toit opened a bank account in your name and placed three thousand pounds in it, to provide working capital until his estate has been wound up and the balance of the money in his account transferred to yours. After death duties and various disbursements and fees, we have calculated that the balance coming to you will be approximately five thousand pounds. The land is currently valued at twenty thousand pounds and the karakul sheep at approximately four thousand pounds.

The will expressly states that the farm and assets are left to you out of community of property, which means you are not obliged to involve your husband in any financial transactions concerning this property or any other assets or properties which you may acquire from this capital ...'

Anna read on in a daze. Eight thousand pounds! A fortune. She was rich and even more important – free. She smiled sadly. Dear Uncle Acker. She had always relied on him in her youth and now, it seemed, he had sized up her predicament. Strange that it was he and not her mother who had cared enough to help her.

Anna walked home in a dream, hardly feeling the weight of the twins on her back. Light as a gazelle.

Then she saw Simon and some of her euphoria slipped away. He beckoned her over. You could not complain that he was lazy, she thought, for he worked all hours. Surely his worst crime was stupidity. He was blind to the farm's disadvantages, like a man infatuated with a worthless woman.

Again she had to control a surge of affection, for surely he was the most handsome man she had ever seen, sitting perched high on the seat of his new toy, king of all he surveyed, laughing, green eyes glinting under a titian halo.

He stopped the harvester. 'Come for a ride.'

'All right.'

He reached down, took her hand and pulled her to the seat beside him. 'You'll do yourself injury carting those heavy babies over the land.'

'We went for a swim in the donga.'

When the harvester started the twins cried.

'I'd better go,' she shouted.

'No, stay. They'll get used to the noise.'

188

'I've had good news,' she yelled after a while. 'I've inherited Uncle Acker's karakul farm.'

For a moment Simon concentrated on the intricacies of stopping the harvester. Then there was silence.

'But that's really wonderful news,' he said solemnly. 'In South-West Africa?'

She nodded.

'When are we leaving?'

She shrugged. 'We'll have to think about it.' She climbed down with the twins.

If it were only so easy, she thought sadly on the way back. If only she could trust him. She began to think about the possibility of living there with Simon. Intolerable, she decided. Just the two of them, shut away from the rest of the world, two hundred miles from the nearest shop. Solitary confinement! No fishing for Simon to run away to, and for her the occasional visit to town to re-stock the larder. Besides, she rationalized, there were no schools and the children would have to be sent away. Still, the farms were profitable, one could become wealthy after years of hard work. Then the thought came: What would be the point of the wealth, for Simon would reinvest in more and more land. Simon's hunger for land was insatiable. No, she decided. She would find a manager. It would be difficult, but not impossible.

The harvest was completed in a record three days. Simon drove slowly back to the farmhouse, put the harvester in the shed and came into the kitchen for coffee. He looked exhausted and no wonder, for he had operated the harvester single-handed from four in the morning until midnight each day.

'We'll celebrate tomorrow, Anna. Tonight I must sleep,' he told her. 'This is a record crop and the harvester has made all the difference. We're finished just in time. You'll no doubt have noticed that the wind changed to north-west in the night. I'll have to get a move on getting the wheat to the millers. Many poor devils'll have their harvest drenched tonight.' Then he smiled. 'Thanks to you and the chickens we've saved ours.'

Ours! she thought. How strange that he could still consider them a team after all that had passed. She never considered anything on the farm to be even partly hers. The farm, the cattle, the sheep and the wheat were Simon's. The chickens were hers and so was the karakul farm.

Looking around, Anna saw the sweeping slopes of wheat stubble glistening golden in the sunlight. Further off she saw a gleam of sunlight reflected from glass and a cloud of dust. A van. Then she saw it was Kurt's van. She walked back arriving in the courtyard as Kurt parked. He looked tired.

'Come inside,' she said. 'I'll make tea.'

'Where's Simon?'

A strange greeting. 'Gone with the grain to the miller's.'

'I've come to tell you that it's all over between us.'

Anna tried to suppress a smile. 'Yes, of course,' she said. 'It was always like that, even before it began.'

Kurt clenched his fist. 'My situation has changed. I had thought that Madeleine and I were divorced. Now she says she loves me.' He pressed his eyes tightly together. 'Oh God,' he said. Anna reached out and touched his hand which was ice cold.

He swore suddenly. 'Even here their evil can reach me, hurt me, destroy my world.'

He smashed his fist on the table. The milk jug toppled and fell and the milk dripped on to the floor.

'God damn them to hell.' To her horror Kurt buried his face in his arm and began to sob: harsh, deep, ugly sobs. Anna stood frozen with embarrassment while Wagter licked the milk from the floor.

'To be so angry and so impotent. She's been interned and there's nothing I can do to help her. That bitch,' he sobbed. 'She deserves almost anything – except this. And I – I am tied to her as long as she stays in that camp – or as long as she lives.' He shuddered. 'You don't understand,' he said eventually and sat up. 'I'm sorry.'

'I'm sorry, too,' she said. 'I know it's terrible. That's why I

190

can't get to grips with it. It's beyond reality.'

'I know, I know.'

He glanced sidelong at her, searching for signs of distress, but there were none. He watched her dispassionately, as if seeing her for the first time, noticing the tension in her like a huge, caged beast. She was statuesque, untamed, still, inexorably feminine, yet devoid of real feeling and therefore unattainable. Velasquez should have painted her. He could have brought out the pallor of her face against the deep brown of her hair, her eyelids, heavier nowadays, glistening in the sun. She was a gypsy woman, wild, cruel, distrustful. Yet he loved her.

'Do you love her?' Anna asked.

'No. I thought I hated her, but now – I don't know any more.'

'She says ... ' he nearly gagged on the words. 'She says she remains alive only to be reunited with me after the war.' He broke off. How could he tell her more? He remembered the last time he had seen Madeleine, her hair more ash blonde than ever in a neat pageboy, blue eyes blazing hate. She was making a new life, she had told him, she had joined the Nazi Party. Impossible, he had told her, since you're Jewish. Religion is a matter of personal choice, she had replied.

Now she was interned in Sobibor, betrayed by Gunther, disposed of in the easiest possible manner, her property confiscated.

'She's interned in Poland,' he said tonelessly. 'She's pregnant and she claims the child is mine.'

'And is it?'

'No.' He flinched and closed his eyes. 'Perhaps Gunther's, or a camp guard's.' He gave a long, shuddering sigh.

'How did you find out?'

'She smuggled a letter to her mother who wrote to me, via relatives in Switzerland. They expect miracles, but there's nothing I can do. That's the worst part, the helplessness. I can't take it.'

Since he had received the letter, three days ago, he had been unable to banish visions of Madeleine from his mind. The firm, pure white flesh, once coveted and finally hated. She was always greedy, demanding more than he could give. He shuddered.

'You look pale,' she said. 'Let's go outside into the sunshine.'

It was difficult to visualize Germany in the blazing midday heat of a South African farm. He tried out a smile, sprawled on the grass, and poured some dismal memories on her.

Later he said, 'You see, Anna, I must wait. I can't divorce her now that she's interned. I'm going away.'

'Where are you going?'

'I don't know. If I could only find a desert island, or anywhere, away from people. Behind their smiling faces lurk the most hideous possibilities.'

She stared at him with her mouth open. Here was her solution. She wanted to blurt out: I have just the place for you, but instead she set about wooing him into the idea.

'Right now I'm beside myself with worry,' she began.

Half an hour later it was all settled. Kurt would run the farm as a partner, sharing the profits on a fifty-fifty basis.

'It's two hundred miles from the nearest shop,' she warned. 'Nothing but sand and bushmen.'

Kurt's eyes glowed. 'Just what I'm looking for. But Simon,' he broke off and frowned. 'What are you going to tell Simon?'

'I can't see that it has anything to do with Simon,' Anna retorted stubbornly. 'Naturally I shall tell him when I am ready.'

It was not that simple, she discovered. November passed and December, heralding the forties; a decade that was to dramatically change their lives, and still she had not told him.

For Simon the New Year was a time for regrets and introspection. He knew that Anna and he had to leave, for it was time to grow. Looking on the bright side it was an adventure, something they could tackle together, a new start. He would lie awake in his single bed night after night and

192

picture them in South-West Africa, a man's world. Anna would rely on him for her security and survival and, so many hundreds of miles from Modderfontein, past sins and disappointments would soon be forgotten, he reasoned.

Yet what a wrench to leave Modderfontein and what should he do with his beloved cows and sheep? He would have to sell them and leave the land lying fallow. Simon was in no hurry to leave, so he waited for Anna to make the first move with her poultry and meanwhile he bought a book on how to speak German which he studied evenings, while another month passed.

On 1 February, when Anna went to the village, she found a letter from Kurt in her post office box. It read:

'*Dear Anna: This is a business letter and what else could it be since I am writing to my business partner? Therefore, I will control myself and not bore you with details of how I miss you (and the twins) or how unendurable the loneliness is, or how much I regret my foolish ambition to shut myself away from the human race. I just thank God that you had enough sense not to come here with Simon.*

My advice to you is sell the karakul sheep and leave the land lying idle for the duration of the war. Currently, there is no market for karakul pelts, nor will there be until Europe returns to normal with money to spend on luxury items. My own opinion is that this will take a decade at least. However, others differ on this point. Most farmers believe that a year will see the end of hostilities and they are hanging on. For this reason karakul sheep are still fetching fair prices, about five shillings each. Which means that you could raise about four thousand pounds, for the stock is excellent and the pelts are of good quality. This capital could be far better invested in a food distribution business, which I believe will boom during the war years, or even in an extension of your own poultry farm.

If you decide to carry on with the karakul, as others here are doing, I will remain on your farm at least until I can find a reliable farm manager. However, if you decide to take my advice, don't delay. My warmest regards to you and the twins. Kurt.'

Anna took a telegram form, and wrote 'Sell immediately' and added as an afterthought: 'warmest regards, Anna.' Then

193

she thought for a few minutes on whether or not to waste the money on those two extra words, but decided that the investment was worthwhile.

20

On New Year's Day the Coloureds explode into an orgy of dancing, singing, drinking and laughter. A diverse group – near-whites and near-blacks; Moslems, Christians and atheists; labourers and teachers – they have little to unite them. Yet there is one common denominator – hope – and the New Year symbolizes hope. A better year, a better decade, a better life. So the streets erupt to the sound of guitars, voices and the pounding of feet.

Next morning Sophie awoke on the floor of the canning factory's bunkhouse with a raging thirst, an aching head and a feeling of martyrdom. There was some wine left by the fisherman who had shared her bed, but no money. She drank the wine, but it did not improve her head, nor her hunger, and succumbing to a feeling of dejection and degradation she swore quietly to herself and began to pick at a corn with a piece of broken stick.

He himself was at the centre of her downfall, and his hoity-toity wife who had let her baby die. Brought up without home or love Sophie had always felt deprived, but she had never known why until the day Simon had raped her. From then on he became the instigator of every woe, the reason for her loneliness and destitution. Her rage increased and, after a while, mumbling to herself, she wove a precarious way towards the village where she tried, without luck, to solicit a loan, a gift or a free breakfast. Feeling more desperate than usual she managed to hitch a lift as far as Modderfontein's gate.

It was noon and hot by the time she arrived at the

farmhouse and, feeling faint, she propped herself against the kitchen door. She had intended to ask for money, but when she saw the food on the table – roast duck, peas, roast potatoes and a huge jug of steaming gravy – she remembered how hungry she was.

'Is the Master in?' she whined entreatingly. 'Is the Madam there?'

There was no answer, but inside she could see the Madam's babies stumbling around on the floor. She took a few steps towards them. My, they were beautiful babies with their shiny red hair. She could not resist walking closer and a desire that was almost lust came over her. She had to touch them. Her little baby would have been just the same age, but as she bent over them the children became alarmed at this stranger who smelt and looked so different from Lena or their mother and they began to scream.

'There, there, don't be frightened, it's only Sophie.' She smiled, showing a large gap where her front teeth had been punched out by a Spanish sailor four months back.

Anna, who had been fetching tomatoes from the shed, raced to the house and flung herself at Sophie, knocking her against the wall.

'Don't touch her,' she shrieked, convinced that Sophie was trying to take her child.

Hearing the commotion Simon, who was returning for lunch, ran to the cottage and paused in horror at the sight of Sophie sitting dazed against the wall, cursing Anna who was clutching Katie.

'Sweet Jesus, help me,' Simon prayed desperately. 'Sophie, what are you doing here?' he said sternly, trying not to show his quaking fear.

'I came to see the grave of my poor little baby,' Sophie sobbed. 'My baby that the Missus left to die. Now she's trying to kill me.'

'I will kill you. I swear to God I will, if you don't keep away,' Anna said, feeling relieved.

'What baby?' Simon stammered turning white.

'The Master's baby,' Sophie whined.

'She's lying,' he said desperately.

'It was your baby,' Anna said contemptuously. 'And it's dead. Now get this whore out of here.' She eyed Sophie repugnantly.

Simon crumpled into a chair and buried his face in his hands. 'Oh God! Oh my God, Anna.'

Sophie began to shriek angrily, 'Who are you calling a whore? You bloody liar.' She let off a stream of abuses in a dozen different languages which she had picked up recently.

'What am I going to do?' Simon appealed to Anna.

'Nothing. There's nothing to do. It's dead and buried.' Anna frowned. 'Pull yourself together and get her out of here.'

'That's right, it's dead,' Sophie wailed. 'The Madam could have saved my baby, but she let it die because it looked just like the Master with long red hair. Just like the Madam's babies.'

'Out! Get out!' Anna shrieked and pushed Sophie towards the door.

Simon took over and, ushering Sophie outside, he called Jan. 'Listen Jan, come here and give Sophie some food and something to drink, and get the driver to take her to the village. Here Sophie, wait.' He ran to the bedroom and returned with twenty pounds which he thrust into her hands. 'I'm warning you, Sophie, if you come back here and make trouble again I'll call the police and have you locked up.'

Sophie stopped sobbing and gave him a crafty grin. 'On what charge, Master? Rape would it be?' Then she shrugged, suddenly tired of whites and the burden of dealing with their strange, hard ways. She turned away, happy to see Jan and pleased with the money and the prospect of food.

Simon went back to the house where Anna was sitting on the floor, rocking the twins and crying quietly.

'Oh my God, Anna. What a terrible thing I've done.' He sat down heavily. 'An evil thing. Because of me a poor baby died. I killed it.' He covered his face with his hands. Then he said: 'Did it suffer badly?'

'It's dead. Let's forget about it,' Anna said uneasily.

Catching the guilt in her voice, Simon was puzzled.

'What did it die of?' he persisted.

'The cold, or starvation. How should I know?'

'Didn't they tell you at the hospital? Surely you took it to hospital?'

She nodded guiltily.

'Anna, you must understand that all this happened before I met you. I swear to God it was only the one time.' He tried to explain, but was unable to convey the terrible physical need which had driven him crazy.

'I don't want to know,' Anna said too quickly. 'Let's forget about it.'

Anna was looking as guilty as she felt and Simon picked up an undercurrent of fear. Besides, it was unlike Anna to let him off so easily. He had committed a crime. Six months was the minimum penalty, but besides his legal crime there was his moral sin.

'So you knew all this time?' he said slowly. 'And that's why you seem to hate me now.'

'Yes,' she said bluntly.

But why was she guilty? What had she done? He began to look at her fearfully, remembering the punctured snake.

'To which hospital did you take it?' he asked, recovering his courage.

'It was late at night,' she said angrily. 'I got back here late and I didn't even know she had left it in the roof. It cried, that's how I knew, you see. I took it to the doctor in the village. He gave me medicine. He said it had pneumonia and other things as well. It had no chance. If you don't believe me go and ask him,' she stammered. But why should she explain to him? It was absurd. He was the guilty one. 'I'm not responsible for your Coloured bastards,' she cried out. 'Why are you getting at me? What are you trying to prove?'

'You're lying! Why are you lying?'

She bit her lip and stared at him.

'God, it's terrible.' He covered his face with his hands and after a while he looked up and said, 'You don't understand me at all. You never have. I would far rather the baby lived. The scandal, maybe even prison, the trouble. That's nothing

198

compared with a life. And it had red hair, just like Acker?'

'No, not red,' she blurted out. 'Black and crinkly.'

'But Sophie said it had red hair and you agreed.'

'Oh, stop it, stop it,' she screamed. 'Stop this cross-examination.'

He stood up. 'I never heard of a woman doing such a terrible thing,' he said heavily.

Anna gasped. Abruptly relief flooded through her. He thought she had left the baby to die, or worse. She burst out laughing and then she called at his retreating back, 'You're right of course. I let it die.'

After a while she began to clear off the table and put the food into the larder. They would not feel like eating today.

For the next few days Simon and Anna behaved like strangers, hardly ever speaking and avoiding looking at each other. They both realized that they could not continue indefinitely in this manner. Anna began to consider divorce while Simon, who felt hopelessly alienated from Anna, pinned his hopes on a new start in South-West Africa and, for the want of something better to do, redoubled his efforts to learn German.

Eventually he could stand it no longer and at supper the next night he said, 'It's time we got a move on. Doesn't pay to leave property in the hands of managers. Who've you got there?'

'What are you talking about?'

'The farm, of course.'

'Oh. Kurt Friedland,' she said, forcing herself to look candidly at him.

'Friedland! He'll rob you blind.'

Her eyes became much colder. 'You would, but he won't,' she said icily. Suddenly she no longer cared how he reacted and thought to herself, I might as well get it over with.

The answer seemed to stun him and he sat for a while, plunging his hands in his pockets and lowering his head until his chin rested on his chest. Then he looked up. 'Well, he'll soon be out of a job, won't he?'

How mean he could look at times, she thought. Great bull

head, eyes that became red when he was angry. He was trying to look calm but the twitch in his cheek gave him away.

'He's out of work now,' Anna said.

'Fell out, did you?'

'No,' she said defiantly. 'I sold the karakul.'

His eyes narrowed slightly. 'Why did you do that?'

'Because Kurt thought the money could be invested more profitably somewhere else.'

'And you believed him?'

'Yes.'

He sighed. 'Did you sell the farm?'

'No.'

Now he appeared to be relieved. 'Easy enough to restock,' he said. 'How much did you get?'

'Four thousand pounds.'

'My father!' He whistled.

'Tell me,' he asked. 'Why did you choose Kurt?'

'Because he's my friend.' Defiantly. 'And because he has a good business brain.'

'You think he's better at farming than I?'

'Not exactly that,' she said slowly. 'You would put your passion for farming and the land first and foremost. Profits don't really concern you. You'd hang on to a poor deal, live on stones and insects if you had to, just to stay on the land or maybe improve it a bit. I want to make money. I can't sit around wasting time. Besides I don't feel like living in isolation with you, and,' she hurried on, 'I can't leave the chickens.'

'One more question,' Simon said, his voice low and hoarse with temper. 'What are you going to do with the money?'

'I'll think about it.'

'I'll look for a better farm in the Malmesbury area,' he said forcibly.

'That won't be necessary,' she cried out. 'Simon,' she went on with an outward show of calm. 'The farm was left to me out of community of property and I intend to leave the land fallow for the children to take over one day if they want to. I've given Kurt power of attorney to act on my behalf and we'll probably go into food distribution.'

Simon stood up and stared at her as if seeing her for the first time and not enjoying what he was seeing. Then he said quietly, 'To you, Anna, life is a balance sheet and you're so short-sighted you can see no further than the figures. Credits and debits! Sophie's baby was in the wrong column, like the hens and the karakul. You're a cruel and stupid woman.'

Then he punched her. She fell back against the piano, tasting blood in her mouth where she bit her tongue and hearing roaring in her ears.

A long time afterwards she went to bathe her face and look at the twins. There was no sign of Simon. He had packed and gone.

The next morning the station master telephoned to ask her to send a driver to fetch the van. Simon had joined up, he told her, his voice tinged with curiosity.

Anna arranged for two drivers to come from the village. She did not leave the house for ten days because she did not want the villagers to see her black eye.

21

Anna walked into the imposing entrance of the Table Bay Insurance Society, and found herself transported into a world of opulence. As her old farm boots sank into the plush pile of the carpet she wondered if she had made a mistake. Perhaps, for once, she should have dressed more becomingly. A gilt and mirror lift brought her face-to-face with herself; just perfect for cleaning out the cowshed, she thought, and emerged faint-hearted on the fourth floor, where a sophisticated receptionist in a superb black dress showed her to a seat in the corner of the foyer adjoining the society's boardroom.

Anna was early and the longer she waited the more uneasy she felt. She leaned back, took a deep breath and for the hundredth time thought: am I doing the right thing?

When Simon had left Anna had walked around in a daze for several days, but eventually she began to miss him, for even when they were fighting at least there was someone there. Uneasily, she wondered if she should have told him the truth about Katie. But no! She reminded herself once again that it was illegal for a white family to bring up a Coloured child and, if it became known, Katie would be taken away and placed with a Coloured family or in an institution. Her Katie! The idea made her feel faint. Far rather let Simon believe that she had murdered the child. But how could he misjudge her so? How could he have punched her? And why had he left? That was the big question which plagued her at nights. Was it anger, because he had been deprived of the karakul farm, or jealousy over Kurt, or was he disgusted with her? She felt she should know the answer to this question, but she did not, and that made her realize uneasily how little she understood Simon. She had married a stranger and now he was gone.

The past six weeks had been the worst she remembered, for shortly after Simon left she discovered that her father had returned to South Africa just before war started. She had been buying provisions in Malmesbury and when she unwrapped her purchases her father's face stared up at her from the local paper which had been wrapped around onions. It was a month old and said simply that André van Achtenburgh had returned to Fontainebleu after an extended holiday in Switzerland where his wife, Maria, had passed away. Anna had smoothed the paper and put it in a drawer. Since he had not tried to contact her, presumably he was still set against her and this, more than anything, increased her bitterness.

Added to this was Kurt's disappearance. He had written a letter stating the amount he had received for the karakul sheep. The money, less his commission, had been placed into her account, but that was a month ago and since then she had not heard from him.

One day when she was feeling particularly low she had tried to trace him. Contacting the lawyers in Windhoek, she had obtained the telephone number of Nick Foley, but he had not seen Kurt since he moved to his own place. The lawyers, too, were mystified. Kurt had vanished. His wages and commission were sufficient for him to fly to England. Perhaps he had managed to join up after all. Daily she went to the post office box hoping for news.

Inquiries to the defence force, the South African navy and the air force had also drawn a blank. Simon had not joined up. There were several Simon Smits, but none from Saldanha Bay. He, too, had quietly vanished.

After three weeks Anna had decided that she would go out of her mind sitting alone at Modderfontein. Kurt had left, but that was not the end of her dreams. She would launch the business herself. Damn him.

After that she had made a few trips around neighbouring farms and then further afield and discovered that Kurt had been right. There was a fortune to be made. Livestock could be picked up for next to nothing in outlying areas and, if reared or fattened nearer to town, the profits would be considerable. She had discarded Modderfontein as a possible stock-rearing area. It was Simon's farm and she would run it for him. Instead she had rented several morgen of good pastureland on the Cape flats and even bought one or two consignments of livestock.

Putting her capital to work made her feel more hopeful. But that was as far as she could go, for the produce had to be available as and when required, and she realized that a warehouse and cold storage facilities near the docks were essential.

For the next two weeks Anna had searched the factory area around Woodstock, the docks themselves and their surroundings for abandoned or unused warehouses suitable for conversion, but was unsuccessful.

Then, at the beginning of March, she had heard a rumour that the Aegis Apple Export Company was going into liquidation. They had a warehouse just outside the docks and conveniently close to a railway station with its own siding. The liquidators were asking an exorbitant price of twelve thousand pounds. If she were to purchase this building it would take all her available cash and she would have nothing left for financing the business. The answer was to obtain a seventy-five per cent bond. After all, she reasoned, they would have the building for security, as well as her farm in South-West Africa. So she had filled in the required forms and attached them to a letter explaining her intention of launching the Southern Cross Ships' Chandlers Company.

It was at that moment that the buzzer sounded and the sultry receptionist rose in a rustle of silk and aura of perfume to usher Anna to the board room.

Five of the company's directors faced Anna around a big mahogany table, three of them she knew, Louis le Grange, Frikkie Geldenhuys and Cobus Fourie, for they were not only directors of this society, but also prosperous farmers and property owners. She had met them on various occasions with her father. All were men past fifty, solid, substantial men and she realized that she was cutting a rather impoverished figure. Le Grange introduced Anna to the other two, Martin Sommers and Clive Duncan. Their faces were impassive and controlled and their eyes were cold and hard as steel. No doubt they had heard about the scandal of her marriage. Well, Anna had not come here on a social visit. She had come to ask for six thousand pounds.

'I have enough cash to purchase the building,' Anna began earnestly. 'They are asking twelve thousand pounds, but they will probably settle for nine. However, you gentlemen know this type of business requires very ample cash flow resources.

'I need a bond of six thousand pounds. The building is an ideal site, with its own railway siding and large deep-freeze storage facilities.'

As there was no word from them she hurried on: 'I don't have to remind you gentlemen how much our Allies and our own forces will depend on reliable supplies of food and provisions for ships rounding the Cape,' Anna said, sitting at one end of the table. 'This vital sea route must also be equipped to supply fresh fruit, eggs, meat, vegetables.' She paused and looked round. Their faces were impassive and somewhat sceptical now.

'We already hold contracts to supply the defence force,' Anna said hurriedly. 'I think you know what kind of money there is in food distribution – just as I am sure that Mr le Grange, here, knows that I have – we have,' she corrected herself, 'the security to back this mortgage I'm requesting, but I have to be very liquid.'

Geldenhuys was frowning; he cleared his throat and said: 'Mrs Smit, why should this business need more cash than any other business?'

Anna was on firm ground here. 'It's a question of buying at the right time, when the stock comes on offer,' she began eagerly. 'If I hear of a trainload of calves available, I can probably pick them up for next to nothing if I'm in the right place at the right time with the cash. Then the warehouse has to be full, you don't always know when the ships are going to arrive or restock. I've been involved in food distribution for the past two years,' she went on.

Geldenhuys looked around at the other four, as if vaguely amused. 'My dear young lady, I would hardly call a poultry farm food distribution.' He grinned. 'All right, so you succeed in making profits and your uncle has left you a farm, but does that really equip you for this type of business? I think not.'

'The mortgage would be based on the security of the building, and in addition there's my farm. It doesn't matter whether or not you think I can run this business,' she argued desperately.

Le Grange shook his head. 'My dear, that is not so. We're not here to loan you money so that we can take your building and your farm. Our job is to guide you and if we feel that you are, well ... ' He cleared his throat and looked at the others for support, which was obviously not forthcoming. 'If we feel that you are biting off more than you can chew, to put it crudely, then it's our duty to discourage you, by not loaning you the money.'

Anna reddened, wishing she could tell them to go to hell, but she could not.

'Mr le Grange, I am going into food distribution with or without your loan,' she said icily. 'Please don't concern yourself as to whether or not I can run the business because I know I can. You can always take back the building, it's worth more than six thousand pounds.'

'My dear, we're not in the business of buying and selling, merely lending money,' le Grange said sternly. 'We could very well find ourselves in an invidious position. The law looks very tolerantly upon women in this country. In nine cases out of ten we cannot even prosecute them. You can always hide behind your sex, my dear, if you wanted to.'

This was not going the way Anna had planned. Stupid old men, she thought contemptuously. Born to riches, affluent all their lives, never ever having to try hard at anything. Anna's eyes narrowed and her chin jutted out determinedly.

'Plenty of men go bust,' she snarled.

'Take it easy, Anna,' le Grange warned. 'We're only concerned at the viability of your plans.'

206

'There's going to be hundreds of ships,' Anna cried out. 'In the docks and at Simonstown and they'll all need food. It's a profitable business. Food has always been a profitable business.'

'You see the war in terms of profit?' Geldenhuys asked.

Anna flushed and bit her lip. 'I was building my poultry farm long before the war began, but now that it's here, why should I not expand my business to the fullest extent?'

'Mrs Smit,' Fourie said brusquely. 'I believe your husband, Simon Smit, has joined up. You have twins, a little over eighteen months. Apart from this you're running a poultry farm and your husband's farm in his absence. Don't you feel that is enough for you?' He frowned. 'You say you have a partner. Where is he then?'

To lose control now was to lose everything. Anna smiled beguilingly. 'I am sure I remember, Mr Fourie, that you have six children,' she said, 'three farms in the Stellenbosch area, a share in the local winery, three buildings in town and in addition, you're a director of this firm. Has anyone ever said to you that running one farm and your six children is more than enough for you?'

Fourie glared and shuffled his papers. Now they were all looking angry. She flushed, pushed back her chair and stood up. 'I've told you everything there is to say,' Anna told them. Taking a sheaf of papers from her file she threw them on the table. 'There are the facts and figures, gentlemen. It lists my assets, the value of the buildings and the security you would have. As for my future, I'll look after that myself. I didn't come here for advice, but for a mortgage and you can grant it or not, just as you please.'

Le Grange hurried after her as she made for the lift.

'Anna, be reasonable,' he began. 'We have our rules and regulations. I don't hold out much hope for you, but I'll tell you this. Just get your father to sign personal security and I promise you there will be absolutely no problem.'

'I have enough security myself. There's no reason for me to bother my father,' she said with as much dignity as she could muster.

Seven days later the dreaded letter arrived and it was no surprise to Anna to read that her application for a loan had been turned down. The letter stated simply that it was not the Society's policy to grant large mortgages to women unless secured by a male in a suitably affluent position to make good his pledge.

That was that! She had an option on the building for another three days.

'We're not beaten yet,' she said to Acker that night as she bathed the twins. It was funny how the babies filled her world and gave her the courage to try harder. For them she would be successful; fulfil the role of mother and father; she would make sure they had the best in life; nothing would stand in her way. 'We're going to get that building,' she told them solemnly. 'You can count on your mother.'

22

After supper the following evening, when the twins were sleeping and Lena had returned to her small cottage beyond the dam, Anna took her notebook and as it was a warm evening, sat outside on the steps with the lantern beside her.

It was a perfect summer night, cicadas chirped shrill and urgent; frogs croaked in the donga; the moon hung low and huge over the hills. Scribbling frantically Anna was intent only on her figures. What to do? Buy the building for cash and leave herself without working capital or let the opportunity slip through her fingers? How could she raise more cash? If she sold the poultry farm what would she realize? Frantic scribblings again – and so it went on.

The venture was beyond her cash resources, but she was afraid to hold back. Nights of loneliness were sucking her courage, and she knew that too long a wait would render her incapable of starting again. The prospect of a solitary future at Modderfontein, alone with the twins and Jan, was too horrible to contemplate. Her life seemed to stretch ahead like a prison sentence. She was sure that she would never see Simon again, nor would she want to. Her father had returned, yet made no move to contact her, and Kurt had disappeared. She was utterly alone, abandoned. For all anyone cared she could rot here, progress slowly from youth to old age with little change between the one and the other.

'God, no,' she would murmur aloud when these black moods of despair gripped her. Far better to try; to hurl everything at one determined thrust towards change, money, a better life. Yet she was just as fearful of taking the first irrevocable step. What if she failed? There was no one to fall back on, no one to advise her. Perhaps she would not cope with the business single-handed. What if she ran out of cash? She stood up and began to pace the path. She would do it anyway, she decided, with or without enough cash or courage. She would offer nine thousand pounds, first thing in the morning.

An hour later she saw lights slowly approaching over the hills. A lorry. No, two lorries. Whoever could it be at this time of night?

It was Kurt and when she saw him her anger surged until she could not control herself.

'For God's sake where have you been?' she shouted before he had climbed out of the lorry. 'What took you so long? You're utterly thoughtless, cruel, spiteful, irresponsible.' She burst into tears and ran back to the kitchen, too relieved and too angry to stop crying.

'There, there, I'm sorry. It's all right. There, there.'

'Stop it, oh stop it. I'm not a child,' she snapped.

'You could have fooled me.'

She laughed and cried at the same time and all at once the burden of her loneliness lifted, she took a deep breath and smiled. 'Oh, but I'm glad to see you,' she murmured. She tried out a smile and flung her arms around his shoulders. 'So what took you so long?' she murmured. 'Why two lorries? What's going on?'

'Food first, talk second,' he said. 'We've not eaten all day.'

'You're in luck. There's mutton stew cooked and cold beer in the ice-box.'

'But where have you been?' she persisted as she fetched the stew from the pantry and put it on the stove. 'You've been missing for over a month. I tried to contact you. Eventually I gave up.' She broke off, remembering the misery of that day.

'I was coming back, as we arranged,' he said.

Looking at him Anna could see how much he had changed: broader shoulders, skin browner, but how thin he was.

'I went down with malaria on the way,' he went on. 'Then we bumped into a buffalo, broke the axle. What a trip. One disaster after the next.'

'You could have flown. You have no idea how worried I was.'

He looked pleased. 'Anna, I could not fly with your uncle's furniture. Oh, that reminds me.' He stood up and hurried to the lorry and, opening the back, he whistled and called, 'Wolfie, come boy.'

'Good God, uncle's dog. Who would believe he's still alive? He must be all of, let me think, twelve years.'

As the grizzled dog emerged Wagter went for him and the two set up a commotion of snarling and yelping until Kurt hauled Wagter off and beat him. The dogs slunk into the kitchen behind Kurt, where they remained on either side of the room, eyeing each other suspiciously.

'Don't worry, they'll have a few fights and then they'll settle down,' she said.

They were joined by a short, lean, ugly man; Coloured, plus Hottentot and possibly Chinese, Anna decided, staring sidelong at him, for his eyes were slanting and his face was cracked and crinkled like old parchment.

'This is Hennessy, my driver – our driver, Anna.' Kurt clapped his hand on Hennessy's shoulder. 'Best driver in Africa.'

It was not until much later, when Hennessy had been fed and given a place to sleep, and they had finished supper, that Anna told him about the building and the disappointment over her failure to obtain a bond.

'You make it sound like a palace,' Kurt said.

'To us it's more useful than a palace.' She frowned. 'Unfortunately five old fools have knocked the idea into a cocked hat.'

'You're a cuckoo,' Kurt said eventually. 'You set about things back-to-front. First buy the building and when you own it apply for a bond. You'll find it's a simple matter. Don't worry, we'll look at it tomorrow.'

She went on to describe the land she was renting to fatten stock and the bullocks and pigs she had purchased, plus the offer of two thousand sheep for which she needed more space.

211

Watching her Kurt could not help admiring her courage, but at the same time she looked tired and depressed, there were dark shadows under her eyes, her skin looked drab and there was an air of sadness about her that had not been so apparent before.

'Now you've told me all the trivial things, tell me the important ones,' he said when she finally ran out of facts and figures.

'Such as?'

'Simon! Where's Simon?'

'He left me,' she said bluntly and went on to explain what had happened. 'I don't know if it was over the farm, or you, or because he thought I'd killed the baby, or deliberately let it die, which amounts to the same thing,' she ended sadly.

'I don't suppose he knows himself,' Kurt said. 'What did happen to the baby?'

She flushed. 'You, too!' she said angrily.

'It's just that you're such a rotten liar,' he retorted.

'Look, the baby's not dead. I swear to you. Sophie wasn't a fit mother for it. There's an end to the matter.'

He raised his hands. 'I give in. I don't want to fight,' he said mildly, assuming she had handed it to child welfare.

Suddenly she burst into tears and crumpled into a chair and, watching her, Kurt wondered what he had done to provoke this outburst. He crouched beside her and put his arms around her.

'What have I done? What's the matter?' He stroked her hair and wiped her eyes with the kitchen towel.

'Don't stick that dirty old cloth in my eyes,' she complained.

He threw it on the floor.

'I'm sorry,' she sobbed. 'It's just that Simon could have reacted like you. That would have been the end of the matter, but he always thinks the worst of me. Why is life so easy and calm with you and so difficult with Simon?'

'Make a swop,' he suggested.

'I don't know why I'm being such a fool,' she sobbed. 'When he punched me I didn't cry, not even when he left.

Then when I couldn't find you I just worked, and Pa came back, oh, and everything! I was so calm and now you're here I go and make a fool of myself.'

He carried her to bed, soothed and coaxed her until she cried out the miserable month she had endured.

Finally she looked up, smiling tremulously. 'Now you're here, you can do all the worrying,' she said and smiled again.

Watching her, Kurt thought how wonderful it must be to let go of problems, trust someone else enough to shed the burden. And she could trust him. He would protect her for the rest of his life. How could the silly child cope without him? It seemed that there was some purpose in coming to South Africa after all. To succeed in business was easy; he was confident of his ability and his experience; but to acquire the desire to succeed – that was the problem. But for Anna he would be prepared to begin again; she would provide meaning to the meaningless disaster. He truly loved her and felt confident that with time and patience, she would learn to love him, too.

He bent down and brushed his lips over her shoulder and suddenly became suffused with desire for the first time for months. He began to feel his body awaken. It was not just an urge for sex, but a resumption of life; a need to smell, to touch; to enjoy beauty again – to be hungry. Anna was his lifeline. Only through her would he ever feel joy.

'Purr, purr,' she said. 'I love being stroked. I wish I was a cat. Did I tell you Simon shot my cat?'

'Hush, don't talk, just purr,' he said and lovingly stroked her back, her breasts and the white soft flesh around her thighs. Something about the neat slash amongst dark hair inspired him with compassion. He could cry for woman's vulnerability, he thought, watching her. He would love and protect her for the rest of her life. She would always be safe with him.

He stifled passion, stroked her arms and neck, kissed her body, slowly letting his tongue stray over every part of her. How beautiful she was, her velvet skin was smooth and unblemished, her eyes dark with faint shadows under them.

213

As his hand caressed her skin, her nipples hardened and turned dark. She stirred and moved restlessly, groaning softly.

He should take her away from here, build her a house by the sea. He imagined her walking barefoot at the water's edge; hair blowing in the wind. A gipsy woman!

Watching her he felt confused; conflicting emotions struggled to gain precedence; he desperately wanted to protect the beauty which she was carelessly squandering; but part of him wanted to ravage her; ensnare her; for he was sure that he could awaken the sensuousness of which she was still unaware and, when he did, she would be his forever.

She moved, groaned, opened her eyes sleepily. 'Don't stop,' she said. Desire flooded his limbs, driving out all conscious thought. Instinct took over. As he thrust into her he knew without a flicker of doubt that she was his. This beautiful, wilful headstrong girl would one day love him as he loved her.

What a difference another human being could make, Anna thought next morning. Her dreams seemed so much more attainable, the future brighter. Even the cottage seemed warmer and gayer and there was a warm glow inside her.

The weather changed during the night and by morning low clouds and thick mist had set in. When Anna woke Kurt at nine with coffee it was already drizzling.

'Last night was lovely,' she said mournfully, 'and I do love you in a way, but I can't divorce Simon for joining up and you can't divorce Madeleine for being in a camp, so we'd best put our emotions into cold storage until the end of the war or we'll end up hating each other. Worse still, hating ourselves.'

'Last night was something special. I've never been so happy,' he murmured, resentful of her change of mood, staring at the window where the drizzle ran down the panes.

'Kurt, am I right or wrong?'

His mouth closed into a tight, stubborn line.

'For God's sake, Kurt, don't you remember that day you came to Modderfontein? The day you heard about Madeleine? You said you couldn't marry me. Well, it's still true, isn't it?'

He groaned and pulled the pillow over his head.

Men! She sighed. 'So we'll wait then, won't we?' she persisted, following him into the kitchen where he fetched hot water to shave. 'A promise between us, Kurt. A pact! We'll cool our feelings until war ends and then sort ourselves out. Forget last night. Do you promise, Kurt?'

'We'll see, we'll see,' he exploded angrily.

On the long drive to Cape Town they worked out their partnership; Kurt would hold fifty per cent and Anna fifty. They would pay five thousand pounds each and Anna would lend Kurt his share, which he would repay at two hundred and fifty pounds a month. In the meantime he would pay interest at the going rate. This was a point which he had insisted upon, in spite of Anna's protestations. Kurt was to run the ships' chandlers, for which he would receive a salary, and Anna would run the stock buying and rearing for which she too would be paid.

Anna was delighted with their agreement and anxious to secure the building, but watching Kurt later as he peered into every corner and crevice, his face grimmer each minute, she wondered if this would ever happen. He was disappointed, furious even, and he showed it. The agent was becoming increasingly nervous. Kurt inspected the roof, the cellars, the windows, the wiring, tapped on walls and floors and as far as Anna was concerned wasted a good deal of time.

Finally he strode into the front yard, cast a contemptuous look at the building as if for the last time, and said, 'I have a better prospect. This building needs too much renovation and time is short.'

Anna scowled at him.

'I quite understand, Mr Friedland,' the estate agent said, 'but I feel you should think again. The building is very solid, very solid indeed and I'm sure my client would be prepared to meet you on the renovations. You see, the liquidators are keen to wind up this affair.'

Kurt nodded contemptuously. 'It's not just a question of money, my dear man, it's time. Time is money and I must have premises in working order.'

'Make an offer,' the estate agent insisted. 'Take off what you think the renovations will cost. The building industry is quiet now, you can have the best firm here tomorrow morning, working at the double.'

'If it were just builders,' Kurt shrugged and spread his hands in a gesture of despair. 'We need refrigeration engineers. Are there such skills in the Cape or must I send to Johannesburg?'

'Indeed there are. I daresay I can have a refrigeration engineer on your premises by eight tomorrow morning.'

Kurt looked confused. 'Well, I don't know ...' he began. 'All right, I'll give them an offer for seven thousand pounds, only for twenty-four hours, mind you. Quite honestly I'll be relieved if they say no. At that price the building's a good buy, admittedly, but a lot of trouble. If it weren't for the railway siding I wouldn't bother at all.'

The estate agent hauled out a sheet of paper and began to scribble frantically. 'Just sign here please, sir,' he said deferentially and Anna was annoyed to remember how high-handed he had been with her.

Kurt hesitated and then signed his name with a flourish. He turned to Anna. 'Come along, Anna, we have four more buildings to see and we don't have all day.'

Anna returned to the lorry in a turmoil. How dare he? It was the only building anywhere near a railway siding.

'You've ruined everything,' she grumbled as soon as they were out of earshot. 'Seven thousand pounds. Ridiculous! It's worth double.'

'We'll see,' was all she could get out of him.

They were hardly back at the farm when the telephone rang, a rare event at Modderfontein, and Anna picked up the receiver, wondering who it could be. It was the agent assuring her that their offer had been accepted. If she would care to call in and pay at her earliest convenience the building was hers. She replaced the receiver and stared at Kurt, feeling embarrassed.

He laughed before she said anything. 'Business lesson

number one, my dear. Things are not always what they seem. Now for your second lesson in business methods and procedures you will go back to the Table Mountain Insurance Company and apply for a seventy-five per cent bond. Do the same with every other finance house and assure them that you will take the first offer that comes through at current rates. We'll have to take two vans, because I'm going to inspect this farm you're renting.'

'We're renting,' Anna corrected him.

'Apologies,' he said and smiled suddenly, and she realized for the first time how truly delighted Kurt was.

'You're a genius,' he told her at supper that night. 'You'll see, together we'll make a formidable team.'

The bond of six thousand pounds, the original amount that Anna had applied for, came through within ten days. Anna and Kurt signed joint personal security, and Kurt paid her one thousand pounds which he had saved towards the five he owed her.

From then on the feeling of sadness and despair that had settled so heavily on Anna in the mornings faded and a feeling of wellbeing took its place. There was no need to feel poor, she would make her own fortune, no need to feel abandoned, she had Kurt to help her with the business. She woke earlier each morning and leapt out of bed with a smile.

What was it, she wondered, that made the sky glow bluer, turned a dull day into a panorama of subtle colours, made each humdrum job seem satisfying? It was, of course, the home-grown, heady wine of success.

23

Their new building was not yet completely renovated when Kurt's demands for more meat, more eggs, more poultry, began to pour in, so Anna engaged Hendricks, a young school-leaver from the village, to write orders and check stocks, but their reserves soon dwindled and from then on Anna's days were spent searching the neighbourhood for supplies. They often had to approach established wholesalers and pay exorbitant prices.

Kurt assured her it was worth the loss. 'The war is only beginning,' he would say. 'New ships are rounding the Cape and once they've received good service they'll stick with us. We must grab every contract we can.'

Anna began to wake at five, and after inspecting the farm she would spend the day purchasing stock.

One evening when she arrived home dog-tired, Koos van Niekerk, poultry foreman, waylaid her.

'What is it?' she asked with a sigh.

'It's like this,' he said nervously fingering his hat. 'Overseas they've got this new system of keeping hens in small cages, each one not much bigger than the bird itself, about a foot by a foot and a half, roughly speaking, Ma'am, and this prevents the hens from moving around too much.'

'Fat hens don't lay well,' Anna snapped.

'Ah, Ma'am, but that's the thing. They feed them mainly protein.'

'No mealies?'

He shook his head. 'Right now we know when a batch is going off, but we never know which ones are doing the laying.

With these batteries, as they call them, you can cull the bad 'uns. Besides, they keep the hens in a long shed and keep the lights on ten hours a day so that the hens get fooled into thinking it's always summer. That plus the heating.'

'Heating?'

He smiled self-consciously. 'It's all in this book.'

Anna took the magazine curiously. 'And what do you think we'd save with this system?'

'Ma'am, we'd double production with the same amount of hens.'

She shrugged deprecatingly. 'Well, maybe we'll try it out.'

'Not as easy as all that. The batteries cost about five shillings each and then there's the shed, the heating, the lighting.' His voice trailed off.

Anna frowned. 'But that's out of the question, Koos. We could never recoup such an outlay.'

'Begging your pardon, Ma'am, but you're thinking short-term. The batteries last at least fifteen years.'

'Well, yes, I suppose you have a point. Give me a few days.' Anna stood up hoping Koos would leave and he did, slowly, still fingering his hat. 'Just think, Ma'am, if you don't change to the new system, others will, and eventually you won't be able to compete pricewise, particularly during winter. It's batteries or bust, you might say.'

What a nerve he had. Anna forced a smile and, shutting the door firmly behind him, she scrambled through the pages, seeing the neat illustrations of hens in their long prison rows. A marvellous idea! Why had she not thought of it herself? She must put out a tender for a thousand.

Next morning, Anna's first call was at a farm three hours' drive from Saldanha Bay, along the west coast past Struisbaai. She had heard the van der Merwes were selling up. You could hardly blame them, Anna thought, observing the havoc wrought by two years of drought in this area.

The wife was a frail creature, shrivelled by years of toil and humbleness; her red-faced, obese husband was in a fine temper as he greeted Anna in the doorway.

'Thought they were sending a buyer from the Southern

Cross Chandlers,' he said angrily.

'That's me,' Anna said lightly with a nervous smile.

'Reckon I don't want no truck with women,' he said, turning away.

'Have you had any other buyers, Mr van der Merwe?' she called into the dark passage, but there was no reply and a few seconds later his wife returned, holding a tray with a glass of water, a cup of coffee and some biscuits.

'Come in the kitchen and drink this,' she said shyly.

Anna stirred three spoons of sugar into the thick black brew and drank it gratefully.

'Have you had any other offers?' she asked.

'Not one.' The woman wiped a tear with the back of her hand. 'The stock's starving, you see. They need fattening. It'll take months.'

'Go and tell your husband I'm the only buyer for Southern Cross Chandlers and he'll either deal with me or no one. I'll give him a fair price.' She smiled to soften the aggression.

Eventually the farmer returned, his face redder, his manner apologetic. 'I didn't mean no disrespect to you,' he said heavily. 'Times are changing, I suppose. What does a woman know about these things?'

It was a long and depressing walk over sandy stretches and meagre pasture. The sheep were scraggy but they would recover with good grazing. The cows were a sorry lot, hardly worth the transport, and the pigs not fit for streaky bacon. What a disaster.

After scribbling in her notebook she said: 'Five hundred pounds for the lot.'

The farmer gasped in annoyance. 'But that's robbery, Ma'am. The sheep alone are worth more than that and as for the cows – why the cows are worth more than the sheep. All they need's a spot of fodder.'

'I'm sorry, Mr van der Merwe,' she said firmly. 'That's my offer. Of course you don't have to accept it. Perhaps you have had a better one?'

He shook his head dumbly, too overcome with annoyance and disappointment to speak.

Anna handed him her card, her usual procedure. 'Please telephone me if you decide to take my offer and if I'm not there leave a message with Hendricks who mans the phone all hours.'

For a while they tramped in silence, Anna shielding her eyes from the sand which was stinging her legs as the wind gathered force. Nearing the farmhouse the farmer said, 'All right, I'll tell you what. It's hard to sell now so I'll accept seven hundred pounds.' He sighed.

'I'm not here to bargain,' Anna told him. 'I offered you a fair price in terms of market conditions. I have to take into consideration transportation costs and the long time it will take to fatten them. You can accept my price or reject it, it's up to you. Good morning to you, Mr van der Merwe.'

She looked in at the farmhouse to thank his wife for the coffee and drove off, sure that he would follow a pattern that had been emerging over the past weeks. Tomorrow he would telephone and offer another compromise deal and the following day he would accept her offer.

It was four in the afternoon when Anna reached her seventh and final farm for the day. By this time she was unenthusiastic about another long tramp over the land. This farm, like the rest in this area, was dry, the sheep skinny. Mr Myburgh, the farmer, was nearly seventy and his wife not much younger. They were looking forward to an overdue retirement and planning to live with relatives in Stellenbosch.

Before long they remembered Anna's pedigree for three generations. Anna was always amazed at the interest people took in the affairs of others. To Anna, strangers were divided into two categories: those who were useful and those who were not. Neither were of much interest to her.

'We might have carried on a while yet,' Myburgh told her, 'but we've done all right. Ever since I can remember the weather's followed a pattern, a few good years and then a few bad 'uns. I want to pull out now before the farm gets real dry like the ones around Springbok.'

Anna pricked up her ears.

'Drought three years running.' He sighed. 'The stock are

dying and farmers are closing. Trekking to town for work. Ruined! If you're looking for sheep to fatten, a trip up to those parts would be worth you while, Mrs Smit,' Myburgh went on. 'But you'd best be quick or they'll be dead before you get there.'

For once her offer was accepted immediately, for he was glad to see the back of the farm and enjoy the few years left in tranquillity.

It was after eight when Anna arrived home and she was feeling exhausted, but the kitchen was warm, the wood stove burning brightly, and Lena had mutton stew with dumplings on the boil and a glass of mulled wine ready for Anna.

Anna leaned over the children's cots to kiss them goodnight. It was all worthwhile, she thought wearily, for she planned to be a millionaire long before they left school.

Two days later Anna set off for Springbok at four a.m. although it was nearly noon by the time she arrived. All around her the fields were dried and shattered with years of drought, looking like gigantic jigsaw puzzles. Carrion crows circled over the disaster area where dead sheep had fallen, picking the bones.

Passing a gate which read: 'J.H. Firth', Anna turned and drove a mile to the farmhouse, a place of shattered windows, peeling whitewash, the dam a dried-out hollow. It was abandoned. She got out of her van and stood watching the scene, trying to quell her mounting depression. This might have been her fate if she had not found water at Modderfontein. She visualized Simon and herself, with the children, trying to live on the modest pickings of a landless farmer, begging for odd jobs.

The next farm was little better, but inhabited, and here there were plenty of sheep, heads drooping, ribs jutting, searching the land. There was a smell of rotting carcasses which turned her stomach. Nature's cruel revenge.

The farmer, Willis Grobbelaar, was a young man, ash blond hair, bitter eyes, his wife joyless and desperate. Two children, small replicas of their parents, stood biting their nails, staring distrustfully.

She wondered whether to leave now. Profiting from misery was not part of her plan, but then she decided that if she did not buy their stock they would be worse off.

They did not offer her coffee, having none, she guessed.

'Vultures from the city,' Willis began with a scowl. 'Picking over the bones. That's all you'll find here. Bones.' He swore and punched his fist into his hand.

Oh my God, Anna thought. What have I let myself in for? And is it worth it?

Mrs Grobbelaar broke in angrily. 'Things are bad enough, Willis, without throwing away what's left.' She turned suspiciously to Anna. 'Mr Grobbelaar will show you the stock.' Her words, commonplace enough, were like an insult.

The same sorry drama unfolded at every farm she saw that day, but by evening she had bought five thousand sheep, yet she would not pay for them until Hendricks and his gang arrived. 'Payment in cash,' she promised them all. 'On the nail when the sheep are put in the lorries.'

Night fell and Anna bought a cup of coffee at the café and asked where she could find a room for the night.

'Mrs Joubert, down the road, lets rooms when necessary,' Jurgens, the café proprietor, told her.

Anna walked along the dusty street to Mrs Joubert's house which looked clean and pleasant enough, freshly whitewashed with a tin roof and bright green shutters.

The woman was pleased to have a paying guest and insisted on moving out of her bedroom. There was no bathroom and by the time Anna had washed in the hand basin and eaten supper she had made up her mind to purchase an additional two thousand sheep for Modderfontein. She had to contact Hendricks and the nearest telephone was at the café, so she hid the money under her pillow and, slinging the canvas bag over her shoulder, set out in the dark.

It was only five blocks, but dark, and halfway there she gained a strong impression that someone was following her. She paused uneasily, peering over her shoulder. The night was full of shapes and shadows, but none were moving.

She went on. Surely soft footsteps were dogging her own. Someone was walking on rubber-soled shoes, or barefooted, on the pavement not more than a few yards away. She heard the crunch of a stone dislodged and then a short hard skid from a misplaced step.

She made a dash for the shop, still three blocks away, but the footsteps were running too, gaining on her.

Her shoulder was pushed hard and then she was sprawling on the ground.

She screamed long and hard and then called out, 'Help! Somebody help me.'

Her bag was wrenched away. Her attacker vanished, but as a car approached she caught a glimpse of ash-blond hair. Running feet. The brakes squealed and she was helped into the car and driven to the café.

'There was only small change in my bag,' she explained after she had refused brandy and accepted a cup of coffee.

'Folks here know you've come to buy the sheep and they know you're carrying a fortune in cash,' Jurgens told her. 'When a man's desperate there's no telling what he might do. It's not woman's work, but if you must do it, get a good dog, or a bodyguard.'

Memories of the next few days would make her flinch for years: resentful, desperate farmers; entire families without hope; the sheep stinking and expiring; Hennessy, with his ten hired lorries, sweating through two trips a day to move the stock. She could smell the fear wherever she went. A buyers' market!

Five days later Anna loaded the remaining fifty sheep into her lorry and joined the convoy for the last trip to the Cape Flats. She felt exhausted. She had spent every penny and bought seven thousand sheep at rock bottom prices.

By dawn Anna was in the Hex River Valley, surely the most beautiful place to be at dawn, she thought, rubbing her eyes. The sky a pale, translucent blue, the mountain slopes purple as they caught the first rays of the sun, the pasture green.

She arrived ahead of the convoy and called the farm workers to help her remove the sheep and clean the lorry. A quick inspection showed the sheep were recovering rapidly. Three months, she thought, and then a fat profit. A highly successful trip if she could just shake off the sadness.

Her lorry was soon washed down, but she felt sure she would never be rid of the smell of rotting carcasses, manure and desperation.

She should go home, but home would be too much of an anti-climax. She wanted to see Kurt's face when she told him about the seven thousand sheep. Besides, it was over a month since she had last seen him. A busy month, for she had been out daily buying stock and Kurt should have completed the building by now. Strange, but she was really longing to see him.

24

Triumph surged in her blood, vibrating to her fingertips, like too much brandy or good music. There was her building, looking twice as large as life in the false winter sunlight. Squinting, Anna read the company's name: 'The Southern Cross Ships' Chandlers', and smaller, '(Pty.) Ltd.' blazoned across the front in dark green against white.

They had fought for days over the outlay for paint. Anna, who had endorsed the cash for reconditioning the freezing plant, had baulked at a thousand pounds just to pretty up the place.

Kurt had insisted, saying: 'Image, my dear. Always watch your image. Something you are inclined to neglect. It can make you or break you.'

At the time she had been furious but now, looking at the building, she had to admit that he had been right, for there was an aura of tradition about the place. Not bad for two months. You could swear it had been there for years.

'Amazing,' she murmured once inside, for the wide, dusty passage was now an imposing foyer in white and green with pillars and – she gasped. Surely not a marble floor! He couldn't be that extravagant. She dropped to her knees and ran her hand over it. Linoleum tiles, but a superb imitation. 'Fantastic.' She spoke aloud and became aware of neat ankles and pale blue court shoes not a foot away. Her gaze travelled upwards. Pale blue suit, frilly cream blouse, azure eyes and ash-blonde hair. Probably a replica of Madeleine. Aware that she was still on her hands and knees and not cutting a very becoming figure she scowled, 'Not very well laid, these tiles. I think you should complain.' She stood up, aware of her new status as employer and held out her hand. 'Pleased to meet you. I'm Mrs van Achtenburgh-Smit.'

The girl did not offer to shake hands, nor did she give her name. Instead, disdainful blue eyes noted the muddy boots, the old slacks. Anna became very aware of her dirty fingernails and the stench.

'What is your business?' The receptionist darted behind her desk and flicked her manicured finger on to her intercom.

'Why, I own this business,' Anna said, unhappily aware that she was lying, throwing her weight around, lacking in manners, and that she was altogether too envious to care.

'There's a strange woman here ...' The woman spoke into the intercom with a trace of German accent.

'Send her up.' Kurt's voice sounded remote.

'First on the left upstairs,' the girl said. As Anna reached the top she heard her say: 'Butch is on the way.'

She flung open the door. 'Did you hear what she said?' she gasped. 'Sack her. I insist.'

'No, of course I won't. Come and sit down. I hope your clothes won't ruin the chairs.'

Anna was caught midway between anger and envy, for while she had been sweating it out in Springbok, amidst the horror of starving sheep and the stench of ruined families, Kurt had made himself very comfortable indeed. The top executive to his manicured fingertips she thought grimly, noting his tailored mohair suit, his suntan, his blond hair gleaming, eyes shining with amusement.

'Damn you, Kurt, you're having a cushy life,' she said, all too conscious of the miserable picture she was making.

Anna walked slowly across the room, eyes cold, lips compressed. 'The place is unnecessarily ostentatious,' she said, 'and so are you.' She sat down, leaning forward, elbows on knees, legs apart, mud from her boots flaking on the carpet. 'I've got seven thousand sheep, damn near starved to death, but I reckon we'll save ninety per cent. Got them for a fraction of their value and in three months we'll have enough mutton to keep the British navy going.'

Kurt clasped his hands together and appeared to be deep in thought. Then he said briefly, 'Congratulations, Anna.'

'Is that all you can say? Just that? I slogged my guts out, worked all hours, drove overnight, helped get them off the trucks, some were so weak we had to carry them, and all you can say is "congratulations".'

'Well, what did you expect me to say?'

Anna smashed her fist on the desk with annoyance. She did not know what she had expected him to say, but not just "congratulations", as if he did not mean it. She took a deep breath and leaned back. 'Well, I guess congratulations just about covers it,' she said. 'Never mind, I came for you to take me to lunch.'

Kurt eyed her coldly and eventually said, 'Not today, thanks, Anna. I'm too busy.'

She gasped, flushed with annoyance. 'I insist you take me to lunch. Damn it, Kurt, I haven't had a decent meal for five days. I've looked forward to getting back. What's the matter with you? Let's go out and celebrate.'

'No, I won't take you.' His voice had an edge of harshness, mockery.

Anna made an effort to control her temper, but her hands were shaking. No doubt about it, he was after that pathetic creature downstairs.

'You work for me and I insist that we go to lunch.'

'I don't work for you. We're partners and what I do with my lunchtimes is my business.' At that moment he could have killed her, not because of her mean temper, but because of the way she looked. Her essential womanliness destroyed. She was deliberately spoiling something he loved. 'My lunch companions usually smell of perfume, not dung, and their language is cleaner than yours and so are their nails.'

'How dare you,' she gasped, taken aback.

'A cowhand couldn't stink worse than you. When are you going to learn to wear a dress instead of trousers?' Quiet words, white face, but inside seething and compressed.

'I'll dress how I please,' Anna shrieked.

'I'll take who I please to lunch,' he murmured.

228

'Like that hoity-toity prissy bitch downstairs, I suppose.'

'If I want to, why not? At least she's not trying to be a man.'

'Damn you, Kurt. You've no right, no right at all. You've got the cushy job while I slog my guts out. You're sacked!' Her eyes glinted with the pleasure of being thoroughly spiteful. 'Sacked!'

He watched her as if in a trance. A stupid child throwing her weight around. For two pins he would throw in his shares and start again. She'd be bust within a month, but he stood imprisoned, victim of his desire and need for her. Almost daily he repented the stupidity of a business based on emotions. Nevertheless he would endure, prosper and drag her up behind him. At that moment she seemed a hundred years younger than he.

She scowled at his tidy desk, put her foot on it and a large lump of dung fell on to his papers.

'Go and find a job somewhere else and take your prissy secretary with you.'

It was not the words, but the dung on his precious contracts which transformed Kurt's seething ill-humour into an eruption of rage. He grimaced with fury, hoisted Anna over his shoulder, flung open the door to his bathroom and, tossing her into the shower, turned the cold tap on full blast.

The squeals and shrieks turned to whimpers as Anna gasped for breath.

He pulled her out and her face contorted with rage. 'I'll get you for this,' she gasped. Pushing her back he turned the warm tap on, his rage cooling at the sight of Anna bedraggled and cold, but still angry.

When he released his grip slightly she stuck her head out of the spray.

'Damn you, Kurt, get out of my bloody building.'

'You can't sack me, Anna. It would cost you more than you've got.'

She lunged forward, punching his face and then dug her fingernails into his cheeks. Kurt wiped his cheek with the back of his hand and it came away bloody.

'I should punch you,' he muttered, shaking her.

Anna fought her way from the jet of water as he tried to push her back. 'You can stay there until you get rid of the stench and cool off your temper,' he gasped.

'You're got delusions of grandeur, Kurt. Who the hell do you think you are?' she yelled.

'And you?' He struggled to wrest off her clothes. 'You have a desire to be the lowest thing on two legs. I can't let you do it to yourself.' He panted with the effort of holding her still.

'Leave my clothes alone.'

'Come on, Anna, don't start playing the virgin if you're finished with your cowboy act.'

He succeeded in tearing her blouse and her bra off; she in turn ground her teeth viciously and tore at his shirt. 'Two can play at this game,' she hissed and the buttons scattered on the floor.

'My shirt, look what you've done to my shirt,' he raged.

'I've just begun,' she snarled and lunged at his waist. Kurt skidded and fell back on to the muddy, drenched floor.

'You bitch! You bitch! Look at my suit.'

'You want to play at undressing, that's OK with me.' She grabbed his shoe and hurled it through the open door, where it landed with a satisfying thud on his desk.

'How dare you!' He grabbed her trousers and hauled them down.

Anna was naked and furious. She flung herself on him and bit his neck and for a moment they were writhing, panting, teeth bared on the floor, but somewhere passion surged, replacing temper, and when Anna caught sight of his body, so virile, so desirable, the force of her need was almost unendurable and she caught hold of him, pulling him on top of her.

'Come here, come here,' she murmured, winding her arms around his neck and her feet around his hips. 'Rape me, rape me.'

'Rape you? My God, I'll be lucky to emerge in one piece.'

He pushed himself back and sat on his haunches and Anna, unwilling to let go of his neck, was pulled on to him. She sat astride and laughed with triumph as his penis pushed between her thighs. 'Pretend you don't want me,' she said and pressed her lips against his. Her breasts were hard against his chest.

He stared at her, caught halfway between anger and desire.

'I love you when you're angry,' she murmured and rubbed her breasts against him. Suddenly she was impaled upon his hard, throbbing flesh. He stood up, carrying her on him, his arms wrapped around her buttocks while she clung to his neck. He set her down upon the desk and pushed her back over the papers.

'Your prissy secretary will have to type everything again,' Anna murmured as she abandoned herself unashamedly to the sheer joy of satisfying her physical lust.

Afterwards Kurt stood back and stared squeamishly at his desk.

'Never mind that. Do you love me?' she asked.

'Anna, I love everything about you, except you,' he said gloomily.

'What a horrible thing to say.'

'I love your face, your incredible beauty, your spirit. But you – you give me a pain.'

Taking a cloth, he wiped the water from her eyes and under her hair and, rolling her hair into a towel, rubbed her briskly, lifting first one foot and then the other, drying her thighs, her legs and between her toes. Then he began to dry her hair.

'Anna,' he sighed. 'If you would only stop punishing yourself, hating yourself. Start riding, enjoy life and get to like yourself.'

'You're being ridiculous,' she murmured. 'We needed the sheep, we almost ran out.'

'You could have flown there, hired a plane. No need for you to stay five days and help lift the stinking things and then drive back. Madness!'

'You don't understand,' she said peevishly. 'They were dropping off as we looked at them. It's a miracle so many survived.'

'Have you never heard the word delegation? It means you pay others to do the dirty work. For God's sake, Anna. Learn to delegate.'

231

'Oh Kurt,' she whispered, winding her arms around his neck. 'Let's have a truce. Stop nagging, I'm so tired. I must sleep.'

'I thought you wanted to eat.'

'I want everything,' she murmured sleepily. 'A succulent steak or fish, a bottle of wine, maybe oysters, or let me think, perhaps crayfish. But what shall I wear? My clothes are wet through. All your fault.'

'I'll take you to eat later. Right now I have an appointment.'

'Promise?'

'Promise. I'm going to lock the door, Anna. Sleep until I get back. I'll get you some clothes, don't worry.'

He dressed.

'You look as if you fell in the drink,' she said, laughing.

He opened the cupboard and took pillow and blanket. 'I often stay here nights,' he told her, 'when I'm waiting for a ship.'

When Kurt returned at six-thirty Anna was still asleep. How beautiful she looked, a faint blush appearing once more on her cheeks, her long lashes quivering, hair wildly tangled in dark brown coils. Kurt loved beauty obsessively.

He went to his desk and, exclaiming with annoyance at the dung scattered over it, he began to clean the papers, dusting the filth into the bin. What an impossible person she was, an unlikely and unfit custodian of all that beauty. God knows how long it would last, the way she was driving herself.

Anna heard the noise, yawned and smiled.

'What time is it?'

'Six-thirty.'

'Mmn.' She rolled over. 'This is the first time I've felt pleased about your carpets and heater.'

'Look.' He stood up. 'I bought you a dress. I've been shopping.' Awkwardly he opened the box.

'Oh Kurt,' she swallowed hard as she gazed at the pure wool dress of palest blue that would obviously mould itself on to her body.

'It looks expensive,' she said.

232

'Yes, it was. You should only wear good dresses.'

'What size is it?' Anna asked, watching it suspiciously.

'Thirty-four.'

She sat up. 'I used to be thirty-four. But Kurt,' she laughed. 'I can't just wear a dress. Things go underneath, stockings, shoes, bras, you know.'

He produced another bag. 'I told the woman in the shop that my wife had fallen into the sea and was waiting for me to bring a complete outfit. I chose the dress. For the rest you'll have to hope for the best.'

'And shoes?' she demanded imperiously.

Anna gasped as he produced boots of beige suede, with high heels and a long zip. She pushed her feet into them and they fitted perfectly.

'Kurt, you've a genius,' she said.

Standing up she walked around the office, staring at her boots.

'I'm a genius, I acknowledge that,' he admitted, 'but I took your dirty boots to check the size.'

They went to a restaurant along the coast, specializing in seafoods and Anna went through the menu enthusiastically, starting with oysters, then calamari and finally crayfish.

'I didn't eat properly for five days,' she told him.

I shall retain this image of her for the rest of my life, Kurt thought morosely, watching Anna fiercely intent on devouring her crayfish. I shall trot it out and drool over it when she's being bloody-minded, when she wants to play the boss and make everyone squirm.

Her eyes looked over-large and deeper violet in the candlelight and her skin glowed so invitingly that he could hardly stop himself from reaching out and touching her. Instead he analyzed her. There was a strange symmetry about her face ... her even features; her classic nose; her strong white teeth. Her face was a perfect oval, with shadows beneath high cheekbones. Her thick, dark eyebrows offset the violet of her wide-set eyes. Quite perfect, he thought dispassionately. And if it had just been that, and nothing more, she would not be driving him crazy now. No, her appeal lay elsewhere. Perhaps

233

it was the way her eyes could gleam with passion one moment and cruelty the next; her mouth could be full and seductive today and tomorrow set in a thin, hard line. That was it, he thought. She was the unknown, unpredictable. Not one woman, but many – most of whom he feared. He picked up his glass and held it out to her. '*Prosit!*'

With a grimace, half-amused, half-irritated, she plunged her hand into the finger-bowl, wiped it hastily on the serviette and picked up her glass.

'Cheers,' she said, far too casually.

'Today was perfect,' he said, trying desperately to prolong the moment, for undoubtedly she had been wholeheartedly his for a while and she had appeared to love him.

'Why use the past tense? Tonight is perfect,' she corrected him.

'Yes, of course,' he murmured.

'That's the trouble with men,' Anna went on. Picking amongst the crayfish claws she snapped them with a precision and determination that was chilling. 'Men think sex is the be-all and end-all of everything, but I like to satisfy all my senses. That's happiness, when all five senses are satisfied at the same time. This evening is perfect because the crayfish is perfect, the wine is perfect, this restaurant, too,' she said with an effusive gesture. 'And then there's the sound and the scent of the sea, the warmth of the fire and the drowsiness of it all, and after sex, too. What could be more perfect after perfect sex... I feel happy.'

'I'm glad I was as satisfactory as the crayfish,' Kurt said, feeling hurt.

'Oh God, don't start again,' she said.

'Well, there's two missing,' Kurt said, trying to enter into her imagery. 'What about touch?'

'Ah,' she gurgled. 'I have a good memory.'

'And sight?'

'Well, I'm looking at you, aren't I, and you are almost the most handsome man I've ever seen.'

'Who did you see who was more handsome?' He laughed as he teased her.

'Simon,' she said.

The laugh faded.

They sat in silence for a while and then Kurt said: 'You know I love you. I want you to promise me you'll divorce Simon and marry me.'

Anna grabbed her glass and gulped her wine. Marry Kurt? Unthinkable! She wanted him just the way he was now, adoring her, working for her, building the business. He was so brilliant, but so unpredictable. How silly she had been to make love with him. She could not afford to lose him.

She put her glass down carefully. 'Kurt, we have no right to think about that sort of thing with Simon fighting a war and Madeleine ... Well, let's hope she's alive.' She hesitated and then went on determinedly. 'We must play our part from now on. No more sex, just friendship.' The war might last for years, she thought.

Her fingers went snip-snap, snip-snap, for all the world as if her life depended on extracting every last shred of flesh from the claws.

'Would you like another crayfish?' Kurt murmured, hating her at that moment.

She looked up and laughed. 'No thanks, I just don't want to waste this one. What's the matter with you, Kurt?' she said, feeling irritated. 'You look so miserable when you should be happy.'

'Why should I be?' he grumbled. 'Empty, sterile years lie ahead.'

'You see what I mean,' she said triumphantly. 'Sex! Just sex. We're going to do everything together, run the business, make a fortune and we'll be friends. There's only one thing we're not going to do, so why should that transform our lives into empty, sterile years? Really, I have no patience with men. The centre of their being dangles between their legs.'

'I hate crudity,' he said and signalled for the waiter.

'I'm not being crude, I'm being truthful,' she argued. 'Kurt, we'll make a fortune. We'll be millionaires. I feel it, I know it. We're a formidable combination.'

'We'll see,' Kurt said, sometimes wishing that she were not

quite so much of a child. And cruel like a child, too. 'I don't think you would be able to handle it. Anyway,' he went on morosely, 'what would you do if you had a million, Anna? You wouldn't have the faintest idea of how to spend it. Spending money is an art. Correction. Enjoying money is an art. You certainly don't have that art.'

Anna fell silent and stared at her wine. What would she do, she wondered, if she were wealthy? She could not think of anything except that she would like to buy Fontainebleu. 'What does it matter?' she said.

'It matters to me,' Kurt told her. 'I like to enjoy what I have.'

'You like to enjoy what you don't have, too,' she retorted.

Suddenly he reached forward, took her wrist firmly and turned her palm uppermost. 'Did you know I can read fortunes?' He smiled; a twisted, mocking smile.

'Oh really?' She laughed. 'Well, read mine then.'

'I see Anna Smit setting off on her insatiable quest for more and more money, but she never gets enough, she's never satisfied, and she never spends any of it, so she becomes old and embittered.'

She pulled her hand away and scowled at him. 'I wish you wouldn't talk so much nonsense,' she said. 'Particularly when you haven't the faintest idea what you're talking about.'

'That's true, and I'm sorry,' he said. 'Forgive me.'

But late that night when Anna lay in her lonely bed at Modderfontein, she could not help remembering his words and thinking: What if he's right? What if his silly prophecy comes true? She shivered and eventually went to make herself some tea. His words seemed to have taken all the pleasure from the evening. She had forgotten the love and warmth, the togetherness and even the triumph of seeing their company building painted and labelled for all the world to admire. All she could remember was Kurt's stupid omen. The words kept knocking around inside her head, ringing a discordant tune, like church bells rung by a horde of idiots.

25

The letter was official, that much was clear, and Anna stared at it for a few seconds before taking it out of her post office box. She knew no one in Britain, yet there it was addressed to Mrs Anna Smit in bold, unfamiliar handwriting with the letters OHMS on top.

The blood surged to her face as she read the first three words. It was from Simon and she was filled with joy which soon faded as she read the brief note. He had worked his passage to England and joined the British navy in order to save her the embarrassment of bumping into him on shore leave. Only at the end he had written: 'I often think of you, Simon.'

She stopped three times on the journey home to read the letter again, trying to glean some affection from the brief message, but eventually she put it away.

'We've had a letter from Daddy,' she told the twins when she reached home.

'Daddy, Daddy,' Acker said, but did not look up as he played with his train.

'I've lost my dolly,' Katie cried, running behind her.

It was only eighteen months since Simon had left, yet they did not remember him, she thought sadly as she gathered them into her arms.

After receiving the letter Anna increasingly began to miss Simon as her imagination gorged itself on happy memories and censored the rest. Simon had never known love, but she could have taught him. Instead, she had driven him away and if he were killed it would be her fault. She admitted she had tried to destroy Simon. Remembering his impotence, his fumbling attempts at reconciliation and his growing sense of inferiority, her guilt began to fester and she likened herself to a scorpion which destroys its mate. Only work dulled remorse, as morphine to pain, and Anna became addicted, rising at five and driving herself relentlessly until nightfall. Days, weeks, months merged into a continuous round, for if she stopped loneliness and guilt became unbearable.

Sometimes at night she would leave the twins in Lena's care and drive to the village, or to Malmesbury, just to gaze at curtained windows, lights shining, to hear voices and music. She lost weight and became quite bony-looking, and her face took on a pinched look with tight lines around her lips and between her eyes.

At first Kurt tried to woo her, arriving with tickets for the theatre or a concert and occasionally she would go – yet she remained beyond reach. Since that last time in the office, he had been unable to break through her reserves. Anna was determined to remain alone and it was clear that she regretted her brief affair with him. She was content with their business partnership and wanted nothing more from him.

Give her time, he told himself, but a year passed and then another and still Anna remained aloof, self-sufficient, untouchable. My God, what was she waiting for, he wondered? She had loathed the sight of Simon when he was home.

Anna was bent on becoming a recluse, shut up on her awful farm. If he could only reconcile her with her father. He tried on a number of occasions, but failed each time. Anna was obdurate.

Kurt's ambitions were not without self-interest and that he freely admitted, for now he pinned his hopes on Simon's return. When the absent war hero was once again a mulish farmer, Anna would seek more compatible company and he would be waiting. At Stellenbosch the misalliance would be even more apparent.

Besides, he rationalized, she was lonely, and Kurt

understood loneliness. Surrounded by new acquaintances, suppliers, customers, new friends, still he missed his home. Yet he had adjusted quicker than Anna, possibly because the change was not so taxing. He had found his rightful place in a new society, still Kurt Friedland, successful businessman. Anna, on the other hand, had become that rare and unpopular creature, a successful businesswoman and she fitted nowhere. Her former friends were leading very different lives from her own, engrossed in husbands and children. The solution was for Anna to be reconciled with her father, but all his persuasion had failed.

Yet they worked so well together, fought together, worried together, planned together. It seemed to be the perfect business partnership and they prospered. By 1943 they owned the largest ships' chandlers in the Cape and controlled over a dozen different companies.

Then, at the beginning of April, 1943, the day before Kurt and Anna were due to meet and examine the previous year's balance sheet, Kurt opened the morning paper to find his rival was featured on the front page. Admittedly it was a small article from Reuters, London. It read: '*South African sailor awarded the DSO for bravery in action. Lieutenant Simon Smit, formerly a farmer from the Cape Province, South Africa, who joined the British navy at the outbreak of war, was awarded the DSO at a ceremony at Buckingham Palace yesterday for bravery in action beyond the call of duty. While his ship was under heavy bombardment some ammunition caught alight and Lieutenant Smit carried the remainder to safety single-handed even though injured, and succeeded in rescuing a comrade from the fire. Smit was discharged from hospital before the ceremony and has now returned to his ship.*'

Anna arrived the following morning with rosy cheeks and a glow in her eyes. No need to ask her if she had read the report.

'Didn't you know Simon was in hospital?' Kurt asked. 'No letter?'

'No,' Anna smiled tremulously and blinked back a tear. The little woman bears up under the strain, Kurt thought furiously. He was jealous, but he consoled himself with the knowledge that Anna was living in a dream world. When the

239

country bumpkin came back she would find she had outgrown him. She wouldn't be able to stand him, not even for a day.

It seemed that whatever they touched took root and multiplied, Anna thought as she examined the figures. To be sure they had cash flow problems, but the bank manager had become most understanding lately. They were paying off three stock-rearing farms on the Cape flats; their new sausage and polony factory was booming, supplying both ships and the city; while Anna's poultry farm was the largest in the Cape Province. Koos' experiment was paying off, and although only five thousand hens were in batteries, it was enough to show the way they would go. Their stock buying operation was extremely profitable and was being run by Hendricks from an office in Malmesbury. As for the Southern Cross Ships' Chandlers, that was the pride of their group and had the lion's share of contracts with the shipping lines, thanks to Kurt.

Uncle Acker should have shared all this, Anna thought, remembering the last time she had seen him. She was brought back to the present by an impatient cough from their accountant. She pushed the books away.

'I think we deserve a celebration lunch. What do you say?' Kurt was grinning like a schoolboy.

'We're doing much better than we planned,' she admitted.

Anna stood up and walked to the window where she could see the ships sailing in and out of harbour. 'Another time please, Kurt.' She summoned a smile. 'You're right, we have something to celebrate.'

Longing and resentful, he touched her arm briefly as she strode out of his office.

Anna drove home in a strange mood for the examination of the year-end balance sheet, though exciting, had also increased her guilt.

At Modderfontein Anna examined the farm with a critical eye, gaining none of her usual satisfaction from her handiwork: the wide even road planted either side with trees; healthy sheep; a dairy for fifty cows; the dam filled to overflowing from new pipes laid down from the hills. Not enough! Nowhere near enough to offset the fortune she was making while Simon was getting wounded at war.

The twins, now four years old, came racing to the courtyard and flung themselves on her. Surely never were two children as beautiful as hers. Acker was a replica of his father and his huge green eyes gleamed with love. Yet it was Katie who caught attention wherever she went, with her long titian hair and huge brown eyes.

The latest issue of the farmers' periodical had arrived and as usual Anna studied it for sales of stock. As she skimmed the columns she noticed that the renowned St Croix breeding stock, including twelve Merino rams, were being auctioned on the following Wednesday. St Croix was one of her father's best friends, an aristocratic old man with beaked nose and shock of white hair. At his Bredasdorp farm he bred the country's best Merino sheep from Southey, Minnaar and Luckhoff bloodlines and now they were for sale. There were only twelve rams and within seconds Anna had decided to buy them for Simon. She wondered how much they would fetch. A packet, she decided. But with them she would eventually double Modderfontein's wool yield.

She leaned back and thought about Simon, how pleased he would be to return and find such magnificent stock on his farm. Would that day ever come? In two years she had received only two letters, both brief and cool.

Many times Anna had attempted to explain her longing and her loneliness, pour out her dream to start again, but desire and regret seemed to fade as she faced the blank sheet of writing paper. All she could think of were facts and figures which she transmitted regularly and sometimes, with an effort, she would write: 'I miss you and the children are well.' Letter writing was not one of her talents, she decided.

As Wednesday approached, Anna's determination to acquire the rams was equalled only by her fear of appearing at the Stellenbosch show grounds. All her family's friends would be there. Unbearable! Fleetingly she thought of sending Kurt, but he judged sheep in terms of mutton on the table and he would not bid enough to acquire them. Without doubt they

241

were the finest in the country, bred from stock imported before the 1929 Australian export embargo. Competition would be intense and she had taken the precaution of cashing three thousand pounds.

The auction was to be held at 10 a.m. and Anna arrived well beforehand with the twins, all three of them in new outfits. They had just left the car when they came face to face with Piet Joubert whom she had not seen since she left home. He nodded coldly and turned away. From then on it was sly nods and digs; murmured whispers behind cupped hands. Well, to hell with all of them. She had come to buy the rams and, by God, she would get them. They would see she was no pauper.

When the first two were led into the camp a gasp of admiration went around the crowd. They were the finest seen in South African, old St Croix' pride.

The auctioneer was selling the first two separately and bidding opened briskly at one hundred pounds but slackened off at four hundred pounds.

Anna could pick out the determined buyers for she knew most of them. Old Viljoen who had three sheep farms at Malmesbury and a vineyard at Stellenbosch; Cronje from Bredasdorp; Joubert; all big sheep farmers.

In no time the bidding reached seven hundred pounds, the highest price Anna remembered for two rams. At the same time, she thought, with the Australian embargo, the chance to acquire Merinos of this quality came once in a lifetime. She began to worry that the three thousand pounds would not secure them all. The bidding began to quiet a bit and the auctioneer searched amongst the faces. Anna decided to enter the fray and called out clearly: 'Eight hundred pounds.'

There was a sudden hush. The auctioneer turned and his face lit up. 'Why, it's young Miss van Achtenburgh. Welcome back, stranger,' he called. 'Any advance on eight hundred pounds?'

There was a hush and then a voice, well-known, once loved called: 'Nine hundred pounds.'

Gasps from onlookers. Father and daughter were bidding against each other. Anna, seeing her father for the first time in nearly five years, felt wounded. Her own father bidding against her. At the sight of his face and his clear blue eyes she could have burst into tears for he looked older, much thinner and quite frail. But here he was, still set against her, and to add to her humiliation all their old acquaintances were gathered around the paddock to watch their family feud finally erupt in public.

Well, she'd show him; he had brought it on himself. Raising her voice and her hand she called out clearly. 'One thousand pounds.'

'One thousand, one hundred pounds!' The quiet voice from the other side of the camp seemed to thrust like a dagger into her. She recoiled with shock and nearly called out, anguished, 'Pa!' but managed to keep her mouth shut.

'One thousand, two hundred,' she cried.

'One thousand, five hundred!'

'One thousand, seven hundred,' she screamed hoarse and furious.

There was a sudden hush and then some gasps and a snigger and even the auctioneer looked taken aback. 'Did I hear you right, Anna?' he called nervously. 'Did you say one thousand seven hundred pounds, for the two rams?'

She nodded firmly. Here was an end to the matter. So it had cost her, she thought feverishly. The rams were worth every penny of one thousand two hundred pounds. She had thrown away five hundred pounds for the incredible joy of beating her father in public. She could afford the best. She'd bid what she liked.

The auctioneer was about to rap the hammer when her father's voice came clear and incisive. 'Two thousand pounds!'

It was a nightmare. Never in her wildest flights of vanity could she see herself paying one thousand pounds each for the sake of teaching her father a lesson. No, she would have to retire in defeat. Sam, the auctioneer, was only too happy to

243

bring his hammer smashing down.

'Sold to Mr van Achtenburgh of Fontainebleu,' he called out.

Well, there were another ten rams, she thought, putting on her sunglasses so that no one could see how upset she was. She would have ten of them, but when the next three were brought in, her father said very clearly: 'Six hundred pounds.' Anna could not endure another competition. There must be a limit to the number of rams he required. She would wait for the next lot. Shortly afterwards her father acquired the three for one thousand pounds.

Let him have them, she thought sadly, feeling twice as rejected and humiliated. What bitterness had caused him to make an exhibition of her in public and deny her the rams she needed so badly. God knows, he did not need them. I shall never speak to him again, she vowed. Never, never, and when he dies I won't go to his funeral. Whatever there was is now irrevocably smashed.

When the bidding began for the final seven, in one lot, Anna began tremulously: 'One thousand pounds.' It was absurd to begin any lower, but the same calm voice said: 'Thirteen.' If Anna could have reached him at that moment she would have smashed a hammer over his head. She was filled with rage, thwarted and bested by a man whom she had hoped still loved her. He hated her. That much was clear enough. He was prepared to go to any lengths to get back at her, and knowing how much he loved money it must be a real sacrifice, she thought. She would make him pay for his revenge. She called out: 'Fifteen.'

'Sixteen.'

'Seventeen.'

'Eighteen.'

'Two thousand pounds,' she cried out. Suddenly she was staring at him wildly across the arena. Oh, what was the use? He had more money than she and little enough to do with it. At three thousand pounds she gave in, grabbed her children and hurried across the grass to the car park.

'Why are we going?' They began to whine. 'Mommy, we

don't want to go. What about the swings, Mommy? Can't we have ice cream? You promised.'

Sullen faces, whimpering mouths. The day spoilt.

Cruel, she thought. A cruel revenge. Worse still, seeing her father so unexpectedly had produced a vivid recall of home and she could not banish the images. At that same showground they had shown their prize cattle, shared the prizes and the triumphs. How hard they had worked together, sometimes up all night with a pregnant cow or a sick horse. All these memories were ruined by today's exhibition of his spite. She smothered her sobs and hid behind her sunglasses.

Once at Modderfontein she called Lena to take the twins and threw herself on the bed.

Around teatime she bathed her face in ice water. What a stupid fuss she had made. After all her father had not seen her for five years and now he could wait another fifty. There would be other rams, though perhaps not as good.

The twins were playing happily at the side of the dam with Lena who had made a picnic. Anna sat down with them and heard the rumble of a heavy lorry coming along the farm road. Who could it be at this hour? As it reached the crest of the hill, she saw the familiar green colour of Fontainebleu flashing in the sun and her heart sank. What new hurt was coming?

Leaving the twins with Lena she ran to the house, arriving as the lorry swayed ponderously into the yard.

She had not seen the driver before. He tipped his cap. 'I'm looking for Mrs Anna van Achtenburgh-Smit.'

Van Achtenburgh-Smit? It had a certain ring to it. 'I'm the daughter of Mr van Achtenburgh,' she said.

'Delivering stock, Ma'am. Twelve rams and two ponies.'

Anna felt too scared to hope. Surely they could not be … No, no, of course they could not be. My God, her father had just paid over five thousand pounds for those rams. Then she thought: It must be a mistake.

'Are you sure they're for this farm?'

'Modderfontein, Ma'am.'

Still she was afraid to hope. She grabbed the delivery book. It said: 'Twelve Merino rams, two Shetland ponies, to Mrs

Anna van Achtenburgh-Smit, Modderfontein.'

Suddenly she was racing to the back of the van, fumbling with the heavy doors, hands shaking until the driver opened it.

Anna clambered in and saw the beautiful Merino rams that she had wanted so much, all twelve of them. A present from her father. She could not believe it. At the back was a young boy sitting between two Shetland ponies and they, too, were delightful, diminutive, piebald, but with long white manes.

Then she whispered, 'Pa, oh, Pa! Thank you.'

Clambering out of the van she yelled, 'Jan, Jan. Come and help me, Jan.'

Jan, catching the tone of excitement in her voice, came helter-skelter from his cottage and whistled up small boys and, with the help of Wagter, they soon had the rams penned in the lucerne camp.

When Kurt arrived the following afternoon he found the twins in Lena's care racing round the front lawn on Shetland ponies, but there was no sign of Anna.

When the twins saw Kurt they clambered off. 'Look what we've got,' Acker yelled. 'Come and look.'

'Mine's called Samson,' said Katie.

'Mine's the best,' Acker yelled. 'He's got a star on his head. He's called Pluto.'

'Mine's the best,' Katie screamed in temper. 'Look, Uncle Kurt, he's got the longest mane.'

Acker pushed Katie over. She scrambled to her feet, sprang at him, holding on to his hair. In a trice they were rolling on the ground, scratching and kicking until Lena pulled them apart.

'Oh, baas, these are such naughty children,' she complained, holding them. 'If you fight over these ponies your Mom's going to take them away from you,' she scolded.

'They are both very beautiful,' Kurt said. 'Where did you get them?'

'From Grandpa,' they said solemnly.

'Grandpa?' Wonderingly. 'And where's your mother?'

'Down at the Lucerne camp, baas,' Lena told him. 'Would the baas like a cup of tea?'

246

'Later, Lena, thanks. I'll go and find Mrs Smit.'

Anna was perched high in the fork of a eucalyptus tree overlooking the camp, eyes blazing with excitement. To Kurt she looked more beautiful than ever. Eyes larger and fiercer and her mouth drawn into a grin of delight. A gypsy woman. The field was full of ewes and boys were sorting them out, pushing in more from the adjoining pen, removing others.

'Hey, what's going on?' Kurt asked. 'Why have you covered the sheep with dye?'

Anna burst out laughing. 'Really, Kurt. You don't know the first thing about farming,' she gurgled. 'If we don't daub the rams with dye we won't be able to remove the sheep they've serviced and they'll keep fucking the same old ewes.' She burst into a peal of laughter.

Kurt squirmed. He hated crudity in women, but he had to admit they were magnificent rams.

One of the ewes trotted off shaking her tail, smeared with red dye, and the boys chased her out of the camp.

'Just watch,' Anna crowed. 'Fucking all that pedigree into Simon's scruffy ewes.'

'Anna!' he exclaimed, feeling annoyed. 'I'm going back to the house. Lena's making tea.'

She laughed at his receding back, hunched shoulders. He could be such a prude. She turned and watched the rams, amazed at their extraordinary virility.

Later, when she joined Kurt at the farmhouse, she found the twins showing off their ponies and Kurt stretched out in the sun.

'Aren't they magnificent?' she said and he thought she meant the ponies. 'The finest pedigreed rams in the country. In a few years the flock will be transformed.'

Kurt felt a twinge of envy at the warmth in her voice. 'I don't understand why you bother. The place was a shambles when you arrived.'

'Yes,' she said uneasily, 'but he had no money to do these things. Now we're getting rich while Simon is at war.'

'It's not my fault, Anna,' Kurt snapped. 'God knows I tried hard enough to join up.'

'I'm not blaming you, Kurt,' she said gently and then told him about the auction and her father's gift.

'But why are you here?' Kurt asked, looking cross again. 'You should have gone to thank him.'

She looked away. Then she said, 'It's difficult, Kurt. So many years, so many grudges. I feel responsible for Mama's death.' There was a long pause. 'I've decided to write and thank him.'

'Oh no, you won't,' Kurt argued. 'You'll go there if I have to take you myself.'

'Look, Pa sent the sheep. He didn't come here, so I shall write back thanking him and telling him how grateful I am, and of course I am.' Looking at Kurt's face she said, 'I'll send him photographs.'

Kurt looked cold and forbidding. 'Anna, I've always known you to be a hard woman, and sometimes a callous woman, but never have I thought you cruel. Life has a way of getting back, Anna.'

'I'm not being cruel,' she flared in temper. 'I'm plain terrified if you want the truth.' She sighed. Why was she wasting her time arguing with Kurt? She knew she had to go.

It was a beautiful autumn morning when Anna set out for Fontainebleu and when she reached the lagoon she parked and walked along the edge of the lagoon with the twins. Five years, she thought. Tough years, but tremendous. She gazed at the blue expanse, remembering the first time she had seen it, frightened, pregnant and in love. Suddenly her spirits soared. She whispered, 'I don't regret anything. I'd do the same again. I have my children and when Simon comes back it will be very different. And I have Kurt, my very dear friend, and the business.'

Suddenly she was impatient to be on her way. When they reached the outskirts of Stellenbosch Anna felt a lump in her throat and she could hardly breathe. Her palms began to sweat and the steering wheel felt slippery. I should have telephoned first, she thought. What if he's not there? What if he doesn't want to talk to me? Then she remembered the rams and she knew without a shadow of doubt that Pa wanted to see her.

She had forgotten how beautiful Fontainebleu was. Acre after acre of vines, the flowers, the stately lawns, the long avenue fringed with oaks, the house with the imposing gables, carved doors and shutters, the intricate paving of the courtyard and the splendour of the old trees.

She could hardly speak and the children were looking out of the window ooh-ing and aah-ing. A palace could not have impressed them more. They trailed behind her, suddenly shy as she walked uncertainly to the front door. Then she saw a shadow move behind the curtains in Pa's study and a few seconds later he stood framed in the doorway.

For a long time father and daughter stared at each other, words unnecessary, for the van Achtenburghs were two of a kind, hard to relent, slow to forgive, suspicious and introverted. Anna searched for signs of reproof, a hint of anger or contempt, but there was only love and a trace of pleading; while André looked for arrogance or self-righteousness in his daughter, whom he knew had progressed so well in the business world, but he saw only his Anna, trusting, seeking love. Suddenly Anna was in his arms.

The twins began to pull at her skirt and whine.

'Oh my,' she said eventually. 'They're jealous.' Standing back she held their hands and said, 'This is Acker and this is Katie. Acker, Katie, say hello to Grandpa,' she went on. 'And this ...' She looked up at the house. 'This is home.'

Part Three

26

February, 1946

Outwardly cool, inwardly quaking, Anna stood on the platform amongst a crowd of hastily assembled dignatories and friends, including the mayor and her father, looking frail, but distinguished. Not bad for five hours' notice, she thought, Pa could get things moving when he wanted to.

Pa had insisted on having a 'hero's welcome', saying, 'Simon's going to have a lot to live up to, but at least he earned the DSO without any help from you. That's why we're going to push it.' For once he had been adamant.

The mayor fingered his gold chain and glanced at his watch. 'Train's half an hour late,' he murmured, 'as usual. I think we'll have another rehearsal.' He turned to the band, pompous in their red and gold uniforms, and for the third time that morning they played the South African anthem, and then 'A Life on the Ocean Wave', followed by 'Anchors Aweigh', all of which were out of tune with the trombone a beat late, a strident cacophony that drowned conversation and dulled the senses. Ideal under the circumstances, Anna thought treacherously.

She looked sidelong at Kurt, who was noticeably upset, and she could guess why. Anna, too, was nervous. So many years apart after such a bad parting. She had forgotten what Simon looked like and could only visualize his hair, a burnished halo in sunlight.

'Mrs van Achtenburgh-Smit?'

Turning, Anna saw a pimply young man with notebook and pencil.

'William Rose, *Stellenbosch Star*,' he went on. 'I wonder if you'd give me some information about your husband's DSO.'

'I think you should ask him yourself.' Anna did not want her ignorance revealed in the columns of the local rag.

'Would you care to add your comments to this article?'

Anna skimmed through the typed sheet and gasped with annoyance: '*Today, the cream of Stellenbosch society opened its arms to welcome its own war hero. Simon Smit, who spent five years in the British Navy, rising to the rank of Lieutenant Commander, DSO, was welcomed for the first time by his father-in-law, André van Achtenburgh, so culminating a long-lasting family feud which had all Stellenbosch agog seven years ago when Anna ran off with her penniless young farmer.*'

'How dare you.' Anna crumpled the sheet. 'There's no family feud. Never was.' She summoned a smile. 'Try again, Mr Rose.'

Turning, she yelled to her father, 'How can the *Star* employ such an oaf?' But the music stopped in the middle of her sentence and everyone heard what she said. She flushed and stared at the ground.

Watching Anna, André felt irritated. Why had she invited Kurt to the station? She should have had more sense. It wouldn't take Simon long to size up the situation. Not that his daughter was having an affair with Kurt; nothing like that he felt sure. Yet she gave him enough hope to keep him hanging around. Easy to see what the fellow was thinking – that Anna would divorce Simon and marry him. André sighed. Personally he did not like Kurt, yet he did not know why, for he couldn't help admiring him. A superb business brain and a cultured man, too. Perhaps he was just too damn perfect.

Kurt edged closer through the crowd and took Anna's arm. She shook him off impatiently. He had become painfully insecure in the past few weeks and she was tired of the pleading and questioning in his eyes each time he looked at her. Simon's homecoming posed a problem. She intended to divorce him, but what would such a country bumpkin think of that? She would probably have to pay him off and then she would have Kurt plaguing her. What a bore men were.

At that moment they heard the train approaching and saw

puffs of steam rising from the trees. The rustling, coughing and conversation ceased; the musicians squared their shoulders; the bandmaster stood with hands poised; only the train moved inexorably closer. Then the bandmaster's baton came crashing down.

After five years spent mainly in the North Sea, Lieutenant-Commander Simon Smit, DSO, was drenched with sweat from the unaccustomed heat and longing for home. It had been a disturbing day. Arriving at Johannesburg at dawn he had telephoned Modderfontein only to discover that Anna had installed a farm manager in his house and was now living at Fontainebleu. He was disappointed, but not unduly so. It could all be rectified now that he was home.

Leaving the manager to telephone Anna, he had spent the next hour walking around the airport in a daze, absorbing the wide horizon, the sense of freedom, clear unclouded skies, friendly faces. At Cape Town he just made the train to Stellenbosch.

Now, drenched with joy, Simon hung out of the window. Otto should be here, he thought, to see the mountains, the vineyards and the colours. Wild Otto! Simon could not suppress a grin as he remembered the night Otto had earned his nickname. It was in a pub in Plymouth and six of them had demolished a squad of US marines. A middle-class British upbringing had not been able to suppress Otto's wild nature and hasty temper which he had inherited from his Danish mother, along with her ash-blonde hair and light blue eyes. Simon had spent most of his shore leave with Otto Tenwick and his wife Edwina – and how they had teased him when he tried to convey the beauty and virility of the country. They had never believed him.

Now, he felt a pang when he remembered how often he had pictured his homecoming, seen the barren hills of Saldanha Bay, the lagoon, heard the baboons barking. Funny how he had missed the baboons. He had vowed never to trap them again. Simon had seen too much maiming and killing; too much for one lifetime. Five years of longing for home: to stand ankle deep in the soil, to till the land, to work from sunrise to sunset and to live in harmony with the beasts and seasons. Five years at sea, and the proximity of death on many occasions, had enabled Simon to clarify his priorities. It was not wealth he craved now, but happiness; a sweet and loving wife; children; a chance to make a living.

The train was almost at a standstill and there was a large crowd on the platform. There must be someone important arriving. He ran his finger round his collar wishing for a pair of shorts and open-necked shirt, feeling out of place in naval uniform.

As Simon stepped out of the train he nearly turned and ran for there was a huge placard saying: '*Welcome Home Commander Simon Smit, DSO.*'

'Damn,' he mumbled. 'How in hell's name did they find out about that?'

The moment Simon stepped on to the platform Anna nearly fell over with shock. He was magnificent. Superbly handsome in his naval uniform, his features were finer, his eyes glowed with intelligence and good humour and his hair was well-cut.

Some of the old magic started flooding through Anna's body as she reacted to the overpowering magnetism of the man. Oh no, she thought, never again. Love was for fools. She set her lips tightly and brought herself under control. Still, as a breeder she could see what an asset he would be to Fontainebleu; even better than the Palomino horses and the Merino rams. Physically speaking, he was the best that homo sapiens was ever likely to produce. All thoughts of divorce vanished. She would be the envy of the neighbourhood. Wealth and Simon, too!

Simon felt embarrassed, but he would have to endure the silly rigmarole. Anna was watching him and so was Kurt. What was that bloody man doing here. He shook hands with a hundred people he had never seen in his life while the band kept up a performance that would have given them twenty days' detention in a British naval barracks.

Anna was saying something, but he could not hear what and then she caught him by the head, stood on tiptoe and

256

shouted, 'Welcome home.' How nervous she was, all shrunken up with tension with tight lines round her mouth.

The mayor said a few words of welcome and clapped Simon on the shoulder and after that everyone stood around looking ill-at-ease, while the band went through their repertoire again and then dispersed.

When at last he could hear himself speak the first thing Simon said was, 'Where are the twins? Where are the babies?'

'Well, they're not exactly babies,' Anna laughed awkwardly. 'They were here.' She had forgotten about them with the trauma of meeting Simon. At that moment Acker came rushing out of the waiting room, clutching a bar of chocolate and looking upset.

'Say hello to your father,' Anna said sternly.

Acker stood still and said: 'Welcome home, sir.'

'Sir?' Simon's voice boomed over the platform as he swung the boy on to his shoulder. 'I'm not sir. I'm your Pa. Say "Pa".'

'Pa,' the boy said softly.

'You know what Pa's are for?' Simon said holding the boy's hands.

'No, sir, Pa.'

'Pa's are for hunting, fishing, boating and riding and we're going to do all those things together, Acker.'

'Have you got a horse, Pa?' Acker asked suddenly, smiling and tightening his grip on this huge stranger's hands.

'Why sure I've got a horse and I'm going to teach you to school your horse properly like a man should. I see you're nearly a man,' Simon went on. 'And where's your sister?'

'Her finger's stuck in the slot machine, sir, I mean Pa.'

'Oh my goodness,' Anna murmured and the family rushed to the waiting room where Katie was standing stuck, trying not to show how much it hurt. Simon swung Acker from his shoulders and in a trice he had extricated her finger and he crouched, rubbing it. 'You're lucky it's not worse, Katie,' he said gravely. 'Next time you want a bar of chocolate you must pay for it.' He fumbled for change and handed the children a handful of chocolate bars.

257

At Fontainebleu the tables were laden with food, there were whole sheep roasting on spits, gallons of home-made wine, mountains of grapes, salads, cold meats, *boerwors*, while all Stellenbosch seemed to be waiting to greet him. The sight of all that food made him want to cry. It could have fed a school or a village in England. Well, he could hardly blame Anna for wanting to go home and presumably he, too, was expected to live at Fontainebleu for André had welcomed him kindly enough. The prospect held no joy.

His attention was caught by the sound of singing. A group of Coloureds burst on to the lawn, snapping their fingers and wriggling their buttocks strenuously to the beat of a strummed guitar.

'My father, if it isn't old Jan. Living in the lap of luxury, I can see and drunk as a sailor.' He clapped Jan on the shoulder.

The old man grinned back toothless and witless. 'Welcome back, baasey,' he crooned.

'You'll have a thick head tomorrow Jan. Hold back on the liquor man.'

'You're not eating,' Anna said when she met up with him shortly afterwards.

Taking her firmly by the arm, Simon steered her away from the crowd. 'Anna, I'm longing to see home.'

'Modderfontein?'

He nodded.

Anna flushed. 'Simon, I'm sorry I didn't tell you I'd moved, but it's difficult to explain in a letter. I don't think I'm very good at letter writing, and besides you never answered. This is our home now. You see, after Mama died Pa needed me and besides I wanted the best for the twins.'

'Of course I realize Modderfontein is not the best,' he said.

Damn! She had said the wrong thing again. 'I think you'll find things quite satisfactory there,' she said stiffly in the manner of an efficient caretaker.

'Let's go and have a look.'

'But Simon, it's out of the question,' she said. 'All our guests are here to meet you.' But Simon persisted and

258

eventually she agreed. 'Very well. I'll go with you.'

'I suppose my van's a bit clapped out?' he said.

'Well, actually, Simon, I replaced it. There's a new one, well two. It's difficult to explain but I've been quite busy while you've been away, building up this and that. You know how things grow, especially in a war.'

Why was she making excuses, he wondered? Apologizing for everything.

She led him to a white Jaguar and opened the door.

'My father!' he laughed. 'What a beauty. Whose is it? Pa's?'

'No mine – ours,' she quickly corrected herself. 'Like it?'

'Sure I like it,' he said uneasily. 'I suppose Pa bought it for you?'

'No,' she said. 'I bought it for myself – ourselves.'

There was a long silence. Simon was feeling depressed, wondering how he had managed to get so out of touch with reality during the war. There was nothing soft or tender about Anna. He had loved the girl once, but realized it too late. Now there was no trace of this girl in the tough woman beside him.

'It's hot in this damned uniform,' he muttered. 'Do you know where my clothes are?'

'Simon, you left one old patched shirt, a pair of shorts and a terrible suit.'

'It's the shorts I was thinking of,' he said.

'I threw out everything, but don't worry, I'll buy more tomorrow.'

'I'll get them,' he answered quite brusquely.

'Well, I suppose it doesn't matter who gets them,' she said after a pause. 'There's no shortage of money here.'

'Anna, this may be difficult for you to believe,' he began determinedly, 'but I'm not aiming to live on your money.'

'Why, whoever said you should?' Defensively. 'You've got plenty of your own in your bank account. In fact the precise balance is six thousand, two hundred and fifty-one pounds, fifteen shillings.'

This time Simon was stunned and he showed it. He jerked upright and glanced at her suspiciously. 'Hey now, how d'you make that out, Anna?'

'Well, the farm's making about two thousand pounds profit each year. It's not much, but I saved most of it.'

'And the upkeep, fences, repairs, roads, fertilizer?'

'That's been paid for, and of course I pay rent for the chickens.'

'Jesus, Anna.' The words came pouring out. 'A wife doesn't pay her husband rent for keeping chickens, nor for living on her husband's land. It's a husband's duty to provide a home for his wife – and her chickens.' He grinned at her but her face was set hard and serious.

'Well, that's so usually, but in the war so many women returned to their families and I don't think Pa could do without us now.'

When they reached Modderfontein Simon was amused to see a brand new gate, with a magnificent archway and beyond it the road, now wide and flat. 'My Father! Anyone could be misled into thinking Modderfontein's a real fine farm,' he said laughing.

'Well it is. Wait till you see the sheep – you've a lovely flock now.'

'They were always a fine flock,' he said defensively.

'Yes, but wait.'

On a ridge of hill overlooking the farm Anna parked the car and Simon admired the vista to the north, row after row of poultry houses, sheds housing batteries and the brooders for the cockerels; to the east the pigsties where prize Landrace sows reared their prize-winning young, and behind them camps of lucerne and barley and he was amazed at the greenness of everything.

To the west, where Simon used to plant wheat, all the hills were contoured, while to the south he could see the sheep, thicker, woollier, and when he caught sight of the rams in the camp he went racing off.

Anna took her wellingtons out of the boot and tramped after him. Simon was fascinated by the rams; he felt their wool, prodded their horns, ran his hands over their haunches and eventually said, 'These cost a packet.'

'Ah yes,' she said nonchalantly. 'The finest in the country.'

'Where'd you get the money?'

'As a matter of fact they were a present from Pa.'

'Ah.'

The twitch in his cheek was working overtime, so Anna told him the story of the auction while they walked towards the dairy. By this time Simon was speechless.

'You must spend a great deal of time on the farm,' he said eventually.

'Koos runs the farm. He's most reliable and I inspect the place once a week. Of course I'm always here at shearing time.'

'It looks as if I'm out of work again.'

'Oh, don't be absurd,' she snapped. 'It's your farm. Do what you like with it.'

Simon rubbed his jaw reflectively, thinking: She hasn't got much sense of humour. I'll have to be careful with her.

When they were walking back from the poultry Simon took her by the hand and pulled her down beside him on a rocky outcrop.

'This used to be my favourite view when I was a kid,' he said. 'It's the only place where you can see the sea through the gap in the mountains there. I used to dream of being in the navy and I can't say I regretted joining up, but it's not for me. I need the land. Look! You see beautiful sunsets from here.'

Anna glanced at her watch impatiently. Sunsets were all right on canvas, particularly if the painter were famous and the paintings valuable, otherwise one was very much like another. By now Pa would be wondering where they were and their guests would be starting to leave. God knows what this bloody rock was doing to her dress.

Besides, there was that sickening lurch in her stomach again, and sharp stabs of pleasure pierced her body each time she felt the closeness of this incredibly masculine man she had married. He was enough to sweep any young girl off her feet, she reasoned, but she was no longer a silly, impressionable girl and she had paid too dearly for past mistakes. Love was for fools and she was no fool. She would take what she wanted, when it suited her, but never again fall under his spell. She had the upper-hand now and she intended to hang on to it.

'When I was at sea I discovered how much I need the land,' Simon went on. 'Nowadays people seem to think they're apart from nature. They talk about the environment as if it's something different from us, like a house or a garden. We're as much a product of the soil and the air as every other creature.' He looked around and caught sight of a dung beetle laboriously pushing a ball of sheep dung larger than itself. 'Look at that,' he poked the beetle with a stem of grass. 'How are we different? It's made up of chemicals from the earth and the air. It performs gargantuan tasks, but using available material, limited by its resources, not by its guts. Just like us, breaking our backs to push a load of shit. We're all part of the whole, interrelated, dependent. I get mad when I hear people using terms like conserving the environment, instead of self-preservation.'

'We really must go, Simon,' Anna said, trying to sound regretful.

The party was still in progress when they returned to Fontainebleu and the music could be heard all the way to the main gate. Lena had put the children to bed, but they had escaped over the balcony and were running around in their nightclothes.

No wonder Simon was captivated by them. They were such beautiful, intelligent children and they had taken to him instantly, which surprised her for they had never grown close to Kurt. Katie in particular was hanging around Simon, clearly fascinated. With a jolt Anna realized she was jealous. She had grown used to Acker adoring André, but until now Katie and she had been inseparable. Anyway it was time they went to bed, she decided, and gathering them up she took them whining and sulking to their bedroom.

When she returned she noticed Simon was surrounded by women. She had to admire his new-found social assurance. Nevertheless, as the evening progressed she found her cheeks were burning and her hands moist at the prospect of the coming night with him.

She began to avoid him, flitting from group to group, and long after midnight when their guests departed, Anna supervised the cleaning up operation, much to the annoyance of Jacob who always coped perfectly well without her.

When she crept into the bedroom she found Simon fast asleep, sprawled naked on his bed. Down his back was a jagged purple scar. 'Damn,' she muttered, regretting her tardiness, but although she clattered in the bathroom for half an hour Simon did not wake up.

Seven a.m. and the alarm began ringing, waking them both from a deep slumber. Anna sat up, yawned and jumped with shock to see Simon watching her. Yesterday came flooding back. Simon was home. Not only home, but stumbling across the room towards her. She sat up, pushing her hair off her shoulders, and swung her legs out of bed, showing pure white thighs. Simon paused. His gaze was snared and he felt overwhelmed by an onrush of desire.

He paused. He had vowed that sex between them would be mutual. Never again would he show his need or his passion. Never again would he rape her. That way led to disaster, for Anna would pounce on any weakness and use it.

How long had it been? He stood irresolute and then he remembered. Six months exactly. She was laying it on the line, although she was loath to admit that she wanted him. Instead she watched him carefully, a touch of shrewdness in her eyes as she peeled off her nightgown and walked slowly to the bathroom.

When Anna returned she saw Simon was back in his bed, watching her, propped on one elbow. Perhaps the accident had turned him into a eunuch.

'Anna, come here.' She sat down next to him and Simon took her hand and pushed it under the blankets. 'You see, it's not that I don't want you. God knows I do, but not like it was before. Never again. You must want me as much as I want you and then, perhaps ...'

Anna had a deep, neurotic need to be desired.

'I want you to make love to me,' she said and meant it.

263

He sighed. 'Let's wait,' he said. 'There's plenty of time.'

But, no. Anna would have none of it. They must make love, there and then, and only then would she feel that she had a hold over this handsome stranger who had suddenly re-entered her life.

She had forgotten the delicious smell of him, the way his flesh was firm and soft over hard muscle, ideal to press and clutch, the delicate pinkness of his body, the sheer overpowering maleness of him. She clung to him ferociously, urging him on to faster movement, taking the lead. He represented maleness. For the time being he was safely anonymous. Soon it would all be spoiled, when he became a person, with a mind of his own, making demands, quarrelling with her. If only she could find a man just like him, as handsome, as virile, and never have to know his name, or anything about him. In ancient times she would have bought a male slave. Ideal! She imagined Simon fettered to the bedpost, turgid and quivering, on call day and night, humbly adoring! The thought brought her passion to a climax.

By eight Anna was dressed and Simon was lying on the bed remembering. Anna was too calculating and too beautiful. She had matched love with need, tenderness with lust. He felt used and abused in a strange reversal of the sexual roles. She had pretended to be gripped with love and passion, but at a quarter to eight she had switched off both, glanced at her Piaget watch, which was all she had on at the time, and told him she must get up at once and go to work.

'Can I come with you?' Simon asked when she emerged from the bathroom.

She flushed with annoyance. Then she thought: What difference does it make? So she smiled and said, 'That would be lovely, Simon, but you'll have to hurry and skip breakfast,' hoping that he had not noticed her reluctance. He had.

The first farm had some fine sheep and cows which Anna intended to turn into mutton and beef if the price was low enough, and it was. There were four more farms to visit and by then they were late, so she rushed to the Cape Flats for a brief inspection of some new acquisitions. Nearby was the land she was hoping to purchase to grow vegetables and she wanted to examine that, too, and lastly she called at headquarters to speak to Kurt.

When Simon saw the building outside the dock he managed to hold back an exclamation of shock and put a brave face on his plight, for clearly the husband of a business tycoon was not to be envied. Anna was clever, determined, hard-headed and rich. He could love her or leave her and either way she would survive.

In the days that followed, Simon's predicament became apparent to everyone, for he had nothing to do at a time when he badly needed to immerse himself in something.

When he visited Modderfontein Koos was obviously jealous and nervous of any intrusion on his territory. Yet Simon longed to return to his home. Eventually he brought up the matter of his future with Anna.

'Anna, you've done a fine job at Modderfontein,' he said one morning as they were having breakfast, 'but now the war's over I should like to go home. Let's go back with the children.'

'Why, that's absurd,' she snapped. 'Where would Koos live?'

'Well, I don't know. I suppose he'd find another job.'

'And who would look after the poultry?'

'Well, I could if there's no one else available.' He looked up, but the contempt on her face made him look quickly away. 'It is my home, Anna,' he said gently. 'I feel out of place here.'

'If you think about it, I'm sure you'll agree that it's a perfectly lousy idea,' she snapped. 'For me, for the children, for Koos and for Pa. As for you, surely you rate yourself a bit higher than a poultry foreman.' With that she hurried off to work.

Simon mulled over the idea and reluctantly decided that he had to think of the children, who were enjoying the best that life could offer at Fontaineblue.

After that he tried driving over to Modderfontein mornings, returning at night, but Koos seemed to have the place well in hand. Unless he started planting wheat, which would mean

265

cutting the number of sheep, there was nothing at all for him to do there. So instead he took the children riding, fishing and swimming, but soon the holidays came to an end and the twins returned to the village school.

In contrast, Anna was the busiest person Simon had ever seen, for apart from the business there was an endless round of social activities, tennis parties, horse shows, concerts, charities. A function or committee was not complete without Anna van Achtenburgh-Smit, as she was now called.

André van Achtenburgh saw Simon's embarrassment and felt sorry for him.

One morning, when Anna had left for a buying trip, André sought out Simon and as usual found him in the stables grooming Vixen.

'She's a fine mare, but she's getting past it,' André said, stroking her head.

'She's old, that's true, but she'd beat most when it comes to dressage,' Simon retorted.

'Simon, I'd like to clear the air between us.' André took Simon by the eblow. 'Come and have coffee with me,' he went on.

'I have misjudged you and I hope you will forgive me,' he said when they were sitting on the *stoep*. 'I was so sure that you were after Anna's inheritance. I'd like to have a talk with you, be friends. Besides, I have a proposition to put to you,' he hurried on when Simon did not answer.

'Mr van Achtenburgh,' Simon said coolly. 'I'm sure you are a very fine judge of character, and you were quite right. I was after Anna's inheritance at the time, although she was also beautiful and desirable. After I married Anna I fell in love with her, but something went wrong and I ran away to war. There's nothing like a war to bring you face to face with yourself. You hope to remain alive and you think about what you want out of life. It wasn't Fontaineblue I longed for.' He gave a wry grin. 'It was a wife who loved me, my own farm, where I could plant things. I shall work towards that aim.' He hesitated and André cut in.

'You don't feel at home here, do you, Simon?'

'No, but that's probably my own fault.

'Nevertheless, this farm will be yours one day.'

'Anna's,' Simon said harshly.

'I have no intention of leaving the farm to her out of community of property. Let's face it, she is a very wealthy woman and likely to become more wealthy.'

'You don't understand,' Simon said harshly. 'I don't want Anna's wealth. I have to make my own way.'

André waited until Flora had put the tray down and left and then said, 'Simon, you're being hasty and short sighted. Forgive me for saying so. You've just come back, things are not what you were expecting. Now give us all a chance. I need you. I can't run the farm single-handed any longer, your children need you and Anna needs you.

'No, don't shake your head,' he went on. 'She does, but she's all bottled up inside and not good at showing her feelings. Give it a chance. I want you to take over as farm manager. After all, eventually it will all be yours. Fontainebleu, the wheat farms in Malmesbury and other holdings.'

Simon looked away awkwardly, trying to find the words to refuse.

'There's a lot to you, my boy, and don't you ever let anyone put you down,' André said. 'You're my son-in-law and I'm asking you to do it. Give it a go for me and for your children. Tell me you'll stay and run the farm for a six-month trial and at the end of that time we'll talk again.'

'I don't think I could refuse that, at least,' Simon said.

27

From the day Simon returned Anna's life became a torment, for she was forever comparing the two men in her life, weighing them in the balance, wanting to be loved and desired, but unable to give love — dividing herself between them and pleasing neither. Both were necessary to her, both had a role to play.

Simon went quietly about his work, saying little, and Anna would often find him watching her intently.

Kurt alternated between temper and black despair, sometimes refusing to talk to her. One day, when they were checking the books in the office, he said, 'Anna, put the books away. I want to talk about you and me.' He folded the sheets and placed them meticulously in the file, taking his time; trying to think how to begin, while Anna fumed.

'Anna, I've always loved you,' he began hesitantly, 'and besides that we have so much in common; we've accomplished so much together; we're a team.' He grimaced. 'Surely you understand … all those war years … the only thing that kept me going was the promise of you after the war. You kept me at a distance with your promises.' He scowled as she started to protest. 'The point is, I can't carry on like this, working together, knowing that Simon and you …' He shook his head. 'I'm not prepared to carry on with you. The tension of it …'

'Unrequited love?' She laughed harshly.

'You like to pretend you're an iceberg, but I happen to know that you're not. We kept the pact, for the good that it did, but now Simon's back and the war's over …' He broke off again. His brows knitted together, mouth compressed. 'You must divorce Simon.'

Her eyebrows shot up, a presage to temper. 'And when I'm divorced do you intend to marry me?'

'Yes,' he said simply.

'Haven't you forgotten Madeleine? What was it you said? "A captive of your conscience." Rather flamboyant, I thought at the time.'

'It's over a year since Germany capitulated and I've heard nothing. She must be dead. Nearly everyone is. Not many survived the camps.'

Anna stood up and looked out of the window. She had enough problems without Kurt pressurizing her. She would work it out herself, in her own time.

'I've spent a fortune trying to trace her, a dozen different agencies on the job,' he went on. 'If she's alive why hasn't she contacted me?'

'Six months isn't long enough, Kurt. People are turning up all the time. You read about it in the papers every day.'

'But if I'm free, will you marry me?'

Anna looked away. 'I don't know. I don't think so.' She scowled at him. 'Why should you pressurize me into making a choice when you yourself don't know.'

'All right, I'm sorry. I have no right, but Anna, I can't wait forever.' He seized her roughly, bending her back over the desk.

Anna pushed him away angrily. 'I never made any promises,' she said.

She forced a smile. Of course she loved him, but she loved Simon, too – as far as she was able to love. How was it possible that a woman could love two men? she wondered. Yet she did. With Kurt there was no frenzied passion to be stemmed at night with tranquillizers; her feelings for Kurt were devoid of sexual passion, yet she trusted him and needed him and she knew she depended upon him. Theirs was a symbiotic relationship, like two oxen in a team. The thought of life without Kurt filled her with despair and the possibility that Madeleine might intrude into her life caused her sleepless nights. She felt she must know whether or not Madeleine was

269

alive, and every time she saw Kurt she tried to persuade him to go and search for her. Only when she heard that Madeleine was dead would she feel secure.

On the other hand, Simon's aggressive good looks, his untamed maleness, filled her with craving. Yet since that first morning she had been unable to succumb to her desires, for Simon had become a real person, no longer just a male body, and she could not open herself to him, or give, or in any way be dependent upon him. When they made love it was Simon who exploded in a paroxysm of passion and she who lay unsatisfied. To depend upon Simon was to invite mental and physical pain. Disillusionment! Yet her nature was passionate and a sudden look or touch could send her body surging with need. Then she would force herself to ignore her passion, to defend herself against him – and her only shield was the contempt which she became adept at using.

In the face of Anna's persistence Kurt agreed to go to Germany and search every displaced persons' camp, but as the time for Kurt to leave drew closer Anna became frantic, and this was expressed in bad temper which she showered over her family. Eventually she decided she must get away, be alone for a while. A few days before Kurt left she told everyone that she was going to South-West Africa to examine Uncle Acker's farm and investigate the possibility of restocking with karakul and employing a manager. Having made up the story, it suddenly seemed like a good idea and she felt ashamed that she had not been there since she inherited the farm.

Simon, who understood her tension, did not offer to accompany her, reasoning that if she wanted him she would ask soon enough.

'Do you want me to keep an eye on the business while you're away?' Simon asked a few days later when they said goodbye at the airport.

'Well,' she said, feeling embarrassed. 'Kurt's assistant, Hans Lombard, is looking after everything, but if you would like to 'phone Hans just to let him know where he can get hold of you.' What possible help did he think he could offer?

She handed him the keys of the Jaguar, which she had insisted on driving herself, and giving him a cold kiss on the cheek, set off across the tarmac.

Simon watched her go, a slim figure in beige trousers and plain cotton blouse, with her hair braided and khaki grip slung over one shoulder. He knew she had a gun in it. Still she was feminine and desirable, he thought. The more she fought against her sensuality the more it blazed out of her, deceiving no one but herself.

From the air the Skeleton Coast was a place of incredible beauty: flocks of several hundred flamingoes spread out like a rose stain to the horizon; bizarre mountains of red and black stripes rose incongruously from the desolation; hills of shifting sands were forever changing their shape in the wind; while occasionally a herd of gemsbok fled from the shadow of the aircraft.

From Windhoek Anna caught the charter flight to Grootfontein, arriving at five. The Land-Rover she had hired from the local garage was waiting and Anna set off for the farm.

In the dusk a herd of wildebeeste surged over the road ahead, churning the ground to dust. Anna braked and then reversed to a safe distance. The sun hung motionless over the horizon for several seconds before plunging out of sight. Shortly afterwards it was dark and the wildebeeste had vanished as if they had never been.

It was midnight before she reached the turn-off to Bosluis, which she remembered so well. The drive to the house seemed twice as long for the road had fallen into disrepair. Eventually she reached the water pump, but as she approached she saw a dim light shining from the farmhouse. She braked violently.

Squatters! But who? Certainly not the local Ovambos, they preferred their own homes. Tramps? Impossible. Tramps could never exist in this inhospitable territory. The local bushmen would rather die than sleep imprisoned by four walls. Perhaps homeless Coloured people, or detribalized Ovambos.

271

She took her gun out of her grip, hid the ignition keys behind the dashboard and crept quietly towards the house. As she approached a figure lurched into the doorway. She switched on her torch.

'Kurt!' she yelled. 'My God! You were so close to being shot.' When relief had flooded through her and receded, anger took its place. She stepped back and said, 'What the hell are you doing here anyway.'

'Waiting for you. What else?' He smiled sadly. 'Want a drink? You look as if you need one.'

'You're well equipped,' Anna said noting the bottle of Scotch and box of provisions. 'Just as well. What a shambles.' She stared gloomily at the dust, the broken windows. 'Ugh!'

Kurt passed her a mug of Scotch. 'I decided to spend a few days here, help you investigate the karakul scene. The truth is I'm too damned scared to go to Germany. I need a few days of peace.'

She stared at him without answering, feeling depressed.

'It's terrible here,' she said after she had downed her drink, shuddered and examined the house, flicking her torch at debris and decay.

There was no answer.

Anna walked towards him and stared at his face in the candlelight. 'What's the matter with you?'

'I'm terrified of going to Germany. Terrified that she may have survived. I may be ...' He hesitated. 'Saddled with her and Gunther's son.' He shuddered.

'Hate is a disease,' he went on. 'I've seen it in action in Germany. Contaminating. Spreading.'

'Sometimes you talk nonsense,' she said uneasily.

'Anna, I hate her and I'm not big enough to stop hating her. Hate corrodes.'

'Let's talk about something cheerful,' she said.

'All right, let's talk about us,' he said. 'Swear to me that you'll divorce Simon when I'm free.'

She gasped. 'Oh no, I won't promise anything of the sort. Besides,' she went on, evading the issue, 'how could any man abandon a woman who's been in a camp?'

272

'How childish you are sometimes.' There was an ugly expression on his face. 'If you wanted me you wouldn't care about respect or what's right. You'd reach out and grab what was yours.'

'Well, I don't feel like that.'

'Then why did you pretend that you did? You kept me hanging on through the war years, saying that we just had to wait, promising love, promising to divorce Simon.'

'I changed my mind.'

He stepped forward and caught hold of her. 'You must love me. For God's sake.' He thrust his mouth on to hers, forcing his tongue between her teeth. Anna stood limp and detached, waiting for him to let go of her.

Eventually Kurt stepped back and when he looked at her the expression on his face was one of hate.

'Don't look at me like that,' she said, feeling alarmed.

'Why not? How do you think I feel when you go to bed with him at night?'

'None of your business. I'm married to him,' she retorted.

'You are my business. I made you, built you up, gave you back your confidence. I've loved you and waited for you for years and you let me wait. Damn you, Anna.'

'You're overwrought. Stop behaving like a fool.'

'You bitch!' With one hand he gripped her throat and squeezed until she was nearly throttled, pushing her back on the dirty ground. She could feel grit and stones against her skin, pressing through her blouse. Kurt violently ripped her panties with his other hand. When he loosed his grip on her throat she screamed and struggled, but suddenly remembered their remote location. There was probably no one within fifty miles.

Kurt was mumbling. 'You must love me. You don't know how I've waited. Six years I've longed for you. You bitch, you never cared, only pretended.'

She could not believe how strong he was. As they struggled on the floor she nearly choked in the dust.

'Kurt, let me go. You're hurting.' She was beginning to panic.

273

His hands were gripping her wrists and forcing them together above her head. He pushed them back on to the floor and held them with both hands.

Anna yanked her knee into his ribs and kicked out with the other foot, but Kurt pressed his full weight on her until she could only take short, gasping breaths. Fumbling under him, he tried to push her legs open.

Anna fought back. He's gone mad, she thought. She pushed her head up and bit him hard on the cheek. She tasted something sweet and salty. Blood.

Kurt wrenched his face away, pulled up her head and smashed it back on the floor.

Anna saw shooting lights and blacked out. It seemed only a split second later that she was lying, legs apart, with Kurt inside her, thrusting hard and deep and grunting like a pig as he had never done before.

'God damn Simon, you're mine, not his,' he muttered. 'You've always been mine. How does he do it to you? Better than this? What's so special about him? It must be a God damn miracle since it keeps you chained to a peasant.' He rammed her harder and she winced.

Anna was suffused with a sense of physical loathing, not directed at Kurt, but at herself. She felt imprisoned in loathsomeness; a sensation akin to pleasure, making her skin tingle and her limbs heavy.

She turned her head and vomited as Kurt came.

Suddenly he pushed himself away. 'Oh God,' he said. 'I wanted to force you to love me and you vomited.'

Anna stood up slowly. Her head throbbed; racing circles of light like gigantic bicycle wheels ran around the edge of her vision; there was a dull ache in her stomach. 'You hurt me,' she said quietly.

She went to the bathroom and turned the tap, but there was no water. Of course not, how foolish of her. She had forgotten where she was. Then she vomited again into the toilet, but there was no water to flush it.

She felt her way through the dark house, found her grip and fumbled for the gun.

When she crept back Kurt was sitting on the ground, his arms around his legs, his face on his knees. He was crying.

She pulled up the gun and pointed it at him. Then she thought, What good is he dead? She put the gun in her pocket.

'I'm sorry, I'm sorry,' Kurt was sobbing. 'It's so long since we made love. I waited for you – years – and you promised. I thought that when we made love you would remember, but you vomited. Oh God! Have you ever thought what I'm going through?'

'Kurt, I once loved you,' she began, 'but maybe not in the way you wanted me to love you. I don't think I can love anyone like that anymore. I admit, Simon attracts me, but when we make love ...'

'Shut up,' he said. 'I don't want to know.' He glanced at her and quickly looked away. 'I'm sorry. More sorry than you'll ever realize.'

'Kurt. Go and get a bucket of water from the pump,' she said gently. 'I must wash and clean this mess.'

Anna sat on the floor. No point in trying to keep clean now. She felt more depressed than ever.

The trouble was, she admitted, she had no deep feelings for anyone – she just needed them. Even more depressing was her lack of physical feeling when she made love. It was as if she had numbed her body while she was deliberately numbing her mind.

She left Bosluis before dawn, creeping out while Kurt was still asleep.

At Fontainebleu Simon thought about his prospects and wondered how long he would be able to endure such a battering to his self-esteem. People he came across in the daily running of the farm were always slighting him, however unintentionally. They would say: 'Helping Mr van Achtenburgh on the farm, are you?' Or: 'I'm sure Anna's glad to have an extra hand.' Even if no sneer was intended Simon saw it, read it in their faces, heard the things they would like to say, or so he imagined; everyone looked down on him and quite rightly so, since he was a man living on his wife.

Sensing Simon's distress, André moved out of his study and Simon found himself directing the old man's farming interests from the very room where he had planned it all six years before. The work was absorbing, but for Simon there was no joy in unearned riches; no satisfaction in reaping a crop that he had not planted. The wealth for which he had yearned with all his heart became a sour taste in his mouth and he could hardly bear to spend a penny.

Driving to the village the morning after Anna left, Simon decided to go to the co-op and order the seed and fertilizer for this year's planting, for it was nearly May.

'Will it be the usual amount?' the manager asked.

Simon gave him the order, increasing the fertilizer and lupin seeds, for he planned to cultivate several low hills on the Malmesbury farms and put the land to use.

'You'd better check this with the old man,' the co-op manager told him. 'Let me know,' and he hurried back to his office.

Simon returned to Fontainebleu and telephoned Hans. 'Just want you to know I'm here if you need any help,' he said.

'I'm sure that won't be necessary, sir, but thanks anyway,' Hans said.

'Everything going as usual?' Simon persisted.

'Better than usual. We've received a contract to supply the Castle liners. Mr Friedland's been after it for years. I've sent a cable, but he won't get it until he arrives in Frankfurt next week.'

'Next week? I thought he'd get there tonight.'

'No, he's staying at Bosluis for a few days.'

Simon replaced the receiver. He had never thought of Anna as a cheat. The day dragged on slowly. At last the time came to fetch the twins from school. At least in Katie's eyes he was the best man in the world.

28

After Anna's visit to South-West Africa, Simon became even
more remote. Inwardly, he was suffering, but outwardly he
maintained a cordial relationship with everyone. Apart from
his despair over Anna and his sense of inferiority at
Fontainebleu he was lonely. During the war he had built
strong, enduring friendships. He missed the comradeship and
he could not help remembering shore leaves: quiet, semi-
detached houses, pubs, darts games. Some people had more
important priorities than profits, he recalled, but in his world
money was the yardstick.

Van Achtenburgh noticed the change in Simon, the pallor,
shadows under his eyes, lips in a tight line, but said nothing.
Anna did not notice. During the two months Kurt was away
she threw herself into her work.

Their company had secured almost every large shipping
contract, but there were still some smaller ships' chandlers in
existence and Anna worked like a mongoose at a hencoop to
get their business.

Nowadays there was no problem with meat supply and
their sausage factory worked round the clock to keep up with
orders, but frequently they were caught in a bottleneck with
dairy supplies and Anna had set her heart on acquiring the
Cape Imperial Dairy. This would not be easy, for the owners
were determined not to sell. Eventually she set up a rival plant
and began to encroach on their milk supplies. With all this
activity she had no time to notice Simon's long face and
strangely distant manner.

277

Night after night Simon lay sleepless, wondering what he would do. His strength lay in farming, mechanics and the sea. During the war he had planned to return to Modderfontein, make a success of the farm and raise children with Anna. He could laugh when he thought of it now. Otto, on the other hand, had been intent on a salvage business and from his letters it seemed that Otto was tired of Britain's post-war austerity and lack of opportunity.

Simon spent a few afternoons in the docks talking to skippers of tramp steamers rounding the Cape. They were all concerned by the lack of facilities for ships and they would welcome service and cleaning facilities. Salvage was also possible, but only when the opportunities arose. In the meantime, servicing ships' engines and cleaning boilers could be their bread and butter. Simon wrote to Otto.

A week later he received a trunk call from Otto who was delighted at the chance of getting out of England and making a new start.

He began to search for suitable premises and eventually found an abandoned pre-fabricated structure which had been erected by the defence force in the war. It was ideal for conversion to a warehouse and small offices.

'And what will you do for cash?' André wanted to know when Simon told him of his plans.

That was their weak point, Simon told him. He had some savings plus his demob pay and he intended to sell Modderfontein. Hopefully he would have thirty thousand pounds and Otto could supply another ten.

'Lack of working cash has been the ruin of too many businesses,' André argued. 'I'd like to lend you the cash on a five-year contract. Naturally this will be strictly between the two of us. Anna mustn't know about it.'

'No thanks, sir,' Simon said, cheek twitching, face reddening. 'Don't think I don't appreciate all you've done for me. I said I'd give Fontainebleu a try for six months, but it's not working out.'

André understood. His daughter had become brutally independent. He would not have cared to have been married

278

to her himself. 'Yes,' he said sadly. 'I see what you mean, my boy.'

'And what will Anna do with her poultry if you sell Modderfontein?' André asked.

Simon stood up and began to pace the small study where he was closeted with his father-in-law. 'I've worried about that, sir. You probably know half her hens are already housed in batteries on the Cape Flats. I believe she only kept the rest there to pay the staff to look after the farm.'

'Yes, you're probably right,' André said. 'I sympathize. If I were in your place I'd sell Modderfontein as a going concern. Except the poultry, of course. Shake the sands of Saldanha Bay off my feet forever.'

Next morning when Simon told Anna of his and Otto's plans her anger was almost uncontrollable. She shouted in a manner most unlike Anna and even resorted to pleading. Simon was shocked, but would not give in.

'You've been treating me like shit,' he said quietly, 'and that was what I deserved. Well, no more of it.'

'If you loved me you'd look after Fontainebleu,' she shrieked, beside herself with temper.

'Why should I, Anna? You've only despised me for moving into a cushy position you felt I didn't deserve.'

'But that's not true,' she stormed, aware that she was lying.

'You use people, Anna,' Simon said sadly. 'Maybe you weren't always like that and maybe I had something to do with it. When I met you ... why, you were so trusting, so vulnerable. That's all changed and I feel I'm to blame, so I hardly ever criticize you, or tell you what an utter bitch you've become, but I think it's time someone did.'

Disbelief and fear showed on her face. 'You mean you're leaving me? Not just Fontainebleu, but me?' she stammered – and even Simon was surprised at her distress.

'Well, maybe not forever,' he faltered. 'But for the time being ... yes.' Simon sat on the bed and looked at her sadly. 'I want to be looked up to by my wife, I want our children to think of me with pride and the only way to do that in this God awful place is to be rich. Surely you can see that? It's your world.'

'But I don't understand.' Anna sat on the bed next to him and began to sob. 'I don't want you to be a success at business. Why can't you breed pigs or make wine, or any damn thing that suits you? Why do you have to compete with me?'

Simon stood up and looked out of the window at the vineyards, a scene he had grown to hate.

He said: 'Do you know how long it is since we made love?'

Anna fumbled for a tissue. She could not remember; some time ago, obviously, but that could be rectified. She had not given him enough attention. 'Maybe too long.' She tried out a timid smile.

'It's two months, damn it,' he said, hitting his fist into the palm of his hand.

She shook her head dumbly.

'Why do you think we never make love? Have you ever thought about it?'

'No,' she said. 'Sex isn't the be-all and end-all of my life, I assure you.'

'I doubt it's of the slightest importance in your life,' Simon shouted. 'How could sex compare with acquiring a dairy?'

'Oh, stop it, stop it,' she wailed. 'All right, I admit I've been wrong. Obsessed with the business. But surely you can look at things my way, can't you? Kurt's overseas. It's a big responsibility. I have to do everything by myself.'

'He'll be back soon,' Simon said. 'Probably with Madeleine.'

His words struck a cold chill into her. Abruptly she stood up, rushed into the bathroom and urgently began applying makeup. It was a routine that she went through every morning without really noticing. First the eye shadow, then the eye liner, face powder, rouge and lipstick, but this time she looked at herself in the mirror.

She saw a hard, decisive, arrogant woman, beautiful, but cold. Walking to the bathroom door, she stared anxiously at Simon. 'You used to say I was beautiful. Do you still think that?'

'Yes,' he said, 'but sometimes the expression on your face is not beautiful. As people get older they begin to look like they are instead of how nature designed them. Then real beauty comes out or real ugliness. If I were you, Anna, I'd watch out.'

She was losing. Simon was implacable. Anna began to feel afraid. 'What will you do for capital?'

'Sell Modderfontein.'

'You can't sell Modderfontein, it's just as much mine as yours,' she shouted.

'Anna. Let's get this farce over, shall we? I have to sell Modderfontein. Besides, it reminds me of my failure.'

'I need it for the chickens,' she lied.

'But I heard you telling Kurt you couldn't move the chickens because "poor Simon needs the rents". Those were your very words.'

'You're always slinking around, spying on people.'

'Maybe I spy on you sometimes,' he admitted. 'I know you went to South-West Africa with Kurt.'

She gasped and turned, pale and frightened. 'That's not true,' she said.

'Don't lie, Anna.'

She buried her face in her hands and gave a long, shuddering sigh. 'It's not true that I went to South-West Africa with Kurt. I thought he was in Europe, but I found him waiting for me. He wanted to talk before he went to find Madeleine.'

'The two of you must have had a fine time while I was in the navy,' he said without emotion.

'No, that's not true.' Suddenly she flung her arms around his neck. 'I want to tell you everything. The whole truth of the matter.'

'I don't want to know,' he said, pushing her away roughly. 'I ran away, whatever I got I deserved. I don't want to hear another word.'

He fumbled in the cupboard and hauled out his battered suitcase.

'God, don't tell me you've still got that old thing,' she said. 'Take mine.'

His eyes blazed. 'You've missed the point,' he said quietly.

Anna grabbed her coat and raced to the car.

'Mommy, Mommy,' she heard the twins running behind her.

She had almost gone without saying goodbye or telling them when she would be back. She felt tension running down her back and into her legs. She wanted to scream.

'Go and tell Grandpa I won't be here for lunch, but I'll be back in time for supper,' she said. 'I'll read you a story tonight, so be good children today.'

'What's the matter? Why are you crying?' Katie said.

'I'm not crying, I've got hay fever.' She wiped her eyes with the back of her hand and said too brusquely, 'Go along now, do as you're told. Go to Grandpa.' She saw happiness change to uncertainty and doubt.

It's his fault, she thought, fighting back the tears. Damn him, he's breaking up our family. He doesn't know what he's doing. Then she thought, panic-stricken, perhaps it's that bloody woman's fault. What was her name ...? Edwina!

Suddenly she turned and raced to the house, through the door, past the maid, nearly knocking her over, and flinging open the bedroom door she said, 'Don't go; you don't know what you're doing. You'll break our lives, Simon.'

'I must, Anna,' he said. 'If you think about it you'll realize that I must.'

The children burst in and began whining. 'Why is Daddy packing his suitcase? Where are you going, Daddy?'

'Tell him not to go,' she said, collapsing on the bed and bursting into tears.

'Jesus, Anna. You're a selfish bitch. Why did you have to drag in the kids? You don't care who you use to get your own way.'

'That's not true,' she wailed and Katie wound her arms around her neck and said, 'If you're horrible to Mommy I won't love you. Don't cry, Mommy.'

Simon swore viciously and sat on the bed. 'I'm not going away,' he told the twins, 'at least not very far. Just to Cape

Town to start a business and make money. I'll see you weekends.'

'We've already got a lot of money,' Katie said gravely. 'We don't need any more money. Mommy makes all the money.'

'Perhaps Daddy wants his own money,' Acker added.

Simon was amazed at the precociousness of his children. When he was seven he would not have understood one word of all this and there they stood, two solemn grown-ups, four foot high. He sighed.

'If you want me, all you have to do is pick up the 'phone and I'll be right over.' This was the worst part of all, he thought. He'd grown to love the children. He'd miss them.

Putting on her sunglasses Anna said, 'Okay, kids, I'm off. But I'll be back soon.'

She could not help thinking of Modderfontein as she drove to town. The first and only home of her own. She remembered what it had looked like when she arrived; her precious hundred pounds that had gone into new floors and paint; Uncle Acker's furniture. She should fetch that. Then she thought about the donga and how the water came welling up, the herons and weaver birds, the contours she had made, the day she had acquired the rams. Suddenly she made up her mind to buy Modderfontein and when she reached the office she telephoned the bank manager at Malmesbury.

'Buy it under a nominee,' she urged him. 'I don't want Simon to find out. Make sure yours is the best offer.'

'And your limit?' he asked.

'There's no limit,' she said after a short pause.

29

Vienna, August 1946

Kurt was spending most of his time alone in a bare room in one of the few houses that remained undamaged where he was billeted on a reluctant Austrian family.

It seemed as if he had awakened from an eight-year dream, for the moment he arrived in Europe, the bitterness and the anger which he had walled up came seething out. Hate flooded his psyche, excluding rational thought. Six million Jews wiped out, but no record of the emotional crippling of those who had technically survived. Kurt was one of them, but he was an intelligent man. He knew that this hatred and bitterness would eventually destroy him and he tried to gain an objective view of what was now, after all, a historical event. He failed.

He found the visits to displaced persons' camps distressing – and he had seen them all. Hundreds of thousands of unwanted people. Flotsam on history's tide. He visited his family home. The gaunt mansion housed troops and the ballbearing plant had been destroyed in the bombing.

Kurt had been told that his search was hopeless. Every person in the camps was documented, their relatives had been contacted whenever possible. If Madeleine's name was not on the list then she was not there. So many millions had vanished. Shrugs and apologetic smiles.

Kurt had been astonished, too, at his own reactions, for as the weeks passed and the chances of finding Madeleine diminished he began to feel relieved. This abominable blot on human history had been caused by ordinary people who had abandoned values built up over the past three thousand years, and blindly done as they were told. Madeleine had been one of them and he hated her as he hated the rest. He wished her dead. The more he recognized this, the more he despised himself and drove himself to investigate every angle, press advertisements, inquiries in Madeleine's home town, her old haunts, even contacting Gunther's family. But Gunther had been killed in the blitz.

Now he had been waiting two days for a last possibility; a train was coming from Budapest returning people to the West. No one knew if they were prisoners of war or displaced persons.

He would wait for the train and afterwards take the first flight to South Africa. He would never set foot in Germany again.

The scene outside the station next morning was unbelievable. Everyone seemed to have lost someone; everyone was hoping. Kurt, who had a pass to the platform, had difficulty getting there. The train was six hours late, but nurses, doctors, ambulance drivers and Red Cross officials waited patiently with the US military police.

Pandemonium broke out when the train finally arrived, but the cries of welcome were quickly hushed, for most of the passengers needed assistance to leave the train. Here were the crippled, deformed, blind or injured, all were in urgent need of hospital care.

'The Russians didn't want this lot,' a Red Cross official muttered to him as she rushed to their aid.

The main station had been transformed into an interrogation centre, with trestle tables, and the passengers were escorted or carried to sit in rows. Those in urgent need of hospitalization were documented first.

Kurt wandered around, feeling sick, until he saw Bud Collier, a Red Cross official whom he had met in his search.

Collier's eyes skimmed the Fs and Gs on his list. 'No sign, but don't give up hope yet,' he said.

Kurt walked around the benches trying to keep calm, but eventually he gave up and waited near the Red Cross information department. It was here that Collier found him.

'Hey, Kurt, Kurt Friedland. Over here,' he called. 'Down that row there's a woman claims she's Madeleine Friedland. Small boy with her. He's deaf and dumb I'm afraid. Shell shock case by the look of things. Just thought I'd warn you.' He smiled sympathetically. 'Don't worry, I'll be right behind you.'

Kurt walked down the row, knees wobbling, mouth too dry to shut, panting a little, trying not to see the shattered people on either side. How could Madeleine be one of these. It was impossible. Insane!

A woman sat where Bud was pointing; thin, but not emaciated, mousy hair hung dishevelled, huddled in a Red Army overcoat. It was very old and she looked old, too. She was clutching a small boy, bony with shaved head and large brown eyes which mirrored all the woes of the world.

'Madeleine?' She looked so unfamiliar.

She looked up and he saw the same blue eyes, defiant now, but not without pride.

'Kurt. My God, Kurt,' she said in German. Then she laughed coldly. 'I see you had a good war.'

She was becoming more familiar by the minute. 'Welcome back,' he said.

'This is Paul,' she said, pushing the boy forward.

As Kurt looked at the boy, his gaze wavered away, frightened and hostile.

She shrugged. 'He's deaf and dumb,' she said without a trace of emotion. Watching her, Kurt caught a glimpse of broken brown teeth.

At that moment a hooter sounded from the station and the boy cowered into the bench.

Dumb maybe, but not deaf, Kurt decided. He turned to Collier. 'I can't think straight. For God's sake help me. I want to get them out of Germany, to Switzerland, to a sanatorium.'

The rest of that day and the next was an eternity of queues, forms, declarations, affidavits and at the end of it Madeleine was a permanent resident of South Africa and both of their photographs were added to his passport. Two strangers dependent upon him. He shuddered and put it away. The following morning they left Germany for a convalescent home in Switzerland. Madeleine tried to telephone her mother as soon as she arrived, but her mother had died during the war.

In the weeks that followed Madeleine regained her former health and Kurt was amazed at her wholehearted dedication to the task. With good food, Swiss air, exercise and handfuls of vitamin pills, her cheeks filled out, her figure blossomed and her eyes began to lose their fear.

While Kurt denied her nothing to help her recuperate he became miserly when she asked for money for clothes or the hairdresser. He had bought her some sensible tweed skirts and jerseys, low heeled shoes and thick lisle stockings. Her hair hung lank and uncut, although she had done the best she could, and while her teeth had been filled, they remained discoloured for several nerves were dead.

The truth was, Kurt liked her just the way she was; dowdy, unattractive and lacking in confidence. He was behaving rather like a victorious army, determined that the enemy remain crushed forever. She was no longer a threat. Pitifully Madeleine tried to resurrect his passion, but was rebuffed.

One night when Kurt was asleep, she crept naked into his bed and tried to tempt him. She rubbed the back of his neck and his back, searching for places where her touch could arouse him, letting her hand drift over his buttocks and around.

Ramrod stiff he awoke and switched on the light. 'Madeleine, the war's over. You no longer have to be a whore,' he said cruelly.

She shuddered and turned her head away, trying to hide the tears. 'I just wanted you to love me,' she said.

'In the only way you know?' He grabbed the meagre flesh on her thighs and pinched hard. 'How many men, Madeleine? How many? Tell me.'

'Stop it, stop it,' she sobbed.

'Poor, weary, pounded flesh,' he said and, holding the lamp up, he pulled back the bedclothes and peered at her, noting the changes the war had brought. 'I could never,' he said and shuddered.

Then, a month after they arrived in Switzerland, the long-awaited letter arrived from her mother's lawyers in Australia, enclosing a bank draft for two thousand pounds, and informing her that she would receive a small gratuity of one hundred pounds a month left by her mother.

Madeleine disappeared for the day and returned with ash-blonde hair in the latest cut. During the next few weeks her teeth were capped by the best Swiss dentist and with good clothes she regained much of her former glamour. Kurt was furious and announced that they would return to South Africa immediately.

'She is far from better,' the psychoanalyst told him. 'Admittedly she looks fine from the outside, but we cannot get her to talk about her experiences in the war. She has buried her wounds deep inside her and they will fester. She should talk about it. Get it out in the open.'

Kurt repeated the conversation to Madeleine, but she said, 'The war's over, let's not prolong it by talking about it.'

Paul was another matter. He would not speak, although specialists assured Kurt that there was nothing wrong with his vocal chords. 'Shock,' they explained. 'We'll probably never know what caused it.'

They questioned Madeleine. Had the boy ever spoken? She pointed out that she had been parted from him most of the time.

'Take him home,' the specialist said. 'There's nothing more we can do. Maybe with love and patience, a stable life, who knows, after a while ...'

Kurt looked down into the brown eyes. Gunther's eyes! The boy's every mannerism reminded him of Gunther – and Madeleine's treachery. He hated them both, jointly and severally.

30

It was the end of September, springtime, and the south-easter was blowing at Force Ten, with gusts of up to eighty miles an hour, so that ships could not enter or leave harbour and the liner remained immobile for twenty-four hours, tossing like a cork in Table Bay.

The hardier immigrants gathered along the rail of the ship, admiring Table Mountain which was half obscured with its thick tablecloth of cloud, but most of the passengers remained below. Edwina had become sea sick the day she set foot on the liner at berth in Southampton docks and the agony of it became worse during ten days at sea. Besides, she was enduring a painful pregnancy, face bloated, brown stains on her cheeks, sunken eyes with deep shadows beneath. She looked and felt years older than twenty-six.

She had seen little of Otto during the past two weeks for she had tried not to be a nuisance. Every morning he collected their daughter, Margaret, who was two, and returned her to the cabin, after which she fell asleep at night. She was so ashamed of herself, the cabin stank and she was so ugly now. As if to accentuate her misery Otto had never looked better. He had acquired a deep tan during the voyage, his blue eyes looked twice as bright and his hair was bleached almost white. Edwina adored Otto but with reservations. She was uncompromisingly English and his threats to emigrate had almost destroyed their marriage. Finally it had been her pregnancy which had led her to capitulate. Now she was timid and insecure, dreading the changes and the dependence upon Otto which she knew would follow, as she settled down with two small children without her parents in a foreign land.

When the wind dropped the following day, they entered harbour to the sound of the ship's siren and delighted yells of passengers, but Edwina had to be helped on deck by her four cabin-mates who packed for her.

It was a lovely morning. The clouds had disappeared from the mountaintops, the sun shone brightly, the sea was as calm as a millpond, but Edwina took one look at the seals floating in the harbour, blacks shouting from the quays, towering backdrop of mountains and shuddered. This foreign country would never be home, she decided.

Simon met them at the docks and, upset by Edwina's miserable condition, rushed them to the Ritz Hotel where as immigrants they were to stay for two weeks with expenses paid by the State. Within days she had recovered her health, but not her spirits. She hated the country and as her pregnancy increased, so did her despair.

Madeleine's first view of the Cape was from 20,000 feet in the first class section of a SAA airliner, and although she said little she was thrilled at the sight of the mountains and the blue sea. Above all it was the space that impressed her, mile after mile of beaches, mountain ranges, vast dams, fertile farmlands. A new world!

Kurt was feeling jaded after an uncomfortable night and endless hours on the plane, but Madeleine looked as fresh as when she left the convalescent home; eyes blazing with curiosity, capped teeth gleaming, wisps of curly hair half obscuring her cheeks.

What's a night's discomfort to a professional like her? Kurt thought.

When they crossed the tarmac, Madeleine looked round at the flat dry grass, the unbroken blue of the horizon, the distant mountains.

'I'm afraid it's not Vienna,' Kurt apologized. 'An outpost.'

'I love it,' she said. 'I love it already.'

Kurt shuddered. Then the boy caught up with him and hung on to his jacket and Kurt had to resist an impulse to strike him. Paul had not benefited from their stay in Switzerland. Never hungry, never happy, he shuffled around getting in everyone's way, dogging Kurt's footsteps. It was hard to know if he understood what was said to him and Kurt was ashamed of escorting this stumbling, starved waif. He explained the circumstances to everyone he met, even complete strangers.

Waiting in the airport lounge, Anna was prepared for the worst. She had even wondered whether or not to bring a wheelchair. She had received only one letter from Kurt, a bad one which she had burnt. He had poured out his distress at finding Madeleine alive, and at her miserable state, as well as her son's affliction, which made it impossible to leave her. Since then she had received only a telegram giving the arrival time and asking her to book them into a hotel. Of course that was out of the question. Instead she had converted the east wing of Fontaineblue so that they could be private, but help would be on hand when needed.

In the past weeks, part of her loneliness and rejection at Simon's leaving her had been lessened as she threw herself into the job of preparing for Kurt's family. Nevertheless, she could not understand Kurt's feeling of responsibility towards this woman who had left him before the war. Why not leave her in a sanatorium? Why must he feel saddled with her?

She saw why a few minutes later when Madeleine burst into the lounge, ash-blonde hair tossed over one shoulder, huge blue eyes sparkling, her model's figure draped in some costly grey woollen affair. A beautiful, vivacious woman with features like a film star. Thank God she had not brought the wheelchair. Hating and resenting this cuckoo in her nest, she braced herself for the meeting.

'I'm so pleased to meet Kurt's best friend,' Madeleine gushed in broken English. She bent forward impulsively and kissed Anna on the cheek. Her voice was low and husky, her manner contrived.

Flamboyant, Anna observed, watching the Friedlands as they waited for their luggage to arrive. She dismissed

291

Madeleine as a show-off and turned her attention to Paul. What a disaster! His feet were too big, his nose too long, his head too large for his slender neck. Painfully thin, his clothes hung as if from a scarecrow and to make matters worse Madeleine had bought everything a size too large for him. He had a strange, shuffling way of walking, as if he dreaded stepping into the future and would rather remain in a place where he had been safe for a while. Add to that his dumbness, Anna thought, weighing him up, and you would imagine him a boy to be pitied. Yet all this was insignificant compared with his eyes – huge, brown and glowing with interest. Right now he was observing Madeleine's efforts to please with distaste. He was painfully insecure, yet trying to preserve some dignity, being coldly indifferent to the children's advances and refusing to hold Anna's hand. Dumb or not dumb, that kid's got guts, Anna decided, and warmed to him immediately. Yet Kurt was visibly resentful of the child and Madeleine seemed indifferent. She could not understand them.

At Fontainebleu Madeleine gushed over everything while Kurt did his best to keep out of the way. 'You'd think she'd never seen a farm before,' Anna said crossly to André. 'I've never seen such an exhibition.' When Madeleine expressed a desire to see the horses, the family accompanied her. She patted one absentmindedly while trying to describe the fashions in Europe in broken English. Paul stumbled behind them. He tripped over cobbles into manure and scrambling to his feet clutched Madeleine's dress.

She said, 'First thing we need is a nanny.'

'I'll find a nanny,' Anna told her impatiently and, taking Paul by the hand, she hurried to the paddock.

Jan was checking the feed. When he saw Paul he pushed back his hat and scratched his head. 'Looks like we'll have to feed him up,' he said, looking upset.

The children came running behind, demanding that Jan saddle their ponies immediately. They wanted to show off to Paul.

'You must go and change your clothes,' Anna scolded them. 'And bring something for Paul to wear. Maybe he wants to ride, too.' She watched them rushing off, arrogant, spoiled,

292

beautiful children – just the way she wanted them. The contrast was shocking; Paul was so forlorn and wary, resting between disasters.

'Would you like to ride?' she asked, guiltily aware that he could not understand English and anyway was dumb.

He watched her, hostile and prepared.

Anna sighed and led him round the stables, calling each horse by name and holding him up so that he could stroke them. He showed no fear. That was a good sign, she thought.

The children arrived with Lena in tow and Paul watched as they leapt on their horses and raced round the paddock.

'We're going down to the river,' they called.

'No you're not, you're going to stay with Paul,' Anna said.

'He can come.'

'Don't be ridiculous. He's never been on a horse before.'

'Saddle Jamie,' Acker told Jan. 'We'll lead him round the paddock, Ma.'

'Perhaps he doesn't want to.'

'Course he wants to!'

He climbed off his horse and approached Paul determinedly. Grabbing Paul by the arm he pushed him towards the stables.

She wondered if she was doing the right thing, but decided that if he didn't want to ride he could always resist. He emerged ten minutes later, slouched on Dobbins, but obviously enjoying himself.

'Sit up,' she said sharply. She sighed, climbed over the fence and gave her first lesson in mime.

Strange how he seemed older than the twins. Admittedly he was skinny and half-starved, but still she was puzzled.

She climbed back again and sat on a fallen tree trunk. When Acker trotted, Jamie kept up and Paul rattled and shook until he fell on the ground. He grinned self-consciously and although Anna called him, shook his head and scrambled back.

She left them in Lena's care. 'Not out of the paddock,' she warned them, and walked back to the house. If they let him stay here, he'll soon be OK, she thought.

A delicious aroma of roast duck was coming from the kitchen. She heard voices raised in the east wing and a door slammed. Footsteps approached, it sounded like Kurt.

Anna sighed. She had not seen Kurt since the night at Bosluis. She knew she should be angry, yet she was not. A moment later Kurt was at the door, frowning and impatient. 'Bloody hell!' he said, slamming the door behind him. He stamped across the carpet and sank into her bedside chair. 'We shouldn't have come here,' he began. 'It was so kind of you, particularly after what I did ...' He broke off.

'It's in the past, let's keep it there,' she said awkwardly.

'Where's Simon?'

'He left me,' Anna said miserably. Where was Simon? She wondered. She had refused to meet his precious Tenwicks, but for them Simon would have been at Fontainebleu. God, how she hated him for leaving her.

Sensing his advantage, Kurt stood up and put his arms around her. 'What a bloody mess.'

'Where's Madeleine?'

'In her room. Really Anna, that suite, it's terrific. So kind of you, but we should have gone to a hotel.'

'The house is empty,' she began then broke off. 'Damn you, Kurt, you made her sound like a bloody invalid.' She glared at him. 'I even hired a wheelchair.'

'Madeleine's resilience is nothing short of miraculous,' he said smoothly.

She moved away from him, but he caught her arm. 'Don't behave like a stranger, please, Anna. I'm truly sorry, you know I love you. Are you still cross with me?'

'Not for the reason you think. It's just that Simon found out we were there together.'

'You told him?'

'No. Hans Lombard.'

'I'm sorry, but it's for the best. Divorce Simon and marry me.'

The arrogance of the man. 'No.'

He swore. Then he took off his jacket, hung it behind the door and sat on the bed. 'I swear I haven't touched Madeleine. You're the only woman for me.'

294

Anna smoothed her hair. Madeleine was no threat after all. She could have Kurt if she wanted him, but she felt no desire, no passion. Yet why not? She needed a triumph however trivial, even over that weird, fragile, laughing woman. To take something that she wanted; to pass on the rejection that hung so heavily upon her. She would hit back at Simon, too. Then she thought: if she rejected Kurt he would turn to Madeleine; they might go away together. Kurt was part of her life, necessary and irreplaceable. His clever business brain was forever thinking of ways to expand, to make more profits.

Fixing Kurt with what she hoped was a voluptuous stare she unbuttoned her blouse, but caught sight of her breasts in the mirror; her joyless flesh, unloved and now to be abused, flaccid, decaying.

She hesitated and seeing this Kurt caught hold of her arm, drew her towards the bed. She felt helpless, a victim of her own rejection, and allowed herself to be pulled and pushed down and down. She was falling, falling, like a leaf released from the tree that had succoured her; swaying in sunlight, all that was left was decay. She cried out and clutched at Kurt, but he let go, pushed off his trousers with unnecessary haste and pounced on her; he the street sweeper and she the leaf, helpless, quivering.

He would not let go of her; she jerked her head aside and caught sight of white buttocks rising and falling in the mirror, a jerking, aggressive rhythm. Why had he not removed his socks? White flesh against black wool. She clasped her teeth together and closed her eyes, blotting out vision. She began to loathe herself, it was a strangely powerful feeling, welling up through her like alcohol in the bloodstream, permeating every part of her; she was drowning in it, emotionally and physically. She could have taken a knife and slashed at her breasts and her stomach, ripped out her womanliness. She began to moan with disgust and Kurt, mistaking it for passion, intensified his efforts.

Long after he left, she remained huddled in the blankets feeling spent, degraded, hating herself.

Left alone Madeleine gazed out of the window. Her room

295

overlooked the vineyards, acres of vines in bud and beyond them woods leading to the mountains. It would be wonderful here, were it not for Anna who terrified her. She was like a gypsy, cruel or kind as the mood took her, a woman of terrible contrasts.

Madeleine felt vulnerable; unarmed in enemy territory. If only she could enjoy the peace of Fontainebleu, but when she shut her eyes Anna's face was still there. Images! They were coming again and she could not escape them. Sometimes she felt she would go crazy. Those terrible, implacable eyes. Now Anna was changing, splitting open like an overripe pomegranate and out of her stomach a bird unfolded, a bird of prey, with Anna's eyes. She smothered a scream and ran to the balcony. There was no one there. No one had heard. She squared her shoulders and took a deep breath. That was better. She would unpack while she waited.

Where was Paul she wondered, without feeling anxious. Strange how Anna had taken to him, picking him up and hugging him as if she had known him all her life. Madeleine could never do that and she often wondered why she was different to other women. It was not that she disliked children, just that she had no maternal feelings at all. Paul would be happy here, she knew. Easy to see he was taken with horses.

Half an hour later she was still waiting. Unwilling to venture out alone, she decided to unpack for Kurt, too. It was in the side pocket of his suitcase that she found a jewel case and inside, nestling in dark blue velvet, a diamond bracelet. It was of delicately wrought gold, fashioned into a design of leaves with six small gold flowers with diamond centres. Exquisite! Was it for her? Surely not? Not from a man who had refused to buy her clothes. Carefully she replaced the box in the suitcase and stood up. Was Kurt in love with Anna?

In spite of Kurt's coldness over the past few weeks she had convinced herself that he still cared for her. Why else had he searched for her? Now she forced herself to remember their marriage as it had really been and not as she had imagined it during the long war years. The truth was too ugly to consider and after a while she gave up and convinced herself that with time and patience she would win him back.

When Kurt returned a few minutes later she was brushing her hair. He hardly glanced at her.

'Surely you should be looking after Paul,' he said crossly.

She started guiltily and went outside.

Paul was in the paddock with the twins. He seemed happy enough. Anything's better than the camp, she thought, so why feel guilty about him?

That night Anna came to dinner wearing her beautiful new diamond bracelet. When Madeleine saw it she fought back an exclamation of dismay and instead sat quietly next to André. Glancing around she saw a malicious gleam in Anna's eyes and secret, tender smiles from Kurt. She was an interloper, unwanted by everyone. Why had he searched for her so long and so hard? The truth hit her viciously: because he had wanted to prove she was dead.

It was an embarrassing evening for everyone and eventually André said firmly, 'Anna, play the piano, dear. You haven't played for months. It would please me.'

She agreed with bad grace and glancing at Madeleine said coolly, 'Aren't you a singer, Madeleine? I believe Kurt mentioned that once.'

'I used to sing. It seems a hundred years ago now.' She was about to explain that she no longer sang when Kurt interrupted.

'Spare us, do. I suggest you practise on your own one day. Like everything else, singing has to be kept up.'

How cruel he could be. She gazed at him, remembering the soft, vulnerable boy she had once know. 'I only know German songs,' she said.

Anna began to play: Heidenröslein.

Why had she chosen that? Madeleine cleared her throat and hummed the opening bars, but suddenly she was in the Europa Club, Germany, 1939. She had been singing that very song when the Nazis had come for her. She closed her eyes, remembering. She had gone quietly, not wishing to make a scene, but outside she had said, 'You're making a mistake. I'm not Jewish.'

'Do you deny this?' They had thrust a letter at her, signed by Gunther, with her birth certificate pinned on it.

Betrayal! That more than anything obsessed her during the nightmare days that followed. She had been taken to a large room where she waited for a day with a hundred other Jews. Eventually the women had been ushered to a waiting room where a black-haired man in uniform sat at a trestle table issuing passes. He had stared too long and too hard at Madeleine.

'Age?'

'Twenty-one.'

'Vocation?'

'I am a singer.'

She and five other young women had been given stamped passes and put on a lorry which drove them over the Hungarian border to a German regiment. They had none of them known what to expect until they were ushered into the officers' mess; from then on it had been all too obvious.

'I am a singer,' she had screamed when she was ordered to stand on the table and strip.

'Ah, a singer, pretty, too. Then sing while you strip, my dear,' the colonel told her.

She forced the memories away, down into her subconscious which she thought of as a fetid bog. Fearsome things lived in the bog, foetuses expelled still moving from the womb, beaten women, troops back from the Russian front.

She looked up to see André bending over her, holding a glass of brandy. 'You nearly passed out. Please drink this,' he said. 'You are far from recovered, my dear.' There was something tragic about her, André decided. She threw herself too trustingly into relationships, like a moth into the flames. She would be burned, particularly by his daughter.

Madeleine went to bed early, but as she walked past the study she saw Anna's beautiful cashmere shawl thrown carelessly over a chair. She caught hold of it. How soft and beautiful it was and she could smell Anna's perfume. She carried it to her room and hid it behind her clothes in the wardrobe.

298

31

Otto and Simon were working round the clock, sometimes snatching a few hours' sleep on camp beds in their offices, offering a twenty-four-hour service to get ships in and out of dry dock in record time.

Simon's Afrikaans connections, and his affinity with Xhosa labour gangs, allied to Otto's shipping experience, proved the ideal combination. Besides, they were both handsome, imposing men with good war records and a sound knowledge of the ships' requirements. The contracts began to roll in.

While Otto was selling their services to the ships that put into Cape Town harbour, Simon was supervising the work, and it was not long before the labour became highly skilled and they appointed two black foremen.

In December they obtained their first big contract to service engines, clean boilers, scrape and paint a fleet of freighters that hauled cargo around the African coast from Walvis Bay to Durban. It was a huge contract, too big for their available equipment and labour. They decided it was too good a chance to be missed and ploughed the rest of their capital into down payments on air compressors and spray painting equipment. Now they were dependent upon their debtors paying in time to cover the mounting weekly wage bill. Before long Simon had to negotiate overdraft facilities for five thousand pounds. The six thousand pounds gained from Modderfontein's sale had not lasted long, and as the money was spent Simon's guilt at selling his heritage increased.

Their acute shortage of cash began to worry them both. They had given quarterly post-dated cheques for building materials for their offices and warehouse, but there were dozens of unexpected expenses that kept cropping up at awkward times.

Nevertheless, business was thriving and the books showed a profit, and both of them were impressed at the value of the orders coming in. Rising at five a.m. each morning, they would work all day until dark and often all night, grabbing a sandwich or a plate of fish and chips from the Portuguese café in the docks when there was a lull. Nights were spent planning, doing accounts, sorting out labour for the next day's contracts. It was becoming complicated.

It was then that the telephone would ring and it was always Edwina, tired of being alone, unwilling to endure another night of it.

Edwina had little to do and as her pregnancy increased so did her loneliness. She longed for gentle English hills and valleys, neat, hedged fields, walking in country roads, country people.

In this raw and frightening country she made no friends, for she met only immigrants and found them unacceptable. They came from every European country and they had in common only their desire to make money fast; a concept as crude and brash as they were, or so it seemed to Edwina.

Even the climate was harsh and unbearable. When the south-easter blew up from the Antarctic she would freeze, but the wind would drop just as suddenly, leaving a heatwave. It was beyond all reason, a cruel, savage, terrible country where no one was safe.

As if to confirm her fears, one evening as she was walking with Margaret along the beach at dusk, two men materialized out of the shadows. In a flash, one pressed a knife against her neck while without speaking the other took her handbag, pearls, rings, watch and even her shoes. The horror of it was to remain in her memory for years, like a silent movie played in slow motion.

After that Edwina never strayed far from home. But what was home? Two bare rooms let by a widow in a small house two blocks from the sea front. She shared the kitchen and bathroom.

Impossible to stay there all day, so she toured the streets, keeping to crowded places, dragging Margaret behind her, but even here the horrors continued, for the sight of a crippled or blind beggar, or a homeless black child, filled her with despair.

'Don't they have social welfare here?' she would complain. 'Don't they have places where these people can live? Don't they have homes for these children?'

The answer was always 'No.'

'It would never be allowed in England,' she would say to everyone she met. It became her theme song and as the weeks passed she became known as 'that English lady'.

Simon and Edwina's friendship grew stronger. He had always been fond of her, even in England, and he could not understand why Otto had so little compassion nowadays. Sometimes Edwina would catch a bus and bring Margaret to the docks, an ordeal which took all her courage, and she would sit around or make tea until one or the other took her home – and it was usually Simon. If she had to go shopping or visit the clinic, Simon would help out.

Simon, who bitterly regretted his failed relationship with Anna and who missed his children, was only too grateful to take Otto's place in these insignificant duties. Besides, Simon could not help feeling flattered by a woman who obviously thought highly of him. With Anna he had missed even a hint of adoration. Now he was swimming in it. During weekend visits to Fontainebleu he felt he slipped out of one skin straight into another. In Anna's eyes he saw himself cruelly; a man who put his own selfish ambitions before the happiness of his family; a man who failed. When he wanted a better image of himself he could find it in Edwina's eyes.

On Christmas Eve Otto rushed Edwina to the nursing home, where after only six hours labour she gave birth to a daughter whom they named Rosemary. A month later, Edwina returned to her routine of cleaning the two rooms and pacing the streets, only now she pushed a pram and Margaret tottered behind her.

It was Christmas day and Anna was lonely although the house was full of people. Simon was late for lunch and the twins were disappointed, but not enough to spoil their day, for there were presents and all the Christmas trappings.

By one o'clock the family was gathered around the tree toasting Christmas, and today the children were allowed some wine. The staff were getting boisterous in the kitchen, Jacob was strumming a guitar and Nella, the cook, was singing noisily. Jan was nursing a sore head from the party they had held for all the farm workers the night before.

'We'll be lucky if the dishes are done before they pass out,' Anna murmured to André.

When Flora tottered in with the turkey on a large platter Anna held her breath.

'Now you watch that boy,' Flora said pointing at Paul and giggling, 'or he'll have the turkey under his bed.'

'Hush, Flora,' Anna chided her. 'Just because he can't speak doesn't mean he can't understand.'

'Oh, he understands me all right,' she said and hiccoughed. 'I'm warning you, my lad.' She giggled and went out shaking her tail like a duck dabbling.

Paul's curious hang-up was a problem to all of them but mainly to the staff for it was Flora who had to clean the mess of mouldy bread hidden in drawers, melted chocolate in the car, cakes in the stable, and placate Nella when the roast disappeared.

'Where's Madeleine?' Anna asked.

'Lying in her room with a migraine. Where else?' Kurt sounded cruel. Lately he had changed, Anna thought, stealing a glance at him. The telephone rang. It was Simon full of apologies. 'An emergency in the docks,' he told Anna. 'I must finish the job by three; then I'm going on to visit someone in hospital; after that I'll drive on to Fontainebleu. Give the kids my love, I'll try to make supper.'

Exasperated, Anna flung down the telephone.

When they heard the news Acker moaned, Katie burst into tears and Anna became even more irritable.

Anna went to fetch Madeleine. She heard Kurt hurrying behind her.

'Anna, I can't keep hanging on here forever. The house was ready to move into weeks ago. I dread leaving, but I'm going to have to take my terrible family and go.'

Kurt had bought an old farmhouse in Constantia with three acres of ground overlooking False Bay and it had been modernized, ruining it, Anna thought.

'But Kurt, you surely weren't thinking of taking Paul away from Fontainebleu?'

'Well, of course I must.' He smiled at her. 'I can't have you looking after my problems forever.'

'I would hardly call Paul a problem,' Anna retorted, feeling hurt.

'Oh come on, Anna, he's impossible. All those visits to the psychoanalyst don't seem to have helped at all. What about the things he steals, food going mouldy everywhere? Anyway he's Madeleine's son.'

'Madeleine doesn't give a damn about him,' she hissed.

'I agree, but that's my problem, not yours. Legally he's my son.'

'But it must be better for him to be with the twins,' she stammered.

'If you mean more enjoyable, I agree, but there's no point in him getting used to this place. The longer he stays the more he'll miss it.'

Anna was unwilling to reveal her feelings for Paul. During the past three months she had grown to love him. She felt she understood him better than anyone. Who else had witnessed his pluck as he learned to jump, who else knew the despair that gripped him when he struggled to speak, or his joy in living at Fontainebleu.

'You only want to punish him,' she blurted. 'Just to get back at Gunther. Why can't you leave him where he's happy?'

'Because life isn't just a question of doing what makes you happy,' he said coldly, 'and incidentally you are quite wrong about my intentions.'

Anna heard footsteps approaching.

'It's Madeleine,' she whispered, but Kurt gripped her and pushed her back against the wall, holding his mouth against hers.

She struggled, pushed him away and saw Madeleine run past them, face averted.

'But you heard her,' she hissed. 'You're not deaf. You did it on purpose.'

'So what.' He scowled towards the dinning-room. 'Serves her right.'

'If you hate her so, why don't you divorce her? I'm sure she would co-operate.'

'I don't want to discuss it,' he said.

'Well, I want to discuss it.' She stared at him quietly for a long time. Then she stepped forward and slapped his face. 'How dare you use me to punish her. Do you remember what you said at Bosluis,' she went on. 'You said "hate corrodes". You were right. You're corroded.'

Kurt's eyes were cold as he turned away.

'Anna, Anna,' she heard André's voice from the dining-room. 'Lunch is getting cold.'

She went in, avoiding Madeleine's spaniel-like eyes. 'Kurt's in the garden,' she said.

'Oh really! Tch!' André went to fetch him.

When he returned with Kurt a few minutes later he poured the wine and picked up his glass.

'A Merry Christmas to one and all,' he said.

Anna and Kurt avoided each other for the next few weeks although the weekly business meetings were essential and embarrassing. Towards the end of January Kurt took Madeleine and a pale-faced Paul to their new home in Constantia and Anna sent the boy's pony after him in a horse box. To hell with them both. They could damn well look after it.

It was midnight when Kurt telephoned her. 'I hold you

304

responsible for this, Anna.' He sounded almost incoherent with rage.

'What are you talking about?'

'Sending that damned horse. I told you I didn't want it.'

'You have a field next to the house. Good God, you've even got stables,' she exploded.

'Paul's run away with the horse. If he's killed you'll have it on your conscience.'

Anna gasped. What if Paul met with an accident, or worse? He could not even call for help. 'It's your fault,' she blurted out. 'You knew he didn't want to leave here.' Then she pulled herself together. 'When did he leave?' she asked.

'I don't know. Some time after he went to bed. I heard a noise in the night and looked in his room, but it was empty. Then I got the idea that he might be sleeping the stable, but the horse had gone, too, with the saddle.

'He'll be thrown under a car, or murdered more likely,' his voice went on gloomily. 'Imagine a small child wandering around in the middle of the night in this country.'

'I don't think you realize just how good a horseman Paul is,' she said.

'At eight?' Sarcastically.

'Yes,' she said flatly. 'Have you called the police?'

'Of course I have.'

Anna replaced the receiver. Paul was coming home. He was more determined than Kurt had realized. Her small flicker of triumph was replaced with fear. Which way would he come? she wondered. Should she go out to look for him? Impossible in the dark. 'Dear God, just let him be all right,' she murmured.

She began to pace the hallway. At least it was summer.

It was five o'clock. Anna and André were sitting on the steps of Fontainebleu watching the sky lighten. Anna had hired a plane from the crop sprayers. The pilots would take off as soon as it was light.

Jan came out with a Thermos of coffee and two mugs. He

had been up with them for most of the night for he had seen the lights and come to investigate. Strangely enough it was Jan's words that comforted her the most. 'Paul's not like other boys; he's tough,' he had told her.

'Oh Pa, I've never known a longer night,' Anna said, resting her cheek on her father's shoulder. 'He's like my own son,' she began.

'It's only thirty miles as the crow flies,' André said. 'But I reckon he'll have about forty miles altogether. He should make four miles an hour. He won't push that pony of his. If you take a look through these binoculars you can see almost to the village.'

Half an hour later she saw him riding along the side of the road, a bag slung over his shoulder.

'It's him,' she said and passed the binoculars. She sighed with relief, stood up and stretched. 'I'll go get him,' she said.

'No, don't do that. He's OK. Doesn't even look tired,' André said. 'He's got this far under his own steam, let him do it himself. Go and make him some breakfast.'

'You know something strange,' André said when Anna returned. 'I could swear he's talking to his horse. Take a look.'

When Paul cantered up the driveway with a flourish he found André and Anna sitting on the steps with coffee and toasted sandwiches.

'Welcome back, my boy,' André said. 'I'm glad to see you're safe. It was very naughty of you. These are dangerous parts at night.'

Paul shot him a contemptuous look.

Anna was too relieved to speak.

'Well, while you tuck into breakfast I'll get on the telephone to cancel the aircraft and tell the police. I guess I'd better let Kurt know, too.'

Paul refused to go to bed until he had groomed his horse, and Anna managed to persuade Kurt to let Paul stay for a few days.

When Paul was sleeping, Anna called the twins to her study. 'I think Paul was talking to his horse. Have you heard him talking?'

They looked away, obviously ill-at-ease. 'We're not allowed to tell tales,' Acker said eventually.

'It's not wrong to try to help a friend,' Anna said severely, but decided not to press them.

Later that day, when Acker was out with André, Katie sidled into the study. 'If I tell you a secret, Mommy, will you swear not to tell Kurt?'

'No,' Anna said.

She pouted. Eventually she said in a stage whisper: 'Paul's been talking for ages and do you know what he told us? Paul's not Auntie Madeleine's son at all. His mother's dead and his father, too. The Germans hung them. Like this.' She twisted her neck, rolled her eyes and stuck out her tongue.

'Don't do that, Katie!' Sharply. 'Who told you this?'

'Paul, of course. They hung them because they were Jewish.'

Anna smothered a cry. 'Dear God, what terrible things children know nowadays.'

'You see,' she explained to Kurt the next day in the office. 'If he's not Madeleine's son then he's not Gunther's either and you can stop hating him. If you don't want him, I assure you I do, but we can't let him carry on like this. It must all come out in the open.'

'I'll have it out with Madeleine,' Kurt said.

Kurt let Paul stay for a while and during that time the boy began to speak naturally, without a trace of an accent. He grew rapidly and his frame began to widen, but Kurt and Madeleine decided to enrol Paul in a college. He was to be a boarder and return to Constantia for the holidays.

Paul was depressed and so was Anna, but she promised to look after his pony and to persuade Madeleine to let him spend some of his holidays at Fontainebleu.

After Paul left there seemed to be another empty gap in the house and Anna missed him more than she had thought possible.

32

It was the twins' eighth birthday, but instead of playing Katie was practising her music and singing. She had talent, there was no doubt about that, but no one could understand what drove her to practise for hours until she was too tired to eat.

Katie was at an age when she felt herself the pivot of her world and if something went wrong then surely she was the culprit. Her beloved father had left home and it was her fault. She was not sure of the crime she had committed that had caused his leaving, but it was she alone who could get him back.

She began to dress with care, brushing her hair until it gleamed, wasting hours at the mirror, and the rest of her time was spent at the piano. She became pale and her eyes looked even larger.

'It can't be helped,' Anna would say to André. 'She's obviously a perfectionist.'

Weekends when Simon arrived, Katie would lead him to the music room and sing and play her latest piece.

Later she would ask: 'Are you staying this weekend, Daddy?'

Invariably he would answer, 'Not this time, Katie; too much work to do.'

She would turn away to hide the disappointment on her face.

On her birthday she practised for two hours, singing the same song over and over again until Anna could no longer bear it. Besides, Simon was late for lunch and there was no point in waiting. With a deep sense of disappointment Anna

308

called the twins to the table.

Not long afterwards she heard Simon's voice booming through the hall. 'Katie, Acker.'

Katie was up in a trice, knocking her chair against the wall, dropping her fork on the floor as she raced round the table and into her father's arms.

Anna glanced at Acker. Why was he not there, too? But he did not look rejected or withdrawn. He put down his fork and stood up.

'Hi, Dad, how's it going at the docks?'

Anna leaned back and took a deep breath. In spite of the break Simon and the twins were the best of friends, she decided.

She was unaware that Acker viewed his father with reserve, for he was an observant boy, watching everything, saying little, and he sensed the unhappiness which his mother tried to conceal. He had often seen her eyes light up at the sound of Simon's car, only to have her hopes dashed, for he only came to fetch the children. Usually Acker stayed with Anna, not wishing to leave her alone, and his excuse was the farm, for there was always something vital to be done with André. He was an independent boy, hard-headed, self-contained, a replica of his father and, like Simon, once he had made up his mind it was difficult to influence him.

Katie, however, would sail off triumphantly on Simon's shoulders, red hair streaming in the sun, eyes brimful of happiness.

Today she was looking downcast as she returned to the table, leading her father.

'You forgot,' she said peevishly after a while.

'Forgot what?'

'You should know what.'

'No,' he said feigning ignorance.

'Dad's teasing you, silly,' Acker said.

Her face lit up.

Why must Simon always tease? Anna thought resentfully, but the twins seemed to love him just the same.

They finished their lunch and Simon took them to the

courtyard and wished them happy birthday solemnly. Their presents were two bicycles and for the next hour Simon ran around the courtyard teaching them to balance.

Katie was thrilled. Her hero was staying for the weekend. As usual Simon was only too happy to spend all his time with the twins, listening to Katie singing, helping Acker school his horse, and that night he read them stories until they fell asleep.

If only he could be with the children always, he thought, as he put the book down and smoothed the bedclothes, but he felt an interloper here, little better than a bum, free-loading meals and accommodation. He knew how much Katie loved him to stay for weekends, but he had done so only because it was the twins' birthday. One day he would be successful, and only then would he be able to endure his formidable wife.

After dinner he seemed embarrassed to be alone with Anna. As soon as the twins went to sleep he began to yawn and complain how little sleep he had nowadays. Then he went off to the east wing where, he said, Flora had made up a bed.

Sitting alone on the balcony Anna felt close to hating him. For the first time she began to toy with the idea of divorce. What was the point in wasting the rest of their lives? Simon had returned from the war a stranger. He was so cool and reserved, always ready to see the worst side of anything she did or said.

She now saw that he was essentially a simple man who viewed life in terms of black and white. To him there were two types of women – good and bad. The things she had done had turned her into a bad woman in his eyes and once cast in this role her mistakes and faults were used to reinforce his image of her, while her virtues were ignored.

Tonight she could not stand being alone. Bad enough when he was working, but now that he was home ... Feeling that she must talk to him Anna hurried to his room.

When she knocked at the door there was no answer so she walked in. As usual Simon was sleeping naked, blankets thrown on the floor, curtains open so that the moonlight streamed in. He did not stir as she approached the bed.

310

What if she were to creep in beside him? The longer she stood there, the more it seemed like a good idea. She took off her clothes and slipped into bed.

At first he did not stir, but as she stroked him, his desire, which was purely physical, began to intrude on his deep sleep. He groaned, rolled over and flung one arm over her.

'Anna?'

She pressed closer against him. Still afraid, her hand began to stroke his chest.

He turned his head and opened his eyes. How strange she looked.

'Anna, why are you doing this?'

'Married people sometimes do,' she whispered. 'I want to be loved,' she went on. 'I know you won't believe me, but I miss you.'

'Why now? Why not before, when I needed you?'

'Let's start again,' she murmured.

He sighed, closed his eyes and pulled her close to him.

Why is he closing his eyes? she wondered. Is the sight of me so hateful? He's doing this out of duty, not because he wants to. There was none of the old passion that used to leave him gasping with desire. She felt horribly ashamed and awkward.

'I want you to want me,' she said miserably.

'Then don't lie there like a log of wood,' he said irritably.

She froze inside. If she could only feel something she would be happy, but as usual there was nothing. Only numbness.

She flung her arms around his neck and murmured, 'I love you.'

'It doesn't feel like it,' he replied.

She gasped and moved her hips, fooling no one.

Simon gave up eventually and came and instead of falling asleep, lay staring at the ceiling.

'Did you come?'

'No, I'm sorry.'

'Don't apologize. Do you ever?'

'Occasionally.'

'With Kurt?'

'Stop it,' she hissed.

'Answer me.' Quietly.

'Except for the morning you came home, I haven't come for seven years,' she said, avoiding a direct answer.

'Jesus!'

After that he lay thinking. She doesn't want me. She doesn't want anyone. She's frigid by nature. Trying to control me. When all else failed women could always fall back on sex and they did so without a moment's hesitation.

'It's not the same any more, Anna,' he said after a while. 'Whatever we had it's gone. I want you to divorce me.'

She sat up and began sobbing quietly. 'What a cruel way to behave. To make love and then to ask for a divorce. Just like that. Boom-bam. Straight afterwards.'

She climbed out of bed and stumbled into her clothes.

'Never!' she said. 'Never! Not if you plead for fifty years. You'll never get a divorce.'

She went out, slamming the door, and the next day remained in her room pretending she had a headache.

33

No one could fail to see the sign on the dining room door for the boys had taken a sheet of cardboard and scrawled in thick charcoal: '*Jews Forbidden*' and underneath '*Juden Verboten. By Order – The Fuhrer.*' It was stuck to the door with four pieces of chewing gum, and two boys from Class I were keeping cave in the corridor in case a master should pass.

It was Paul's third month at school and during that time he had not made a friend. He kept himself apart and committed the unforgivable sin of trying hard at his lessons and coming top in arithmetic. But it was his passion for food which prevented him from fitting in and earned him the nickname of 'Piggy', or as an alternative 'Jewish Pig'. Although he ate little at meals he would carefully wrap bread, or a piece of meat, in his handkerchief and store it in the dormitory. Bits of mouldy bread were always being found by the housekeeper who moaned bitterly. Twice he had been caught red-handed in the kitchen and he had taken to hanging around the tuckshop after hours. At first the masters expressed concern and patience, but Paul was a difficult boy to love and eventually they gave up and ignored him.

Paul walked along the corridor to the dining-room feeling not so much hungry as permanently unsatisfied, and consequently he was looking forward to lunch. Then he saw the sign hanging in the doorway and for a second he paused, pulling up his socks to give him time to consider. It could not be meant for anyone else since Paul was the only Jewish boy in the school. It was one of many practical jokes they had played on him.

This time, however, a variety of images flashed through his mind, more feelings than thoughts, as memories of degradation were recalled by that crude sign written in German.

He was late. The headmaster walked in, followed by the remainder of the staff in strict pecking order. The boys shuffled to their feet and stood waiting for grace, but the headmaster glanced irritably towards Paul. 'Come along Paul, take your place please.'

There was a gasp as Paul scrambled on to his chair and stood on the table. He held up the notice for the headmaster to read and one or two boys made a grab for it, but suddenly they froze.

Paul had no conscious action worked out, he only knew that this was filth being shovelled at him and he, in turn, must shovel filth on their gesture – like against like. The boys gasped and stood open-mouthed while urine splashed over the tablecloth, dripped on to chairs, sprayed the boys, drenched the bread plates.

Then there was pandemonium. Shouts of rage from masters, glee from the boys who, jumping back, knocked over chairs, making it more difficult to reach the villain. Paul, who had neglected to empty his bladder before lunch, felt a tremendous outrush of tension as he hit back for the first time in his life. Turning with a triumphant yell, he sprayed the boys and the masters, who retreated to a safe distance until he ran out of ammunition.

Anna and Kurt were meeting in the office when the call came from the headmaster.

'It's the most disgraceful behaviour that I have seen in thirty years at this school. The boy's mad. Take him away and get him the right treatment. We should never have accepted him, knowing his background.'

'It's all your fault,' Anna stormed at Kurt. 'You had no right to send him to school. I told you so.'

'Something or someone must have provoked the boy,' Kurt said, wondering why he should feel obliged to defend the boy.

'I'll fetch him myself,' Anna insisted.

314

The headmaster was waiting in his study, an irate and anxious man. 'If this should get back to the parents,' he kept repeating. 'There'll be an inquiry. My dear Mrs van Achtenburgh, Paul needs psychiatric care. I believe they have excellent facilities at Valkenburg.'

Paul was sitting on the end of his bed, fully dressed and ready to leave with his suitcase beside him.

'Paul, why did you do it?' Anna appealed to him, but he would not answer.

Absurd, Anna thought, looking at the starkness of the room, ten iron bedsteads with curtains pulled back for the night. Nine heads turned her way, eyes gleaming with suppressed amusement.

Paul picked up his case. 'Dirty pisspot,' one of the boys hissed as they left.

They walked along the corridor and heard bare feet on the linoleum. Anna turned to see a small, freckle-faced boy with soft brown eyes.

'Please, Ma'am, I'm Rodney, Ma'am.'

'Yes, Rodney?'

'I want to say I'm sorry, Ma'am.'

'Sorry for what, Rodney?'

'We put a sign up saying Jews Forbidden, outside the dining room. Everyone knows how Paul likes food.' Suddenly he burst into giggles and struggled to control himself. 'He put the sign on the table and he ...' Rodney burst out laughing again.

'Where's the sign?' Anna asked.

'The headmaster took it. I saw him burning it.'

'Thank you, Rodney. I accept your apology,' Anna said. 'But that was a very bad thing to do.'

'Yes, Ma'am.' He stood there looking grave.

Two minutes later Anna was back in the headmaster's office. 'There's no question of your expelling Paul,' she said. 'I am removing him until I receive your written apology. Furthermore I shall bring up the matter of anti-semitism with the board.'

'Quite unnecessary. Just a childish prank, I assure you.'

Anna was adamant and there was little point in taking on Mrs van Achtenburgh-Smit. The headmaster knew of her reputation.

'I want you to know that I'm glad you fought back, Paul,' Anna told him on the drive to Fontainebleu. 'Your method was a little unusual, but effective, let's face it.'

She felt a small hand grasping hers.

34

The following spring, almost a year since Kurt had brought his family back to Fontainebleu, disaster struck both the Friedlands and the van Achtenburghs. André awoke one night with a desire to pass water and found that he was unable to do so. By noon he was in agony, but not wanting to cause a fuss he called Jacob to drive him to the doctor. Acker, a sensitive and perceptive boy, sensed that his Grandpa was frightened and insisted on going with him. After a brief examination, the doctor sent André to the casualty ward of Bellville's general hospital where, he said, they would examine him properly and administer a catheter.

Acker sat beside André in the back of the car, holding his hand. At eight he knew he was too old for holding hands, but he felt his responsibilities keenly. Besides, who else was there? Mama was away on business as usual and Katie was frivolous, as girls always were.

For two hours, Acker sat outside the curtained cubicle and afterwards followed his Grandpa as he was wheeled to the urology ward and there he stayed, refusing to leave, until André called the sister to fetch Jacob from the car park to drive the boy home.

Early the following morning Anna and Acker returned to the hospital, but André was in the operating theatre.

'Your father had a growth we removed half an hour ago,' the doctor told Anna after a long wait. 'Don't worry, he'll be fine. You'll be able to take him home in a few days.'

'A growth?' Anna queried. 'Surely not malignant?'

'Tests will tell,' the doctor answered evasively.

Five days later Anna was taken to the professor of the department who told her that André had cancer of the prostate. 'Don't worry, we've removed the growth. He'll be fine. Another ten years ahead of him,' the doctor said.

'Money's no object,' Anna began. 'Is there anything that can be done to cure cancer?'

The doctor smiled sadly. 'We can arrest it, we believe, but not cure it. I'm sorry, there's nothing more we can do.' He turned away, unwilling to face her grief and Anna took Acker's hand, feeling that the main pivot of her world had come adrift.

A week later they took André home and within weeks he had forgotten about the operation and appeared to have recovered his former health and vigour. Once again he went riding with Acker and even invited a neighbouring widow to the theatre several times.

For the Friedlands disaster arrived in a most embarrassing manner, for after a day spent at Fontainebleu Kurt noticed Madeleine was wearing Anna's Piaget watch. He knew it well enough for he had bought it for her twenty-fifth birthday during the war.

'Ag! What a fool I am, I took the wrong one. I was helping Anna in the kitchen,' Madeleine said. The watch was sent back with a note of apology and Anna spent the day searching unsuccessfully for Madeleine's watch, but feeling puzzled because hers had been left on her dressing table.

After this Madeleine's bedroom began to get crowded with gloves too large for her; boxes of white sewing cotton, although she did not sew; silk scarves; necklaces; and a week later, when she was arrested for shoplifting, Kurt's hidden fears were realized.

It was a simple matter to have Madeleine released. Kurt paid for the goods, bribed the store manager and tried to persuade Madeleine to see a psychiatrist. The problem was taken out of his hands a week later at the races when Madeleine stole a mink coat belonging to the wife of a well-known trainer. Madeleine was released on bail and Anna set off one Friday afternoon to see the woman, whom she had met once or twice. How satisfying it was to sit and play God. Neither of them liked Madeleine and finally Anna persuaded her to discuss the theft with Kurt and agree to drop charges on condition Madeleine entered a psychiatric clinic for observation and treatment.

Anna drove home feeling pleased that she had solved the problem in a manner that was beneficial for everyone, not the least herself, but satisfaction fled when she saw Simon's car parked in the courtyard.

The blood surged to her face, her eyes watered as she rushed into the house.

'Where's Simon?' she asked André who was sitting on the *stoep*.

He watched her compassionately. 'Down in the kraal with Acker. He's come to take the children for the weekend.'

Curbing her dismay she rushed down to the kraal. Simon was helping Acker to groom his pony.

'Hello, Anna.' He straightened and gave her a cool smile. His shirt, buttonless, fell open, revealing red hairs curling on his chest. The sheer, overpowering maleness of him struck her like a blow in the stomach.

'Have you come for the weekend?' she faltered.

'No,' he said gravely. 'I came to fetch the twins.'

'Oh, well, I don't think you should take them away from Paul. He's a lonely boy, he needs their company. After all he's just come back from school.' She smiled artfully. 'Rather stay here, it would be so pleasant to have you for the weekend.'

'No,' he said firmly. 'If it's inconvenient I'll leave them.'

She fled to the house, but heard footsteps running behind her. 'Can't we go, please, Mummy. Please!' Katie looked as if her heart would break at such a disappointment.

'Of course you can go,' she said, swallowing the hurt aching in her throat.

Anna endured the lonely weekend by taking Paul swimming and riding. It was just one of many lonely weekends the two of them spent together. During the day Anna would throw herself into the absorbing task of watching

319

Paul grow and learn, but one of the hardest lessons to teach him was to be happy.

At night, she would try for an hour or two to dismiss her fears, her loneliness, her guilt and sense of failure and for a while she would succeed, but after Paul was put to bed and André was sleeping she would prowl around the lounge, walk outside, see the lights of Stellenbosch twinkling in the distance, hear the occasional car pass, the whoosh of its tyres on the road a sudden comfort, leaving her twice as lonely in the silence that followed its passing. Then suddenly she would sense the reality of the planet revolving in space, the pitifully thin atmosphere that enclosed her and safeguarded the human condition, the emptiness beyond. She could almost feel the earth revolving. Her feet were resting on the soil; the rest of her stretched out towards an alien world; there was nothing between her and the endless vacuum of space. How frail our human security, how transient the air and earth, how cruel a plan that gave each one an evanescent glow of life; a sense of immortality.

Eventually she would succumb to her fears and, fumbling in her handbag for her tranquillizers, always handy, she would swallow one precious capsule with a glass of neat whisky.

Six hours' oblivion. A priceless pearl!

Madeleine was voluntarily committed to the Alphen clinic outside Cape Town the following week. Kurt took her to a private ward and left her. She stood puzzled and depressed in the joyless room. Two days later she had a nervous breakdown and Kurt was summoned to see Doctor George Warring, head of the clinic. The interview was traumatic for Kurt.

'I can't believe,' the doctor said, pointing his finger at Kurt, 'that a man as intelligent as yourself could allow this poor woman to go straight into the business of living without psychiatric help after five years in a camp.'

'I didn't know there was anything wrong with her,' Kurt mumbled.

'What about this child, Paul? You say she pretended it was her own. Didn't that tell you something?'

'No,' Kurt answered angrily. 'You see they gave priority to women with children, particularly maimed children, and she was desperate to get to the West. Madeleine is one of the world's survivors.'

The doctor watched him shrewdly. 'In many cases, people who steal, and particularly women, are really taking symbols that represent something they need badly, but are unable to get, like love or security. Do you think your wife lacks love?'

Kurt's eyes glinted angrily. 'Why ask me? You're the shrink,' he said.

35

It was late January, the south-easter had dropped the previous evening and the docks were sweltering. Simon was in his office when the mail arrived and when he saw the bank envelope his hand shook so much he could hardly open it. His fate hung in the balance. Inside was a death sentence or a reprieve.

They had started the business a year ago, and for the first few months they had been delighted with their progress, for there was no shortage of work and they were making a profit. It was over-rapid expansion that had caused the problems, for they soon found they needed more equipment and more labour. Their wage bill soared and so did their paint bill, for which they had to pay in thirty days, whereas shipping companies often paid as late as a hundred and twenty days. Most of their equipment was bought on hire purchase and the repayments were a burden that the business could hardly sustain.

Simon endured sleepless nights, particularly before pay day, and towards the end of November he had approached the bank for a long-term loan. The manager had told him to prepare a cash flow budget for the next two years and an anticipated profit and loss sheet for the next five. After many failures he and Otto finally succeeded in doing this and from it they discovered that they would need twenty thousand pounds to survive the next two years. After that most of the equipment would be paid and they would have a very profitable business.

Since then Simon had lost weight as he worried about the loan. Of all the things he had done – whaling, farming, being torpedoed in the war – he had never experienced anything quite as destructive as business. He wondered why he had imagined businessmen to be ninnies. He was desperate for the loan, desperate to succeed.

Now he held the letter in his hand. Damn it, they had taken long enough to reply, he thought as he drew out the sheet. His eyes skimmed through the typed message. The board had decided to lend them five thousand pounds, a quarter of what they needed. It would get them through for a while, but then?

That night Otto and Simon's weekly business meeting was a sombre affair, for the five thousand pounds would stop the gap, but only for six months.

Finally it was Otto who thought of a solution. They would start a separate salvage company. They had some of the equipment, they would need more, but the bank loan would be enough for a boat, air pump, diving suits and divers' wages for several months. They would go for one of the many prizes littered around the coast, and by the end of the year earn enough through salvage to finance the service business.

Simon was unwilling to take the gamble.

'All right, I admit it's a bit of a gamble,' Otto retorted, 'but that's what business is about. If we pull it off we could make enough out of a single salvage operation to pull us out of the shit.'

It was one in the morning before Simon agreed, and then only on condition they obtain a contract for the salvage and that he inspect the site himself before investing in diving equipment.

While Simon continued with servicing and painting ships, Otto went looking for salvage contracts and before long he found a promising one: the *George M. Livranos* which had sunk off Mouille Point lighthouse and scattered its three thousand tons of nickel cargo worth half a million pounds over the ocean bed. Lloyds had already put out an open tender for five thousand pounds.

'An easy job,' Otto assured him. 'It's not more than two hundred yards off-shore.'

'If it's so damned easy,' Simon grumbled, 'how come it's been lying there all this time?'

'Who else is there besides us?' Otto said grinning.

Next morning at dawn they took the longboat and set off from Number Five Wharf, past the colony of seals flapping lazily in the harbour, and rounded the jetty into the open sea. They chugged past rocky outcrops towards Mouille Point lighthouse where the wreck was situated.

They dropped anchor, four hundred yards off-shore and Otto hung over the edge of the boat, looking into the crystal-clear water. It was a beautiful day and the water rippled gently into the narrow mouth of Three Anchor Bay not far off. Around them seaweed rose and fell in the swell.

Simon knew the sea intimately. Instinctively he felt that this would be more difficult than Otto predicted. It was a particularly dangerous stretch of coastline, where at least a dozen wrecks from recent times lay just below the surface. The rocks stretched up almost to the surface and far out to sea, and without warning the south-easter could whip the bay into a frenzy within minutes. The backwash in this area was particularly strong and the bay was thick was gigantic fronds of seaweed, like huge banana plants, limiting visibility, and this would hamper the search.

Otto was fighting to control rising panic as he watched Simon lazily donning the scuba gear. There had been plenty of opportunities to dive in his father's salvage business and he had received a thorough theoretical training, until they found out about his claustrophobia. When the water closed over his head panic would send him kicking blindly to the surface. Now his mouth was dry, palms sweating. He turned away so that Simon would not notice and studied the coastline.

'Let's split up,' Simon said. 'I'll go for the wreck and you have a look round for the nickel.' He watched Otto strangely. 'Or hang on there, if you like, till I get back,' he added. Adjusting his mask he swung over the edge of the boat and disappeared. Otto watched his dark shape, looking twice as large as life, disappear into the tangle of seaweed.

There was plenty of nickel scattered over the seabed, lying in piles amongst the rocks. Simon swam north, noting that the ingots were scattered hundreds of yards away from the supposed site of the wreck. With a gang of black divers who would work, the job would be finished in a few months, but there were no black divers available and with one diver God knows how long it would take. He was filled with foreboding as he turned and swam back to the wreck. He found it more or less as it had been described to him by local skin divers, impaled on a high rocky outcrop, lying sideways with a gaping hole in the hull. There was little left of the Greek freighter and most of the barnacle-encrusted hulk was almost indistinguishable from the rocks. Underneath were signs of a much older wreck. He turned and slowly swam back to the boat.

Otto was crouched on the seabed fighting wave after wave of nausea and struggling to keep control. Fear enveloped him like a fog; fear of the unknown; fear of an icy death in an alien world; fear of sharks and of suffocation. As if in answer to his fears a long grey shape came nosing its way amongst the rocks and seaweed. It approached cautiously. Otto took his knife from his belt, but three metres away the shark veered off and shot into the silvery, dancing waters above. Still Otto sat on and eventually returned to the boat, forcing himself to go slowly. Seconds later he was panting as he hung over the side.

'For Christ's sake,' Simon said. 'What's got into you?'

'A shark,' Otto said clambering over the side.

'At this temperature they're not a danger,' Simon said. 'It's too cold, man, besides there's so many seals around.'

But Otto was still gasping for breath. 'God, it's eerie down there,' he said. 'Great towering rocks, dirty great shadows, huge seaweed. Ugh!'

'Come off it, Otto, you've been down enough times. You were brought up in salvage.'

Otto nodded and shook himself like a wet dog. 'It's different in England,' he lied.

'It's not going to be as easy as you imagine,' Simon said later when they were sitting in the office. 'The backwash is tremendous. On rough days it can chuck a diver a hundred yards and bash him to bits on the rocks. That's why the nickel is spread all over the place up to a kilometre away. We'll be lucky to find half of it. We'll only be able to dive on calm days.'

'Well, we've got to take it on,' Otto persisted. 'If we get half of it we're well off.'

Simon shrugged. 'I'm willing if you are. It's a good chance, but we need a professional diver.'

'I know one,' Otto said quickly. 'Name is Jim Perry. Worked with my father's outfit couple of times and he's out here now, doing odd jobs in the docks at Port Elizabeth.'

'What's he doing here?' Simon asked curiously. 'If he's any good, you'd think he'd be where the action is.'

'He came to survey that wreck past Durban that's supposed to be full of treasure. The deal fell through but he liked it here. Found a job stevedoring.'

That night the partners worked late, estimating the probable cost of equipment, diver, linesman and boys, the diving gear, the pumps, the pipes and another sturdy longboat. They called their new company Table Bay Salvage.

36

'Why don't you visit Madeleine?' André suggested one morning at breakfast when Anna announced that she was going to the office to inspect the balance sheet. 'It's almost on the way.' He shot her a shrewd glance. 'She's been in that place for four months. Don't you think you should ask if she wants to see Paul?'

'Does Paul want to see her?' Anna replied defensively, watching the children through the window. The boys were racing round the paddock on their ponies while Katie hung over the fence.

'You could ask?'

'Oh, Pa,' Anna grumbled.

She drove to the clinic with mixed feelings. In the four months since Madeleine had been in hospital Kurt had become a different man, eyes once again gleaming, his sense of humour returning, and Anna herself, who was no hypocrite, admitted that she hated Madeleine and was in no hurry to see her recover.

Half an hour later, she could not repress a surge of satisfaction, for clearly Madeleine was no longer a threat; just a sad woman with dirty fingernails and two inches of mousy hair above the straggling ash-blonde wisps, listlessly staring out of the window. Had she ever been beautiful, or gay? Drab was the word that came to Anna's mind.

The drab eyes stared at her resentfully. 'Now you have Kurt and Paul to yourself. I expect you feel happier.' The drab face took an expression of dislike, startling Anna who stood up and shook her head vehemently.

'You mustn't say things like that,' she said. 'It's – it's mad.'

'Do you know what you remind me of?' The drab mouth kept moving while drab sounds thrust at Anna. 'A queen bee, surrounded by your workers and drones.'

'You're crazy,' Anna said. 'Look at you. Anyone can see you're crazy and you're saying crazy things. I shan't bring Paul to see you, not until you're better and I can see that's going to take a long time.'

She rushed out, blocking her ears to the sound of laughter.

Kurt was pleased Anna had visited Madeleine. How was she? he wanted to know.

'Oh, as fine as can be expected,' Anna said vaguely.

'Did she seem all right to you?'

'Well, no, not really. Quite mad in fact.'

'Maybe it's me that's crazy,' Kurt said, 'but I can't help thinking that this is too terrible a punishment.'

'She's being treated, not punished.'

'I wonder if I should take her away.' Kurt stood up and stared sadly at Anna.

'You don't have the right to make that choice, Kurt,' Anna answered. 'Leave her where she is.'

Shortly afterwards the accountants arrived and they examined the books. At least on paper they were millionaires, for they had added six companies to the group since the war's end: a spares division for ships' engines; the long coveted Imperial Dairy; a cartage contractor whom they had been using a great deal and a rival poultry farm. During the past year the group had made two hundred thousand pounds' profit before tax, and increasing its net asset value to two million pounds.

'This deserves a lunch. We must celebrate. Don't you think so, my dear?' Kurt asked, looking pleased.

Anna nodded and put on her gloves. She could not help wondering why Kurt gained so much satisfaction out of the business while she gained so little. Admittedly, she worked as hard as he did, but however much money she made she was still left with an empty feeling.

'What is it?' Kurt asked, putting one hand on her shoulder.

'Nothing. Do you know what I'd like?' she said on impulse. 'I'd like to go to that old Portuguese café on the docks where they have such super shellfish. Is it still there?'

'Of course. I still eat there sometimes. Don't you want to go somewhere better?'

'I just feel like it. Do you mind?'

He smiled. 'You find you're a millionaire so you want to eat with the deckhands. It figures.'

They chose a table in the corner and Anna sat with her back to the wall where she could watch the café filling with noisy seamen and fishermen and beyond them, through the glass shop front, the busy wharf where fishing boats were moored.

Today there were oysters, calamari, grilled crayfish, prawns. Kurt ordered a small plate of smoked salmon.

Watching him, Anna could guess why, for Kurt still looked like a fashionplate. He wore his clothes superbly and his figure was still slender and muscular. She knew he spent an hour in the gym every day. He had turned forty a week ago and it showed, she thought treacherously. His blond hair was fading, his face was lined. Only his eyes were unchanged, those clever, calculating eyes that missed nothing. There was something about his mouth which upset her; it had become a thin line across his face.

If I had to tell Kurt his fortune, she thought inconsequentially, I would say that he had gained all the things which are unimportant and missed all that he cared about. Momentarily she felt guilty. She turned her attention to the food and ordered a gigantic platter for one, containing everything, with ice-cold Portuguese wine. She had no problems with dieting, perhaps because of the farm work, she thought, whereas Kurt sat at his desk most of the time.

Anna was halfway through her meal and drowsy from the wine when she saw the door open and Simon standing framed in the entrance. For a moment her face lit up with pleasure and then she saw that he was beckoning someone. He ushered

329

in a blonde woman, pale skin, long straggly hair, big dreamy eyes peering myopically around. Anna froze, mouth open, too horrified to look away.

Kurt glanced over his shoulder and then reached out and pressed her hand. 'Let's ignore them, shall we?'

But from then on lunch was a nightmare as Anna talked too fast and too loud about nothing in particular and all the time thinking: So that's why he wanted a divorce. Damn him! She had guessed who Edwina was. Simon had spent his leaves with the Tenwicks – no wonder he had returned a stranger. Now she understood Simon's coldness. All her loneliness and humiliation were suddenly attributed to this insipid young woman.

Simon was not splashing out himself, she noticed. They ordered two Cokes, fish and chips for Simon and she chose frikadels with mashed potatoes. It seemed that this was a daily affair and not a special occasion.

How poorly dressed she was, Anna noted with satisfaction. Yet there was something about her blue eyes and the expression on her face which showed a certain class 'If I had to describe her in one word,' she suddenly said aloud, 'I would choose "refined".'

'Forget her, can't you?' Kurt was annoyed. He had something important to say to Anna and he wished he had chosen another restaurant.

Anna was becoming so strange lately, Kurt thought, looking for slights where none existed. She was short-tempered, particularly when she did not get her own way, and she would not be pleased at his news.

'Anna,' he said. Reaching forward he took her hand. 'I want to thank you for all you have done for Paul.'

'Don't thank me,' she said, pulling her hand away. 'He's like my own son.' In fact, she thought guiltily, he was so much closer than her own son. Acker was a strange boy, independent, observant, wise beyond his years, and he went his own way. She had no influence over him at all, but Paul was different. Paul clung to her, made her feel like a real mother. With Acker she felt like a very temporary guardian.

Kurt was speaking. Her mind registered alarm although she had not consciously heard what he said.

'What did you say?'

'I said, all the more praiseworthy, my dear, considering that he is not your son.'

'Not yours either,' she said too quickly. 'God knows who his parents were.'

'Jewish martyrs,' he said sombrely.

She flashed a glance of sudden dislike. When Kurt was pompous he was irritating.

'Well, at least Paul is a very happy boy now, where he is,' she said defensively, sensing an unwelcome change.

'That's what I want to talk to you about. I've engaged a young woman to look after Paul on a full time basis. She is a particularly gifted young woman and thoroughly recommended by the rabbi. She has a degree in child psychology and she specializes in gifted children. We both know that Paul is far advanced mentally.'

'A hired hand cannot replace a mother,' she said, realizing her mistake too late. God knows she felt like his mother.

'Exactly.' He gave a theatrical sigh. 'We can but try our best and you, Anna, have been so kind.'

Here we go again, she thought. She felt an urge to start laughing: at Kurt and his clumsy efforts to disguise his cruelty; at Simon trying to play Big Daddy, a role for which he was particularly unsuited; at that silly woman gazing at him as if he was some sort of God. The entire man-woman tradition was such a bloody farce.

'Ha!' she said too loudly and smashed her fist on the table. A glass toppled, rolled, smashed on the floor. A few heads turned. One of them was Simon's. He flushed, called the waiter and left. Edwina seemed surprised at their hurried retreat.

Kurt was behaving as if she had stripped in public. Well, damn him and damn Simon.

'Show me a real man,' she said inconsequentially, 'and I'll behave like a real lady.'

'Anna, you've drunk too much. Never mind, it was a

celebration. It's not every day one becomes a millionaire.' He called for the bill. She noticed his tips were becoming meaner as he became richer.

37

The salvage operation began in May and by July the nickel ingots were piling up in the stockroom. The first ton brought in one hundred and eighty-six pounds. It was too good to be true, like finding money in the street. Simon and Otto were more optimistic now as they paid the cash into the bank. They began to look less haggard and even smiled occasionally, but from then on the weather worsened and recovering the nickel became hazardous. Nevertheless, during the first three months they had lost only nineteen working days. Not bad for winter, they thought.

Spring came, bringing the south-easterly gales which gathered their strength in the Antarctic and hit the southerly tip of Africa with all the ferocity they could muster; trees bowed before the gales, huge breakers mounted the sea wall and smashed over the beach road, flats and hotels were drenched with salt spray. Then the ships would lie at anchor, well out to sea, unable to enter or leave harbour.

For fourteen days they could not dive. Jim hung around the pubs restless and angry, hoping to work the next day. On the fifteenth day the wind fell and Capetonians awoke to a glorious spring morning, calm and crisp.

Otto and Jim were keen to get back to work and when Simon arrived at six a.m. they were stacking the boat.

'Hey, not so fast,' he warned. 'The gale's not over yet. You see those clouds on Table Mountain, that means the south-easter is on the way again. A bad one, too, by the look of things.'

'I've never seen anything quite as cock-eyed as the weather predictions in this country,' Otto told him. 'Everyone treats

333

Table Mountain like a big bloody weathercock.'

'That's what it is, mate,' Simon retorted. 'Normally I wouldn't give a damn if you want to get yourself caught in a storm, but with all our equipment on board, there's no way you can go.'

Simon went into the shed to clock in their labour.

'What d'you say, Perry? Looks like the finest day we've had for weeks. D'you think he's right about the wind coming back?'

'Search me,' Perry said. 'But I can't see what he's worried about. We're only ten minutes from harbour and if the worst comes to the worst, we could put into Three Anchor Bay within a minute.'

'Idiots!' Simon muttered when he saw the boat skimming across the calm harbour waters, with Otto, Jim, Tom, their linesman and two Xhosas. He'd half a mind to go after them, but that would make him late at dry dock.

About noon, when Simon was packing up, there was a sudden strong blast which sent the paint pots flying and knocked a ladder on top of a painter. The wind always began with one hell of a big bang and today it was worse than usual. Within five minutes they were coping with a Force Ten gale. Huge breakers splashed over the harbour wall. Damn! No hope of getting the Castle liner in on time; he might as well let the gangs go off early. Briefly he thought about Otto. They'd be on the way back by now, if they had any sense.

Five hundred yards from Mouille Point lighthouse, Otto, Tom and the Xhosas were hanging on as the longboat raced over thirty-foot breakers that had suddenly appeared from nowhere. It took the full force of the engine to keep the boat pointing out to sea, off the ragged, razor-sharp rocks obscured now by boiling foam.

We'll land up on the rocks, Otto thought desperately. What the hell was Perry playing at? They had signalled to him when the first gust blasted the boat and felt his answering tug on the life-rope, but Perry had not surfaced. Since then they had signalled twice.

'In another five minutes,' Otto told the linesman, 'we'll haul him up.' But he was loath to take the risk for if the airpipe twisted round a rock, Perry would suffocate. At the same time, if the ship foundered there was no hope for Perry. His life was dependent upon his rubber umbilical cord supplying air from the pump in the boat.

The Xhosas bailed out desperately as wave after wave splashed over the gunwale. The sea was a cauldron of bubbling froth, gigantic seaweed plants, like small trees torn out by the roots by the force of the water, were tossed in the air by hurtling breakers. The air was thick with ice-cold salt spray.

'Three pulls! Three pulls! I felt them,' the linesman yelled and began pulling Perry's liferope. The Xhosas rushed to his aid.

A helmet bobbed up thirty yards from the ship and on a rising wave they saw Perry floating like a corpse. 'Haul him in,' Otto yelled thinking: What the hell has he blown himself up for? The fool would have broken his neck if he'd come up under the boat.

Three of them pulled at the rope until Perry was bobbing like a bloated whale at the side of the boat. They nearly capsized getting him in, while Otto fought to control the boat, one moment so deep in the trough of the waves they could not see the lighthouse and the next hurtling up the next glittering slope of water, like a green glass mountain. On wavecrests they could see the breakers riding over the railings of the beachfront.

'We won't make it,' the linesman said. He was fumbling with the glass front of Perry's helmet.

'Hurry, damn you,' Otto yelled. 'Keep on pumping,' he screamed at the Xhosa who had left the pump to bale out. 'Take over,' Otto said to the linesman. 'Make for Three Anchor Bay. We'll never reach harbour.'

A second later Otto had unscrewed the facepiece. Perry was half unconscious and Otto removed the helmet and fumbled in the kitbag for a flask of brandy, which he poured between blue lips.

Perry choked, opened his eyes and said, 'Don't worry about

me. I'm all right. D'you think we'll make it?'

'Sure we'll make it. We'll put into the bay there. What happened to you? You took so long.'

'I got thrown.'

'You shouldn't blow yourself up, Perry. I've seen divers break their necks coming up under the boat.'

'No other way, mate.' He screwed up his face as a wave smashed over them. 'Here, Otto. Help me out of this damn gear, if the boat founders I'm a goner in this lot. Every time I got towards the boat I was thrown, one time the backwash took me three hundred yards. The swell down there is bloody awful,' he went on as Otto stripped off his heavy boots and began to unfasten the thick suit. 'It's suicide. I'll never go down there again as long as I live ...' He broke off as the longboat hurtled over another crest and for the few moments they were straddled with the outboard motor lifted from the water. The boat swung sideways in the swell.

'Get her round.' Otto grabbed the tiller and headed the boat to shore as another wave toppled over them.

'It's like a whirlpool down there,' Perry shouted, 'sucks you out by the feet. I was riding out to sea, feet first, expecting to be chopped to ribbons on those bloody rocks. You should've hauled me in sooner.'

'You didn't signal.'

''Course I signalled. All the bloody time. You couldn't feel it against the swell. Jesus, I thought I'd reached my last hour.' Suddenly he vomited over the side.

One of the Xhosas was shouting above the roar of the wind. 'Wrong way, baas. Wrong way.'

'D'you know where the rocks are?' Otto yelled.

The narrow opening to the bay was somewhere to starboard, but the rocks were obscured in the boiling surf. The Xhosa pointed, but at that moment a huge breaker, the largest yet, caught them up. For a brief, terrifying moment they seemed to be held in mid-air by a gigantic hand, the swell surged back and the boat landed with a shattering crack on the sand, beneath a concrete ledge in front of the beach huts.

For a few seconds they all sat stunned. Then Otto stood up.

336

'Tidy,' the linesman muttered, 'very tidy.'

'Well, that did us a good turn,' Otto said, wiping the sweat off his face. 'Home and dry. Anything lost?'

'Nothing, baas.'

'You all right, Perry?'

Perry was fighting the pain flooding his limbs, for as the numbness receded agony set in. His fingers were crushed where he had hung on to the rope and clutched at the rocks, nearly all the skin was gone and several bones were broken.

'Give him some more brandy,' Otto said. Perry's body was black and blue.

'Just bruises. Nothing broken except your fingers, by the look of things,' Otto told him, but Perry was swearing, making an ominous deep noise like an animal at bay and then he began to groan.

'We'll get you to a doctor,' Otto told him.

'I don't need a fucking doctor, I need a fucking drink,' he said. 'Here, you bastard, get that bloody brandy out before I swipe your fucking head off.'

The words came pouring out, torrents of abuse as Perry struggled against the pain and shock.

'I'm going back to England,' Perry told them that night in the pub where they were celebrating their safe return from the freak storm. 'You can stick your sunshine and your cheap booze. Back home I might reach old age.'

For days they tried to dissuade him while searching for a replacement, but Perry was determined and left on the next Castle boat. There was not another trained diver south of the Equator.

Anna was in the paddock helping the children school their horses, when Vera Mankowitz came to take Paul to Constantia. Anna had not expected her because Kurt had ducked the issue and left Vera to cope as best she could.

Anna watched the unappealing young woman lean over the paddock and wave. Earnestness was oozing out of her. Another enemy, Anna thought, but one she could easily dispose of. Certainly not in her class. She loved Paul as much as she loved her own children; she understood his fierce ambition to win at all costs; he was a survivor like herself.

How cruel of Kurt to take him away.

'Would you care to ride?' she asked Vera maliciously. For a moment she pictured this lump of lard balanced on a horse. She would simply slide off and melt away in the sun.

'I never learned, unfortunately,' she called out.

'Really. You don't ride? What a pity, Paul loves riding.'

'Perhaps he'll teach me,' the girl said smiling, and to Anna's annoyance Paul smiled back.

'Such a waste,' Anna went on. 'All those stables at Constantia and the land and no animals.'

'Paul can keep his pony and dogs and anything he likes.' Vera's brown eyes beamed behind thick steel-rimmed glasses. 'Can't you, Paul?' she called excitedly.

There was no answer.

'The trouble is,' Anna's voice sounded hard even to her, 'someone has to know how to look after them.'

'Well, if Paul can't look after his animals then he doesn't deserve to have them,' Vera added.

''Course I know how.'

'Will you teach me, Paul? I've never had a horse or a dog.'

Paul was very still. He looked Vera up and down curiously. Anna had warned him of Vera's engagement and he had expected someone much older, more like a school teacher. Not this plump, pimply woman with the thick-lensed glasses. There was something bookish about her. Her eyes glowed with an intellectual zeal. Compared with him she was a child, he decided. Paul felt very old, older than the twins, older than any boy in the school. He understood the games that grown-ups played, but was unwilling to become involved in them. He preferred simplicity, hated emotional involvement. He did not know the reason for this, but any attempt to breach his defences was defeated by withdrawal. If a woman tried to love him, or a child to make friends with him, they would seem sloppy to him, sickening even, and if they tried further, they became repulsive, like Madeleine. Only Anna had succeeded because she was hard and stern and only warm occasionally.

He had never thought this out, he did not understand that the war had left him too maimed to risk any further involvement. That was all buried deeper than his consciousness. All he knew was that friendship was sickening, mawkish, vomit-stuff. Vera was a simple woman with a good brain carrying a load of learning which she wanted to try out on him. He could have been a rat in an experimental laboratory; she posed no threat. She would not want involvement, only success.

'Maybe,' he said. He turned and cantered to the other end of the paddock where they had arranged the jumps. The twins followed him.

Why ever would he want to show off to her? Anna wondered. 'Come up to the house and have some tea,' she said quickly.

Vera smiled. 'Thanks, but I'll watch Paul first, then I'll come on up.'

Anna walked back to the house feeling puzzled. Kurt had won, she thought sadly. But however could he have known that Paul would take to such a plum pudding?

It was Sunday evening and as usual Otto and Simon were sitting in their office, planning next week's work. Not the least of their problems was where to find the cash to pay for the labour and the paint they would need.

'It's no good putting it off,' Otto said abruptly. 'We've got to salvage that nickel. Think of it, lying under the sea, just waiting to be picked up. Damn it, Simon, it's our nickel; we've paid for it. My God, if Perry can do it, I damn well can.'

'Yeah, that would be OK if you didn't get claustrophobia.'

Otto glared at him. 'That's a lie.'

'Come off it, Otto. You don't have to kid me. I saw your face when you came up.'

Simon poured out some beer. 'You're right, it's our nickel and we need the cash, but I'll do the diving. I'm good at it. Been diving since I was a small kid. My Ma used to send me down to get crayfish for supper and I wasn't allowed back until I had it. Boy, the water used to be cold.' He took a mouthful of beer from the can. 'Admittedly I don't know much about pressure suits, but I'll learn.'

Otto sighed and shook his head. 'Messy,' he said. 'I know nothing about servicing engines. You're a genius at mechanics. We'd be bust in no time if I had to run that gang of black labourers you've got eating out of your hand.' He thought for a while and then shook his head. 'No, it's impossible. I must do the diving until we can replace Perry.'

Simon kept quiet. He had no idea what Otto went through when he was under water, but he was talking sense. They were running a tidy operation with the painting and servicing. If it were not for the cash payments for their initial capital investment, they would be laughing. They had a book of fifteen thousand pounds that was killing them.

'All right, but promise you'll rely on me for weather reports,' he said. 'I know the sea hereabouts and the tides.' After all, he thought, Otto could not come to much harm in such shallow water.

Edwina had left a pile of bills discreetly on the table. Otto felt ashamed when he saw how unhappy she looked. For months his family had been deprived of luxuries; even basic necessities were often beyond their resources. He knew she only produced the bills when she had to; most of them were hidden. He stood up and put his hand on her shoulder. 'Don't worry, love, things are coming right. In two years' time we'll reap the rewards of all this scrimping.'

She smiled, looking pale and glum. Her hair was a mess and so were her clothes. She had tried to find a nursery school for her daughters so that she could work, but there were none available. Other working women left their children with black nannies, but Edwina refused to do this. Rosemary was eighteen months and Margaret three and a half. Unthinkable to leave them in untrained hands.

'We're getting the nickel up again, starting tomorrow, that's if the weather holds. Everything's going to be all right.' He expected questions but Edwina did not ask about the diving.

It can't possibly be as bad as I'm imagining, Otto thought

when he lay in bed that night. A couple of days and I'll be used to it.

But he was wrong. It was far worse than anything he had imagined. The terrible feeling of isolation and helplessness when he allowed himself to be sealed into the cumbersome suit from which he could not extricate himself without help. Incarcerated! When they placed the helmet over his head and prepared to screw on the glass plate he wanted to beg them not to, plead with them, but none of it showed as he stared sombrely at the horizon.

He stood up, dragging his feet in the heavy suit, and Tom steadied him as the boat heeled over. He wanted to say something, but could not. His world was seen dimly through smeared glass and communication was reduced to pulling on a rope.

The pressure was singing in his ears, making them pop and hurt, and he paused for a minute to adjust the valve. With a gigantic effort of will he let go of the ladder and watched the surface, a white bubbling ceiling, slowly recede. He landed, tipped forward and fell on his hands. The sediment rose around him in a thick cloud and slowly settled. The noise of the air whistling in his ears was distracting and the stench overpowering. Good God! How Perry had suffered and he had never given it a thought. Next time the bloody labourers would bathe before they hung over the air pump or, better still, knock them in the drink. The air was foul with the smell of stale sweat. His hands were beginning to burn, for the Antarctic currents were near freezing summer and winter. Soon they would be numb.

Now the fear worsened. Sweating and shaking, he visualized the tons of water above wanting to crush him and the dangers that lurked around. The urge to blow himself up to the surface was almost irresistible.

'Dear God, give me strength to stick it out.' He made himself think of Edwina and the children trusting him. 'Without this nickel,' he said to himself and his voice sounded odd, vibrating and highpitched, 'we're sunk.'

Slowly he circled, looking at his airpipe, a thick rubber

tube, reinforced with steel mesh, that was slowly undulating in the waves. He must be careful not to snare it. The rope was tied to his waist. His lifeline! Three sharp pulls on that rope would have him hauled instantly to the surface. The thought gave him a certain comfort. He looked down at his hands; they looked so white and vulnerable. Fish fingers for passing sharks. It was time to walk, but his knees were weak and kept giving way. Then he realized it was fright and pulled himself together, forcing his legs to feel their way over the uneven surface on the long, tedious search for nickel.

It was a few minutes before he found the first large pile and giving one sharp tug on the rope he waited and watched the bottom of the boat, a huge dark shadow, slowly move overhead guided by the bubbles from his helmet. He could see the oars rising and dipping. The basket came drifting down. Otto filled it with nickel and watched it go up to the surface. Down it came again and Otto picked up the nickel slabs, so light in the water, and placed them in the basket. The nickel was soon finished and he began to search for the next lot. He made towards the huge outcrop of rocks where he knew the wreck lay. There was probably far more nickel there, but not today. Oh no! Some other day when he was stronger and more used to the job. He veered south and five minutes later found quite a large pile and once again the boat came skimming overhead and the basket drifted down.

The day passed slowly. Otto was praying for it to end, to get back into the air, yet he seemed to have gained the upper hand over his claustrophobia.

Exactly at three, he turned down the valve, and the trapped air sent him floating slowly to the surface. Seconds later he clambered into the boat and Tom took off the facepiece.

'Jesus, I made it,' Otto said gasping in deep lungfuls of pure, fresh air.

'Tom, you've got to be careful who you put on the air pump in future,' he said. 'The stench nearly knocked me out.' He swore and Tom was surprised. Otto had never sworn before. 'I've got to have clean air,' he said.

Tom looked at him in surprise. 'I never thought of that,' he said. 'Perry never complained.'

Now that he was safe Otto began to shake, at first a little and then a lot. His hands were numb, bruised and scraped. Later when his hands came back to life the pain was agonizing. By four that afternoon it seemed that every nerve-end was raw and ultra-sensitive. His legs began jerking like a puppet on a string and one eye began to twitch.

Simon returned from the dry dock. 'My father! You look a sight,' he roared. 'Give it up, for God's sake.' He passed the brandy bottle and Otto drank deeply. As the rough, raw alcohol went down his throat it gave him a certain measure of relief, but not enough. He poured another glass.

Edwina was surprised to see Otto home so early and she could tell something was wrong. 'What is it? What's happened?'

'Nothing,' he snapped and turned on her furiously. 'Everything's marvellous.'

'But what's wrong with you?'

'I wish to God you'd stop whining,' he said.

He had never spoken to her like that before. Well, at least they had two rooms and she could go into the other one to put the girls to bed, spending much longer than usual reading Margaret stories.

When she returned to the living room Otto was drinking neat whisky and she could see from the bottle that he had drunk several. That was not like Otto. 'You'll get sick if you drink on an empty stomach. Would you like fried eggs? I'm sorry, it's all we've got. Or omelette?'

'Don't apologize,' he snarled. 'You're always damn well apologizing. Why don't you say it? Come out in the open and say: "We've only got eggs because you don't give me enough money for food".'

'I'm not complaining,' she said gently, feeling thoroughly alarmed now.

'Well, complain then, damn it,' he yelled. 'I'd feel better if you complained.'

He poured another drink, but Edwina reached forward and took it from him. Placing the glass on the mantelpiece she said, 'Eat first, drink afterwards if you must drink. Whatever problems you have, drinking won't help.'

'You're wrong there,' he mumbled. Drinking was definitely helping, for the millions of nerve-ends which had been alive and shrieking were becoming pleasantly dulled by the soporific effect of the alcohol. Tension was receding from his legs and his back. He knew he was drunk, but better to be drunk than terrified, for ahead of him stretched another day and then another and each day he would spend eight hours underwater, four hundred and eighty minutes, each as long as a hundred years stretched ahead of him day after day. He knew, too, that he would continue diving until every available slab of nickel was recovered.

'I wish I was dead,' he muttered. Suddenly he flung his glass against the wall. The glass shattered and the pieces scratched the wallpaper and scattered on the floor. To his surprise, Edwina said nothing, but took the dustpan and brush and began to clean up the mess.

'Oh God,' he said slurring his words. 'Please, please, don't do that.' He took the brush out of her hand and started to pick up the pieces, but cut himself.

Edwina suddenly lost control. 'For God's sake, Otto, you're drunk,' she sobbed. 'Leave it alone. I'm not complaining. Just let me do it, but please, please tell me what's the matter.'

But Otto went into their bedroom and shortly afterwards fell asleep.

For Otto life had turned into a nightmare, but he was so ashamed that he would not have admitted it to anyone, least of all Edwina and Simon. How could a grown man be afraid of the water? A sailor! He would rather face a dozen U-boats than one more day in the dreaded diving suit. Yet although they tried agencies all over the world they could not find a diver willing to come to South Africa and without the nickel they would go broke. He should step up recovery. Tomorrow, he decided. He must go to the wreck.

The following morning Otto descended into the depths and as he hit bottom a shark ripped past him, knocking him on the shoulder, leaving him swirling in the wash. He sank to his knees and held his knife ready. When the fish turned he intended to sink his knife into its guts, but the shark kept out of reach circling, but not approaching. The water was unusually clear and Otto filled several baskets with nickel before venturing towards the ridge of high rocks. With the boat following him, guided by bubbles, Otto picked his way along the lower ridge and began climbing to where the wreck lay.

The hulk was lying on its side in the midst of a rocky outcrop that stretched from the lighthouse. Beneath it were remnants of a much older wreck. There was a deep gash in the hull, but the stern was almost intact. The rest of the freighter had been broken up and destroyed by the force of the currents. Slowly he picked his way through the barnacle-encrusted wreckage. The nickel lay scattered, but there was not much of it. A few days' work maybe. The rest, presumably, lay in the hold. Reluctantly he approached the gaping hole and clambered inside. As he did so a huge cloud of sediment rose, clouding his vision completely. He trod on something thick and squirming that moved under his feet.

When the sediment cleared he saw dozens of eels wriggling amongst the debris. He could guess why and he felt sick. Something about the place filled him with loathing. He signalled for the basket, stepped out to the rocks and when the basket swung down took it back into the wreck and filled it rapidly.

Outside the sharks kept up their circling as if waiting. Like vultures circling a dying man, Otto thought.

After the third basket he lost control and, closing the valve, blew himself up. Arms and legs spreadeagled, he hurtled into the bow of the longboat, bruising and almost dislocating his shoulder. They pulled him into the boat with difficulty.

'What's up?' Tom asked when they had removed the facepiece.

'Sharks,' Otto said. 'And eels, hundreds of them.'

'Never heard of sharks attacking a diver. They're scared of

the bubbles, but you want to watch your fingers with the eels.'

'Yes,' Otto said and shuddered.

'Well, I reckon you've had enough for today, haven't you?' Tom went on, but Otto felt ashamed and insisted on going back.

There was no sign of the sharks now, but the second descent was worse than the first as he forced himself to climb inside the wreckage and fill several baskets with ore. Once again the eels squirmed around his feet.

That afternoon Otto began to drink as soon as he arrived home. Even before saying hello to the children or to Edwina he poured out a glass of neat whisky and drank it at a gulp. After that he drank steadily until bedtime. Then, eyes heavy, voice slurred, he said goodnight. The nightmares began as soon as he slept. He groaned, tossed and turned, and once struck Edwina as if fighting off unseen attackers.

In desperation the next day Edwina poured all the liquor they had down the drain. When Otto returned he found the cupboard bare.

'I've thrown it away,' she said primly. 'I'll have no more liquor in this house. You're becoming a drunk.'

Otto stared at her long and hopelessly. Could she not grasp that it was hard enough to survive until the job was finished? No, he could see by her face she would never understand. He turned and went out very quietly without a word and returned at midnight. From then on he spent his evenings in a nearby bar.

38

She was in a long tunnel; a long, grey, lonely tunnel through which she had to walk alone, maybe for years and she was tired of loneliness. After a while she began to cry.

A nurse came past and said, 'This won't do, Mrs Friedland. Cheer up. You're getting better. You know that, don't you?'

Getting better, she thought scathingly. She was getting worse; worse by the day. She dabbed her eyes with a tissue, went to the mirror over the washbasin and stared at herself. Disdainfully she examined the straggly hair, half platinum with two inches of mousy brown at the roots; the dull, lustreless eyes, sagging eyelids. If this was getting better, she'd rather stay sick, she decided. She sighed, fetched a comb and tried to do something with the stringy mess, but there was really no hope without a shampoo and after a while she went back to bed.

She had several books at her bedside which she had asked Kurt to bring and he had been very good about it. He would give her anything she asked except the one thing she craved – love. The books showed the incredible number of cul-de-sacs she had traversed since arriving in this place. *A Jewish Woman and Her Home*; *A Christian Duty*; *Teach Yourself French*; *Teach Yourself Shorthand!* How could she ever have wanted to be a shorthand typist, she wondered, as she gazed in despair at this large pile of books and the discarded typewriter.

She felt that the doctors, nurses, Anna and Kurt were all in a conspiracy to destroy her and they had succeeded with shock treatment. Yet, somehow, deep inside her, far beyond the traumas and the hang-ups, there was something which told her she could never be destroyed. They had destroyed Madeleine Grass, the beautiful, carefree, ash-blonde Viennese socialite and they had finally succeeded in destroying Mimi the singing whore who had entertained the troops back from the Eastern front; perhaps they had also destroyed Maria Grass.

She lay in bed for a while, staring at the ceiling and thinking about Madeleine Friedland née Grass. She had hated her since the day she had created her and she could remember to the minute when that was. Before that she had been Maria Grass, a mousy-haired, plump pin-cushion into which her mother thrust her barbs. She had been fifteen years old, vulnerable, sensitive, and lacking a strong self-image and she had stood one day in the living room listening to her mother talking to a neighbour.

'She's such a disappointment to me,' her mother had said. 'No ambition, no looks, no brains. She'll be lucky to get a husband; a career is out of the question. Who'd want her? The trouble is she takes after her father. When he left I said "good riddance to bad rubbish" but I found myself landed with the daughter.'

Maria had grown up when she realized that she had become a failure to please her mother. The realization was not all that sudden, it sank in gradually as she looked at her mother with new eyes. So she took her pocket money and had her hair dyed platinum blonde. It suited her and the boys at school began to notice her. For the first time she was dated. Within three months she had lost twenty pounds and the following year she won a local beauty competition. After that there was no holding her back and she rode roughshod over her mother and everyone with whom she came into contact. Until the war.

As time passed Madeleine realized that she was not in a tunnel, but a cocoon, hanging poised midway between the past and future. Timeless!

She slept and grew and slowly her depression lifted. She went to the hairdresser and began to care for her nails. Her hair was not really mousy, she decided, but a pretty light brown. She began to plan for the future, trying to imagine how she would emerge, but the future still frightened her.

'You're getting better, Madeleine,' Dr Warring had told her at least three times that month. 'There's little more we can do for you.'

She laughed. Her laugh had taken on a new quality in the past few weeks. She was more positive, yet there was still so much fear in her eyes and she was concealing a great deal. After all the horrors of the war, which she had recounted vividly, Dr Warring could not imagine what worse experiences she could be holding back. It was a miracle she was not insane. Once again he marvelled at her resilience. He had little doubt that she would make the grade eventually, but not if she returned to people who hated her.

That afternoon she was sitting in the garden when the waiter came by wheeling a tea trolley. There was nothing threatening about him, but something in his eyes made her glance back. She saw a man alienated from his fellow men. Beady, cruel eyes. As she watched, his head changed, darkened, altered shape. A carrion crow! The beak opened and he squawked while his hands passed the sugar.

Madeleine bit back the scream; forced herself to see him as he really was. I'm not mad, she thought. It's only my imagination causing hallucinations. After all, I can make the pictures go away. She decided to tell Dr Warring her problem.

She tried to explain later that day. 'Faces seem like masks that people hide behind. When I look at them the masks melt away and I see horrible things, horrible cruel faces, sometimes animals ... I've never told anyone before,' she finished lamely.

'Draw them,' he said. 'Bring them out into the open. Expose them.'

He decided to engage an art teacher and sighed. If all his patients had wealthy husbands their treatments would be greatly simplified.

It hurt Simon to see how badly Otto was treating Edwina, for hadn't he made the same mistake with Anna before the war? It was none of his business, but his sympathies were with

Edwina and when he found the opportunity he would put in a good word for her with Otto. He helped, too, with gifts of food from the farm, grapes in season, sometimes a small sucking pig and always dozens of eggs. He drew the absolute minimum so that Otto could take most of the available cash. After all, Otto was his best friend, apart from his business partner, and Edwina was a woman he treasured, perhaps because she was Otto's wife. It hurt him to see the two of them so disillusioned, hating each other.

After Edwina tipped the liquor down the sink Otto was seldom home in the evening. She endured this final betrayal with a mask of stoic indifference, ignoring him when she saw him, walking around permanently red-eyed, afraid to ask for money, yet desperately in need.

'I don't know him any more,' she confided in Simon. 'He's not the man I married. It's like living with a stranger, and he seems to hate me.' She said nothing about the drinking, hoping that no one would find out.

As the months passed Simon and Edwina drew closer together. She needed a shoulder to lean on and he was delighted by her dependence, her need to be looked after, her gentleness.

The New Year heralded a month of superb weather. A week before Edwina's birthday there was a heatwave which lasted for several days. The Berg wind drifted over the land, filling the air with the scent of herbs and flowers. Edwina spent days on the beach until she and the children were golden brown. At dusk the Coloureds would stroll along the seafront, strumming their guitars, singing strange, haunting songs. Voluptuous evenings! Restless nights! Edwina, a pale flower from colder shores, began to tremble and pine; she uncurled her petals and became a victim of hidden desires, but Otto was never home.

She decided to have a party for her birthday, just the three of them, since she knew no one else and she bribed the old lady to let her have the kitchen to herself for the afternoon. By seven the children were in bed and Simon and she were

350

waiting for Otto.

Eventually Simon volunteered to go and search for him, but Edwina refused and burst into tears. Simon clasped her in his arms to comfort her and she whispered, 'Make love to me, please, please Simon. I've wanted it for so long and Otto never does, not any more, not for months. I just want to be loved.'

Simon gently smoothed her hair, wiped her face with his handkerchief. He was in a quandary. Never once had he desired Edwina. After all she was Otto's wife, she was like his sister, but here she was peeling off her dress and her bra with the utmost confidence. To refuse would be an insult. The sight of her pure white breasts, sagging over suntanned skin, aroused him. She was slightly bow-legged, but her faults seemed to make her more appealing, she was so very vulnerable. When she took off her glasses, her eyes seemed huge and defenceless.

He made love gently and softly at first, which presented no problem for she lay spreadeagled on the bed, gentle moans being all that she contributed to the union.

Eventually he asked, 'Have you come yet?'

'Why, yes.' She smiled happily. 'Didn't you know?'

'No,' he said. He closed his eyes and grasped her tightly. It took great imagination to feel Anna's hard body impaled beneath his instead of this pliable flesh. He pictured Anna as she was before the war, breasts pushing into him, hard nipples, blue eyes like pools of deep water. Oh God! He groaned as desire flowed through his limbs. The anguish of it. Well, to hell with Anna. He was no gigolo. He would not be used as a stallion for servicing purposes. If she could not need him as a husband, then there was no hope for them.

His desire was melting. He felt Edwina stir, her eyes opened questioningly.

A poor substitute. Yet he loved her in a way. He felt protective. Brotherly! Yes, that was the right word. Oh God, he would never make it.

He shut his eyes tightly and remembered Anna, years ago, by the river, wanting him, leading him on, demanding more

351

than he would give. What a fool he had been. He should have given it to her then. Thrown her on the sand and hammered away, purging his lust. She had been so beautiful, desirable, passionate, sitting naked by the river. He would never forget that day.

When he exploded at last, he buried his face in the pillow, unwilling to come to terms with reality.

'My, you're really something,' Edwina said after a while.

Simon quickly tired of the affair with Edwina. The clinging woman charade was becoming tedious and he could never quite satisfy her needs for transport, for help, for sex and overwhelmingly for reassurance. Edwina was so demanding. There would be a flood of tears if he was late for supper, tantrums if he was missing for an evening, jealousy when he visited the twins. Simon felt she had confused his role with Otto's, while Otto got off scot free. Besides, his guilt was getting the better of him. He began to wonder how he could end something that should never have begun, but the decision was taken out of his hands because one evening Otto returned unexpectedly early.

They caught sight of a white face looking down at them and then he was gone.

'Oh my God, what are we going to do?' Edwina sat up looking horrified. Her blue eyes were too brilliant; her cheeks too pink; hair too yellow. To Simon she had seemed pretty once, now he was surfeited. He scrambled into his underpants and trousers.

'Come on, Edwina, you know I'll look after you,' he said gritting his teeth. 'Don't be a fool.' It was he that was the fool, neatly trapped.

'Two small children,' she wailed. 'How will I manage?'

'Oh, God.' He patted her shoulder. 'Look, don't worry. Everything will be all right. I'll go and find him; talk to him.' He grabbed his shirt.

'What are you going to tell him?' she whispered.

'I'll tell him, I'll do the right thing. Whatever that is,' Christ, it was a bloody mess.

'You do love me, don't you?'

'In a manner of speaking,' he mumbled.

'Are you going to marry me?'

The little woman had her head screwed on the right way even in moments of crisis. Simon glanced at her, feeling shocked. 'I must be honest, Anna has refused to give me a divorce, but that doesn't stop me from looking after you and …' he nearly choked on the words, 'living with you.'

For a moment her face registered shock and then she covered her eyes with her hands. 'Poor, poor Otto,' she began. 'Did you see the look on his face? I don't want to lose him. Will he ever forgive me?' she wailed.

'How the hell should I know.' He went out slamming the door.

Simon did not have far to look, for Otto was sitting on the bottom steps of the front porch, head in hands.

'It's no good fighting.' Simon began hating himself at that moment. 'I wouldn't hit back anyway. Let's talk it out like civilized people.'

Otto stood up. 'Civilized people do not talk on a doorstep. I'll buy you a drink. Come on.'

They walked side by side in silence. Simon was trying to work out a way to explain, but he could not remember why the affair had started in the first place.

'Strange thing,' Otto began, 'but I went home to tell her how sorry I am. I didn't tell you this, but we've recovered nearly five thousand pounds of nickel. Not bad really. I thought I'd give it a break for a bit.'

The quietness of his voice filled Simon with bitterness. He could have sat down and cried. Pity he hadn't thought of that before.

They reached the bar and sat on two stools near the wall and argued about who was to pay. When the drinks came they picked up their glasses, avoiding each other's eyes.

'Well, what shall we drink to?' Otto asked. 'We've been good friends for a long time. You saved my life once. God, but that was a rum do. Let's drink to that.'

'Don't feel sorry for me, old man,' Otto went on, staring at his glass. 'Edwina's the sort of woman who has to cling to someone and I was gone, or so it must have seemed to her. I deserve it.' Suddenly he straightened up and grinned. Clapping Simon on the shoulder he said, 'I'll arrange for a divorce right away and who knows, we may even land up friends. How's that for civilized behaviour?'

'Hey, not so fast,' Simon cut in. 'You can't wipe out five years just because of a ...' he fished around for the right words, 'because of a temporary lapse.'

'Temporary lapse?' That seemed to amuse Otto. 'Just how temporary was it?'

'Couple of months,' Simon mumbled.

'Not long enough really. I found out too soon.'

'Otto, I want you to know that I deeply regret ...'

'You sound too bloody silly for words, Simon. Drink up.' He called the barman and ordered another round.

Simon sat fumbling for words. They did not come so he drained his glass at a gulp and ordered again.

'You must forgive my curious silence,' Otto went on, his words now rather slurred, 'but my education did not prepare me for this social occasion. Should I offer to fight you for her?'

'Now who's sounding bloody ridiculous?'

'Yes, you're right, Simon,' Otto said. 'She's not exactly Helen of Troy.'

'I didn't mean that,' Simon said, defending her. 'I meant ... Oh, for God's sake, I don't know what I meant.' He beckoned the barman.

'My turn,' Otto said.

'She still loves you,' Simon said somewhere around the sixth drink. 'That's how we got together in the first place. Trying to save your bloody marriage. Sounds ridiculous, doesn't it? All she used to talk about was you, at first.'

'Forgive me for jumping to conclusions,' Otto said, 'but tonight I assumed that she loves you, now, and that you are anxious to step into my shoes.'

354

'Well, I don't think so,' Simon stuttered.

'In other words it was just a slice off the loaf, so to speak.' He sighed. 'I've done it myself, but it's odd to be on the receiving end. No, I've got that wrong, haven't I?'

'If you can believe this, in a way I was helping out,' Simon said miserably.

'Helping out?' He burst out laughing.

'I've tried to tell you a hundred times. Of course the fact that you've been a bastard to her,' Simon went on, 'doesn't excuse my actions.'

'I know I'm a bastard,' Otto said, slurring his words, 'because she's told me so many times. Has she told you what a bastard you are?'

'Frequently,' Simon admitted.

'No one, but no one can live up to Edwina's expectations. You don't know what it's like coming home without enough cash, having to look at those tragic blue eyes. Come on, drink up, we're getting morbid.'

'My turn,' Simon said, beckoning the barman.

'How is it you and Anna don't get on so well?' Otto asked. 'I saw her once. A really stunning lady.'

'Yes,' Simon said, 'but tough. I once made a bad mistake and Anna never forgave me. She's like that. Never lowers her standards, never gives in.' He was slurring his words, too. Without really meaning to he told Otto about Sophie and her child. 'Left the baby to die because it would have been embarrassing. Gave me the creeps when she told me, so I joined up. You get a different perspective on things when you're out of the country. She never forgave me for Sophie. I never forgave her for killing the child.'

Otto shuddered.

'Edwina and I were washed up before we came out here,' Otto went on. 'Don't get me wrong, she's a very fine lady. Her father was a clergyman in Kent. Never been a passionate woman. Was she with you?'

'No,' Simon said. 'Quite the opposite.'

'Exactly.' He had trouble saying the word. 'Well, let's be

355

straight about it. You don't really want her, do you?'

'No. After all, she's your wife.'

'Well, she's your ... whatever they call these things.' He laughed without humour. 'I don't want her much either, but one of us must have her. We're into this thing together, as they say in the States.'

'Otto, shut up for Christ's sake.'

'I could make an honourable retreat and leave you to run the business. It's on its feet. The nickel saved us.'

Simon's cheek began to twitch harder. 'When I told Edwina that Anna would not give me a divorce she didn't seem too keen to live in sin.'

'No, Edwina wouldn't like that. I'll toss you,' Otto went on. 'What d'you say? Loser takes Edwina.'

'I'm on,' Simon said gloomily.

'Couldn't be fairer,' Otto said as he fumbled for a coin.

Simon won. He felt relief sinking into every pore like a damp wind in a drought.

Otto looked stunned. 'Let's go home and have a drink,' he said.

To her horror, Edwina saw the two men stagger into the lounge, propping up each other. Otto took two glasses and filled them with neat whisky which they tossed back. Watching them she felt used and rejected.

'You two bastards ...' she began. 'You two bastards ...' but the landlady came knocking on the door to complain about the noise.

'I can't say I'm sorry, Otto,' she said a few minutes later when Simon had left. 'You've been a swine to us, but I still love you and I'm prepared to try again if you promise to give up drinking and not to throw this in my face for the rest of my life.'

'I won't mention it again, but don't expect anything from me until I finish salvaging the nickel.' And then he told her of his fears; of eels that wriggled and squirmed amongst dead men's bones, of the water crushing down on him, of the frailty of his precious airpipe.

When he had finished she said, 'Oh, my poor Otto. God forgive me, I never understood.'

For the second time that night Edwina found herself on the bed, arms and legs entwined.

39

The next morning Simon drove to Fontainebleu. He had
decided to dispense with goodbyes, reasoning that the
previous evening had been one long goodbye. There was
nothing left to say.

He parked on the crest of the mountain pass and looked
back. A mistake, he decided. He was leaving too much behind:
the beautiful city hemmed between mountains and the sea,
friends he had made; all his cash; worse still, his only hope of
meeting Anna as an equal.

It had all been for nothing and his guilt at selling
Modderfontein was accentuated.

Anna was sitting in her study, totting up figures. She looked
up and smiled nervously. He had decided to tell her the whole
story, exactly as it had happened. He felt it imperative to
produce a reasonable excuse for abandoning the business, but
he was unprepared for the tantrum that followed.

'You bastard,' she screamed, her face contorted and
unrecognizable. She picked up a vase, flung it at him and it
glanced off his shoulder as he stood rooted to the floor with his
mouth opened. For a few seconds the room rained pencils,
glasses, books and ashtrays. Then, in three quick strides,
Simon reached her and pinned her arms against her sides.

'Cut it out, Anna. This wronged wife act doesn't cut any ice
with me. You've been screwing around. How do you think I
felt when I found out about Kurt at Bosluis?' He shook her
and pushed her away so that she spun across the room, hitting
her hip against the desk, but she turned, quick as a cobra.

'You fool. Now you've thrown away the business, as well as

Modderfontein, like you threw away our marriage. All for a stupid, whining woman. Good God, she's not even pretty. I saw the two of you together. I know what she's like. Why did you do it? Why?'

'Because she needed me,' he said quietly. His words were like a slap in the face.

She struck out blindly.

'Let up, will you?' He caught her arms again. 'I'm going away. Maybe Australia. I shall work my passage on the next available boat.'

'Yes, run away why not?' she said. 'Ever since I met you, that's all you've ever done.'

Anna sat in a chair and covered her face with her hands. Why am I upset? she asked herself. What difference would it make if he were in Cape Town or Australia? Then she remembered the children; they loved him so. Why should they be deprived?

To Simon's surprise she burst into tears. 'You're always whaling or fishing or joining up, never around to sort out the mess. Now it's Australia. Just because you can't face Otto. It's yourself you're running away from. When are you going to face up to that? Why can't you stay here? I need you and God knows the children need you.'

'You want me,' Simon said quietly, 'like you want a pet dog, someone to bark around the place.'

'That's a lie,' she said. 'You're always against me. You punish me because I'm rich.'

'Maybe I do,' he mused. 'If I asked you to come with me, live on whatever I could afford, help me build a new life, would you come?'

'No! of course not. Don't be so selfish; think how the children would suffer. Stay here.'

'No,' he said.

'Oh, I don't care.' Suddenly the will to fight evaporated. 'Do what you want.' She buried her head in her hands.

He walked out and sat on the grass. When he thought about it he decided that she was probably right. He always ran away and he resented her wealth. She always made sense; he had to admit that.

He was sitting on the grass when Katie rode back from the village on her bicycle. 'Daddy.' The bicycle rolled on but Katie had flung herself on her father.

Later when he told her he was going away, her face changed and she stopped following him around and went outside. Acker came home and when he heard the news his eyes blazed with anger.

'Where's Katie?' he wanted to know, but no one could find her.

Eventually Wagter found her, for she had crawled into a hole at the edge of the vineyard and covered herself with leaves.

'If you go I shall kill myself,' she said melodramatically.

'Don't be ridiculous,' Simon said, trying to brush the earth from her face and her ears. 'What you need is a good shower.'

'You've got your mother, and your brother and your Grandpa,' he said later when he had put her in the bath and was sponging away the dirt.

'Grandpa's old,' she said sulkily.

'Well, that doesn't make him any less nice, just because he's old.'

'All the other little girls have a daddy and I want my daddy.'

'I'm not going forever,' he replied. 'Just a year or two.'

'To a little girl two years is forever,' she said with a wisdom beyond her years. He turned and gazed at her for a few minutes and then brushed the leaves from her hair.

Eventually she won, as she always won. How could he possibly have considered leaving, he wondered? Was any other man blessed with such beautiful children?

Anna went to bed early and Simon and André were left alone in the lounge.

'It's not often I see you, Simon. I wish it were more often,' André said and meant it. 'What brings you back at this time of the week?'

Simon told him.

360

'Well, we must either celebrate or commiserate and both occasions deserve a bottle of the best.' He took a key out of his pocket and opened a large *kist* in one corner of the room.

'I often wondered what was in there,' Simon said.

'Only the best, Simon.' He took out a bottle of brandy, held it up to the light and then poured. 'This was bottled before you were born, my boy. Just think of that.'

Simon did not want to think of it. It meant wealth. A dirty word to him nowadays.

'I think you might be able to help me,' André said much later. 'I have a farm, enormous place, up Namaqualand way, called Luembe, about fifty miles south-east of Pofadder. Desolate area, as you know. It's been on the market for the past five years, but no buyers. Trouble is, there's no farmhouse and no water pump. Never looked for water. I'd like to interest you in the venture. Go up there, have a look and see if it's suitable for karakul, if you can find water, that is. Build a farmhouse. I'll put up the capital, you do the job. Later we'll sell out and split the profits fifty-fifty. It'll do me a favour and, who knows, you might land up with some capital. Of course if there's no water there's no deal. Are you interested?'

'Am I interested? I should think I am.'

It was midnight and Anna was still awake. Her mind was in a turmoil. Surely, if she only had time, if he would give them a chance, they could get along well enough. If they could only discuss their problems without both of them flying into a rage, and she was the worst culprit.

She must talk to him. She crept along the passage, but Simon's door was locked.

'Let me in,' she hissed.

Eventually the door opened. Simon stood there looking tousled and sexy.

'Why did you lock the door?'

'For obvious reasons.'

'You're trying so hard to keep us apart. Why is that, Simon?'

'Because every time you demand sex you make me feel like a

stallion put out to stud. Sort of compulsory; earning my keep. It puts me off.'

She gasped and hurried away.

She sat for hours at the window, while Simon's words kept echoing in her mind. A stud horse! My God. Compulsory! The words were like blows. How could a man say that to a woman? Any woman! There was too much cruelty between men and women. She thought of Kurt at Bosluis and afterwards the way Kurt had used her to wound Madeleine. Most of all she remembered Modderfontein.

In her lonely room, in the night, despair chilled her. From now on she would be inviolate.

The wind was getting up and it was a cold wind. The grapes were harvested, leaves falling. Something inside Anna died that night.

Madeleine was dressed, packed and ready to leave, feeling a little scared as she walked into Dr Warring's room.

'I'm glad you came. I wanted to have a last talk with you.'

'I couldn't leave without saying "thank you". Could I?'

'What are your plans now, Madeleine?'

She shrugged. 'Keep painting. I'll flow with the current. My mother left me a small income.'

'And Kurt?' he asked gently.

She smiled sadly. 'I'll have to see if things work out.'

'Sit down, relax. Coffee's coming,' he said. 'Did no one tell you of your exceptional painting talent when you were at school?'

She smiled. 'Yes, almost everyone, but I wanted to be a singer, and I hoped to become an actress, but I wasn't much good.'

'Madeleine,' he began slowly when the coffee had come. 'You're going back to the same world, the same people who feel, rightly or wrongly, that you have harmed them in some way. Face up to their hatred, their cruelties, and accept them. Fight back, but don't try to kid yourself.'

She shrugged. 'I'll try, but it's not easy to accept that you

362

are not a likeable person, that people hate you.'

'I like you. It's hard for me to say this to you when I'm talking to you in a professional capacity. Just remember that I'm here. If you want dinner or a trip to the theatre, or just someone to talk to, I won't be Dr Warring any more, but George.'

'Goodbye, George. I'll phone you.'

Filled with enthusiasm she ran down the steps and almost fell into the arms of Kurt, looking furious as he leaned against his Jaguar.

'You're late,' he began. 'They said ten and it's past eleven.'

'I'm sorry Kurt, Dr Warring wanted to talk to me. I had no idea they said ten. I didn't even know you were coming.'

He scowled at her. 'These fellows don't have any idea how important time is. They wouldn't survive five minutes in the commercial world. It's virtually sheltered employment. Get in the car, I'm late for a meeting. I'll have to rush you home to the nurse and rush back to the office.'

'Nurse! But Kurt,' she began hesitantly, 'I can look after myself. I'm going to start again. I told you that. You've been so kind, but now I'm better.'

He frowned and opened the car door. 'Time enough to look after yourself when you're well again. We'll talk about it then.'

'They wouldn't have discharged me if I weren't better.'

'Come on, Madeleine,' he repeated. 'Don't start an argument standing on the steps. You haven't even got out of the place. You're overwrought. You know what a state you get in. I don't want you to upset yourself.'

She took a step back and looked at him coldly. 'Why did you say that? I'm not arguing. I merely said …'

'I heard what you said. Are we going through all these scenes again? Now Madeleine,' he said as if speaking to a child, 'be a good girl and get into the car.' He took her firmly by one elbow and pushed her in.

Dumb with misery, she allowed herself to be driven to Constantia.

After a while she plucked up courage to start again. 'Kurt,

363

we must talk. Our marriage ended long ago. I want to be alone for a while, get a job and start again. If you thought you loved me – well, you'd know where I was, wouldn't you?'

He turned and she was stunned by his coldness. 'Let's get one thing straight, Madeleine. You've been ill and I intend to look after you. It's quite unthinkable that you should try to live on your own. You'd be in prison for shoplifting within a week. You don't understand what it's like not to have everything you want.'

'Oh,' she leaned back, understanding at last that Kurt was determined to be the 'good guy'; she was to be the bad one, and if not bad, mad. She smiled.

Watching sidelong, Kurt said, 'Do you always laugh to yourself, Madeleine? I think I should warn you against it. People might talk. Especially knowing where you've been.'

'If I smile occasionally people might think I'm crazy?'

'Well, you and I both know you're crazy, but we might as well keep the news in the family.'

Suddenly it was all too much and she burst into tears.

They arrived home at that moment and Kurt solicitously helped her out of the car, and stood holding her arm calling, 'Nurse! Nurse Philips! Mrs Friedland is overwrought this morning, nurse. Not a good day I think. Please take her to her room and give her a sedative.'

Bewildered, Madeleine allowed herself to be guided into a sterile room rather similiar to the one she had just vacated.

'Take this, my dear.' The nurse held out a pill and a glass of water.

Madeleine heard the sound of Kurt's car driving away. 'I'm going to see Paul,' she said firmly. 'If I need you, I'll ring. Thank you, Nurse Philips.'

Paul was in the garden. He had grown so much she hardly recognized him.

'Hello, Paul.'

The boy looked over his shoulder. There was no welcoming smile, rather a look of studied exasperation. 'Oh hello,' he said. 'Are you back for good?'

364

'No,' she said. 'I came to say goodbye.'

The relief was like a slap in the face.

'Where's my car?' she asked.

'In the garage. Vera's been using it.'

'Who's Vera?'

'My teacher.'

'Do you like her?'

'She's not bad.' He paused and then he said, 'She's all right, but I'd rather stay with Anna.'

'Could you find my car keys while I pack a few things? I'm leaving now.'

His face lit up. 'Sure.'

Ten minutes later she drove out of the house forever. It was a beautiful day and she could drive in any direction; go wherever she pleased; start again; make new friends. She felt there were no limits to what she could do. She decided to drive around the mountains before finding accommodation. Suddenly, for the first time in her life, she was free. Without even noticing she began to sing.

40

It was the beginning of winter, June 1949, and their rooms were draughty and cold. Margaret and Rosemary had permanent running noses, but none of this worried Edwina for she and Otto were becoming a unit. Since that night, which neither of them mentioned, they had begun to pull together. Edwina handled the accounts, Otto the labour gangs and ships' contracts. Tom, the linesman, had proved a good foreman in place of Simon, but now the full burden of administration fell on Otto's shoulders and he worked late every night in order to cope with stocktaking, reordering spares and paint, and planning the labour gangs.

The weather had been foul for the past month and Otto had been unable to recover the nickel. It irked him to think of the rest of it lying under the sea. So far they had sold over twenty-six tons at one hundred and eighty-six pounds a ton, reducing their overdraft by over five thousand pounds. Somewhere, scattered amongst the wreckage was a fortune of nickel. He guessed that part of it was lying under the debris inside the hold.

At the end of July they would have to pay the salvage fee as well as several more down payments on building materials and equipment, and they could easily cover this if they salvaged the nickel. Otto had repeatedly tried to obtain a diver, but still none were available. There was no alternative; he would have to dive again as soon as the weather improved.

On the first calm winter's day in June, Otto set out through the chill early morning mist with Tom and two deckhands.

The sea was like a metal sheet, calm, grey, deceptive. The

mountains were obscured by cloud, not the frilly tabletop cover that heralded a south-easter, but thick black rain clouds. A cold wind started from the north-west, driving a fine drizzle as they reached a spot roughly above the wreck and began to unfasten the chests of diving gear.

Otto was never warm enough.

Lately Edwina had knitted him thick polo-neck jerseys, vests, long woolly pants and socks out of natural wool with the grease of the sheep still in it, but still he shivered.

When Tom screwed on the glass facepiece, the deckhands began to turn the pump handle and Otto heard the familiar sighing and hissing of air through the valve, a sound that was now as well known to him as the beating of his own heart.

There was no point in delaying the descent; the sooner he went the sooner he would be back. He gave Tom the thumbs-up sign and clambered over the side, hanging on tightly to the iron bars of the ladder until he reached the bottom one, then he let go and sank quickly through the water to the seabed.

He began searching the perimeter of the wreck and found several large piles of ingots which he despatched into the baskets. When he was fifty yards from the wreck a sudden strong current washed him off his feet and flung him against the nearest rocks. He hung on and sat there for a few seconds watching the water swirling, seaweed pulled to its furthest extent, like palm trees in a gale. He saw several fish swimming past: steenbras, rock salmon, he could recognize them all nowadays, and the thought flashed through his mind that if he weren't so damn scared he could enjoy this job.

He wondered if he should get back to the boat, but there were no further eddies and no urgent tugs on the rope from above, so he assumed that it had been a stray wave. After this he approached the wreck and stood staring at it, feeling puzzled. The large, gaping crack seemed to be in a different place. An optical illusion, he thought. Still he hesitated, but eventually he eased his way over the barnacled hulk and lowered himself into the hold.

Kicking his feet around to frighten the eels and crabs, Otto waited for the sediment to clear. After a while he found he could see for about four yards around him. Above, everything that floated was pressed against the uppermost side of the hulk; the nickel lay in piles around his feet amongst the debris, but when he took a step the sediment rose in a black cloud.

Further away from the gap in the ship's side, the hold was as black as night and, using the torch, it took half an hour before he had completed a casual search, enough time to convince him there was plenty of nickel to cover their debts.

He was about to make his way towards the aperture when the wreck gave a long shudder and slipped at least two feet to starboard. Panic-stricken, Otto sensed that the wreck was not impaled on rocks, as he had imagined, but could be shifted by the backwash. No wonder the hole had appeared to have moved! Then he realized that if the hulk keeled over much further it would shift the break against the sand, blocking his only escape. A second later another big wave set the hold shuddering, sediment washed around him making the torch useless, while boxes and heavy bars bounced in the water. He blundered into the debris as he fought his way back.

The wreck shuddered and swayed as wave after wave smashed against it. There was a clamour of grinding and cracking, huge floating objects bowled him over. Otto fought back and eventually the hold lightened as he reached the gash. Now he could see he had been right, the ship was swinging like a pendulum on the rocks and half the hole was hard against the seabed.

Thank God he was in time. He clambered through the opening and half running, half crawling, moved away from the wreck. Then he turned and stared at it. For a moment the sea was calm, sand, sea shells and stones were slowly sinking to the seabed, like a snowstorm, he thought. The huge hulk towered above him, rusted and old. A macabre picture.

'You nearly got me, too,' he murmured, but as he moved back to the boat he was suddenly held fast and, turning, he saw that his airpipe and lifeline were caught on something inside the wreck. He swore, retraced his footsteps and, catching hold of the pipe, yanked it to him, but it was stuck.

He would have to go back inside and unravel it. A

dangerous operation and for a moment he hesitated, but then another heavy swell hit the wreck and he watched as it keeled right over, squashing his airpipe against the rock.

The air supply stopped immediately, but Otto had a few seconds left and from then on everything happened in slow motion. He closed the outlet valve, conserving the trapped air in his suit, took his knife and cut through the pipe. He could have saved himself then by pulling on the rope, three sharp pulls for an emergency, but the rope, too, was snarled and useless.

With the pipe and the rope cut he tried to rise, but he was trapped on the ocean floor by his heavy suit and boots. Now his head was hammering, his body felt limp and exhausted, his movements were shaky, unco-ordinated. He could feel the pressure of tons of water pressing in on him as he had always known that it would, but it was worse. He succeeded in getting one of his boots off; already his suit was waterlogged. When he reached down for the second boot he lapsed into unconsciousness. Slowly his body drifted in the swell, swirling around the wreck, while the gale worsened.

During the sad months that followed Edwina was too proud to contact Simon. She had never been a very capable woman and now, incapacitated by grief and anxiety, she was almost useless. Tom did his best and succeeded in finding a buyer who offered Edwina ten thousand pounds for the business and equipment. She accepted, but as the weeks went by the money dwindled; there were so many claims to pay as well as the bank overdraft and salvage fee.

By the end of September, Edwina was left with three hundred pounds, two daughters aged six and three to bring up and no friends or relatives in the country. For a while she thought of returning to England, but her mother had died and she could see little point in going back. It was enough to survive.

Edwina had worked as a teacher in England, but local schools were full, although some offered her the next vacancy for an English teacher. Eventually she took a job at the haberdashery counter of a local department store which brought in thirty-two pounds a month.

She was forced to leave the children with the maid, which she had always dreaded, and returning home one evening she found the girl drunk on the floor with Margaret squatting beside her, bathing her face with a wet sponge. It took two days to replace the maid and when she returned to work the supervisor threatened her with dismissal. She endured the reprimand in silence and worried all day in case the children were being neglected.

Anna was in a quandary. She had read in the newspaper about Otto's death, but it seemed that Simon had not heard, or surely he would have rushed to Edwina's rescue, or so she imagined. What was she to do? She pondered on the problem for several weeks, hoping that Edwina would simply disappear. Various alternatives were open to her; she could give her the cash to go to England, but Simon might follow her. Anna felt sure that eventually Simon would find out about Otto's death and go to the aid of his widow. No, that was no good, nor could she leave her destitute, for Simon might feel obliged to support her. Eventually she decided that Edwina should become self-supporting and the safest place was right under her nose in Stellenbosch.

She set out accomplishing this in her usual practical manner.

Edwina's lawyer contacted her and told her that he had been approached by the board of the private school in Stellenbosch who had seen the advertisements he had placed on her behalf in the newspaper. They had a vacancy for an English teacher. The salary was on the low side, but a house went with the job. She applied and was accepted immediately, and when she learned that Rosemary could attend pre-school classes while Margaret would start Grade I she burst into tears of relief and spent the next ten minutes apologizing. She was to begin in January and in the meantime she could move into the cottage. The house had three bedrooms; she could hardly believe her good fortune – she fell in love with the old pressed ceilings, the antique carved door, the funny cobbled

370

yard in front.

There was only one drawback; the school was in the same town where Simon's wife lived and her children also went there. That was really upsetting but where else would she find such a suitable position?

'It's not England,' she told her daughters. 'This could never, never be England, but it will do for the time being until we've saved enough to go home.' Then she set about buying the furniture they needed with the remains of her money.

It was Friday afternoon and Anna had been waiting for almost an hour in the doctor's consulting rooms.

'Well, and how is she?' She put on the false heartiness that adults use when dealing with sick children as the doctor emerged at last.

Katie followed listlessly. For days she had been moping around the house, looking wretched, with big shadows under her eyes. Clearly she was sickening for something and Anna prepared herself for the worst.

'Fine, fine, fine,' the doctor said echoing Anna's tone. 'There's nothing physically wrong with her. If you ask me, Katie's trying to dodge school.'

Surely he should know it was holiday time, Anna thought peevishly.

Katie shot him a look of dislike. She turned to Anna. 'I told you I'm all right. You wouldn't listen.' She smiled wanly.

'Now you sit there a few minutes, Katie, while I talk to your mother. Won't be long.' Anna's stomach contracted as she followed the doctor into his surgery.

'As I said, there's nothing physically wrong with her.' Anna felt her muscles let go and she exhaled audibly. 'It's just that she's a very unhappy child. Do you have problems in the home? What could upset her so? Her father's away in Namaqualand, she tells me. Perhaps she's pining. Is she close to her father?'

'Perhaps,' Anna said uneasily, 'but he's always been away — on and off.' She leaned back and closed her eyes, thinking that the tragedy of rearing children was that you could not create a

371

perfect world however hard you tried. They missed him badly, she knew, but he never failed to telephone twice a week and he drove down every month to see them. She had no complaints of Simon as a father. She knew how much he loved and missed the children.

Besides, lately she had been able to spend more time with them. Koos was running the poultry superbly with Pa supervising; the stock buying was handled by a team of men on commission; Kurt needed no help to run the business and for the first time Anna had time on her hands. She lavished it all on her children. Perhaps because Katie was her stolen child she felt doubly responsible, showering her with gifts and new clothes, and she seldom went out without her.

Every free afternoon Anna took the children riding, swimming or fishing, depending on who pleaded the hardest. Katie had to be shuttled to and from ballet, piano, gym, drama, and singing lessons; Acker preferred farming. How could Katie be unhappy? Yet something was wrong.

Anna took Katie home, stopping to buy a rubber dinghy on the way. They could play on the dam, they were both good swimmers.

'How would you like to go for a holiday with your father?' Anna asked Katie in the car.

'Oh no,' the girl opened her eyes in mock horror. She was always acting and often it was hard to know when she was sincere, but this time she seemed genuinely upset.

Anna was puzzled.

It rained the next day. No problem for Acker, he had a million things to do, but Katie hung around looking depressed until her mother volunteered to play the piano while Katie sang. Usually it was Katie's favourite occupation, but this time she was unenthusiastic. They went through all their favourite songs, but Katie sung dutifully with none of her usual sparkle.

When she broke off and burst into tears her mother led her to the couch, pulled her on her lap and hugged her.

'Now look here Katie, that's enough of your nonsense. I

want to know what's wrong. You're eleven years old. Good gracious, almost grown up. Far too old to cry. You know you can trust me,' Anna persisted, after a long silence.

Katie began in a roundabout way. 'Uncle Kurt's getting divorced because Aunt Madeleine left the house. What will happen to Paul now?'

'Why nothing. Paul will live with Uncle Kurt. A nice governess called Vera is coming to look after him.' She stared uneasily at her daughter.

'But if you divorce Pa and marry Kurt, will Pa still be my Pa?' she burst out.

'But I'm not going to divorce Daddy and I'm not going to marry Kurt either,' Anna said and laughed. 'Whatever gave you such a silly idea ...' She broke off, feeling alarmed. It was only a few days since Kurt had told her of the pending divorce. No one else knew, so how had Katie found out?

It was Sunday when Kurt came, she remembered, and she was schooling a new mare in the paddock. He must talk to her at once, he insisted, so she took him into the stables and he stood watching impatiently as she rubbed down the horse. She tried to recall what he said, but could only remember the gist of the conversation.

He was furious because after seven months Madeleine still refused to go back to him. He had discovered that she was living with an artist. Madeleine was painting, too, and planning an exhibition.

'I'll be the laughing stock of town. I'm divorcing her. In fact, the summons has been issued. In three months it will be finalized. Just like that,' He snapped his fingers. 'So easy in this country.' He grinned. 'Now that your peasant has left you, too, there's nothing to stand in our way.'

He began to pace the concrete floor and his tension was transmitted to the horses, who became restless. 'You've been dilly-dallying for years, Anna, but I've reached the crossroads in my life. Either you divorce Simon and marry me, or I'm selling up and returning to Germany.'

Anna groped for excuses; anything but the truth. The children needed Simon; André needed his family; she could not face the scandal.

Kurt was at his most persuasive. 'Scandal! My God, Anna. D'you think Simon is leading a monk's existence! D'you think no one knows about Edwina. There's a woman up at Springbok right now …'

'Stop it, stop it,' she cried. 'It's none of your business. I don't want to know.'

'What about Paul?' Kurt had thrown in. 'He needs a mother, you said so yourself.'

'He's welcome here always,' she said sullenly.

'Come to your senses, Anna, before it's too late. Simon married you for your money. He never cared for you, but I've always loved you. We used to be happy and we can be happy again. I'll give you a week to think it over.'

Frowning and resentful, he had pushed her against the wall and kissed her. 'I'll never forget the nights we spent together,' he murmured.

'I'll never forget Bosluis,' she flung at him. 'It was your fault Simon left.'

He stormed off, leaving her puzzled. Perhaps the divorce was affecting him more than he would admit, or perhaps it was the trauma of passing forty.

She had not seen him since Sunday, but every time the telephone rang she expected it to be Kurt, demanding, questioning, upsetting her.

Anna could hardly wait until Flora called the children for their supper. Instead of sitting with them she ran to the stables and looked around. Perhaps the loft, she thought. Climbing the ladder she peered around and there in the corner she saw a house made out of straw, complete with books, sweets, Cokes and André's binoculars. How awful! They had heard everything.

That night, when she read them a story, she rifled in the cupboard until she found the children's version of Hercules. The stories seemed to go on forever, but she was determined to reach Penelope's tapestry before they fell asleep.

'So you see,' she told them seriously. 'Everyone wanted to marry Penelope while Hercules was away, but she was only pretending. She was waiting for Hercules to come home.' But perhaps that was a little subtle for eleven-year olds.

'Men often want to marry women who don't want to marry them. Of course it's best not to be rude, but just to put them off. I certainly don't want to marry anyone but your father,' she said gently.

Acker turned to Katie. 'I told you not to tell Ma, you silly little ninny,' he exploded.

'I didn't tell,' she yelled.

''Course you did. You always do.' He stared at his mother thoughtfully. He loved her for her frailties as much as for her virtues. It was a strangely adult love.

'Women are so silly,' he said. 'All you had to say was: "Kurt I don't love you enough to marry you." Do you think he's going to pack up the business? Really mother, it's his life. And if he did, who cares?'

'You don't really like Kurt, do you?' she said, feeling silly.

'No, not much.'

'Is there some reason why you don't like him?'

'Nothing you'd understand,' he said and turning, pulled the blankets over his head.

Anna sat and held Katie's hand until she fell asleep.

41

England, or 'home' as mother called it, had become a sort of fairyland to Margaret, where the weather was never too hot, nor too cold, the snow fell in December to make Christmas pretty, a queen lived in a castle and everyone was always safe.

But it can't be prettier than Stellenbosch, Margaret thought. No place could be prettier than here. She had said very little when they arrived, but behind her solemn grey eyes was a mind that drank beauty like a thirsty horse gulps water; she would scoop it in at every available opportunity. Margaret was an over-sensitive girl, loving everyone, expecting to be loved in turn, and as this was not often the case, life was just one trauma after the next.

This morning she was terrified for it was the first day of school. Knees tight with tension she had trailed behind her mother who kept repeating, 'Hurry up Margaret, please dear, we can't be late. Poor darlings. If your dear Father had not drowned at sea you would never have had to attend an Afrikaans farm school, but I promise it won't be forever, Margaret. Keep your head high and never forget you're English. Don't let them bully you because you can't speak Afrikaans.' So they continued with warnings, threats, promises and advice until Margaret was as confused as she could possibly be.

Her teacher tried to make her feel welcome, but Margaret was unable to understand the Afrikaans lessons. So she gazed out of the window at mountains and deep blue sky. Even the classroom was beautiful: tall ceilings, flowers on every windowsill, walls covered with the children's drawings. They were all farming children so they drew donkeys, horses, cats, sheep, fathers on tractors and Margaret loved every one of them.

At break the children ran into the field behind the school leaving their shoes and socks under their desks. Margaret, not wishing to be different, took hers off, too, and tried to ignore the sharp stones and thorns. Her feet were too sore to play tag so she sat on the edge of the field watching while she munched her sandwiches. Soon a scruffy dog with short legs came slinking on its belly through the long grass towards her. It was a funny looking dog, with long, pointed nose, floppy ears, a bushy tail and a skinny body with ribs jutting out. She offered a piece of cheese and the dog dashed forward, snatched it out of her hand and retreated a few yards to swallow it ravenously. 'The poor thing's starving,' she said to herself and gave it her sandwiches.

When the school bell rang, the dog, whom she called 'Sandy', trailed at her heels, but the children would not let him in the school. The dog retreated and crouched on its belly, eyes pleading, so she sat with it.

Teacher came out. 'Come along Margaret, you're late.'

Caught halfway between fear and determination Margaret burst into tears and clasped the dog's neck so tightly that he was nearly throttled.

She was conscious of a great shadow blotting out the sun and, looking up she saw two green eyes, a freckled face and big white teeth laughing at her. He must be the biggest boy in the whole world, she thought, and his hair was the brightest red she had ever seen. 'Why are you crying? What's the matter with you?' the boy said.

'I don't want to leave my dog. It'll run away.'

'No it won't, it's always here and it's not yours,' the boy said. 'What's your name?'

'Margaret.'

'Ah, you're Mrs Tenwick's daughter.'

Margaret nodded.

'I've met you before,' the boy went on, 'but you were smaller and you won't remember. My name's Acker Smit. My father and your father were in business together.'

'I remember him,' she blurted out.

'What are you doing with this dirty thing? Just look at your dress.'

She was covered in dirt and grease, for the dog had been hiding under cars. Its eyes were filled with mucus and its coat was encrusted with shiny black knobs.

'It's starving,' she said. 'I just found it, but I'm keeping it.'

'Of course it's starving,' he said. 'Because it's a kaffir dog.'

'What's a kaffir dog?' she asked.

'From the blacks' village. They've turned it out, so now no one wants it. It'll starve.'

'No it won't, 'cause it's coming with me,' she said angrily.

'D'you know what these things are?' Acker went on taking hold of one of the round shiny knobs and pulling hard. The dog winced and suddenly Acker was holding an obscene insect with six waving feet and no head. 'Look, see? Its head's still under the dog's skin and now it's going to get a sore,' he went on.

'No, it's not. I'll take it out,' she said.

Three small girls appeared on the front step. 'Margaret,' they chorused in English. 'Teacher says you must come now.'

'Tell you what,' Acker went on. 'It won't run away, it's been here for days. I'll take it home after school and clean it for you. Then I'll bring it to your Ma's. Sure you want it?'

'I want it,' she said firmly.

'Do you know him?' the girls asked, wide-eyed as they linked arms with her. Acker was their hero, Margaret discovered. He was head boy of the primary school as well as captain of the rugby and swimming teams and when he befriended Margaret some of his aura rubbed off on her. Every girl in the school wanted to be friends with Acker and so they made friends with her instead.

As the weeks rolled into months Margaret began to love the school and surrounding countryside with a passion that was unusually intense for someone so young. She loved the heat, the smell of damp earth when the early morning sun made it steam, the mountains, wild flowers, the vineyards and the

378

people, particularly the farm workers for they seemed so natural and warm-hearted.

One afternoon she returned home to find her mother digging up the poinsettia in front of their cottage with the help of the school gardener.

'How could you? How could you?' she cried and burst into tears. 'That beautiful, beautiful tree.'

Edwina, who loved her children, was upset and hastily trampled the roots back into the earth.

'Run and get a bucket of water, child,' she said quickly. 'I'm sure I haven't killed it.'

When the roots were carefully pressed back Margaret said, 'Why, Mother? How could you spoil something so lovely?'

'I wanted to make an English cottage,' Edwina explained, suddenly on the defensive and wondering why. 'I bought some rambling roses. Look how lovely the lavender is and the Michaelmas daisies.'

'But this is not England, Mother,' Margaret said slowly. In all her life she had never had to explain anything so difficult; she fumbled for the words and eventually, knowing that she was not succeeding at all, she said, 'It belongs there. That tree belongs there,' and went off in a huff to take Sandy for a walk. How could she explain feelings and thoughts just taking root? A sense of belonging.

Two months after school began Edwina received a letter from the school board welcoming her and requesting a meeting. Edwina arrived at the school's common room, where the meeting was to take place, and found that Mrs Anna van Achtenburgh-Smit was the sole representative of the board.

Anna frightened Edwina from the moment she saw her; those huge blue eyes flashing coldly like the diamonds she wore, the extravagant silk dress, the blood-red, long nails. She uncoiled herself from the battered sofa and formally welcomed Edwina to the school. 'Do sit down,' she said. 'I hope you like the cottage.'

Edwina murmured her thanks.

'I expect you're wondering why I called this meeting,' Anna went on while Edwina sat poised on the edge of the chair, eyes watchful like deer that has sensed a leopard.

'I wanted to warn you of the school politics,' Anna went on. 'You see, the staff were very much against the appointment of another English teacher; after all Miss Joubert was coping adequately, so I suggest you tread softly. Perhaps you could start a few joint projects, make a friend of her. It's not easy to fit in where there's no real need, but you can count on my support. To all intents and purposes I am the school board.' She smiled coldly.

Edwina gasped. 'But I don't understand. I thought this position, I mean, it being in the same town as you, well, I thought it was just a coincidence.'

Anna pressed her fingertips together. 'Oh, come now, surely you discovered what a dearth of teaching positions there are at present. After all you took a job in a haberdashery department. You worked as an English teacher in London, I believe, although unqualified, and this is the only place where I have any influence. What else could I do?' Her mouth smiled again, but her eyes were cold.

Edwina shivered. 'I had no idea … I don't know what to say.'

'Oh, my dear, how naïve you are, no wonder you believed all Simon's silly stories.'

Edwina stood up, nervously rubbing her hands together. 'I don't think we should discuss …' she began.

'No, sit down,' Anna said sharply. 'I really haven't finished. If we're going to work together for years we may as well understand each other.'

'But we don't work together,' Edwina retorted coldly.

'Oh yes, in a way we do. I'm very involved in school activities. I don't know if you've heard that my family founded this school. It's practically our school, although other families are represented on the board.' Anna stood up and began to pace the carpet. Hate was rising like flood waters as she talked to Edwina. She could not help imagining her in bed with Simon.

'We have a lot in common,' she went on. 'Simon took us both for a ride, the only difference being I married him,' she

380

shrugged. 'You'll probably think I'm mad, but the fact is I still love him in spite of all the women he's had. I'd never give him a divorce. Not that he's ever asked for one,' she added quickly.

She glanced at Edwina, who was sitting bolt upright, stony-faced.

'He's always breaking women's hearts. He told me Otto surprised you both and the two of them could not decide who was responsible for you, so they tossed up and Simon won. Not very gallant of him to tell me, was it?'

Edwina began to sob quietly, covering her face with her hands.

'But then, he isn't a very gallant person,' Anna went on and for a few seconds she stood in front of Edwina, staring down at her.

Edwina looked up and shuddered. 'I loved my husband,' she said softly. 'It was only because ...'

'Don't tell me, Simon already has. You needed someone to look after you.'

'Why are you telling me all this?' Edwina looked up hopelessly.

'I just want to clear the air between us. I want you to know that you are quite secure here, unless, of course ...' The unspoken threat lay heavily between them. 'I just wanted to warn you about Simon.'

Anna left suddenly in a rustle of silk, leaving a trail of perfume behind.

After the meeting Edwina spent a few months trying to find another post, but was unsuccessful.

From then on, she lived for the day when she could take her children home to England, but each year her goal receded as British housing prices increased and her savings dwindled. Besides, she would need more than a house to start again with two growing girls. At least in Stellenbosch they were secure, although there was no cash for luxuries.

Besides, the children were happy. Margaret became brown and sturdy. She was always running barefoot over the veld and by the time she was eleven she was fluent in Afrikaans and involved in wild life, horses, farming and subjects that were of no interest to Edwina. She was seldom home except to sleep or to deposit another strange creature in their midst. They had three tortoises, two dogs, a bush baby, and an assortment of birds, scorpions, crickets and even a meercat. Margaret wanted a horse and Rosemary wanted a piano, but both demands were equally unrealistic. It hurt Edwina to have to say 'no,' but there it was. She knew it was hard on the children, being the only family without a car, without a large garden and horses, the only ones who never went for holidays. Still, they survived, and that was something to be thankful for. Edwina scraped and scrimped to pay for Rosemary's piano lessons and Margaret worked at the local stables where they gave free tuition in return for her labour.

The one big annoyance for Edwina was 'that woman' who seemed to overshadow her life. When, at the completion of two years, Edwina applied for a rise, the school board turned down her application on the grounds of lack of qualifications and her need for matric-level Afrikaans. She began to study at night. When the board decided on fund-raising activities Edwina would be sure to land up with the brunt of the labour; when she raised a bond from the local building society and attempted to buy her cottage, the board refused to sell. The board, or Anna, became a stumbling block for all her aspirations.

Worse still, it was always Anna who gave the prizes at the end of each school year and Edwina would usually find herself detailed to fetch and carry for her. Even more annoying was Acker's friendship with Margaret – at least three times a year an invitation would arrive for Margaret and Rosemary to attend a garden party or a birthday party and Edwina would endure the humiliation of walking the children two miles to Fontainebleu and trudging up the long driveway while other families swept past in cars. Always refusing to stay, she would leave the children at the door and return later to collect them, again enduring the humiliating walk. She would have liked to forbid Margaret to play with Acker, but could not bring herself to do that. Eventually their friendship ended without her interference.

Walking up the mountain path one day, Margaret heard a shot and saw a hawk swoop down. Panting with dismay she ran to the spot hoping the poor creature was dead, but it was cowering in some dense bushes while Acker and three friends tried to beat it out.

'You mustn't kill,' she shrieked. 'Acker, how could you? You, of all people. I'll never speak to you again.' She sat on the ground and burst into tears. Acker fought off the boys, caught the hawk and dropped it on to her skirt. She caught its body while the shattered wing hung over her knee.

'Have the damn thing for all I care,' he said looking shame-faced as he stalked off with his friends. The following month she was not invited to Acker's birthday party.

The bird mended with a good deal of care and expense from the local vet and for a few weeks sat on a perch behind the radio in the living room, devouring minced meat, until one day the vet pronounced it to be healed. Margaret took it to the top of the mountain where it flew away.

Margaret, however, did not mend quite so easily; she became more introverted, more involved with her animals and less able to make friends.

It was shortly afterwards that André van Achtenburgh had a recurrence of his old trouble and because Anna and Katie were spending a week at Knysna, Acker called Jacob to drive the car and took André to casualty. He looked so frail and bewildered when he was transferred to the urology ward on a stretcher.

Acker was fifteen, but looked older, for he was over six feet tall, with broad shoulders and deep-set, dark green eyes.

The young nurses giggled and flirted with him. Acker stayed by the bedside all day, talking about plans they had made for the farm, and when at last André fell asleep he fetched Jacob and drove home to telephone his mother.

'He's dying, Mom, I just know it. You must come home.'

They arranged to meet at the ward at ten, but when they arrived André was being X-rayed and they sat in the empty ward for an hour, feeling depressed. Eventually he was wheeled back and Anna was distressed to see how his strength had waned in the past few days.

The doctor took Acker aside, assuming him to be older than he was. 'I'm afraid it's bad news.'

Acker nodded. He knew already that André was dying.

'The cancer has blocked the tube from the kidneys so that he cannot pass water and he will die soon of renal failure.'

Acker glared at the doctor. 'Surely you can cut out the growth, or put him on the kidney machine?'

'Prolonging life in cancer areas simply brings terrible pain when the cancer reaches other organs. We try to avoid this.'

'How long?' Acker asked.

'About five days, maybe seven ...' The doctor shrugged apologetically.

'That's impossible,' Acker stammered. 'Yesterday he was walking.'

'But today he can't,' the doctor pointed out. Adding, 'He'll lapse into a coma which could last up to ten days.'

'But can he come home?' Acker persisted. 'We don't want him to die amongst strangers.'

'Either way it can make no difference to the outcome. If you'll excuse me ...' The doctor left; his limited time was for those who could be cured.

André was still sitting up looking depressed, but cheered up when he heard he could go home.

Late that night Anna burst into tears when Acker told her the doctor's verdict. 'You had no right to keep this to yourself,' she stormed.

'But I knew you would cry,' he said, 'and then Grandpa would see.'

Of course he was right. How was it possible that Acker had grown so responsible, she wondered? Of all the men she knew Acker was by far the most dependable. Always there when you needed him. She went sadly to bed and cried all night. Life would never be the same again without Pa. In the morning she spent half an hour washing her eyes with eye drops before she could face her father. From then on Acker stayed at his grandfather's side, sleeping in an adjoining room, watching the old man sinking.

André, puzzled at his failing health, began to imagine in turn that he had been poisoned, that he was dying of starvation, that he had not been given the medical attention he deserved. Finally he clutched Acker's hand and said, 'I don't want to lie down. I'm afraid to sleep in case I drift into unconsciousness and never wake.'

By the seventh night André was very weak.

'Acker, I'm dying, aren't I?'

Acker looked away.

'Yet I can't think why,' he went on as Acker did not reply. 'I feel no pain, just a bit uncomfortable, but I'm so weak.'

He smiled, but looked so sad.

Watching him Acker had to fight to control himself. 'Don't give up, Grandpa,' he said, not wishing to lie.

'It's the modern trend nowadays,' André complained. 'Treat old people like babies; lie to them. You know something Acker. You don't even have to tell me. I can see it in your eyes, and your mother's eyes, too.' He sighed.

'Strange, but I don't feel any older than when I was thirty,' he went on. 'It's only that lately I remember my youth so well, and it's so much closer than it's been for years.' He pressed his lips tightly together. 'Well if this is all there is, I can't really complain. I've had a good life, but still, it seems wrong somehow.'

He blinked and then closed his eyes and for a while Acker thought he was sleeping, but André was wide awake. After a while he reached out again and pressed Acker's hand.

'Times like this you can't help looking back and thinking about what you've done and what you haven't done. Nothing else to do, I suppose. I made one big mistake, my boy, and it's bothered me for years.'

Acker hung on, trying to swallow past the lump in his throat. He loved his grandfather more than he loved his father, even more than Ma. The thought of him not being there was almost more than he could bear.

'Why Acker,' his quiet voice went on. 'If I'd had my way all those years ago, you'd have been adopted. Yet you're the best thing that's happened in my life. We get on fine, don't we?'

The feeble hand squeezed Acker's again.

'You see I was deadset against Simon – tried to stop the marriage, but your mother was determined. But later, when Simon came back from the war, he had grown up, he didn't want to be beholden to us. He couldn't live here, but if I had acted different in the first place, who knows, they may have been happy.

'Funny thing about your mother, she was always such a sweet girl. She's not tough really, not as strong as you are, although she likes to make out that she is. You'll have to look after her when I'm gone.'

'Don't talk like that, Grandpa,' Acker said, staring hard at the wall.

'You know Acker, I've been thinking about life and it seems to me there's more to morality than we're taught. It's not enough just to be good – the absence of sin – why that's nothing. You have to be good to yourself, too. Be fulfilled! I want you to find out who Acker Smit is before it's too late; live your life as you feel it should be lived. Your mother hasn't found out who she is and it hurts me when I see how unhappy she is.'

'Grandpa, why don't you sleep?' Acker said. 'You haven't slept for nights. No wonder you're exhausted.'

'No,' André said obstinately. 'You lift me into my wheelchair, Acker. I've plenty of time to sleep ahead of me. Right now there's nothing I want more than to stay awake.'

He insisted on being wrapped in blankets and wheeled on to the balcony.

'You'll catch a chill,' Acker argued.

'At this stage do you really think it matters?' André said softly. 'Now you go away. Have a sleep. I want to sit here alone and watch the vines in the moonlight. I've always loved them so; listen to the owls and the frogs down in the river; hear the wind in the leaves. That's life, Acker. That's life.'

Acker was exhausted and slept until dawn. He awoke with a fright and raced to his Grandpa's room to find he was dead and already stiff. The corpse did not even look like André; a rigid, discarded shell frozen into a macabre sitting position.

The boy flung himself on to the bed and began to sob and the torrents of grief were as much for the human race as for André. After a while he called his mother and went outside, leaving her to cope with death. He sniffed the fresh air. How fragrant it was, cool and fresh; the grapes were half picked and André was missing all this. He walked through the vineyard and the woods to the mountain slopes.

'Oh God,' he whispered. 'If I could only understand. One day I too will not be able to put out my hands and touch the leaves and the bark of trees.' He caught hold of the tree trunk and pressed his body against it. Then he stepped back and sat on the earth, covering his face with his hands. Man's perennial question possessed and eviscerated him. He felt himself burdened by the grief of the human race; for those who would one day die and those who had died before. If there was a God, if there was immortality, then why were we left in ignorance, hoping, imagining or blindly believing? Surely it would have been far better never to have been created than to face extinction, he thought. Like flowers in the Garden of Eden, one brief burst of life, an evanescent glow. 'Oh God,' he muttered. 'If I could just believe.' But solace would come only with intimacy. So he sat on, pleading, cajoling, threatening, hating, while the sun rose and fell and darkness came.

42

The rain fell in torrents, churning the ground to mud. Simon was standing in a large crater he had dug over the past few days with the aid of five workers. He stared around moodily. There had been no rain for months, so why could it not have waited another week until the sides of the dam were reinforced?

Even as he watched, the sides of sloping earth were slipping back. They would have to start again when the rain stopped; that was his fate, a perpetual wrangling with nature, he thought, but God knows, they needed the rain.

He bent over and took a handful of soil and rubbed the texture between his fingers. With regular rain it would be fertile soil, but stony. The soil drained between his fingers leaving three stones in the palm of his hand, splashed by the downpour.

He was about to throw them down when his gaze was snared by one of them. It looked so much like a rough piece of shattered glass the size of a pea. A diamond! Impossible! He had never heard of diamonds in Namaqualand, yet this *was* a diamond. He was sure of it. He put it thoughtfully in his pocket and glanced round to see if anyone had noticed.

He drove the workers back to the settlement, for there would be no more work until the rains finished, and went on to the nearest co-op to purchase a large sieve.

'Going prospecting?' the manager joked.

'No, building,' he said.

When he returned he was in a quandary. Should he call the farm workers? The job of sifting the soil in the crater would be completed that much faster, but they would be bound to talk. Finally he decided to do it himself and he stayed all day in the summer rain, sifting, examining, hoping against hope that he had found one solitary diamond, never to be repeated, but by nightfall he had five and one was as large as his thumbnail.

He drove home sodden and depressed.

It was five years since Simon had moved to Namaqualand and during that time he had grown to love the place; it was a hard, merciless land where man pitted his ingenuity and his courage against overwhelming odds. In this man's world Simon had been able to lick his wounds, regain his pride after the loss of Modderfontein and recover from his guilt over Otto's death.

It had been months before he had heard about it, the news had arrived belatedly on an old newspaper wrapped around a piece of farm equipment he had ordered from the Cape. He had driven overnight to Cape Town, met the new owners, visited Otto's grave, and eventually, feeling guilty and useless, driven to Fontainebleu where the twins had been overjoyed to see him.

Frantic inquiries to find Edwina had met with no luck until Acker, walking into the study the next day and hearing his father on the telephone, had said, 'But, good heavens, Father, Auntie Edwina is teaching at the school and they live in the cottage Mama bought from old Joubert's estate down by the stables.'

'Your mother bought them a cottage?' Simon had asked incredulously. When he tackled Anna she had merely smiled and said, 'It was the least I could do in your absence, dear.'

Simon had telephoned Edwina after school, but she had told him to keep away and put the telephone down on him and after that he had heaved a sigh of relief and taken the twins for a short holiday.

Since then he had worked night and day to build up the farm hoping to gain enough from his fifty per cent share of profits to start again with a farm in Malmesbury. For once his prospects had looked good until now. He sighed.

For the next few days Simon sieved the soil alone in the rain until he had a bad attack of flu and over twenty diamonds in his pockets. It appeared to be a particularly rich mine and he planned to make sure that the van Achtenburghs owned the mineral rights before the news leaked, present Anna with the bag of diamonds, and leave her to worry about the wearisome business of marketing them.

February was the time that Anna loved best, for then the vines would be burdened under their heavy harvest of thick, glossy grapes and an air of excitement would hang around Fontainebleu, infecting everyone. The family, the workers, the kitchen staff, would dash around in a frenzy; there was so much to do and each day Coloured farm folk, tramps and schoolchildren would come from miles around, traipsing up the lane to help harvest the grapes. The export shed would be opened and the best Hanepoot and Waltham Cross would be lovingly laid in trays on tissue paper and nailed up for export to Europe. The wine grapes were sent to the winery and the grapes for home consumption to market by the lorryload.

This year, however, the excitement was lacking, the mood subdued for André was dead and buried.

Anna spent most of her time closeted in the study trying to get to grips with the estate that André had run together with Acker and it was here that Simon found her.

He looked so tired, she thought, and downcast, dressed in dirty khaki trousers and shirt. Nevertheless at thirty-eight he had reached a peak of physical fitness, broad shoulders, skin burned almost black by the sun, and now that he had matured he looked even more handsome.

She was startled to see him and said, 'My God, you look ...' She had wanted to say 'magnificent', but bit back the word and substituted 'tired'. 'We've been trying to get hold of you. Where were you?'

'Busy,' he said evasively.

'Pa died. We buried him yesterday,' she said without a sign of emotion.

'Hell, I'm sorry. I should have been here. I'm really sorry. I liked the old boy. We had a bad start, but we got on just fine.'

390

'I know,' she said. 'He liked you a lot. Told me so before he died.' She turned away, blinking, and stared out of the window at the harvest.

'We've had a particularly good year,' she went on. 'With the wheat and the grapes. How's it going your end?'

He dropped a bag on her desk. 'This is for you,' he said without answering.

'Is it a present?' Her face lit up.

'No.'

'Oh.' She bit her lip.

'It's your property, from the farm.' Still she stared at the bag. 'Go on, open it,' he said impatiently.

She opened the box and found it full of stones. 'Uncut diamonds,' she said wonderingly. 'Did you say from Luembe?'

'Yes.'

She tipped them on to her desk and ran her fingers through them. 'Fifty. I can't believe it. Look at this one.' She picked up the largest which he had found on the first day. 'It's enormous. I don't even know if we have the mineral rights.'

'You do, or rather André did. I've been checking. That's where I've been the past two days.'

Suddenly she yelled and flung herself at Simon. 'Rich, rich, we're rich.'

He disentangled himself from her arms. 'You mean you're richer,' he said. 'I'm still a bum.'

It did not take long for rumours to race around the village; Anna van Achtenburgh-Smit had scored again and was a multi-millionairess with a pit full of diamonds you could dig up with a spade; or, she had sold the mining rights for ten million pounds; or else, the biggest diamond mine in Africa. Stories blazed like veld fires, getting bigger and better and no one knew how they started.

The truth was Anna had negotiated a very good deal for the family. She had leased the mining rights for ten per cent of turnover. Her joy quickly evaporated when she and Simon had a last, bitter fight. Anna insisted that Simon was entitled to half of the proceeds of the farm according to the terms of their contract. He, however, said the contract stipulated karakul sheep, not diamonds, and refused the money she tried to shower upon him. To Anna it seemed that Simon was spitefully thwarting and wounding her. Simon, however, had learned the hard way and knew that to him unearned cash was unrewarding. He wanted to succeed on his own. Eventually he agreed to take half the cash from the sale of the sheep and he rented a small shack in the village and began a service and repair business for farming implements and vehicles.

Anna was furious when she found out. How could he make such a fool of her, and the children? There was Anna in her mansion and Simon in a small rented room downtown. Their fight was long and devastating. At the end of it Simon told her to go to hell and Anna watched his battered car leave for the village.

From then on she discovered that she had no idea what to do with her wealth. To be sure Fontainebleu needed air conditioning and heating and she installed it, but she could have afforded it years before. She added another wing to the farm workers' school and employed a second teacher, but this was insignificant, for Anna's spending power was colossal.

Anna became the target for numerous charity collectors. Hardly an evening passed without the front door bell ringing two or three times until she employed a secretary to deal with these irritating nuisances.

Anna never forgot her first year at Modderfontein when, alone and penniless, she had battled to survive and today, far from being enriched by hard times and her achievements, she was deeply scarred, insecure and bitter. As the years passed the trauma increased. Deep inside she was still the friendless Anna Smit, and all that her wealth had done was bring numerous acquaintances. Nowadays she was seldom alone; always needed for committees, fund raising, school functions. But if acquaintances tried to get closer they would be rebuffed, for to Anna a hand stretched out in friendship was a beggar's supplication. Sooner or later she would find out what they wanted. She became increasingly suspicious, unable to be herself, for after all what was herself? Poor Anna Smit. Her wealth became a barrier and soon she began to richly deserve her reputation as a hard and bitter woman for Anna learned to use her wealth as a weapon, bludgeoning everyone with it.

To Kurt, Anna was a big disappointment. The camaraderie of their early business days had long since disappeared. Unable to come to terms with Anna's rejection of him, Kurt now found her vain, self-opinionated and ostentatious.

In 1956 Kurt turned forty-eight; time to sweep away illusions. Paul was eighteen and studying overseas and Kurt was lonely. He decided to marry. But who? He had to admit that he had become used to having his own way. His home was like a museum, containing priceless collections of paintings, sculpture and carpets. He hated the thought of a strange woman moving things around, introducing cats and potted plants, cluttering the place with female paraphernalia.

His thoughts turned to Vera Mankowitz, Paul's former tutor. She was now thirty-one and still a spinster, a plump girl, always smiling, obsessed with books and studying; demanding little from life and giving little in return. She had lived in his house for years and never once interfered; never thrown her weight around, or moved so much as a vase. Her personality did not intrude and it was easy to forget she was there. It did not take Kurt long to admit that she was the obvious choice.

He gave up bullying Anna and married Vera.

Anna was now alone apart from her children, yet at thirty-seven she was still a striking woman with hardly a line on her face; her hair still dark without a trace of grey. She looked in her early thirties, but there was something cold about her, a certain frigidity that aged her and marred her beauty. Only with her children was she still a warm, loving and feeling woman. She loved them as passionately as when they were young and when she looked at them her face lit up with joy so that she appeared years younger. She spoiled them both, particularly her daughter. What else could she do with all that money?

Only one person in the family knew how to make the most of their wealth and that was Katie who, as she grew older, enjoyed every penny of it. She flaunted wealth like a peacock flaunts its tail, never being seen twice in the same outfit, discarding cars on a six-monthly basis and her chauffeurs with them. She began to give mad parties and threw herself into orgies of extravagance. Stories of her exploits began to circulate and they were never to her advantage.

Still, mother and daughter were inseparable, for while Acker showed a stolid indifference, both to their wealth and Anna's ambitions for him, Katie clung to her mother. They were friends; together they won the trophies at the horse shows; planned the hunts and hunt balls and went shopping. Katie was the best-dressed girl in town. She was also beautiful, talented, vivacious, arrogant and hopelessly spoiled. She loved to be the centre of attraction; at parties and gatherings she was always asked to sing. If her mother was present she would be persuaded to play the piano. Anna was not fond of public performances, but for her daughter's sake she gave in and soon the two of them were much in demand.

They were the envy of every woman in town and particularly Edwina, for she could not help enviously comparing her own daughter's prospects with Katie's. The sight of Katie regularly winning the English prizes, taking the lead in school plays, giving concerts at the school and even in the town hall increased her anger. How unfair it all was. Katie was vivacious, intelligent, a beautiful actress, an accomplished pianist and singer. She was also an outrageous snob and far too disdainful to speak to Edwina or Margaret. She overshadowed every other girl in the district and to compare her with Margaret was absurd for Margaret was gawky, awkward, too plump for her age and her blonde hair was always in a mess. She had difficulty communicating and all her pent-up emotions were directed towards animals, which she loved passionately.

Two major disasters occurred in Margaret's cloistered upbringing. The first was the discovery that she did not like her mother. Admittedly she loved her because she was her mother, but like – well, that was another matter.

Edwina had never succeeded in adapting herself to South Africa. She had learned enough Afrikaans to hold a conversation, but she would deliberately falter over the words and the women would switch to English for her sake. Although Edwina was fluent in both French and German she made a point of not being able to cope with the Afrikaans language or the local way of life, feeling that her English heritage gave her a sense of superiority over the rest of the townspeople. They were rich, but she was English; they travelled extensively, but she was still English; they wore the latest fashions, but her clothes were good, solid and made in England. She clung to her Englishness as a shipwrecked creature will cling to a raft.

Edwina kept apart from the other women and had no friends, but she had many acquaintances and was the main source of gossip in the town. She was feared for her sarcastic tongue, for her scathing observations of the frailties of human nature.

As a widow she felt her position to be impregnable, for she hated men now and there was no chance of her being involved in scandal. Her needs were few, she was mean to the point of obsessiveness and she hoarded their savings, which grew slowly each year. She would frequently tell her daughters how they stood in relation to 'going home'.

As her daughters began to ripen she began to feel uneasy that they might marry here and hamper her plans to leave, or worse still, that they might become the source of scandal. Consequently in 1957 when Margaret was fourteen she had only two short school dresses, flat black shoes and bobbysocks. She had never been out in the evening, never visited a restaurant or the theatre other than performances at the school, never had a date. Margaret did not mind, but the restrictions on her liberty irked her.

The second major disaster was when Margaret discovered that she would not be able to be a vet. She brought up the question of a future career one morning, and learned that her mother was impatient for the day when Margaret would join her as a wage earner. Years of studying were out of the question; one year at a teachers' training college might be possible. They'd have to see. It was the first time Margaret felt the impact of their poverty and her mother's obsession with saving. She began to work harder at the stables and saved the money she earned giving riding lessons. Maybe in a few years' time it would be possible, she hoped.

Katie had a different problem – for to indulge yourself from morning to night with the wholehearted pursuit of happiness is as tiring as any other task and far more boring; the worker can quit his job at five, but Katie spent all her waking hours at hers. She became tired and listless and began to look further afield for her entertainment.

Finally she decided upon a Swiss finishing school and after a little research discovered one attended by daughters of oil sheikhs and film stars.

She set about wooing Anna into agreeing to let her go. She knew it was not the expense that would worry Anna, but Katie's absence, so Katie prepared her ground as thoroughly as any general, mustering her reserves, setting out her front line of attack and when she marched in for the kill her mother was easily vanquished. Within twenty-four hours she had sadly agreed.

At first Anna was depressed about it, but the children deserved the best, she reasoned, and it was only for a year or two and then they would be home again. Acker, too, should have the best that money could buy. She decided to discuss it with him and sent Flora to bring him to the study.

As usual the boy looked like a tramp, which always annoyed Anna.

'There's a hole in your shorts,' she said irritably, 'and look at your shirt, it's filthy. Don't you have something better to wear?'

'Yes, I suppose I do,' he said with a smile, 'but it really doesn't matter, Mother, because I'm working in the stables today.'

'Something wrong?'

'Yes, bit of trouble with Katie's mare, but nothing that won't come right.'

It was his usual answer.

'Well, sit down,' Anna said and then called: 'Come in,' as Flora knocked on the door. Flora was getting old. They'd have to pension her off one of these days, as they had Jan who was living in a cottage on the estate. Jacob could only manage to hobble round the garden and prune the fruit trees. The place was turning into a home for the retired. She watched as Flora bent with difficulty to place the tray on the desk.

'Coffee?'

Acker was in a hurry and would have liked to refuse, but his mother had obviously planned this conversation in advance, so something must be bothering her. He concealed his impatience and sat down.

'Acker, I've been thinking how wrong it is for me to let you waste your days pottering around the farm. After all, you did brilliantly at school.'

'Well, hardly pottering, Mama,' he said shaking his head. 'I'm running the estate as well as the Malmesbury farm, then there's Modderfontein, the winery, the karakul ...'

'All right,' she interrupted him, unwilling to be sidetracked. 'The point is any farm manager could do what you're doing. You should be studying overseas.'

Acker leaned back and took a deep breath. So that was it. He knew Katie had been pestering Mother to go to a Swiss finishing school, which was all right for a girl, but he had more important things to do.

'I want you to study economics,' Anna was saying. 'You'll get an excellent degree overseas. One of these days you'll be inheriting the farm, the diamonds, our half of the Southern Cross food distribution group; fourteen companies there alone. It's going to be difficult for you without the right grounding.'

Acker sighed. For years he had known that one day he and his mother would have precisely this conversation; his world was not his mother's world and he doubted whether she

397

recognized the gulf between them – for while she was obsessed with her ambitions, he had none at all. His interests lay in quite another direction. He was content with farming, and whether it was his own farm or someone else's made little difference as long as he was close to the soil with time to think and to grow. But how to explain this to his mother without hurting her? Instead he confined himself to a simple, 'No mother, not for me. I prefer home.'

'But Acker,' she persisted. 'Just think. You'll be in partnership with Paul and he is getting the best education money can buy. He's at Cambridge.'

Acker sighed. 'Mother, I wish sometimes we had more time to get to know each other. If you knew me at all you would never suggest that I should go into business. I'm not interested.'

Anna bit her lip in vexation. 'Well, what do you want to do?' she asked impatiently.

Placing his hands on his knees Acker stared sombrely at the carpet. He had always been a slow talker and Anna was often impatient with him. Now he was going to take his time considering his reply. She wondered if that was why she spent so little time with the boy. She had hardly had a conversation with him over the past two years, except to discuss the state of the farm. 'It's amazing how you've grown,' she said. He was massive, as tall as Simon, but even broader, as if hewn from a block of granite, with craggy features, jutting nose and chin, huge hands and shoulders broad enough to carry an ox. He was earthy, she realized, there was no other way to describe Acker.

'Acker, you have duties and obligations to your family. You will be the custodian of the family fortunes and you'll probably have to look after Katie's affairs as well as your own. It's up to you to get as good an education as you can.'

Acker stood up and smiled slowly. Then he bent over and kissed her on the cheek. 'Ag, Mama, you're wasting your time,' he said and squeezed her shoulder. 'I'm a farmer and that's final.'

Anna knew he would not change his mind. Acker took after his father; his obstinate, proud, insufferable father.

43

When Katie heard the bell she wanted to scream with suppressed temper. The Swiss school was not the least bit as she had expected and although she was pampered and treated with respect she was also disciplined for the first time in her life. She fretted with the restrictions; when she felt like skiing it would be time for reading; when she had to wear evening dress that was the time she wanted to wear slacks and a sweater; she missed her car and chauffeur, midnight gallops over the estate. She had been as free as it was possible to be and she had exchanged it all for this web of petty restrictions and the companionship of a few conventional, unfriendly girls. Above all she hated the school bell; the sound of it dominated her life, regulated her thinking, the chimes jangled on her nerve-ends sending currents of rage surging through her. 'God damn it!' she said, kicking the chair.

The temptation to walk out of school, bus to the airport and catch the next flight home was almost irresistible, but to return after only six months was unthinkable, for she was far too vain to admit failure.

There was a knock at the door; one of the maids had been sent to find her.

'Enter,' she called.

The maid wore a severe navy uniform and a severe expression to match. 'Excuse me, Mademoiselle, but you are late for your music lesson. Monsieur O'Carrol is waiting.'

Muttering under her breath, Katie grabbed her music book and flounced along the corridor, down the wide marble staircase and across the hall to the music room. Slamming the door behind her she thumped her book on the piano.

Looking up, Michael could see the rage in her. He frowned. A spell in Ireland earning her own living would be of enormous benefit to the girl; of all the spoiled brats in the school she was by far the worst. To make matters worse she had one of the finest voices he had ever heard. It was untrained, but it was there. Wasted! Katie had no intention of even practising her scales.

'Well now, Miss Smit, it's a fine temper you're in this morning. I suggest you pick up your book and replace it more gently this time.'

'You can go to hell,' she said, tossing her fine red hair over her shoulder.

Katie stared into his deep blue eyes and momentarily flinched. All the girls in the school were crazily in love with their handsome Irish music teacher. Katie loathed him. It was rumoured he was a composer who earned his keep by teaching until he succeeded.

Watching her Michael yearned to box her ears, but he needed his job. It was his own fault he was burdened with her for three hours a week, for when Katherine Smit had arrived at the school he had been overjoyed to find talent at last and he had persuaded the school secretary to write to her parents, informing them of her extraordinary talent and requesting that she have her voice trained. Her mother had written back immediately giving permission and that was when the troubles began, for Katie had been furious. The singing lessons interfered with skiing, he discovered. He had tried persuasion, pointing out that her voice could earn her a fortune and bring pleasure to everyone.

'I already have a fortune and I look after my own pleasure and so can everyone else.' She was a determined young woman bent on having her own way.

Watching him now, and his taunting smile, Katie felt an irresistible urge to wipe the smile off his face.

'Pick it up, Katherine,' he repeated, 'and put it down gently.'

400

Katie picked up the book and brought it down none too gently on top of his curly black hair. 'I already told you what you can do,' she said. 'Music lessons are terminated, as of now.' That was that, she thought, she would not endure another hour of this nonsense.

She turned and smiled spitefully, yet when she saw his expression she made a dash for the door, but she was too late. Catching her by the arm he sat heavily on the chair, hauled her over his legs.

'I'll scream,' she hissed, but his hand came down hard on her rump.

'You bastard. You'll get the sack for this.'

His hand pounded rhythmically while Katie struggled, kicked and bit. 'I'll get the sack for sure,' he panted, 'and it'll be well worth the effort.' He was out of breath with the struggle.

He let her go and she scrambled to her feet.

'Poor little rich girl got what she so richly deserved,' he said. 'Why didn't you call for help?'

'I don't need help to deal with you,' she gasped. 'I'll get you myself.'

'Well said, Miss Smit,' his mocking smile was back in place, adding, 'now's your chance.' Footsteps were hurrying across the hall towards the music room.

Now that his temper had cooled Michael regretted his action. Absurd to lose this job because of a brat he detested. The two stood frozen in the centre of the room as the door opened.

It was the English teacher whom Katie disliked and her unattractive face was twisted into a look of suspicion and envy. Easy to see what she was thinking and on the spur of the moment Katie decided to play up to her. He'd get the sack either way.

She flushed, straightened her skirt and her blouse and smoothed back her hair. Then she groped for her book on the floor conscious of girls giggling in the doorway.

Michael ran his fingers over the piano keyboard. 'Are you

ready?' he said and for once he sounded unsure of himself.

The bastard! 'Yes, darling,' she said meekly and burst into song.

Anna missed Katie more than she had thought possible; the two years that she would be away stretched ahead endlessly and after the first few months Anna was feeling desperate. Besides, Acker was seldom with her; he travelled to the various farms they owned and when home he spent his evenings in the stables or catching up with accounts and administration. He had become a solid, dependable man; she could rely on him for anything except company. Paul was at Cambridge, Kurt seldom visited Fontainebleu nowadays and Simon still rented a room in town. Anna had never visited him there. Fontainebleu seemed larger and emptier than it had ever been.

It all began very casually, just to pass the time, but as the weeks passed Anna became increasingly involved in the welfare of the pupils at her farm school. She had always loved children and because of Katie she felt involved with the children of the farm workers. She found that when she was worrying about 'her children' as she called them, her own loneliness seemed to melt away until finally she became so busy there was no time left to worry about herself. She set up a job agency for school-leavers, and after this she decided to run an after-school recreation club in an abandoned hall which she purchased and renovated. All of a sudden the farm folk lost their suspicions and she earned the nickname of 'Auntie'. Being liked was a feeling that Anna knew little of and she found that it was a warm, pleasant inner glow. Some nights she even forgot to take her tranquillizers.

The farmers commented favourably on the recreation centre. Who knows, it might keep some of them out of the bars, but the job agency was criticised for it encouraged the youth to seek work away from the farms and labour was scarce. Anna received several critical letters.

Next Anna became involved in prison reform and child

welfare. After that it was only a small step into politics. When the local MP died, shortly afterwards, after a good deal of heartsearching, Anna decided to stand as an independent candidate in the by-elections. By now her liberal views were becoming well known.

Suddenly the town's business and farming right-wing echelon was set firmly against her. This was no mere pastime, Anna was on dangerous ground; the invitations stopped rolling in, she was no longer in demand for charitable functions and she was openly snubbed by one or two farmers' wives.

From morning to night Anna was obsessed with planning her campaign. She intended to gain a seat on the local council at the forthcoming election nine months ahead and characteristically she planned with precision, working at it from morning until night, so she was not really pleased when Vera Friedland telephoned asking if it would be convenient for them to visit her on the following Sunday.

'Do come for the weekend,' she said, adding falsely, 'it would be lovely to have you.'

The weekend was a disaster from the first dinner. Anna was woefully aware of her lonely state at the head of the long table with Vera and Kurt on either side and she became brittle and over-gay, laughing too loudly and drinking too much wine. Kurt seemed to delight in setting Vera up in order to knock her down. 'In the light of your training Vera,' he would ask, 'how do you see the current wave of crime amongst our youth?' Vera would blush happily and reply and Kurt would pounce on her, 'For an expert on child psychology that was the silliest remark I've heard.'

Vera never seemed to learn. After dinner she excused herself and went to bed.

'I'm afraid we're inclined to talk shop,' Kurt said. 'It bores Vera.'

'Yes,' Anna said, feeling glad that she had gone. 'How's Paul?'

Kurt frowned moodily. 'That's why we wanted to see you. Paul's left Cambridge. Refuses to go back.'

They were in the lounge huddled in front of a roaring fire, but its warmth seemed to extend only a few yards on this particularly cold winter's night. Kurt nursed his cognac in silence while Anna waited.

'The boy's a great disappointment to Vera,' he blurted out eventually. 'I can't say that I've ever really felt very close to him, but Vera has devoted her life to him.'

Her sympathies were with Paul. 'Perhaps he doesn't want to be Vera's life's work,' she said.

He glowered at her. 'We need your help. You've always had a great influence over the boy. We want you to persuade him to go back to Cambridge. Finish his education.'

'What does Paul want to do?'

'Such a lot of nonsense. Just wait till you hear it. He's coming for lunch tomorrow.'

Anna felt hurt that Paul had not telephoned her. They had always loved each other, although over the years Vera had done her best to keep him away from Fontainebleu.

Anna went to bed at eleven and after lying sleepless for an hour got up and hunted in her drawer for the sleeping pills. She took two, to be on the safe side, and slept deeply for six hours, but awoke at dawn with a headache. Early mornings were the worst and she always began by counting her assets on her fingers to reassure herself that all was well. Only then could she face the day.

Paul was late for lunch. By one-thirty Kurt was pacing outside the courtyard glancing at his watch, looking pale and disdainful. When Paul arrived on his motorbike he revved up and made as much noise as possible before parking. Then he took off his helmet and for a moment looked at Kurt with something close to hate in his eyes.

Anna was peeping through her study curtains and she thought Paul looked far older than his supposed eighteen years. He had developed into a short, stocky man, brown, with black hair and slanting eyes. Like a cossack. She felt resentful: unfairly burdened by this family drama thrust upon her for the weekend. Now she felt responsible, through no fault of her own. After all, it was Kurt's private disaster with his son. She watched Paul look away from his father, thrust his hands into his leather jacket and saunter nonchalantly up the steps to the hall. With a sense of being trapped and suffocated, she hurried out.

He greeted Anna rather formally and then said, 'Am I on time?' as if daring them to contradict him.

'Any time's all right,' Anna said. She went into the dining room and rang the bell for lunch and stood in the empty room waiting for the Friedlands to join her.

It was so cold. She shivered and looked out at the wintry scene; the bare branches of the old gnarled oak tree, the vineyards, gaunt and ugly. The mist obscured the mountains; drifted in valleys.

When Paul arrived five minutes later he joined her at the window. 'What this place needs,' he said, 'is more life. A good shopping centre, entertainment.'

'Don't start,' Kurt said from the door, and even Anna could hear how angry he was. She wondered what had caused the family drama, but it did not take long to find out.

Halfway through lunch Paul said abruptly, 'Have you told Aunt Anna about my plans?'

'Day-dreams, you mean?' Kurt smiled. 'No.'

'It's lunchtime,' Vera said.

'So?' Paul scowled at her. He hesitated. Then he said, 'What the hell. I might as well fight you as well.' He glanced briefly at her and for the first time Anna realized that he was an extremely tough individual. Paul was no longer a boy, but a hard, shrewd man determined to get his own way. She wondered if Vera realized this and why they were wasting their time arguing with him.

'This guy's trying to hold me back,' Paul said gesturing towards Kurt.

'How dare you?' Vera spoke in an unusually high-pitched voice and two red spots appeared on her cheeks. 'This guy is your father and you'll address him that way.'

'Come off it, Vera.' Paul subsided into sullen silence.

'Do you sleep at night?' he asked Anna abruptly.

'Yes,' she said, remembering the phial of yellow pills in her drawer.

'I don't,' Paul said gloomily. 'I lie in bed, think and plan; I've got everything mapped out; I know exactly what I'm going to do. All I need is a start.' He looked at Anna and a smile appeared and left just as suddenly. 'Lend me the cash I need.' He was suddenly cocky, over-confident. 'It's worth your while. You see I don't intend to inherit the family fortune or run the business. It will all be Acker's.'

Anna was taken aback by the brazenness of the boy. 'Paul, there's something I think you should know,' she said eventually. 'Acker is not going into the family business. He wants to be a farmer.' She smiled a little sadly. 'If it's Acker you're worried about, forget it.'

'Not me, Ma'am.' He began to attack his food ferociously.

Any minute now he's going to spear his tongue, Anna thought. Had Vera not taught him manners? She glanced slyly at her. Vera's face was tinged with red and she gazed at Paul as if mesmerized.

'Well, early days,' Anna went on with forced cheerfulness. 'I agree with your father. Get your degree first.'

'I don't have time,' Paul muttered.

Anna noted the big, powerful nose, the brutal neck, the sensual, self-confident mouth. 'What do you want to do?'

'I want to get hold of fifty thousand pounds,' he said flatly. 'If you won't lend me the capital I'll get it somewhere else.'

'What on earth is going on?' Anna said urgently. 'Will somebody tell me?'

'He wants to buy a small shop. My son, the small shopkeeper without a degree. He'll start there and he'll finish there. Wiped out! The age of supermarkets is approaching. Without a degree or a trade he won't even get a good job. He'll be begging me to take him back into the business without a formal training. He's mad.'

'Well, maybe it's not as bad as all that,' Anna murmured.

'What I want,' Paul began, 'is to buy the controlling interest in five or six small shops. I've got my own ideas on retailing. I'm going into the franchise business. Once the five

406

are doing well others will be begging to join the group. Mass buying, that's the new trend.' Paul stood up and began pacing the room. 'You're so stinking rich, all of you, you wouldn't even notice the money. I'll do it anyway, Aunt Anna, but with backing I'll do it quicker.'

'I don't understand the hurry,' Anna said.

'Perhaps you don't want to, you're so busy siding with them, perhaps you can't think straight.' He hit his fist on the table, plates and glasses clattered, a glass toppled over and the deep red stain spread slowly over the tablecloth. Anna picked up the salt cellar and began spooning salt on to it.

'You'd think I was asking for a million,' Paul grumbled. 'My God, Anna, that bracelet you're wearing would set me up.'

It was made from the first fifty diamonds found at Luembe, a cobblestone effect, for they differed in size with the larger stones set in the middle. It reminded Anna of Simon who had brought the diamonds in a bag and left them on her desk. Not a happy memory.

Anna took it off slowly, reached across the table and dropped it beside Paul's plate. 'It's yours,' she said.

Paul looked embarrassed now. 'I was speaking allegorically, of course.' He picked it up as if it were a snake and handed it back, but Anna smiled and moved away.

Kurt stood up looking stricken. 'Don't come crawling to me when you're broke,' he said and walked out.

Vera glanced at them both, half angry, half hurt and hurried after him.

'Come down to the stables with me,' Anna suggested. 'I have a new stallion I want to school.'

It was a beautiful creature, but nervous; sidestepping, kicking and rolling its eyes. Paul watched the stallion curiously, admiring the sleek black coat and the strong legs. 'Mind if I ride it?'

Paul was a superb rider and, watching him, Anna could not help admire his drive. To Paul every challenge must be met head-on and conquered personally. Kurt was wasting his time trying to control the boy. Still, she could not help feeling guilty for they had relied on her to persuade Paul to complete his education. But what right did they have to drag her in, she thought resentfully? For years they had deliberately kept Paul away from her.

The stallion was rearing and kicking, tossing its head and rolling its eyes. Old Jan came hobbling along to watch. On pension now and growing more peculiar each year, he was the self-appointed family guardian, involving himself in all their activities whether or not he was invited. He had taken to strolling around the estate dressed in a starched white collar, black tie, black suit and bowler hat with an ebony stick which had belonged to André. When the youngsters at the settlement played up, the stick would land swiftly on their buttocks.

'Keep his head down,' Jan called waving his stick. 'He's a bad one, the Missus should never have bought him.' He flashed her a look of annoyance and hobbled off grumbling to himself.

After an hour the stallion was trotting diligently around the paddock, obedient to every movement. Paul, too, seemed to have expended his aggression.

It was not until they were walking back to the house for tea that Anna said, 'I meant it, Paul, but there is one condition.'

'Oh hell,' Paul said, 'you sound like my father.'

She ignored that. 'If you fail then you complete your university course. Furthermore,' she went on, 'when you have your degree you will join the family business.'

'Jesus, you people get your pound of flesh, don't you? I suppose that's how you got rich in the first place.'

Anna decided to ignore his rudeness.

'What makes you think Kurt'll have me?'

'There's my half,' she said and smiled. 'If he won't, then I'll take a chance on you.'

He laughed harshly. 'You really mean that, don't you?'

'Yes, I do,' she said.

Suddenly he put his arm around her. 'You're a good-looking woman. Wasted to be alone here. You might as well be in a museum.'

408

She stared coldly at him.

'Don't give me that frigid look.' He chuckled. 'I'm very fond of you, Aunt Anna. I'd be happy to escort you until you find someone more suitable. D'you mind if I cut out the Auntie crap?'

Little pipsqueak! He'll be all right, she thought. His preposterous cheek will carry him through.

She had not really wanted them for the weekend, but still the house seemed twice as empty when the Friedlands had left. The clock's chimes echoed sadly every quarter hour, but for the rest there was only silence.

Anna paced the lounge nervously, wondering how to pass the evening; then she decided to plan her posters for the coming election campaign. Might as well get them done well beforehand, she thought. She fetched some paper and pencils from the study and sat by the fire.

Vote Anna van Achtenburgh-Smit for a new deal. Bit of a cliché. She crossed it out. What about: Join Anna Smit for farming reforms? She scored it out and chuckled. ' "Vote for Anna and join the twentieth century." That'll make them fighting mad,' she said. Then she stopped short. Lately she had started talking to herself and it was becoming a habit. 'It's the loneliness getting me down,' she went on.

She was right on both counts.

44

Under the leadership of arch-conservative, Conrad Pietersen, a committee was formed to try to persuade Anna not to fight the election. The first meeting was held at eight p.m. at the offices of the *Stellenbosch Star*. Pietersen owned this paper as well as the printing works and a chain of grocery shops.

Six men were seated at the table headed by Pietersen, florid-faced, with heavy jowls and bulging eyes. 'A blameless life,' he was saying with exasperation. 'No hint of scandal. Nothing to work on.' No one was listening.

Next to him sat the editor, William Rose, no friend of Anna's since their first encounter when Simon returned from the navy. A skinny man, nicknamed 'Ferret-face', he was frowning now as he noted the attitudes of the men around the table. On Rose's right was old man Joubert. Apart from the winery he owned several butcher's shops in the northern suburbs. 'She should have stuck to farming,' Joubert kept muttering, obviously feeling guilty. He turned to his friend and colleague, Eugene van Breda, chairman of the winery. 'She breeds the finest damn Landrace sows in the country.'

Eugene shrugged. 'Who cares,' he thought. If Anna got on to the council she would back the winery workers who were trying to form a trade union. She had to be kept out at all costs.

Opposite Joubert was John Ross, who owned a large vineyard. He had lost several of his best youngsters to jobs in town, thanks to Anna. Beside him, Jack Tassetti, originally from Italy, owned the only big competition to Anna's poultry farm.

Yes, Pietersen has picked them well, Rose thought pensively. They all had vested interests in seeing Anna defeated.

Pietersen rapped on the table. They had had time enough to booze and swop jokes. 'I suggest we get started. The purpose of this committee is to ensure that Anna van Achtenburgh-Smit is defeated at the polls, or better still, defeated before the polls. What do you rate her chances?' He turned to Joubert.

'Good,' Joubert said sombrely. 'Very good indeed. She's respected in the town, she practically is the town. She's an institution; not a person. There isn't an organization that hasn't benefitted from her money. Money tells.'

'As for her-a liberal ideas-a,' Tassetti cut in waving his hands in the air. 'They're-a nothing. No one's-a going to be put off by that-a.'

'Besides,' Ross went on, 'she's born lucky. Whatever she touches goes right for her.'

The conversation droned on, but nothing was achieved.

Eventually Rose broke in. His voice was dry: wind on dead leaves. 'The point is she will win because she is admired. Her views don't count at all. The only way to beat Anna is to destroy the admiration. She has to be smeared, dragged through the mud. That's our job.'

'Oh, come now,' Joubert cut in. 'That's dirty work. What about a fair fight, hey? What about that?'

'Politics is dirty,' Pietersen said. 'It's winning that counts, not how. She has to be defeated, preferably before the elections start.'

'Correct-a.'

'Hear, hear,' said van Breda, 'but tarnishing Anna's reputation? That's a problem. Anyone heard of anything we could work on?'

There was silence around the room.

'Maybe it won't come to this,' Joubert said. 'Let me go and see her. After all, I knew her family well when her father was alive. I'll try to talk her round.'

'Bloody woman's like a robot,' Pietersen said. 'No smoking, no men, no scandals. Just work. What can you do with a woman like that?'

'There's-a always something,' Tassetti began. 'Always-a. There's-a an expression in Italy …' Nobody wanted to hear it.

Rose said carefully, 'She's had her problems like everyone else.'

'Yeah,' Ross said, 'but she and Simon are ancient history. If she hasn't got a scandal we're not going to find one.'

'Fair enough,' Pietersen said. 'But if there is one Rose will find it. He's an expert. Meantime we'll start the campaign by attacking the profits she's making. The diamonds? She's worth a fortune. What she gives to charity is a mere bagatelle compared with what she's worth. Start off like that, Rose.' He clapped his editor on the shoulder and drained his glass. 'Write a few editorials; make her generosity seem like meanness.'

Rose nodded.

'I needn't remind you, gentlemen,' Rose said, 'that we have the editorial columns of the *Stellenbosch Star*. Whatever we find will be plastered from page to page, even if it's not derogatory. Anna's a very private person, I've heard. She may well decide that public life is not for her after she's read a few of our comments.'

'Mr Joubert, how nice to see you again, and you've come on the right day, too. Nella has baked a milk tart. I seem to remember it's your favourite.'

Anna stood at the front door, feeling agitated, as Willem Joubert arrived. He was late and she had an appointment with her lawyer at five.

'Yes, yes, dear, but I have to be careful nowadays.' He thumped his fist against his heart and grimaced.

He looked old, she thought, as she led him puffing through the house; his face an even deeper shade of cerise. Anna had seen little of the Jouberts since her father died. Today his visit was curious and quite out of character. He had telephoned the previous day, telling Anna that the family winery was going public and he wanted to offer her the chance to purchase shares.

Anna led the way to the patio and sent Jacob to ask Nella for tea.

'How very kind of you to think of me,' she said. 'Of course I'd like some shares; as many as possible. What a question!'

Right now his shrewd eyes were watching her guardedly. The man was on edge, but surely not because he was going public. The shares would be snatched up as fast as they were offered.

'Wine distribution is big business nowadays,' he complained. 'I'm keen to get out of it. Farming, growing grapes, that's a job for gentlemen, not the cut and thrust of marketing.'

'However,' he went on as she sat silently, 'the family are still holding a good interest. We're keen to retain as much as possible and as far as I'm concerned, Anna, you're "family" too.'

'That's very kind ...'

'After all,' he broke in on her. 'I once hoped you would be my daughter-in-law. André and I were very close, particularly in our young days. I don't know if your father ever told you, but many's the time we were out on the tiles when we were bachelors.'

Anna smiled politely. It was just a matter of time, she thought, before he came to the point.

It was only after tea that Joubert brought up the subject of his visit. 'I've always admired you, Anna,' he said. 'You built the first farm school against a lot of opposition and, let's face it, the value of the community centre you've established can't be under-estimated.

'Of course we don't agree on how to treat our Coloured workers. You believe in education. Fair enough! But I say what's the point in education if the workers can't satisfy their ambitions? Makes them discontented.'

He sighed. 'Still, you went ahead and did what you thought right and I've always admired you for that. I suppose we have to move with the times. Nowadays the government is spending a fortune on black education.'

Anna was unwilling to be drawn into the conversation. She

413

was well aware of Joubert's patriarchal views. After all he had fought her tooth and nail, particularly over the employment bureau.

'Anna, I came to warn you,' he said, placing a hot hand on her arm. 'This time you're making a mistake. You'll be an outlaw amongst your own people. God knows what mischief you'll make and the end result will be trouble for you and everyone else.'

'Why, whatever are you talking about, Mr Joubert?' Anna asked sweetly, although she knew well enough.

'Standing for Parliament as a liberal. Folks around here won't stand for it. Everyone's against you. Surely you realize that?'

'Then there won't be a problem since I won't be elected,' she retorted.

'Some people just vote without knowing what they're voting for.' He frowned. 'I feel I must warn you, for André's sake.' He was looking embarrassed now. 'The Liberal Party is going to be banned. Full of Commies.'

'But I'm not joining any political party, Mr Joubert. I'm standing as an Independent.'

'With liberal leanings.'

Anna laughed, 'If that's what you call helping people.'

'When women start meddling with things they don't understand there's always trouble,' Joubert said heavily. 'You know nothing about politics, Anna. You're one of these goddamn do-gooders. And you're lonely. Now you give me one good reason why you should be in Parliament. What good do you think you're going to do?'

'Do you think I haven't given the matter a lot of thought?' Anna glared at him wondering why she was enduring this lecture from a silly old man. 'I assure you I have.' She paused. Why should she bother to explain? Still, he meant well. 'I'm totally opposed to racialism,' she began slowly. 'It's not something I've always felt, but something that's crept up on me lately. Mainly because of the children and their lack of prospects. You see I can't help seeing these dirty, lousy, dumb kids and thinking that I could have picked any one of them

414

and brought them up as my own and who would know the difference – other than colour of course,' she added hastily.

Joubert exploded with laughter. 'Anna van Achtenburgh-Smit in Parliament isn't going to change their home environment one jot. You're wasting your time worrying about racialism because it's only a myth – an excuse.'

'I don't think any of our workers would agree with you,' Anna said coldly.

'Anna, listen to me,' Joubert went on more gently when he saw how angry she was. 'Long ago the Nationalist Party decided that colonialism was finished. A disaster! As they saw it they had only two choices if they wanted the Afrikaner to retain his home in Africa: complete integration or complete separation. They chose the latter course – "apartheid" as we call it. Deliberately and gradually they reinforced racialism to keep the two groups apart. Not just racialism, it's total economic, geographic and cultural separation.'

He took a deep breath. 'You and so many others are taking a small-minded view of the situation. D'you suppose it would change anything if all blacks had white skins? Not at all, I assure you; we'd call it a religious war, or a class struggle. Whatever! The bare bones of the matter are two opposing groups struggling to survive and grow – in the same territory. To us apartheid means survival, it means splitting up the country and retaining a part of it. Listen to me Anna, don't try to gatecrash the party because you don't understand politics at all.' He took out a handkerchief and blew his nose long and vigorously.

'The liberals want to give the country away, hand it to them on a plate. Is that what you want?'

'Is that a rhetorical question or are you going to let me say something?' Her smile was forced, transparent; blue eyes glittering. 'I think you're forgetting my family came here a couple of hundred years before yours,' she said haughtily. 'I'm not interested in party politics – perhaps I don't understand, as you said, but I do understand human aspirations. When you say politics, I say food, when you say long-term solution, I say a minimum wage; you want to push apartheid, I want to

415

see more happiness. I'm not joining any party and I'm not reaching for the moon. I'll be content with small victories: schools, enough food, a chance to learn. My God, that's our birthright …'

She jumped up nervously and hammered her fist into her palm.

'Save it, save it, Anna, for your election platform.'

Joubert stood up and for a moment the two of them peered angrily at each other like two fighting cocks about to strike. Then Joubert laughed and patted her on the shoulder.

'You must understand Anna, your precious Coloureds have little to do with the politics of this country. They are the casualties; a small minority group. Why can't you be content with community centres and social services. Use your common sense, girl.'

'I've thought about it long and hard, Willem. I'm putting common sense aside. I'm listening to my conscience instead.'

After he left she found herself too angry to concentrate on the meeting with her lawyer. She telephoned and cancelled. Instead she spent the evening planning posters for her campaign. To hell with everyone, she thought.

On Friday morning, Acker returned from their Malmesbury farms to find Anna in her study, pale and angry, as she read the *Stellenbosch Star*. 'Bastards,' she kept muttering. She looked up and saw Acker. 'Welcome home. Look what these bastards have written.'

There was a complete listing of the profits Anna made, exaggerated tenfold.

'These figures are distorted and horribly exaggerated,' she said. 'We don't make anything like this, least of all from the diamonds. He'll have to print a correction.'

Acker looked at her sympathetically. 'You can't force them to, and would we really want to publicly air our assets? Leave it alone. But Mama, what prompted this virulent attack on you? On us,' he corrected himself.

She sighed. 'Oh, Acker, we hardly ever talk to each other any more. You're always away, or busy. I'm fighting the next

416

by-election as an Independent, but with liberal leanings. A most unpopular move. This is their way of throwing down the gauntlet.'

'Rather effective,' Acker said. 'Still, they've shot their bolt. You're rich and they've said that. Your only crime as far as I know.' He smiled and put his arm around her. 'Just forget it.'

'Surely you can think of something, Acker?'

'Buy a rival newspaper and start digging up muck about them,' Acker suggested.

'Oh, honestly, Acker. Do you know who their candidate is? Old Major Barrett. Can you really see me embroiled in a mud-slinging competition with that poor old bird?' She stood up and thrust the newspaper into the bin. 'Maybe you were right first time.' She smiled. 'How's the farming going?'

Acker took the question seriously. He opened his briefcase and Anna was bombarded with statistics going into the minutest details on all their farms.

'Only the poultry is a problem.' Acker came to that last. 'So many hens in batteries nowadays that egg prices have fallen drastically. It's no longer worth keeping hens unless they're in batteries.'

'Half our hens are still in the chalet system,' Anna said. 'Are you suggesting I close down this operation?'

'Undoubtedly, the sooner the better, and expand the batteries.'

'Go ahead then.'

'And now for the good news,' Acker said with false heartiness. 'I've just spent two nights with Pa and you'd be amazed how well he's doing.'

'You're right, I'm amazed,' she said icily.

'His service department is worth a packet nowadays. Why don't you go and take a look? You'd really be impressed.'

She shrugged. 'He didn't have to make a martyr out of himself. We were married in community of property, you know that. Everything that's mine is half his, but he would never take a penny of it.'

'Well, a man's got his pride,' Acker went on. 'It was his birthday yesterday. He's forty-three.'

417

Anna sensed a reprimand in the boy's words. and looked away. 'I'd forgotten,' she said. Her voice was suddenly tinder-dry. 'Any more accounts?'

'No,' he said, sensing her mood. He hunched his shoulders, thrusting his hands in his pockets. He never gave up trying to reconcile his parents with each other, but he never succeeded. 'Heard from Katie?' he asked.

'No, Katie can't be bothered to write letters, but I heard from the headmistress. She wants Katie to study opera seriously. Evidently she's very talented.'

'I'd hate to think of her staying overseas,' Acker began.

'Don't worry.' Anna laughed. 'She's not the least bit likely to do anything useful. She's one of life's decorative assets, here for humble folk to adore. She'll be back for the summer holidays. Only eight weeks to go.'

William Rose was obsessed with the problem of smearing Anna. His need was threefold: he hated the establishment and anyone with wealth was his natural enemy; secondly, Anna had been responsible for his first reprimand at the newspaper; lastly, should he succeed he would receive a very substantial rise. Pietersen had said as much to him, and so, like a dedicated speleologist, he decided to explore every tunnel, every cul-de-sac and delve deep underground into Anna's past.

His expense account soared as he bribed his way from servant to servant, but Pietersen kept his cool, sensing that if there was something to be found, Ferret-face would find it.

He found that the story of Anna leaving home, although much bandied around, was basically the truth. He even discovered the date that they were married, when she was three months pregnant with twins, but that was common knowledge and Anna had lived it down. As for Simon, past sins had been forgiven, particularly with his war record – he was one of the most popular men in Malmesbury. It seemed there was nothing to find there. Still, Rose was not a man to give up easily so he went off to Saldanha Bay, booked into a room and sat around in the bars night after night, questioning, hinting, paying for drinks and before long discovered that there had been a certain amount of gossip about Kurt calling on Anna during the war. This could be played up to its fullest extent, but Rose, with the instinct of a good sleuth, sensed a better story.

One night he decided to visit the fish factory and talk to the fishermen about Simon, if any still remembered him, and it was there he met a Swedish fisherman called Carl, who knew a Coloured man called Hendrickse, who had shacked up for a while with a woman called Sophie, who claimed that Anna had murdered her child. When Rose asked around he found that the story had been heard frequently over the years and discounted by everyone, for Anna was a woman of impeccable character, whereas Sophie was a drunken whore who would tell any story for a drink and go to bed for another.

Nevertheless the tale sent adrenalin surging through his veins, the hair stood up on the back of his neck and his fingers positively itched to get to a typewriter.

This one was a peach of a story; front-page photographs of Sophie crying for her lost child; he could see it all. But first he must find Sophie.

He began with the fishermen living in the shacks around the lagoon, but there was no joy there. Sophie had disappeared about two years ago and no one knew where she was, although several of them had known her well. No one knew why she had left, but there was some story of a liaison with the pay clerk at the factory.

Two days later Rose cornered him in a bar and he was strangely reticent, but after half a dozen brandies he admitted that Sophie had given him a dose of clap. He was cured, now, he claimed, but he had given her a beating she would not forget in a hurry and she had left the district.

'Where would she go?' Rose asked.

The man shrugged. He was not interested as long as she never came back.

Rose returned to Stellenbosch and called a meeting of the committee.

'I don't suppose there's much truth in it,' Pietersen

growled, 'but find the woman and bring her to Stellenbosch. Er – clean her up first.'

No easy task, Rose thought next morning as he packed his bag, but he knew there was a clinic near the docks and that would be a good place to start.

'They seldom tell us their real names,' the doctor told him the next day, 'but we get to know most of them by sight; they're back time and again. It's a hazardous occupation.'

Rose began to haunt the docks, the cafés and pubs; he even ventured into District Six, a no-go area where thieves, pimps, murderers and gangsters terrorized local inhabitants.

Three weeks later a call came from the clerk at the clinic. Sophie was in the queue, he remembered her from two years back because she was always drunk.

Rose felt embarrassed going in. There was a crowd of women in one room. When he peered through the doorway his heart sank; Sophie was one of life's drop-outs. Years of excessive drinking were stamped upon her face; her skin was criss-crossed with lines; her voice was raucous and she was very drunk. She looked sixty, but if she really was Sophie Jasmine then she was close to thirty-five.

Rose hung around the outside and eventually Sophie came out. Jumping out of his car he called, 'Sophie Jasmine?' then reeled from the odour of stale sweat and stale wine.

'Twenty pounds,' she said firmly. 'Double for whites, see? And if we do it in the car it's five pounds more.'

Rose shuddered and said, 'Sophie, get in the car.'

'Let's see your money first,' she said triumphantly.

45

Late November and the Cape was blistering in a heatwave that had lasted two weeks. Katie, who had recently returned from Geneva, left the house early for Muizenburg beach. She was anxious to regain her deep tan; a year in Switzerland had left her skin looking sallow.

At noon the heat became unbearable and for the third time Katie went into the sea to cool. This time the surf was crowded, so she set off in a lazy crawl to deeper waters where she lay floating on the surface, filled with a sense of peace and freedom that she had not felt for a year.

Above the sky was hazy blue, with the deeper blue of the sea around her, ringed on three sides with low purple mountains. Excited screams of children playing in the surf reached her softly as she abandoned herself to the pleasure of rolling up and down slopes of unbroken waves.

Memories of Geneva were fast fading, but she could still see the face of her enraged music teacher and his strange, burning eyes. She had manipulated his dismissal and succeeded in getting herself expelled in one brilliantly executed confession of love – totally fabricated – which the headmistress had believed. Europe and the cold, damp winter winds must surely belong to another planet, she thought. Slowly, lazily she began to swim backstroke, eyes closed. When she opened them later she almost missed the black triangular fin skimming past two yards away. It was so close she could have touched it. One split second it was there and then it disappeared under the water.

Shark!

She jolted into activity as her body reacted to the proximity of deadly danger. Death, the cruellest death, was there beneath her; she could picture the shark coming up out of the depths to take her now.

She screamed, one long, agonizing scream and then realized that no one could help her. She set off at a fast crawl towards the shore, but suddenly it was there again. The nightmare monster came with tremendous speed, hitting her with its nose so that she was flung half out of the water, then it surged by, a victim of its own momentum. Suddenly she remembered reading that sharks bumped their victims before coming in for the kill.

She glanced wildly over her shoulder and changed from crawl to breaststroke. Somewhere she had read that splashing reminded them of a fish in distress.

'Oh God, oh God,' she was murmuring, 'get me out of this,' but the shore seemed to have receded.

The shark was now circling twenty yards off, its fin making smaller circles as it moved in for the kill. Frantic, half out of her mind with panic, her movements seemed futile against the distance and the speed of the savage creature bearing down on her.

There was a sudden commotion and she screamed as the shark surged out of the water in front of her. This was it. Terror gripped her and she could no longer swim, yet she saw the shark fall back, spattering blood, harpooned through the head. Still she screamed. In the same awful split-second she was encircled by strong, black tentacles and for a moment she fought frantically even though she could see that it was a skin diver.

He pushed back the mask and said urgently, 'Keep moving, doll, keep moving, back to the shore, quick as you can.' He pushed her violently in that direction. With one hand gripping her bikini they moved rapidly, helped by the impetus of his flippers. Then he muttered in her ear, 'I'll have a look underneath. Just keep going, fast now. There's more than one shark here today.' He plugged in his mouthpiece and sank out of sight and once more she was alone, fighting a sense of shock that was deadening her limbs so that she could hardly move. If she could only sleep, she thought. She had to sleep. Then she felt a hand firmly grasp her and push her on.

'Sharks,' she yelled to the bathers as she stumbled out of the breakers. All of a sudden she passed out, and her rescuer carried her up the shore.

'Clear the sea,' he yelled to the lifesavers, ripping off his gear. 'She got bumped, but not badly. I got a lucky shot in. These stupid girls. If they knew what they looked like from below. Whitebait, splashing away invitingly.'

Bathers clustered around Katie murmuring sympathetically. The lifesaver produced some brandy and Katie found she could stand up, although shakily. Her side was grazed from her elbow to her thighs, as if rubbed by sandpaper.

'Pull yourself together,' the diver said harshly. 'It's over, you're safe. Next time be more careful.'

She shuddered and said, 'Where's Jacob?'

'Who's Jacob?'

'My driver.'

Jacob was found and Katie was helped to her car.

'But you can't just walk out of my life,' she began. 'Please come and meet my mother.'

'Look, I don't want a lot of fuss,' he said.

'Well, at least tell me your name.'

'Anton de Waal,' he said reluctantly and helped her to the car. Katie gazed at his ash-blond hair, deep blue eyes and huge, bronzed figure thinking that in Switzerland he would have seemed almost God-like, but here he was commonplace.

'I owe you,' she said. 'Please do come for dinner.'

He looked at her doubtfully and eventually smiled. 'OK. How about Sunday?'

She nodded and gave him her address.

It was not long before reporters came knocking at Fontainebleu for the story had all the drama needed for a front-page picture. A beautiful girl nearly taken alive. When the papers arrived next morning she read that her rescuer was heir to the Dewaal Estates, mainly apples and citrus fruits for export.

'Well, he comes from a nice enough family,' her mother said.

'We'll have something special on Sunday.' But on Saturday evening Katie received a curt telephone call from Anton apologizing that he would not be able to make dinner after all.

'Well, next Sunday,' she said gaily.

'I'm afraid not,' he replied and rang off.

It was the first time Katie had been rebuffed and while she had been only mildly interested in the man, other than expressing her gratitude, she now began to fume over his hard-headed attitude. By Tuesday she was determined to seek him out so she dressed simply in a blue and white dress and calling Jacob, set off for Elgin.

The Dewaal Estate was spread over several thousand morgen and seemed to include the village as well. The homestead was situated well back in a valley, a huge, whitewashed manor house with the largest oak doors she had seen, at least twenty feet high. There was an old slave bell hanging outside which she rang and the sound echoed in the hallway beyond. A moment later she heard footsteps on stone and the doors were opened by a young maid in starched uniform.

'I've come to see Anton de Waal,' Katie said and, stepping inside, she admired the old paintings and intricate marble floor.

A few minutes later she was shown into a large room overlooking the orchards. A woman hurried towards her. Anton's mother, she guessed from her ash-blonde hair, wide cheekbones and large, pale blue eyes. She was an impressive woman with strong features and broad shoulders. Her accent was Germanic.

'How do you do,' she said. 'I am Anita de Waal and you, I can see, are the young lady Anton saved from the shark. I recognize you, my dear, from the pictures in the newspapers.'

Katie held out her hand and explained that she had come to thank them all and to see Anton.

Anita smiled slowly. 'He's supervising in the packing sheds,' she said, 'but he is very cross with you, I'm afraid. That's why he didn't go to dinner. He hates, in fact we all hate, newspaper reports or any type of publicity. We're a very private family, you see. Well, never mind, since you're here let's have some coffee.'

She rang a bell and the starched maid came hurrying in.

Katie was impatient to see Anton, but thought it politic to win over his formidable mother first. Only when Anita had decided that she approved did she send the maid to fetch her son – her only son, she was careful to explain.

Anton was cool and almost rude, indifferent to Katie's fetching ways. After coffee, in response to her pleading, he reluctantly agreed to show her round the apple sheds.

'The newspaper reports weren't my doing,' Katie explained as she trailed behind. 'My mother gave a reporter a photograph the next morning.' She gabbled on, hoping he would not see how boring she found apples. Somewhere between the washing tanks and the crating department, Anton relented and agreed to come to supper.

In the weeks that followed Katie and Anton saw each other daily and slowly Anton fell in love, while Katie idolized him. Nevertheless he was a serious boy and spent most of his time supervising the farm. Katie ruined several new outfits tramping around with him.

It seemed only natural that the apple orchard should provide the setting for their romance.

Katie, who was despairing of ever being kissed, grabbed an apple from a tree and handed it coquettishly to Anton. She leaned towards him alluringly, apple balanced on her outstretched palm. 'You're invited to eat this forbidden fruit.'

'Really Katie,' he said angry and unthinking, 'you've torn off half the branch; that damages the tree.'

'Two leaves and a small twig.' She pouted.

'Enough to let microbes into the wound. If you're going to marry me you'll have to learn to be more careful.'

She gasped, for once speechless.

Watching her Anton slowly flushed scarlet. 'I spoke out of turn,' he said.

'Was that some sort of proposal?' she said eventually.

Anton's eyes became a trifle colder. 'I was planning to propose on your birthday,' he said stiffly. 'You'll be nineteen. Quite a suitable age for a girl to be engaged. I'm twenty-three. We come from similar backgrounds. As a matter of fact ...' He faltered. 'Well, I spoke to mother about it and she approved.'

'What about my approval?' Katie said quietly.

'Well, you can think about that when I ask you.'

Katie turned away angrily, but Anton caught her arm.

'Will you say "yes"?' he asked.

'You'll find out when you ask me,' she hissed. 'Here, take a bite.' She passed him the apple. He dusted it carefully and put it in his pocket. 'I hate eating apples,' he said sombrely.

'All right then – will you? That's a proposal,' he went on after a long silence.

'I can't possibly decide unless you kiss me,' she said. 'I'll see how it feels.'

Very correctly he leaned forward and brushed her lips with his. Katie stood with her eyes closed. Was that it? she wondered, but then she felt his lips softly against hers again; one arm circled her back and his lips pressed harder; then his other arm caressed her shoulder, moving down and around her neck. He pushed harder into the small of her back, bending her over while his lips wandered over her cheeks. His hand had found her breasts and suddenly Anton was gasping. Then he pushed her back against a tree trunk, his body taut and hard against hers.

As the bark scraped her back she pulled her mouth away. 'What about the microbes? You're damaging the tree,' she gasped.

'Damn the tree.' He pressed closer and Katie began to struggle. He was human after all.

'Yes,' she gasped. 'Yes, I'll marry you.'

When they announced their engagement that evening Anna was too upset to speak for a few moments. She had nothing against Anton, although she knew Simon detested the boy, but to lose Katie again so soon was unthinkable. Besides she was only eighteen, far too young for marriage. Remembering her own rebellious youth Anna was too cautious to oppose them. Instead she had coffee with Anton's mother and unbeknown to their children they agreed to try to postpone the marriage for at least a year.

46

The following day Anna received a call from the *Stellenbosch Star*. 'Hold on for the editor, William Rose,' the switchboard operator said.

'News spreads quickly,' Anna thought, composing a piece about the engagement as she hung on.

Then she heard Rose say: 'Mrs Smit? Good morning, Rose speaking. Would you care to add your comments to a short article we're publishing in the next issue?'

'Certainly, go ahead,' she said graciously.

He read: 'The plight of a penniless widow and her eighteen-year search for her daughter has been taken up by the *Stellenbosch Star* who are assisting Sophia Jasmine in her investigations.'

Anna reeled with shock; the room began to spin.

'Seventeen years ago,' the voice continued relentlessly, 'Sophie left her baby in the care of a farming family because she wanted to seek work. Since then she has not seen her daughter in spite of continuous inquiries. The *Star* questioned Mrs Anna van Achtenburgh-Smit who was the last person known to have seen the child. She said …' He paused.

Anna gasped for air, flung down the receiver and sat pale and shaking. Disastrous! She had thought the affair forgotten. How had he found Sophie? What had Sophie told him? And why had she thrown down the telephone? Fool! She would have to pretend they had been cut off.

She picked up the receiver; laid it on the table. She needed time to compose herself. Calling Flora for a cup of coffee she rushed to her room, grabbed the phial of tranquillizers, threw some into her mouth; then she returned to her study, drank her coffee and dialled the newspaper's number. She was put through immediately.

'We were cut off, I was expecting you to ring back,' she said icily.

'Engaged,' the dry voice crackled.

'Whose baby did you say?'

'Sophia Jasmine.'

'Sophia? I don't really think ...' she paused, 'unless of course you mean Sophie, the Coloured girl, who used to work on my husband's farm?'

'Yes, indeed.'

'Well, what about her?'

'I believe she left a baby with you.'

'Certainly not with me. I wouldn't have taken it. She left it in my loft without telling me and it died the following day.' She broke off feeling that her voice was too high-pitched; she knew she sounded nervous. 'It was some time ago, I don't remember when.'

'Eighteen years to be exact.'

'So long? Good heavens.'

'What exactly did the baby die of, Mrs van Achtenburgh-Smit?' His voice sounded cruel now.

'Who knows? There's a wide choice: starvation; pneumonia; exposure. According to the doctor she was suffering from all these things. He told me she had no chance of survival.'

'You took the baby to a doctor?' Rose sounded disappointed.

'Well, of course.' She gave him the doctor's name and address. 'I don't know if he's still there,' she went on, 'but I suggest you find out and address your inquiries to him. As for Sophie, she knows very well where her child is buried. She's visited the grave a number of times.'

'I see.'

There was a long pause.

Then Rose played his last card. 'Are you aware that Sophie is accusing you of murdering her child?'

Anna laughed. 'Please, Mr Rose, don't waste my time. Check with the doctor.'

'One last thing,' he called as she was about to replace the receiver. 'We should like to photograph Sophie at the grave of her daughter.'

'Please do,' Anna said feeling that she had easily won. 'Sophie's welcome there whenever she likes.'

She forced herself to replace the receiver gently and went outside to wait for the tranquillizers' first heady wave to pass.

It was February; the vineyards were overflowing with chattering pickers; baskets were being passed up and down rows. This year was a particularly good year; the boughs almost cracking under the strain of the heavy bunches.

When Katie came out half an hour later she was surprised to see her mother sitting on the balcony doing nothing. 'Are you ill, Mama?' she asked.

'No,' Anna said smiling fondly at her. 'Just watching.' She would rather die than let Katie discover her parentage, Anna thought, watching Katie race to her car. If only she could squash the story, but any attempts to do that would provoke Rose to further prying. Best to ignore it.

When Katie had left, Anna telephoned Simon and told him about the call. 'This could get nasty,' she warned him. 'Sophie's bound to have told him who the father was. He'll try to implicate you.'

'Don't worry,' Simon said. 'I shall deny everything. After all there's no evidence, just her word. You took care of that, didn't you?'

Strange how he had managed to swing the guilt on to her, she thought as she rang off.

It was a long day, but eventually she came to a decision. At four she telephoned Parliament and told them she was giving up her candidacy due to ill-health; that she had suffered a minor heart attack the previous day and was acting on doctor's orders.

As soon as the news was out, telegrams and flowers came from all over the Province; visitors arrived hourly and Anna did her best to look sick, feeling a fraud as she accepted the gifts.

On Friday, the newspaper appeared with a photograph of Sophie at the bottom of the front page, with a heading: 'A wooden cross ends an eighteen-year search,' followed by a lurid piece describing how the baby, unchristened and without a funeral, was unceremoniously dumped into the ground; plus an interview with Sophie who was quoted as saying: 'If only my little baby were alive today to comfort me. She was so beautiful with her light skin and her deep red hair.' Right next to it was a small article announcing Anna's retirement from the political arena.

The farming folk began to prick up their ears. 'A red-headed light-skinned baby from Modderfontein. What a scandal!'

In the village Simon found himself avoided by some of his acquaintances, while friends advised him to confront Rose and threaten to sue. 'She can make up any hair colour she likes, since the child's dead,' they told him.

Simon went to his lawyer who wrote a letter to Rose threatening action. The answer was a brief note to Simon saying: 'If the cap fits, wear it. You're not the only red-headed man in South Africa. Sophie was well known in the docks and canning factory.'

Acker and Katie were up in arms about the report which, they felt, pointed a finger at their father. Privately they decided that Anna had given up politics to protect the family from further attacks by Rose; they knew she had not had a heart attack.

There the affair seemed to rest and probably would have died, for there was little more that Rose could squeeze out of it in view of the doctor's report. To hint at murder was absurd. He gave up supporting Sophie; let her go and Pietersen gave him the promised rise. Sophie made for the nearest bar, happy to be free again.

Two weeks later, Mother Superior of the Woodstock orphanage saw the report lying in her dentist's waiting room.

She decided that in the interests of truth and good order, she should point out to the editor that the child had not died. So on her next free afternoon she took the convent's station wagon and drove to Stellenbosch and, to the surprise of Rose, walked into his office without an appointment.

He jumped up, wishing that his secretary was more efficient. 'My dear Sister ...'

'Mother Superior,' she said with a gracious smile.

'My dear Mother Superior,' he persisted. 'My secretary handles all charities and we make regular donations to any cause we feel worthwhile.'

'I have been following one of your worthy causes,' she said dryly. 'Sophie Jasmine and her lost daughter. I saw the photograph of her crouching over the grave. Very touching, but not very factual.'

Rose, who at first was too taken aback to comment, began to feel excitement surging through his limbs. 'Please sit down,' he said and rang for coffee.

'Tell me about it.' Rose rubbed his hands. The Mother Superior leaned back, closed her eyes and remembered almost to a word what had passed eighteen years before when Anna had snatched the baby from the cot and fled.

When she had finished Rose asked, 'Then in your opinion, she was not willing to have a red-haired baby in a neighbouring foster home?'

'No, I didn't say that,' the Mother Superior said crossly. 'In fact I suggested this to her and she was quite annoyed. She had imagined that our home was very much more pleasant than we are able to make it. Unfortunately funds ...'

'Yes, yes,' Rose interrupted impatiently.

'We try our best.' Then she began to ramble on about changes in child welfare over the years. Rose listened and eventually steered her back to the present.

'So she said she'd find a foster home?'

'Yes, and she must have done so. I never saw her again. I'm sure you'll find the child safe and sound and better off without its mother.' She sighed. 'Mr Rose, I think you should think before rushing in for the sake of a headline.' With that she swept out.

On Friday, the *Stellenbosch Star* burst upon unsuspecting townsfolk with banner headlines: 'Mystery deepens – Mother Superior tells her story.' This was followed by Rose's imaginative prose telling the nun's story, which proved that the baby did not die in its first three days as Anna had claimed nor in its first three months.

Anna was bombarded with questions, not only by the *Stellenbosch Star*, but anxious friends and curious acquaintances. 'The baby died. It's buried there,' she told everyone. 'I can't remember exactly when it was. After all, Jan buried the baby, not me, and it's so long ago he can't remember.'

Jan appeared to be senile. No one could get any sense out of him.

When Anna went to the horse show on the following Saturday she found her friends strangely distant, but she pretended not to notice.

However, two mornings later, when a police officer arrived at Fontainebleu 'to clear up these ridiculous rumours' as he put it, Anna panicked. She told him that the child had drowned in the farm's dam. When he asked why she had not called the police to search the dam or notified the authorities of the child's death, Anna had no answer. She apologized for lying and claimed that she had only assumed the baby had fallen into the dam. In fact, she had given it to her farm workers to look after and it had disappeared. She had forgotten about it until the day the newspaper editor telephoned, she claimed.

When the police officer left, Anna locked herself in her room and refused to talk to anyone.

The next meeting of Pietersen's committee was a triumphant one. Rose was congratulated by everyone. This time, Pietersen's cousin, Sidney Johnston, senior prosecutor for Stellenbosch, was there. The two were partners in many of Pietersen's business deals.

'Now look here! You guys better understand Anna's down, but she's a resilient woman,' Pietersen told the committee. 'She's got something to hide; why else would she have resigned so promptly? But what's to stop her from coming back next election? I say we go the whole hog now; with Johnston here we can persuade the police to open a murder docket and the publicity will tear the family to shreds.'

'But I say,' Joubert said, blushing scarlet. 'That's a bit much. After all she's resigned and that's what we wanted. Let her alone now.'

'She resigned because she's got something to hide,' Johnston put in.

'But murder?' Joubert persisted. 'There's no evidence. I never heard anything so silly.'

'True,' Johnston said. 'But we don't want to hang her, do we? We just want to keep out the Independents. We haven't had a liberal in the district since 1938. Let's keep it like that. Smear Anna, prove her a liar and the liberals won't stand a chance here.'

The meeting was long and unruly, but eventually Pietersen won, as he had known he would, and Johnston promised his support.

'I'll have a battle to push it through,' Johnston told them, 'and I'd need some co-operation from the press.' He nodded to Rose.

'You can't incriminate Anna in so many words,' he went on. 'But I've unearthed statistics on the number of child crimes which remain unsolved; particularly concerning murder cases of non-white children. Blame it on the police! In fact, make your whole article, plus editorial, a vicious attack on the authorities for their laissez-faire attitude towards child abuse. I've got some beauties for you. Somewhere in the article, link the disappearance of Sophie's child to the long list of unsolved crimes. Don't accuse Anna of murder. Better still, don't even mention her name. Got it?'

Rose assured him that he understood perfectly.

'You couldn't hang a cat on the evidence you've got,' district commandant, Colonel Ted Prinsloo, told Johnston ten days later at the end of a stormy half-hour meeting.

'We all know Anna's lying,' Johnston told him. 'Let's find

out what the truth is. That's all I'm saying. Did you see the article in the latest *Stellenbosch Star*? They quoted fifty unsolved cases. That sort of thing is not doing your reputation much good,' Johnston went on.

The district commandant shrugged. 'I am most unwilling to become involved in this eighteen-year-old rumour,' he said primly.

However, after three more virulent editorial attacks on the police, the district commandant reluctantly opened a docket on Sophie's missing child and put Sergeant Jamie Fourie on the case. Fourie was an ambitious young man and this was his first big chance. He began by checking birth certificates and discovered that Sophie had registered the birth of her child, whom she had named Lettie Jasmine, but that there was no death certificate. Undoubtedly a child was missing.

After this Fourie took statements from Sophie, the Mother Superior, Anna, Simon and Jan. He felt suspicious of Jan who was unusually dim-witted for a man of his age. Jan claimed he could not remember who had looked after the child. 'So many workers on the farm,' he kept muttering. 'They never stayed long.' Fourie plodded on. He was intent on an early promotion.

47

On the Saturday following Rose's third editorial on child abuse, Anna was at the races and found, to her shame, that she was ostracized by almost everyone. She left early, but a crowd gathered around her car which had been daubed with red paint. Amongst the abuse, the word 'Murderer!' stood out clearly.

Very early on Sunday morning, Sergeant Fourie, taking with him two constables, picks and spades and the necessary documentation, drove Sophie to the site of the grave at Modderfontein, where Jan had claimed to have buried her baby.

Sophie was half demented with fear. To the sound of her wails and hampered by snarling dogs, they unearthed the skeleton of a small baby which they carefully excavated piece by piece and transferred to a box. Sophie passed out and had to be carried to the police van.

Fourie did not need the pathologist's report to tell him that the baby's skull was fractured.

The following morning, at six a.m., heavy boots trod the driveway of Fontainebleu and Anna was arrested for murder, cautioned, taken to the police station and charged.

'You're lying,' she screamed when they told her about the corpse. 'How could you find a skeleton when the baby's not buried there. You're trying to trap me.'

Even Fourie was impressed by her earnestness. She was so obviously baffled, angry and very scared. 'Then where is the child?' he wanted to know, but Anna remained obstinately silent. She was let out on bail the same day and Kurt engaged Thomas Quinn, the best defence lawyer in the country. A month later a preparatory examination was held in the Stellenbosch Magistrate's Court.

The examination was over within the hour. The prosecutor presented the facts in a matter-of-fact tone. Quinn stated that Anna would reserve her defence.

The case was referred to the Attorney General in Pretoria, who decided that the State would prosecute. The trial was set for 13 May – four months ahead – to be held at Cape Town's Supreme Court.

During this difficult period Anna's family presented a united front to the world at large; but at home everyone was in a turmoil. Simon moved back to Fontainebleu and constantly harangued Anna to tell him what really happened. Simon had always believed Anna allowed the baby to die of exposure, imagining this to be only a matter of hours after it was abandoned. Anna had told him as much years ago, but the Mother Superior's story proved that the baby was alive and healthy at three months. Now it had been found with a shattered skull. So who had killed her? Simon felt sickened by the whole affair.

Besides, it all seemed so long ago. Looking back, his own actions seemed outrageous, something performed by a stranger, for although he could clearly remember what he had done, he had forgotten the terrible sexual frustration which had driven him to do it.

Acker knew that his mother would not deliberately kill a child and for the first time father and son were at loggerheads. Acker resented his father's implied accusations and the two had several fights. At the same time Acker felt that his mother was lacking in trust for not telling them what had happened and he pestered her constantly.

Katie added to the confusion with daily tantrums. Never for a moment could she imagine that her mother would hurt any child, so there was all the more reason for Anna to tell them what had happened, she reasoned. Her obstinate silence was embarrassing. What a scandal! And it was all her mother's fault.

437

Kurt kept rushing over and trying to do something useful. He flew in experts from Germany to date the child's skeleton, but they came close to the date of Lettie Jasmine's disappearance. Next he engaged a private detective agency to track down every family who had ever worked at Modderfontein. That, too, proved costly and useless. At Quinn's suggestion he engaged a leading psychoanalyst to question Jan, but the doctor could not coax anything out of the old man, although he was convinced that Jan was not senile.

'Whatever happened, they're in it together,' Quinn told Kurt. 'If only Anna would tell me. Once I know what I'm dealing with I can make a plan. I hate nasty surprises, particularly during a trial. As things stand now, her attitude will prove more damning than the evidence.'

Quinn was thoroughly put out by his uncooperative client. Daily he threatened to resign from her defence.

Anna remained silent.

The one morning Anna broke down. 'Everyone thinks I murdered the baby,' she sobbed to Quinn. 'Even my husband! Even you! I don't care. I shall carry my secret to the grave. No one will ever know where the child went, but I'll tell you this. I don't know how that battered skeleton got into the grave. It's not Sophie's daughter.'

Quinn, who was an excellent judge of character, believed her. He drove home thoughtfully.

Anna lost weight and became increasingly withdrawn and, watching her, Simon was overcome with guilt. It was as much his fault as hers. He should be standing trial with her. The family was being punished for his sin of raping Sophie, nineteen years ago, and Anna would bear the brunt of the punishment. Worse still, he could not help her.

The days passed; the date of the trial drew closer, and everyone in the family greeted each morning with dread.

Hands were pushing her, the priest was praying, the hood descended, she felt the rope around her neck. Anna gasped and cried out: 'I didn't murder her; I swear I didn't. Katie is Sophie's daughter.' Too late! She

438

was falling, falling ...

She awoke.

It had been so real; it took a few seconds to realize that it was only a nightmare and a bad one; she was drenched with sweat and she sat up waiting for reality to banish her dread. Then she remembered that today was the start of the trial. It was real after all.

Was her dream a warning, she wondered, as she got out of bed and opened the curtains? The dawn sky was visible behind the mountains. In less than four hours she would be standing in the dock. Perhaps she had been wrong to lie, but how could she avoid it? She knew that the stigma of being Coloured, the daughter of a dockland whore, would break Katie. Her daughter was so proud, so self-assured. She might be reclassified as a Coloured. And even if she were not, her engagement to Anton would be broken; her life ruined.

What if she were to choose her own security before Katie's happiness? Anna asked herself constantly. She might face kidnapping charges. Besides, Simon might be imprisoned for immorality. There was no way out, she decided.

The minutes passed slowly; she heard the servants arrive, curtains being opened, doors slamming. It would be so much easier to fall asleep and never wake. She clasped her phial of sleeping pills and shook them. There were enough! No, never, she thought eventually.

At seven-thirty the family met in the hall. It was a strained, sad greeting. No one wanted to look Anna in the face.

Anna was filled with dread as she sat in the back of the car beside Simon, with Katie in front, next to Acker who was driving. Oh God, she thought, what if I am locked away in a dark place with no sunlight, no flowers.

As they approached the main street of Stellenbosch the car halted at traffic lights and a group of labourers recognized Anna and jeered; one of them threw a stone which shattered a side window. A crowd gathered and surged around the car. Katie screamed.

'Keep quiet,' Anna snapped as another stone glanced off the bonnet.

The car began to rock as hands grasped and pushed. One of the labourers stuck his head through the window and Anna was appalled by the hatred in his eyes.

Simon hurled the door open, leapt out, grasped the two nearest to him and banged their heads together. Seconds later father and son were fighting back to back, a good head and shoulders above the crowd. Acker was grasping men by their shirt fronts, shaking them, and throwing them aside. Anna had never seen him in a fight before, she doubted he had ever been in one. The crowd quickly dispersed.

'I needed that,' Acker grunted as he started the engine. His hair was ruffled, one coat sleeve was torn. Simon was rearranging his shirt collar.

'Good work,' he said briefly.

'You'd think it was a carnival,' Katie wailed as they neared the courthouse. It was an hour before the trial was due to begin, but already crowds were converging and there were many familiar faces from Stellenbosch.

By half past eight the courtroom was packed and the crowd spilled on to the pavements. The Smits were sitting in the front row next to Thomas Quinn. They looked pale and fearful, Simon gazed at the ground, too embarrassed to look up and his children, too, were suffering.

The trial opened at nine a.m. on the morning of 13 May 1957, before Judge Cornelius Collins, a plump and stern jurist. The Public Prosecutor was Louis Bester.

It was obvious that the defence lawyer, Quinn, wanted no reformers on the jury for he had dismissed two women, one a doyenne of child welfare, another well-known as a foster-mother of several orphans. He had gone to great lengths to select the most right-wing jurors he could, preferably with no children. From his choice of a mainly male, right-wing farming jury his line of reasoning was becoming clearer. He would concentrate on Anna's lack of responsibility. 'Are we our brother's keepers?' would be his main line of defence.

Opening for the prosecution Bester gave a lucid description of the known incidents of the supposed tragedy followed by a dispassionate demand for the death penalty, perhaps more

440

forceful and deadly because of the lack of dramatics or emphasis.

The prosecutor recounted that Sophie Jasmine had left her ailing daughter, Lettie Jasmine, with Anna van Achtenburgh-Smit because she felt that the baby would die; when she returned to see the child, she was shown a grave where, it was claimed, Lettie was buried. There was every reason to believe that the child would have died, for the doctor's report showed that she had little chance of survival. For eighteen years Sophie had been convinced that her baby had died of natural causes.

Then, William Rose, editor of the *Stellenbosch Star*, had begun a campaign to trace the missing child. Whereupon several facts had come to light. The most damning was that the child had survived infancy and been seen by the Mother Superior when she was three months old. Taxed with this evidence, Anna Smit had made a number of conflicting statements. The police eventually investigated, exhumed the grave and found the corpse with a broken skull, Bester recounted at length.

'Other than pleading not guilty, the accused has never denied that the child is dead, but she will not say how the child died, merely that it disappeared.' Bester's voice rose slightly. 'In view of the Mother Superior's sworn statement that the child was thriving at three months, Mrs van Achtenburgh-Smit's claim that it had died of exposure or starvation shortly after it was abandoned cannot be accepted.

'There is no shadow of doubt that Anna Smit is guilty of murder,' he went on. 'The evidence will show that when faced with the unwelcome realization, put to her by the Mother Superior in all innocence, that the child would be proof of her husband's immorality and infidelity, she decided to destroy the evidence by destroying the child. That is what this trial is setting out to prove.'

The jury listened thoughtfully to this tall, soft-voiced man. His manner was confident and contemptuous. It was obvious that he felt he had an air-tight case against Anna and that he despised her and everything she stood for.

441

When he had finished, Quinn rose and opened for the defence. He outlined the defence he proposed to follow, saying, 'My client is not a cruel woman, nor is she a vicious one. She is well known for her good deeds in Stellenbosch.' He explained at some length the time and money Anna had put into the Coloured school, the recreation centre and the cottages on the farm. 'Yet she is in court today accused of murder under the most bizarre and ridiculous circumstances; a murder which, it is claimed, took place eighteen years ago.

'What are the facts?' He paused dramatically.

'A child was abandoned in Anna's barn. She took it to her doctor who refused to accept it; after that she took it to Woodstock orphanage which was desperately overcrowded. She tried, unsuccessfully, to find a foster home amongst the fishing folk at Saldanha Bay. What else was she to do?' he asked and paused dramatically. 'You know as well as I do that it is illegal for a white woman to bring up a Coloured child. So Anna did the next best thing, she handed the child to her farm workers to rear and supplied its food and clothing.'

Quinn turned to the jury. 'The child disappeared.' He shrugged. 'To try to make something more out of this is ridiculous. Perhaps it was neglected, possibly it met with some misfortune. Who knows? The farm workers who minded the child cannot be found.

'Now a child's skeleton has been found. Was it the same child, or another? No one knows – least of all my client, Anna. She admits that she does not know what happened to it. To put the blame for the child's demise on her is ridiculous. To accuse her of murder is insane.

'Anna van Achtenburgh-Smit is a woman of impeccable character.' His voice was full of drama now. 'This case is just one woman's word against hers. Plus the vicious campaigning of the local press for their own political ideologies.

'Are we our brother's keepers?' he went on to a hushed courtroom. 'Some of you will answer "yes", others "no". Your viewpoint is a matter of personal choice. Anna was not obliged to look after that child; it was not her child; she had not accepted it; she did not want it. When the child died –

442

accidentally or because of the negligence of her farm workers, Anna was no more responsible than you or I when we pass a newspaper boy shivering on street corners and look the other way, or when we see waifs sleeping in bus shelters and hurry to our warm homes. If Anna is guilty of murder then we are all guilty.'

Quinn finished in a flourish and for a moment no one spoke, then there was a low murmur of voices.

It was good theatre, but was it good legal tactics, Kurt wondered? Squashed into the back row he studied the public's reaction. Clearly the question in everyone's mind was: 'How did she kill her?' There was hardly a man or woman in the courtroom who had not read the *Stellenbosch Star* and who did not believe that Anna had deliberately brought about the child's death. Kurt pursed his lips wondering if he had made a mistake in choosing Quinn.

Principal witness for the prosecution was Sophie Jasmine. She had been kept in 'protective custody' which everyone knew meant she was being dried out; consequently she was suffering badly from withdrawal symptoms, hands shaking and sweating profusely. Whispers ran around the courtroom when Sophie took the stand.

The clerk called for silence.

Bester lost no time in getting to the point. 'Is that the man who fathered your child?' he asked pointing at Simon.

'Yes,' she answered.

There was an excited whispering from the court until the clerk succeeded in restoring order.

'Tell us, in your own words, exactly what happened,' Bester went on. 'Start from the beginning.'

With a good deal of prompting Sophie explained about her life-long devotion to Simon's mother, who had never failed to give her bread and jam and a glass of milk at night when she returned from her wanderings behind the turkey flock with the eggs she had retrieved from their hidden nests. After 'Mama' died there was no more bread and jam, but Jan would share his mealie-meal in the evenings. Eventually she decided to go to town and seek work and she begged a lift from the young

443

master. She described the rape with such clarity that no one doubted her word. Then Sophie described how she had dressed and hitched a lift to town, and found a job as a maid, but was turned out when her pregnancy became apparent. After that she had met a man in a bar by the docks who had agreed to keep her until the baby was born, but in return she would have to go into business with him.

'Sophie, tell the court what happened when you returned to the farm with your baby.'

'She was there.' Sophie pointed at Anna. 'She went white when I showed her the baby's hair. I thought she'd faint clean away.' She paused and then added, 'I left the baby in the loft while she was in the village.'

She broke off and stared defiantly at the jury. Then she said, 'Later, when I went to fetch my baby, she told me it had died.' She pointed at Anna, her face contorted with fury. 'I thought she was lying, but Jan showed me the grave, so I went back to Cape Town.'

Simon sighed, feeling ashamed and desperately sorry for Anna and the children. Anna was like a statue – pale with staring eyes, lips tightly compressed. For the first time he came close to understanding her; all that hardness, her icy calm; it was only a front, for he knew that Anna was sick with fear.

Quinn rose to cross-examine Sophie. 'Why did you leave your baby in the loft, Sophie?' His kindly voice and gentle manner calmed her fears and some of her aggression subsided.

'It would have died,' she admitted. 'I had no milk, no money ...' her voice trailed off. She looked sidelong at the jury, but their faces were impassive. 'White people are clever,' she whined. 'They have medicines. I thought she would save it, but the Madam didn't want my baby to live.' She burst into loud wails again.

When she had quieted, Quinn asked, 'You've had a hard life, Sophie?'

'A terrible hard life,' she admitted.

'How many children have you given birth to?'

Her eyes narrowed. 'Just the one,' she said.

'Come now Sophie, I have some birth certificates here …' He picked up his file and riffled through it. 'Daniel, Gina …'

'Only one child whom I loved so much,' she said quickly, 'but besides the first there was another three.'

'I have records of four here, registered by you.'

Sophie took out a dirty handkerchief and wiped her face.

'Four is it? It's hard to remember.'

'I'm not surprised, Sophie. It was a long time ago. Tell me Sophie, of your five children how many are alive today?'

'Just two,' she said angrily.

'I believe they were placed with foster families in infancy. Is that correct?'

'I don't know why the master is asking all these questions since he seems to know the answers better than poor old Sophie,' she whined.

'Sophie, answer the questions put to you,' the judge said sternly.

She shrugged angrily.

'At what age were they placed, Sophie?'

'I can't remember. They were very young and it was long ago.'

'Was it two months or six months?' Quinn persisted.

'Two months,' she said angrily.

'No, not so, Sophie.' One was placed in a foster home at one year after recovering from second degree burns in the children's hospital and the other, an infant, was removed from your care by court order at the same time.'

'I don't remember,' she muttered.

'Now, let's take Daniel Jasmine, deceased, the only son you gave birth to. How old was he when he died?'

'Only a few months,' she said angrily. 'He fell.'

'No, wrong again. He died of pneumonia at the age of one year.' Sophie began to mutter, but Quinn pressed on relentlessly.

'Tell me, Sophie, it's rather unusual for a mother to run out of milk so soon after the birth; particularly a strong woman like you. I suggest that the baby was closer to two months or even three when you abandoned it in Mrs van Achtenburgh-Smit's loft.'

Bester complained bitterly to his assistant that Quinn was virtually making Sophie his own witness. Quinn hammered away at Sophie for another hour and by the time he was finished not one member of the jury would believe Sophie's statement that her daughter, Lettie, had been only a few days old when she abandoned it in Anna's loft.

Eventually Sophie collapsed into loud, uncontrollable wails.

'I've finished with this witness, your Lordship,' Quinn said and Bester allowed Sophie to stand down.

Bester called the Mother Superior to the stand and led her through the evidence. With a little prompting she told the court of Anna's visit, of the little girl Anna wanted to hand over, but finally she snatched back, and of Anna's conviction that Simon was the father of the child.

Cross-examining the Mother Superior, Quinn brought out the fact that the baby had been well wrapped against the cold. 'In other words,' he asked, 'the defendant had ample opportunity to allow the baby to die of natural causes without the necessity for violence?'

'I gathered she was fond of the child,' the Mother Superior said. 'She could not bring herself to leave the baby.'

'You stated that the child was at least three months,' Quinn went on. 'Yet you state that the baby was well wrapped for a windy day.' He paused and peered at her intently. 'I put it to you, that not even a doctor could pick the precise age of a young baby swaddled against the cold.'

'I said about three months,' the Mother Superior replied coldly.

'Are you prepared to swear on oath that the child was older than two and a half months?'

'No, of course not, how can I be sure?' she said, looking cross now.

'Or two months?'

'Certainly more than two months.' She was more positive now.

446

'Then you admit that you cannot pinpoint the age of the child to within a month, or even six weeks?'

'It certainly wasn't an infant of a few days,' she said tartly.

'That will be all.'

'Thank you, Mother Superior, you may step down,' Bester told her. She left in a crackle of starched robes.

Bester called Dr Ben Whysall. He was over eighty, crippled with arthritis and had to be helped to the witness box. He seemed to be suffering from a chest ailment and wheezed badly so that everyone was gasping for breath before he was halfway through his evidence.

He stated that Anna had telephoned him on the night of 15 February 1939, but that he had been unwilling to visit the farm. Eventually Anna had arrived with the baby, woken him and tried to leave the child with him, but he had refused to accept it. 'There were dozens of abandoned babies in those days,' he explained.

'Too many women used to hang around the fishermen. There weren't the jobs there are now; they used to dump their babies on the farms. Well, I was a doctor, I wasn't running a creche.' His voice petered off.

'After that I never saw her,' Whysall went on after a spell of coughing. 'But one day I met her in the village and asked her what became of the baby. She told me she had taken it to hospital and that it had died there. I wasn't surprised at all,' he said.

A low ominous murmur ran through the court. Anna was staring hard at her hands, gripping the rails. She seemed unwilling to look at her family.

Quinn stepped towards the witness box.

'Could you describe to the jury the condition of the baby when Anna brought it to you?' he asked.

'Well, as I recall, it was in the last stages of dehydration,' Whysall said. He glanced at Anna and frowned. 'She'd done what she could. Cleaned it up, bought some clothes, smothered it in ointment. You've never seen such a mess, but she told me that when she fed it, all the food was vomited up again. Happens sometimes. The child was allergic to cows' milk and to baby foods. Anna, that is Mrs van Achtenburgh-Smit, had tried both.' He looked around at the stony faces of the jury.

They gazed back impassively.

In the cross-examination Quinn tried to show that the child must have been a weakling even if it had survived the first three months. He tried to break the doctor's insistence on the baby's age, but Whysall insisted that the baby was only a few days old and could not have survived without its mother and breastfeeding. With that Quinn gave up and Bester let the witness stand down.

The jury were left to puzzle over the frail, emaciated baby that became the chubby little girl the Mother Superior had described.

Next, Bester called William Rose and led him step by step through the drama that had led to the trial. Rose spoke concisely, pointing out that Anna had deliberately misled him, telling first one story and then another and because of her evasiveness he had decided to proceed with the newspaper investigation.

Quinn's cross-examination of Rose seemed too brief and ineffectual to Kurt. He merely tried to suggest that the newspaper campaign had been politically motivated.

After lunch Sergeant Fourie took the stand and explained the facts about Anna's conflicting stories and the reason why the police opened a docket for the case.

Bester asked Fourie to describe the exhumation of the child's grave. The witness told his story simply, obviously impressing the jury with his zeal and straightforward manner. There were several gasps from the court when he explained how Sophie had passed out when she had seen the baby's battered skull and had to be carried to the police van.

It was Quinn's turn. He asked Fourie what evidence led him to believe that the child's skeleton was in fact that of Lettie Jasmine.

'None at all,' Fourie answered. 'We merely exhumed the grave where Mrs Smit told Sophie her daughter was buried eighteen years ago.'

'Would you say that Sophie was a reliable witness who could remember the exact position of an unmarked grave eighteen years later, in a state of extreme distress and, what's more, in pitch dark?'

'We found the corpse, didn't we?' Fourie retorted disdainfully.

Quinn hammered away at Fourie's evidence for the next hour, but was unable to shake Fourie's calm assurance.

When the first day ended, everyone seemed to be caught up in the atmosphere of tension. Anna was obviously worn out, close to collapsing, and the family watched sadly as she was led away for a night in the cells. Bail had been withdrawn; an ominous sign. The long walk to their car without their mother was agonizing. Anton came hurrying after them. He put his arm around Katie and tried to comfort her. 'All this fuss about a Coloured child; and eighteen years ago; really it's absurd,' he said. 'Who cares what happened? Not the jury I assure you. Too many Coloureds anyway.'

'Hush, Anton,' Katie said anxiously. Anton's racial views were something she had managed to conceal from the family, or so she thought. Secretly she agreed with him.

'Come for supper,' she urged.

He shook his head. 'I can't, sweetheart. I must drive mother home. Chin up!' He kissed her on the cheek and hurried away.

Simon's cheek was twitching. Katie knew Pa disliked Anton, but other than an initial warning not to trust the boy, Simon had kept his feelings to himself.

Katie ate supper alone. Acker remained in the stables and Pa shut himself in his room. Everyone felt depressed and frightened.

When court opened at eight the following morning the seats were rapidly filled. Later, when Anna appeared it was clear that she had not slept. Her face was haggard, with deep shadows under her eyes and she looked nervous.

Feeling unusually optimistic Bester watched Anna clutching her wet handkerchief. She would be a poor witness in her own defence. He could hardly wait to get her on the

449

stand. She'd be lucky to get off with ten years.

The State called Dr James Smythe, a forensic expert who testified that the fractured skull on the corpse could have been caused by a fall or a deliberate injury. Smythe was a small, precise man with a soft voice. Hardly anyone could hear what he was saying.

Quinn's turn came and he repeatedly asked the doctor to speak up. 'Would you say it was within the bounds of possibility that the child could have sustained such an injury, as indicated by the state of the skull, and have lived on for a day or even a few days?'

'Why, yes, certainly it's possible,' Smythe replied. 'That happens frequently. The child may or may not have been conscious. Without an X-ray it's difficult to tell whether or not the brain has been damaged.'

'Would you please speak up and repeat that to the jury,' Quinn said. He darted a glance of satisfaction in their direction, but noticed that most of the jury looked disappointed. They had set their minds on conviction.

Katie twisted her handkerchief nervously as she sat in the front row. Anna looked frightened and close to collapse. Katie, too, could not help wondering if Kurt had been right in his choice of Quinn for the defence. He had not succeeded in convincing anyone of her mother's innocence. Guiltily Katie realized that now even she believed that Anna had done something wrong. Occasionally she looked over her shoulder at Anton. He was beginning to look worried.

'I put it to you that the child could have sustained such an injury by the mother falling, perhaps as she carried her baby to the loft. Then is it possible that it could have lived another day or even more in Anna's care, without her being aware of the injury?'

'Yes, that is quite possible.' Dr Smythe said.

Everyone was waiting for Anna to be put on the stand. She was a pathetically pale and unhappy figure and spectators were commenting on her appearance and her lack of resolve. She appeared to be resigned to the worst. They were all disappointed when Bester called Jan to the witness stand.

No one had been able to determine Jan's second name, so he was called 'Smit' after the family who cared for him.

Jan was old now although no one knew how old. He had to be helped to the witness stand and he stood there, swaying and munching with his toothless mouth. Yet he was soberly dressed in a neat grey suit with a starched collar and black tie.

Watching him, Katie was becoming increasingly nervous. Her father's reputation had been ruined, now what was going to happen to her mother?

Acker put one hand on her shoulder. 'Everything will be all right, Katie,' he said, but Katie knew that was not so. She could not shake off a sense of approaching disaster.

When Bester prodded Jan into giving his evidence the old man hesitated and stared imporingly at Anna. Eventually she nodded at him, as if to give him the go-ahead. There was a murmur in the court and one member of the jury began to scribble in his notebook.

Quinn sighed. Only Anna and Jan knew the truth. He waited impatiently while Jan described how Sophie had been brought up on the farm, how she had returned and brought her baby back and abandoned it in the loft. Then the Madam had cared for the baby for several days and one morning found it dead in its crib. She had called Jan to bury it. He had done so, and later, when Sophie had visited the farm, he had shown her the grave.

Eventually Bester sat down looking pleased.

Quinn began softly as if speaking to a child. 'Jan, you've known the Madam a long time, haven't you?' he said.

'Yes,' Jan said. 'A long, long time.'

'What was she like when you first saw her?' he asked.

Jan's face lit up and his eyes glowed. 'She was beautiful,' he said. 'Like an angel come out of the Bible. She cleaned up the farmhouse and bought me new clothes.'

'You often worked together, didn't you?'

'Yes,' Jan said, warming to the theme. 'We built the chicken farm. We used to work hard in those days. The Missus and I were always together.'

'Jan, tell us about the day when Sophie came to fetch her

451

baby,' Quinn began.

Jan closed his eyes, rocked backwards and forwards and said, 'It's so long ago, it's hard to remember.'

Quinn sighed. Then he called for a glass of water for the witness.

'Jan,' Quinn went on more gently. 'You love the Madam don't you?'

Jan bowed his head. 'Yes,' he said after a while. 'I love the Madam. I miss the old days. I don't see her much now.'

'Well, Jan. She has a lot of businesses to run, but she's looked after you well, hasn't she?'

'Yes,' Jan said.

'You have a cottage on the estate?'

He nodded vigorously.

'And a pension?'

He nodded again.

'Jan, your Madam is in trouble,' Quinn went on. 'She stands accused of murder. Do you know what that means?'

Jan began to hum to himself.

'The people here think that the Madam killed Sophie's baby. Is that true, Jan?'

The judge leaned forward, frowning. 'I don't understand your reasoning. You seem to be trying to incriminate your client,' he said sharply.

'Your Honour, I just want to impress upon Jan the seriousness of the charges against my client, in the hope that it may help his failing memory.'

'I told all I know,' Jan said too quickly.

Quinn looked at the judge. 'Your Lordship, if you will excuse my using an unorthodox method I believe that this witness might be persuaded to amend his testimony and tell the truth. That, after all, is what this court is after.'

The judge nodded gravely as Anna gripped the rail. 'Jan,' she called, losing her control at last. 'Don't tell them. I beg you. Don't tell.'

There was a hubbub in the courtroom as the judge called:

'The accused must remain silent or be removed from the court.'

She gazed desperately at Quinn. 'I demand ...' she began, then paused, looking dazed.

To Katie, Anna looked like an animal at bay: eyes wild and staring, hands gripping the rail. She pulled out a handkerchief and began to dab her eyes. Then she felt Acker's hand gripping hers.

Quinn mopped his brow and turned to Jan.

'Poor Mrs Smit,' he said. 'Jan, do you know the penalty for murder?'

Jan looked around uneasily and for a moment his eyes rested upon Katie.

Why is he staring at me? Katie wondered, for his gaze had been questioning.

'Jan do you know what will happen to your Madam if you don't tell the court the truth?' Quinn persisted.

Jan stared obstinately in the other direction.

'She will be taken in a van to a special prison and there they will put a rope around her neck and hang her until she is dead.'

Katie screamed. Anton put his arm around her and glared at Quinn who had turned apologetically to the family.

As the judge rebuked Quinn for his melodrama an angry hissing ran around the court.

Jan crumpled and buried his face in his hands. When he looked up there were tears in his eyes.

'Jan, you've been lying, haven't you?'

The old man nodded.

'You know what happened, don't you?'

'Yes,' Jan said.

Suddenly the courtroom was so silent Katie could hear the birds in the trees outside and the sound of the clock ticking in the passage.

'What became of Sophie's daughter, Jan?' Quinn said gently.

'The Madam never killed her,' Jan began slowly. He hesitated and glanced at Anna. Her eyes implored him to be silent. He looked away, at Katie, at Acker and Simon and lastly back to Quinn. 'She brought her up like her own.' He stretched out his his hand and pointed a finger at Katie.

'He's mad,' Katie murmured. 'Senile! Why is he pointing at me?'

'Breastfed her to keep her alive,' Jan was saying, 'but then she couldn't part with the baby, so when the boss came back she passed them off as twins. She was afraid he would be angry you see,' he said nodding towards Simon. 'I've seen him knock her headlong many times. The boss never guessed the truth and old Jan never told him.' Then he laughed.

It seemed to Katie as if his laugh was from the devil itself.

She was suddenly tossed headlong into a nightmare of terrible proportions. She! Sophie's daughter? Never! It was insane.

'Well, I knew she wouldn't like it,' Jan apologized to a silent courtroom. 'The Madam told me never to tell, Katie being so spoiled and everything ...' He gazed pleadingly at Simon. 'The Madam will be angry, that's the truth. Only last week she made me promise never to tell anyone.'

He looked around the courtroom, tears rolling down his cheeks. Then he gazed at the jury. 'Well, it's better than the Madam being hung, isn't it?'

Suddenly there was an uproar in court. The clerk called three times, 'Silence in court or I'll clear the court.'

Anna was sobbing in the dock.

Katie clung to Simon. 'It's not true, is it Pa?' But Simon was gazing from her to Sophie and back again with horror in his eyes.

Katie was filled with terrible shame.

How could they all have overlooked the obvious? She had been blinded by her own self-confidence. Unprepared for destruction. She, the envy of the neighbourhood, talented, clever, an heiress, reduced to the position of the charity foster-daughter; her mother a drunken Coloured whore.

Coloured!

The full impact hit home and Katie held up her hands and examined them as if seeing them for the first time. This dusky pallor, where did it come from? What ships had carried foreign seed into Table Bay to be deposited there – just as

454

birds deposit seed from other continents? She felt exposed; stripped, dissected. The shame of it! She turned and clung to Anton, but he stood up, pushing her away. His face registered shock and something else ... loathing!

Anton was running up the aisle. Katie saw his mother, a flash of blue chiffon and ash-blonde hair, slip silently through the doorway, followed by her son.

Suddenly there was a hand on her shoulder, a breath of stale wine stole over her. She half-turned, her heart pounding.

It was Sophie and her grip was hard and proprietary.

'My little daughter,' she said. There was no welcome in her words. Just a statement of fact.

Acker caught hold of her, but she pushed him aside frantically. As the full force of her position hit home, shame burst upon her. She gasped for breath and ran headlong out of the court.

When silence had been restored, Anna stopped crying and wiped her eyes. 'Now are you all satisfied?' she said in a cold, stricken voice.

Quinn turned to Jan who was crying weakly, unable to look at Anna.

'Jan, do you know which baby was buried in that grave?' he asked.

'Ask Sophie,' he said. 'The next time I saw her she was expecting again.'

'No more questions, your lordship,' Quinn said.

Bester stood up, scowling ferociously, and Jan was visibly cowed.

'Jan, I'm going to read the court your original statement made to the police and signed by you,' he said. He read the statement and went on, 'Do you now admit that you were lying; that in fact the baby lived and was brought up by Mrs van Achtenburg-Smit and passed off as her own daughter and that you lied to Sophie in showing her the empty grave?'

Jan mumbled unhappily, but no one had any doubts about the truth of the matter.

When Jan was dismissed Quinn stood up. 'Your Lordship, I move that the Prosecution has failed to present a case to

455

answer and that the charge of murder against my client, Anna van Achtenburgh-Smit be dismissed.'

Five minutes later it was all over. Anna was escorted from the courtroom by Simon and Acker amid cheers and well-wishing which upset her more than the booing had done.

Johnston, a bad loser, had Sophie rounded up by the police and brought to the charge office the following day.

'You'll be glad to hear that we are looking after your interests, Sophie,' he began. 'We intend arresting Mrs van Achtenburgh-Smit for her part in the kidnapping of your daughter.'

'How can you do that, Master?' she retorted, 'when I gave her my child to look after.'

Bester eyed her shrewdly. She was drunk, but not besotted.

'Yes,' he agreed, 'but when you returned to fetch your baby, Anna told you she had died. It's a crime to steal someone else's baby, Sophie, didn't you know that?'

'She didn't steal her,' Sophie persisted. 'I won't let anyone say a word against the Madam. I left my baby there for the Madam to look after – and she did.' Two large tears rolled down Sophie's cheeks.

'Sophie, perhaps you'd like to tell me how the skeleton got into the grave,' Bester said, trying another approach.

'It was my second baby that died. It wasn't my fault. I was drunk, I fell against a crane. My little baby,' she wailed. 'I took her home to be with Lettie. I thought … You see …'

'Then there's Simon,' Johnston went on. 'You'd like to get even with him, wouldn't you? Rape? Well, maybe not, in view of your profession, but immorality. Don't worry, Sophie, I'll see you get off.'

'I'll swear it's all a lie,' she said. 'May God strike me dead if I ever harm that family again.' She scowled at him. 'Forget it.'

'Come now Sophie. You've caused a lot of trouble with your evidence of child-stealing and rape. If you don't co-operate I'll send you to a rehabilitation centre for alcoholics. Pity you didn't go there years ago. They'll dry you out and put you straight. Think of it – five years without a drink.'

Sophie watched him carefully. She was a shrewd judge of men by now, part of her instinct for self-preservation. She could see he meant what he said.

'You're a nasty bit of work,' she said. 'If I met you in the docks at night I'd give you the go-by.'

Watching her retreating back as she was led off, Johnston muttered, 'You won't last five days without a drink.' He leaned through the doorway.

'Remember Sophie, when you feel like a tot, just ask for me.'

A stream of abuse echoed along the corridors.

There was no understanding these people, he thought, as he lit a cigarette.

Part Four

48

April, 1961

Autumntime and the storks were leaving earlier this year; it would be a harsh winter. Every day Acker watched them circling overhead before flying north to Europe and sometimes he would think of Katie and wonder where she was.

Four years had passed since the trial, but to Acker it seemed much longer. At the time the case had proved a major sensation and Katie's disappearance had prolonged the speculation, making it so much worse for his parents, particularly for his mother. The family had not stinted in their efforts to find Katie, but it was as if she had never existed. She had fled from the courtroom and vanished. Anna had flown to Europe at least eight times following false alarms from the many agencies engaged to find her daughter – after each trip she had returned even more depressed. Nowadays she spent most of her time in her study, curtains drawn, the telephone her only link with the world outside.

The aftermath of the trial had disrupted their lives for nearly a year. There had been hundreds of calls and letters – abuse and praise – many of their close friends had shunned them and Simon in particular had been strongly criticized. Jacob spent much of his time painting out slogans which appeared overnight on Fontainebleu's walls.

The police had continued to call for some time. There had been talk of arresting Jan for perjury and Simon for immorality; Anna had broken the law on two counts: kidnapping and harbouring a Coloured child in a white home.

The family engaged a team of top lawyers who succeeded in squashing all charges, while Katie was officially declared white and later legally adopted. Evidence that she looked white and had been accepted as white in the community was all that was required. Once again the grumbling had rumbled around town, but eventually it had all fizzled out.

It had been a traumatic period for Acker, too. He had never been able to view people in terms of race or colour. To Acker, people were people: good, bad, likeable or unpleasant, a point on which he and Katie had always disagreed. If only he had been Sophie's child instead of Katie.

At first he had blamed Katie and his anger had been hard to live with. She had run away, unable to face the ridicule of a small and unimportant community, leaving her mother pining and embittered, widening the rift between their parents and not even having the decency to let them know where she was. She was a coward, he told himself daily. After all, she was Simon's daughter and his half-sister and, God knows, his mother had loved her the best.

As he matured he sympathized more with Katie's reaction to the discovery of her true parentage at the trial. She had to find herself, he could understand that and sensed that her separation from the family would help her to do this. But still he could not overcome his resentment. She had rejected them all and Anna was inconsolable.

Sometimes Acker wondered if it was Katie's disappearance or the booing and stoning that had damaged her the most. After the trial Anna had cried for days, and at the end of the month she had become alienated from everyone, even Pa and himself. She had engaged a team of private investigators, led by Mervyn Morris, the sharpest, meanest lawyer in the district, and embarked on a series of reprisals. The townsfolk rested uneasily under Anna's wrath.

The farm workers who had stoned her car were the first to feel Anna's rage, for she had closed the community centres, the job agency and the many social centres which she had previously supported. When she tried to close the farm school she had clashed bitterly with Acker and he had won; afterwards she had stayed in her room for a week refusing to talk to him.

Edwina had received her share of retribution, too, Acker knew, for he had seen the letters. Applications for rises had been turned down; repairs and renovations to her cottage had been refused; Edwina was looking as dilapidated as her home. One day, when Anna seemed better tempered than usual, Acker had taxed her with it, but she had merely laughed coldly.

'She hates me,' she had muttered.

'Mother, for goodness' sake, Edwina doesn't hate anyone,' he had argued.

'Then why was she in the front row day after day?'

Acker had lost his temper; a rare occurrence. 'Can't you forget the damned trial? It's you that's being harmed, not them; this hate; this meanness; you're destroying yourself. Surely you can see that?'

Anna had avoided Acker for days afterwards.

Yet for all her vindictiveness Anna had staunchly defended Jan. After the trial Jan had remained in the village for three days, dead drunk and refusing to speak to anyone. On the fourth day he had staggered back to Fontainebleu, collected his meagre possessions and called at the front door to say goodbye with tears streaming down his cheeks. It had taken Anna all afternoon to persuade him to stay. Acker had never been able to understand the strange bond his mother shared with this drunken old Hottentot.

Anna was pacing the darkened room, feeling tense and anxious. Eventually Mervyn Morris called.

'What took you so long?' Her voice grated into the receiver.

'My dear Mrs van Achtenburgh-Smit, the party has just this very minute left my office.'

'He signed?'

'Come now, we both know that he couldn't avoid signing, but he took his time about it; wanted guarantees for his staff and so on.'

'Which you refused.'

'I carried out your instructions to the letter. You are now the sole proprietor of the *Stellenbosch Star*.'

'Carry on as arranged,' she said bleakly and replaced the receiver.

Within twenty minutes the editorial and clerical staff of the *Stellenbosch Star* had been sacked with the exception of William Rose, editor. Fear smouldered in his eyes as he dialled the number he had been given. It was no secret who owned the paper now.

'I intend raising the level of news coverage in this paper,' Anna told him coldly, 'and I shall keep close control. How much are you earning?'

He told her sullenly.

'The type of editor I had in mind would earn treble that figure,' she went on, 'but you're welcome to try.'

This was the time to resign, but treble the salary! Worth putting up with that bitch, or so Rose thought at the time.

'You will deliver your editorial plans in writing each Sunday evening and copies of the main features and editorial every Wednesday evening. I'll telephone if anything is unacceptable. Oh, and Rose, I notice the *Star* has ignored the change-over from pounds to rands, other than increasing your price to five cents. Make the next issue a special one on decimalization; effect on farmers, that sort of thing.'

'Impossible,' he snapped. 'Deadline's Thursday. Today's Tuesday.'

'For the type of salary you'll be earning, Rose, impossible's a word you'd best forget.'

The conversation terminated with an impersonal click.

On the first day of May the weather changed abruptly. Cold winds came racing from the south-west and the first rains fell, presaging an early start for planting.

Simon was inundated with calls to service tractors and orders for new ones. Two years previously he had secured the sole franchise for one of the best names in American-made agricultural machinery. Sales had boomed and he wondered how they would cope. There was a three-month waiting list and his four servicemen were working round the clock.

When a call came from the Goedgeluk farm no one was

available, but it was an emergency so he went himself. The farm was eight miles beyond Malmesbury on the road to Riebeek Kasteel, the sort of place Simon had dreamed about in the war; well over fifteen hundred morgen. It bordered the slopes of a low range of mountains where several rivers plunged into the farmlands. All the farms around the mountain slopes were known for their exceptionally high yields. Simon's eyes gleamed with envy as he gazed around on the long drive from the gate to the farmhouse.

Paul Bosman was waiting in the yard. He was an old man and looked upset.

'Don't worry, we'll have it going in no time,' Simon assured him.

It took two hours, but when Simon was finished he was still not satisfied. 'It's an old tractor and several more parts are about to go,' he told Bosman. 'Looks like a profitable place you've got here, why not invest in a new tractor?'

Bosman shrugged. 'I'm selling out,' he said. 'My son's wife refuses to live here. That's the trouble with youngsters nowadays, they're afraid of a bit of work. I shan't be planting much, so just patch it up, best you can. Then come and have a bite of lunch.'

'Thanks; I'd rather get done,' Simon told him. 'I'll fetch the parts you need. No point risking another breakdown.'

What a waste, he thought as he drove to the village. The farm was one of the most fertile in the district, perfect for wheat and dairy farming. There was a huge orchard behind the dam and irrigated, too, by the look of things. Besides, the place was beautiful, the house nestling amongst trees on the mountain slopes with a magnificent view. If he could own such a place his life's ambition would be realized.

He returned with the spare parts, fixed the tractor and stayed for supper with the family. Bosman's only regret was the prospect of selling the farm.

'Reckon I'll give it another few months, see if Piet won't come to his senses,' Bosman said. 'If not we'll put the place up for sale.'

Simon could not sleep that night thinking about Goedgeluk,

465

yet he knew that a farm without a farmer's wife was a lonely place. Since the trial there was no hope of reconciliation with Anna. She had been furious when she found out that he, too, had thought she had murdered the child, or at best abandoned it to die. He reasoned that it was her own fault since she had told him as much. Why had she said so, all those years ago?

For Simon, Anna's image had undergone a sudden transformation. He had to admit she was not the hard bitch he had imagined. Quite the opposite, for hadn't she risked the gallows to protect Katie? Overnight Simon's preconceived ideas on the female sex were shattered. There had been the good woman: kind, soft, endearing, pliable and needing a strong man to lean on; and the bad woman: hard, spiteful, frigid and self-sufficient. Now he saw Anna as a strange mixture of both, but overwhelmingly her fierce love and loyalty to what she saw as her duty set her apart from others. It had taken Simon twenty years to learn to love her as she was and it was too late. She would not speak to him, or see him, although he had tried persistently for several months after the trial.

He sighed. Anna lived by her own rules, set her own standards. She was intent on ruining everyone who had harmed her.

A month later Simon was contacted by McCullum and Robb, a firm of attorneys in the Cape who, acting as nominees, offered him a substantial sum for his business.

'Don't sell,' his lawyer advised him. 'You'll make a fortune with your business.' But Simon was interested in farming, not fortunes. He went to the Land Bank and arranged to borrow the remainder of the cash he would need and drove straight to Goedgeluk.

It was springtime when Simon took possession of the farm; a day that he would remember clearly for the rest of his life. Dew sparkled and steamed; wild flowers bloomed pink and white on the fallow land; a grysbok plunged out of the glade and fled to the donga; guinea fowl scampered through the stubble; doves called in the trees.

Simon walked shyly, softly, like a boy in church, for this was hallowed land – God's own earth and it was his, too, bought with the labour of his hands. All his dreams, his hopes, his longings were satisfied that day.

'He's mad,' Anna said when Acker told her the news. 'Your father's always been mad. He was sitting on a goldmine with that business; he'll never get the same returns with farming. He'll be walking barefoot soon. When Simon gets a piece of land he becomes its slave.'

'He's not mad, mother, he's a farmer,' Acker said.

'Farmer! Ha! A farmer has to make a profit from the land, your father bankrupts himself, putting more back than he gets out.'

'Better to be a giver than a taker,' Acker retorted gravely. 'Anyway I'm going to give him a hand for a few days. Will you be all right here by yourself?'

'Of course,' she glowered at him.

'Well, you'll know where to find me if you need me,' he said lamely.

Two mornings later, Acker's prize Palomino stallion erupted in a frenzy, bit Jacob who was feeding him, and kicked his way out of the stall. When Jacob tried to catch him, he reared up, catching the old man on the hip. Jacob rolled out of the way and hobbled back to the house to get help, but when he knocked on Anna's door she would not answer.

'In one of her fits again, I suppose,' Nella, the cook, sighed. She telephoned the local stables and asked them to send a stable hand to Fontainebleu.

Pat McGregor, owner of the stables, looked around for someone to send and saw Margaret grooming a fractious mare.

'Look, you're not a stable hand, but please help out. I've no one else I can spare. A horse kicked the groom and there's no one to cope. I don't know why these people keep horses if they can't look after them.'

'Oh, but they can,' Margaret said. 'Acker Smit's an expert,

you know that as well as I do.'

'Yes, but he's away somewhere and his mother's gone batty since her daughter disappeared. Shuts herself up, they say and today she won't come out at all.' She frowned. 'The cook phoned. She says the stallion bit another horse, but she doesn't want to call the vet if it's not necessary. Be a pet, Margaret. After all, they'll pay you.'

That was good enough. Margaret had only a small portion of the money she would need to be a vet.

When she arrived at Fontainebleu the gardener took her to the kitchen where the cook made her a cup of coffee. Jacob was hanging around with a hang-dog look about him.

'They need a younger man to look after the stables,' he told her. 'Normally the master and Franz do everything, but we don't know when they're coming back.'

'Here,' Nella said to a maid, as she put the coffee on a tray, 'take the Madam to the lounge with her coffee.' Turning to Margaret she said, 'We was expecting a stable hand, you see.'

'Please,' Margaret said. 'I'll sit here,' but they looked embarrassed and guilty so she allowed herself to be led from the kitchen, along a corridor to the house. It was a dark and desolate place, curtains drawn, a smell of dust and a sense of emptiness and sadness hung around. Not a bit as she remembered Fontainebleu. A portrait of Anna above the fireplace scowled at her intrusion. Margaret drank quickly and left.

At the stables Margaret discovered a mare had come on heat. The stallion was doing his best to kick down the gate to the mare's box. Really an ugly customer in his current mood, she thought, eyeing him warily, but a shot in the rump would quiet him, so she took out her bag and eventually managed to inject him with a tranquillizer. Half an hour later he was as quiet as the geldings and she led him to graze in a field beyond the paddock, which seemed well enough fenced to keep him out of trouble.

She spent the morning feeding the horses and exercising them. She had never roamed around Fontainebleu and she was amazed at the extent of the estate and the beauty of it all.

Lunchtime, Nella sent Lena to fetch Margaret and she found herself sitting alone in the dark, empty dining-room. Stray sunbeams penetrated between the shutters, glittered on chandeliers and beautiful old silver. The world of the rich was completely foreign to Margaret. She was filled with awe. If she should live in such a place, she would throw open the shutters and fill the house with sunlight and laughter, she decided. How could Mrs van Achtenburgh-Smit shut herself up for days at a time?

Margaret was a simple, straightforward girl, honest and uncompromising. To her neurosis was unnecessary; self-pampering, emotional outbursts were the sign of a weak, undisciplined person. She had no patience with weakness.

The doctor arrived shortly afterwards and decided that Jacob must stay in bed for at least a week and because there was no one available to look after the stables, Margaret agreed to come twice a day until Acker returned. When he arrived on Friday at noon, Margaret met him in the courtyard and told him what she thought of the way he ran his farm and his stables in particular.

Acker smiled calmly and when her annoyance was spent said, 'You're quite right to be angry and I'm still sorry about the hawk.'

She flushed. 'I must get back,' she said awkwardly.

'Let's look on the bright side. Jacob's accident brought us together again.' He put one hand on her shoulder and Margaret's throat constricted, remembering how she had idolized him.

'I don't have time. Sorry,' she said firmly and hurried to the station wagon.

Acker was intrigued by Margaret who had grown from a podgy child into a capable young woman. She was grave and honest; she would be like a rock in times of disaster, no need for tranquillizers, sleeping pills, no spite. No one could call her pretty, her face was too square and too strong, her skin too freckled; she was too tall and too broad, but her eyes were large and beautiful and even when she was angry her face was full of good humour. He sensed the hidden passion in her

469

nature. Instinctively, he liked her and wanted to be friends with her.

Over the next ten days he telephoned frequently, but each time Margaret refused to meet him. Finally, he went to the stables on Saturday afternoon, and found her giving lessons in the paddock.

Margaret was annoyed to see him hanging over the fence and glad that she was looking her worst. After five hours of teaching she was covered in dust and drenched with sweat for it was a particularly warm spring day.

'What time do you finish?' he called out.

She shrugged. 'When there's no one left to teach.' She turned away and ignored him for the rest of the afternoon, but when the sun set and Margaret was supervising the grooms she found Acker in the stables examining Ponty.

'This one should be put out to graze,' he said. 'How old is he?'

'I don't know, maybe twenty. He was old when I first came here. Pat doesn't put them out to graze, she sells them to a factory that makes pets' mince. I'm afraid I've been persuading her to hang on to him a bit longer. I know it's cruel, but he doesn't get ridden often. Maybe three times a week.'

'Arthritis.'

'Oh I know, I know. God, it's awful.' She sank on to a stool in the doorway. 'The pounds shillings and pence oi ..ie get me down. I just don't understand people; people with money, that is. I'd buy him if I could.'

'He can't be worth much.' Acker gazed at the old horse sombrely. 'How much will he fetch?'

'Ten pounds I think.'

'Twenty rands, you're out of date.'

'I keep forgetting,' she smiled sadly. 'Twenty rands doesn't sound like much, but I've nowhere to keep him.'

'What are you doing with yourself nowadays? Finished school, haven't you?'

She nodded. 'Fighting with mother mainly. She wants me to teach kindergarten. I want to be a vet. Meantime I'm working here and saving, but it will take me years to save enough.'

He grinned. 'That would be ideal for you.' He stood up and walked out of the stables and, following him, Margaret was struck by his air of gentleness. His eyes shone with friendliness.

'I came to ask you to supper,' he said. 'Don't say no this time. We used to be friends. Why can't we be friends again?'

'I'm sorry, I have a date,' she said and turned away, but when she glanced back at him, Acker looked so surprised she burst out, 'Don't you believe I could have a date?'

'Well, I don't know,' he said. He wrinkled his forehead just as he always had when he was embarrassed.

'Oh, Acker,' she said. 'You've got to stop this nonsense.'

'Why nonsense? Friends are important.'

'Yes, but you and I. I mean it's just ridiculous. We're not kids any more. Besides, I'm studying evenings and working all day. I just don't have time for dates.'

He gave in eventually and drove home and Margaret walked through the streets feeling sad, but how could she have gone, she reasoned, when she did not possess one suitable dress. She had her old school dresses and slacks and blouses, flat-heeled shoes and white socks. Absurd to dream of going to dinner.

Margaret was depressed for the next few days, but not once did she regret her decision. Lately she had begun to hate herself. Each night when she fell into a deep sleep, after hard physical work at the stables, her dreams were always the same; she was a beautiful, slender girl and Acker was always pursuing her, wanting her; the dreams always culminated with marriage. What came afterwards was shrouded in mystery, for when he began to take off her clothes in some fairytale hotel she would wake up with the intensity of her feelings that drenched her body, and she would find her nipples taut, her thighs sticky and she would cry tears of despair into her pillow, very quietly, so that no one would hear. Consequently her face was always red, her eyes always swollen and when she looked into the mirror she saw herself ugly and unlovable. She hated her body, too, and began padding her bras with cottonwool to hide her nipples that would show through her bra, petticoat, shirt and sweater, which she wore even on hot days. She hated the shooting swords, half pleasure, half pain, that plunged through her stomach if a man were to brush close to her by mistake, or when she saw love scenes at the cinema. How could this be her – solid, reliable, hard-working Margaret? She began to hide herself in her work.

On Monday morning Pat was waiting outside Ponty's stable and Margaret felt a lump forming in her throat when she saw Ponty being led into the horse box.

'Anna's not the only batty one up at Fontainebleu,' Pat told her. 'Her son Acker just bought Ponty. Says he's starting a rival processing plant for pets' meat.' She glanced shrewdly at Margaret, who gazed agonizingly at Ponty, trying to hide her emotion.

'Look here, Margaret, none of my business, but after all I've known you for a long time. Tell him to get lost. You don't need a disaster at your young age.' Margaret glared at her, but Pat hurried on. 'Acker's got everything, he's handsome, rich, clever. He's already broken a few hearts around these parts. Don't know why he's wasting his time with you, but in the end you'll get hurt. All men are bastards by nature,' she went on, 'But the rich ones are the worst.'

She walked off, leaving Margaret to shake off the hurt.

49

Was it worth it? Anna thought as she examined progress reports from the twenty-eight missing persons bureaux that she employed in various parts of the world to search for Katie. She had received a paltry assortment of rumours and hoaxes over the years at a cost of thousands of rands. She sighed and began to pace her room. Common sense told her to give up, but she knew she would never do that. She saw mankind as a pack of hunting dogs, cowards individually, but ferocious and mean-minded together. Katie and she had been savaged by the pack and Katie had panicked and run. Her disappearance was a pain that thrust into her each morning when she awoke and remained with her until she succumbed to the soporific effects of butyl barbiturate at midnight; and she had to increase the dose continually as her resistance grew and oblivion became harder to achieve.

She was still pacing her room, frowning and intent, when there was a knock at the door.

'Go away, I'm busy,' she called.

The door opened and Paul stood there. 'Take it easy, Anna.'

'I do donations at the end of each month, right now I want peace ...' she said, but Paul walked in and shut the door softly behind him.

'Time for peace when you're dead, Anna. You're alive, although sometimes it's hard to believe.'

She glared at him, then sank on to the settee. Why was she so much closer to Paul than Acker? she wondered. She could understand Paul's neurosis, his uncontrollable ambition, but not Acker's preoccupation with philosophical problems.

'I suppose you want something, since you've bothered to come and see me.'

'I wouldn't mind a drink.'

'It's three o'clock in the afternoon.'

'So?'

'Are you turning into a drunk?'

'Do I look like a drunk?'

Anna laughed coldly and pressed the button for Flora and for a few minutes they sat silently staring at each other. Anna saw a stocky, confident, handsome man, with black gleaming eyes and a Roman nose. There was something irrepressibly appealing about him.

Paul was saddened by the sight of a distraught woman, too thin and pale with hate in her eyes. After a while he said, 'You can't carry on like this, Anna.'

Paul took a package out of his pocket and placed it on the table. 'Don't say I never pay my debts,' he went on.

Anna opened the box and was astonished to see the bracelet that she had thrown at him in a temper years before. 'I'd forgotten how beautiful it is,' she said. 'All that time ago. I thought you had sold it. When was it?'

'February, 1956,' he said gravely.

'Seems like a hundred years ago. Don't you think it's beautiful?' She put it on her wrist. 'It's a collection of the best stones ever found at Luembe.'

'Beautiful, but flashy,' Paul said. 'It's valued at a hundred and fifty thousand pounds. I've insured it for you. The bank have been hanging on to it for security. They gave me an overdraft of fifty thousand rands and it's taken five years to get it back.'

'Congratulations,' she said. She pulled back the curtains and stood watching the stones sparkle in sunlight, but she was thinking about the small boy who had grown into a man she admired. In the beginning, more by cheek than anything else, he had lured twelve grocers into his franchise group with promises of cheaper produce, better shop displays and he had done the buying and the displays himself. Slowly he had built

474

his franchise organisation, *Better Buys*, bullying and begging for publicity in the local press, touring the country giving lectures on inflation. Paul had been first with self-service, first with mass buying techniques, first with pre-packed fish, meat and vegetables. Now he had fifteen retail outlets. Like all pioneers, Paul had paid for the mistakes that his competitors could avoid and at least two other chains had erupted like mushrooms. She turned and watched him shrewdly. 'You've got competition nowadays.'

He grinned wryly. 'I aim to keep ahead. Next stop is to convert the stores to supermarkets. I'm worried the opposition may get started first.'

'You should have sold the bracelet and used the cash. How much will a supermarket cost?'

'Depends.'

'Depends on what?'

'What sort of a property deal I can get.'

'I'm going to back you,' she paused. 'In return for certain favours.'

'For goodness sake, Anna, you don't have to pay me for favours. You brought me up.'

She ignored him. 'I pay for what I want,' she said coldly, 'and I want Pietersen and his piddling grocery shops put out of business. Two supermarkets should do it. I'll sign personal security for the cash you'll need. Pietersen had to sell the *Stellenbosch Star* after his printing works closed. He only has the grocery chain left.'

'I heard a rumour that you bought the paper wholesalers and a rival printing shop.'

'Well, you can't believe all you hear.' She laughed coldly.

'Perhaps there's something wrong with me, but I see you as a beautiful, desirable woman. Get out and enjoy your life instead of moping around planning your vendettas. For God's sake, be enthusiastic about something.' He sprang up, too tense to sit still, hands thrust in his pockets. 'Come in with me, Anna. Get enthusiastic about the stores. Instead of signing personal security, buy shares. In five years time I'm going public and we'll both make a fortune.'

475

'I've too much money and no talent for spending it,' she said sadly. 'My husband won't touch a penny, my son is disinterested, Katie's run away. Why should I want more?'

'All right, forget the money, think about the public. I'm going to drop prices to the minimum, cut the cost of living, fight inflation. I can see it all: vast stores filled to the ceiling with food at cut-rate prices, thousands of shoppers rolling it out in their trolleys. Can't you see it?'

'I see a small boy hiding cakes and bread under the mattress,' she said carelessly.

'Damn it, Anna,' he exploded. 'You have a rare talent for making men feel small. I'm beginning to understand your problem. Ten years ago you made me feel this high.' He pushed his finger and thumb towards her. 'But today you've excelled yourself. Congratulations, Anna, and goodbye.'

She laughed triumphantly as he left. 'I'll sign anyway,' she called down the corridor.

It was probably Pat McGregor's advice that made Margaret say 'yes' the next time Acker telephoned – that plus gratitude for Ponty's home. She withdrew some of her precious savings from the building society and bought a dress and shoes. Then she spent the next day regretting it, for the dress made her look plumper and squarer. Ridiculous! She combed her hair in a dozen different ways, but it seemed to look best in a mess. As evening drew nearer she panicked.

Edwina watched her uneasily. She had always been sure that Margaret would not cause her problems; no boys had ever been interested in her, not so much because she was unattractive, but because she repelled their advances. She was too cool, too reserved, uninterested in their problems and conversation, and too straightforward to pretend. She was just right for teaching, it would be her vocation. But whoever could be calling for her?

When she opened the door at seven and saw Acker, Edwina could not control her annoyance, while Rosemary was overcome with awe and hung around him. Somehow, Edwina thought, I've got something all wrong.

Acker seemed to fill their small lounge to overflowing and had to stoop to enter the doorway. He exuded masculinity; his head, shoulders, hands, were all larger than life. His hair was too long and he looked as if he had crawled out of a barn five minutes before. He reminded Edwina of Simon and she was filled with anxiety for her daughter.

Margaret emerged from her room looking pale and unhappy, clutching Edwina's cheap evening bag and smoothing her hair. Acker glanced at her in surprise. How awful she looked in that frilly dress, he thought. Not that it mattered.

'Would you mind bringing your jeans and hurry,' he said quickly. 'I thought we could have a hamburger and get back to the stables. There's a mare about to foal ...' He broke off suddenly, wondering if he was insulting her. He knew the old Margaret well enough, but not this rather distant young woman. Then he saw her grey eyes were gleaming with amusement.

It was three a.m. before the foal emerged and nearly dawn before they left the stables. It was a night in which Acker and Margaret had worked together without saying much, yet they both knew they were a team, at home with each other, friends. They made coffee and breakfast in the kitchen before Acker drove her home.

Edwina was waiting in the lounge, dozing in an armchair. She stood up, grey-faced, looking her age.

'I've been worried sick about you,' she began.

'Mother, whatever you're thinking, it's nonsense,' Margaret said.

'Yes, I know you well enough,' Edwina retorted, 'but what will the town think?' She turned to Acker. 'What you did was wrong. I'm counting on the school offering Margaret a position in kindergarten. She can't afford a scandal.'

'Oh mother, don't start again,' Margaret said and shook hands with Acker.

'I'm sorry if you were worried. Next time we'll phone you,' Acker said.

Over the next few weeks Edwina became quite frantic at Acker's constant calling, yet the two never seemed to want to be alone. It was a strange, unnatural relationship, Edwina reasoned, and one day she decided to talk to her daughter.

'If you're setting your cap at Acker you can forget it,' she told her. 'You're making a fool of yourself. The whole town is talking about you. I've told you before, the rich marry the rich and anyway, his mother would never allow Acker to marry you. She's a spiteful woman and she hates me, so forget him, my girl, the sooner the better.'

'For goodness sake, Mother, I can hardly talk to anyone without you imagining that I'm trying to marry them,' Margaret said and burst into tears, which was very unlike her.

For Acker the weeks slipped by in a pleasant daze until he began to worry about Margaret and from then on the relationship became a nightmare. Acker was obsessed with right and wrong and the meaning of existence. A free thinker, he was contemptuous of blind faith, or simple acceptance of another man's creed. He discarded the religion in which he had been raised and he doubted the existence of God. But if there was no God, then there was no purpose in life and although he did not believe, he kept up a dialogue with the non-existent; haranguing, blaming, criticizing, accusing.

When Acker saw processions, or a brass band marching in the town, or any sign of tradition, tears would come to his eyes and he would feel sad for people who so trustingly spent their lives thrusting meaning into a meaningless disaster. When he saw children he could hardly bear the pain of their eventual disillusionment, for was there anyone to testify to the existence of God? So what did life hold – a brief taste of paradise on earth before extinction; a false sense of immortality? Life was a confidence trick perpetrated by an idiot; no, worse than an idiot, a chemical reaction; and mankind, at the pinnacle of life, was the victim. And so Acker reached the lowest depths of the human mind, fighting with himself and God. One thing he knew – he would never perpetuate the farce, he would bring no children into the world, nor would he expect another person to share his doubts and sufferings.

One morning Margaret's mother announced, 'I've decided to pay for you to go to college and become a vet.' She made the unsolicited statement at breakfast and Margaret gaped at her.

'You'll be catching flies any minute,' Edwina said.

Margaret slowly put her spoon on to her plate. 'But why, Mother? Why now? Why not before?'

'Don't ask so many questions,' her mother said.

Margaret's first reaction was anger. She had been desperate for this and her mother had refused. Now, in order to break her friendship with Acker, her mother had found the money that previously had been so unobtainable. Then she decided she was being uncharitable and ungrateful and she said, 'Thank you' abruptly and went into the garden to consider the matter.

Could she leave Acker? Over the months they had developed a sense of comradeship, yet she could as well be another boy. For the first time she realized how dependent on Acker she had become; all their interests centred around Acker's horses, Acker's farm. What if he should marry someone else? How empty life would be with no wheat to worry about, no grapes to harvest, no Landrace sows to tend. Eventually she decided to speak to Acker.

When she saw him that afternoon she mentioned her mother's offer and to her dismay his eyes shone with happiness. 'How marvellous,' he said. 'You must do it.'

Suddenly her heart seemed to turn to lead and she had difficulty holding the horse's reins, but what exactly had she hoped for? She had never really imagined that he would marry her. She had just wanted their friendship to go on forever, just as it was.

'You see, Margaret,' Acker was saying and she forced herself to listen. 'We have a friendship which is going to carry on,' he broke off, looking embarrassed. 'Ag, I don't want to spell it out. I love you, but I'm never going to marry and I shall never have children.'

'Because of your mother?' she asked stonily.

'No.' He looked surprised. 'It's not something I can talk about.'

'I didn't ask you to marry me, Acker,' she said. 'Nor did I ever imagine that you would do so, but, oh dear, what a pig-headed fool you are.' She burst into tears and, turning her horse, galloped back to Fontainebleu.

Nevertheless, Acker sensed that she would take his words as a sign of rejection, which they were not, and he set about convincing her of his sincerity. He offered her a loan for the university fees, which she coldly refused. He even tried to explain the reason why he would not marry, but found it difficult to do so. Instead he simply hung around, bringing little gifts, trying to ingratiate himself in the family, until everyone became fed up with his great hulk filling their tiny house so that there was no room to move.

50

Paul spent weeks finding the best area for his first supermarket, but eventually he chose an empty field at the crossroads to four large suburbs. It was simple enough to secure the site, but the next step proved more difficult than Paul had anticipated.

'OK so you've got fifteen small shops. So what?' argued Jonathan Pinn, managing director of R & P Property Developers. 'You want me to build a supermarket and shopping centre so you can rent the store. I take the risk. Have you any idea of the cash involved? Millions!' Jon was unimpressed by Paul's protestations of his expertise.

'Jon, if you don't come in with me someone else will and you'll lose out. This is the coming trend. It's done in the States and it's bound to come here.'

When, eventually, Paul was shown out he consoled himself by remembering that not once in the exhausting four-hour meeting had Jonathan said 'no'.

The following week Paul arrived early and was shown into the boardroom. There, on the long table, was a papier maché replica of his project – exactly as he had described it. Paul began to feel hopeful, but it was only after an hour of wrangling that Jon said, 'We're prepared to go in with you, but if we take the risk we expect profits. We'll put the stores up at our own expense and rent them to you for five per cent of turnover.'

Paul swore. 'Five per cent! That's ludicrous. Don't you know how these stores operate? I won't take more than five per cent markup. That's the business: high volume, low markups.' He pleaded his case for an hour and eventually insisted on seeing the company board.

Jon said: 'Look, shove the board. I'm the board; you know that as well as I do. I'm not taking risks without a slice of the action.'

Paul's eyes blazed as he walked out. The bastard! He was being screwed, he knew, but he had no other options.

51

It was midday, late November. The sun was hot enough to roast a scorpion on a stone; it beat upon lethargic, half-grown lambs as they stumbled behind sleepy ewes; it sent the somnolent cattle to seek shelter in dongas where doves, their crops filled from gleaning, cooed in the shade; it baked the earth and ripened the wheat. Perched high upon the harvester Acker could feel the sun burning his shoulders through his cotton shirt. The metal was hot enough to blister his skin.

This was a period of fulfilment for Acker when the year's toil and anxiety culminated in the harvest. As always, he reaped in a circular motion, starting on the outside so that eventually there would be a patch as big as a room left in the middle where an assortment of wild creatures would be sheltering, bewildered by the noise and the destruction of their environment. Then Acker would stop the harvester and trample through the patch. Today, three hares, two rabbits and a meercat scampered away, but a fieldmouse hovered close to her nest where six young, each as big as his thumbnail, crawled.

'Ag! Who needs this last small portion?' he murmured and clambered on to the harvester.

Gazing around he experienced a feeling of intense happiness; he loved the land sensually and intellectually; he loved to walk barefoot over the soil so that he could feel the ploughed earth against his skin; he had a deep emotional need to work with the earth and an intelligent appreciation of its capabilities; the sight and the smell and the touch of it could give him physical spasms of joy.

483

In the distance, he saw a small figure approaching along the farm track. It was Margaret. He smiled as he watched her enduring the noon heat to bring him grapes or coffee. Birds were skimming over the land; around him stretched mile after mile of ripened wheat undulating in the hot summer breeze; beyond the mountains shimmered. How he loved this scene and Margaret he loved even more passionately. As he watched her the love seemed to start in his stomach and swell out, filling his body, to his toes and his fingertips, until the act of loving drowned every thought and action.

Suddenly his consciousness surged out of the shell that was Acker Smit and became free. He was the wheat and the soil and the flies that buzzed over it; he was the rocks and stones; the birds that swooped over the stubble; and he was the stubble. He was like a drop of rain which falling into the ocean becomes the ocean; no longer a single entity, but part of the whole, lapping against ships, smashing on rocky shores, swirling softly into lagoons. He was part of a living force pervading the universe; indivisible with God; part of an endless, formless mind; a font of energy; overwhelmingly that force was love and he was indivisible from it. Ecstasy!

Then Margaret was standing in front of him and he was suffused with a sense of loss; isolated and imprisoned in the illusion that was Acker Smit. He stretched out his hands and gazed at them. 'Acker Smit,' he murmured. Then, slowly a sense of joy dawned, for now he knew without doubt that he was part of that vibrant, living force of energy that was within everyone and everything. He remembered that there had been no time and no boundaries; he had been as much a part of the flies and sheep and farm workers as himself and he thought: every living thing is part of me and 'I am indivisible from every other living thing'. God was there – around and within.

He looked up at Margaret and saw anxiety and sadness so he reached out and caught her hand.

'I've just discovered,' he said, laughing like a schoolboy, 'that God is love.' Then he realized that he had heard that trite phrase enough times, it went with the rest of the meaningless mumbo-jumbo; yet how else could he describe the

484

force which he had just encountered? Was it possible that men who had first coined that phrase had experienced what he had experienced? Surely he was the first and he must tell everyone, but when he tried to put his experience in words for Margaret, he could only think of long worn-out phrases: God is love, God is within you, every man is your brother. Words that had been toted around for nearly sixty centuries.

Margaret looked at him doubtfully. Had he been dreaming? 'I'll fetch you a soap box if you're going to talk like that,' she said pertly.

He stood up grinning and catching hold of Margaret whirled her around. 'Will you marry me?' he asked.

'Marry you?' she gasped. 'You're not teasing me?'

'Will you marry me?' he shouted.

'Marry you?' she shrieked. 'Of course I'll marry you.' And they stood in the field gazing passionately at one another.

For Margaret, the need, the longing and the desire that she had buried so deeply surged out until her breath came in short, sharp gasps, her skin tingled and she began to unbutton her blouse while her eyes were locked with Acker's — both were mesmerized by their all-consuming need.

'We'll breed dozens and dozens of children,' Acker panted. Abandoning himself to his unbridled passion he undid his belt and threw off his shorts and his shirt. He stood astride, bracing himself against the storm of emotions that were sending his blood racing through his body. 'Margaret,' he said hoarsely. 'Later we'll go to the village and sign some papers and that will seal our bargain, but now, on my land, I shall take you as mine and we'll stay together all the rest of our lives.'

'Oh, yes,' she murmured.

Every part of his body ached and trembled; his fingertips tingled; his hair rose as if electrified; his thighs and his stomach began to stiffen while he trembled with anticipation. He wanted to throw her back in the earth, hurl himself on to her, but he was shy and afraid of frightening her.

Margaret threw her blouse down and tugged urgently at her skirt. How huge he was, how handsome, how stable, how dependable. A man among men with his wide shoulders and large head jutting against the sky. The dreams and longings which she had suppressed began to surge to the surface, her face was bright red, her eyes stinging. She felt like an overripe pomegranate, about to split open and spill her vital juices into the earth.

Watching her, naked in the field, Acker was so happy it nearly took his breath away. How fair she was, how strong; yet her skin was soft and white and her breasts were thrusting up as if reaching out for him and her hands were groping for him. He felt drenched with desire and flung himself on her.

Together they loved boisterously, laughing, touching, coupling, nuzzling and then rolling over the earth until they were covered in it. Then they lay quietly for a while, arms around each other, eyes full of wonder, until they began all over again.

The fieldmouse plucked up courage to grab some grain, the birds pecked around them, a grysbok passed close by, and hares ventured out of the patch to glean the wheat. The sun sank behind the mountains, dusk came, plovers swooped down to the donga, their mournful cries echoing over the land and then the bats began to swirl after gnats while night fell.

Acker sat up and said, 'I'm hungry.'

They began to hunt for their clothes which were scattered over the field. Acker put his arm around her and said, 'Perhaps I'll never know why I'm here, or why life was ever created, but I do know that I shall love everything and you I will love most of all. And now we shall go and see your mother and tell her we'll be married the day after tomorrow. Tomorrow I'll get the licence.'

'It won't be so easy,' Margaret told him later when they had trudged to the farm gate where Acker's car was parked. They were covered in dust for they had lain and sweated in it. 'She'll never give her permission,' she went on. 'I'm nineteen and she hates my mother.'

'She can't refuse.' Acker put his arm round her. 'By now you're undoubtedly pregnant with quins.'

She giggled and snuggled into his shoulder, laughing with happiness. When they reached her home she burst into the house calling, 'We're going to be married, Mother, the day after tomorrow.'

Her mother froze. Appalled! Dreams of taking her daughters back to England evaporated. Besides, the sight of them standing together was like a spear thrust into her entrails. They were as married now as they would ever be, so she said, 'Yes, I think you'd better do that as soon as you can by the look of things and you'd best go and bathe. And you Acker,' she went on, 'please go and shower. Whatever will the neighbours think?'

'Does it matter?' Acker said laughing.

'Not to you, obviously, but to me it matters.' Edwina went into the bedroom, shut the door and cried. A few minutes later she muttered, 'Goodness, this won't do. I'm being selfish; the girl will be the envy of the neighbourhood. Who would have guessed he would marry her?' So she bathed her face, powdered her nose and came out saying, 'Well, let's have a drink to celebrate. I think we have some sherry in the sideboard.'

Anna was not so easily placated. 'That woman's daughter,' she said incredulously. 'You want to bring that woman's daughter into this house. Your father had an affair with her and that was the rift which ruined our lives.'

'It's none of my business, Mama,' Acker said gravely, 'but you didn't have to let your life be ruined. Even now Pa would be glad to come back if you would meet him halfway.'

'Don't you preach to me. Why, you've never known misfortune. You've had it easy.'

'That's true,' he acknowledged, 'but what has that to do with Margaret and I?'

'I won't have her living in the house,' Anna said.

'Then we'll live somewhere else,' he retorted. 'There's a house on one of the Malmesbury farms. I can do it up, or if you want I'll make my own way. I can get a job.'

Anna was taken aback. She had been mentally slapped in the face and for a moment she was unable to reply or to think coherently. Jealousy flooded through her. For the first time she could ever remember, her son was not on her side. She had lost him forever. For a few mad moments she felt she was being hurled back and away like a discarded husk of fruit. Sadness welled through her and she nearly cried out. From now on he would be half of another and together they would watch her with alien eyes.

'I'll disinherit you,' she cried, but even as she uttered the words she knew she had made a mistake.

Acker shot her a contemptuous look and walked out angrily.

Suddenly Anna was running after him. He was, after all, the very last one. She loved him. 'No, no, all right, bring her here if you must,' she said. 'Let her run the house, it'll put a bit of life into the place. I'll take the east wing.'

Acker had turned and was watching her compassionately. She hated that look. 'Don't expect me to come to your wedding,' she flung over her shoulder as she hurried back. Anna locked herself in her room, feeling uneasy. The pack was invading her home.

They were married in the Magistrate's Court on the last Saturday in November. Only Simon, Rosemary and Edwina were there and it was a quick, simple ceremony, but when they returned to Fontainebleu a crowd of farm workers were waiting to greet them with baskets of flowers.

'They're expecting a party,' Acker said feeling embarrassed. 'I didn't think of them and that was wrong.'

Flora and Jan organized the workers to bring out barrels of wine and light the spits while Margaret walked shyly into Fontainebleu. Would it ever feel like her home? she wondered. The house was dark and gloomy; sadness hung heavily around her.

'Where is Mrs van Achtenburgh-Smit?' she asked Flora, who was carrying in baskets of flowers.

'Ach, the Missus is shut up by herself like she always is.' She gave a theatrical sigh.

'Come,' Acker said, taking Margaret by the arm. 'Let's find her.'

Anna was sitting in her parents' old bedroom, now converted to a lounge. It was a pleasant room with high ceilings, a large balcony and steps leading to the vineyards, but it was dark; Anna had drawn the curtains.

'Mama, you're not going to shut yourself away,' Acker said. 'You'll love Margaret.'

Anna turned and stared coldly at the girl.

A chill ran through Acker as he wondered for the first time if there was something wrong with his mother; the rigidity of her body and the intensity of her wide, staring eyes seemed strange.

'I want you to understand that the house is yours and the wing is mine,' she said by way of greeting to Margaret, ignoring Acker. 'You respect my privacy and I will respect yours.'

Margaret's cool grey eyes appraised Anna and found her wanting; a spoiled, rude, arrogant woman, pandering to ancient sorrows, unable to forgive or relent.

Give them a month or two and they'll get used to each other, Acker thought, but he was wrong.

Nevertheless the year that followed was one of intense happiness for Acker and his wife. Margaret threw herself wholeheartedly into running the house, the stables, the accounts and the winery. She became plump and merry, content in her partnership with Acker and everyone was amazed at her strength, for she gobbled work as a locust gobbles the crops. She even coped with her social activities and soon Fontainebleu was once again the scene of garden parties, tennis parties and hunt balls. The house was always crowded; Margaret was always smiling and Fontainebleu began to bloom again.

Only Anna resented the change. What right had Margaret and Acker to be happy when Katie was deprived of her home? she thought.

And where was Katie? Anna worried about her constantly. If only her daughter were happy. Instinctively Anna knew that Katie was alone and afraid. The sound of laughter merely increased Anna's grudge and she kept to the east wing, refusing to take part in any of Margaret's parties.

As the months passed, Anna's unhappiness and guilt increased. But she never gave up hope. One day, Anna knew, she would find her daughter.

52

LONDON, November, 1960

There are few less prepossessing sights than London's grey streets in pouring rain at dusk, Michael O'Carrol decided as he left the recording studio. He was later than usual; he felt depressed and his mood was mirrored in the faces of pedestrians hurrying past.

When he had time, he enjoyed a quiet beer in the Red Lion before going home to work and on this particularly depressing evening he felt he deserved at least two. He sat in the corner; a tall, hunched figure, bearded to disguise his fine features; his face too sensitive and too thin. It had been a rough day: Robin Meakin, the studio head, was dissatisfied with his latest song and they had fought over it. When he knew he was right and the song was a good one Michael usually shrugged it off, but this time he had been on the defensive for the song lacked magic; like morning without sunrise, or better still, he thought, like a woman without tits. Flat! Not just flat, but faked.

And why?

He knew why. He had been abandoned by the muse who doled out creativity. Night after night he burrowed head-first into her store – eager as a kid into a tub of lucky dips – but for three weeks he had emerged empty-handed. Where did they come from, these lucky dips? Not from him. He'd always lived in dread that one day he would ask and be refused. Now it had happened; so he had cocked a snoot at the bitch and composed the tune himself.

So what? One bad song amongst so many good ones, but if she were to turn her back on him forever?

Michael tried not to think about it.

There was a sudden halt to the hum of conversation and clinking of glasses. He sat up and looked round.

Everyone was gaping at the door and it was easy to see why. A girl stood there; a girl whose features had been etched on his mind these past five years, but now she looked pale and frightened. Her huge, brown eyes seemed too big for her face; she was clutching a large handbag and her sodden fur coat tumbled over one shoulder like a half-drowned animal clinging to her. Her dress was drenched and stuck to her body, making it all too apparent that she was braless. She knew that every man in the pub was ogling her and that seemed to make her more nervous. Then she sneezed.

She turned hesitantly to the publican; whispered to him. His face registered first disbelief then pleasure. He could not believe his good fortune.

Michael stood up and went to the bar. He ordered another beer and stood listening.

'Here, drink this before you start,' the publican told her. 'You should wear a raincoat; a fur's no good in pouring rain. Catch your death, shouldn't be surprised.' He poured some barley wine into a glass and handed it to her.

She nodded numbly, unable to control her chattering teeth. Her long fingers clenched the glass as she sipped the drink. She did not look happy, but she was still the most beautiful woman he had seen in his life. Her hair was dark red and very wet, dripping down her back, her eyes were amber-brown, her skin was flawless ivory and she had the unique aristocratic appearance of Castillian women portrayed in old Spanish paintings.

What was she doing in London? he wondered.

After a while she assured the publican that she was sufficiently recovered and went over to the piano. She began to play and sing, but the songs were badly selected for the clientèle, too sultry for the jovial, hurried atmosphere. As if sensing this she changed to Country and Western, but that was too unsophisticated for their taste. Her voice faltered and she looked miserable, sensing that no one was listening.

After a while she caught the barman's eye and he smiled. A nice enough man, Michael thought, embarrassment was dripping out of him.

She flushed with shame and was about to stand when she felt a hand grip her shoulder pushing her down on to the stool.

'A terrible rendering, Miss Smit.'

Her eyes looked up and Michael could not suppress a feeling of mounting desire.

'You should have paid more attention to your singing lessons, Miss Smit. Or may I call you Katie?'

She scowled at the tall, bearded stranger. 'I don't know you,' she said.

'Michael O'Carrol. Surely you haven't forgotten your singing teacher from Zurich – your very first lover, or so you told the headmistress and she was fool enough to believe you.'

'My name is Veronica Smith,' she said. 'You've made a mistake.' She glanced anxiously over her shoulder.

'Mistaken?' He laughed. 'Never, Katie Smit. I'd know your voice anywhere; a thin wailing to which you've added a strong nasal intonation, like a cross between a Korean vocalist and a cow in labour.'

She flushed and turned away, but he held on to her elbow.

'Katie, what's the matter with you? Where's your spirit, girl? I prefer to see you bad-tempered as a bull at a toreador instead of cowering like a whipped puppy.'

Katie glanced at the bar again. 'Please go away. I need this job. I'd best go and help.'

'Don't heed the old bugger; I'll cheer him up.'

He sat down and began to play, long brown fingers racing over the keys, bursting from one song to the next: jazz, pop music, old melodies. She could hardly believe it was the same man. He had played only classics at school.

The conversation flagged and then the pub was quiet. He finished to shouts of applause.

'Now,' he said, snapping his fingers.

How she had detested him when he did that.

'You once gave a fine rendering of Schubert's 'Wiegenlied'. We'll try it now.'

She shook her head. 'I must get back to the bar,' she said.

'Come on, girl.' He played the opening chords.

There was a smattering of applause, but Michael looked over his shoulder, one black eyebrow cocked. 'If you want Katie to sing you'll have to applaud a bit better. She's a fine, proud girl, that she is.'

Katie flushed and buried her face in her hands. 'Go away,' she hissed between her fingers.

'Katie, take some good advice. If you want to sing for your supper have done with tantrums. Put your temper into your singing.'

He played and she opened tremulously on the first bar.

'Jesus,' he muttered. ''Tis an air raid siren they've dug up from the war. I can't believe it's really you.' Her voice had eloped with her courage.

She tried harder, anger flushing away nervousness.

Clearly the girl was down on her luck. 'You have a rare natural talent, Katie,' he said. 'No one can deny that, but it's waiting to be developed.'

'When you've finished making a fool of me, I'll get on with my work,' she said and flounced back behind the bar. She saw his mocking smile and glint of compassion which was worse. She wished she could die there and then. Instead, she forced herself to go on wiping glasses, smiling. It was her first night there, and her last, she promised.

Closing time, he was still there.

'Tell him to go,' she hissed at the publican.

'Time to go,' he called cheerily into the stale fumes and cigarette fog.

'I'll wait for you outside,' Michael called and left.

The cheek of it, she thought. Why would he think that she would want to talk to him?

She left by the back entrance, hurried to the tube station and caught the last train to her dingy Chalk Farm room.

Another job gone, another trip to the labour exchange. What did it matter? They all ended the same way. They always would. A man would look at her with lust and mirrored in his eyes she would see herself – a Coloured whore.

She kept running but her problem was always with her.

She had been in London for two years now and while she never allowed herself to think about home, she longed passionately for the sun. London gloom was depressing and her dingy room was horrible, but it was all she could get for four pounds ten a week. An old mirror took up one wall, reflecting the room in shades of murky green, so that she seemed to be living in a shipwrecked cabin fathoms under the sea.

It was the room that drove her to work the following day; that and a promise Michael had once made years before. 'Study with me,' he had said, 'and you'll be a star one day.'

She knew it was ridiculous even to remember his silly boasting, men would say anything. To think of the times she had tried to earn her living singing was too humiliating. Now she was tired, but she had not given up.

Michael was in the pub, as she had known he would be; he seemed to take her presence as an indication that she wanted to see him. When he was leaning over the bar for his third beer she hissed, 'I only came because I need this job.'

'I can't think of another reason for you to be here. Broke, are you?'

'Yes,' she said huffily.

'And your rich parents?'

'I left home.' Adding defiantly: 'Years ago,' as if time had set a seal on it.

After that he sat in the corner for the evening and the publican did not suggest that she should sing.

At eleven she took her coat and scarf and stood undecided, then followed Michael into the street.

It was raining, the pavements slippery underfoot, sounds deadened.

'I hate the cold,' she said.

'Hmm,' he responded and that was the extent of their conversation as he walked her home.

'You can't stay here,' he said after a quick glance around. 'Pack your things.' He called a taxi and she followed him, not curious enough to ask where they were going. She was like a stray cat, he thought. Interested in him only as far as he affected her survival.

His home was in a massive block of flats off East Heath Road, backing on to the Heath and it was surprisingly large and comfortable, with antique furniture, thick velvet curtains, and central heating.

Katie went to the corner of the room and sat on the floor next to the radiator.

'Oh, how wonderful to feel warm,' she said.

Sensing her embarrassment and shame, he left her there and began to work, but as he became absorbed in the intricacies of the melody he was seeking, he forgot about her.

Time speeded up when he worked; often a night would pass in two or three hours – or so it would seem to him, but suddenly he had the melody by the scruff of the neck. It would not escape him again. He was sorely tempted to play it and risk the wrath of his neighbours, but then he remembered Katherine van Achtenburgh-Smit, spoiled, vicious, vain and heedless of her talent, last seen crouching gratefully in front of the radiator. Well, he had tried to warn her years ago; talent must be shared with the world, ignore it at your peril. Sooner or later you'll be forced to use it.

He went to look for her. She was asleep, legs astride too close to the radiator, skinny shanks burned pink. He swore quietly. She would require tender loving care, feeding, teaching. Worst of all she would demand time; and time was the one commodity he was short of.

He sighed, went over to the airing cupboard for sheets and blankets and dumped them on top of her, but she slept on. He bent down and shook her and when she opened her eyes, said, 'This fine deep sleep of yours deserves a better bed.'

She flushed and he saw fear starting up, so he held out the bedding. 'Make your own bed. It's a job I detest.' Taking her by the elbow, he hoisted her to her feet and pushed her to the spare bedroom.

When he went back ten minutes later, carrying a glass of milk and a plate of sandwiches, she was sitting up in bed, eyes wide, a look of frantic determination on her face. She could have been waiting at the dentist. Rape was expected of him. Terrible people, women, he decided. Whores by instinct – every last one of them. 'You'll forgive me if I don't seduce you,' he said. 'I'm tired and to tell the truth it's not my style at all. But I'll teach you to sing, if it's humanly possible. Just so you can go and earn your own living, mind you.' He smiled with his lips, but his eyes gleamed with compassion.

'Why?' he heard as he got to the door.

For a moment he stood poised thinking: because there's no one else, because she had crossed his path. But he called out, 'I hate a job left half done. We were going fine in Geneva, till you ran away.' He closed the door firmly.

53

Midwinter in the Cape; the rains had fallen in torrents for twenty-six consecutive days; rivers had burst their banks; several farms on the Cape Flats were flooded, but still the rain fell until even the farmers began complaining.

Fontainebleu was smelling of wet dogs; burning pine logs; and simmering mutton stews. Acker was seldom home, for the bridges and dams needed constant attention and Margaret divided her time between running the home and supervising the stables.

On Saturday morning she made a huge steak and kidney pie. Acker was mending a bridge across the river to the labourers' settlement. He would be drenched and frozen when he returned.

He arrived late, dripping mud over the kitchen floor. She helped him out of his boots and oilskins and hung them in the gun room.

He reached out and hugged her, rubbing his hand over her stomach. She was big for five months. 'And Mama? How's Mama?'

'I'm fine. I feel guilty.' She smiled self-consciously. 'No morning sickness, no aches and pains. I never felt better. I have to look in the mirror to persuade myself that I'm pregnant.'

Acker rubbed his hands when he saw the gigantic pie being carried to the dining-room.

'Flora, have you called the Madam for lunch?' Margaret asked.

'The Madam's not hungry, Miss Marg.' Her voice sang in a

497

dozen different tones, but managed to imply extreme disapproval. 'She's got a headache.' She sniffed. 'She says she wants to be alone.'

Acker sighed.

'Oh, stop worrying about your mother,' Margaret grumbled. 'She uses her slimming sprees to make everyone feel guilty.'

'You're not being fair,' Acker said. Still, who could blame her, he thought. Anna spent days secluded in the east wing but would emerge as shrewish as ever.

They had nearly finished lunch when they saw a small figure take the turn-off from the road to Fontainebleu. Hardly anyone walked up the driveway; the labourers took the short cut through the vineyard to the Coloured settlement beyond the river; everyone else drove.

'Who do you think it is?' Margaret asked, and stood up to see better.

'Goodness knows. Maybe someone looking for work.'

'In this weather? Don't be silly.'

The figure was bent forward against the gale force winds and driving rain.

'It's a Coloured woman,' Margaret said with a feeling of unease. 'Curious.'

Ten minutes later they heard the bell clang through the house and then Jacob's footsteps walking across the hall. Shortly afterwards he came into the dining-room.

'There's someone here to see Mrs van Achtenburgh-Smit, senior,' he said and they could see from his face that something was wrong.

'Well, who is it?' Margaret asked.

'Sophie Jasmine,' he said disdainfully.

'That terrible woman,' Margaret gasped. She hurried to the front door where Sophie was leaning against the wall, looking wet and exhausted. Her eyes turned bleakly towards Margaret. She coughed and said, 'I want to see the Madam.'

'She's ill,' Margaret said sternly. 'If you want money you can speak to my husband.'

'No, I must see Anna Smit,' she persisted. She crouched

498

down on her haunches as if prepared for a long siege. 'Has the Missus got something for Sophie to eat?' she whined.

Margaret called Jacob. 'Take Sophie to the back door and tell Flora to give her some stew,' she said.

She returned to the dining-room and stood in front of the log fire for a few minutes, trying to warm herself. 'I've never seen her before,' she said. 'Of course I heard about her. Incredible to think that she's Katie's mother. She's so – so horrible.'

Acker looked at her reprovingly. 'You didn't have to send her outside to the back door. She could have walked through the house.'

'She smells,' Margaret said sternly.

Acker felt uneasy; the torch of women's compassion burned so fiercely for their families, yet not a flicker escaped beyond those narrow confines.

'I'll tell Mother,' he said. He hurried to the door dividing the house from the east wing and unlocked it with a key he kept for emergencies.

'Mother, it's Acker,' he called. It was so dark. The day was dark enough, but every room was shuttered. 'Mother,' he called again and then walked along the passage. He knocked at Anna's bedroom door.

'Go away,' he heard a muffled voice say. He opened the door and saw Anna lying on the bed, wrapped in an old dressing gown, a wet flannel on her temples.

'How cold you are,' he said taking her hand. 'Silly of you to lie here freezing. Why didn't you get the fire lit?' He stood up, fumbled for matches and lit the fire which was ready laid.

'If I wanted the fire lit, I'd light it.' She sat up and glared at him. 'I have a headache,' she said, as if that explained everything.

'Sophie's here. She wants to see you.'

Anna sprang up. 'That cow! She'll be after money. I've expected her for five years.'

'I sent her to the kitchen to eat. Will you see her?' Acker watched her worriedly.

'Yes, I suppose so.' She squeezed his hand. 'Everything all

right – I mean on the farm?'

He nodded, wishing there were something he could say or do that would bring his mother back to the family, but after standing undecided in the doorway he left.

Sophie was obviously ill-at-ease when Flora left her at the door and she seemed afraid to walk in.

'What do you want?' Anna said. 'Don't you think you've caused enough trouble?'

Sophie watched her cautiously and walked inside.

'You're five years too late,' Anna went on. 'I expected you. Oh yes, I knew you'd come one day. You think you've found a gold mine here, don't you? You think I'll pay, and keep on paying to stop you from laying a charge of kidnapping. I understand you, Sophie, you and your kind, but you've left it too late.'

Anna watched the Coloured woman coldly, clenching her hands until the nails cut into her palms. She hated Sophie and not only for what she had done, but for what she had become – a blight on the human race, a flaw in the female sex. She saw the hard, drink-thickened features; the defeated eyes; the cowed demeanour. That was something new, she thought, Sophie had never been cowed. Anna observed it all without compassion or understanding.

'I've come for news of Katie,' Sophie began hesitantly.

'How dare you, how dare you ask,' Anna muttered. 'You ruined her life, spoiled her engagement, made her flee from her home and you dare to ask how she is. Well, I can't answer you.' She paused and took a deep breath; tried to control herself. 'Perhaps she's starving, or lost, or a prostitute like you. I've spent a fortune trying to find her.'

She broke off, bit back her tears and began to hammer her fist into the palm of her hand. 'You disgusting, drunken old whore; it's all your fault.'

Sophie did not want to understand. 'So how is she managing without money or a place to stay?'

'I don't know,' Anna exploded. For a moment the women were gripped by a mutual fear, but only Sophie understood the peril of being abandoned in a hostile environment; the

500

slow, relentless downhill path when survival is the only creed. She sank into a chair and Anna could smell her fear. It was a dank, filthy odour.

'Go away, go away,' Anna said. 'You'll get nothing out of me. I don't care what you do.'

'I only came to thank you,' Sophie said. 'For saving her life and bringing her up so well.'

'It's not for you to thank me,' Anna cut in angrily. 'You're not her mother. You lost the right when you abandoned her. She nearly died. It took three weeks to nurse her back to life.'

Sophie was not listening. She rambled on, 'I used to watch Katie at the trial, thinking what a lucky girl she was. She had everything and I used to hate you for it. I never understood, but if only I'd known. I'd rather die than harm her.'

'You are disgusting,' Anna said, watching her tears take a zig-zag course down the eroded cheeks. 'No wonder Katie ran away. She'll never come back while you're around.'

The woman flinched. 'My own child brought up as a decent white girl; that's something I used to dream about. Free, she'd be; free to take a good job; live where she liked – perhaps a nice place by the sea; to hold her head up and feel proud. When you find her,' she went on, 'tell her how proud of her I was. She was everything I always wanted to be.' She stood up, went to the French door and opened it. A blast of cold air sent smoke billowing into the room. Anna locked the door and held a newspaper over the grate until the fire settled down. When she looked out of the window she saw Sophie hurrying through the vineyard. She went back to the fire and huddled there.

It was four in the afternoon when Jan came running to the house. 'Where's the baas?' he said to Margaret.

She called Acker from the study.

'What are you doing out in the storm, Jan? You're too old for getting drenched.'

'It's Sophie, baas. She fell in the river. Drowned for sure. The boys made a chain, tried to find her, but it was no use. The water's this high,' he pointed to his waist. 'Getting worse by the hour.' He lost his breath, then he said, 'The boys are still looking.'

Acker took a rope and set off at a run. Margaret took oilskins and boots and followed him.

The river was a raging cataract, cascading from the hills, tossing tree trunks. Acker tied the rope around his waist and the other end to a tree and waded in, groping around under the bridge and down the riverbed. Ten minutes later it took all his strength to haul himself out.

'Terrible,' he muttered. 'I couldn't keep my feet on the ground. She'll be miles downstream by now. Drowned! It's hopeless.' He split the young men into two groups to search on either side of the bank and they set off, but an hour later at dusk when there was still no sign of Sophie, Acker called off the search.

The story soon raced around that Sophie had thrown herself into the river. Three boys swore they had seen her jump and later her body was found two miles downstream.

When Anna heard she felt a thrill of satisfaction. 'I killed her,' she thought.

Sitting in his warm, wood-panelled office beyond the boardroom, the editor of the *Stellenbosch Star* smoked his cigarette and sipped coffee. The warm, heated air ruffled his newly-dyed hair. The editor licked his moustache and smiled, enjoying his quiet reflection. On his right was an intercom, which could summon Adele, his secretary and mistress; long-legged, high-busted, wicked as a monkey. On his left was a private line with which he could speak to his new, young pregnant wife, reassure himself that she really existed, that it was not just a dream. He called Adele who hastened to fill his cup, light his cigarette, brush her lips across his cheek and discreetly disappear.

The editor half-shut his eyes and savoured this new and exquisite life into which he had been propelled by Anna van Achtenburgh-Smit when she bought the newspaper. The trebling of his salary had enabled him to pay a deposit for a Mercedes; the Mercedes had attracted Tina, his dumb, but well-stacked wife, seductive and eager; his position had enabled him to pick a suitable secretary on terms to please himself; and now he had purchased a house – a beautiful villa on a hilltop overlooking the town. It was far beyond his means and he had only been able to pay a ten per cent deposit from his savings. Admittedly the payments on the car, the bond, the furniture and his wife's clothes nearly equalled his salary, but he was confident of another rise soon. Anna liked him; encouraged him in all his indulgences.

Life was good to him and he felt filled with tenderness; he pressed a manicured finger on the intercom. Adele popped in immediately.

'Lock the door,' he said eyeing her lecherously. 'There's just time before the meeting.'

'But Mr Rose ...'

Protesting was not part of the deal. She scowled, locked the door and unfastened her skirt.

The next meeting was with Anna van Achtenburgh-Smit and it took her half a second to destroy his world beyond repair. Not another editor in the country earned the salary he was paid, if he could find a job at all.

'But Mrs van Achtenburgh-Smit,' he stammered. 'Please reconsider, my wife is pregnant, I have just bought a house, I have commitments, how will I manage?' As the full scope of his dilemma sunk in he realized he would go personally bankrupt, but by this time Anna was halfway back to Fontainebleu.

54

Rosemary smirked at her reflection in the mirror; she saw clear, slanting green eyes, a heart-shaped face, pale smooth skin and brown hair. She had heard herself described as a beauty any number of times, but that did not lessen her discontent.

At eighteen she found life dull, for she disliked teaching kindergarten and her social life was unsatisfactory.

It was so unfair, she thought several times a day. Margaret, her dumpy sister, whose greatest delight was to clean out the stables, had landed the best catch in the Cape. Yet she, the beauty in the family, had no prospects. The farmers' sons who courted her were not at all suitable. Nice enough boys, but no wealth behind them. Manure and milk churns were not for her.

'Are you ready, Rosemary?' Her mother's impatient voice broke in on her thoughts.

They were going to the christening of Margaret's son, Otto. Such a bore! Margaret and Acker would be cooing over their latest; Auntie Anna would be in a fever of impatience to crawl back into her shell; her mother would be irritable and ill-at-ease as she always was when Anna was around.

She had nothing suitable to wear, but what did it matter? She took out her blue and white woollen dress with lace collar and cuffs. It made her look sweet and demure, not the kind of image she desired.

'Rosemary!'

'Coming, Mother,' she called.

There was the usual crowd at the church; farmers and their

504

families; ogling eyes and shiny red faces. She ignored them.

For once Aunt Anna had an escort; a dark, handsome, thick-set man; aggressive-looking, Rosemary thought, like a Roman gladiator she had seen at the cinema last week.

The ceremony took half an hour, then everyone went to their cars to drive to the reception at Fontainebleu. Acker and Margaret took Rosemary.

'Who's the man with Aunt Anna?' she asked.

'Kurt's son, you know, Anna's partner; the one who runs the business with her.'

Rosemary gasped. 'Then he must be very rich,' she said.

'I don't suppose he is,' Margaret went on, 'but he intends to be one day. He walked out of the family business and started on his own. He runs that discount chain, *Better Buys*. It's rumoured Anna backed him.'

The baby began to cry and that was the end of the conversation.

As the car drew up in the courtyard Margaret peered over her shoulder, already sticky from the baby's burps. 'Just forget it, Rosemary. He's Jewish. Jewish men marry Jewish girls.'

'I don't think he's the marrying kind,' Acker added.

Rosemary looked politely confused. 'Whatever are you two talking about?' she said.

Fontainebleu was overflowing with flowers and champagne.

'Damn,' Rosemary muttered as she glanced at her old dress. 'What a disaster.' Nevertheless she often glanced round to find Paul watching her intently.

She was a natural, Paul thought. Knowing she was being watched she became more vivacious. Laughter floating over the guests. She had marvellous legs, too. Long and supple with a golden tan and high-heeled white sandals. He liked the dress; it was exactly right. He would find her eyes gazing at him, lids half closed; a teenager's impression of a provocative stare, he decided. Suddenly he grinned, made up his mind and walked over to her.

'Hello Rosemary, I'm Paul Friedland, we're almost related,' he began.

505

She turned her body away, twisted her head and smiled over her shoulder, a pose that had obviously been perfected in the mirror. He gained the impression that she seldom did anything else.

'How do you do,' she murmured.

'Have you done any modelling?' Paul asked.

'Why no,' she said and smiled again, thinking it was a curious way to start a conversation. 'I teach at kindergarten.'

'The sweet smile suits you better,' he said perfectly seriously. 'The sultry look is definitely not your style.'

For a moment Rosemary was thrown off balance, her eyes clouded, her mouth stayed open.

'I didn't mean to offend you.' He patted her arm. 'I'm looking for a face; a beautiful face,' he added placatingly, 'but someone who's not a model; someone I can sign up for *Better Buys*. If I find the right girl I want a fifteen-year contract, which means she'd never be able to model for anyone else. If you have any ideas about a modelling career forget what I said.'

Not a modelling career, she thought, but I certainly have ideas. He was obviously obsessed with his business. 'I'm quite devoted to teaching,' she lied. 'And of course I study evenings. Later I intend ...'

'Think about it.' Paul was not interested in her plans. His hand dropped momentarily on her shoulder. 'Let me know if you're interested. Now if you'll excuse me.'

For once she had been very wrong. He just wanted her face, on bags of oranges, frozen foods, advertisements ...

She quickly moved towards one of the gawky youngsters and pretended he was the man she most wanted to be with, but her thoughts were fixed on Paul Friedland. Without any doubt he was 'Mr Right', she decided, and business was obviously the best way to get through to him.

How could she have been such a fool, she told herself miserably three months later, when she had not seen Paul since the christening.

First, a photographer had arrived at their house and spent

two exhausting hours taking photographs of her.

Then a lawyer came and after some fruitless arguments she signed on the dotted line. For fifteen years she would be available when required after school closed, and she could undertake no other modelling commissions. For this she would receive the fee of a hundred and fifty rands a month. It was more than she received as teacher.

It was not long before Rosemary regretted her contract, for she felt that portraying a hard-working housewife was ruining her image. There was nothing sultry or sexy about the face that peered over a tub of wet washing, or smiled gaily, kids in tow, holding up special offers from *Better Buys*.

When she complained her mother snorted, 'What image? You're a kindergarten teacher and one day I suppose you'll get married. What could be more natural than for you to be seen running a family? Of course it's not spoiling your image. Now, if you were modelling bikinis or some of this horrid new make-up ...'

After this Rosemary made several unsuccessful attempts to see Paul, but he remained elusive, protected by his business commitments and a bodyguard of secretaries.

55

For weeks Rosemary searched for an excuse for a family get-together. Hearing that it was Anna's birthday in February she persuaded Margaret to hold a surprise party. Paul could hardly refuse to go, Rosemary reasoned.

Borrowing Margaret's car she drove to a Cape Town boutique and bought an emerald green silk dress. It was so daring that even she hesitated. The back hardly covered her buttocks; it clung to every curve, with a plunging neckline to her waist and halter neck.

At last the day came. Rosemary had no wish to be cluttered with an escort, so Margaret sent Jacob to fetch her.

The women gasped when she walked in, the men's eyes swivelled to watch. Apart from being revealing the dress set off her amazing green eyes and black hair – which she had dyed. One gauche farm lad told her she looked as if she had walked straight off the cinema screen and into Fontainebleu.

When Paul arrived an hour later he found himself next to Rosemary, but could not think who she was, although there was something familiar about her.

'Why Paul, you've lost your tongue,' she laughed triumphantly.

'Rosemary?' he queried. 'Good God. I hardly recognized you. Where's your apron?' Then he scowled. 'I hope you aren't thinking of keeping your hair that colour and you're much too thin. Why can't you just be yourself?' He nodded coolly. 'Well, have a good evening,' he said and moved away.

Rosemary gasped. How dare he cast her in the role of a low-class housewife just to suit his bloody business? She drained her champagne glass and would have followed him, but Margaret cornered her.

'That dress,' she muttered. 'It's too much, Rosemary. How could you? You'll be the scandal of the neighbourhood. Is that what you want?'

'I'm sick of being seen in an apron surrounded with dummies and detergent,' she said and gulped another glass of champagne.

Margaret stared intently, then she smiled. 'Oh Rosemary. I told you not to set your cap at Paul. He has no heart, just a computer in its place.'

There was a child's wail and Margaret hurried away.

From then on the evening became a nightmare. Rosemary had no idea how many glasses of champagne she had drunk and she began to feel ill. She went outside, carrying her glass, and wobbled unsteadily down the balcony steps towards the bench in the rose garden. Paul was there, staring at the mountains and the moon.

Perhaps she had imagined his slight, she thought, and putting one hand on his shoulder she said, 'Penny for your thoughts?'

He looked up and smiled. Taking that for an invitation, Rosemary sat on the bench beside him as close as she dared.

'I was thinking,' he said, 'that if I were to take over the packaging of soap powders I could cut the price by at least ten cents a packet.'

'My God,' she scowled at him. 'You look at the mountains and the moon and you think about washing powder?'

Momentarily Paul's eyes skimmed over her nubile body. Urgent breasts and fluttering lashes. He grinned. 'The power of the press, I suppose. When I look at you I can't help thinking of washing tubs and detergent.'

For a moment Rosemary was too horrified to move. The man was a monster, a cruel, insulting monster. The champagne heightened her disappointment and her anger. Another time she might have laughed, but now she gasped and flung the contents of her glass into his face. She heard a low

509

chuckle as he returned to the house.

Oh, how miserable she was. She sat shivering in the rose garden as nausea spread through her. When she tried to stand up she could not. Eventually she vomited into the roses, feeling ashamed of her drunkenness, her dress and her schemes; just wishing she could crawl into a hole and stay there forever. 'Oh, oh, oh,' she moaned.

Anna, who was walking in the garden feeling hostile at this ridiculous charade for her birthday, heard everything and then, finally, soft sobbing. The sounds expressed her feelings exactly, yet she was unable to cry. She approached quietly. The girl was crumpled on the bench, smelling vilely; her head in her hands.

'Rosemary, what's the matter?' Anna asked, although she knew. She wondered why she was feeling so sorry for the girl. After all she was 'that woman's' daughter.

'Go away,' Rosemary blubbered. 'I'm sorry I've ruined your roses. Just go away.'

'Nonsense – very good fertilizer,' Anna said. 'You may come and fertilize the roses every night if you wish.'

Rosemary looked up suspiciously. She had never had a conversation with Anna before, but she had heard so much about her from Margaret. Compassion had never been mentioned. She shivered.

'Come with me,' Anna said. She supported the girl around the side of the house to the vineyard and up to her bedroom. Then she ran the bath and called Flora. Together they forced Rosemary to drink a glass of foul-tasting medicine which made her vomit more than ever. Afterwards she felt weak, but not quite so drunk. Then she passed out.

The next morning she awoke in the guest bedroom. Margaret was bathing her face. She groaned when she tried to move her head.

'What a disgrace!' her sister said. 'In future kindly limit your drinking to two glasses of anything. I telephoned mother to say you had food poisoning and she blamed me for everything.'

Rosemary murmured her thanks.

510

'Anna wants to see you. Serves you right,' Margaret said before she left. 'Don't forget.'

Anna was in the paddock schooling a new black stallion. Watching her, Rosemary thought that the animal's restlessness and temper seemed to reflect Anna's personality. She hung on to the fence waiting for the lecture.

'You're not a very good saleswoman,' Anna began severely. 'It's not much point making the package look pretty if your buyer hates prettiness. What if he only likes brains? Or guts? You'll never get Paul with sex appeal.'

She prodded the stallion more fiercely than she had intended and the beast reared.

Rosemary's cheeks were burning and she was glad Anna could not see her as she struggled to regain control of the brute.

'The psychology of selling is to give the buyer what he wants together with whatever you're selling. In this case – you. Usually the buyer doesn't know what he wants, but subconsciously he'll recognize it, and grab it when you offer. I found that out myself through business,' she said.

Suddenly she smiled. It was the first time Rosemary had seen her smile and she felt quite dazzled. She wondered why she had not noticed how outstandingly beautiful Anna was, perhaps it was because of the scowl she usually wore. Yet her eyes were brilliant blue and they seemed to have infinite depth. You could get lost in those eyes, Rosemary thought enviously. Her thick eyebrows almost met over the bridge of her delicate nose and then slanted up to the side of her forehead. Her mouth was full and sensuous, her neck smooth and unlined, while her hair hung straight over her shoulders. Yet she must be over forty, Rosemary quickly calculated.

'Paul is looking for the security of love from a strong woman and a partner in his business.' She laughed curtly. 'Enthusiasm and guts will stand you in better stead than sex appeal. I doubt it's worth it. Take my advice. Find a nice man.'

Was it possible that Paul and Anna had something going between them? Rosemary wondered. She could certainly outshine a far younger woman.

Her eyes revealed her thoughts. 'Don't be a fool, Rosemary,' Anna said sharply. 'Go home and use your brains.'

Rosemary waited impatiently for the school holidays. On the first day she set off for *Better Buys* in Stellenbosch – Paul's biggest failure. As usual the store was nearly empty and the buyers looked poor. They had come for the loss leaders. She spent the day questioning shoppers as they left. The following day she tackled the Bellville store and by the end of two weeks she had completed a survey of all Paul's stores in the Cape. It was then that she received an irate telephone call from Paul telling her to lay off and stop harrassing his customers.

'You're ridiculous,' she snapped. 'You don't know much about your customers. You don't even know what they want. You can only think as far as pulling down prices. Besides,' she went on, 'I questioned them outside your store, and you don't own the pavement, much as you would like to.' She slammed down the telephone.

Paul replaced his receiver thoughtfully. Who the hell did she think she was? Upstart, prissy little miss who thought she could teach him about marketing. Yet it was true that he was attracting only the lower income groups, not the big spenders. All the same, he'd be damned if he'd telephone her again.

But he did the following evening.

'All right, what do you want?' he said.

She grinned. 'Nothing. But maybe you want something I have. We can discuss my research during dinner and dancing.'

'Lunch,' he barked.

'Dinner,' she said.

There was a long silence. Then he said, 'It'll have to be next Saturday. I can't make it before.'

'Hold on while I look at my diary,' Rosemary countered. 'I'm afraid it will have to be the following Saturday,' she told him.

Paul replaced the receiver and sat gazing out of the window

512

for a few minutes. All the bitch wants is a good screw and all the rest that goes with it, he thought, but she was too young and she was too close to home; much too close to Anna. He said aloud, 'I shall avoid her like the plague,' startling his secretary, who was waiting to resume dictation.

56

It takes a harsh winter to appreciate spring, Katie discovered. Outside their flat was a concrete gully and, beyond, a five-yard slope to the heath. It had been filled with rubble three months before, but painstakingly she had cleared the mess away and planted some bulbs. Afterwards the snow had obliterated everything.

Now the air was sparkling, several green shoots were sprouting and the hedge had burst into white blossom. She became quite giddy with joy, opened the windows and climbed through. Then she hurried to the nursery by the village and spent some of the housekeeping on erica, lavender and some flowering bulbs.

'And how did you find the time with all your hours of practising?' Michael wanted to know when he came home, but instead of scolding her he stood at the window, staring intently at the flowers. Something about the way he was looking made her think: It's as if he's seeing them for the first time – or the last time. As the thought fell into place she felt cold and puzzled. Why had that thought invaded her calm, untroubled existence? She thrust it aside.

'They're lovely, aren't they?' she said.

'A fleeting glimpse of paradise.' Michael turned away quickly and she heard the door of the music room shut.

Surely to God he wasn't ill? No, of course he wasn't. She continued admiring her flowers and thought how light the room looked now with the heavy net curtains drawn aside. She had wasted the day, but it was worth it. She had spent most of the housekeeping money, too. They would have to eat eggs and chips for a week. She laughed and went to the kitchen.

Later, at supper, she said, 'Why are you doing all this for me?'

Michael looked up, startled. 'Agh, Katie, I've thought about it often enough. It's not to eat eggs and chips, I assure you.' He laughed.

'But tell me?' she persisted.

He reached forward and pinched her ear. 'Perhaps I want to tell people: "She's only a famous singer because of me".'

'Be serious, will you.'

'Why, why, why; always questions. Women are like children. I told you before, I hate leaving a job half done.'

'That reason is no longer acceptable,' she said.

'Well, think of a reason that's acceptable and perhaps you can sell it to me.'

'What do you mean?'

'I mean that I don't know the answer to your question. Perhaps it's because you represent life.'

'What else is there, but life?'

'Oh God, Katie, have done with your badgering, will you?' She pouted.

'I'll tell you what; we'll swop information. You tell me why you left home and I'll tell you why I'm doing it.'

She flushed scarlet, bit her lip and rushed to the kitchen to make tea.

She was a lovely girl, he thought, and if things had been different he would have married her. He wondered what had happened to make her so ashamed. Well, easy enough to find out. He had friends in Cape Town, teaching at the School of Music. He would write and ask them to inquire.

The spring flowers grew, blossomed and died, and as the days lengthened Katie did not have the heart to plant anything else. There was something wrong, she knew it. He was so thin, and why was he always working, hardly ever sleeping, as if he couldn't waste a moment? There was a sadness about him. More than that, he hardly ate. And what about all those pills he was always forgetting to take?

One day she took all his pills out of the bathroom and went to the chemist.

'My father died,' she lied. 'I want to throw out the pills I don't need, but I can't remember what all these are for. Can you help me?'

He began to sort them. 'You can throw these away. Your father died of cancer, did he?'

'No,' she said. 'A heart attack.'

'Well, perhaps it's just as well since he had cancer. Didn't you know?'

She nodded, too upset to speak.

'These are for pain,' he went on, 'and these are for nausea. You can keep these,' he said, 'if you ever get hay fever, that is. I'm sorry about your father, dear.'

Katie hardly knew what happened the rest of that day. She wandered over the heath and through the streets. When night fell she returned home, numb with sadness.

Surely not Michael! Not her Michael, with his sense of fun, his glowing eyes, his incredible creativity. She realized then that she had loved him for a long time.

57

At last Saturday came. Paul and Rosemary were having dinner at Angliotti's where Paul was obviously well known; he was studying the results of her market research and scowling intently. The evidence roared loud and clear: *Better Buys*' image had been gauged too low; 'cheap' had been the only message. Rosemary wanted a new campaign showing her as the up-and-coming professional's wife. The emphasis, she felt, should be on better hygiene, better quality, saving time. Admittedly, cheaper prices were the draw, but they should be pushed indirectly.

'I'm curious,' he said eventually. 'Why are you doing this?'

She smiled. 'How about a job? Public relations officer perhaps? I'd be good at it.'

'No, really.' He reached over and gripped her hand; for a moment she was overwhelmed by the force of his personality. Then she stammered:

'I want to be part of whatever you do.' She regretted the words as soon as she had said them.

'Why?' He said fiercely.

Rosemary laughed falsely. 'Don't you know?' she said overbrightly, trying to recoup her position. 'You were quoted in *Femina* last week as the country's second-most eligible bachelor.'

Paul scowled and turned his attention to his food.

'Only the first,' she went on, unable to stem the babble of words that was making everything worse instead of better, 'was so ugly.'

Paul was really angry. He ignored her throughout supper.

Yet when he took her home that night he caught hold of her and kissed her. A savage, unexpected gesture.

'I'll be seeing you,' he said.

From then on Paul called her frequently, but only to help him with business problems, usually market research or personnel. He often took her to business dinners and introduced her proudly as 'Miss Better Buys'. She helped him write his speeches, but he was always very correct and businesslike. She began to despair of ever getting through to him.

'I don't know why you bother,' Edwina kept saying. 'After all, he doesn't pay you extra. Your time would be better spent studying.'

It was the opening of Paul's latest supermarket. As usual the event was turned into a 'happening' with a brass band, competitions, dancing and drinks.

For the first time Rosemary had been invited by the store manager and, to her surprise, found herself beside Paul throughout the noisy ceremony.

'How about lunch?' Paul suggested when the store settled down to normal trading.

He took her to a tiny Hout Bay restaurant, overlooking the beach where they ate fresh, grilled lobsters. Afterwards they went for a walk along the sand and sat on a rock watching the fishermen haul in their long, curved nets.

After a while Paul said, 'I expect you're wondering why I didn't offer you a job.'

Rosemary shrugged and looked the other way.

'I'm about to offer you a position,' he went on. 'It's a long-term project; the financial rewards are good, plenty of hard work and no set hours.' He paused and sat scowling at the sand for a while. 'I want to put it to you straight,' he said. 'No mincing words. I don't want you to get the wrong impression.'

She felt bewildered and a little sleepy from the unaccustomed wine. Today, for some reason, Paul frightened her.

'I've been thinking about this for weeks,' Paul went on. 'I

can't help remembering that dinner we had and what you said that evening.'

Rosemary tried to remember, but could not.

'I'm twenty-six.' He laughed shortly. 'Short of cash, but in terms of assets, worth a million. The point is, my agency advised me to get married. They think it'd be good for the family image, *Better Buys* being a family store. I'm always plugging the housewife and they feel I should have one of my own, by my side.'

He picked up a handful of pebbles and began to hurl them into the sea, venting his spite on the calm waters.

Rosemary began to feel dizzy with shock. Surely he was not proposing? Her eyes began to smart with tension. If only he would get to the point.

'I talked about it to Anna,' he went on. 'She's very much in favour of the idea. The point is, everyone seems to think I should get married and I too ...' He broke off. 'I have a gut feeling about it. Looking around for a suitable candidate, I picked on you.'

Rosemary began to say: 'Is this ...?' but he gripped her wrist tightly. 'Wait a minute,' he said. 'I want you to know that I will never love you and I can't pretend I'm fond of you. There'll be no children. I'm offering you a straight business deal, hard work, entertaining, opening stores, checking, supervising. We'd make a good team; both ruthless, both ambitious. You won't be short of money.'

He looked at her for the first time and his coal-black eyes bored into hers. There was no love there, only his usual cynical humour.

'I accept,' she said. Later, she thought, once they were married, she would be able to reach him.

He shook her hand.

'Isn't it more customary to kiss me?' she stammered.

'Rosemary,' he said chidingly, 'don't let's begin on the wrong foot.'

The wedding was held at Fontainebleu and was one of the biggest events of the year. Acker gave the bride away and

Margaret arranged the catering.

The ceremony was held at ten o'clock in the morning and the local magistrate came to the house to marry them in the main reception room overlooking the vineyards.

Paul was curt, abrupt and obviously ill-at-ease and, when they were pronounced man and wife, he gave Rosemary a cool peck on the cheek and went to the bar.

The wedding party began shortly afterwards and went on throughout the day. At sunset, when there was still no sign of anyone leaving, Acker produced more mutton for the spit, more kegs of wine and the bottle store rushed over with reinforcements; the band were persuaded to stay on for as long as they were needed for double the pay and fairy lights were hastily erected in the trees. The lunch party was still in full swing by midnight, but long before then Rosemary and Paul had driven to the airport where they caught the Johannesburg flight. From there they joined a special charter plane to Paradise Island.

For Rosemary, the island was exactly as its name implied: white sandy beaches, seclusion, bathing within coral reefs, underwater swimming and a quiet hotel owned by an old Portuguese couple who cooked for them.

Each morning they awoke early, raced to the sea and afterwards roamed the island, returning at nine ravenously hungry for breakfast. Then they would go out in glass-bottomed boats with their diving masks and snorkels to explore underwater reefs. Lunch was usually fish or steak cooked on the beach over a fire with ice-cold wine and salads; afternoons they would laze in the shade, awake at four, and wander over the island until it was too dark to see. Then Paul would teach her to play chess or cards and they would eat succulent calamari, crayfish and shellfish. At midnight, drowsy with wine and the warm, somnolent air, they would go to bed and sleep soundly until morning.

For Rosemary, that was the only snag in an otherwise perfect holiday. The absence of sex filled her with anxiety. She was a virgin and although she was not a warm, sensuous creature like her sister, she knew that sex and marriage were, or should be, synonymous. Edwina had never discussed sex with her daughters and while Margaret had the mating instincts of a supremely physical woman to guide her, Rosemary was far more finely balanced, intellectual rather than physical. She looked forward to sex as a child will look forward to punishment, wishing she could get it over with and the longer it was delayed, the more she worried.

On the fifth day of their honeymoon, Rosemary broached the subject. They were sitting on a rock inside the barrier reef after a lazy swim from the shore.

'Are you a virgin, Paul?' she asked.

He frowned at her. 'No, did you expect me to be?'

'No,' she said, 'it's just that ...' She broke off, stuck for words and Paul gave her no help.

Pointing out to sea he said, 'Look, a fin. There're plenty of sharks outside the reef.'

The fin disappeared and she shuddered. 'I'm a virgin,' she blurted out.

'Bully for you.' He stood up. 'Come on,' he said. 'Time to go.'

'No, please, Paul. I want to talk about it.'

'Why?' he asked and looking up she saw repugnance on his face instead of his usual cool friendliness.

'Well, I'm scared,' she said. 'The longer you put it off the more scared I get.'

'Is that all?' He laughed curtly. 'It wasn't part of the deal, was it?'

She gasped. 'Were you expecting me to remain a virgin all my life?' She blushed as she spoke.

Paul's eyes travelled over her trim figure, her breasts half exposed in her fragile bikini, her long shapely legs. 'I guess not,' he said. 'Is there a special hurry?'

'No hurry,' she said timidly.

Was he impotent? she wondered that night when Paul fell asleep earlier than usual and this time without his customary peck on her cheek. Perhaps he was a homosexual and had married her for propriety's sake, or did he hate women? She could not stop worrying. At midnight she got out of bed, tiptoed across the room and, taking off her nightdress, scrambled under the sheet beside him.

Paul awoke instantly, she could tell from the change in his breathing and the tension in his limbs, but he was pretending to be asleep. She snuggled against him, feeling his hard back against her bare breasts. It was a delicious feeling and she pressed closer. He was wide awake, yet he made no move to reject her. How warm he felt. Her husband! It was wonderful to be so close to him. Filled with bliss she fell asleep.

She awoke an hour later to find Paul lying propped on one elbow watching her.

'Tonight's the night, is it?' he said.

Rosemary was overcome with embarrassment and burst into tears.

'Please, please don't cry,' he said. 'When I hear a woman crying I just want to run away – and never stop.' He sighed. 'Go to sleep. I'll never do anything …' he fumbled for the words '…that you don't want. Please feel safe.'

'That's the trouble,' she sobbed. 'I don't want to be safe.'

Moonlight was streaming into the room. Paul pulled the blind and then the curtains. To Rosemary's surprise he returned to bed and in the dark made love furtively and quickly. For Paul it was a savage, shameful act and Rosemary guessed some of the anguish in him when he buried his head in the pillows to stifle his groans.

Afterwards Rosemary felt lonely and restless. She stood up and pulled back the curtains. It was full moon. The balmy air was carrying the scent of ozone. Phosphorescence shimmered on the sea. She longed to walk barefoot on the sand, the breeze rustling her nightgown. She could have taken any fisherman, then. Instead she sighed and sat watching for hours. She would play the part of the happy wife, she decided. No one would ever know how lonely she was.

A thousand miles away Anna, too, was disturbed by the full moon and the warmth of the night wind. The Coloureds were singing and laughing beyond the river. Margaret and Acker had retired early, but a soft light was still shining from their window. All the world seemed to have someone to love, except her.

What was Simon doing now, she wondered? Then she wished she had not thought of him for she could not help remembering how she had loved him once, on just such a night. Absurd to think about it. The man was an oaf and thoroughly unreliable; like everyone else she knew. Since the trial the human race had become unacceptable to Anna – a cruel and grasping crowd. She was lonely, she admitted, but the alternatives were far worse.

To while away the night she walked down to the vineyard, examining the budding grapes in the bright moonlight. It would be a good year again. Then she went back and sat on the steps, leaning against the wall.

She began to think about Katie. How she had loved the child, and later, when she had turned into a lovely girl, she had loved her even more. Anna felt that if she could just know whether or not Katie was alive and well, she would be happy.

'I'll find her,' she whispered. 'Some time, somewhere.'

58

June, 1964

'There's a letter for you from South Africa. Now why would
you get a letter from South Africa? It's there on the table by
the door.' Katie's face was clouded with suspicion.

Michael picked up the envelope. It was bulky. No doubt she
had prodded and pushed at it. 'I have a friend at university
there.' he said. 'Possibly some of his compositions to market –
if I can. I'll read it later.' He thrust the envelope into his
pocket. 'Ach, Katie, it's worse than any housewife you are,
with your black looks and brooding suspicions. You'll have me
explaining to you like any yokel still wet behind the ears. Now
will you stop this foolishness.'

Lips compressed, she fled to the kitchen and Michael went
into his study and quietly locked the door.

When he had slit the envelope he drew out several sheets of
newsprint and before he had even found the letter his eyes
were caught by the headlines: *Mother's eighteen-year search for
lost daughter.*

He scanned through the first paragraph and glanced at the
photograph of a bedraggled Coloured woman. The next page
showed her kneeling at the side of a grave.

What had all this got to do with him? he wondered. Then
his eyes were snared by a picture of Katie – the old Katie –
dressed to the nines and glaring contemptuously at the
camera, a tall, blond man at her side. Carefully he laid down
the press cuttings and took the letter. The Hardys had put in
some sterling work going through newspaper libraries.

'Dear Michael, Jenny and I are filled with curiosity about your

inquiry, for the "Smit case" as it was called, caused a major sensation in Cape Town in 1957. This was before our time, but as soon as we received your letter and mentioned the names, our colleagues were only too glad to tell us the story, plus some extra embellishments. It's all there in the cuttings from the first suspicions until Katie was identified as the missing woman's daughter. After that she ran away. I telephoned her brother who confirmed that no one knows where she is. Hope this helps. We'll be in London next Christmas. Hope to see you then. Best regards, Claude.'

Obsessed with the reports, Michael hardly noticed the time passing, or the clattering Katie was making in the dining-room as she tried to attract his attention. So that was the reason for her hang-dog air; she was ashamed of herself. He understood why she had lost her flamboyance. Success was the last thing Katie needed. She craved a hole to hide in, not a platform on which to reach out to the world. But what an incredible reaction to something so trifling, he thought.

Her mother's name caught his attention. Sophie Jasmine! 'Katie Jasmine,' he murmured. Better than Katie Smit.

There was a loud knocking on the door.

'For goodness sake, Michael, are you going to eat supper or not?' Katie called.

It had been a week of misery for Katie, for it was clear that Michael's illness was getting the better of him. She had watched him surreptitiously disappearing into the bathroom to take his pills; his sad attempts to be happy; his feverish anxiety to write more and more songs.

He was going to die; maybe not this year, but soon. The thought filled her with sadness for Michael and terror for herself. She knew that she loved him and she was sure that she would not survive without him.

Sometimes, in the night, she would lie awake and remember those terrible years before she met him.

It had taken only a few months to discover that, untrained and without influence or a band to back her, she was merely one amongst thousands who wanted to be stars. She would have been content to earn a modest living, but even that had

525

proved unattainable. She became aware that third-best was beyond her reach. Singing in pubs she had reached a new low, unable to charm the patrons from their sausage rolls and beer, however fleetingly. Since leaving home all her energy had been devoted to survival.

Repeatedly she told herself to give up singing, learn a trade and earn a decent living, but she always gave herself one more chance. Only when she was successful would she be able to show Anna and her former friends that she could make it on her own. Singing was the only thing she had ever been good at. Now Michael had given her new hope.

Watching him as he picked at his food she wondered if he still believed she could succeed. He worked her hard enough and paid for extra tuition, but he was no longer so enthusiastic.

'Michael,' she began. 'You once told me you could turn me into a star. Do you still believe that's true?'

Michael was about to fob her off with a touch of harmless flattery, but seeing the earnestness in her eyes, he said, 'Well, I don't know, Katie. I don't think I ever had the right to say that anyway. What I should have said is that I could turn you into a good singer.' He hesitated. 'Being a good singer doesn't make you a star. For that you need a hell of a lot of luck and you haven't been very lucky lately. Besides you need something else – a certain personality which you once had.

'You've lost your self-assurance,' he went on. 'The magic's gone.'

'So should we go on?' she asked, swallowing hard. 'All this work; all this trouble and expense for you.'

'All I can say is – we'll give it a try. You won't be worse off, will you?' He looked so sad that she felt anxious for him.

'You're wrong about one thing,' she said.

Michael looked up, eyebrow raised.

'I'm lucky. After all, I met you, didn't I?'

He glanced away, frowning.

'I know you love me,' she burst out. 'Why can't I get through to you?'

'My interest in you is purely paternal, my child,' he said.

She thought about that for a while and then she said, 'No, I don't believe you. You're not that old and I'm not that childish. You're making me feel very undesirable.'

'My dear Katie, if I'd had the slightest idea that I was the object of your attentions I would have been frothing at the mouth. Where sex appeal is concerned you have no equal.'

'Well then!'

'Well then,' he mused. 'You said that with such conviction one could be forgiven for thinking that it made sense.'

'Michael, you can be very irritating,' she said.

'And you, too, my dear. Talk about your singing, or my songs.'

'I want to talk about us.' She stood up. Clattering the plates with unnecessary vigour, she stalked into the kitchen and dumped them there. 'I'll do them tomorrow,' she said when she returned to the lounge.

'The wine's got into you,' he said. 'Tomorrow you'll be sorry.' He stood up, sat beside the fire and began to fill his pipe.

'Do you know how old I am?' she said.

'I've a very good idea.'

'I'm twenty-six,' she went on. 'I'm a virgin at twenty-six. It's a disgrace nowadays, did you know that?'

'Well, that depends on how you view life,' he began.

Michael, is there something about me that puts you off?' she said.

'Why no, your looks could coax a bishop into purgatory.'

'Then maybe you have a sex problem?'

'By God, I do not.'

'Then tonight you will sleep with me.' She felt better when she had said it.

'Sure, I have a right to choose my own woman,' he said. He stood up, pushing Katie away, for she had been shifting closer to his knees.

'Katie,' he said none too gently. 'You're here to learn to sing and I'm going to teach you and we can't have any distractions. Besides,' he went on, 'I have a wife in Ireland.'

'Oh nonsense,' she said. 'You'll have to think of something

better than that, Michael. You have no wife in Ireland, nor anywhere else for that matter.'

'No,' he agreed cheerfully enough. 'Nor will I have, nor mistress either.'

'Yet I know you love me,' she said sadly.

'Katie, there's something I haven't told you.' He looked serious for a moment. 'One of these days I'm going away. I'm not the sort of person who can be tied down. It's no good loving me. You'll just get hurt and what will become of you when I've gone?'

'Michael,' she said. 'I know you have cancer.'

He stiffened and then she heard an almost imperceptible sigh. 'The world's too full of mourning widows, don't you think?' he asked.

'Better a mourning widow than a sterile old maid,' she replied.

That night he came to her, as she had known he would. He took her in his arms and drew her to him and for a while they lay without moving, content with the warmth of their bodies and the joy of being together at last.

She knew that all her life had prepared her for this moment. She and Michael – that was the only thing for her.

'You know I love you,' he said eventually. 'You've always known that. Isn't this enough then, just to be close, to work together?'

'No, oh, no.' She sat up, pulled off her nightdress and flung it on the floor and impulsively undid his pyjamas and snuggled back under the bedclothes.

He gasped with the force of his passion, which was stronger than he had ever known for she was – had always been – infinitely desirable to him. Her soft and silky skin, her hair spread over his shoulder, her tender eyes, and sweet, shy glances. Yet she was a poor broken thing compared with the Katie he had known in Switzerland. Poor, forlorn, lost creature. Compassion welled out of him, too. What right had he to take and not to nurture, to bite the apple and discard half eaten, but she was pressing, wanting, gasping. He let his mind flow with the passion of his body.

528

She felt his desire rise against her with amazing strength. This was life – her life – to yield, to hold, to keep – all the rest was nothing. She felt helpless, open, acquiescent. He could take her gently or cruelly, love her or kill her. She was his only. She was like a placid secret pool; rippling, waiting, ready for the man, the only man, who would dive deep into her secluded waters, explore the hidden recesses, touch the sea anemones, find the pearls.

Now waves were rising, swelling, eddies and swirls, as the current reached that deep and secret cave. A thousand sea creatures became alive, writhing, tingling, throbbing with passionate feeling; they quivered and murmured as the diver fell and fell and rose and fell. Sea anemones shuddered and closed and opened again, drunk and craving more of the swirl and flow of passion; waves rose and splashed against a shore of pleasure, each sparkling drop a spasm of pure joy.

It began softly, something new and unknown, a feeling more sweet than she had dreamed possible. This strange body of hers, which she had never known until this night, was a vessel bearing pleasure, and it was pouring, pouring away, and the joy and the ecstasy was more than she could bear. She sobbed: 'Michael! Oh Michael. Oh Michael hold me, hold me.'

In the morning, when she was lying drugged with the langour of satisfaction, Michael said, 'It won't help us, Katie. The inevitable result of this night's work will still be you – on your own and even more lonely than when I found you. You must work harder. I want you to succeed.'

59

In 1962 Paul's first supermarket proved an outstanding
success, but at the time he knew that his opposition was not
far behind. Afraid that they might become entrenched in the
prosperous Transvaal before him, he borrowed heavily from
several different merchant banks and over the next twelve
months opened three more supermarkets in Johannesburg
suburbs. All were successful and in 1963 Paul's next step was
to buy out his partners in the *Better Buys* grocery stores, some
of which were then converted to supermarkets. By the end of
June 1964, Paul had nine thriving supermarkets and in
October *Better Buys* went public.

Paul's merchant bank offered forty-nine per cent of the
equity to the public, which was over-subscribed threefold in a
mad scramble as nearly every investor in Johannesburg and
the Cape tried to get in on the ground floor.

Only Paul knew that he was on a treadmill that was
beginning to spin at an alarming pace and he had to keep his
footing or go under. His prices had to beat those of the
opposition or his faithful consumers might turn fickle.
However there were also investors to be placated, so growth
must continue to improve, which meant more and more
profits. His profit margins were so narrow there was only one
way to do this and that was to sell more – and more. If the
growth rate were to fall investors might lose confidence and
share prices would dip. This would be catastrophic, for Paul's
shares were pledged to merchant banks for overdrafts with
which he expanded his group. At all costs share prices must
rise.

The treadmill spun faster and faster.

There was one area where Paul could score and that was with suppliers.

He would begin by wooing them as assiduously as any suitor until he was responsible for most of their output, then he would turn the screws. Finally he would leave them so minute a profit that it was hardly worthwhile continuing their enterprise. '*He who feeds the crocodile gets eaten last,*' the Africans say.

So it was with Kurt and Anna.

One day Kurt awoke to the realization that seventy-five per cent of their poultry production went to *Better Buys*. It was not long before Paul pounced and announced to an astounded Kurt that he was going to reduce the retail price of poultry by twenty-five per cent. As for eggs, he explained, they had been over-priced for years. He could see no reason why Kurt and Anna should make more than ten per cent on their poultry operation and he had worked out to the nearest cent what to pay so that they received their ten per cent. Paul withdrew his order and waited for Kurt to meet his prices. Father and son were locked in a feud far more destructive than at any time in the past.

Eventually Kurt went to see Anna, hat in hand, bowed with sorrow and embarrassment, and explained to her what his son was doing to them.

To his surprise, Anna smiled and then burst out laughing.

'You old fool,' she said. 'He's just a baby. You're so cluttered with emotional hurt that you can't think straight. Play him at his own game. Behave as if he were a stranger.'

A week later they offered Paul even lower prices than he had demanded, explaining that they were planning for higher turnover at lower profits. In return Paul was to buy only from them and run a six-month hard-hitting advertising campaign with eggs and poultry as his loss leaders. He, too, was to take no profit on these items.

Paul was surprised and agreed enthusiastically.

Six months later Jack Tassetti, Anna's only big competition and a former member of Pietersen's committee responsible for

Anna's political downfall, went under. Anna bought his batteries, sheds, poultry and land for a song and an astonished Paul found egg prices raised fifty per cent overnight. He shopped around, but there was no one else with the production capacity available.

Paul learned a lesson and was more careful in future.

Six months had passed since Rosemary's wedding, yet she could hardly claim to know Paul better than on the day she had married him. By tacit consent they presented an image of the happy young couple to the outside world. Otherwise she hardly saw Paul, for he worked all the time.

Usually Paul would come home after midnight and their furtive sex life took place only at dead of night, when Rosemary was half asleep – a hurried act which would leave her feeling disturbed and very lonely.

Rosemary yearned to be loved, but it seemed that this would never be. She decided to join the local amateur theatrical society and was soon drawn into a new set of friends, an endless round of parties. Every week her face appeared in the social pages of the press and always with a different escort.

Paul did not care how she spent her time as long as she was there when she was needed – and she always was.

The weeks passed. On Rosemary's first wedding anniversary she received flowers from the family, a telephone call from her mother and cards from several business acquaintances, but nothing from Paul. She telephoned him at the office.

'Darling, I thought it would be nice to have an evening at home together, dinner for two. Could you make it by seven?' She waited anxiously for his reply.

'Whatever for?' He sounded annoyed at the interruption.

'Well, today's our wedding anniversary,' she began timidly. 'I thought ... '

'Today's a working day, like any other day.' A brief click ended the conversation.

Rosemary replaced the receiver more slowly. Why cry? she

asked herself, wiping her cheeks with the back of her hand. She had achieved exactly what she had set out to achieve. To cry about it was absurd. At that moment it seemed to Rosemary that she had taken a great deal of trouble to walk down a cul-de-sac. What good was wealth if you were lonely?

She spent the evening alone, sitting on the patio overlooking the bay. There were so many alternatives open to her. She could take a lover, but what was the point when she loved Paul? She could be content with all the pleasures wealth brought: her boat, her riding, her friends, her clothes – but she knew that this was not enough. It all seemed trivial. Then she thought that since she had achieved her ambitions once, she could do so again, but this time it was love she wanted, not wealth, a friend at home, someone with whom to share her life.

She had no idea of how to reach Paul, but she would try and the first step would be to stay at home. At least when Paul was at home she would be there, too.

From then on, Rosemary intensified her efforts to penetrate his defences, but without success, until eventually she became suspicious, for Paul was hardly ever at home.

She began to check on his movements, and this was not an easy task for Paul had numerous commitments; but still there were inexplicable absences, and always on Friday evenings and Saturday mornings. Perhaps he had a secret vice such as gambling, she guessed. Eventually it seemed to Rosemary that another woman was the most likely cause of her troubles and, once she had made up her mind, it was just a short step to employing a private detective to discover where he went each week.

The report was brief and arrived two weeks later. On Fridays at five-thirty in the afternoon Paul went to the synagogue and remained there until nine, after which he returned home. On Saturday mornings he did the same thing and sometimes Saturday afternoons as well. On Yom Kippur and other holy days he remained there all day and occasionally all night as well, according to others who knew him. Did she want them to take the matter further?

She paid the fee, feeling foolish, neurotic and ashamed.

How odd, she thought. Paul had never given any indication that he was religious or even interested in being Jewish and if that were the case, why had he married a gentile? Vera had been so upset at the wedding, complaining of Paul's lack of Jewish feeling. Yet, unbeknown to them all, he held something dear. She guessed that his secrecy was something to do with his childhood and instinctively she knew that she would never be close to Paul unless she could share this with him.

Rosemary had always disliked Vera and she suspected that her step-mother-in-law reciprocated this feeling, but eventually she found the courage to go and ask for her help.

Vera's home was like a museum, with every available space crammed with works of art. Rosemary hated it, but today she was too intent on her problem even to notice as she poured out her troubles to Vera.

'I don't know what to do any more,' she concluded. 'There's an impenetrable barrier between us. I'll be living with a stranger for the rest of my life, and to make matters worse I love him.'

Vera watched her coldly. 'My dear,' she said eventually. 'If you wanted an emotional attachment you should have secured it before marrying. You entered the relationship through the back door and now you want to change everything. I've always believed that you two deserve each other.'

'You've never liked me, have you?' Rosemary said sadly.

'It would be more accurate to say that I've never understood you. Paul told me that it was a marriage of convenience. He needed a wife and you needed a rich husband.'

Rosemary blushed. 'I told him that long ago,' she said defiantly. 'But then I fell in love with him and took him on any terms.'

'Well, I don't think you stand much chance of getting through to him,' Vera went on. 'After all, I didn't and I was trained in dealing with Paul's kind of problems. That's how I met my husband. I was engaged to help Paul.' For a moment she seemed to let go. 'I can't say I ever succeeded with either

534

of them. You would think he really was Kurt's son. They are both alike, so' – she searched for the right word. 'So remote,' she said flatly. She stood up. 'I'll accompany you to the door,' she said formally.

'Bitch!' Rosemary muttered as she drove home. Suddenly she braked, turned the car and drove towards Stellenbosch.

It was noon when she arrived and instead of looking for Margaret she went around to the east wing and knocked on Anna's door.

There was no answer, but when she tried the handle the door opened. She found Anna alone in her lounge, sitting at her desk, scribbling in a ledger.

'Why didn't you answer when I knocked?' Rosemary asked.

'Because I'm working,' Anna retorted rudely.

'Anna, I need your help.'

Anna glanced irritably over her shoulder. 'How much?' she asked.

'You can be really mean sometimes.'

'I'm learning,' Anna said. 'I suppose Paul sent you to try to get round me over the egg prices?'

Rosemary looked bewildered.

'No? Oh, all right, what is it then?'

Rosemary was only too grateful to pour out her problems. 'If I could only get through to Paul,' she said finally.

'The result of loving someone is disillusionment,' Anna said. She closed her ledger with a bang. 'Leave the situation as it is. There's nothing to spoil. Just have a good time. As for children – if you don't have them they can't disappoint you – or run away and break your heart.'

'Vera was awful to me,' Rosemary went on. 'Really nasty.'

'Yes,' Anna said thoughtfully. 'But she wasn't always like that. When I first met her she was soft as butter; fat as butter, too. She's changed.' She broke off thinking that it was Kurt who had damaged Vera; he had never loved her, only tormented her.

'Why not carry on as Cape Town's answer to Jackie Kennedy,' she said. 'You do it so well.'

Rosemary felt angry. No one cared. 'You're supposed to be fond of Paul,' she blurted out. 'You're as heartless as Vera.' Her eyes glinted. 'I beg you both for help, but you couldn't give a damn.'

'Rosemary,' Anna said gently. 'Whatever happened to Paul, it was before he came to South Africa. Only Madeleine knows and she won't tell. She's a perfect bitch, by the way. But suppose you were to find out – how would that help you? He'd still have the same hang-ups.'

'Maybe I'd be able to help if I understood.'

Oh God, Anna thought, nagged by memories and guilt. I wish she'd hurry up and go.

Paul knew where Madeleine lived; he sometimes visited her, but Rosemary dared not ask him. Instead she went to the dealer where Madeleine's paintings were sold. It was an imposing gallery, situated near the law courts and one room was devoted to Madeleine's work.

Walking around gave Rosemary a queasy feeling. The paintings disturbed her. One, in particular, was of two women in a garden, but their faces were masks that had slipped. Behind were fierce, predatory expressions; one of them looked like Anna. In Madeleine's paintings the human race appeared diseased and horrifying. Prices were even more breathtaking; not one under two thousand rands.

Eventually the dealer arrived and told her that Madeleine had married a specialist called George Warring and was living at Bloubergstrand. Rosemary telephoned and was asked to tea the following afternoon.

The house was old and rambling; the studio was situated at the bottom of a sandy garden. Rosemary was surprised when she saw Madeleine, a plump, grey-haired woman in a smock, smeared with paint, with glowing blue eyes and a cheerful expression.

'You're not a bit like your paintings might suggest,' Rosemary stammered.

'Well, I try not to paint myself. I might frighten myself too much,' Madeleine said. She put an old kettle on to a handigas ring and a few minutes later handed Rosemary a mug of tea.

After a while Rosemary found the courage to ask Madeleine about Paul's early life. 'I want so much to make my marriage work,' she went on shyly. 'We never fight – we don't know each other well enough to fight. He's always polite, but we're only playing at being married. I feel so undesirable and I'm losing my confidence.'

'I've always felt involved in Paul's destiny,' Madeleine told Rosemary, 'but he's never liked me. He feels happier when I'm not around. George, that's my husband,' she explained, 'has helped me to understand. He says I remind Paul of the past – something he wants to forget, but can't.

'I'll tell you what little I know,' Madeleine said sadly. 'They were terrible times. I was interned at the beginning of the war because my mother was Jewish. I am alive today only because I was young enough to be sent to a camp as a troop prostitute.' She smiled apologetically. 'It was a strange situation; captors and captives became inextricably bound in the same destiny. I cried when the troops were killed; they shared their last rations with me and the other women.

'At the end of the war I was liberated by the Russians and put in a camp with hundreds of refugees. It was a time of confusion; no one had papers; no one knew who anyone was. After a month I heard a rumour that they were planning to repatriate the sick to the West. I was not sick, but there was a young boy – Paul I called him – who was deaf and dumb.'

Rosemary gasped.

'Yes, he was at the time,' Madeleine frowned. 'He had been brought to the camp by an old Polish woman, a former maid in his parents' house. She told the camp guards that she wanted him to go back to his own people. She claimed he was Jewish. His father had been a doctor, but the Germans hung him when they invaded Poland. His mother was raped by the troops and then hung. The maid found Paul wandering around and hid him for four years. He never spoke. She was

537

not aware that he was deaf, too. More tea?'

'No – thank you,' Rosemary whispered.

'There wasn't much control at the camp. No one had papers. We were all intent on getting home. It was easy to pretend Paul was mine. He was so skinny I thought he was about five, but later I realized he was at least two years older than that.

'I can't see the point in crying about it now,' Madeleine went on as she handed Rosemary a tissue. 'It was so long ago and Paul recovered completely. Anna helped him far more than I did.'

'Please excuse me, but I'd like to go,' Rosemary said blowing her nose. 'I'd like to come another time, but now I feel so upset.'

She left by the garden gate and walked along the deserted sand dunes for an hour, battling against wind and sand.

Did Paul remember any of his early experiences? she wondered. Probably not. Yet it was all there under the surface. No wonder he hated sexual aggression. She remembered how he reacted to tears, he just wanted to run away. What right did she have to demand more than he could give?

When Paul returned for dinner on Friday there were two candles burning on the table, but Paul did not notice.

After a while Rosemary said, 'Paul, I'm going to become Jewish.'

He put down his fork and scowled: 'You don't become Jewish,' he said. 'Either you are or you aren't – and you aren't.'

'Not true,' she argued. 'I know a woman who converted and I'm going to.'

'Forget it,' he said. 'A converted "shiksa" is in no-mans's land.' He left the table abruptly and went to his study. Rosemary did not see him for the remainder of the evening.

The following Monday Rosemary telephoned the Jewish Board of Deputies and was given the telephone number of a

538

rabbi in the Reform Movement who dealt with converts. She felt sure that eventually this would bring them closer together.

60

Nancy Meredith was a shrewd show-business personality,
famous on both sides of the Atlantic for the fastest-ever climb
to the top. She ran her own television variety show and had
gained a reputation for being clever, warm and
compassionate. Michael was counting on all of her attributes
to help him.

It was a relief to enter her over-heated studio on this
freezing November morning. Lately, the cold seemed to bite
into the heart of him.

Nancy was sitting in front of the mirror, looking impatient
while her hairdresser wound her long hair into rollers. Her
pianist, Duke, was trying out a new song. He seemed
dissatisfied with the beat, strumming it over again and
frowning. Ike Cherbar, her agent, was drinking coffee on the
other side of the room.

Nancy caught sight of Michael, jumped up and kissed him.
'Well, here's that famous composer,' she drawled.
'Congratulations, darling. "Autumn Evenings" reached the
Top Ten yesterday.'

He nodded, smiled, and huddled into a chair, shuddering.
'Your voice pushed it there. By God, it's cold outside.'

She nodded. Her shrewd, compassionate eyes noted his
weight loss, the pinched mouth, huge, luminous eyes. She
said, 'What's a famous composer doing here so early on a cold
morning? Not to sell me a song, I'm sure, since I launched
your last two. You know I'll take whatever you have.'

'There's something else I want you to launch,' he said. 'But
I haven't come empty-handed.'

540

'Well, warm up first, for goodness sake. I think you need a dose of your own home-brew.' She poured some black coffee out of a Thermos, fumbled in the cupboard for a bottle of whisky and poured in a generous measure. Two curlers came unwound and fell on the floor. The hairdresser swore.

It was Scotch, not Irish. Michael drank without pleasure but, not wishing to offend her, accepted another.

The pianist was strumming a tune, lips pursed, unwilling to comment until Nancy had set her seal of approval or disapproval.

'Well, what do you think?' she asked Michael uncertainly.

'Hard to tell unless you sing it,' he said. 'Your voice could push Humpty-Dumpty to the top.'

Nancy was unwilling to be flattered. 'You Irish live on your wits,' she said. The hairdresser pushed her into the chair and began winding, but Nancy brushed him aside again.

With half her hair straggling wet down her back and the rest in curlers, she still looked desirable as she bent over the piano, Michael noticed, as she first hummed and then sang the new song. Whatever else had failed, his sex drive had not.

'Whose is it?' he asked.

She shrugged.

'Never mind whose it is,' Ike called out. 'What do you think?'

'Charming and catchy,' Michael said. 'You'll do well with it. Take it.'

'Are you sure?'

'Sure, I'm sure.'

Hunched over the keys, the pianist said, 'I like it baby, I like it.'

She looked over her shoulder at her agent. 'Okay Ike, we'll take it.'

Michael fumbled in his briefcase, took out his score and handed it to her. 'Try it out. See what you think,' he said.

She was impressed, he could see that as she hummed the melody. Her pianist knew from her voice that she liked it. He said, 'This is for you, baby.'

Nancy pulled a face at Michael. 'I suppose your prices have

soared since I made you famous.'

'That would be true, in a straight business deal, but this is a gift, in return for a favour.'

'A gift from you?' Nancy winked at her agent. 'Don't make me laugh. Come on! Exclusive rights, Michael.'

'Would I be fool enough to offer you anything else? It's like this, m'darling,' he said deliberately exaggerating his Irish brogue. 'I've got a young singer and I want her launched. I'm her agent.'

He broke off as Ike laughed. 'You've reached the top in the song-writing business so now you want to be an agent. Pull the other leg.'

'It's someone special,' Michael said. Nancy felt a twinge of envy. Whoever she was, she had Michael in her pocket.

'You want me to launch a singer on my show in return for this song?' she asked incredulously.

'Yes.'

'You know what you'd get for this song?'

'Yes,' he said.

'Then she must be bloody awful,' Nancy said petulantly.

'No, she's not. By God, she's tremendous.' He stood up. 'She's brand new, too. Unbelievable talent. I would have preferred her to start the hard way, but it's a long haul and I'm in a hurry.'

'If she's any good she'll get there anyway, Michael,' Nancy said sternly.

'Come on, Nancy,' Michael said suddenly feeling impatient. 'You know how tough it is. It might take years. She hasn't got your drive or your confidence. A helping hand from you would make all the difference.'

'Oh, Michael,' she said, looking cross. 'I can't launch just anyone on my show. Bring her round.'

'I've brought a recording,' Michael said. He went to the recording equipment and found his hands were shaking. Ridiculous to get so uptight, he thought.

Nancy shrugged and returned to her hairdresser who was close to losing his temper. He grabbed her hair and began to wind it quickly as the sound of Michael's piano flooded the

542

room.

'Be reasonable, Henri,' Nancy said as he tried to thrust her under the dryer. 'I want to listen.'

It was a short, sad song and the voice sounded sad, too, Nancy thought. A superb voice, but short on confidence, holding back. She lacked the training to bring out her emotions.

When it was over she said, 'Michael, there's nothing wrong with her voice but she doesn't seem to have the rest of it.'

'It's coming,' Michael said.

'Yeah, when?'

'Six months,' he said.

'All right,' she said. 'Six months it is.'

Michael's face lit up. 'A straight swop. Okay.'

'Okay.' She frowned at him as she went under the hood.

'Thank you,' he began and then broke off, realizing that she could not hear him, so he blew her a kiss and left.

61

November in the Cape is harvest-time. This year, as if to repay Simon for his perseverence, nature had made amends and it had been a magnificent year.

In May, the rain had flooded the earth, day after day, soaking deep into the earth's bowels; filling underground caverns of water; flooding rivers; coaxing the grain to send up tall, proud shoots.

In June the wheat had sprouted thickly, covering the land with a carpet of green and daily showers pampered the shoots, so the wheat grew taller and thicker than ever before.

In October the ears were plump and long; all that was needed was the hot summer sun to ripen the grain. Nature fulfilled her promise. Day after day the wheat ripened and rippled in light summer breezes.

The harvest was bountiful; sacks of thick, luxurious grain. The farmers smiled and said there had never been a year as good as this one. Not in living memory.

Simon experienced a feeling of deep gratitude and well-being. Each day he stood barefooted, ankle deep in the loam, watching the labourers bind the sacks and transport them to the lorries. He saw contented sheep gleaning the grain, plodding patiently amongst the stubble, while the heat beat upon his head and shoulders, flowed through his limbs and down into the earth.

His land! He would rather die than part with an acre of it. He knew he was in partnership with the soil, for the soil needed him, craved his ploughing, raking and fertilizing, only then could it reach fulfilment; and Simon needed the soil to be fulfilled; to be real. The farmer and his land! A curious symbiotic relationship. Without the land he was nothing.

62

Better Buys was riding the crest of a wave, or so it seemed to onlookers. Shoppers were surging to the stores in their tens of thousands. Backed by expensive advertising campaigns Paul was conducting in all the main centres, he had become the blue-eyed boy of the press.

Only Paul and a few trusted advisers knew how top-heavy the group was. The structure had grown too big, too fast, without a strong enough foundation of solid cash beneath it. For every asset Paul controlled there was the equivalent overdraft. Even his glittering stores were owned by the rapacious property company which backed him.

R & P Properties were a source of continual annoyance to Paul for they gobbled up five per cent of turnover. Paul felt that it was they and not he who were enjoying the profits from his stores.

R & P were keen to expand in Johannesburg and so was Paul. Jon claimed to have found the right site for a hypermarket and was nagging Paul daily.

Eventually, Paul flew to Johannesburg to examine the place. It was perfect; poised equidistant between five great suburbs.

Paul dilly-dallied, would not give Jon the go-ahead. Instead he cancelled his return flight and spent the next few days touring suburbs, looking for an alternative site to go it alone.

Two days later he found a field in an ideal position, offering better access to the motorway and more space for parking.

On the flight back he could think of nothing but his gigantic new shopping centre. There would be twenty-four shops, he decided, and the largest hypermarket the country had ever seen. He made sketch after sketch. He could already see the shoppers, the cars, the bustling activity. He decided to call the centre *Southways*.

When Jon heard that Paul was turning down his offer he laughed. 'You smart alecs should learn to stick to subjects you know something about,' he said.

Paul soon discovered that *Southways* would tax his resources to the limit. When his architect had completed the drawings and costing, the estimate was five million rands; far in excess of anything Paul had planned. But as the architect pointed out, when *Southways* was completed it would be worth eight million rands at least, and over the years its value would keep on appreciating – as would the rents.

Paul spent an agonizing ten days worrying about it, but eventually made the decision to go ahead. The following day he endured an embarrassing hour with Leonard Kingsley his banker.

'But five million rands, my dear Paul, it will be very difficult. We've backed you all the way in expanding your supermarkets. I, for one, have always admired your decision not to go into property, but to stick to food merchandizing, something at which you're an expert.' He broke off, looking embarrassed, ran his hands through his hair and smiled apologetically as he showed Paul to the door.

For ten days, Paul tramped from bank to bank, pleading, arguing, showing his plans and cash forecasts. He worried and became a victim to all the aches and pains caused by tension. Were it not for R & P's decision to go ahead with his opposition, he might have given up *Southways* then. He had developed an ulcer before the loan was granted. Strangely enough granted by the General Merchant Bank of South Africa, a very traditionally minded institution, and he was surprised. It was the bank which had backed him with the loan for his first supermarket. He decided that this was a good omen.

'The loan is a personal one,' the credit manager said. 'You sign personal security and the loan is valid for five years, renewable on a five-yearly basis. Anyway I won't bore you with the details. Our contract's on the way to you. You can read it yourself. As soon as you sign, we'll go ahead.'

Paul signed and delivered the contract by hand the following day.

Paul's tension was expressed in irritability at home. He preferred to keep his problems to himself and, not knowing the cause of his unkindness, Rosemary assumed that their marriage was breaking up. Paul was so remote and everything she said or did seemed to annoy him. She decided to press on with her plans to convert.

63

Katie had dreaded her coming ordeal for months; now it was almost upon her. She stood shivering in the wings, clutching Michael's hand.

When Michael had told her about her coming debut on the *Nancy Meredith Show*, she had tried to look pleased and had taken comfort in the fact that it was six months ahead. Anything could happen in six months. But nothing had turned up to save her and the time had moved inexorably closer.

She tried to control herself as she listened to Nancy go through her opening gambit of wisecracks, winding up with a song before she introduced the show's new discovery. What a fraud she had been, allowing Michael to waste time and money training her voice when all she really wanted was to remain hidden from everyone. At least she had insisted on a stage name; she was to be introduced as Vera Rose.

Glancing sidelong at her, Michael wondered if he was doing the right thing. Katie was so pale and her mouth was set into a grim, tight line. Suddenly he was frightened for her. Yet her voice was trained to the finest peak. If she did not succeed now, she never would. Michael knew how superb her voice was. He had heard her at her best only once. One morning, when Katie had thought he was at the studio, he had returned for his scores and heard her voice pouring out of their small garden in a spontaneous burst of joy. If only she would sing like that tonight. She'd be made overnight.

Michael squeezed her hand. Looking past her he noticed that Nancy seemed strained, too. It was not like her. The two women had met a few times at rehearsals and they did not like each other. Yet he knew that Nancy's personal preferences would not influence her in the least. For Nancy only the show counted. But why was she looking so uneasy?

Nancy had stopped singing and was accepting the applause in her usual casual manner.

'Ladies and gentlemen, tonight I am very pleased to introduce my own discovery from South Africa. A young woman who, I know, will go straight to the top. I predict that the name Vera Rose will hit the headlines.'

Michael watched Katie walk forward as if in a trance. She seemed to have difficulty in putting one foot in front of the other. When she reached the microphone she stood poised and still like a bird before flight.

'Hit the headlines!' Katie shuddered. She was transported back to those dreadful days, just after the trial, when she had hidden in a dingy room in Johannesburg. Each morning, when she walked to the bus stop, she had been determined to avoid the newspaper stand, but she had been drawn to it as if hypnotized to read: *Abandoned Coloured Girl Flees White Foster Home*; and: *Jet-Set Socialite's Secret Revealed*. Suddenly it all came flooding back so vividly.

Nancy was prodding her foot urgently. But what was she supposed to say? She tried to think. Then she remembered: *Good evening, ladies and gentlemen, I'm going to sing a new song written for me by Michael O'Carrol. It's called "Spring Rain". I love it, and I hope you will, too*. Her words had been kept to a minimum, but when Katie opened her voice only a croak came out.

Nancy came to her rescue. 'She's a bit shy talking, but just wait till you hear her sing. She has a brand new song for you, written by Michael O'Carrol. You'll remember his "Autumn Evenings" and "Lost Again" ' – she waited for the applause to die down, taking the opportunity to whisper: 'For God's sake pull yourself together.' She was all smiles as she went on, 'The song is called "Spring Rain". I love it, and I know you will, too.'

Nancy floated off to another round of applause and the

band played the opening chord.

Katie was intent on the faces staring at her. Hostile, derisive faces! Oh God, what was she doing here? Suddenly there was laughter in the audience. The band played the opening chord for the third time, but Katie was back at the trial, watching the staring eyes. An expression of horror came over her face and when she heard the laughter shame burst upon her.

Suddenly Katie was running away from the audience, away from Michael and Nancy, to the wings on the other side of the stage. She fled from the theatre and, heedless of the rain, kept on running.

Michael waited for two hours, sitting tense and withdrawn in the dressing room. After the show he sought out Nancy and tried to apologize, but she brushed his apologies aside.

'Michael, you're being a fool,' she snapped. 'It takes more than a good voice – you need desire – tremendous desire to reach the top. Katie doesn't have that desire and you can't do it for her. Why don't you marry the girl? You're obviously in love with her.'

'It's not that simple,' he said as he left.

It was the coldest April he could remember, the leaves not yet in bud. Hunched against the cold, Michael was sweating as he made for the nearest pub.

He ordered a pint and sat in the corner, obsessed with his problems. Marry her? Why, that would be a sin. She'd be a widow months after she became a bride. A coffin to cherish instead of a cradle; weekly visits to the cemetery.

He thought of home where his parents had a snug farmhouse of cut stone and six children to warm the long winter evenings. They used to sit for hours around the hearth, discussing Ireland's perennial problems or, for a change, poetry or music, while his mother joined in between stitches. The years had mellowed his parents. Now, with their children successfully launched, they were as healthy as two farm horses, plodding through their quiet days, at peace with the world.

Michael had spun through youth's cybernetic maze, guided

by soft reprimands and stern assurances, to emerge at adulthood shaped in their mould. Marriage and parenthood had fulfilled their lives, but this was not for Katie ... not for him ...

Michael left the pub at closing time and caught the last tube home. The flat was empty, Katie had flown. She had a bad habit of living out clichés, he thought, as he took the note from the mantelpiece.

'*Dear Michael, I'm leaving. Thanks for everything. I'm sorry I let you down. Love, Katie.*'

Michael sat there until his blood had quieted and his hands had stopped shaking. Then he went to the telephone and spent the night checking the YWCAs and the cheaper hotels in the neighbourhood. At dawn he set out to search for her.

He had been puzzled for hours by the moving patches of light. Now he realized it was sunlight through branches, reflected on the ceiling. It reminded him of home, only there the ceilings were always cracked and he used to make up patterns out of the cracks. Sometimes an entire feature film would emerge if he lay there long enough.

There was a rustle beside him, and turning he saw a nurse.
. 'Welcome back,' she said. 'I'll fetch the doctor.'

The grey-haired doctor was wearing the regulation optimistic smile. 'Well, I see you're back with the living,' he said. 'For a while I thought we'd lost you.'

Michael shrugged. 'Now or later. There's no great difference.'

The smile faded. 'There's a young woman been waiting outside for two days. I think she would disagree with you. A beautiful lady!' He looked at Michael quizzically. 'I suppose your type of business attracts beautiful ladies. There's been another one here. Nancy Meredith. Fancy you knowing her. Well, I'll send Katie in. She'll do you more good than any medicines, I think.'

Michael thought: If I weren't so damn tired, I'd sit up. Then he fell asleep.

He awoke feeling better. Katie was holding his hands, her

552

long hair falling over his face as she peered at him.

'How did you know I was here?' He tried out a smile.

'It helps to be famous,' she said. 'It was in the papers. You collapsed in Camden Town. Now what were you doing driving around Camden Town in the middle of the night?'

'Looking for you – what else? When I'm stronger you'll be beaten for this.'

'Michael, I'm sorry. Honest to God I'm sorry, but I felt such a failure, such a burden to you. It was all those faces. It brought back the trial to me. I'm sorry, you don't know what I'm talking about.'

'Oh yes I do, Miss Jasmine.' He paused. 'It has a nice ring about it. I like that name.'

She expelled her breath in a long sigh. 'How long have you known?'

'Months. That bulky letter you were so suspicious about contained the press cuttings. What a little fool you are. All this fuss about your predecessors. Seems weird to me. It's time you stopped running away.'

She clasped his hands and buried her face in them.

'Anyway,' he said. 'I've decided to change your name again. What do you say to Katie Jasmine O'Carroll?'

Katie's strong fingers bit into his arm.

'Don't tease me, Michael,' she warned.

'It's not a tease,' he said, 'but you'll have to wait till I'm stronger.'

They were married in May and Michael snatched a holiday – the first in five years – to take Katie for a honeymoon in Corfu. For two brief weeks they stayed in a villa that was situated between a mountain and an isolated beach.

Michael's strength returned as they basked in the sun and took long walks by the sea. Watching Katie, Michael was puzzled by her new-found confidence. A three-minute marriage ceremony and a licence tucked into her handbag had achieved more than two years of painstaking care, he thought, feeling unusually critical. She had a bourgeois sense of respectability. Now she was gay, flamboyant even, and she began to sing like a lark, piping out joy wherever they went.

'Why are you so remote today?' Katie asked when they were waiting on the steps for the car.

Lingering, regretful, he stared across the garden to the sea rippling against white sand. 'I don't want to go,' he said. 'We'll come back in a year for our last holiday.'

He closed his eyes in pain, shutting out the image of her shocked, wide eyes, mouth open in a silent scream.

'What can I do?' she asked. 'For God's sake, is there nothing I can do?'

He kept his eyes closed and shook his head.

'I've made up my mind,' she said over-brightly as the plane came in to land at Heathrow. 'I'll be a singer after all; I'm not afraid any more. I want you to be proud of me.'

'I'm proud of you now,' he said gravely. 'I wanted you to succeed for my own selfish reasons.'

'Whatever your reasons, or mine, I'll do it anyway,' she said. 'I promise.'

She sighed. In her double bed, a year later, she considered how she had failed to keep that promise. While Michael had scored with a dozen songs, she was still struggling with half a foot on the bottom rung of the ladder.

It was 1966. A time when only Newcastle and Liverpool could rival London's new-found cultural energy. While the Beatles were belting it out in the Cavern, the Animals were presenting their own tough version of rhythm 'n' blues. Katie was singing blues and pop with strong jazz undertones.

During February, Katie had worked around Tyneside clubs and discothèques with a modern, Coloured group called the Cobras, each with their own indigenous contributions. Their sophisticated soul sound was well ahead of its time. Together with Katie the group cut their first album, which was a flop, and after this they split up.

Katie had been glad to be back in London. Time spent away from Michael could never be recaptured.

Since then she had appeared with an American group singing soul in clubs and gained a few appearances singing Country and Western.

Nowadays, most evenings were taken up singing in one of the many London clubs and discothèques while Michael worked. She spent her days at home with him. She had begun to lose weight with the rigours of her lifestyle and the worry of Michael. In May, she had been offered a chance to sing with a leading group called the Dreamers, about to tour the north, but she had turned them down, not wishing to leave Michael alone again.

Now she was lying in bed feeling guilty. The night before she and Michael had fought bitterly for the first time since they were married and he had slept on the couch. Michael had composed a dozen or more songs which, he said, were only for Katie to sing. Katie insisted that the songs, which were his best, deserved a famous singer. Nancy, for instance, could send them to the top of the charts almost overnight. Michael had blamed her for being selfish enough to want to succeed alone, which she knew was true, too.

Then she heard his footsteps outside the door. A moment later he carried in a tray of coffee.

'Ach, Michael, I would have done it if you'd waited awhile.'

'Sure and you're beginning to sound like any Irish wench,' he said, but when he glanced over his shoulder she was struck by his haggard expression. Some mornings he was like that. She would wake and find him lying so still, so thin and white, that she would have to nudge him to assure herself that he was still alive.

'Michael, have you been to the doctor for a check-up lately?' she said, scrambling out of bed to pour coffee.

'I have indeed,' he replied gaily enough.

'And what did he say?'

'He said a year ...'

She stopped pouring and thrust the clattering cup on to the table. 'Dear God,' she murmured. 'How is it possible they can know for sure? They've been wrong before. They can be wrong again. God damn them,' she said loudly. 'A year?'

'Of course they're wrong,' he said. 'But all the same, let's take that holiday while we can.'

'Of course, we must,' she said.

'But first, there's something we're going to settle,' he went on more firmly. 'I want my songs recorded, but if you don't sing them, they'll never be heard.'

'But Michael ...' She stopped and stood up. 'I'll pour the coffee. It's not like you to stoop to moral blackmail.'

'I'm serious, all the same.'

She put her hand on his shoulder. 'And what if I spoil them for you? What if they flop because of me? Such lovely songs. Your best, you know that.'

'It's what I want.' He shook his head obstinately. 'They were written for you.'

Kevin O'Neal ran the best recording studio in London, according to Michael, but none of the groups he worked with were right for Michael's new songs. They were soulful ballads with a strangely ethereal quality, all with strong, intricate melodies and elusive lyrics.

Kevin set out to create a new group for the recording and engaged a classical pianist and a classical guitarist.

All the musicians talked the same language, understood Michael's music perfectly and were totally committed, so preparations proceeded in an atmosphere of exhilaration. Katie, sensing that this would be the last time she would work with Michael, put her heart into her work. The cover of the album featured one photograph that filled both sides: grey skies, molten sea, white sand with Katie and Michael, two figures in the distance, walking away from the camera. It matched the album's overall mood of loneliness and sense of doom and it was titled after one of the songs: 'Scent of Jasmine'.

It was released at the beginning of September, on the day Michael and Katie flew to Corfu.

They returned two weeks later to find that their album had reached the top of the charts. Jasmine O'Carrol was an overnight celebrity. A large pile of mail was heaped on the doormat. They opened a bottle of champagne and sat at the table going through the mail, jumping up every few minutes to answer the telephone. All Michael's London friends were thrilled at Jasmine's success.

It was cold for September, particularly after Corfu. Katie lit the central heating while Michael went through the press clippings from his agency. The *New Musical Times* enthused: 'Altogether this is the finest album I've heard this year and the best "first" I can ever remember.' Other newspapers reiterated these sentiments.

There was an American television offer to film Katie singing the most popular track: 'Nevermore' backed by a full-scale orchestra; plus a short note from Nancy Meredith inviting 'Jasmine' to try again on one of her forthcoming TV shows.

Katie returned to the table and opened another letter. 'Ike Cherbar wants to be my agent. What do you think?'

'Grab him,' Michael said. 'He's Nancy's agent. Bloody good.'

'He wants me to go on a European tour to promote the album.' She tossed the letter aside, frowning.

'You couldn't look gloomier if the album had flopped,' Michael said, glancing sidelong.

'It's not that. It's just that ... I want to be with you.'

Michael closed his eyes, but he had never felt more awake. He could remember every part of the holiday in the minutest detail. The delightful expression on her face in the morning when they went down to the sea; he could picture her sprawled on the sand, somnolent, sexy, ready for plucking; and evenings, moist-eyed as she clung to his arm. He remembered, too, those secret early mornings when she would lean over him, searching for his breath and agitated, poke at him. He always pretended not to know. One morning, one day ...

Oh no! There would be no hanging around together waiting for that last nudge when she found she was alone. Instead she would be working, rushing breathless from one show to the next. Michael smiled, pushing death out of sight as he picked up Nancy's offer.

'We'll play this my way,' he said.

64

It was early in the morning and Paul sat at his desk staring horrified at the newspapers. The headlines read: *Top Johannesburg builder goes bust*, followed by: *Twelve builders topple this year as fiscal controls slam the economy*. Paul had to race through a column of political criticism before he confirmed his worst fears. Neppe, *Southways'* builder, was bust.

Paul sat staring at the wall in a state of shock, remembering the evening, two months before, when Neppe had flown from Johannesburg to see him.

It had been the day interest rates had risen by a further one per cent and Paul had been sitting worrying about how he would meet the next quarterly interest bill when Emmanuel Neppe had walked into his office. Paul had been shocked to see him. The fat, jolly little man had become gaunt overnight. Eventually Neppe had come to the point. If he did not get an immediate loan of at least a million he would not be able to complete *Southways*. He faced ruin.

At the time Paul had lost his temper. 'I'll sue you for breaking contract,' he had yelled, careless of being overheard.

Neppe had crumpled. 'And of course you will win, but I'll be bust, so how will that help you?'

Paul had calculated swiftly. Undoubtedly he would find another builder just as good, but it would take time. A six-month delay would cost him one hundred and twenty thousand rands in interest, and the new builders would probably increase the price by at least half a million. Prices had soared in the past two years. Even worse, he would lose the race against R & P with their new hypermarket.

Instinctively he knew that the first centre opened would get the business – and keep it.

'I can't raise the cash,' he had said, 'but if I were to sign personal security for a loan … How much would you need to guarantee completion of *Southways* on time?'

Eventually he had signed personal security for one million rands. Now Paul sat staring at his desk, smiling ruefully. Only he knew just how delicate his operation was. He owned fifty-one per cent of the stock of his company with only ten shares to tip the balance to majority. When he went public most of that became collateral for the various bank loans. Now it was only a matter of time before Neppe's bank came down on him for the one million. Two years ago he could have raised the cash. Right now it was out of the question, unless he sold the remainder of his shares. The next interest payment was practically breaking his back.

Over the next few days Paul tried to remain calm, at least on the outside. Inside he felt punch-drunk. His architect put out quotes and eventually Paul engaged Hamish Cochrane and Partners, old, established, conservatively-minded builders with a good reputation. They quoted an additional half a million rands to complete *Southways* by March. The price and the contract, they said, were subject to a thorough investigation into the project. Paul felt he was in costly but reliable hands and wondered where he was going to find the extra half million.

Next, Neppe's bank demanded repayment of the million rand overdraft he had secured. Paul flew to Johannesburg and bargained for time, but the best he could get was twelve months to pay. And this at the going interest rate.

But once back in Cape Town reality hit home, for the next interest payment was due, plus the interest on Neppe's million – an extra fifteen thousand rands, as well as eighty-four thousand rands for the first month's repayment.

Paul was still trying to raise the cash for these payments when another blow came in the form of a letter sent registered express with Cochrane's logo on the back.

Paul opened it curiously, but blanched as he read the brief

report. Their structural engineer had discovered subsidence on the site due to the subterranean collapse of an old, disused gold mine in that area. The wing of peripheral shops would have to be demolished in order to put down a different type of foundation. Paul's eyes raced over the technical details ... Raft construction ... Distributing the load evenly ... 'Get to the point, man,' he muttered feverishly. The point was an additional one million rands and another six months to complete the project.

September!

In desperation, Paul went back to the General Merchant Bank of South Africa for an additional one and a half million rands to complete the project, plus one million to pay off Neppe's overdraft. 'I must have the cash or *Southways* will never be completed,' he told the Board. 'The interest on the four million I've already drawn, plus the repayments of Neppe's overdraft, will put me under.'

The bank's Board shopped around and managed to raise a private loan on the grey market for two and a half million rands at ten per cent; the loan would be handled through the bank. On Friday evening he telephoned Paul at home.

'I thought you'd like to know, rather than sweat it out for the weekend,' he said.

Paul hardly knew whether or not to feel relieved. He would have to pay six per cent on five million rands – the amount that Neppe had originally quoted – and now a further ten per cent on two and a half million rands. He was calculating feverishly as he pretended to listen to Rosemary. His interest payments alone would amount to over half a million rands a year. How would he raise the cash? If he could just survive until *Southways* was completed ...

65

The downturn in the economy began to reach the man in the street and shoppers cut their purchases, even going easy on food. *Better Buys'* turnover shrank by ten per cent. Consequently, all available cash was needed for paying suppliers.

Paul began to cut costs frantically. He even cut advertising, a fact that was noted and commented upon by the press.

Paul engaged a property company to let *Southways* shops and offices, but partly because of the recession and partly because R & P's complex had filled the need in that area, they could not find tenants.

Paul pushed ahead with the opening with fanfare of trumpets, competitions and massive loss leaders while the rest of the building was still being completed. This time he faced daunting opposition and as the days passed it was clear that local shoppers were choosing his opposition.

Paul had to admit that *Southways* was not only a failure, but fast becoming a nightmare.

In desperation, Paul went cap in hand to Jonathan Pinn of R & P, who laughed him out of the office.

Sadly Paul realized that he had missed out by only six months. R & P's centre was a thriving metropolis, yet Paul had only ten per cent of office and shop space let. *Southways* had a mournful air.

In September, 1967, the third quarterly interest payment on the General Merchant Bank loan fell due. Paul began to feel like a shark caught in a net, for with every twist and turn the

561

net tightened. Finally the thought came: he might never escape.

Stealthily, he began to sell the remainder of his *Better Buys* shares. At first he was cautious, but as share prices fell and the bank increased the pressure, Paul's selling became frantic.

'*Better Buys' managing director off-loads shares*' the headlines read next day, and in the afternoon press: '*Southways pulls down an empire.*' Paul was plunged into a maelstrom of horror. Suppliers wanted immediate payment; some held up deliveries awaiting the outcome of the rumours; shareholders raced to the Stock Exchange to offload shares; Paul was unable to meet the next interest payment and, in December, the General Merchant Bank of South Africa succeeded in putting *Better Buys* into liquidation and Paul into personal liquidation.

Emotionally Paul was unable to handle this defeat. His personality was *Better Buys*. Without his business he was nothing. He wondered whether or not to kill himself, but discarded the idea. What was the point? He lacked the passionate self-hatred that leads to self-destruction.

One morning Paul packed a suitcase and walked out on Rosemary. He moved into cheap lodgings and left his wife to cope with the liquidation of their private assets.

Rosemary took the loss of her house, her car and her jewellery stoically, but was broken by the loss of Paul. Margaret insisted that she return to live with them at Fontainebleu until, as she put it, Paul came to his senses.

Paul spent the last of his cash on a train fare to Johannesburg and took a job selling second-hand cars which, he thought, was a good way to avoid meeting anyone he knew.

After a few weeks Rosemary borrowed the money from Margaret to fly to Johannesburg where she begged Paul to return. He was like a stranger.

He did not want a divorce; no, he did not hate her; no, there was no one else. Yes, he did want to be left alone. If she wanted a divorce he certainly would not oppose it. He did not think to ask her how she was managing for money or where she was living.

Rosemary returned to Cape Town, passed her exams and

converted to the Jewish faith. She badly wanted to be married in the synagogue, but she no longer had a marriage or a husband. Instead she returned to teaching kindergarten at the local school.

66

Five days after the *Better Buys* group was placed into liquidation a registered letter arrived for Anna. Margaret signed for it and sent it to the east wing with Flora.

The back of the envelope had the stamp of the General Merchant Bank of South Africa. Curious, Anna thought, she did not deal with this bank. She opened it and after reading the first few words collapsed into a chair. 'Insane!' she murmured.

The letter called upon Anna to make good her pledge of unlimited personal security for *Better Buys*. Currently *Better Buys* was indebted to the bank for an amount of eight million rands.

'I never signed,' she muttered angrily. 'They'll try anything,' and picking up the telephone she dialled her lawyer, Mervyn Morris, who agreed to investigate the matter.

Anna decided not to tell the family; after all, it was probably a false alarm and there was no point in worrying everyone.

The following afternoon she arrived in her lawyer's office, feeling fairly confident, but soon discovered that her confidence was ill-founded.

'This morning the bank sent me a copy of the Deed of Surety you signed in July, 1961.' He slid a piece of paper across the desk. 'Do you remember this?'

Anna picked up the sheet and suddenly recalled the day Paul had walked into her room to return the diamond bracelet. She was wearing it now. She fingered the stones nervously.

'I ... Well, yes, I remember,' she began.

'It's not a forgery, perhaps ... is it?' Mervyn asked hopefully.

'No, but good heavens, that was six years ago. It was to cover the launch of a new supermarket. Fifty thousand rands. The money was to be paid over five years.'

'What a pity you didn't limit your security to that amount.' Mervyn fidgeted with the pencil on his desk, feeling uncomfortable. 'Evidently Paul did repay the overdraft as stipulated, but in 1964 he applied for five million rands to build *Southways*. Then, in 1966, another one and a half million to complete the project.'

'Surely my security can't be expected to cover these huge loans borrowing six years later,' Anna faltered. Her hands were shaking so badly that she laid the document on the desk and thrust them out of sight on her knees. 'But eight million rands,' she said feeling ready to pass out. 'Surely they can't make me ... They don't expect me to pay it all?'

'They can,' he said, 'and they do. And there's no way out of this, Anna. You're not the first person to be caught by any means. I expect they took your security into consideration when they gave Paul the loan. I wonder if he remembered it?'

'He would have checked with me if he had,' Anna said, defending him.

'Well, it may not be as bad as it seems,' Mervyn said. 'His company's financial position still has to be investigated. Perhaps the shortfall won't be all that bad. Let's wait and see what happens.'

He watched Anna leave sadly. He had very little doubt that she was ruined.

Anna went home and kept the news to herself. She was hoping that her problem would go away and that something would turn up to save her.

A few days later, Anna received a letter requesting eight million rands, payable within fourteen days. She dialled her lawyer immediately; she could hardly speak she was so upset.

'They can't expect me to find the money within fourteen days,' she wailed. 'I'll never be able to raise it. In any case I'm

565

ruined. Ruined, I tell you.'

The lawyer calmed her as best he could. 'They don't expect you to pay, Anna,' he pointed out. 'What they're after is a court order. Then they can put in their own manager to wind up your affairs and sell your estates. I've already spoken to the liquidator and he expects that the company will be able to pay a dividend of only fifty cents in the rand. I'm afraid that's the procedure.'

For three weeks, Anna stoically kept the news to herself, knowing she was doomed ... They were all doomed. Ruined! A lifetime's work destroyed. Even more than that, she thought, her heritage, Fontainebleu. It was Acker's heritage, too. They were penniless because of her carelessness. It was the loss to her family that caused her nights of tossing and turning. If she could only save Fontainebleu. She would wake in the night and feverishly jot down her assets, tot up figures, and each time she would come to a different amount, but it never came to nine million. Her poor, poor children. How they would despise her.

Every morning she tried to bring herself to tell Acker what had happened, but each time she lost her courage.

The day before the court case, she felt like a condemned prisoner, for now she had to tell the family. She could not delay it any longer for they might read the news in the newspapers the following day or hear gossip in the town. Finally she asked Margaret to telephone Kurt and Simon and ask them to come round that evening, because she had something important to tell them.

Vera and Kurt arrived sharp at eight. Vera was carrying a flower in a pot. She made a big fuss about the silly thing, putting it on the antique table in the hall. Anna made a mental note to have it removed later before it ruined the table. Suddenly the full impact of her disaster hit home. Within a few weeks she would not own that table, nor anything else in this home – the horses, the vineyards, the pigs and all her beautiful breeding stock that had taken her family three generations to build. 'Oh God help me,' she whispered.

Simon was late and Anna's small talk was soon depleted.

Vera was antagonistic and as usual Kurt was irritated by her. He snarled each time she reached for a nut or a sweet. Since Vera had married Kurt she had been kept on starvation rations; consequently she was slender, deprived and always resentful. Kurt was looking old. Anna calculated swiftly; good God he was turning sixty this year. He looked it, too. As usual, Margaret sat smiling like a satisfied Cheshire cat and had nothing to say while Rosemary was moping. As for Acker, if he were not talking about farming then he had no conversation. That evening Anna came close to hating them all. She was curt to the point of rudeness when Simon burst in, half an hour late, looking twice as large as life and aggressively handsome. He was fifty-three, but looked at the peak of life, hair still red, though fading slightly, eyes still large and brilliant.

He flushed angrily. 'The rebuke is noted,' he said and sat sulking in the corner. 'In future I will try to be on time.'

A bad start for what she had to say, Anna thought.

For a few minutes they sat quietly waiting for Anna to begin, but she had no idea how to.

As if sensing her difficulty Margaret jumped up and made a big fuss about refilling their glasses and pouring Simon a beer.

'I called you all together because of something that has happened ... Or rather something that happened six years ago ... But in fact it's something that is happening now ...' She broke off. 'Oh my God,' she said and pulled out a handkerchief. 'We're ruined, all of us ruined, and all because of my stupidity.'

Anna made a tremendous effort to control herself, took a few deep breaths and then thrust her handkerchief into her sleeve.

'Six years ago,' she went on, 'I signed personal security for a business. It was supposed to cover an overdraft of fifty thousand rands, but the company has just gone bust and the bank is calling on me to pay eight million rands ...' She choked on the words. 'Really absurd. Far more than I own, far more than I can raise.'

By now they were all talking at once, but having started

567

Anna could not stop and she gabbled on louder, 'There's no way out of it, I've seen my lawyer and the court case is tomorrow.'

Suddenly there was dead silence.

'I don't think I have to tell you all how very sorry I am and how much this means to me and I know to all of you. A disaster ... for all of us!'

'Tomorrow?' Kurt said ominously.

'I don't believe it,' Vera said, her voice shrill. 'I don't believe you could sign unlimited personal security and then forget about it.'

'Yes,' Anna said heavily.

'Impossible, madness! Well, that's not going to affect us, is it, Kurt?'

'Vera, keep quiet, won't you. Tomorrow, you say?' He turned to Anna. 'Why didn't you tell me before?'

'I was too ashamed,' she said flatly.

'It's Paul, isn't it?' Kurt asked.

'Does it matter who it is? It wasn't intentional.'

'Does it matter? Are you crazy? He's my son, isn't he?' Kurt began pacing the room. 'We're in this together, Anna.'

'But I signed. You didn't,' she said.

Rosemary began to sob and Margaret put her arm around her, whispering, 'It's not your fault, love. Why don't you go to bed?'

But Rosemary insisted on staying and wailed, 'We've ruined you all.'

'Oh God. It's beginning to sound like a bad opera,' Kurt said angrily. 'Can we stop trying to take the blame and get the facts, please?' He wiped his face with his hand, a gesture Anna had not seen for years.

'I told you not to back the boy,' he went on, losing his temper. 'The boy's an emotional cripple; he's flawed; acts impossibly and emotionally. He's got his Achilles heel ... That's what built him and that's what's broken him.' Suddenly he was shouting. 'His insatiable urge to grab more and more ... Never satisfied ... Didn't I warn you?'

'I won't hear a word against Paul,' Anna shouted back. 'He

didn't ask me to sign. I insisted.'

'You've always hated him,' Rosemary flung at Kurt. 'Never accepted him. He tried his best.'

'He tried his best?' Kurt said angrily. 'But he's lost eight million, ruined four families. But he tried his best.'

'But how does all this affect us, Kurt?' Vera was whining.

'Will you keep quiet,' he shouted. Turning to Anna he said, 'You're a fool.' He glared at her. 'You should have come to me right away; given me a chance to plan something; just a few days would have been enough.'

'But, Mother,' Acker added his voice to the throng. 'Why did you insist on signing?'

'Because I wanted to ruin Pietersen and his chain of grocery stores,' she shouted.

Acker sighed and turned away. If only he could find the words to express himself, if only he could help his mother. Thoughts! Creative, potent, dangerous thoughts were like atomic power used by children. Anna had used her creativity to surround herself with revenge and destruction and the irrevocable result had been destruction for Anna.

Kurt hunched his shoulders and thrust his hands into his pockets. 'A lifetime gone down the drain for both of us, because you want to play Big Mommy to the world. Compensation, that's all it is; because you can't give, because you can't be a wife, you play with power and money. Well, now you've come a cropper, Anna, and we're all going to pay.'

Simon, who had been watching quietly and saying little, took two steps across the room, caught Kurt by his tie under his collar and shook him. For a moment Kurt's face went blood-red. It seemed to be happening in slow motion and Anna watched as if mesmerized while Simon brought back one hand and punched Kurt on the side of the face. As he let go, Kurt toppled backwards, striking his head on the side of the table. Then he sprawled on the carpet.

In that brief moment of incredulity Simon said, 'That's for Bosluis, Kurt, that's for the war, that's for every bloody time you fucked Anna. I should have done that years ago.'

Suddenly he felt as if a load had been taken off his shoulders and he laughed.

Vera was on her knees clutching a handkerchief, dabbing Kurt's face where the blood was trickling out of his mouth. She sobbed, 'You brute, you lousy brute. Look what you've done.'

Kurt pushed her aside, scrambled to his feet and moved towards Simon, but Vera clung to him and by the time he had pushed her off he had lost the urge. Instead he laughed curtly and said, 'You're twenty years too late, Simon.' He nodded to Anna and she followed him to the front door, apologizing all the way.

'I'm sorry, too, Anna, we're going to lose a packet. Nevertheless I'll do what I can. Tomorrow morning I'll have the business valued, obviously at the lowest possible valuation I can get away with, and I'll make them an offer for your half-share. I'll play for as much time as I can to pay it off. Then we'll get a lease-back on the building, sell the polony factory, the dairy and the poultry ... Poultry's a pain nowadays anyway ...' He broke off, thinking that he could probably raise that much cash within a year.

'The position depends on what we can get away with,' he went on quietly. 'Basically we're worth about three million, but I'll offer them one million.' He had been about to tell her that he would retain her half-share of whatever was left – as he would – and that they would be back on their feet in a few years, but he decided to keep quiet about it. Let her suffer for a while. Bloody bitch, he thought, she hadn't even tried to stop Simon from punching him. She'd always preferred Simon. He remembered that first night when she had clung to him in her funny little farmhouse yelling, 'Simon, Simon,' as she came. He had never forgiven her for that.

Vera was hooting impatiently from the car. Suddenly Kurt caught hold of her, gripping her shoulders tightly. 'You should have stuck with me, Anna.' He kissed her on the cheek. 'Well, goodbye and good luck, I'll leave you to your Neanderthal man.'

Anna stood dazed in the doorway, watching the car drive away until she heard footsteps behind her and, turning, saw

Simon. He put one arm around her.

'You don't need him,' he told her. 'Never mind what he said; he did all right out of you. Come and talk to the kids, they're worried about you.'

Anna decided for once in her life she would keep quiet.

'You'll lose your home,' she told them in a small voice when she returned to the lounge.

'Not my home,' Margaret said firmly. 'I've never regarded this place as home. I don't want to hurt you, Anna, but I only stayed here to keep you company.'

'Yes,' Acker said. 'We stayed here for you, Mama. We didn't want you to be alone, you see.'

Margaret sat motionless, staring at Anna. Then, with a brisk movement, she jumped up and busied herself refilling Simon's glass. 'Some days I feel I'll go mad here. Everything, but everything is you. I want a home of my own. I've always dreamed of going to live at Malmesbury on one of the farms Acker owns.'

'We own,' he corrected her.

Simon looked surprised.

Belatedly Anna remembered her mother's will. Well, thank God for that, she thought sighing with relief. Something would be saved. She turned to Simon. 'I don't think I ever told you ...' she broke off, looking awkward. 'It was so long ago, I really can't remember.' She glanced apologetically at Simon. 'Ma never forgave me for leaving home. She left her property to our children, to be divided equally between them. Acker's been looking after the farms. I had forgotten they were not part of the estate ...' Her voice trailed away. Margaret had not forgotten, she thought. All these years she had been longing to go.

'There's always Goedgeluk,' Simon told them. 'There's room for all of us there.'

'But all this ...' Anna waved her hand thinking of the stables, the horse shows, the travelling, the servants and all the trappings of wealth they seemed to take for granted.

'Mama, don't get me wrong.' Acker stood up, looking embarrassed. 'I'm very upset for you and I know how much it means to you to be rich but I'd just as soon be a farmer. All I want out of life is my own piece of earth, my wife and children. I know I speak for Margaret, too.' He gave her a hard look as if willing her to speak.

Margaret hesitated and then said, 'I want you to know, Anna, there will always be a home for you with us.' Her face was mask-like; her voice too high-pitched.

'Thank you,' Anna said, noting the effort.

Watching them Simon realized that Anna's wealth had not ruined Acker, as he had always imagined it would. He was a fine boy! What a fool he had been to let the family grow away from him. Well, soon they would be living nearby and with luck Anna would visit him.

Simon stood up, went over to the cabinet and said, 'Let's drink to the future. It can't be all bad. What'll it be, Acker?'

Anna could not remember him doing that before. He had never felt at home here. Suddenly she knew what was going through his mind. How can I tell him, she thought, panic-stricken. 'I think I should be straightforward and remind you that we are married in community of property,' Anna said slowly.

'We've been through this enough times,' Simon began, he broke off as the implications sank home. He said nothing else, but poured the drinks. When he carried them over he said, 'Anna, we're not kids any more. I don't know about you, but I learned a lot about myself over the years. If I lose my farm I'll start again.

'All these years,' he went on quietly, 'I've blamed myself for selling Modderfontein. My father and his father tried to make a living there. I've often wondered ...' He broke off and gulped his beer. 'Now, I guess it doesn't really matter any more.'

'Another thing I failed to mention,' Anna said quietly, 'was that I bought Modderfontein. I wanted to keep it for our children. I couldn't bear to think of strangers owning the old place.'

She laughed awkwardly. 'Now I suppose it will go with the rest.'

She buried her face in her hands. How forlorn she looked.

Simon was longing to comfort her but did not know how to begin. She was all crumpled and beaten. Life had not brought her much joy, he thought.

He held out his hands as if offering them to her; it was a strangely humble gesture and Anna felt embarrassed. 'There'll always be a place for you wherever I am,' Simon said. 'I want you to know that.'

Anna shot him an angry glance.

Simon noticed her expression. 'If you want me, you know where to find me,' he said and, slamming down his glass he left,

Watching them, Acker began to understand his parents' separation. Mama's financial brilliance and her success had made Pa afraid of her. Now she had failed and he could face her, but how would his mother cope? Her personality, her power and her self-confidence depended on her money.

After Simon had left Anna found she could no longer face the children. She went to bed, but it was a long and frightening night. Occasionally she fell into a restless sleep only to dream that she was already at the auction; as Fontainebleu and all her possessions were taken away she clutched at each last item. In her dream she knew that when everything was gone she, too, would no longer exist.

She awoke sweating with fright; if only she could save Fontainebleu, she thought, and once again she took her notebook and began to total all her assets.

Anna did not succeed in keeping Fontainebleu. In the nightmare months that followed the bank auctioned first Bosluis, then Luembe. The diamond mining company paid a record two million rands for the ten per cent of profits which Anna had originally retained; Fontainebleu was bought lock, stock and barrel including the vineyards, the breeding stock, the stables, the antique furniture and everything else on the property, by the Jouberts, who had always coveted this estate. The bank accepted Kurt's offer of one million rands payable over two years, plus interest on the outstanding money, and Anna's jewellery fetched two hundred and fifty thousand rands; the auction turned into a carnival as half the district arrived to bid.

The horror of it all! New employers for her staff; Flora, Jacob and Nella in tears; the prize Landrace breeding stock sent to the market; the oak glade destroyed to make space for vines even before Anna had moved out; the dogs auctioned and separated from each other; Fontainebleu's school closed and the mothers in tears; there seemed to be no end to the individual tragedies that Anna had caused and she suffered with each of them. Lena and Jan went to Acker's farm, but Margaret's beautiful Palomino mare whom she loved so much was too costly for Acker to buy.

Kurt, too, was working from morning until night negotiating deals to sell up many of their assets.

One morning late in March Acker and Margaret moved to their Malmesbury farm where they were to live in the cottage until Acker built a new house. For the last time Acker insisted that his mother accompany them, but she refused saying, 'I'm not a child, Acker, and I'm quite capable of looking after myself. I shall remain here until the last moment to look after the property and then I will decide where I'm going to live.' After that she shut herself into her room and refused to talk to anyone.

67

For Anna the horror ended abruptly one morning in May, 1968, when the liquidator, who had master-minded the winding up of Anna's estate, called her lawyer to tell him that the bank had succeeded in recovering the total debt of eight million rands through the sale of Anna's and *Better Buys'* assets. He asked her lawyer, Mervyn Morris, to remove Anna from the premises.

'What's left?' Anna wanted to know when Mervyn arrived.

'Things could be worse,' he said feeling guilty. Her calm was worse than tears. 'You still have Modderfontein and, of course, your husband has his farm, which was kept until last as you requested.'

Anna was left with a van, her clothing and costume jewellery, plus a few personal items and that was all. She felt dazed as she walked with Morris to his car.

What a ghastly morning, Morris thought, noting how pale and dishevelled Anna looked. He left as soon as he could.

Anna wandered around disconsolately while Nella packed the last of her possessions and put them into the back of the van.

An hour later Anna drove out of Fontainebleu for the last time.

She went through Malmesbury and, taking the road to Riebeek Kasteel, drove as far as the mountains where she could see Simon's farm, Goedgeluk, in the distance. His life's work! Five kilometres back was Acker's farm which he had inherited from her mother; over three thousand morgen of fertile wheat land. Thank God they had survived the liquidation.

575

She returned to the village and took the road to Saldanha Bay.

An hour later, the view changed dramatically: sandy soil, poorer houses, scrawny sheep. How long had it been since she had driven along this road? she wondered. Maybe ten years.

She could not help remembering the first time she had seen Modderfontein.

Bitter thoughts preoccupied her. Her life's work was wasted; her family heritage squandered. She was forty-nine and she had exactly three hundred and fifty rands.

Still, she was thirsty, so when she reached the village store she drew up and went inside. She was surprised to see Olivier's daughter sitting behind the till. She had grown gross and looked like a large, ginger toad. Had she sat there for thirty years? Her husband, looking pale and tired, was shifting sacks in the storeroom adjoining the shop. He might have been Kurt.

She would have to live off the land, now. It was the first time she had thought of the future, or her survival. Lately she had been preoccupied with the past; of all she was losing and not the least the finance to search for Katie. For the first time she began to lose hope of finding her daughter. She felt a failure; old before her time.

For years Anna had repressed her emotions. The petty acts of vengeance she had carried out had been the result of a promise she had made to herself at the trial. There had been no passion, no hatred, and worse still, no satisfaction.

Now, for the first time she was angry, with the bank and the liquidator, with Paul, with herself for her carelessness and most of all with fate which had dealt her such a crushing blow. Her hands shook, her eyes watered, she wanted to punch someone. Instead she gritted her teeth, but when she reached the farm gate and saw the large, shiny 'For Sale' sign she broke down and her rage came bubbling and seething out of her. She had watched the liquidator and his two assistants hammering posts around every last thing she owned and loved.

Well, Modderfontein was not for sale. Not any more. She

had paid every last penny.

She slammed on her brakes, leapt out of the van and wrestled with the sign, but it had been hammered into granite-hard ground. Panting with rage Anna picked up a stick and battered it. 'Bastard, bastard,' she sobbed. The sign was bent, but still standing, when Anna flung herself on it and smashed it over with the force of her body.

Anna was shaking as she drove to the house. After a while she recovered sufficiently to notice that the trees had grown well, but the road was once again falling into disrepair. What a sad, abandoned air the place had, she thought a few minutes later when she parked in the courtyard. Unlocking the door was like a journey into the past.

The dog was whining uneasily at her feet. Never another Wagter, she thought, for in all the years of breeding from his stock she had never produced such an intelligent dog, but then she had never spent much time with them. She looked at the dog for the first time and he gazed back earnestly, putting his head on one side. Then he whined and she stroked him. How long had it been since she had bothered to stroke a dog?

Along the kitchen wall was a wooden board with a number of keys hanging on hooks, each carefully labelled.

She took the pantry key and opened the door slowly. This was where she had kept her day-old chicks. What a mess it had always been, but now it was lined with shelves and stacked with linen and cooking utensils, all perfectly preserved, but dusty.

She would miss old Jan, she decided, when she considered lighting the wood stove.

Well, she was alone now and she would live out her days here until she died. She felt overcome with misery and thrusting the dog out of the house she bolted the door, rushed to the bedroom and flung herself on the mattress in the shuttered room where she relived the past few weeks and the auction of Fontainebleu.

Was it hours or days? Anna could not tell. It seemed that she lay in that dark room for an eternity. She had an uneasy feeling that she was gripped by unknown forces, that she was no longer in control of her destiny, for she heard the same sounds and smelled the same smells as thirty years before. It all came flooding back so vividly and she knew that she had walked a full circle, returning to the spot where she had begun, like a man lost in the desert.

She analyzed her past, day by day, seeking the watersheds that had changed the course of her life and she decided that it was here, in Modderfontein, that she had stamped out joy, stifled passion and love, learned to distrust. One night a thought struck her as forcibly as a light switched on in a dark room: to reject joy and love was to reject God.

Later, she heard a lamb crying in the hills. Impossible! There were no sheep left at Modderfontein. She had sold them years before. Yet there *was* a lamb crying. Whatever had become of Hansi? Then she remembered she had slaughtered him because he was always in the way. She was filled with remorse for an ancient crime.

Eventually the dog's howling drove her out of the bedroom. She discovered it was dawn. How many days had the dog been without food, she wondered? She drank some water, feeling guilty, and unpacked the bags to find the pet food.

She decided to call him Wagter and shortly afterwards the two set off to explore the farm in the soft, early morning light.

How could she ever have found this place ugly, she wondered, as she crested the second range of hills. Admittedly it was infertile, sandy and windswept, but it had a strange, wild beauty. From the hilltop she could see the lagoon stretched out like a sheet of silver and through a break in the hills she could glimpse the sea. The hilltops were bathed in a strange rosy glow, mist lingered in valleys.

As the sun rose the farm began to come alive; a row of turkeys came up from the eucalyptus grove and set off towards the hills.

Amazing, Anna thought. They must have bred over the years from a pair left behind by mistake. Guinea fowl were scampering through the grass and there were patches of wheat, lupins, lucerne and barley, self-sown from the old days.

Below she could see the dam which was bigger now and a

troop of baboons came scampering down from the hills to play at the water's edge. Two grysbok passed quite close to her and a family of herons soared out of the donga.

With the land lying fallow for years, the abundance of water and the absence of man, she had unwittingly created a game reserve and she decided to keep it like that.

The lamb was not lost after all. Anna saw a small flock of sheep plodding over the hills down to the dam where the lamb emerged from the donga. It had fallen asleep and been left behind. How hungry it was, tugging at its mother.

The flock, which numbered twenty, must have been hidden in dongas when they rounded up the sheep years ago. Now they were enjoying an idyllic existence with so much grazing and water.

Watching them made her feel lonely, so she stood up and walked back to the house, but when she reached the last hill she saw a cloud of dust rising from the farm track.

It was Simon and when she saw him her heart beat faster and the blood surged to her face.

'My father,' he began. 'So you were here all the time and Acker and I have been out of our minds with worry. Why didn't you answer the telephone?' He looked so relieved and happy to see her.

'It didn't ring,' she said. 'And no wonder. Look! The wire's down. I expect it was disconnected years ago.'

'Not according to the exchange,' he said. 'They were trying to ring you.'

'I'm sorry I can't make you coffee,' she said too quickly, wishing to get rid of him. 'I forgot to buy a primus.' How absurd to feel this way about a man who had spurned her for years, and she him.

'I'll light the wood stove for you,' he said.

He walked around the house, throwing the shutters open. It was five days since Anna had left Fontainebleu and he noted the dent in the unmade bed, and no sign of unpacking.

'Anna,' Simon said later when they were eating the eggs he had fried. 'Come back with me.'

'We're thirty years too late,' Anna said sadly. 'Besides, I

579

don't need your pity. I'm fine here. How could we possibly start again,' she went on. 'Too many wrongs, too much confusion, too little trust. We've damaged each other.'

'Forget the past,' he said urgently.

'It's not that easy.'

'It is, Anna.'

Anna watched him gravely, thinking that they had not talked to each other like this in thirty years.

'I'm sorry, Simon. I have so many things to think about now.'

'Alone?'

'Yes, alone,' she said softly.

68

The family met one evening to decide what to do about Anna for she was becoming a recluse. She spent her time roaming over Modderfontein sketching birds and wild life and if one of the family visited her she was never around.

It was a particularly cold late-autumn night and as they sat huddled around the hearth in Acker's cottage, they were all worrying about Anna's survival in the coming winter.

'Mama needs help, she's becoming very odd.' Margaret voiced the thought that they were all thinking.

'She's been strange for years,' Acker agreed. 'Ever since Katie ran away. We should have done something then.'

'She needs psychiatric care,' Simon said gloomily, 'but she won't accept it so I can't see there's much we can do.'

'What she needs is happiness,' Acker said bitterly. 'She never got over Katie and the people at the trial. Everyone was against her. She can't forget that.' He glanced apologetically at Margaret. 'We must try to persuade her to live with us.'

Simon drove home feeling frightened and sad; even driving into his farm failed to cheer him.

There was a handful of mail for Anna, but as she never opened her letters, there was little point in taking them to her. He dumped them on the dining-room table and later, in his dressing gown, with a cup of cocoa, he went through them.

Apart from a handful of accounts which he would pay in the morning, there were twenty letters from overseas Missing Persons Agencies acknowledging the termination of their services and sending a resumé of work to date.

'Precious little for the cash she laid out,' Simon muttered.

581

There was a last letter from America. Simon opened it impatiently and read the letterhead: '*Donavan Launderettes Inc.*' and an address in Florida.

The letter read: '*Dear Madam, Recently, I read your advertisement in the personal columns of the local newspaper and the description of your missing daughter reminded me of a nurse who was working in the local hospital here four months ago when I had my appendix removed. She was in her late twenties and said her name was Katie Smit. She told me that she came from South Africa and that she was leaving shortly to work in a hospital in Los Angeles. We had many talks and I am convinced that she is your missing daughter. Unfortunately I cannot follow up this matter for you, but I can put you in touch with an excellent missing persons agency in Los Angeles, whom I use to trace debtors from time to time.*'

The address followed and letter was signed by managing director, Hal Donavan.

Sounds genuine, Simon thought, feeling puzzled. After all, he was not asking for money.

'I'll write tonight,' Margaret said when Simon telephoned her. 'But let's not tell Anna unless we get something positive. She's had enough disappointments lately.'

They all felt happy that there was something they could do.

'Still,' Acker mused that night in bed with Margaret, 'I just can't see Katie as a nurse. Not her style. I suppose people change. What do you think?'

'I never knew her,' Margaret murmured sleepily, tucking herself into her accustomed position with her knees under Acker's and one arm wrapped around his waist.

'It's all Simon's fault Anna's so odd,' she muttered before she fell asleep.

'Why?' Acker wanted to know.

'He's too soft with her. He should grab her, carry her back to his farm, rape her if necessary.'

Acker turned and ran his hand across her back. 'You'd recommend rape as a cure for anything, wouldn't you?'

'Mmm,' she said as he snuggled closer.

Two weeks later Simon's reply came from the Los Angeles

detective agency. The writer, a man called Hank Lawson, who signed himself 'managing director', stated that they had made inquiries and found that a Miss Katie Smit had worked as a nurse in one of the local hospitals for four months, but had left five months previously and taken up a position as a private nurse somewhere in Vancouver. To trace her would require an advance fee of five thousand dollars to cover travelling expenses and time.

Simon had five thousand rands in the bank. He set about obtaining permission from the Reserve Bank to transfer the money and was able to send the fee five days later. Then he sat back impatiently waiting for the reply, planning how he would break the good news to Anna.

Not before time, he thought, for he feared for Anna. She was so thin and spent most of her time wandering around Modderfontein. She hardly ate or bothered to light the wood stove. How would she survive a severe winter?

Acker was right, he thought, what Anna needed was happiness. If they could only find Katie. But as the weeks passed and the report did not come, Simon became increasingly uneasy. Eventually he made inquiries through the South African consul who reported that they could find no trace of the company and presumably it had closed down if, indeed, it had ever existed.

Simon was enraged, not so much for his missing cash as for the disappointment.

He spent several agonizing days soul-searching, but made up his mind abruptly after visiting Anna one day, for she was walking outside in the drizzling rain in a light blouse and she seemed so remote.

He knew he had a chance of finding Katie and saving Anna, the two people he loved most. How could a farm compare with their lives? Once he had made up his mind he could hardly believe that it had taken him so long.

Goedgeluk was auctioned lock, stock and barrel and a month later he received the balance of forty thousand rands, after paying his bond. Simon packed his clothes and fled leaving the keys with Acker, who agreed to act as caretaker until the new owners moved in.

As usual there was no sign of Anna. Modderfontein was deserted. The hens he had given her were pecking around in the yard.

Simon set off over the hills and eventually found her sitting on the beach, watching the waves break against the rocks. Plovers were racing up and down the sand at the water's edge, searching for shellfish abandoned by the receding tide and he could see a seal bobbing in the surf only a few yards off shore.

For a moment he stood watching her and then she sensed his presence and turned and smiled. Simon shivered as he looked at her. She was so pale nowadays, yet at forty-nine she was still beautiful. Her face looked squarer than he remembered when she was young, but her eyes were deep blue and looked even larger since she had become so thin. There were crowsfeet at the corners, and deep lines on her forehead, but she did not look her age, he decided. If anything, since the crash, she looked younger. A certain brittleness had disappeared and now that she no longer went to the hairdresser her hair hung soft and loose around her shoulders. He liked it better like that.

'Why are you staring?' she asked.

'I was thinking that Modderfontein agrees with you. You look younger.'

She grimaced. 'Modderfontein is to be expropriated.'

Simon looked at her in amazement. 'You're joking.'

'No. I'm sure you've heard they're going to build a railway line from the Sishen orefields to Saldanha Bay and they must enlarge the harbour. Well, Modderfontein will be needed.' She tried to swallow the lump in her throat. 'Lately I loved the place so.'

'All the same it's not worth much,' he said gloomily.

'On the contrary, they're going to pay enough to buy a good farm elsewhere.'

'My father!' Simon laughed. 'So the old place was useful for something after all.'

'Come and sit beside me,' Anna said. She pointed out to sea.

584

Simon saw the black shape of a whale emerge from the water followed by another.

'There's a pod of them,' she said. 'I've counted eight.'

Simon felt her hand. 'You're not even wearing a coat,' he chided her. 'Come back to the house.'

'I've been sketching the birds,' she said shyly as they walked back. 'Do you know there are eleven different types of seabirds alone? I've even seen black oyster-catchers nestling along the reeds by the lagoon.

'You mustn't worry about me so much, Simon,' Anna went on as they neared the farmhouse. 'I'm getting along just fine. I'm teaching myself to live again. I'm fifty next birthday. I always thought fifty was very old, but lately I feel younger than at any time since I was married. Does that sound mad to you?' she asked shyly.

'No,' he said gruffly. 'You look younger. If only you weren't so damn thin and white.'

'A wonderful thing happened yesterday,' she said, feeling more confident. 'I stood on some leaves and enjoyed the crunch. I haven't enjoyed crunching leaves since I was a teenager. I jumped all over them and they made the most delicious crackling noises. Then I collected some pine cones for the fire. The house smelled delicious. Flowers and things are starting to smell like they used to and sometimes I feel such a glow. I'd forgotten what it was like to feel happy.' She smiled at him, glancing sidelong over her shoulder.

She looked so much like the shy young girl Simon remembered so vividly from long ago.

Anna's smile faded when they reached Modderfontein and she saw Simon's suitcases dumped in the lounge.

'I sold the farm,' he said and showed her the letter from Hal Donovan.

Anna could smell a fraud a mile off. She had experienced so many of them.

'You sold your farm to follow up this lead?' she asked incredulously.

'Yes,' he said glaring at her, his cheek twitching violently.

Anna watched him sadly. Parting with his land must have

been like dying, she thought.

'Why, Simon? Tell me why?' she whispered.

'Because ...' He sat down abruptly and then slammed his hand on the table.

'Why? Damn it, Anna, don't ask me why. Because Katie's lost and you're going crazy here. If I don't find Katie, and I pray to God I do, well – maybe at least I'll find you.' He buried his face in his hands.

After a long silence Anna said: 'I've got a feeling you may just do that.'

She watched him silently, checking an impulse to catch hold of him.

'I'll go and fix supper,' she said.

69

To Paul rehabilitation was a long and painful process. At first he hardly noticed the days and weeks passing. He simply existed. In the morning he woke, showered, went to work and spent the day with strange companions selling seond-hand cars. In the evening he bought a hot dog at the café downstairs, read the paper, returned to his small room and fell asleep.

Yet, without noticing, he was slowly recovering. One day the thought came: I'm still Paul Friedland. I've as much brains as the rest, and I'm twenty-eight. I can start again. But how? Not with food. The sight of food sickened him. Property, he decided. That was where his heart lay and Johannesburg was a hive of activity – on the threshold of a boom.

At the end of that month, when Paul received his pay cheque, he put the money in the building society and told his astonished employer that he would not be returning. He knew the second-hand car market like the back of his hand, but it was not a job he enjoyed. Instead he went downtown and had cards printed: *Paul Friedland, Estate Agent*.

Business began to multiply, for Paul worked from early morning until late at night.

Paul had to return to the Cape and he knew that it would soon be difficult to leave the business, so he bought a second-hand car from his former employer and drove back.

It was nine p.m. when Paul arrived at Acker's farm. For a moment Acker was too surprised to greet him. Whatever anger he had felt towards Paul had long since disappeared, but he still felt ill-at-ease, sensing the effort it must have taken for Paul to face the family.

'Rosemary's in the living room with Margaret,' he said, trying to smile. 'They've had a letter from their mother. It seems to be amusing them.'

They heard peals of laughter from the next room. 'Come in,' Acker urged as Paul hesitated in the doorway.

'Thanks,' he stepped inside timidly. 'Where's Anna? I went to Modderfontein … I thought she was there,' he went on.

'She and Simon went to America,' Acker said. The satisfaction showed in his eyes. 'They're looking for Katie.'

'Just give me a few seconds,' Paul said. 'Suddenly I'm scared.' He grinned self-consciously. 'I'll hang on here.'

Acker smiled, pressed his shoulder and left him.

'What's all the laughter about?' he asked Margaret.

'It's mother,' she said. 'A letter full of woe. Just listen to this: "*England doesn't seem much like I remember it,*" ' she read. ' "*So many people – crowds wherever you go and the traffic is terrible. I'm afraid to cross the roads. Everyone here has a hard time compared with home.*" '

Margaret nearly choked. 'You'll notice England is not "home" any more,' she said, smiling at Acker. She read on: ' "*I miss the sun and I miss Stellenbosch. I think I've grown away from England. Can't wait to get back next month.*" '

'What a shame,' Rosemary said. 'All those years of scrimping to "go home" and she finds home has shifted. It's funny, but it's sad, too.'

'Who was at the door?' Margaret asked.

'Paul,' Acker said.

Rosemary was sitting absolutely still, too scared to hope.

'My Paul?' she asked.

Acker nodded.

She raced along the hall and they heard shouts and murmurs and then footsteps going down the passage. Finally the door closed.

'I don't think he should come here,' Margaret said primly. 'He's only going to break her heart when he leaves. That man's a monster.'

'He wouldn't come all this way for nothing,' Acker said.

588

'I've come to fetch you,' Paul said quietly as she closed the door.

She looked at him coolly. 'Just like that?'

Paul stiffened with annoyance. 'Well, I'm not begging you to come. I thought maybe ...' His voice tailed off. What had he thought? That she would cry with happiness. Rosemary seemed to have changed. There was a strength about her that he had not noticed before.

Rosemary watched his face darken and began to feel desperate.

'Don't get me wrong,' she said. 'I love you. I doubt there'll ever be anyone else for me, but living with you – like it was before – no thanks. There was no joy in our lives. No togetherness. I simply combined the function of housekeeper-mistress.'

'What else is there?' he said.

Rosemary's temper flared, but when she turned on him, he was smiling. She could not remember when he had last smiled and she was thrown off balance.

'Why don't we put the past behind us?' Paul said. He wondered why he was arguing. Why he didn't just drive back to Johannesburg. Perhaps because lately every working hour had been filled with thoughts of her and everything he had done had been for her. Then he felt a sense of well-being sinking into him. All he had to do was wait until she calmed down.

'Do you know what's wrong with you?' she said.

'I'm sure I will, in just a moment or two,' he murmured facetiously.

'You're not Jewish enough for me.'

His eyebrows shot up dangerously.

'You don't know the first thing about your own religion.' She was warming to her theme. She hit her fist into the palm of her hand and began to pace the small room. 'You're supposed to be so bloody religious, but don't you know Judaism frowns on asceticism. My goodness, nowadays people seem to think there's a virtue in unhappiness. But you're worse! For you, joy is a vice. Don't think I didn't notice. You feel guilty when you feel happy.

'The Talmud says that not to participate in the legitimate joys of life is an offence against God,' she watched Paul hopefully, but his expression gave nothing away. 'Do you think I enjoyed our sex life?' She was shouting now and Paul heard a door close softly at the end of the passage. 'You used to take sex like a thief. Stealthily. At dead of night. Well, to hell with all that.'

'To hell with all that,' he replied, kicking off his shoes. He stood up and began to take off his suit.

'Jesus!' she said.

'Uh-uh, Rosemary. Don't spoil it all now. You were doing so well.'

'I don't care if you make fun of me,' she sobbed. 'I'm not the pushover you think I am. I'm not coming back with you unless you share your business and your religion with me and learn to share your life.'

'Well,' he began slowly, 'I've started up as an estate agent and prospects are good.' He grinned as he took off his shirt. 'However, I can't afford a secretary, so I've come for you. I've made an appointment for us to be married at Temple David, which is just around the corner from our flat, and as for sex – I'm as randy as a goat, so if you'd just shut up and undress, we might be able to solve all our problems.'

She stared at him with her mouth open. This was a new Paul. Infinitely more desirable, but nevertheless a stranger. Suddenly she felt shy.

70

Anna was dreaming. Strange night noises of an alien city blended with her fears: *She was alone in the grey dawn light, lost in the streets of Los Angeles. She heard soft padding and the deep-throated grumble of a wild beast pacing her steps. Glancing sidelong she saw a leopard, a powerful brute, its breath steaming in the cold morning air. She knew that it had come down from the hills of Modderfontein to show her the way, but she felt afraid and turned aside. The beast glanced reproachfully at her and went ahead into the morning mists. People were shouting. Still she hesitated until she heard shots. Then she ran ahead. 'Don't shoot, don't shoot,' she cried, but the beast lay mortally wounded. When she bent down she saw that it was Simon.*

She awoke sweating with fright and rushed to the door between their rooms, but paused there, unwilling to take the last irrevocable step between the safety of indifference and the fear of caring. She did not know how long she stood there shivering with cold; it seemed hours. Then she thought: the sum of my life is here – middle-aged, but still afraid of love. Eventually she returned to her single bed. Unable to sleep she considered the past traumatic six weeks which had been one disappointment after the next.

It had been morning when they arrived in Los Angeles. Before checking into their hotel they had taken a taxi and driven to the address on the detective agency's letterhead. Downtown. Seedy buildings and small shops. There had never been a detective agency in that building according to the caretaker, nor a Hank Lawson.

Unwilling to accept defeat, they pinned their hopes on the first letter and spent the next few days checking every hospital and nursing home in the district. It was a bigger task than they had realized and after the second day they split up, dividing the photographs between them and meeting for dinner.

When they reached Florida three weeks later they discovered that Hal Donavan, too, was part of the fraud. By now neither of them were surprised.

From then on Anna had watched Simon come to terms with reality; he had been defrauded of five thousand rands, sold his farm, and Katie was as lost as she had ever been. But his disappointment was much greater than this. As she watched him withdraw more each day her longing increased. If he would only make the first move, but he was waiting for her and she had not been able to show him even a glimmer of affection. They had spent six weeks together as travelling companions, sharing meals, chores and disappointments. They spent hours discussing the sights and the people they met, hurling words like logs to bridge the silence between them, but the silence remained. Anna felt that she was beginning to understand Simon. He was over-sensitive, much like herself, afraid to give in case he was hurt.

When they had assured each other that Katie had never worked as a nurse in Florida they returned to Los Angeles and Simon spent the next week haunting the post office. Inquiries had revealed that the ownership of the post office box to which he had mailed his bank draft had not changed in the past twelve months.

But why must she keep worrying about him? she asked herself as she lay in her cold hotel bed. It was an unwelcome feeling.

On impulse she flung back the bedclothes and went into Simon's room. It was empty, the bed unmade.

Anna panicked. She dressed and rang reception for a taxi.

Simon was cold and tired of pacing post office corridors waiting for Hal Donavan to open his box and take out the letter he had addressed to him a few days previously.

Sooner or later he would come, Simon knew that, but he

wished it would be sooner for he was longing to go home. The trip had been a fiasco from the beginning. Still, he decided, if he had the choice he would do it again, for undoubtedly Anna was changing. She was beginning to feel again. He saw it in her face; in her curiously childish habit of biting her lip when she was disappointed; in the shyness of her; her excitement at seeing new places. She could feel again and if there was no warmth for him, well that was not really important, he reminded himself.

Simon intended to take her for a holiday, maybe the Seychelles Islands, before returning home. As to the future, he would set up a small service plant and work towards a farm again.

He was startled then by the sound of high heels clattering along the passage. It was Anna.

'Oh God, Simon, I was so worried,' she said breathlessly as she ran towards him.

'Everything's all right. What are you doing here?' He grinned apologetically. 'He hasn't come.'

'Let's go,' she said awkwardly.

Anna heard him first. Rubber soles on the steps. She tightened her grip on Simon's arm. 'Let's go.'

Simon pushed her down the next long corridor. 'Hang on,' he said. He grabbed letters and keys from his pocket and walked slowly away as if he had just emptied his box.

A short, slight man approached. Not him, Simon thought, looking sidelong. His long curly hair, fleshy lips and huge brown eyes gave him a cherubic appearance, contrasting with his horn-rimmed glasses, grey suit, pink shirt and black tie. Yet he was going straight to the box. He opened it. There was only one letter and Simon recognized it. The cherub smiled a beatific smile, ripped open the letter, pocketed the cheque and discarded the rest. 'Sucker,' he murmured.

Simon's eyes narrowed as he moved forward. The man was cornered in a cul-de-sac of post office boxes.

'Hank Lawson,' Simon began, 'or should I call you Hal Donavan. You guessed my name correctly – "sucker"!'

The cherubic expression gave way to fear as Simon closed

593

in. Lawson made a dash past Simon who caught him by his tie. He shook him slightly and drew back his arm for a punch.

'Hey, you can't hit a man with glasses on,' Lawson murmured.

Simon reached forward, removed his glasses and stamped on them.

'But you can't hit a man who can't see,' he added plaintively. He blinked up at Simon looking curiously defenceless.

Simon struck him a half-hearted blow and, catching him by the collar, sent him sliding along the floor to the end of the passage.

Then he leaned against the wall and sighed. What an anti-climax, he thought. Revenge is for life's failures, a substitute for success; the week should have been better spent.

'Look out. He's got a gun.' Anna froze with fright then and stood staring stupidly at him, mouth open.

Simon pushed her back down the long, narrow corridor. A shot rang out.

'He's coming after us,' Anna gasped.

'Jesus, Anna. Why did you come here?' He peered around the corner and ducked back as another shot exploded. 'Anna, get down,' he said. 'Right down on the floor. He's in a temper and he can't see straight without his glasses. Don't worry.'

He crouched behind the end of the boxes, ready to spring, listening to footsteps creeping closer, trying to judge the distance.

'Simon, I think you should know that I love you,' Anna mumbled from the floor. 'I was coming to tell you, but your room was empty.'

'Shut up, Anna. Just keep quiet.' He crouched lower.

Like a baboon, she thought. 'Simon, do you love me?'

'Keep down,' he whispered.

'Why can't you say "yes"?'

'The right words at the wrong time. You have a talent for it. That's the story of our lives.'

'Don't blame me for everything,' she whispered urgently, 'you were always too eager to accept defeat.'

'With you, maybe, but not with this guy.'

He was close now. Simon sprang forward with a roar. The gun went off as he dived forward in a rugby tackle, catching the man's legs, knocking him forward. As they fell in a heap Simon caught him by the back of the neck and slammed his head on the ground.

'It's OK. You can get up,' he panted, reaching for the gun.

Anna ran forward and stifled a cry. 'You're hit,' she cried. 'Oh Simon. You're bleeding.' As she bent over him he pushed her away. 'Go get the police,' he murmured. 'Hurry! It hurts like hell.' Then he passed out.

When Simon awoke it was light. He opened his eyes and examined his position without much interest. His head ached intolerably; his shoulder seemed filled with molten lead.

He was in hospital. When he tried to sit up, Anna jumped forward with a clatter of high heels on the floor. She leaned over Simon, her deep blue eyes oozed concern; her mouth was slightly open. She licked her lips, then smiled hesitantly.

'Everything's all right,' she said. 'Flesh wounds. You'll be better soon.'

Lying bandaged in the hospital, Simon had a happy feeling of being detached from his world. He regarded himself dispassionately. I am a farmer without a farm, he thought, but I can start again. He felt confident of his chances. I am a husband without a wife, but in a while I'll get her back; I am a father with a missing child, but I will find her eventually. From now on I will create my own world and this woman will be a part of it.

He looked at Anna for a long time. Then he said, 'Do you remember what you told me? It was the wrong time.' He reached for her hand. 'Now would be a better time.'

'I love you,' she said, blushing like a teenager.

Simon pulled himself to a sitting position.

'It's burning like hell. I hope they put him away.'

'They will,' she said.

'I have a great longing to go home,' he told her.

'We can't. Not yet. We have to testify. The police will let us know when. They're trying to hurry.' She bent forward and kissed him. 'Let's turn it into a holiday,' she went on. 'We've never had a holiday together and I like it here. It's a lot like home.'

71

They were returning from a day's sightseeing in Hollywood.
The traffic was noisy; the radio blaring; they were both tired.

Simon had insisted on driving, although he had not yet
recovered. Anna was looking forward to a Scotch and soda
which she intended to drink in her bath. She was half asleep,
anticipating this when, amongst the crackle and static of the
radio's harsh blare, she caught the tone of a well-remembered
voice and for a moment she was so startled that she clutched
Simon's good arm and they swerved out of their lane.

The next few seconds were pandemonium. Simon swore;
struggled for control and returned to his lane. The cars
around hooted and the man on his right leaned out of his
window yelling: 'You stupid son of a bitch!' While Anna
cried: 'It's Katie, Simon.'

'What's got into you, Anna?' Simon shouted.

'It's Katie,' she insisted. 'Can't you hear? Get off the
highway. Please Simon.'

'Calm down, love.' He switched on the indicator and made
for the next exit. When they had left the highway, he parked
by the roadside. The song came to an end and Anna crumpled
with disappointment.

Then the announcer said: 'That was the sweet sound of
Jasmine O'Carrol in one of the cuts from her latest album:
"Jasmine Again". The song was called: "Loving You".
Jasmine will be making her first appearance in America next
week when she sings at Caesar's Palace. She will be
accompanied by her songwriter-husband, Michael O'Carrol,

who composes all her songs. You'll remember his 'Autumn Evenings' which reached the top of the charts for ten successive weeks. Welcome to America, Jasmine O'Carrol. Well, now we have a new singer …'

Anna switched off the radio and burst into tears.

Simon put his arm around her. 'Don't cry, love. One of these days she'll come home – or she'll write. You'll see.'

'But it's her,' Anna insisted. 'It's Katie.'

Anna had been walking around in a state of shock for days. It was not so much the discovery that they had found Katie at last and she was a successful pop star; or her new-found happiness with Simon which had caused it. Rather it was the sudden change from depression to happiness. She was not used to being happy and it took a while to cope with the transition. Happiness, she discovered, like pain or grief, can only be endured in short bursts. And so it was with her. While bathing, or walking around doing nothing in particular, a sudden shaft of joy would thrust deep inside her and she would feel like laughing aloud or bursting into song.

Because she was happy everyone else must surely be happy too, so she was taken aback one evening when they had just returned to the hotel, to see Simon scowling as he pretended to read the paper.

'Does it hurt badly?' she asked.

'What?'

'Your shoulder.'

He frowned. 'No, of course not. I wasn't thinking about it.'

He and Acker were so much alike, she thought. 'Well, what were you thinking about?' she persisted.

'Nothing … nothing at all.'

I bet, Anna thought, regarding the sorrowful face quizzically.

'Look,' Simon said, hoping to sidetrack Anna. 'Here's a piece about Katie's latest disc. The publicity men are working overtime for the show. It's the fourth piece I've seen in two days.'

Anna sat beside him and wound one arm around his neck.

598

'Hmm,' she said, when she had read it. Watching Simon, she suddenly knew what was wrong. 'When we've seen Katie we'll go home,' she said.

He pushed her aside and stood up. 'You're right. I'm homesick. I can't wait to get back. To get started. In five years I'll have a farm again. I still have some capital, so it won't take as long as it did before.'

He stared out of the window at the fog and shivered. 'It's damn cold outside, but it's harvest time at home,' he said softly. 'Right now I bet you could fry an egg on the harvester.'

'We'll be back soon.'

'But not to Goedgeluk. There'll never be another farm like that. Well, I guess I've had one good wheat crop in my life. The best! That's enough.'

'Simon, you've a different kind of harvest coming,' she persisted, trying to cheer him.

He stood staring moodily out of the window.

'Besides,' she persisted. 'Between us we can raise enough cash for another good wheat farm. Let's start off together this time.'

Simon looked at her for a long time. Then he took her wrist and pulled her towards him. 'That's a deal,' he said eventually.

Suddenly Anna wanted him so. She buried her face in the thick red hairs of his chest. Looking up at his green eyes, the strong, sun-tanned throat, memories welled up of their first days at Modderfontein.

Simon bent over and kissed her throat and her cheeks. 'I have a long-standing dream,' he said huskily. 'I'd like it to come true. I used to think about it during the war.' He grinned. 'You'll laugh when you hear it. It involves me sitting on the tractor on a hot day and you walking over the fields with a jug of lemonade.'

'It will be like that,' she said softly.

She clasped him tightly, thinking of the letter she had received from Kurt only that morning. She was back in business again, but this time there would be a time for making lemonade, a time for working and a time for loving. Each in its own time. She felt she had her priorities in order.

She stood up, went to the bathroom and stared in the mirror. Here, at the age of forty-nine, in a foreign country, I have joined the human race, she decided. Her face was lined, but not badly so; her hair was flecked with grey, but only slightly; her eyes were still large and deep blue. Eyes that could love and be loved, she thought. The young girl with the shy smile and graceful figure was gone. Someone new stared back at her. Someone she liked at last.

There was a knock on the door.

'I'll go,' Simon called. Minutes later she heard the chink of glasses. 'Come and get it,' he called. But still she lingered, watching her reflection. I've improved, she thought, and so has everyone else I know. We all benefit from our short stay on a small planet.

She thought of Paul, who had found that he was still a person when his business collapsed; of Acker, making his peace with God; of Katie, spawned in a donga, surviving by chance to be a star; of Simon, imagining himself to be a taker and finding he was a giver; of her own personal disaster which had turned to joy and of the late flowering of her passion, all the more fierce and satisfying.

She walked into the bedroom. Simon was holding out her glass. 'Cheers,' he said.

She took it and smiled. 'Here's to life,' she said.

He stared at her quizzically for a few moments. 'To life,' he replied.

That night they made love trustingly, as two friends, happy in their sensuality. Simon's arm was still in a sling and Anna crouched over him, smothering him with kisses, making sharp piercing cries like a bird.

Afterwards she lay beside him feeling at peace with the world. She thought: because I feared pain there was no joy; because I feared hurt there was no love; I made my own prison and locked myself into it.

Then she fell asleep, clutching Simon.